Chance Encounters

Linda Wells

To

Tania and Catherine
Bill and Rick

And to all who supported me at the Meryton Literary Society while creating this story.

Chapter 1

lizabeth was thrilled with the invitation to visit her Aunt and Uncle Gardiner for the month of February. She had long been weary of her mother's endless complaints after she rejected Mr. Collins' offer of marriage, and she was dying to get away. Her sister Jane had been invited as well, but since she had enjoyed a visit to the Gardiner's recently, she felt that it was only right for Lizzy to go on her own. It was the first week of the Season, when London was repopulated by those residents who were fortunate enough to own country estates. Uncle Gardiner had purchased tickets to the Season's first performance of a renowned orchestra, and was taking his niece and wife as a special celebration of her visit to town.

Elizabeth, though not particularly fond of shopping, had purchased a few new gowns while in London and chose to wear one of them that night. It was a lovely pale yellow silk, with small capped straps which allowed her shoulders to be essentially bare, and was cut to daringly display her décolletage. Her aunt's maid wound yellow and green ribbons throughout her hair, and left three long curls down to hang over her left shoulder. She felt beautiful and was guiltily glad for once not being in the shadow of her sister, since as her mother was so fond of pointing out; her beauty was nothing to Jane's.

The three arrived at the theatre and took their seats on the floor. It was an intimate setting, with private boxes above, but not too far from where they were seated. Elizabeth, always curious to observe people and their idiosyncrasies, spent the time before the concert began perusing the crowd.

She smiled to herself. *Oh, how I wish that Papa could be convinced to come to London, he would love the great variety of personalities available for sketching characters. I think that I would enjoy listening to his commentary as much as watching the performers on stage!*

Mrs. Gardiner was sitting to her right and noticed Elizabeth's amusement. "What has struck your fancy, Lizzy?"

She laughed, "I was just thinking of how Papa would love this atmosphere. I think that he would find it even more entertaining than watching the antics of his silly daughters!"

Elizabeth's attention was suddenly taken by a flurry of activity in the private box above and immediately to her right. A man wearing the scarlet uniform of a soldier had entered with a broad smile; he had piercing blue eyes and tousled blond hair which fell just upon the gold braid on his shoulders. She looked at him with interest, wondering what his rank was and enjoying his obviously jovial countenance when her attention quickly riveted to the soldier's companion. An impeccably dressed, tall, broad shouldered man had joined him. Elizabeth's eyes travelled up his form to see his face. Nothing was out of place on this exceptionally handsome man, at least until she reached the unruly mop of black curls atop his head. Then her gaze fell to his face. She was not sure what she had expected, but it certainly was not the expression of utter sadness that his dark, soft eyes expressed. She was moved to know why his eyes, such a mirror into his soul, were so troubled, and inexplicably, she wanted to be the one who made him smile.

Fitzwilliam Darcy kept his gaze down. He had no desire to catch anyone's eye and therefore be forced to socialize. He hated crowded rooms. He hated being an object of matrimony for every matchmaking mother and her desperate daughter of the *ton*. He was simply tired of the game. He was also very troubled about his sister. Eight months earlier, he had fortunately paid an unexpected visit to her and her companion on their holiday at Ramsgate. There Georgiana had confessed to him that she was about to elope with George Wickham. Darcy was able to stop the scheme, and banish Wickham, who at twice the young girl's age, was obviously only after her dowry. His sister was devastated, realizing what her foolish actions had almost cost her and dwelled on how she had hurt the brother she almost regarded as her father. She was a shell of the girl she once was, and it was tearing Darcy apart in his feelings of helplessness.

He watched his cousin talking amiably to the people in the box adjacent to theirs, marvelling once again at his ease in company with not just a little jealousy. He looked out onto the crowded floor of the theatre, not fixing his gaze on anyone in particular, until he suddenly realized that he was undergoing close scrutiny by a pair of sparkling, dancing eyes set in the face of a lovely girl in a yellow gown. At first he had the urge to glare at her with his best hauteur to encourage her to desist, but then his eyes travelled to her mouth, and then took in her entire expression; and what he saw made him draw in his breath. She was looking at him, not with the calculating view of someone estimating his worth, nor with the simpering compliance of someone wishing to please him to gain favour. She had such an expression of simple kindness on her face, and perhaps even concern.

Elizabeth saw that she had caught the young man's attention, and putting her nervousness aside, decided to go about the task of cheering him up, albeit silently and from nearly thirty feet away. She took a deep breath and relaxed, and looking directly at him, smiled gently. His brow furrowed, as if he was wondering what exactly she was about, so she nodded her head and broadened her smile a bit more. Darcy was fascinated, and involuntarily, he felt the corners of his mouth rise slightly.

Encouraged by her success, Elizabeth nodded her head again, gave him a full smile, including her pearly teeth, raised one delicate brow, and tilted her head to the side. *Come on, you are almost there; show me you can do it, sir!*

To her absolute delight, Darcy finally realized that he was being challenged to follow her lead, and to his amazement, he was enjoying playing along. When he broke into a full-fledged grin, his entire countenance changed, his face was graced by two gorgeous dimples, and his eyes held a warm glow that took her breath away. Trying hard to keep her wits about her, Elizabeth laughed, and mouthed the words "Well done!"

Darcy, now presented with the sight of this stunning creature laughing up at him, her whole body shaking with the joy of her triumph, mouthed back, "Thank you." He was utterly bewitched. *Who was this siren?*

At this point, the lights dimmed and the performance began. It was far too dark to see her, but Darcy stared directly at the spot where she sat, hoping to see any movement, or catch any trace of her voice.

Colonel Richard Fitzwilliam was not unaware of his cousin's behaviour. As they were seated in the box, he saw that Darcy had no intention of being sociable with their neighbours beyond a curt nod to acknowledge their presence. Richard took it upon himself to perform the niceties, but being a watchful soldier, kept an eye on Darcy's behaviour as well.

He noticed Darcy's perusal of the crowd and his usual subsequent staring, but he was surprised when the staring became fixed on a particular point. He began his own search to see who had captured his reticent cousin's eye, and then observed the entire smile exchange between Darcy and Elizabeth. Never had he seen his cousin behave in such a way, and seeing his face just before the lights dimmed, he wondered if he had just been witness to the oft-mentioned, but seldom occurring strike of cupid's arrow, and love at first sight.

The performance was broken into two sections, and with the intermission and reillumination of the room, Darcy and Elizabeth were equally thrilled to see that each had immediately sought the other's face. Both of them sat, hearts pumping wildly, smiling like fools, trying hard to read the other's mind.

Richard leaned over and whispered, "She is quite beautiful, is she not? I would like to meet her and know her better." Darcy instantly broke his gaze with Elizabeth and delivered a glare that would have sent any other man running for his life, but all it served with his cousin was to inspire a lifted brow. "Feeling possessive, are we Cousin?" He laughed, "Well, what are you waiting for? Go and introduce yourself."

"Introduce myself?" Darcy said incredulously. "I have never done such a thing. A gentleman simply does not walk up to an unknown woman and greet her! What would she think of me? I would be considered nothing less than a rake!"

"Surely you cannot be serious! How else do you expect to further this acquaintance? Or are you willing to be satisfied with the memory of smiling at the first woman who I have ever known to catch your eye and turn you back into a blithering schoolboy? How do you expect to propose if you cannot muster the courage to tell her who you are?" Richard was thoroughly enjoying discomposing Darcy.

Meanwhile, Elizabeth's attention was drawn by her aunt and uncle who were wondering why she kept smiling and laughing up at the private boxes. "What are you looking at, Lizzy?" asked Uncle Gardiner.

"Do you see that box just above you? The one with the man dressed in black and the soldier? The gentleman and I have been having a challenge of sorts. He has been determined to be sombre, and I have been attempting to make him smile." Elizabeth was thrilled with her success, and it showed on her face. "I, apparently, have won, because he has displayed the most enticing set of dimples I have ever seen!"

"Lizzy! What has happened to you? If I did not know better, I would think that I was sitting next to Lydia to hear about you flirting so! What must this man think of you?" Mrs. Gardiner was torn between horror and amusement at her irrepressible niece's behaviour.

"Oh Aunt, it is fine. Look at how the two men are arguing, I think that the gentleman's friend is trying to encourage him to come and speak to me. I think that the gentleman is terribly shy."

At least I hope that is the problem, and that he is not too embarrassed with his own behaviour to come and meet a woman who is no doubt his social inferior. To know that she would be rejected for such a reason would be devastating, no matter how likely it was. She very much wanted to know this man.

Unfortunately, the bell rang signalling the end of intermission. Soon the house was plunged back into darkness, leaving the couple both regretting the missed opportunity. Darcy again sat, not listening to the performance, and chastising himself for not acting on the impulse of greeting the woman in yellow. *After all, what harm could come from an introduction? It is not as if I am proposing marriage. It would just be to learn her name, and thank her for her kindness.* Yes, that was it, just a polite thank you. And if he happened in the process to learn her address, and her fondest hopes and dreams, and discover her scent, and the taste of her lips; and to touch the silk of her sweet shoulders . . . *Get a hold of yourself, man!*

Richard watched his cousin argue with himself and finally leaned over, "Perhaps we should depart from our box a bit early to avoid the crowd. Then we might be able to spot any friends who we possibly missed greeting when we entered the theatre." His lips twitched with a smirk and he raised his brows. "What think you, Cousin?"

"I think that is an excellent idea, Richard. You have planned the campaign well, and I am proud to call you family."

"Ha! The campaign may be planned, but it is up to you to execute it!"

"Then success is guaranteed!"

Unfortunately, the best laid plans do not always succeed. When the concert neared an end, the cousins rose to depart their box and began to walk to the stairs leading to the theatre lobby. The plan was to position themselves near the door so that they could easily capture the young lady's attention. When the lights came back up, Elizabeth looked up to the box to find it empty. Disappointed and confused, she gathered her shawl and reticule and followed her aunt and uncle up the aisle to the doors, wondering if the men had left early to avoid meeting her.

Darcy's plan to quickly descend the stairs was thwarted by his suddenly being surrounded by acquaintances vying for his attention. He tried valiantly to shake them off, but was devastated to see his lovely lady in yellow emerging through the doors below him. He and Richard saw her at the same time, and called out, "Wait!"

Elizabeth looked up towards the sound and first spotted Richard's red coat and then Darcy, trapped in the crowd of people. She saw someone approach him and wring his hand while exclaiming, "Darcy! How are you?" She tried to gain her relatives' attention to slow them down, but she felt the grip of her uncle's hand on her wrist, pulling her out the door to the street.

Darcy heard the man say, "Come on Lizzy, we don't want to lose you in this crowd!"

They locked eyes, desperate, searching, for one more moment, and then she was gone.

Chapter 2

"**B**ingley!" Darcy looked down with frustration at the hand that was preventing his pursuit of the bewitching lady in yellow, and then up into the beaming face of his closest friend.

"Darcy! I have not seen you in an age! Luckily Caroline spotted you or I would have missed you entirely!"

With an eye on his cousin who, unencumbered by acquaintances, was rapidly descending the stairs, Darcy removed his hand from his friend's grasp. "Forgive me, Bingley, but I must leave immediately. Call on me tomorrow if you can."

Darcy flew down the stairs, leaving a bemused Bingley in his wake. His sisters, Caroline Bingley and Louisa Hurst had just reached them, delayed in their approach by Gilbert Hurst, who had fallen asleep during the performance. Caroline possessively demanded to know where Darcy had gone, and was thoroughly dissatisfied with her brother's lack of knowledge.

Darcy finally escaped the theatre and looking quickly from side to side, he gratefully spotted his cousin's uniform. Richard had managed to halt the progress of the lady and her companions.

Elizabeth's uncle had pulled her through the theatre doors and out into the scattering crowd. Once beyond the noise of the carriages at the entrance, she finally managed to gain his attention.

"Wait, Uncle, please!" she cried.

"What is it, Lizzy?" Mr. Gardiner slowed and looked at her, noticing the expression of distress on his niece's face.

"The gentlemen from the theatre, they were trying to reach us. They were caught on the stairs, but I heard them call out for us to wait for them. Please could we just stand here for a moment?"

"We do not know these men, Lizzy." He said with some concern.

"But we will never know them if we give them no opportunity to speak to us, will we?" Elizabeth's voice was pleading.

"Come Edward, it will not hurt to wait here and see what the gentlemen have to say, and besides, it will be a while before our carriage appears." Madeline Gardiner looked at her niece; then met her husband's glance. Silently they agreed to indulge Lizzy's request.

Just then they spotted the scarlet uniform of the soldier approaching them. Relieved, Richard let out a breath and gave them a wide grin. "Well, did you hear us calling, or are we merely very fortunate?"

Elizabeth smiled brightly up at him, "I think that it was a bit of both, except you seem to be alone. Where is the other half of your 'we'?"

Richard laughed, "My cousin was waylaid by far too many interested acquaintances, but I assure you, he will join us very soon." He turned and noted Darcy's rapid approach. "Ah, he has escaped!"

Darcy came to a stop, glanced at his cousin, and bowed to the waiting party. "I hope that you will forgive us for delaying your exit, but I could not miss the opportunity to make the acquaintance of the young lady who so kindly lifted my spirits this evening. I know that this is an entirely improper way to make an introduction, however, desperate times call for desperate measures." He took a deep breath, attempted to ignore his cousin's growing smile, and swallowing his extreme nervousness, looked into Elizabeth's sparkling hazel eyes. Gaining courage from her welcoming smile, he said, "My name is Fitzwilliam Darcy, and this is my cousin, Colonel Richard Fitzwilliam."

"I am very pleased to make your acquaintance, sir. I have no hesitation introducing myself to others, and a little bending of the rules of propriety never hurt anyone." Darcy gave her a grateful look, and the corners of his mouth lifted. "My name is Elizabeth Bennet." Darcy's smile grew, *Elizabeth!* She continued, "And this is my uncle and aunt Mr. and Mrs. Edward Gardiner."

Darcy and Richard bowed, "It is an honour to meet you all." At a loss for words, Darcy had no idea how to continue the conversation. Desperately he looked to Richard for help when Elizabeth's warm voice interrupted his panicked musings.

"I am sorry to have my suspicions confirmed that your spirits required improvement, sir, however, I hope that the beautiful performance and the atmosphere of the theatre aided in your recovery."

Regaining his equilibrium, Darcy daringly replied, "I believe that it was the excellent company of the persons attending the concert who gave me the encouragement that I required." Elizabeth and Darcy both blushed.

Mrs. Gardiner, sensing the gentleman's embarrassment, and Elizabeth's sudden shyness decided to forward the conversation. "Mr. Darcy, do you and your cousin frequently attend concerts?"

"I do own a box at this theatre; however it has been some time since I have had the opportunity to attend. My cousin and I share the guardianship of my young sister, and we hoped to have her company tonight, but she unfortunately was unable to join us. Are you often in attendance?"

"No, this evening was a special event for us. We always try to take our niece to a few performances whenever she comes to visit."

Sufficiently recovered, Darcy smiled and addressed Elizabeth, "So, I am to understand that you are not a resident of London, Miss Bennet? May I ask where you are from, or is it a secret?"

Elizabeth laughed, "No, it is no secret. I live in Hertfordshire. My father has a small estate about a mile from the village of Meryton, called Longbourn."

"Meryton?" Darcy's eyes opened wide. "Is there an estate near there called Netherfield?"

"Yes, it borders Longbourn; the houses are about three miles apart. Do you know it? It is being leased currently by a man named Bingley, but he has yet to make an appearance."

"Charles Bingley is my great friend," Darcy said quietly. "I was supposed to join him at his estate in September, but family obligations kept me from coming. I was to stay there two months. When I could not come, Bingley decided to wait to take possession until I could be there. This is his first time operating an estate, and he was hoping for my guidance." Darcy saw that she had come to the same realization. "If I had come to visit my friend when I had planned, we would have found each other months ago."

They stared at each other, inexplicably sharing the same thoughts, *How much time have we lost? Well, let us not waste any more.*

While Darcy and the ladies were talking, Mr. Gardiner and Richard stood off to the side, each closely observing the conversation.

Richard turned to his companion. "Tell me about your niece, Mr. Gardiner."

"What would you care to hear about her? Her character, her home, her . . ."

"Anything you are willing to tell me, sir."

"Well, Lizzy is twenty years old, and one of five daughters to my sister and brother Bennet from the estate of Longbourn, in Hertfordshire." He paused, and noted Richard nodded his head, but kept his eyes on the trio before him. "She is kind, intelligent, well-read, and fiercely loyal to her family and friends. She does not suffer fools, and has a very sharp wit, which is known to scare men away." Here he noted Richard's sardonic grin. "She also is a girl of good sense and despite her expressions of self-doubt in comparison to her sister, Jane, she is quite lovely."

Richard looked at Mr. Gardiner, and grinned. "Well, my cousin did mention her eyes once or twice." He tilted his head. "What of her circumstances?"

"Dowry?" Seeing Richard nod, he said, "You do not hesitate, sir. It is small. She will share five thousand pounds among her sisters upon her mother's death. Their estate is entailed away to a distant male cousin. She has little but herself to offer a man."

Richard raised his brow to Mr. Gardiner, and simply said, "Oh, I see."

"Before you grab hold of your cousin and drag him away from us, you should know one more vital piece of information about my niece. She is no fortune hunter." Richard gave him a sceptical look. "No, I can assure you of this. My niece has stated many times that she will not marry without love and respect for her husband, and would prefer a life as a spinster, reduced to living as a governess than to settle for a marriage of convenience." Richard shook his head disbelievingly. "She has rejected an offer of marriage from the cousin who will inherit her father's estate because she thought him loathsome and ridiculous, despite the fact that even now, as he eagerly awaits her father's demise, he has a comfortable home as the recipient of the living at the Hunsford Parsonage, at Rosings Park in Kent."

Richard looked at him with utter astonishment. He was not sure which piece of news surprised him more, the fact that this girl was so determined to marry on her own terms as to reject a life of relative comfort in favour of felicity in marriage, or the news that the man that she rejected was in fact his aunt, Lady Catherine de Bourgh's, parson. It was incredible! His respect for Miss Elizabeth Bennet rose considerably, and he looked forward to telling this information to his cousin.

Mr. Gardiner registered Richard's reaction, "Sir, I see that I have perhaps convinced you that my niece is no ordinary woman."

"Indeed you have, sir."

"So, I hope that you might indulge me in telling me of the worthiness of your cousin?"

"Ha!" Richard laughed, "Well done, sir! I can assure you that my cousin is no fortune hunter. He has a house here in London, and has inherited his father's estate in Derbyshire, and is quite financially secure. I have never seen him approach any woman before, and he has completely fascinated me this evening. Seeing him smile at your niece does my heart a great deal of good, since it is an expression that I have rarely seen on his face, particularly since the death of his father. He and I share guardianship of his fifteen year old sister, and the description that you provided of your niece's qualities could just as easily be said about him. He is a good and liberal master and loyal friend. Duty and honour are deeply ingrained in him, and I would trust him with my life."

"Thank you for your reassurance, Colonel. I take the care of my niece very seriously, and I will not tolerate anyone trifling with her."

"As I said, my cousin Darcy has never approached a woman before, much less flirted with one and chased her out of a theatre, but I think that it is very safe to say that if he were to pay a call to your niece, he would treat her with the greatest respect."

Mr. Gardiner was pleased. Mr. Darcy was apparently a man of great consequence. His cousin was obviously being careful not to tell too much about his wealth, however, he did seem quite adamant about his worthiness. He decided that if Mr. Darcy did get his courage up to request permission to call on Lizzy, it would be granted.

"Perhaps we should rejoin the others, Colonel?"

The two men stepped back up to the three, just in time to hear Mrs. Gardiner realize that Darcy was the Master of Pemberley, and exclaim with delight that she grew up in Lambton.

Darcy was happy to have an easy topic to discuss with the ladies. He could easily extol the virtues of his estate and Derbyshire without once tripping over his tongue. He asked Mrs. Gardiner if she had ever visited the estate, and she said that when she was a girl, she had taken a tour of the house and grounds during the Christmas season.

She turned to Elizabeth, "The park around Pemberley is lovely, Lizzy, I think that there are enough pathways and trees that even you would be satisfied!"

Darcy looked into Elizabeth's eyes, "Are you fond of nature, Miss Bennet?"

Elizabeth laughed, "Indeed, I am sir. I walk every morning, often for miles, and quite enjoy losing myself in the woods. I have several favourite pathways from my home, and often take a book or simply find a good rock to rest upon and enjoy the time to contemplate life, or more often than not, escape the noise of my sisters and mother!"

"You must be quite disappointed in the loss of your daily walks while staying in London."

"While it is true that I do not have the opportunity to wander as far, there are still many charming parks here in town. I was hoping to take in Hyde Park during my visit, if the weather is favourable, but I do visit the small park near my aunt and uncle's home daily, and sometimes in the afternoons with the children."

"Miss Bennet, with your aunt and uncle's permission, perhaps I could be so bold as to request your consent to pay a call on you, and we could take a walk in this pleasant park together. I find beauty in nature at every time of year, and I would enjoy seeing it with someone who shares my view."

Elizabeth blushed and studied her hands. "I would like that very much, Mr. Darcy," she said shyly.

Elated, he looked at Mr. Gardiner, who nodded his permission. "Then, may I inquire where I might find you, and please tell me when we could meet?"

"We live in Gracechurch Street, in Cheapside, Mr. Darcy. I am a tradesman, dealing with textiles, and it is convenient to the warehouses." Mr. Gardiner regarded Darcy closely.

Darcy quickly hid his surprise in learning that Elizabeth's family was in trade. He thought that they were people of fashion. He certainly never expected them to reside in Cheapside. But then he thought back to his earlier words to them about Bingley, whose fortune derived from trade. Perhaps he was in need of rethinking the way he judged people, simply based on their address.

"Well then, may I call on you there Wednesday morning, Miss Bennet? Would eleven o'clock be convenient?" He looked at her hopefully.

Elizabeth finally met his gaze, and seeing such a look of pleading in his soft brown eyes, she blushed again, bit her lip, and whispered, "I would be honoured to receive your call, sir." She was happy to see the corners of Darcy's mouth lift slightly, and his sombre face lightened with the movement. *He is so handsome when he smiles, I must think of ways to encourage it!*

The parties took leave of each other, and found that the theatre crowd had thinned, and their carriages had arrived. Darcy took the opportunity to hand Elizabeth into her uncle's carriage, and watched while it pulled away. He turned to face the wide grin of his cousin.

"Please, Richard, let us return home and pour a brandy before you start on me."

"Who, me? Not a word, Cousin, I will not say a word!"

Chapter 3

*D*arcy settled back into the soft leather chair in the library of Darcy House and sighed. His mind was full of Elizabeth Bennet. *Elizabeth.* Never before had any woman so instantly captured his complete attention. He was relieved to have finally pushed Richard out the door and on his way back home. He endured an hour of his amused baiting, merrily describing Darcy's tongue-tied, nervous attempts at conversation, and finally relented when he noticed Darcy's gaze continually travelling to the set of fencing foils mounted on the wall. Taking his leave, Richard promised to say nothing to his parents about Darcy's budding courtship, in exchange for full details of their first meeting. He did share with Richard the incredible news that Elizabeth lived next to the estate leased by Bingley. Richard, in turn, gave him verbatim the conversation he had with Mr. Gardiner. Darcy was deeply grateful and thoroughly impressed with all that he had learned. From her uncle's description, Elizabeth was a treasure. He only hoped that he was worthy of her.

When he learned that she had refused to marry her cousin, his respect for her grew rapidly. For a woman in her obviously diminished circumstances, despite being a gentleman's daughter, it was a very brave decision. Learning of the connection to his aunt was somewhat disconcerting, but at least they had never met. So, he reasoned, she could not hold that particular unpleasant connection against him. *Hopefully*, he thought wryly, *I can make a sufficiently good impression on her that she will be able to ignore the offensive behaviour of my most-vocal relation.* He smiled again. How he had changed in this past year. Georgiana's experience last summer and his continuing disenchantment with the people of so-called higher society had made him so much more aware of his and his own family's behaviour.

Cheapside. Her relations are in trade. Never before would he have considered associating with anyone from that part of town. How can a smile and a pair of warm eyes, placed so perfectly in the face of an absolutely lovely woman so affect him? He thought about it, and again realized that so much had changed for him over the past year. He had been trying to aid Georgiana through her recovery from Ramsgate, and feeling so terribly helpless. In addition, bearing the loneliness that had been his constant companion since his parents' deaths had somehow become a smothering burden that he desperately wanted to remove. He had finally recognized that he needed more in his life than duty. The strange spark of hope that he felt when he met Elizabeth's kind eyes in the theatre was something that he wanted to nurture. He decided that he would put aside his prejudices of the past and grab onto the joy that he sensed she could offer.

DARCY FOUND HIMSELF at the breakfast table Tuesday morning feeling better than he had in months. He was not blind, he knew that the only thing different in his life was the introduction to Elizabeth. He was amazed at how a single evening and a brief conversation could so alter him. He realized that he must have been long ready for such a change, and that meeting her was the impetus that he needed to begin. He felt impatient for their visit the next morning, and mentally kicked himself for not arranging it for this day.

Georgiana Darcy quietly entered the room and murmured a good morning to her brother. To her surprise, he returned her greeting with a warm smile, and lightness in his voice that she did not recognize. Finally raising her eyes to his, she tentatively asked, "Are you well, Brother?"

"Quite well, Georgie. I had an enjoyable evening last night. I only regret that you did not come with us. The music and atmosphere was quite soothing to the soul."

"What an interesting description. How was your soul affected?"

Picturing Elizabeth, he smiled a bit more, "I think that the best way to describe it is to say that I was in the mood to not enjoy myself at all when I arrived. I was feeling quite at odds with having to be once again on display, and listening to Richard's happy talk was annoying me. However, a few minutes after taking my seat, completely prepared to be miserable, I observed the kindness of a lady extended to another, and that simple act allowed me to open myself to rejoicing in the pleasure that civility, without expectation of any return, can allow. Then I permitted the music to surround me and take me away from myself. I discovered a way to let go of thoughts which were weighing on my mind."

Darcy looked at his sister, wondering if his words had broken through the cloud that seemed to surround her. Georgiana stared at him, trying to understand what he was saying. "Do you mean that the music gave you a means to escape your thoughts?"

"No, the music enhanced the escape. What augmented my ability to recognize the beauty of the music was recognizing the goodness of one person helping another. For too long, our circle of friends has consisted of people whose only concern was increasing their income, status, or vanity by their connections to us and others through means conducted under the guise of civility and propriety. It has always bothered me, but even more so in the past few years. I have come to the conclusion that I want to be valued simply for being myself, and the way I behave towards others. I want to be assessed for my own inherent goodness, and not judged solely on a few mistakes that I may make along the way to discovering who I am. I think that is a lesson that you would do well to consider."

"That it is not what I have and how I am named that is valuable, but my own goodness, and the way that I influence others with it that matters?"

"Yes, Georgie, that is exactly what I am saying." Darcy was relieved. He hoped that his words had given her something to dwell on other than her perceived misdeeds in allowing Wickham to attempt his seduction. At least she was thinking about it. He was truly at a loss as to how to help her. Her self-recrimination had been going on for so long, it had almost become a part of her, and he desperately wanted to help her to let it go before it became permanent. He realized that the first step to her doing that was to show her that he could let it go as well.

Darcy settled into his study, and spent the morning discussing estate business with his steward. Georgiana had retired to the music room to practice the pianoforte, and with his study door ajar, he was able to listen to her efforts. He was happy throughout to recognize that Georgiana's choice of music that morning was not quite as ponderous as it had been for the past few months. He took it as a hopeful sign.

He was pleased to receive a note from Bingley saying that he was not able to pay a call that day. He missed his friend, but he knew that he would want to ask when Bingley intended to take up residence at Netherfield. That would inevitably bring up questions of why, and then would lead to his meeting with Elizabeth. He was not ready to share her with anyone else just yet.

ELIZABETH SPENT Tuesday anticipating Wednesday. Her uncle told the ladies of his conversation with the Colonel, and Mrs. Gardiner and Elizabeth spent a great deal of time dissecting the conversation and behaviour of Mr. Darcy. Unknown to Elizabeth, her aunt had also set about writing a few discreet letters to friends in Derbyshire, casually asking about Mr. Darcy and his estate. She knew that her friends would hardly be well-acquainted with him, but no doubt, the reputation of the man would be known throughout the area simply because Pemberley was the source of income to so many.

Elizabeth asked her aunt if she would allow them to walk in the park, as Mr. Darcy suggested. She was a little hesitant to grant her permission, but she said that as long as they kept to the very public pathways, and did not stay out too long, she would let them go alone. It was not as if they were engaged, and therefore expected to flaunt the rules of propriety. She fondly remembered her days of courtship with Mr. Gardiner, and realized how much sooner they would have come to an understanding if they had simply been allowed some uninterrupted time on their own.

ELIZABETH DRESSED carefully Wednesday morning, wearing a simple burgundy-coloured muslin gown, decorated with a scattering of embroidered flowers around the hem, and an ivory ribbon around the waist. The colours accentuated the pink of her cheeks and brought out the highlights of red in her dark hair. She perched herself in the window seat of the front room, pretending to read, while scanning the street for any sign of her visitor.

Darcy spent the morning in such attention to his attire that even his valet, who was used to his master's fastidious nature, was quite bemused. When Darcy finally approved of his appearance, it was with great relief that Rogers saw the back of him through the dressing room door.

A magnificent coach arrived at the house on Gracechurch Street, precisely on time. Inside, Darcy donned the gloves that he had torn off on the trip there. His hands were sweating, and he found great relief in torturing his gloves into a twisted mass. His nervousness was taking him over, and he had almost convinced himself that he was being the utmost fool to be paying a call on this practically unknown young woman, when he found himself standing at the bottom of the front steps. The sight of her smiling face in the window instantly calmed him, and with a sense of newfound confidence, he knocked on the door.

"Good morning Mr. Darcy, welcome to our home, I hope that the day finds you well?" Mrs. Gardiner thought it was best that she begin the conversation, since the young man looked so nervous, he might just run back out the door as much as sit down.

Darcy put to use his years of good breeding, and performed the perfect bow, remembered to breathe, and responded, "Good morning Mrs. Gardiner, Miss Bennet. Indeed, I am quite well, and most pleased to be spending the day in your company."

"It is we who are honoured by your visit, sir. I must say that I have been quite looking forward to it." Elizabeth gave him an impish grin that filled him with delight. "You see, my aunt and I were talking about your estate's location in Derbyshire, and thought that you might be familiar with the Lake District, since it is not too far from my aunt's former home in Lambton." Elizabeth had taken note during their first conversation how Darcy had relaxed when the topic of Derbyshire had been raised, and she was trying to get him to that level of ease at the beginning of his visit.

He gave Elizabeth a small smile, "Yes I am familiar with that area, having visited many times over the years. Is there any place in particular that raises your interest?"

Elizabeth continued her smile, "My aunt and uncle have been kind enough to invite me to accompany them this summer when they tour the area. We will, I believe, be passing through Lambton to visit her old friends. I was wondering if there are any sights that should not be missed along the way."

"In all honesty, Miss Bennet, I may be the worst person to ask. I think all of the North Country to be breathtaking and am quite biased in my opinions. If you enjoy viewing large estates, there are several to take in, and if you prefer scenic vistas, there are simply too many to name."

"So Mr. Darcy, you are forcing me to visit book shops to look for my guides to the area?" She accused him.

Laughing, Mrs. Gardiner turned to Darcy, "Oh please, Mr. Darcy, give her some advice, if Lizzy is forced to visit bookshops, I am quite sure that I will never see her again during her visit. Once she enters, it takes a great deal of persuasion to entice her back out again!"

"Short of threats, you mean." Elizabeth said with satisfaction. Her laughing eyes met Darcy's delighted ones.

"So you are a great reader, Miss Bennet?"

"Indeed, I am very fond of books. My father gave me free access to his library, and I have been allowed to read anything and everything, from literature to poetry to histories, and of course the current news. I am also known to read agricultural reports to tell my father of the latest advances in farm management. Not that he implements them though," she added ruefully.

Impressed, and adding this information to the catalogue of Elizabeth that he was keeping, he asked, "And who are your favourite authors?"

"I enjoy Shakespeare, of course, his plays and sonnets, and Blake and Donne, for poetry. I also occasionally indulge myself in a novel by Mrs. Radcliffe when I am feeling particularly melancholy."

They all laughed at that. "Well Miss Bennet, I wholeheartedly support your father's desire to further your reading skills. I encourage my sister in the endeavour, and she is quite well-read for being so young. We often choose a book and debate it together. As she grows older, her arguments are improving."

"I do something similar with my father, Mr. Darcy, and I can say that I take great enjoyment in besting him more and more often!"

"Perhaps we will have to have a debate some time, Miss Bennet. I think that my library will provide a wealth of subjects for us to attempt." Darcy was becoming more fascinated with Elizabeth at every moment, and she was thrilled to see a man who was not intimidated by an educated woman. They were beginning to learn about each other.

"Mr. Darcy, perhaps we could continue our discussion on our walk. My aunt has said that she must stay inside with the children, and has been kind enough to let us go on our own."

Turning to Mrs. Gardiner, Darcy nodded to her, "Thank you for your generosity Mrs. Gardiner, I assure you, your niece will be quite safe with me."

She smiled, "Of that I have no doubt, sir, and I know that Lizzy can take care of herself."

Elizabeth and Darcy stepped outside of the house and with a glance up at his face; she smiled and led the way across the street to the park. Darcy felt that it was too soon to offer her his arm, but that did not stop him from wishing that he could.

"I must say, Miss Bennet, I am a little surprised that your aunt has not insisted on accompanying us."

Elizabeth eyed him, "Are you disappointed, sir? Do you prefer her company to mine, or do you simply prefer to be surrounded by ladies as you walk?"

Darcy's eyes grew wide with surprise, "Neither of those answers is correct, I am quite satisfied with your sole company, and was happy with the kindness of your aunt to allow it."

"Yes, my aunt is very kind."

"I see that what I heard of you from your uncle has proven to be true."

Elizabeth looked at him warily, "I am almost afraid to ask, but being of a curious nature, I cannot let well enough alone. Please enlighten me of my uncle's words, since I am sure it will not be a good reflection of my character."

"Do you doubt your uncle's ability to praise you?"

"No, I doubt his ability to colour the truth. Now, what did he say?" She looked at him with a smile, but he could see the trace of anxiety in her eyes and teased her.

"He merely said that you had a sharp wit, and have been known to scare men away with it."

"Do you feel frightened, Mr. Darcy?"

"I am not afraid of you, Miss Bennet." He smiled down into her sparkling eyes, and saw the relief within.

"Well I am pleased to hear that you do not frighten easily, Mr. Darcy. I do not either, in fact I have a reputation for being able to care for myself with unworthy young men who try to press their unwanted attentions upon me. Perhaps that was why my aunt was so easily persuaded to allow us to walk alone today."

"Did you do the persuading, Miss Bennet?"

She tilted her head and raising a brow, grinned, "I did!"

Darcy gave her a brilliant smile and laughed, once again flooring her with how handsome he could be. "I am duly impressed with your powers of persuasion. Now, since your reputation in self-defence has not as yet reached me, could you share your story, even if it will only help me to learn how to avoid your wrath?"

"Somehow Mr. Darcy, you do not strike me as a rake, but if you would like to be entertained, I will oblige." Darcy noticed that she was staring off into the distance, and that the mirth had left her face. She was lost in the memory.

Wickham entered Longbourn with a hungry look in his eye. He had been laying the foundation of his seduction for weeks, slowly ingratiating himself with the Bennet ladies. He had centred his attention on two of them. Lydia was exactly what he usually looked for, young, stupid, easily flattered, and buxom. She would be an easy mark, and he knew that he could compromise her at the time of his choosing. But Wickham, although a rake of the highest order, was not unintelligent. After all, he had benefited by the education paid for by George Darcy, and he loved the challenge presented by Elizabeth Bennet.

"Miss Elizabeth, might I tempt you to join me in a turn about the garden?"

"Certainly, Mr. Wickham, I am happy to take advantage of this lovely weather while it lasts."

Elizabeth found Wickham's company pleasant. He was certainly handsome, and his manners were everything that was charming, but something about him just did not strike her as true.

"Have you ever been to Derbyshire, Miss Elizabeth?"

"No, I have not, although I know people who have been there, and I understand that it is very beautiful area, why do you ask?"

"Oh, well that is where I am from. I grew up on the estate of Pemberley, owned by the Darcy family."

"I have never heard of either the estate or the family, were your family tenants?" Elizabeth was curious, Wickham had all the manners of a gentleman, and seemed to have been educated well, but how is this possible if he were a tenant's son on a great estate?

"My late father was steward for the late Mr. Darcy. He had a son and heir, but he did not have any affection for him, and looked at me as his own. He gave me the same education as his son, and provided for me in his will."

"You are most fortunate; however, I wonder why if you were so cared for, how do you find yourself in the militia?"

"Ah, well, it is a sad tale, and I should not want to burden you with it." Wickham glanced over at her thinking that his story was working, and that by playing on the lady's kind heart, he was slowly reeling her in. He had no doubt that she would soon be offering to comfort him.

Elizabeth, however, was nobody's fool, and she was not about to take the word of a man whose acquaintance she had barely made. Mr. Wickham's story may have a grain of truth to it, but she was feeling an uncomfortable sensation that this man was attempting to play on her sympathies for nefarious reasons. She decided to let him continue to weave his tale and draw her conclusions from there.

"Well, Mr. Wickham, I appreciate your care for me, but perhaps we should talk of more pleasant matters."

Feeling that he was losing ground, Wickham quickly responded, "Oh no, I think that it would be a great help to me to speak of it, sometimes sharing a memory with a good friend relieves the pain. I have come to regard you as a particularly close friend, Miss Elizabeth."

"Have you, Mr. Wickham?" Elizabeth *thought; "*Now I KNOW that he should not be trusted." *She spoke. "I am gratified that you think that well of me, please continue."*

"Miss Bennet?" Elizabeth startled and was met with the concerned expression of her companion. "Are you well? You seemed to have left me for a moment."

"Forgive me Mr. Darcy, I was lost in an unpleasant memory and I suddenly realized that it has a connection to you."

"To me?" Darcy frowned. "Now I am the one with the curiosity that must be satisfied. Please tell me how anything that has to do with me could have ever touched you?"

"Do you know a man named George Wickham, Mr. Darcy?" Elizabeth was stunned by what she saw. All manner of emotions played across his face. Anger, disgust, and mostly a deep look of anguish were displayed. Disregarding propriety, Darcy took Elizabeth's gloved hands in his.

Searching her face he whispered, "Did he hurt you?" The care for her well-being in Darcy's face filled her with a feeling of comfort and safety that she had never experienced before. His deep brown eyes, so full of concern and fear were boring into her, pleading with her to tell him what had happened. It was overwhelming.

Darcy was trying his best to maintain his composure. *Wickham! Always Wickham! Will I never be rid of this man, and why must he always find the people that I care about? If he hurt Elizabeth . . .* It took every bit of strength he had not to pull her into his embrace at that moment, she looked so vulnerable, and he wanted to protect her.

Finally gathering herself together, she gave his hands a squeeze, and with a very soft voice reassured him. "No, Mr. Darcy, I was not hurt. I managed to get away in time."

"Thank God." The anguish was still in his eyes. "George Wickham has taken advantage of my family for years, and continues to torment us. He attempted to elope with a very close, very young relation of mine to gain control of her fortune, and she has not yet recovered from the experience even though it has been nearly eight months. Every day I am faced with the results of his behaviour when I look into her expressionless eyes. The girl that I was charged to protect has had to bear the burden of my mistakes." He stared down at their joined hands.

Now Elizabeth knew the reasons for Darcy's sadness at the concert, and she had no doubt that the girl who he referred to was, in fact, his own sister. Elizabeth, without regard for anything other than his comfort, reached up and gently caressed his face, drawing him back to her. He did not shrink away or even look surprised. The gesture was done in kindness, and shared understanding, and seemed perfectly natural between them.

He took her hand and gently kissed it. "Thank you, Miss Bennet. Perhaps we could sit down; it seems we have things to discuss." He led Elizabeth over to a bench, bathed in the warming rays of the sun.

Elizabeth told him of Wickham's appearance in Meryton and joining the militia regiment that was quartered there for the winter. She told him of his charming manners, and his interest in her family, and how he seemed to pay particular attention to her. She then told him of his tale of preference by old Mr. Darcy, and his subsequent degradation by Darcy.

She noted his look of disgust, and he murmured, "So he is still spinning that story."

She then told him that she had felt something was not quite right with the tale, and had an uncomfortable feeling that he was trying far too hard to get her in his good graces. She said that it was nothing easily definable, almost an instinctual response that he should not be trusted.

"And then," she continued, "he walked out with me one day in the garden, leading me away from my sisters and other visiting officers to a secluded area. He was quite firm in his grasp of my arm, and since I did not think that he would do anything too daring with all those people about, I did not feel afraid. He must have thought that I was putty in his hands, and," here she paused; her voice broke, and she looked off into the distance.

Darcy took hold of her hands again and gently squeezed. "Go on, please."

Still looking away from him, she spoke quickly, "He pushed me against a tree, and kissed me. He pushed his body against mine, and started rubbing his hands along me. He kept his mouth on mine so that I could not call out for help, and he was so big and strong that I could not push him away." Her voice was a whisper, quavering, and tears ran down her face.

Darcy could stand it no longer. He dropped her hands and pulled her into his embrace, holding her tightly to him. He whispered fiercely into her hair, "It is well, Elizabeth, it is over. I am here. I will let no harm come to you."

She looked up into his compassionate eyes. She felt so safe, like she had found her home in his embrace, and believed him. He watched her face, willing her to trust him, and saw the same dawning of homecoming in her eyes that he was feeling with her in his arms. She was the woman he had been waiting for. It took every ounce of restraint he possessed not to kiss her at that moment.

They drew apart, but remained holding hands, now aware of the new unspoken understanding between them. Then Elizabeth looked down and up into Darcy's face. She wore an expression of defiance and pride, and her entire body straightened.

"I took care of him. I made sure that he would never do that again."

Fascinated by her change in attitude, Darcy asked, "What did you do?"

Elizabeth broke into a gleeful, almost evil grin, "I forcefully took my knee to his most sensitive area!"

Darcy looked at her in disbelief and awe, and dawning understanding. "Do you mean that you kneed him in his . . ." he glanced down at his lap, embarrassed.

"Yes!" Elizabeth laughed in triumph. "He doubled over on the ground, clutching himself and groaning. I ran away as fast as I could and returned to the house. I saw him limping out from the garden about twenty minutes later. He could barely mount his horse! The other officers kept asking what had happened, and I heard him say that he had a bad leg cramp."

"Well, having experienced that particular painful condition, although it was from sitting on a fence railing and not at the hands of a lady, I know exactly what he was feeling, and a leg cramp would be pleasant in comparison." Darcy was smiling so broadly at the downfall of his most bitter enemy that his cheeks hurt.

"And how particularly humiliating to have such a blow be delivered by you! I am extraordinarily proud and envious of you, Miss Bennet!"

"Thank you, sir. I am rather proud of myself! I did, of course tell my father what happened, and he forbade my sisters from ever speaking to him again, although he did not tell them why. He also paid a call to the militia's colonel, and told him privately of the incident. Mr. Wickham was transferred to another regiment within the week."

"Oh Miss Bennet, I cannot tell you how wonderful this story has made me feel. With your permission, may I tell it to my sister?"

"Of course, Mr. Darcy, I am always happy to have my praises sung!" Elizabeth's triumph calmed, and she asked, "Am I correct in concluding that your sister is the member of your family who Mr. Wickham tried to seduce?" Darcy quickly became sombre, and nodded his head. "She has not recovered after all of these months?"

"No, she blames herself, and she has decided that she has disappointed me. I cannot seem to convince her otherwise, although, I do think that I made a small improvement in her yesterday morning." He looked up at her shyly.

Elizabeth gave him a smile, "What did you do?"

"I told her that it is her own goodness and how she treats others that matters, and not her status or money or name. Her value is in herself. She is so worried that she has disappointed me and dishonoured our name. I admit that I was inspired by the unsolicited kindness of a young lady in a theatre, who tried very hard to lift the spirits of a very sad man." He continued to look at her, but now with a small, hopeful smile on his face.

"That young lady would be very happy to know that she was so able to help that man, and I imagine she would like to have the opportunity to do so again in the future." Elizabeth gave him a reassuring smile, her eyes dancing, thrilled with how quickly he had come to regard her as someone special.

"I can think of no greater reward than to spend time with that lady, and benefit from her attentions." Darcy's heart was thumping hard in his chest. He had never been so bold, had never had reason to speak to any woman like this before. *This is happening so fast!*

The two sat smiling at each other, and finally, Elizabeth indicated that they should probably return to her aunt's house, as even her kindness had a limit, and they had been in the park for some time. Darcy instantly offered his arm to Elizabeth, which she happily took. They both let out a sigh of contentment, and looking at each other, surprised, they laughed.

"This has been a most wonderful visit, Miss Bennet. I was so nervous to come here, and now, I think that this has been the happiest day that I have spent in a very, very long time." He smiled down at her lovely face. "When may we repeat this? May I visit tomorrow?"

"Yes, please! I have no engagements tomorrow, and would very much enjoy your company again. Will the same time as today suit?"

"Yes, that will be fine. I am expecting a caller early, but I will happily send him on his way in good time to come to you. As a matter of fact, I will look forward to telling him about you. He is your absent neighbour, Mr. Bingley."

"Hmmm. If you could, ask him when he intends to come to Netherfield, and I will inform my mother. She would love to be the first in the neighbourhood with fresh gossip!"

"Oh no, Miss Bennet, I will protect my friend from matchmaking mamas!"

"Well, maybe I will just have to mention his presence here, and ask Mama to send her daughters to London! Mama will not be stopped!" Elizabeth raised her brow to him and grinned.

Darcy let out a long sigh, "What am I going to do with you Miss Bennet?"

"I am sure that you could think of something, Mr. Darcy."

Chapter 4

*D*arcy stood in his library, scanning the shelves. With a cry of triumph, he found what he was searching for. Carefully opening the cover of the large book, he gently lifted the first page and looked at the beautiful illustration.

"What have you there?" He looked up to see Richard strolling into the room.

"It is a book of landscapes depicting the Lake District. The area came up in conversation today, and I remembered that I had this here."

"In conversation?" Richard smirked, "Who were you speaking with?"

"I was in pleasant company."

"I can well imagine, Darcy." Richard regarded his cousin carefully. Darcy had a slight smile on his face, his eyes were warm, and his posture, usually so stiff, was relaxed. "Will you tell me about your call to Miss Bennet?"

Seeing Richard's concerned expression, he surprised him with a growing smile. "It was wonderful. I was so nervous on my way there, but when I arrived, she was sitting in the window watching for me. I caught her gaze, and I felt like I had come home."

Richard looked at him with awe. "Do you hear yourself? I was joking with you when I spoke about proposing, Darcy."

"I am aware of that, Richard, and no, I have not proposed. But, I have no doubt in my mind that I have found the woman I will someday beg to be my wife." Darcy spoke with conviction, and Richard had no doubt that he spoke the absolute truth.

He sighed and dropped into a chair. "Tell me about your visit."

"Just let me say that she showed herself to be a woman of magnificent kindness, and fortitude." Richard waved his hand, showing that he wanted more. Darcy continued, "If you join Georgie and me for dinner, you will hear a story. I will not mention the woman's name to her, but you will know that it is Miss Bennet."

"That is all you will say?"

"Believe me, when you hear the story, it will be enough."

"Hmmph." Richard looked sceptical, but did not press him for more.

THE THREE COUSINS sat down at dinner, and Darcy, after making inquiries after Georgiana's day, was happy that she asked about the call he had paid that morning. "It was very pleasant. In fact, I heard a fascinating story involving a young lady and George Wickham."

Georgiana gasped, and Richard stared at him in disbelief. Darcy disregarded them both and continued. "It seems that Wickham joined a militia regiment last autumn, and sought to gain favour with the ladies of the neighbourhood. He selected one young lady as a particular favourite and endeavoured to curry her favour by telling her his tale of misfortune inflicted on him by myself." Richard's eyes narrowed and Georgiana hung her head, remembering Wickham's persuasive manner. "The young lady, who was twenty years old, and more experienced with men," here he met his sister's eyes, "felt that although his manner was everything charming, resolved to remain wary of him. This served her well when Wickham pulled her to a secluded area of the garden, and attempted to seduce her." Darcy paused. Richard's fists were clenched, his face red with fury.

Georgiana broke the silence and whispered, "Did he ruin her, Brother?"

"No, he decidedly did not ruin her. She did not give him the chance." They both looked at him as he broke into an enormous smile. "She could not move her arms or cry for help, but she could, however, use her knee, as she said, to strike him in his most sensitive area."

"NO!" Richard cried with delight.

"YES!" Darcy crowed. "He was doubled over with pain and did not move for twenty minutes. When he finally reappeared, he could not mount, and blamed a leg cramp!" The men howled with laughter.

Georgiana, finally realizing what exactly had befallen Wickham allowed a slow smile to spread across her face. "What became of him?"

"Her father informed his colonel, and Wickham was sent packing to another regiment. I have no doubt that his new colonel was fully informed of his behaviour, and I am sure that his other vices were quickly exposed upon his departure."

Richard and Darcy were positively gleeful. Richard said thoughtfully, "I think that I just might have to write to his former colonel and see what became of old George."

Darcy studied his sister, and was gratified to see brightness in her demeanour that had not been present in a very long time. She said softly, "That young lady was very brave."

Darcy regarded her seriously. "Yes she was. She had the advantage of experience to guide her, and a rather fierce streak of independence to help her."

"Maybe if I had been older, I would have seen through him, too."

Taking her hand, he gave it a squeeze. "Yes Georgie, I am glad you see that now."

She jumped up from her chair and fell into his embrace, sobbing. He looked at Richard. They both had tears in their eyes. Maybe this was the breakthrough that she needed. He whispered to her, "It was not your fault, Georgie. It was all him. Please understand this." He hugged her, and her sobs quieted, "Would you like to meet her?"

Georgiana pulled away from her brother and regarded him with a mixture of wonder and anticipation. "Do you know her?"

"Yes, I do. I will call on her tomorrow and invite her to come for tea on Friday. Would you like that? I know that she would be very happy to meet you."

"Oh yes, please invite her!" Georgiana was ecstatic. "What is her name?"

Delighted, Darcy gave her a huge smile and spoke proudly, "Miss Elizabeth Bennet. I cannot wait to introduce her to you." Richard looked on with amazement. In a matter of days the influence of one woman had turned the lives of his cousins around.

THAT NIGHT when Darcy finally fell back into his bed, he smiled at the canopy, marvelling over the events of the day. Georgiana had left her brother and cousin immediately after dinner, wishing to retire to her rooms and think about the bravery of Elizabeth Bennet, and reevaluate her own behaviour when she responded to the advances of George Wickham. Richard and Darcy had spent several hours on the same subjects, both hopeful that meeting Elizabeth would further help in Georgiana's recovery. Richard could not help but tease Darcy about him falling instantly in love, but on a very serious note, performed what he felt was a family duty to remind him of her poor connections, lack of dowry, and the likelihood of not being accepted by their relatives, let alone the first circles of society.

As much as Darcy disliked hearing his cousin's words, he could not discount them. He knew very well that he would receive the approbation of family, particularly Aunt Catherine, and society if he continued to court Elizabeth. Then he laughed out loud at the absurdity of his thoughts. "*If* I continue to court her?!" For a man who had resisted every approach by every woman since the age of seventeen, the simple fact that he was finally courting *any* woman was a wonder unto itself. The thought of even considering rejecting following his desires after instantly succumbing to the beautiful, enticing, fascinating Elizabeth Bennet was absolutely inconceivable to him. A year ago he might have been tempted to reject her simply based on her unworthiness of station, now, he saw her with the clearer eyes of a man who had grown weary of suffering alone burdened with responsibilities, tired of the conceit and pretence of society, and who was able to recognize the happiness that loving her would bring. She had already proven that in the smiles that he and his sister now wore.

He thought over their walk in the park that day, and was suddenly struck with the realization that he had compromised her. Perhaps, it was not so much when they held hands, but without question, their embrace had been absolutely against the rules of propriety. If they had been in a more fashionable part of town, where he would have been recognized, no doubt the news would have been published in the gossip columns the next day. But, because they were in a small park in Cheapside, where both he, and since she was a visitor, perhaps even Elizabeth were unknown, their indiscretion had happened unnoticed. Thinking about it some more, he realized that he would not give up the feeling of Elizabeth in his arms for anything. The moment that he pulled her to him, he knew that she belonged there, and he felt her acceptance of it, as well.

She was the first woman, other than Georgiana who hardly counted, that he had embraced in such a way. The most he had done with any woman of his acquaintance was perhaps to bestow a kiss upon a gloved hand. Unlike the typical behaviour of men of his times, he did not visit brothels or keep a mistress. His father took him to a gentleman's brothel when he was seventeen to be initiated thoroughly, and upon leaving delivered a very stern and adamant lecture that he was never to repeat the behaviour that he had enjoyed there until he was married. His father impressed upon him most emphatically that he wanted no chance that a child with the Darcy blood would be conceived outside of marriage, and furthered his point by telling his son what would likely become of a child born of a woman who sold herself. The mere image of a child of his, even illegitimate, being left to grow up in the slums of London, and if to survive, grow to toil in a workhouse, or if a girl, become a prostitute herself, was enough to keep Darcy from participating in such activities, much to the amusement of his friends, and not with a little personal suffering. He also rejected all of the ladies of society, married or single who offered themselves to him, which may in fact have made him all the more hunted. He kept his private life extremely private.

THOMAS BENNET had received no such admonition from his father, and during his university days made full use of the brothels located near the school, and on occasional visits to London. He felt no remorse for it. The behaviour was generally expected of young men, and thoughts of consequences, other than the passing consideration of disease, really never crossed his mind. Perhaps once he had a thought about it, when he visited his friend John Markham's home in Sussex on holiday and was subtly directed with a wink to the location of the chambermaids' bed closets. He learned upon visiting again six months later that the maid in question had been dismissed, and it briefly occurred to him that unintended births did happen, but in his typical fashion, he did not let it bother him for long.

Early Friday morning found Mr. Bennet where he could be located at just about any time of the day, any day of the week, in the library of Longbourn. He had received the day's post, and knew that Jane had received a letter from Lizzy. He sat back at his desk, waiting for the knock on the door that would tell him of Jane's arrival to share with him Lizzy's news.

He was a man of fifty years, an Oxford educated gentleman, owner of the respectably-sized, but poorly-producing estate. The fact that the estate was poorly producing due to his negligence was not lost on the intelligent man. However, he found that since he had made the rather foolish and impulsive decision to offer marriage to a beautiful but empty-headed fifteen-year-old Fanny Gardiner, a girl twelve years his junior and below him in station, he had increasingly spent more of his time retreating from the realities of the world and instead hid amongst his books. He loved his five girls, especially his second child, Lizzy, but after her birth, and not producing a son and heir, he had essentially lost patience with anything and everyone that did not challenge his sharp wit. Since the estate suffered under the rules of entailment, and would eventually go to a distant cousin, he felt no particular motivation to expend his energy and funds on a property that none of his family would ever inherit. As a result, the estate, the marriage, and the children languished out of a lack of attention and complacency. Only the two eldest daughters, Elizabeth and Jane, had managed to make the most of their gentlewoman's heritage and sought to improve themselves, to be recognized by some accounts as the "brightest jewels of all Hertfordshire."

JANE EAGERLY OPENED Elizabeth's letter. She had begun regretting her decision to stay at Longbourn instead of joining her sister on the trip to London. She read with astonishment the news that Elizabeth was apparently being courted by a handsome wealthy man, who somehow had connections to Mr. Wickham, not pleasant connections she gratefully noted, and was, although shy, everything kind and amiable. She felt the desire to go and join her sister and was relieved to read that Elizabeth felt the same way, and begged Jane to seek her father's permission to come to London. She said that talking things over with Aunt Gardiner was everything wonderful, but it was not the same as discussing things with Jane. Everything seemed to be happening so quickly, she felt that she needed Jane's calm influence to help her truly sort out her emotions.

Elizabeth had received a note from Mr. Darcy that evening, inviting their aunt and her for tea with his sister on Friday afternoon, and reconfirming that he would again pay a call to her the next day, Thursday. Jane could almost feel the nervous anticipation of her sister through the letter, and she determined that she had to speak to her father immediately and gain his permission to go to her.

Jane knocked on the library door, and upon hearing her father's call, she entered. Mr. Bennet sat back in his chair and smiled. "Well my dear Jane, I understand that you received a letter from Lizzy, what mischief has she found in London?"

"Oh Papa, you know Lizzy, she has always been such a well-behaved girl, she could never get into mischief," Jane teased, smiling at her father who knew better.

Mr. Bennet laughed, "Quite so." Then noticing Jane hesitating, he asked with concern, "Is she well?"

"Yes, she is well in fact; I have never received a letter so full of joy from her before." Jane looked up at her father. He was now sitting up, his elbows resting on the desk, hands steepled together, and regarding her with great interest.

"Joy? Please do not keep me in suspense, child. Tell me of your sister."

"It seems that Lizzy has made the acquaintance of a gentleman, a Mr. Fitzwilliam Darcy, and he has asked Uncle Gardiner for permission to call on her. They met at a concert on Monday, and she was introduced to him and his cousin, Colonel Fitzwilliam. Mr. Darcy visited on Wednesday morning, and they took a walk in the park in Gracechurch Street. While they talked, Lizzy realized that Mr. Darcy was the man that Mr. Wickham accused of denying his inheritance. Mr. Darcy told her of how Mr. Wickham had imposed himself upon his own family, and even told her of another young girl that he had attempted to hurt. Mr. Darcy was to come and visit again Thursday morning, and had sent a note over inviting Lizzy and Aunt Gardiner to his home for tea today, so that they could be introduced to his sister. She said that his parents are passed, and that he is the master of his estate, Pemberley in Derbyshire."

His face carried an expression of concern, and she thought; trepidation. "And, she seems to be full of joy?"

"Yes, Papa, I truly think that she is very happy with this young man, and is hoping for a future with him. She asks that I come to London, to lend her my support and opinion. May I go, Papa? I think that she needs me."

Mr. Bennet sighed. He knew that this day would come, and he would have to start to accustom himself with the loss of his daughters' hearts to other men. It did not make him in any way happy, but it was inevitable. He expected his daughters to leave home, but he wished to keep Lizzy with him, always. To know that a man of Mr. Darcy's wealth would be interested in his Lizzy was gratifying; he had after all educated her almost as he would a son. He would not, however, let her continue with this relationship without meeting the man himself, and assure himself of his worthiness, and he hoped, would find him lacking enough to end it altogether. He looked up at his other dearest daughter, and noting her anxiety, smiled. "Of course you must go to town, and as a matter of fact, I will accompany you. I have some business to take care of, and I can deliver you to your aunt and uncle safely, and meet this young man. I will send an express telling my sister and brother of our plans, and we will depart tomorrow morning. Does that satisfy you, my dear?"

"Oh yes, Papa! Thank you! I will go and tell Mama, and start packing!" Jane was relieved, not only was she escaping Longbourn, but she was going to join her best friend.

Mr. Bennet quickly prepared the letter and called for a servant to send it on its way. He put his head back on the chair and closed his eyes, and thought, "Well, Mr. Darcy, let us see of what you are made."

DARCY FINISHED his breakfast Thursday morning and was ensconced in his study when Mr. Bingley was announced. The two friends greeted each other and settled themselves comfortably to catch up on each other's news. They had not spent any time together since before Christmas.

"Well Bingley, how was Scarborough?"

"Oh, you know the same as usual, distant relations, asking annoying questions." He grinned, "When will you marry? When will you buy an estate? Why are you so thin? When is Caroline going to marry Darcy?" Darcy looked up and glared, and Bingley laughed, "It became a bit wearing."

"If that was your entertainment, I am surprised you stayed away so long. By the way, did you answer all their important questions?"

"You know that I did not, simply because I have no answers."

Darcy looked at his friend, then down at his desk, casually drawing a circle with his finger on the polished wood. "When do you intend to take up residence at Netherfield? That might quiet down your relatives' concerns."

Bingley raised his brows. "Ah, you do remember that I leased an estate. By your asking, may I hope that you are at last ready to accompany me there?"

"Perhaps, not right away, I have some important work here in town, and of course, I am due to visit Aunt Catherine for Easter. I would, I think be able to come to Netherfield in say, mid-April for a time, before I would have to return to Pemberley for the spring planting."

"Excellent!" Bingley said excitedly. "I was thinking that I would do well to move in at the end of March. I could have the house opened and ready for guests by the time that you arrived." He looked at his friend, "Of course, you know, Caroline would be there as well."

Darcy sighed. "Forgive me Bingley, but that is not going to encourage me to visit."

"Ha!" Charles knew quite well that his sister's single-minded pursuit of his friend was most unwelcome, and no matter how many times he had told her that, she absolutely refused to believe that she would not win him in the end. "Well, perhaps I can convince her to stay in town for the Season a bit longer. It should be in full swing by that time. But, if her choice is the frivolity of London versus pursuing you, it will be a hard call!" Bingley laughed at the grimace on Darcy's face. Realizing that he had pushed his friend far enough, he changed the subject. "It was a surprise to see you at the theatre the other night, did you ever catch up with you quarry?"

Bingley's mouth almost dropped open with astonishment when he saw a slow warm smile spread over Darcy's face. He had known him for nearly seven years, and such expressions of happiness on his friend's countenance were rare, and always worthy of note.

Darcy looked up and spoke softly, "Yes, Bingley, I caught up with my quarry."

"And??"

"And what?"

"Come on Darcy, you never smile like that."

His assertion just made Darcy's smile broaden. "You are quite right, I do not, but I have a feeling that it is an expression that you will just have to accustom yourself to seeing." He met Bingley's eye, "And I have nothing more to add at this time."

"You cannot just leave me hanging like this!" Bingley was almost whining.

"I can, and I shall. Now, I am very sorry, but I have an appointment at eleven o'clock, and I must prepare to leave. Perhaps you could join us for dinner on Sunday? I am sure that Georgiana will be happy to see you."

Looking at him suspiciously, he tried once again, "You will not even give me a hint?" Darcy's smile barely lifted the corners of his mouth, but his eyes twinkled merrily. Shaking his head, he sighed. "Yes, I would be very pleased to join you for dinner on Sunday. Perhaps your sister will be able to shed some light on this mysterious happiness you are displaying." Darcy just looked at him, his expression staying the same. "Shall I bring my sisters and brother along?"

The smile instantly disappeared, "No. No offense Bingley, but I would very much like to have a very select company at this dinner."

Now it was Bingley's turn to grin. "Oh ho! Well this could be quite an interesting evening, indeed! Very well then, the secret is safe with me. I am looking forward to it."

THURSDAY MORNING Elizabeth again sat in the window and watched for Mr. Darcy's carriage. Her thoughts drifted back to last autumn, and the reality of her life as she had come to finally understand it. She realized that she had come to more frequently rely on taking long solitary walks through the countryside, both for exercise, and escape. She alone had inherited her father's intelligence and curiosity for the written word. They spent many long hours discussing and debating books and newspaper articles. Elizabeth devoured everything that she could get her hands on. This made her a brilliant conversationalist, quite regularly besting her father in her arguments, but at the same time, it was making her painfully aware of how limited and hopeless her life would be. She could not delude herself into thinking that she would ever find a man in the small society that was Hertfordshire who could match or exceed her in knowledge, wit, and interest in the world. Where her personal qualities were assets, lack of dowry and connections had doomed her to a poor selection of suitors. It was unlikely that she would ever receive a decent offer of marriage, let alone the one that she and her sister Jane craved, from a man she could respect, esteem and love for himself, and not for the value of his pocketbook. She knew that it was a rare marriage indeed that was based on love, and she had a daily example before her on the risk of utter failure that was a marriage of indifference. She would prefer a life alone rather than settle for that. She was feeling increasingly trapped, and lonely.

She remembered attending the autumn assembly in Meryton. Presented with the same faces, and general lack of men and good conversation, Elizabeth took the event in stride and simply enjoyed the companionship of her friends and neighbours, even if they did not fill her dance card. There was just nobody special, new, or different present, a disappointment again. She realized that she was ready for a new life, and hoped that when the opportunity presented itself, she would be able to recognize it.

The sound of an approaching carriage brought Elizabeth's thoughts back to the present. Seeing it come to a halt in front of the house, she felt her breath catch when Darcy's tall figure emerged. Placing his hat on his head, she watched him carefully adjust a large book and his walking stick in his grasp. When he looked up to her window, she saw the expectation in his face and delight that suffused his countenance when their eyes met. He hastened up the steps. Elizabeth quickly stood, smoothing her skirts and hair, finally desisting when she hear her aunt's amused laugh.

Darcy entered and bowed, "Good Morning Mrs. Gardiner, Miss Bennet, I hope that you and your family are well?"

"Yes they are, thank you Mr. Darcy," smiled Mrs. Gardiner after the ladies rose from their curtsies. "Would you please take a seat?"

After taking his place on the sofa next to Elizabeth, he carefully set down the book. Elizabeth's dancing eyes met his hopeful ones. "May I ask after Miss Darcy?"

"I am very happy to tell you that after speaking to her of the bravery of an astonishing young woman, her spirits are so roused that I hardly recognize her."

Surprised and gratified, she looked at him. His expression had become serious. "Truly, Mr. Darcy? I am so very pleased to hear this news."

"I cannot begin to tell you how pleased I am to bring it to you." Then looking first to Mrs. Gardiner, he added, "I am looking forward to introducing you both to her tomorrow afternoon. Shall I send my carriage to pick you up at three o'clock?

"That would be very kind of you, sir."

"It is my pleasure, Mrs. Gardiner." Glancing again at Elizabeth's gentle smile, he took a breath and added, "I would also like to take the opportunity now to invite you and Mr. Gardiner for Sunday dinner. My cousin Colonel Fitzwilliam will be there, as well as my good friend, Charles Bingley. You may remember that Mr. Bingley has taken the lease for Netherfield, and it will be an opportunity to meet your new neighbour. I am also hoping that my aunt Lady Elaine Fitzwilliam, and my uncle, Lord Henry Fitzwilliam, the Earl of Matlock will be able to attend as well.

Elizabeth blushed and looked down. She was well aware of the honour he was bestowing on her, and the value he must have for her if he wanted to introduce her to his relatives. Mrs. Gardiner observed her niece; and realizing she was overcome with emotion and did not dislike the idea, accepted on their behalf and thanked Darcy.

When Elizabeth had gathered her wits, she met Darcy's anxious eyes, and immediately smiled to reassure him. She felt her heart jump when he smiled, seeing how a simple gesture from her so quickly made him happy.

Her smile growing, she teased, "Mr. Darcy, should we be worried that you were concerned about being bored during your visit, or do you always bring reading material on calls?"

Darcy laughed, "No Miss Bennet, I assure you, I had no fear of discontent in your company. I was thinking of our conversation last night, and remembered I had this book in my library." He moved slightly closer, "This was a gift to my mother from my father on the occasion of their first anniversary." Opening the cover carefully, and paging past the inscription from his father, he revealed the first illustration. Elizabeth's gasp of delight sent a shiver up his spine

"Oh how beautiful! Is this the Lake District?" She was beaming.

"Yes, my parents spent their honeymoon there in a cottage we own." Stealing a glance into her eyes, he continued, "It is a Darcy tradition to bring a new bride to this magical place to begin their new lives together." He was thrilled to see Elizabeth's deep blush, the tingle in his spine spread over the rest of his body.

Mrs. Gardiner, closely watching the conversation, felt it was time to step in. "This seems to be a very special volume Mr. Darcy, and we are most grateful that you would wish to share it with us."

Returning from the joyful place his thoughts had taken him, he looked to Mrs. Gardiner. "You are welcome to keep it as long as you like. I am sure that it will be safe in your care."

"That is very generous of you, sir. It is obviously valuable for both monetary and sentimental reasons. My husband and children will enjoy it. I will make sure that only adults will turn the pages."

Elizabeth, again recovered from a blush, "Mr. Darcy, we seem to be blessed with lovely weather again today. Shall we begin our walk in the park and enjoy this sunshine?"

Darcy instantly agreed. Soon the couple had donned their outerwear and were standing on the sidewalk. Mrs. Gardiner, from her post at the window, saw that he did not hesitate to offer his arm to Elizabeth, and she likewise did not hesitate to accept it. Watching them thoughtfully, she decided that it would be a very good thing for Jane to come and visit, and help her sister sort out all of the different emotions she must be experiencing. Mrs. Gardiner knew many couples who married after only weeks of knowing each other, and some who only met on the wedding day due to prearranged marriages, so it was not too unusual to see a courtship proceed so quickly. She just wanted to be sure that both Elizabeth and Mr. Darcy were certain of their feelings. She looked forward to observing his family's reaction to her and her lower connections on Sunday. That would be a good indicator of how she would be received by society, and whether it would be with the family's support. This might also show how happy Mr. Darcy would be with her in the future. Surely his relationship with his family would have to affect the marriage on some level. She saw perhaps what Elizabeth was only beginning to realize, that Mr. Darcy was her match in every way.

Setting off briskly, Darcy was pleased to see that Elizabeth's claims of being a good walker were quite true. "Miss Bennet, if you keep up this pace, we will have completed the circuit of this park in mere moments; and I will be forced to return you to your aunt entirely too soon."

Elizabeth looked up with surprise, "Forgive me Mr. Darcy, I did not realize that I was tiring you."

"I do not believe that was what I was implying, Miss Bennet."

"No?"

"No."

"Then perhaps you should speak more clearly, Mr. Darcy." Elizabeth was flirting shamelessly, and Darcy knew it. Deciding to strike back, he spoke boldly, "If you insist, Miss Bennet, I shall. I find you everything that is lovely this morning, and I wish to prolong my time in your sole company as long as possible. If that means slowing down our walking pace to a crawl, then so be it." He gave her a devilish grin, noted that her face had turned beet red, and raising his eyebrows, asked, "There, was that plain enough?"

"I believe you have won your point, sir," she whispered.

Smiling to the sky at making *her* uncomfortable for a change, he asked. "Do you fence, Miss Bennet?"

"What a silly question to ask a woman!"

"I did not mean with foils but verbally. You seem to enjoy twisting words to great effect. Could this be the sharp wit that your uncle spoke of?"

"Oh no, I see that I am going to have to corner my uncle in his library tonight and find out exactly what he told your cousin about me. I seem to have a great deal of ground to make up. And speaking of that, I think that it is quite ungenerous of you to make verbal thrusts at me when I am at a great disadvantage. I have yet to have a conversation with your relatives to reveal all of your faults!"

"Ha!" His eyes shined with glee, "I must take advantage while I can Miss Bennet. Right now I intend to exploit your weakness until you learn mine!" They both laughed and smiled, "I take it that you learned the art of repartee from your father?"

"Yes, he enjoys a good verbal fight, and often will take a contrary point of view just to disconcert someone."

"Do all of your family members share this talent?"

"No, just me. I am the son he never had, I guess."

"Then he must miss you a great deal when you are away from home."

"Yes, I know he does, especially when he actually exerts himself to write to me and complain of my absence."

"He will not let go of you easily." Darcy looked at her very seriously.

"I think that he will always support me in whatever decision I make. He has proven this already." She spoke softly, looking away.

"May I ask what happened?"

"He supported my decision to reject what would appear to be a very good offer of marriage, one that would have benefited our entire family, simply because I did not value the gentleman." She saw Darcy's fixed attention, "I have vowed to only marry a man who I could hold in esteem, who respects me, and who I love."

Darcy's gaze did not waver. "I think that is the most admirable statement I have ever heard from a woman. I know that the choice of marrying for convenience can be hard when one's own survival is to be determined, but I can do nothing but respect and support your opinion on this most important decision of your life."

"Thank you, sir. I cannot express how that makes me feel."

They turned their gazes forward, both absorbing what had been said, and walked on silently. Finally breaking the companionable moment, Darcy asked something that had been concerning him. "How long do you intend to stay in London?"

"I will be here for three more weeks." His heart sank. "Then I will be travelling to Kent for a month. I am to visit the home of my cousin, Mr. Collins and my best friend Charlotte, whom he recently married. My cousin has the living at Hunsford, attached to the estate of Rosings Park. I will return to Longbourn after Easter."

Darcy could hardly believe his ears. He had begun to despair of losing her so soon, and realized he was going to gain an almost better situation. He smiled at her. "How fascinating, I am to spend Easter at Rosings Park as well. It is the home of my aunt, Lady Catherine de Bourgh."

Elizabeth's astonishment was complete. "You are her nephew?" She said incredulously.

"Indeed I am. My cousin Colonel Fitzwilliam and I spend every Easter at Rosings with my aunt and cousin, Anne. I will be arriving there; it seems, two weeks after you do. We will have a fortnight in each other's company; because I have no doubt that my aunt will invite the parsonage party to visit her frequently." Smiling sardonically he added, "My aunt so enjoys attention."

Still recovering from this shock, Elizabeth nodded, "I understand from my cousin that the parsonage is very close to Rosings, and that your aunt seems to have a rather forceful personality."

"Quite." Lifting a brow to her, he grinned, "I will greatly enjoy seeing you trade verbal barbs with her. Very few people are capable of taking her on, but I think that you just might win a challenge. In any case, I very much look forward to it." Then speaking softly, "I think that it will give us an opportunity to know each other much better if you like. I also look forward to showing you the many paths and trails of Rosings. It should be lovely with all of the spring flowers in bloom at Easter."

Elizabeth blushed again. "Mr. Darcy, I would not wish to offend your aunt by trading barbs with her, but I have a feeling from what you are saying, she will not give me a choice. As for taking advantage of the opportunity to forward our friendship while in such easy company, I would like to do that very much." *If I could just stop blushing!* She smirked, "Perhaps you could show me the chimney piece in the drawing room, or the glazing of the many windows. I understand that they were quite expensive!"

Darcy's heart was beating hard, but he had no choice but to laugh at her words about the expense of the house. "I have a feeling that your cousin was quoting my aunt to you?"

"Yes, Mr. Darcy, my cousin is a perfect sycophant."

"My aunt would have never given him the living if he was not, Miss Bennet."

"That speaks volumes of your aunt, Mr. Darcy."

"So it does. I see that we are on the same page."

They smiled at each other again.

"Miss Bennet, I was wondering, my sister was very impressed with your story about Mr. Wickham last night, and since she will not speak of it to anyone, I thought that perhaps you could…"

"Offer to talk to her privately if she wishes?"

Relieved, Darcy nodded.

She regarded him carefully, reading both seriousness and hope in his expression.

"Absolutely, Mr. Darcy. Sometimes speaking to another woman, one nearer her age, helps. If the opportunity does not arise tomorrow at tea, you know that all she has to do is ask, and I will gladly pay her a private call in your home."

"Thank you Miss Bennet, I cannot tell you how happy it makes me to have your support."

"I am glad to give it, sir."

The two continued to walk slowly around the park, finally turning the conversation to less serious subjects, like books and plays, comparing their favourite composers, and rapidly finding that they shared similar, but not completely complimentary views.

"Perhaps you could play for us tomorrow, or after dinner on Sunday, Miss Bennet. I would very much enjoy hearing you."

"Do you think that we could convince your sister to play?"

"I doubt it. She still will only play for me or select family members. She is not at all confident, but she is very good."

"Well, I am not very good, but far too confident. Perhaps between the two of us, we might both do well!"

Laughing again, and feeling better than he had in a very long time, they returned to the Gardiner home. Upon arriving they found that Mr. Bennet's express had arrived, and Darcy instantly extended the Sunday dinner invitation to include Elizabeth's father and sister.

Elizabeth accompanied him to the door to watch him take his leave. He bowed, and taking her hand he softly kissed it. Looking into her eyes, he whispered, "Until tomorrow, Miss Bennet."

Chapter 5

lizabeth spent Friday morning with her young cousins walking in the park. The children loved Elizabeth. She was willing to join in their activities and was not afraid to get dirty. When they started a chasing game, she took a seat on a bench with their governess, and quietly contemplated the gentleman who had taken over her every thought. Her aunt asked her the night before how she felt about Mr. Darcy, and she had no ready answer.

He was certainly handsome, *that* she had noticed immediately. His dark brown eyes made her knees weak. His soft deep voice sent shivers up her spine. When he tried to comfort her and impulsively pulled her into his embrace she felt . . . well she did not know what it was, but she knew that it ended far too soon, and somehow, she sensed that no one else could ever recreate the sensation.

She had slowly begun to gain a sense of the responsibility that he carried on his shoulders. Her aunt's description of Pemberley helped her to realize that a great many people depended on him. Neither of them had opened up about their families yet. Although she was nervous, she was looking forward to meeting his sister.

They certainly shared a great love for reading and she enjoyed the debate on poetry they held the day before. She laughed remembering his argument that poetry was the "food of love" and her assertion that it would advance a strong relationship, but a poorly written sonnet would surely kill an inclination quickly. He was correct when he discerned that she liked to profess opinions that were not her own. That was a habit that she had learned from her father. It made her think that the practice was dishonest, and she should try to catch herself before repeating the behaviour.

Fitzwilliam Darcy was certainly a puzzle. She now knew for certain that she wanted to have the chance to understand him, no matter how long it took. *Maybe even a lifetime?* She could hardly believe she allowed the thought. *But why,* she kept asking herself, *Why me? Why?*

While Elizabeth contemplated Darcy, he was sending his housekeeper to Bedlam. He was always fastidious, but made his requirements for a well-run household with a firm but reasonable attitude. Today, Mrs. Harris was sincerely wondering if his cousin had slipped something odd into his brandy the night before. Whoever the two ladies were who were coming to visit that afternoon must be very important because he left no subject untouched in his demands for absolute perfection. He was obviously reacting out of nervousness, but his behaviour was setting everyone, including Miss Darcy, on edge.

Darcy arrived at the Gardiner home in a state of extreme tension. He so hoped that Elizabeth and Georgiana would like each other and could not wait to observe them together. He had been dreaming of Elizabeth every night and thinking of her during every unoccupied moment of the day since they met. His dreams had begun to drift into thoughts of making his life with her.

Darcy exited the carriage to again see Elizabeth in the window, wearing a look of delighted surprise. She did not seem to have expected him to personally escort them to his home. After the parties performed the necessary courtesies, Darcy helped them into the magnificent carriage. He smiled inwardly at the ladies' attempt to conceal their reaction to the plush interior.

"I do not believe you mentioned where your home is, Mr. Darcy, is it very far?" asked Elizabeth.

"Not too far, it is located in Mayfair, in Park Lane, across from Hyde Park. My great grandfather built it many years ago."

"Oh how wonderful to have access to such a grand park!"

"Have you had the opportunity to visit it yet, Miss Bennet? I remember you mentioning a hope to walk there on the night that we met."

"No, I am afraid that I have been spending time in only one particular park this week." She gave him an impish smile.

"Well perhaps after you and my sister become acquainted, you could pay her a call, and we could both show you its beauty." He suggested hopefully.

Elizabeth looked to Mrs. Gardiner, and seeing her smile and nod, she smiled widely. "I look forward to it, Mr. Darcy."

Darcy allowed his mouth to curve up while inside he was rejoicing. He had found a new way to spend time with her, and help further her anticipated friendship with Georgiana.

The carriage stopped in front of Darcy House, and Elizabeth and Mrs. Gardiner could not disguise their pleasure. The home was amongst the largest on the very fashionable street, constructed of gray stone, four stories high with rows of arched windows. A footman held the door open and Darcy, after personally handing them out, offered his arms to each lady and brought them into the house.

Their outerwear was removed quickly by the waiting servants. Elizabeth and Mrs. Gardiner were introduced to Mrs. Harris, and Mr. Franklin, the butler. Elizabeth could not help but notice the close scrutiny both servants were giving them, and wondered wryly to herself just what Mr. Darcy had demanded from them in preparation for the visit.

He led them upstairs to the drawing room, enjoying the ladies' exclamation of pleasure with what they saw. "This is beautiful, Mr. Darcy. It is furnished tastefully with very excellent quality, but without the gaudiness that is so often seen," said Mrs. Gardiner.

"I agree Aunt, the impression I had when I entered was that this was not a house, but a home. It certainly reflects the character of the owner, instead of the advice of a decorator. It is most pleasant."

Darcy's chest was swelling with pride. "I cannot thank you enough for your kind words. I have always wanted the place where I live to be comfortable, and I am thrilled that you sense the warmth of this being a home. I have been told many times by visiting ladies that the house was lovely, but needed just a few touches. Gilt and gaudy decorations would make me think of a gambling house, not a home."

The three of them entered the drawing room laughing. Georgiana stood, surprised at the uncharacteristic behaviour of her brother. Smiling his encouragement, Darcy took her hand and led her to Elizabeth and Mrs. Gardiner.

"Georgiana, may I present Mrs. Edward Gardiner and Miss Elizabeth Bennet. Ladies, this is my sister, Miss Georgiana Darcy."

The ladies curtseyed, and Elizabeth and Aunt Gardiner strained to hear Georgiana whisper, "I am so very pleased to meet you." She did not lift her eyes above her toes.

Elizabeth said with a smile, "Miss Darcy, we are delighted to make your acquaintance. Your brother has been most vocal in singing the praises of your accomplishments, and I admit a burning curiosity to meet such a talented young lady."

"My brother is most kind." She whispered again.

"Will you please be seated," invited Darcy. Elizabeth noted that he took a chair next to his sister, and decided to boldly sit next to her on the sofa she occupied. Mrs. Gardiner sat across from them.

Leaning in conspiratorially, Elizabeth said to Georgiana, "Miss Darcy, your brother has shared a very great secret of yours with me."

Georgiana lifted her head and stared into Elizabeth's dancing eyes, not seeing her smile. "He tells me that you are excessively fond of Mrs. Radcliffe's novels and has caught you hiding them under pillows when he enters a room unexpectedly."

Incredulous, she turned to Darcy. "William! How could you say such a thing!"

Darcy, at first surprised at Elizabeth telling his confidence, immediately saw how effective it was in jolting Georgiana out of her shyness. He smiled widely, "Did I not speak the truth?"

"Well, yes, but that was not the point!"

Elizabeth touched her hand, and caught her eye. "Please forgive your brother Miss Darcy. We were discussing our mutual taste in literature, and when I admitted to my fondness for the occasional romantic novel, he could not resist telling his story of you."

She turned to glare at her brother. "It is well, Miss Bennet. My brother seems to have forgotten that I am full of such tales of him!"

Darcy, although thrilled to hear his sister speak, began to feel a little uncomfortable. "Now Georgie, I am sure that Miss Bennet and Mrs. Gardiner are not the slightest bit interested in my indiscretions. They are far too proper to ask about them."

The three ladies exchanged smug expressions, and finally Elizabeth teased him, "Why Mr. Darcy, surely you know that a lady is *always* interested in hearing stories of the gentleman's exploits. The information can be used to such advantage in the future." Noting his wide-eyed look of surprise Elizabeth decided to relax him. "But of course, I doubt that you ever have done anything that might prove useful to a lady's wiles, Mr. Darcy. You are everything proper."

"I am relieved to hear you say that Miss Bennet."

Nodding to him, Elizabeth returned her attention to Georgiana. "Miss Darcy, I understand that you have a great love of music. Do you play and sing? And which composer do you prefer?"

After the unexpected frivolity of discomposing her brother, Elizabeth had managed to calm Georgiana's nerves. She was able to converse very well on the subject of music, imploring Elizabeth to play for her. Darcy explained that he had already requested that she play on Sunday and Georgiana was thrilled. Mrs.

Gardiner introduced the topic of Derbyshire, and Georgiana was very happy to discuss her home. Darcy had not seen her so animated in months, and he knew that it was due to Elizabeth. They finished their tea, and Elizabeth made certain to compliment it within the hearing of the housekeeper. Georgiana asked that she and Elizabeth address each other by their Christian names.

"Elizabeth, I know that his might seem a little soon to ask, but I have enjoyed your company so much today. I was wondering; if my brother approves, could you please come and visit me again tomorrow?" She looked hopefully between the two of them, flushed with the exertion of making an invitation.

"I think that is a wonderful idea!" Darcy turned to look hopefully at Elizabeth, "What do you think Miss Bennet? Are you available? I will gladly provide transportation."

Returning Darcy's steady gaze, she smiled and looked to Georgiana, "My sister and father will be arriving after one o'clock tomorrow, but I would very much like to spend the morning with you."

She clapped her hands. "Oh yes, Elizabeth that will be wonderful. Could I have the carriage pick you up at ten o'clock? I promise to return you in time to meet your family." Elizabeth smiled and nodded.

"Excellent, then it is settled." Darcy declared.

They soon rose to take leave of each other, and while Georgiana was speaking to Mrs. Gardiner, Darcy pulled Elizabeth aside. He took her hands in his. "Thank you so much for everything you have done today. My sister has not been so alive in years, let alone since Ramsgate. I am delighted that you will be visiting tomorrow. I cannot wait to see you here again." Then raising her hand to his lips, he kissed it, and noted her blush. "You are bewitching both of the Darcys Miss Bennet, and we are grateful."

Elizabeth was flustered by the warmth that spread up her hand and arm from the touch of his lips, and finally managed to say a coherent sentence. "I am honoured by your opinion sir, but I do believe that both you and your sister are hardly under the power of bewitchment, you both are too intelligent for that. I think that you are both simply in dire need of some teasing, and that I am happy to provide."

"Miss Bennet, you may choose to hide behind a delightful mask of impertinence, but I am growing increasingly aware of the very kind, thoughtful, and exceptionally intelligent and beautiful woman that you are. I am grateful that you have become a very welcome part of my life." Elizabeth had no chance to respond other than to momentarily lose herself in the deep dark warmth of his gaze. She could drown in there. Before she knew it, they were in the carriage, and on their way home.

CHARLES BINGLEY sealed the letter to his housekeeper at Netherfield and sat back, contemplating the study of his home. *Leased home,* he thought. *Everything in my life is leased.* He was looking forward to finally moving into the Netherfield estate, and beginning his tentative steps to becoming one of the landed gentry, fulfilling his father's dreams. He knew that it would be years, probably not until his grandchildren were grown, that the Bingley name would be considered anything other than "new money", but he thought reasonably, it had to start somewhere. He had considered purchasing the London townhouse, but that would have left less money for the estate he hoped to someday buy.

Looking again at the room, he noted the fine interior. It was a large home, *Not as big as Darcy's, but then, nothing seemed to be as big as he, including me!* He laughed, thinking of his friend's towering height. His musings were interrupted by the distinct cackling of his sisters from the drawing room down the hall. He sighed. His sister Caroline's single-minded and unwelcome pursuit of Darcy was a problem. He knew that his friend put up with his sister's company for his sake alone, but Darcy was becoming increasingly vocal in his distaste for her behaviour.

Charles wondered about Darcy's own behaviour over the past months. Something had changed. He had always been impatient in company that he found distasteful, often hiding away silently in a corner or at a least speaking very rarely. Lately he had noticed a greater effort to at least try to participate in conversations, although at the same time, he seemed increasingly disgusted with higher society in general. Bingley knew that he found the matrimonial pursuits of the ladies distasteful. He had also noticed the extraordinary change in Georgiana. She had become more withdrawn. He could not help but wonder if the changes were connected. Both of them seemed to want to stay home more often than not, however, and it was with great happiness that he observed his friend's improved spirits Friday morning. He wondered what had sparked his happy demeanour, and looked forward to Sunday's dinner.

Charles got up and walked to the drawing room to greet his sisters. "Caroline, I thought you would like to know, I have written to the housekeeper at Netherfield, and have asked that the house be prepared for occupancy at the end of March. I realize that it will be in the true beginning of the Season, and you do not have to accompany me at that time if you do not wish."

"Thank you for taking the Season into consideration, I really would hate to leave London so soon. Perhaps if you think that you can spare me, I will wait to join you. Would that be agreeable? You were not planning to entertain, and would not need a hostess right away."

"No, I do not expect to be entertaining. I just want to observe the planting, and of course gain Darcy's thoughts on the estate and if I should consider it for purchase."

Caroline and Louisa exchanged glances. "Oh, I did not realize Mr. Darcy would be accompanying you. In that case, you will need me sooner. I will gladly forgo the rest of the Season to see to your comfort."

"That will not be necessary, Caroline. I have no wish to have you suspend your pleasure prematurely. Besides, Darcy will not be coming with me right away. He has continuing obligations here in town, and then must visit his aunt in Kent for Easter. I do not expect him to join me until late April. Then of course he will be returning to Pemberley to look after his own spring planting. At least that is one responsibility that I do not have to take on. Since I am only leasing, Netherfield's owner is still in charge of the true obligations of the estate."

"So you do not know exactly when Mr. Darcy will come?" She asked, disappointed at the lost opportunity to be in a secluded atmosphere with her quarry.

"No, I do not." Charles was not quite telling the truth, but he clearly saw the mercenary glint in his sister's eye and had no desire to further her machinations for his friend.

"I wonder what made him run away so quickly on Monday. Have you called on him since we saw him at the theatre?"

"Yes, I saw him yesterday morning, and he was in good spirits. I did not see Miss Darcy, but he told me that she was well."

"Oh, yes, we must pay a call on Miss Darcy, Louisa!" Louisa nodded, and she continued her effusions, "Yes, it has been far too long since we saw the dear girl." *And perhaps we can speak to Mr. Darcy as well.*

"I understand that they are busy today, and I know that they are entertaining family on Sunday for dinner, so I would not bother to stop by until Monday at least, Caroline." He was well-pleased with his subterfuge, and knew that Darcy would appreciate the delay in their call. "Speaking of Sunday, I will be dining out, so do not include me in your dinner plans."

"Where will you be, Charles?"

"I have been invited to meet some new acquaintances at a small dinner in a friend's home." He gave his beguiling smile, and left before she could press him for more details.

"Do you think that he is trying to keep me away from Mr. Darcy?" Caroline asked petulantly.

Louisa appeased her sister, "I cannot imagine why he would, Caroline, you would be a perfect Mistress of Pemberley."

SATURDAY MORNING the carriage arrived precisely on time to collect Elizabeth. She knew that Mr. Darcy would not be able to escort her by himself to his home, and she was not surprised to see a maid sitting in the carriage to accompany her. She made some friendly conversation with the young girl, who seemed genuinely surprised to be spoken to by a gentlewoman.

Upon arrival, Elizabeth was met by Georgiana, who was waiting for her with anticipation, and led her to the music room. Elizabeth exclaimed over the lovely pianoforte. "Will you play for me, Georgiana?"

"Oh I do not know, Elizabeth. I have never played for anyone who was not family before." She looked shyly away.

"How old are you Georgiana?" Elizabeth asked.

"I am nearly sixteen, why do you ask?" She said curiously.

"I ask because at your age, my mother had declared me out, and I had no choice but to make my debut of playing in front of a room full of people. I did not have the opportunity to slowly become used to playing for strangers, and was simply thrust into it. I also did not have the benefit of masters to teach me, which I suspect you have." She looked seriously at her. "Your brother has spoken very highly of your talent, Georgiana, and I do not doubt his sincerity. I think that you should start exhibiting your skills to small groups of friendly listeners. When you do come out; and no longer have a choice to refuse exhibiting, you will be confident in your ability."

Georgiana stared. "I wish that I had your confidence, Elizabeth."

She laughed, "You must remember that I am a few years older than you. I would not even recognize the person I was at the age of sixteen now, and to be honest, I would not want to be that girl again."

"Were you naïve at that age, Elizabeth?" Georgiana was thinking of her behaviour last summer.

"I certainly was, with many things. In some areas I am still naïve, even at my advanced age." Elizabeth smiled at her and was happy to see her laugh. "Is there anything that you have questions about, Georgiana? Is there some subject that you would feel more comfortable speaking to a woman about, instead of your intimidating, frustratingly serious brother?"

Georgiana whispered. "Yes." She paused, gathering her thoughts. "Elizabeth, my brother told me about your experience with Mr. Wickham."

"He said that he would." She looked at her encouragingly.

"I had an experience with him as well." She closed her eyes and confessed her secret. "Last summer my companion, Mrs. Younge went with me to Ramsgate on a holiday. Mr. Wickham was there. I remembered him as being so kind to me when I was younger, and when he started paying particular attention to me, it so turned my head that I fancied myself in love. Before I knew it, he had convinced me that we should elope. If William had not arrived when he did, we would have married." By now she was sobbing. "William sent him away. I found out that he did not want me, he just wanted my dowry."

Elizabeth wrapped her arms around the girl and held her, gently rocking her while she cried. When Georgiana stopped, she pulled away and tenderly wiped away the tears with her handkerchief. "Georgiana, what did your brother tell you about what happened?"

"He told me that it was not my fault, that Mr. Wickham is a cad, and that he has done many terrible things to many girls. He said that a man twice my age would not approach a girl of fifteen without nefarious reasons and that if he did love me, he would not have wanted to elope, but would have asked for my hand."

"All of those things are very true, and certainly explain Mr. Wickham's actions. I can attest to his scandalous behaviour myself. Now, what I want to know are your reasons for agreeing to the elopement in the first place." Elizabeth looked at her very seriously.

"What do you mean? He used me." She asked defensively.

"Yes, he did. But what was it that made you willing to listen to his lies?" Elizabeth held her hand.

"I guess that I liked the attention." Georgiana admitted.

"Ah, and why was that?" Elizabeth encouraged.

Suddenly it all spilled out in a rush. "I was feeling lonely. You see, William is wonderful, but he is so much older, and I was taken out of school last year, so I did not have any friends to talk to anymore, and I liked hearing him tell me that I was beautiful." Speaking very softly she added, "I truly miss my father."

"And your brother is not quite the same, no matter how hard he tries. Did you think that doing this would win you more attention from him? Were you unhappy with the time he spent on his other duties?" Elizabeth asked.

"I do not know. I have been so confused." She cried.

"Well, let us forget about your desire for attention for a moment. Let us talk about your other behaviour." She looked at her again. "Did you know at the time that what you were doing was wrong, against everything that you had been taught?"

"Yes."

"But, you did not write to your brother and ask for his help when you felt overwhelmed by Mr. Wickham's attentions? You know that he would have been at your side in an instant do you not?"

"Yes."

"I understand that this happened nearly eight months ago, and you have been completely unlike yourself since then. I wonder, are you upset over what happened, or are you feeling guilty about your own culpability?"

"William says that it was all Wickham's fault, and will not listen to me taking any blame on myself. He has been so unhappy since it happened, and I know he is disappointed in me."

"I think that he is disappointed in himself."

"But he did nothing wrong!"

"He hired Mrs. Younge. He let you go to Ramsgate. He did not expose Wickham years ago."

"That is ridiculous! He had no control over what happened!"

"So you agree that he is not disappointed in you?"

"Of course!"

"Then, you should let go of your guilt over his feelings. He will return to himself when you let this go. But I think that you have a lot to think about yourself. You were raised with certain values, and you went against them for your own selfish pleasure. Luckily your brother came in time, but this whole situation could have been discovered if you had just listened to your inner voice that was telling you that it was wrong."

"If I was older, I would have seen through it sooner."

"Probably, and you would have handled it differently. I do give you credit for realizing that you are young and have much to learn. And I am glad that your values and dedication to your brother allowed you to realize before it was too late that you needed to admit the scheme." Taking her hand again, she continued. "Georgiana, I think that you have much to consider. I do believe that much of the fault lies with Mr. Wickham, but you must realize what you did and why. When you have accomplished that, you will be able to forgive yourself. But do know this, you brother loves you very, very much and wants nothing but your happiness. You, however; have reached the age where your happiness depends upon your own behaviour, and not on the people who are responsible for your care. It is part of maturing. If you wish to be given the privilege of being treated as an adult, then you must prove that you are worthy of it."

Georgiana simply sat, gazing into Elizabeth's sincere eyes. Nobody had ever spoken to her so frankly before. As wonderful as William was, he was always trying to protect her. Elizabeth expected her to be an adult. She appreciated it more that she could say. Suddenly she threw her arms around Elizabeth's neck "Thank you! I wish I had a sister like you!"

Surprised, Elizabeth returned the embrace, "I am honoured that you would think that of me, Georgiana, thank you. But you do have a wonderful brother, and I know that he will welcome you talking to him about this."

"I will, Elizabeth, soon."

DARCY, OF COURSE, knew the moment that Elizabeth arrived. A footman appeared at his study door announcing the carriage had pulled in front of the house. He left the door open, and listened for her warm voice greeting Georgiana, and strained to hear their conversation as it faded down the hallway. He listened for the sound of the pianoforte, but when no music came he began wondering what they could be talking about.

After an hour, his curiosity got the best of him. He knew that Elizabeth was there for Georgiana, but he could not help his feelings of jealousy. He knew that he was being selfish and ridiculous, but he was beginning to feel very possessive of Elizabeth and her attention. He made his way to the music room in time to catch the extraordinary sight of Elizabeth embracing Georgiana, and hear his sister's fervent wish that they were sisters. His heart nearly stopped at her words. He was hoping for the same thing.

Darcy knocked on the door. "Excuse me, ladies, I do not mean to interrupt, but I did want to greet Miss Bennet."

"William!" Georgiana leapt to her feet and ran into his arms, hugging him tightly. Confused, Darcy looked to Elizabeth who met his questioning eyes with a smile and a shrug.

"All is well," Elizabeth mouthed.

Relieved, he kissed Georgiana's head and spoke softly, "Thank you for the wonderful greeting, dear, but I cannot help but ask what has moved you to it?"

Georgiana let go and looked up to her brother's face. "I am just so happy that you have introduced me to Elizabeth. She is a wonderful friend!"

More than pleased, he smiled and touched her cheek. "Do all of your wonderful friends cause tears?" He teased, and then smiled at Elizabeth.

"Oh no, these are tears of happiness!" She realized her dishevelled appearance and blushed. "I must look terrible! Will you please excuse me for a moment while I wash my face?" Darcy instantly agreed and she flew out the door.

As soon as she was gone, he was at Elizabeth's side. "What has happened?"

"Georgiana confided in me her experience with Mr. Wickham." She noted his relief and looked at him carefully. "Do you know she admits that she enjoyed the attention, and chose to disregard her upbringing in order to enjoy Mr. Wickham's advances?"

"She did?"

"She also said that she missed her father very much." Darcy nodded his head, and furrowed his brow. "I told her that she alone is responsible for her own behaviour and that if she wanted to be treated as an adult, she must earn that respect by behaving as one."

"Miss Bennet, I am overwhelmed by what you are telling me! I shall be forever grateful for you drawing her out. I did not even consider that she had any culpability in the matter. Did she act out of loneliness or a desire to be thought of as an adult?" He asked almost to himself and then remembered his companion. "You have made changes in her in minutes where I have failed for nearly a year. How can I ever thank you?"

Elizabeth smiled at him. "Your friendship is thanks enough, sir."

Darcy boldly took her hands. "I have very rapidly come to treasure yours." Elizabeth did not look away. Entwining their fingers, he took a breath. Haltingly, he spoke his thoughts. "Miss Bennet, while we have this moment alone, I want to tell you . . . in the short time that we have known each other . . . I have experienced so many feelings that I, I, I have never dared hope to . . . I hold you in the highest regard and with your approval, may I speak to your father on Sunday and ask for his permission to court you?" He looked at her anxiously. "I assure you Miss Bennet, my intentions are strictly honourable, and I have never done this before."

Elizabeth's face coloured, and she was sure that the rest of her body matched. They were squeezing each other's hands so hard that they were losing feeling. She could not have looked away from him if she tried. "Mr. Darcy, I . . . I am overwhelmed. I never expected your attentions." Suddenly all of her fears came pouring out. "I have hardly allowed myself to dream that a man such as you would ever consider someone like me. I am so below you. I have nothing to offer. It would be a degradation to your name, your family would reject me, and your friends would leave you. Why Mr. Darcy? Why me? Why would you want someone like me?"

"Oh Elizabeth," he thought, desperate to hold her. "Never, ever let me hear you disparage yourself like that again!" He loosened his grip and drew her hand to his lips, kissing it tenderly. "You ask me why? Because you are the only woman who has ever touched my heart and challenged my mind, and did it without asking for anything in return. I also find you the most enticingly beautiful woman I have ever met. With such a combination, how can I not wish to court you? Now Miss Bennet, will you please answer my question?"

Elizabeth was trembling, wishing desperately for him to hold her again. "Yes, Mr. Darcy, my answer is yes. I welcome your courtship, and your honourable intentions." She gave him a small smile, but her eyes were sparkling with joy. Darcy felt like jumping up and shouting his happiness, but limited himself to a kiss to her palm. "Thank you, so very much." Fortunately, they heard Georgiana's approach, and quickly drew apart, releasing their hands.

"I apologize for taking so long." She looked at her friend. "Elizabeth, are you well? Your face is flushed."

Elizabeth's hand flew up to her face, "Is it?" Her eyes met Darcy's, "I suppose that I am a little warm." He smiled at her, nodding his head in agreement.

Mr. Franklin knocked on the door. "Excuse me sir, the carriage is ready to return Miss Bennet to her home. Shall I ask Sally to ride with her again?"

"Oh! I did not realize that it was time to leave already!" Elizabeth exclaimed.

Darcy's disappointment was intense, he swallowed the urge to ride with her and speak to her father the moment he arrived. Instead, he looked sadly to Elizabeth. "It seems that time has slipped away from us today." He turned to the butler, "Yes, please ask Sally to be ready to accompany Miss Bennet in ten minutes." Mr. Franklin bowed and left.

Georgiana expressed again her happiness with her new friend, and her regret at her leaving. "I cannot wait to see you tomorrow and meet your family!"

"I hope that your family will like me."

"Oh how could they not? William, do you not agree?"

His eyes full of open admiration, he replied, "I certainly do." Georgiana looked between the two of them, comprehension dawning on her. They both walked her to the door, and Darcy handed her into the carriage. With the maid present, he could only squeeze her fingers for a moment. "Until tomorrow, Miss Bennet."

"Until tomorrow, Mr. Darcy." She sat back in the carriage, smiled at Sally, closed her eyes and sighed.

Chapter 6

*I*t was a dreary winter morning, and it showed the promise of continuing on as a dreary winter day when Mr. Bennet and Jane boarded the family carriage for the trip to London. The expectations of the two passengers could not have been more diverse. Jane, of course, was full of hope that her sister and best friend truly had found a man worthy of her affection and was determined to be at her side to provide whatever support she needed. Mr. Bennet was worried that Elizabeth had found a man who she would not reject out of hand, and who he could not easily dismiss.

He looked across the coach at Jane, quietly tending her sewing. He loved her. She was a good girl, beautiful to be sure, and never a moment's trouble. She was loving and sensible, and he enjoyed her companionship. She would make someone a fine wife some day, but she did not have the wit and fire of Lizzy. No, she was nothing like his Lizzy. She could spend hours debating a book or playing chess, or join him in his observations of other's character. She was his favourite companion and had long been his closest friend. The thought of losing her weighed heavily on his mind.

The carriage arrived at the Gardiner house only a half hour late. Elizabeth was sitting in her window watching for them, and dashed out the door to welcome them inside.

There was no opportunity for a private conversation that afternoon, or even after dinner. Mr. Bennet took the news of the invitation to Mr. Darcy's house for dinner with a sigh, and decided to speak to Elizabeth early in the morning.

Elizabeth and Jane would share a room until their father left, and they immediately began sharing their news when they retired for the night.

"Lizzy, you must tell me everything! Your letter was so happy, but I was worried for you, this has happened so quickly, I just want to be sure that you are thinking clearly. Now I insist, tell me everything, from the first moment, and please, I have spent hours trapped in the carriage with Papa, so I have had quite enough wit for one day. Please be serious!"

"Jane, I promise I will be serious, and I will tell you all. But first you must know that Mr. Darcy is everything I have ever hoped for, and he becomes more so every day." Elizabeth spun around the room with her joy. She then sat up on the bed with Jane. She told her everything from how they first saw each other and met, *How romantic!* Their two walks in the park, leaving out the embrace, tea with Georgiana, his home, the visit with Georgiana that morning, and finally his beautiful, heartfelt request for courtship. "Oh Jane, if he had kissed me I would not have protested at all. He kissed my hand and I was so flushed that his sister asked if I was ill!" She laughed.

"Lizzy, if it were anyone else I think that I would be green with envy right now, but since it is you, dear sister, I can only express my joy. I so look forward to meeting him and his sister tomorrow. I am sure that Papa will be most impressed with him."

"Yes, I think that he will like him very much, and we will meet the rest of his family. I met his cousin the colonel, of course, but we will be meeting an earl and countess, too."

"Did he satisfy your worries when he explained why he chose you?"

"Yes, I think so, but it is all so hard to believe that of all the hundreds of women he could ask, he would choose *me!*"

"I think that it shows his remarkable taste and good sense!"

"Oh Jane, you are too good!"

MR. BENNET did not have an opportunity to speak alone with Elizabeth until after church the next morning. He asked her to join him in Mr. Gardiner's study. Taking a seat behind the desk, he regarded her face carefully. She was smiling at him with anticipation.

"Papa, what is it? You are being far too mysterious!"

"I wish to speak to you about your friendship with Mr. Darcy." She smiled widely. "You have known him barely a week and you are accepting a great deal of attention from him."

"Yes, Papa, I know that it seems to be developing very quickly, but we seem to have . . . I suppose connected . . . formed a bond . . . It is as if we have been waiting to find someone and recognized each other as that someone immediately."

"Lizzy are you out of your senses? Did he put these notions into your head? How can you accept the word of a man you have known for one week?"

"I trust him, Papa." She said defensively.

"How can you trust him? He is a rich man, Lizzy. What does he want with a girl as lowborn as you?"

"He told me that I was the first woman who asks nothing of him. He has been hunted by mercenary women for years, and . . ." She faltered. She did not like having to explain Mr. Darcy's feelings for her.

"I imagine that he tells many young girls a great many of his pretty stories to catch them unaware and then uses them for his own pleasure."

"Papa! How can you say such things! He is an honourable man! You do not know him!"

"Neither do you, Lizzy. There is no reason why such a powerful man would lower himself to gain the attention of a girl with no dowry, no connections, and no great beauty. He sees an opportunity to advance his baser instincts, and that is all. He would be ashamed to show you in public. He will take advantage of you and move on to the next unwitting girl."

Stung by his insults she shot back, "If I am so low, why did he introduce me to his sister? Why has he invited his uncle, an earl, for dinner tonight?" Elizabeth fought her angry tears.

"Perhaps they are simply humouring him. They all share the same habits." He knew that he was hurting her, but he wished to plant the seeds of doubt.

"Mr. Darcy is a good man. He is not ashamed of me! You will see, Papa. There is nothing to fear. You will see tonight how honourable he is!" She spoke fiercely.

"I fear, daughter, you will be very disappointed. He will prove himself to be like every other man, fond of the sport, and ready for the taste of new blood."

Elizabeth was appalled by her father's words. "I will listen to this no longer, Papa. You will see for yourself. He will prove your fears wrong tonight." She ran from the room, and grabbing her bonnet, continued outside to walk in the park. Never in her wildest imaginings could she think that her father was purposely trying to separate her from Mr. Darcy by creating fictional tales about him. She tried to justify his reaction and words by colouring it as genuine concern for her well being. After walking in the park for some time, she returned to the house, determined to help Mr. Darcy win her father's good opinion that evening.

After she left the room, Mr. Bennet sat contemplating his efforts. He felt that he had been quite effective in confusing her, and was pleased. He hoped that the confrontation he planned with Mr. Darcy would scare him off sufficiently to make him drop his interest in his daughter as not worth the effort. He was momentarily disgusted with himself for his desire to end his daughter's happiness, but soon recovered from it. It was too soon for Lizzy to leave him.

MR. GARDINER graciously declined Darcy's offer to provide transportation to his home for Sunday dinner. The five guests squeezed into Mr. Gardiner's carriage and were soon on their way to Mayfair. Elizabeth was now accustomed to the sight of his townhouse, so her eyes were on her father and sister to register their reaction upon arrival. She was not disappointed. Jane gave a gasp of surprise and her father a wry grimace, which turned into a slow shake of his head as they entered the house and he took in the beautiful interior.

Darcy stood in the foyer nervously awaiting them and gave a small smile of welcome as they entered. As Mr. Gardiner introduced Jane and Mr. Bennet, he forced himself to tear his eyes from Elizabeth. She was stunning in a gown of deep green silk.

"I am pleased to welcome you to my home. If you will follow me, I will lead you to the drawing room. My other guests have only just arrived." He offered his arm to Elizabeth, and she smiled up at him, accepting it. With her touch, his tension disappeared. He leaned down, "You look breathtaking, Miss Elizabeth." He revelled in the new freedom of using her Christian name, with her elder sister's presence; she must relinquish the title of Miss Bennet.

"Thank you, sir. I was afraid that you would no longer notice me now that my sister has arrived." Although she said it with a laugh, her insecurity in her own appearance was clear.

Darcy, becoming more sensitive to her emotions, leaned down and said very softly, "Your sister is very lovely; Miss Elizabeth, but I only see you."

Blushing, she gently gave his arm a squeeze, and recovered her humour, "Mr. Darcy, if you do not desist in these compliments, I am afraid that I will be permanently blushing. I will have to adjust my wardrobe to anticipate my reddened face!"

He was delighted with her confession that he affected her so easily, and laughed. "Now that is a trip to a modiste that I would enjoy!"

"Do you mean that you send your sister to shop alone?" She asked, arching her brow.

"Indeed I do, Miss Elizabeth. I learned years ago, a man's place is to provide the funds and stay clear of the dress shops."

"Oh. I must speak to Georgiana about this!"

"She will no doubt be happy to share many stories with you, to my chagrin, I am sure." They shared smiles, and entered the drawing room.

Mr. Bennet had been directly behind the couple, escorting Jane. He could not catch their soft conversation, but he could not ignore the expressions of mutual enjoyment and happiness on their faces. He realized that he had failed to dissuade Elizabeth from her attachment.

The rest of the dinner party was gathered in the drawing room, sipping small glasses of wine. They all looked to the door at the sound of Darcy and Elizabeth's laughter, and smiled with the entrance of the glowing woman on his arm, and the unusual sight of Darcy beaming down on her. Suspicions about the couple were instantly aroused.

"Ladies and Gentlemen, may I present Mr. Thomas Bennet, Miss Jane Bennet, Miss Elizabeth Bennet, and Mr. and Mrs. Edward Gardiner." Turning to his newly arrived guests, "Mr. Bennet, Miss Bennet, Miss Elizabeth, Mr. and Mrs. Gardiner, this is my uncle, Lord Henry Fitzwilliam, the Earl of Matlock, my aunt, Lady Elaine Fitzwilliam, my cousin, Colonel Richard Fitzwilliam, my sister, Miss Georgiana Darcy, and my good friend, Mr. Charles Bingley."

For a few moments after the introductions were made, silence reigned over the two disparate groups, and they simply looked at each other. Elizabeth glanced up at Darcy's anxious face and her soft laugh filled the air. She smiled warmly at him, her eyes sparkling and declared, "Goodness that was quite momentous!" The frozen moment was broken as smiles formed on everyone's faces.

Richard crossed the great divide between them and stepped up to Elizabeth. "Miss Bennet, it is a great pleasure to see you again! My cousins have spoken of little else than you this past week!"

"I can only hope that their words were kind, sir. But I must take this moment to correct you. The title of Miss Bennet belongs to my sister, Jane."

"Ah, forgive me, Miss Elizabeth. My parents will be most disappointed in my error. Come; let me take you over to them, so that you can observe their chastisement at close range." Darcy reluctantly nodded his agreement and watched with some apprehension as the couple approached his relations.

Bingley made a beeline to Jane, and engaged her in his usual enthusiastic manner. He had been momentarily struck dumb when he caught sight of the angel with the golden tresses and large blue eyes who had entered the room, but he quickly regained his composure and strode to her side. Jane in her turn was overcome with admiration for the striking, green-eyed, widely smiling man with the wildly unkempt blonde hair.

Mr. and Mrs. Gardiner were engaged in quiet conversation with the nervous Georgiana, which left Darcy alone with Mr. Bennet.

"I hope that your journey to London was pleasant, sir." He began. "It is a welcome surprise to meet you sooner than I expected."

"Our journey was uneventful, sir, so as journeys go, I would say that would qualify as pleasant." He eyed Darcy, trying to take his measure. "As for our early meeting, I am not sure what you mean. Did you have plans to visit us in the future?"

"I will be joining my friend Mr. Bingley at Netherfield after Easter, and he is planning to have the house opened by the end of March."

"Ah, well it is good to know that our missing neighbour has finally decided to enter the vicinity. It will certainly please my wife. But do you not have your own estate to care for, Mr. Darcy? How can you afford to spend your time visiting?"

Darcy tried hard to suppress his affront to Mr. Bennet treating him like a school boy. He could not understand his sardonic tone. "My estate, as you may not be aware, is located in Derbyshire, sir. Our growing season is much shorter than that in the warmer climate of Hertfordshire. I can afford to spend a month in my friend's company and return in good time to observe the spring planting. I have been working for months on my plans, and my steward is quite capable of implementing them in my absence."

"I am surprised Mr. Darcy. I would expect a man such as yourself to leave all of the work to your steward, and simply reap the benefits of his labours."

"I am afraid that I do not understand your meaning, sir. I was raised to take interest and control of every aspect of my lands, from the planting to the tenants. A man such as myself would never abdicate his responsibilities to an employee and take credit for work that is not his own."

"Forgive me, Mr. Darcy. I meant no offense."

"Not at all, sir," he demurred.

The dinner bell rang, and Darcy immediately called for everyone's attention. He made his escape from Elizabeth's contentious father by leading the group to the dining room.

Mr. Bennet caught sight of the library on their way, and his hands itched, wishing to leave the group and enter. His jealousy over Darcy's riches increased. He resented Darcy implying that he was neglectful of Longbourn, while failing to realize that he had just accused him of that very act to Pemberley. He refused to recognize the truth of who was the better man, but did see already that Darcy was a man who would not be easily manipulated.

The guests took their places at the table. Darcy at the head, his uncle on his left, and indulging himself, Elizabeth was on his right. She was followed by Richard, Jane, and Lady Matlock. Beside his uncle were Mr. Bennet, Mrs. Gardiner, Bingley, and Mr. Gardiner. Georgiana was in the mistress' place.

Darcy leaned over to Elizabeth. "I am so pleased to have you here at my table, and with so many members of your family, Miss Elizabeth."

"I am pleased as well, Mr. Darcy, especially to see my sister, Jane."

"I imagine that you have missed her."

"Yes, but that is not why I am pleased, now."

"Why then?"

"Because with her present, I have the pleasure of hearing you say my name." She smiled directly into his eyes. He stared back, trying hard to control his desire to leap across the table and kiss her. Their intense stares did not go unnoticed by the rest of the table.

"Miss Elizabeth!" Boomed Lord Matlock.

Startled, Elizabeth jumped slightly, and looking to him, she smiled, "Yes, sir?"

"I understand that you met my nephew and son at a concert on Monday."

"Indeed I did, sir. My aunt and uncle were kind enough to take me."

"And how did you find the performance?"

"To be honest sir, I am afraid that I did not pay close attention. The music served as a pleasant background to my thoughts." She said, glancing briefly at Darcy.

"Is that so, Miss Bennet? And what were you thinking?"

"Surely you know better than to ask a lady her innermost thoughts, Lord Matlock!" She tilted her head and grinned at him.

Laughing, he nodded. "Quite so, quite so, it was foolish of me to ask!"

"I am pleased that you recognized that so easily sir, it shows a reasonable mind."

"Never let my father be accused of being unreasonable, Miss Elizabeth." Richard jumped in.

"Thank you, Son." Lord Matlock nodded his head at Richard.

"Not at all, Father," said Richard, smiling with delight at Elizabeth's repartee. He turned to her, "Well Miss Elizabeth; let us choose a safe topic, what say you of books?"

Darcy had remained silent during Elizabeth's exchange with his uncle, watching with growing admiration her easy handling of the intimidating man. He was less pleased with how his cousin smiled at her. With the subject of books now started, a lively debate ensued between the guests at that end of the table, with all participating equally. Darcy and Mr. Bennet both looked at Elizabeth with pride as she supported her arguments with passion and wit. Mr. Bennet was enjoying watching his Lizzy so much that he momentarily forgot his objective to end her acquaintance with Mr. Darcy. Lord Matlock and Richard were impressed with the country girl.

When Darcy mentioned a story about Napoleon he read in the *Times* that day, Elizabeth asked Richard if he had ever faced his troops. When he nodded and mentioned his regiment, he was amazed when Elizabeth instantly recalled the details of their exploits.

"I cannot imagine the tragedy that you witnessed, Colonel."

"It is refreshing, Miss Bennet, to meet a woman who is informed of both the details and horrors of battle." He looked at her with new respect, to accompany his already growing admiration.

"Will you be returning to battle, sir?"

"Ah, that is up to our little French friend across the channel." They laughed, lightening the mood.

Elizabeth noticed that Darcy frequently looked down the table, checking on Georgiana and sending her smiles of encouragement. She was pleased with how well the dinner had proceeded. She had kept a close eye on her father, and felt that Mr. Darcy had made a good impression on him. Her fears of her father's dislike and distrust of him eased. Bingley was quite happy entertaining Jane and Mrs. Gardiner, who in turn was enjoying watching the blushes of her other niece. When dinner ended, the gentlemen retired to Darcy's library and the ladies left for the music room.

DARCY OFFERED brandy to the men, and watched Mr. Bennet as he wandered through the library, perusing the shelves. Richard, Bingley, and Mr. Gardiner began a debate over piracy and its effect on trade.

Lord Matlock drew Darcy aside. "Tell me about Miss Elizabeth, Darcy." He said in an uncharacteristically quiet voice.

Startled by the question and his uncle's tone he did not know how to answer. "Has Richard spoken to you about her?"

"No, your aunt and I were completely surprised, but your favour for her is very obvious. I hope that you are aware of it, Darcy, and are not raising her hopes without cause."

"No, I have given this great consideration, and yesterday I asked her for permission for courtship. I intend to speak to her father tonight."

"Are you sure of this Darcy? Your honour is not yet engaged."

"My heart is, uncle. I was sure the moment I first looked at her, and what I have learned of her this past week makes me all the more positive. I hope that you will not try to dissuade me."

"You are not a child. You are a man who has been dealing with the marriage mart for years. You can spot the genuine article when you see it." He looked at him appraisingly. "I made a promise to your father that I would attempt to stop you if you tried to make a marriage of convenience. He told me specifically that he wished for you to marry for affection above all other considerations. It seems that my services will be unnecessary. Good luck, my boy!" Lord Matlock clapped him on the shoulder, and Darcy, his eyes bright, gratefully smiled at him.

LADY MATLOCK had not the opportunity to speak to Elizabeth during dinner, but she did catch the conversation. She had also closely observed her nephew's open admiration, and her son's apparent growing appreciation of her. She was delighted to see Darcy so ridiculously smitten. Now she was observing Elizabeth and Georgiana's interaction with great interest. Her niece became animated with Elizabeth's company in a way that she had not seen in years. Elizabeth told Jane of Georgiana's shyness, and all of the ladies took great care to include her in the conversation, drawing her out. Lady Matlock was pleased to see her go to the pianoforte and discuss which pieces they would perform when the men returned.

"Your niece is a lovely young woman, Lady Matlock," said Mrs. Gardiner.

Smiling, she replied, "She is. I am astonished with her behaviour tonight. She has been very withdrawn for some years since her father died, but your nieces, especially Miss Elizabeth, seem to have reawakened her spirits."

"Yes, I noticed that she was intensely shy when we met on Friday. Lizzy has a talent for drawing out the best in shy people. I have observed it many times. Does Miss Darcy have many friends her own age?"

"No, she was taken from school last year, and she is not yet out. I am afraid she may have suffered more for losing the companionship of other girls." Watching the girls look over the music, she continued, "But your nieces seem to have worked some magic on her."

"Lizzy had a long talk with her yesterday and she indicated that Miss Darcy was quite emotional."

"Georgiana confided in her?" Lady Matlock asked, surprised.

"I do not know, I did not ask for details, but Lizzy did say she thinks that she helped her."

"Remarkable." She sized up her companion. "Mrs. Gardiner, was it my imagination, or did I observe a certain intimacy between my nephew and your niece?"

Mrs. Gardiner looked her directly in the eye. "Yes, Lady Matlock, I believe that you did." Lady Matlock smiled with satisfaction. "I believe that I would like to know your niece better, Mrs. Gardiner. Are you ladies available for tea on Wednesday?"

Mrs. Gardiner graciously accepted and Lady Matlock gave her a card from her reticule and noted the address of Matlock House. If her suspicions were correct, she wanted to know all that she could of Miss Elizabeth Bennet.

AS THE MEN moved to rejoin the ladies, Darcy touched Mr. Bennet's arm, halting his progress. "Mr. Bennet, may I ask for a few moments to speak to you privately?"

Mr. Bennet sighed. He anticipated this moment without eagerness. "Certainly, Mr. Darcy, I imagine you have something of import to say."

Darcy was a little confused, but he was too nervous to dwell on Mr. Bennet's enigmatic remarks. "Mr. Bennet, as you know, I met Miss Elizabeth last Monday, and since then we have spent a great deal of time together, with the permission of Mr. Gardiner." Mr. Bennet nodded gravely. "Each time that Miss Elizabeth and I met, my appreciation of her increased, and I have come to the conclusion that we are very well suited for each other. I would like to take this opportunity to ask you for permission to court her." Darcy finally took a breath, and looked expectantly at Mr. Bennet. He was surprised at what he saw.

Mr. Bennet was not smiling. Any other father with a daughter to marry off would have welcomed him with open arms, thrilled that a man of such consequence would turn his eye towards his child. Mr. Bennet did not have the appearance of happiness. He just looked at Darcy.

"Is that all, Mr. Darcy? Do you have any other intentions towards Lizzy?"

Furrowing his brow, Darcy said, "I assure you sir, my intentions are strictly honourable."

"Of course they are." He said sarcastically.

Becoming angry, Darcy replied icily, "I am sorry sir, but I do not take your meaning."

"I find the assertions of your intentions difficult to believe. You are a rich man." He waved his hand, encompassing the room. "Your wealth is displayed quite effectively. No doubt you are quite accustomed to dazzling young girls, promising a courtship to appear proper, and then when you achieve your goal, you send them off, with a tidy little payment for their family."

Shocked and furious, Darcy faced Mr. Bennet. "Sir, I fail to understand you, what exactly do you take me for?" If this was not his Elizabeth's father he would have thrown him from his home immediately.

Mr. Bennet shrugged. "You are a rich man who is used to getting his own way. My daughter is not for sale to satisfy your whims."

Darcy drew himself to his full imposing height and glared at Mr. Bennet. "For your information, sir, I have never asked to court *any* woman before. I sincerely hope to win Miss Elizabeth's heart and hand."

"Why?"

Is it possible that this man is toying with me? Is he amused? Remembering his goal, he swallowed his urge to strangle Mr. Bennet and answered sincerely. "I have never met any other woman like her. She is kind, gracious, sincere, intelligent, witty and loyal. I have been chased by conceited, mercenary, overindulged ladies of society since I came of age. I am tired of fending off their so-called charms. I know that your daughter would be the partner in life of whom I have dreamed. My parents married for love, and I had the privilege of observing the joy of their union for twelve years, until my mother's death. I have always hoped for a marriage of the same calibre, not one of convenience. No woman has ever come close to my vision for my wife until I met Miss Elizabeth. She has not only met my ideal, I know that she will exceed it. She makes me happy, and I hope that someday she will say the same about me."

Mr. Bennet knew listening to Darcy's speech that he was speaking sincerely, and his own argument that Darcy only wished to use Lizzy for his own pleasure would not work. He changed tack.

"I grant your sincerity of motive, Mr. Darcy, but what of Lizzy? She has never been exposed to such riches. How do you know that *she* does not have a mercenary motive?"

Incredulous, Darcy stared at him. "Forgive me sir, but do you really know your daughter?"

Affronted, he shot back, "What do you mean, sir? I raised her did I not?"

"You certainly did, and I am grateful for the access to your library, and your guidance that helped create the extraordinary, intelligent, fascinating woman who is your daughter. That is why it is quite beyond my comprehension that you could stand here before me and accuse her of mercenary motives. You are the man who supported her decision to reject the proposal of her cousin, Mr. Collins."

"You know about that?"

"I do."

Mr. Bennet remained silent.

"Mr. Bennet, your arguments against this courtship have been ill-founded and weak. I wonder if the reason you supported Miss Elizabeth's rejection of Mr. Collins was more for your own selfish reasons." Mr. Bennet stared at him. "I believe that you do not ever intend to let Miss Elizabeth leave home. You see her as your companion, and now that she has met a man who is truly worthy of her, your weak arguments of the past are proving ineffective."

Mr. Bennet was stunned, Darcy was clearly very clever. The belief he held that Darcy would easily give up on Elizabeth after being accused of assumed misdeeds had failed. He knew that he had no grounds for refusing the courtship, but he was not willing to let go of his own desires. He still had time and would search for reasons for Elizabeth to reject him, and even refuse consent for marriage if it went that far. His daughter would never go against his will. "That is enough, Mr. Darcy. I will not listen to any more of this argument. I will grant you permission to court my daughter, and in the end you will see that you will grow to be ashamed of her low connections and will abandon her. I only wish to protect my daughter from pain."

"Thank you for your permission sir. I am sure that you will find that your daughter will never require protection from *me*." Darcy coldly showed Mr. Bennet to the door.

WHEN THE MEN returned to the ladies, Elizabeth looked up eagerly to see Darcy, and was confused that he and her father were absent. Noticing her frown, Richard made his way to her, and quietly told her that Darcy had asked for a private conversation with her father. Seeing her eyes grow wide, and a blush touch her cheeks, he laughed and gave her a reassuring smile.

Nearly a quarter-hour later, Mr. Bennet entered the room alone, and red-faced. He approached Elizabeth and informed her that he had given permission for Darcy to court her. That he was upset and unhappy was clear. He refused to be drawn into any conversation and instead took a large glass of port and began wandering around the room, taking everything in.

It took ten minutes longer for Darcy to regain control of his emotions. To say that he was angry and offended would be an understatement. He had been insulted and degraded in his own home by a country squire. All of the changes that he made to his behaviour over the past year to see the good of people and not to judge them based on their status were dissolving. *How dare he!* He thought angrily. *Who is he to accuse me of such things? He should be grateful for my interest, instead he spat on me, as if I were nothing more than a cad wishing to take advantage of his daughter! The advantage is all for her!* He paced around the room furiously.

Then, through the slightly open door, he heard the sound of Elizabeth's warm, bubbling laughter, and suddenly his fury for himself evaporated. He recognized in time the reappearance of the man he used to be, and returned to the man he was striving to be, the man who would be worthy of Elizabeth. His anger for Mr. Bennet's insult towards him was redirected towards the insult of his own daughter. This woman spoke so glowingly of her love and appreciation for her father, a man who would prefer to see her live a life without love to satisfy his own desires. He could not understand what lay behind Mr. Bennet's actions, but he was sure to be thinking about it frequently.

At least I have his permission to court her. If I do win her hand, no, WHEN I win her hand, he will not welcome my application for his consent to the marriage. I will need to learn when Elizabeth comes of age so that she will be able to make her decision, regardless of her father's feelings. He and Elizabeth had a great many things to discuss, and he would not hold back any part of his confrontation from her. He respected her too much to withhold the truth.

When Darcy finally entered the drawing room, he knew that all eyes were on him, but he only sought one pair. He looked to Elizabeth, and her concern for him was evident. He smiled slightly and went straight to her side. He needed her presence to calm him.

"Are you well? Papa told me that he gave you his consent to court me, but he did not seem pleased. What has happened?"

Darcy disregarded propriety and quickly kissed her gloved hand. "Miss Elizabeth, please, it was a difficult conversation. I do not understand at all your father's reluctance to grant his permission, but for tonight, let us simply rejoice in winning it, and I promise you, I will tell you our entire conversation when we next have time alone. I promise to never lie or conceal anything from you." She continued to look very concerned and caught herself just in time before she reached up to stroke his face. Darcy did not mistake the gesture and smiled at her with gratitude. "Now, Miss Elizabeth, could you please grant me a dear wish? May I hear you play for me? You did promise, remember?"

Still confused, and feeling a burgeoning angry suspicion of what happened, she convinced herself that this was not the time to discuss her father further. She smiled warmly, "Of course, I will play for you, sir. I always keep my promises, especially when I am assured of an appreciative audience." She gave him a cheeky grin, and was happy to hear his soft laugh. Settling on the bench of the pianoforte she played while he leaned against it. They were alone in their own world. She played with feeling, and he felt his emotions soothed by her sweet voice.

THE REMAINDER of the evening was pleasant. Darcy endeavoured to avoid Mr. Bennet and stayed by Elizabeth's side. He only managed to smile for her though, and only with a small lift to the corners of his mouth. What he needed was to take her into his embrace and bury his face in her hair. Unfortunately he was limited to simply drinking in her scent. After his guests departed, with many genuine expressions of gratitude, and another blushing kiss to Elizabeth's hand defiantly delivered directly in front of Mr. Bennet, Darcy found himself ensconced in his library with Richard.

"Well Cousin, what think you of the evening?" Richard had not failed to notice the change in Darcy and Mr. Bennet's demeanour after their conference.

Darcy took a long sip on his brandy and looked at Richard thoughtfully. "I think that it went very well. Miss Elizabeth was as lovely and engaging as I knew she would be. Her growing friendship with Georgiana was a pleasure to observe, and it was gratifying to see how open your parents were to meeting her and her family. That was a wonderfully unexpected surprise."

"I think that my parents have been so concerned that you would never marry, that they welcome seeing your interest in any woman. They know that you have never desired a match with Cousin Anne, despite what Aunt Catherine claims, and they also know that she would not be healthy enough to be a wife for any man. They were concerned at first about you being taken in by a fortune hunter, but quickly realized that you are well-versed in the machinations of those women. I think that their desire for this evening, once they realized that you were introducing them to your potential wife, was to simply observe."

"I imagine that you will be talking to them about it most thoroughly tomorrow." Darcy said dryly.

"Ha! I will be surprised if they are not laying in wait for me tonight!" They both laughed at the truth of his statement. "Bingley seemed rather taken with Miss Bennet," he said grinning, "I did not think that I would ever see a man so instantly struck by love again after your reaction to Miss Elizabeth." He chuckled at Darcy's glare. "You cannot deny it, Darcy. You were fascinating Monday night. Was it not even a week ago? Amazing!"

Darcy ignored Richard's barbs. "Yes, Bingley was quite enamoured of Miss Bennet, but we should, however, note that he is frequently in and out of love. I will take care to observe his sincerity. I would not wish her to be hurt."

"Because it would hurt Miss Elizabeth," suggested Richard sagely. Darcy made no reply. "The Gardiners seemed an excellent couple. If I did not know the truth of his circumstances, I would have said they were members of the *ton*, not the first circles, but they could easily fit in. Excellent conversation from both of them, and Georgiana seemed to respond favourably to them, to all of them, Bennet and Gardiner alike."

"She seems to be returning to herself." Looking at Richard, he added, "She had a long talk with Miss Elizabeth yesterday, and spent the time after she left deep in contemplation. Miss Elizabeth did not have a chance to tell me everything about the talk, only to say that she challenged her behaviour with Wickham and had her consider the reasons behind her response to him. I hope that Georgiana opens up to me about it soon. But in any case, I cannot deny the positive affect that a few hours in Miss Elizabeth's company have made on her, and I am grateful to her for it."

"She is a remarkable woman," agreed Richard.

"She certainly is; which makes her father's reaction to my request for courtship so odd." Darcy proceeded to tell Richard of the entire confrontation with Mr. Bennet. He was astonished with the man's attitude.

"I wondered what happened between the two of you when he returned to the room. What is your assessment of his behaviour?"

Shaking his head, Darcy showed his frustration. "I truly do not know. At first I thought it was him simply being overprotective, but when he began questioning Miss Elizabeth's motives, I began questioning his. I am suspicious that he is jealous of her."

"Really? Interesting. I would have thought that he was selfish, and did not wish to lose her companionship."

"I considered that, but now after having a little time to think about it, and also taking into consideration some statements that Miss Elizabeth has made about the failure of marriages of convenience, and their negative impact on the family, my assessment has changed. I wonder if he is looking at the possible love match of his daughter to a man who can give her financial security as well as access and exposure to people and culture that he would not ever experience."

"It may very well be a combination of the two."

"You may be correct. He really had no reason to deny my request for courtship, but he may be very difficult for future requests." Richard raised his brows at that.

"Fortunately he is returning to Hertfordshire on the morrow, and you will be free to court Miss Elizabeth. Mr. Gardiner seems to be supportive."

"I would not let that keep me from Miss Elizabeth if he were not."

Richard chuckled. "My, my, Cousin, you are lost."

Chapter 7

"Edward, I gave permission for Mr. Darcy to court Lizzy tonight. I think that it was a grave error, and that I should take her back to Longbourn in the morning." Mr. Bennet was pacing in Mr. Gardiner's study after their return from Darcy's townhouse.

"I do not understand, Thomas. What do you suspect? Mr. Darcy is a fine young man."

"I think that he only wants to ruin her and then abandon her!"

"That is unfounded! He would not have asked for your permission to court her if he was not serious! He introduced her to his family, as well as introduced our family to them. He is a man who could have any woman, any heiress, and he chose Lizzy. It is a great honour! Do you not see this?"

"I do not trust him. I think that Lizzy should be at home where she belongs."

Beginning to suspect his motives, Mr. Gardiner asked, "What about Jane?"

"She may stay here. She seemed to enjoy the attentions of Mr. Bingley, and if they form an attachment here, it may continue when he comes to Netherfield."

"I am confused. What is the difference between Jane and Elizabeth?"

"I just do not think Mr. Darcy is good enough for her."

"My Lord, Thomas, what more do you want? A title? Royalty? Mr. Darcy is an exceptional young man. I think that you have a problem letting go of Lizzy." The statement was met with silence. "Thomas? You must realize that she will leave you someday. How can you deny her a possibly extraordinary future with a man such as Mr. Darcy?" Again there was silence. "Thomas?"

"She may stay." Mr. Bennet strode out of the room.

ELIZABETH TRIED to speak to her father about his meeting with Mr. Darcy early Monday morning. He refused to answer any of her questions. In the end, he told her that he trusted her to do the right thing, encouraged her to remember that she knew very little of him, and told her she would be always welcomed back at Longbourn, no matter what happened. Mr. Bennet soon took his leave and returned home.

Elizabeth knocked on the door to Mr. Gardiner's study, and entered when she heard his call.

"Lizzy! What brings you here?" He knew it would be about her father. He stayed home from work that morning, hoping that she would seek him out.

Elizabeth looked confused. "Uncle, I am so unsure of myself. I have been asked to enter into a courtship with the kind of man I have only dreamed of knowing. I already respect him, and hold him in esteem, and I am astonished at my developing tender regard for him."

Gently, Mr. Gardiner asked, "Then what is confusing you, Lizzy?"

She looked up into her uncle's kind, concerned face. This was the relative who she respected more than her father. She always hoped to find a man like him as her husband. The Gardiner's marriage was the one that she wished for, based on love and mutual respect and support. Her parent's marriage was an absolute failure.

"Papa. He had some sort of confrontation with Mr. Darcy last night. Mr. Darcy said that he would tell me everything about it when we could have some privacy, but I think that I have an idea what they discussed. Papa has been saying such odd things to me about him. He keeps implying that Mr. Darcy will hurt me. If he said something like that to Mr. Darcy, I can understand why he was so upset. I just do not understand why he would want to convince me that Mr. Darcy was an unworthy man."

Mr. Gardiner sighed, and walking to Elizabeth, laid a hand on her shoulder, "You know that your father thinks of you as his favourite child, do you not?" She nodded. "And, living there, you know how unhappy your parents' marriage is?" She nodded again, sadly. "I am only surmising this, but I think that your father is afraid of losing you to marriage and that he would behave this way to any man who you accepted."

"He would wish me to remain unmarried and at home?" She demanded.

"Perhaps not married so soon, and then to someone close to home."

"I cannot believe this! That would be so . . ." She searched for the words, "selfish!"

"Yes Lizzy." He sat next to her and took her hand. "I will not stand in the way of your courtship, and you are welcome to stay here as long as you wish. Mr. Darcy is an exceptional young man, and you should not let your father's insecurity and unhappiness end this dream of yours."

"I hardly know what to think." Coming to a decision, she drew herself up. "Thank you for your kindness, Uncle. I will stay here. I will continue my courtship with Mr. Darcy, and we will see where it leads. I will do what I feel will constitute my own happiness, without reference to my father."

"Good for you Lizzy, and remember, on April 4th, you will be of age, and you will legally be able to make your own decisions."

She smiled. "I think that is something I should mention to Mr. Darcy!"

BINGLEY BURST into Darcy's study shouting with excitement. "Darcy!"

"Good morning, Bingley," Darcy grinned at his friend and leaned back in his chair. "What brings you here this fine day, as if I did not know?"

"She is an angel, Darcy! Did you not see her?"

"Who are you talking about?"

"Miss Bennet! Miss Jane Bennet! Oh, Darcy, she is everything lovely!"

Darcy chuckled, "Are you in love again, Bingley?"

"Yes, and for the last time. She is the one. I know it!"

Darcy shook his head. "I have heard this all before Bingley." Then regarding him very seriously, "I will not have you trifling with Miss Elizabeth's sister."

Bingley had been sitting, smiling off into space, with a vision of Jane Bennet in his mind. Darcy's last words snapped him out of his reverie. "Is there something you need to tell me Darcy?"

"Only that I am courting Miss Elizabeth Bennet." Bingley stared at him. "I have every intention of winning her heart and marrying her. This means that someday, hopefully soon, Miss Jane Bennet will be my sister. I know you Charles. If you are truly serious about Miss Bennet, I will support you. All that I ask is for you to take this very slowly. Do not declare yourself or give any indication of your intentions until you are absolutely sure of both your and her feelings."

Bingley regarded him steadily. "I know that I have behaved impulsively in the past, but I think that I am ready to enter into a serious courtship. I spent last night almost exclusively talking to Miss Bennet, and she has met my vision of the woman I would someday marry."

"All I ask is that you take it slowly, Charles."

Bingley started, "How long have YOU known Miss Elizabeth, Darcy?"

Darcy smiled. "One week, today."

"And you have the audacity to tell ME to take things slowly!"

"Touché, Bingley, but you can hardly compare my amorous affairs with yours."

Bingley smiled. "Touché, Darcy."

"So you will take it slowly?"

"I will."

"I am happy to hear it."

Leaning forward, Bingley grinned. "When will you next call at the Gardiner home?"

"MY DEAR MISS DARCY it has been far too long since we have seen you! My, how you have grown!" Caroline Bingley smiled her most simpering smile to Georgiana, winked at Louisa, and sipped her tea.

"Thank you, Miss Bingley. I do not believe that I have grown at all since I last saw you." Georgiana was careful not to mention that she was happy to see her, because she was not. She knew that Caroline Bingley was there to catch a glimpse of her brother, who had no desire to catch a glimpse of her. Georgiana looked nervously at her companion, Mrs. Annesley.

"We saw Mr. Darcy at the theatre last week, but did not see you there. I was surprised that he did not bring you along for a musical performance. You are so accomplished at the pianoforte that I would think he would be sure to invite you."

"I was invited to attend, Miss Bingley, but decided to stay home that evening. I felt a headache coming on. My brother said that he and my cousin, Colonel Fitzwilliam, had a very enjoyable time." She hoped that ended the inquiry, but of course, it did not.

"Yes, I saw that your brother was smiling a good deal during the intermission. I do wonder what could have brought him such happiness? I meant to ask him after the performance, but he dashed away before we could catch up."

I am not surprised. Georgiana thought. "I am sorry Miss Bingley, but since I was not there, I cannot begin to speculate about my brother's behaviour."

"Of course not." Caroline hid her frustration. "Is he at home today? I would be happy to greet him now, since we missed each other before?"

"I am sorry, Miss Bingley, but I believe that he and Mr. Bingley left some time ago."

"My brother was here? And they left together? Do you know where they went?" Caroline glanced at Louisa, who shrugged her shoulders.

"I know that they were to pay a call on some friends."

"Charles did not mention that he was paying calls today. I wonder who they went to visit."

"I am sorry; Miss Bingley, but I cannot help you." Georgiana smiled to herself. *That was truthful enough!*

Caroline and Louisa soon departed, but they both found the idea of Charles and Mr. Darcy paying a social call together very odd. They planned to speak to Charles that evening.

"LIZZY, I have received some letters from my friends in Derbyshire. I think that you should read them." Mrs. Gardiner walked into the sitting room where Elizabeth had been quietly discussing Mr. Bennet's behaviour with Jane.

"You wish me to read your friends' letters, Aunt?"

"Last week after we met Mr. Darcy, I wrote to my friends in Lambton, and asked after Mr. Darcy's reputation. I knew that they would not personally know him, but an estate the size of Pemberley touches many lives, and the character of its owner is reflected in the comfort of his tenants. Since we really knew very little of him when he first asked to call on you, I thought that this would be a good way to get to know a little about him from neutral parties."

Elizabeth looked at her aunt in amusement. "That was rather creative of you, Aunt."

"Yes, it was." She said with a little satisfied grin. "Would you like to see them now?"

"Of course!" Elizabeth took the small stack of letters. "Help me Jane, if you read some, we can learn of his character so much faster!"

"Lizzy, this is wrong! I feel like a spy!" Jane fretted.

"Oh, and you are not curious, either!" Elizabeth accused.

"Oh, give me the letters!" Jane grabbed them out of her hand.

The girls settled down to read and soon they shared the results. As Aunt Gardiner said, none of the writers personally knew the Darcy family. Occasionally Mr. Darcy was seen in town, but never Miss Darcy. His reputation was that of a very good employer to his servants, who were well-compensated. His tenant's homes were repaired when necessary, and he was always first to help those families that had suffered some sort of tragedy, whether fire, illness, or death. He provided food baskets and medicine if a family was struggling. He was considered very stern, but fair when resolving disputes, and did not tolerate tenants ignoring his orders. He was seen as proud, but in a way that was acceptable. Pride in his family and his estate was understandable. The history of how he paid merchants for the debts left by George Wickham was well-known. All in all, he was regarded as a man to respect.

Elizabeth was very gratified to read of the high esteem that Mr. Darcy's Derbyshire neighbours held him. It confirmed her own intuition over the goodness of the man who had singled her out. As she and Jane exchanged letters, her justification for agreeing to her courtship became stronger, and her anger with her father's false accusations grew.

"MR. DARCY and Mr. Bingley," announced the maid.

The gentlemen entered the room and bowed, and the ladies dropped the necessary curtsies.

"Ladies, I know that we did not make any arrangements for a visit today, but we thought that we would take a chance and see if you would be home. I hope that we are not interrupting anything?" Darcy focussed on Elizabeth's smile.

"No, you are not interrupting at all, gentlemen. We were just enjoying some correspondence that I recently received from my friends in Lambton." Mrs. Gardiner winked at the girls.

"Ah, and I hope that all is well in Derbyshire? I imagine that the snow is quite heavy there right now." Darcy still had not torn his eyes from Elizabeth.

Amused with his distraction, she smiled to herself. "From what my friends have said, the winter is unusually mild this year."

"That is good news to all of Pemberley." Still fixed on Elizabeth, he delighted in her growing blush.

Shaking her head, Mrs. Gardiner suggested that the four young people take advantage of the sunny day and walk in the park. They all gladly agreed, and donning their outerwear, set off. Darcy confidently took Elizabeth's arm and they set off at a brisk pace, leaving Bingley and Jane to their own devices.

"Mr. Darcy, may I enquire after Georgiana? She seemed to be in good spirits last night. I tried to convince her to play, but she would not be moved."

"She is well, Miss Elizabeth, I will tell her that you asked after her. In fact, she wanted me to arrange another visit with you. Are you available to call on her Wednesday?" He looked at her hopefully.

"As a matter of fact, we were invited to tea with Lady Matlock on Wednesday."

"You were?" He asked, surprised.

"Indeed. She made it clear that she wished to know me better."

"I am very pleased to hear of this. I always hoped that I would receive my family's support when I finally decided to enter a courtship, but to have it displayed so easily is a great and wonderful surprise." Darcy was truly amazed. He was sure that her lack of connection and fortune would have been a problem with his family, despite what his uncle told him. It was so ingrained what it meant for him to do his duty by his name that he still expected a great fight to have Elizabeth accepted, even after they received her so well at dinner.

"Did you think that they would oppose you?"

"I frankly did not know." Seeing her concern, he smiled. "You must realize, I have never brought a lady home to meet the family before, and I did not know what to expect. Acceptance is unexpected. They must have truly enjoyed your company, which I admit is gratifying to my confidence in my discernment." His smile grew wider, exposing the devastating dimples.

"You sir, are entirely too self-assured!" She lightly slapped his arm. He laughed but his smile was erased as she spoke quietly, "I wish that my father was as accepting of you."

"He was very adamant last night. He seemed to feel that I was going to hurt you and walk away. He did not think that I would lower myself to someone of your station. His arguments were weak and ridiculous. When I did not respond to them, he suggested that you had a mercenary motive for accepting my attentions."

Elizabeth was appalled. "He said those things to you?"

"Yes, amongst others, but that was the general idea. After thinking over the conversation last night, I could not decide if he wished to prevent you from marrying anyone at all to keep you at home, or if he was jealous that you were being courted for reasons of affection." He fixed his intense stare on her.

She disregarded the rest of his statement for the moment. "Affection?"

"Yes, Miss Elizabeth, a very steadily growing affection."

"Thank you for telling me that, Mr. Darcy. It is good to know that my opinion is shared." She had looked down, but now peeked up at him quickly. He drew in a sharp breath, and raised her hand to his lips, kissing it. They walked silently, both suddenly warmer.

Just then, they came around the circle of the path and met Jane and Mr. Bingley. "Darcy, Miss Bennet and I had a wonderful idea! Let us attend the theatre on Friday! I think that a new production is opening. Do you still own a box?" His enthusiasm was boundless, his grin was huge, and Darcy noted that Miss Bennet did not seem at all opposed to the idea.

Darcy looked at Elizabeth, who was staring at her sister with expressive eyes and glancing at Mr. Bingley with a smile. He knew that he would love to attend the theatre and sit in a darkened box next to Elizabeth for hours. "What an excellent idea, Bingley! Do you agree, Miss Elizabeth?" She nodded at him happily. "Perhaps we should invite the Gardiners, as well?"

"I am sure that they would be pleased, sir." Elizabeth nodded.

"Then it is set! To the theatre we will go!" Bingley took Jane's arm in his and merrily led the way back to the Gardiner home.

"Poor Jane, I think that your friend overwhelms her!" Seeing Darcy's look of concern, she added. "She was quite impressed with him last night. She thought he was just what a young man ought to be."

"You mean a fool?" He said, sharing her smile.

"We are all fools in love, Mr. Darcy."

Chapter 8

*A*lmost the moment that the gentlemen took their leave, Mrs. Gardiner ordered the carriage and insisted that Elizabeth and Jane visit her modiste to purchase new gowns for the night at the theatre. Both sisters protested that the purchase was unnecessary, but Mrs. Gardiner knew better. The girls, especially Elizabeth, would be under very close scrutiny that night. They were unknown women, being escorted by well known rich men who had been the subject of matchmaking mothers' machinations throughout London for years. It was important that they look very well indeed.

The modiste promised that she would have the gowns ready by Friday morning, with a fitting on Thursday afternoon. While Jane looked at the dress patterns, Elizabeth chose her fabric, and thought ruefully to herself that she should take her own advice and choose something that would compliment a blushing face.

RICHARD ENTERED his father's study with the air of a man expecting an inquisition. The message that he received upon returning home from his post was to present himself as soon as possible.

"So what inspired this invitation?" Richard asked as he walked over to the sideboard to pour himself a brandy. He held up the carafe to Lord Matlock, questioning him silently, and seeing his nod, filled a glass for him as well.

"Please close the door, Richard, and take a seat." Lord Matlock watched as his son settled into the leather armchair opposite his desk and began. "I imagine that you know the subject of our interview?"

"Could it perhaps have something to do with my cousin?" He asked, smirking.

"It does." Lord Matlock looked down at his steepled fingers. "We were quite taken by surprise last night, Richard. Your mother and I had no idea that we were coming to dinner to meet a possible wife for Darcy, let alone her family. Did you have any prior knowledge of this?"

Richard could not tell if his father was angry. "I knew that they were invited, yes. I also knew that Darcy felt himself instantly smitten with Miss Elizabeth when we first saw her last week. He has stated that he intends to win her. I did not know that he was going to propose a courtship to her father last night. He asked me to keep his confidence. He did not want you or mother to form any opinions before meeting her yourselves."

"By our appearing in his home with the Bennets and Gardiners, we give implied consent to the match. If your mother and I were not so impressed with Miss Elizabeth, we would be very unhappy to have been so deceived." Lord Matlock looked very sternly at his son.

"But you did like her?" Richard focused on the positive.

Lord Matlock sighed. "Yes, we did. Very much. She is quite an engaging young woman. Beautiful, lively, good mind, and from her interaction with

Georgiana, I would say very good-hearted." He thought some more. "It was extraordinary to see Darcy smile and laugh, and to see Georgiana drawn out from that burden of shyness she carries."

Richard nodded. "I can attest to it all beginning the night that Darcy met Miss Elizabeth and chased her down outside the theatre to learn her name."

Lord Matlock raised his brows. "Really? Richard I would appreciate it if you could tell me all that you know of the situation, including Mr. Bennet's odd behaviour."

Richard proceeded to tell his father the events of the last week, ending with the discussion he had with Darcy that night. Lord Matlock was even more impressed with his nephew's behaviour, his niece's response, and the fascinating creature that was Elizabeth. Her father bothered him, though.

"He actually fought the attachment? The idiocy of the man! To have one of the richest young men in England offer to court your daughter and to accuse him of God knows what just to keep her to yourself is the greatest lunacy I have ever heard! He has next to nothing to offer her and he disparages Darcy!"

"Darcy is undecided if he is selfish or jealous."

"Or fit for Bedlam!"

The men shook their heads and laughed. "If anything, Darcy expected the objection to the attachment to come from *our* family." Richard looked at his father intently.

Lord Matlock smiled. "He has good reason for that. As the head of the Fitzwilliam family, I am naturally concerned with maintaining the fortune of the estate, including the connections made upon marriages. A potential wife for you, your brother, and Darcy should have something to offer besides just herself, otherwise it would be a degradation, and she would be rejected by society. At least that is how I used to see it." Richard sat up, very interested. "Your brother is well married, so it does not affect him anymore. You need to marry with fortune in mind since you will not be inheriting the estate or title, although you should know that I do have something set aside for you *if* you ever do marry." Richard tilted his head at his father, and raised his brows. "We will discuss that another time, Son. We are concerned with Darcy now. But for him, when he came of age, I had the same expectations, until I spoke to his father. His father learned that he was dying, and he charged me with the task of looking after Darcy's self-interest when it came time to choose his wife. His attitude towards marriage as a duty to honour the Darcy name had changed significantly. He wanted him to marry for affection. He did not care if the girl had a fortune or title or any of the rest of it. He wanted more than anything to see his son love and be loved equally. He wanted happiness for him, because he knew what his son had suffered after the loss of his mother, and what Darcy would be taking on upon his death. He wanted Darcy to have the marriage that he experienced with my sister, Anne."

Richard could not withhold the expression of surprise on his face. "So he asked you to make sure that Darcy did not settle for a marriage of convenience?"

"That is it, exactly. If he seemed to be heading in that direction, I was to dissuade him from it. My sister Catherine has been bleating for years that he was to marry Anne. I knew that Darcy did not want it, and I told her so, but she is headstrong, and would not hear of him rejecting her. He has been alone for a very long time, and if he thinks that Miss Elizabeth Bennet is the woman he wishes to make his wife, and I see that she returns his affection, I will not stand in their way. Your mother and I will support them, and make it clear to society that our family has accepted her, and will help to introduce her to the first circles. It is the last favour that I can do for my sister."

Richard sat looking at his father, feeling new respect rising for him, as well as an uncomfortable jealousy of his cousin. "I think that is the greatest gift you can ever provide Darcy, Father. I hope that you can tell this to him yourself. He has declared that he will pursue Miss Elizabeth regardless of what her father or our family thinks, but I know as well as you do that he will truly wish for your support."

Lord Matlock stared down at his desk, his eyes shining, thinking of Darcy's parents and their hopes for their son. "I already have." Then thinking to himself he wondered, *But shall I tell him the rest of George Darcy's story?*

TO ELIZABETH'S SURPRISE she and Jane received an invitation from Georgiana to come and visit Tuesday morning. Darcy was attending to business away from home and she would enjoy their company. The carriage had been sent, and if the ladies were available, they were to take it to Darcy House. Aunt Gardiner was happy to send them on their way.

When they arrived, they met in the music room, drinking tea and discussing the dinner party. Jane asked Georgiana how long she had known Mr. Bingley.

"Oh, he has been friends with William for seven years, but I do not think that I really started seeing much of him until about three or four years ago, after my father died. For the first few years after William took over Pemberley, he was so busy learning everything that he hardly ever came into town, and of course, I was in school. But once he seemed to be confident in his work, he started socializing more, and he came to London again. By that time Mr. Bingley had graduated from Cambridge, so he became a regular visitor. We saw him often at Pemberley, too."

"I understand that he has two sisters?" Jane asked tentatively.

Georgiana tried not to look unhappy with the mention of the ladies, but her expression was not missed by either Bennet sister. "Yes. There is Mrs. Hurst, his eldest sibling, and Miss Bingley." Looking at Elizabeth, she said, "Miss Bingley is quite adamant that she is going to marry William."

Elizabeth raised her brow. "Is she, now?"

"Yes, and I know that it is rude to speak ill of another person, but. . ." She hesitated.

"But?"

"Oh Elizabeth, she is just awful! William tolerates her because she is Mr. Bingley's sister, but she pays me calls and looks around the house as if she is redecorating it in her mind. I have heard rumours that she uses William's name to be invited to parties where she would otherwise never be asked to come. And when she is here, she almost attaches herself to him! It is so upsetting! I was afraid for some time that he would give in and marry her, but he assured me that would never happen, thank goodness!"

"Is she rude to you?" Elizabeth asked, considering just what lengths this woman would go to achieve her goal, and wondering how many other Miss Bingleys were wandering around town with the same ideas.

"Oh, she is never rude to me; she wants my favour, after all. No, but I have heard that she is quite rude to any other woman who tries to catch William's attention. She has a very sharp tongue."

"Hmm. Well, I am sure that I shall meet her at some point, but I thank you for putting me on alert!" Elizabeth smiled.

"If anyone can stand up to her, you can, Elizabeth. She quite frightens me!" They all laughed, but Jane's face showed her concern.

"I wonder what her hopes are for her brother?" Jane asked, almost to herself.

"I think that she hopes he will marry me." Georgiana said quietly

Jane and Elizabeth gasped. "But you are so much younger than he!"

"Yes, but if he married me, it would bring her closer to William." Georgiana said, displaying great understanding. The ladies all nodded at the veracity of her statement. "I am not at all interested in him. He is very nice; and friendly, and I like him very much, but I see him as another brother, and nothing else."

Jane was relieved to hear this news. "It seems that the brother is nothing like the sister, then."

"Well, if you think about it, Jane, I am nothing like you and we are nothing like our other sisters. Simply having the same parents does not guarantee that the children will be exactly alike. Each has their own experiences which form their character."

"In the case of Mr. Bingley, I think that the experiences that formed his character must have been very good indeed!" Jane declared. Elizabeth and Georgiana exchanged knowing smiles.

The sisters encouraged Georgiana to play for them, and after hesitating, she finally agreed. She became comfortable after receiving their sincere praise played several pieces and insisted that Elizabeth play as well.

Darcy returned home from his morning at the solicitor's tired but happy with the results of their work. He was told that Georgiana was entertaining some callers when he heard Elizabeth's voice floating down the hallway, singing a love song. Walking to the music room, he stood unnoticed in the doorway and listened to her lovely voice as he watched her play. Her eyes were closed, and she was swaying slightly. He imagined walking up behind her, and gently placing his hands on her shoulders, then bending to trail kisses down her neck. As he considered where those kisses might lead, the song ended and Georgiana noticed him.

"William! I did not expect you home so soon, what a nice surprise!"

Elizabeth instantly blushed. *Not again!* Attempting to regain her equilibrium, she rose from the bench and greeted him.

Darcy smiled to see her blush and bowed. "It was a most pleasant surprise to enter the house to hear such enchanting song filling the air. It instantly relieved the tension left from my business. I thank you Miss Elizabeth."

"I am pleased that I could bring you such relief, sir. And I thank you for your compliment. I do not speak Italian, so I hope that my pronunciation of the words was not too ill."

Darcy looked deeply into her sparkling eyes. "I assure you, Miss Bennet, the meaning was perfectly clear."

The sisters stayed a little longer, but they had promised their aunt to not overstay, and to Darcy's great disappointment, he soon found himself handing them into his carriage for the trip home, holding Elizabeth's hand a little longer than was necessary before reluctantly, he let go.

TEA WITH Lady Matlock was not what they had expected. She was gracious and solicitous, not at all intimidating, at least to Elizabeth, who answered her questions with humour and fortitude. Jane was relieved that it was her sister who was being interviewed and not herself. Upon learning that they were to attend the theatre on Friday night, Lady Matlock was pleased to learn that new gowns had been ordered for the occasion. She agreed with Mrs. Gardiner that the sisters would immediately attract attention. Jane asked why.

"Are you aware of the income of the gentlemen who will be escorting you Friday?"

Jane looked at Elizabeth, and said, "No, your ladyship, I never thought to ask. Have you, Lizzy?"

"No, I have not really considered it. I supposed that Mr. Darcy was comfortable, since he has both an estate and a house in town, and that Mr. Bingley was doing well since he had taken the lease on Netherfield and was considering purchase of his own estate. I know that with our background it is wise to be prudent financially when considering an attachment, but speaking for both of us, we are not interested in fortune as much as felicity."

Lady Matlock was impressed, and she had seen enough of the ladies to know that they were being honest. "Well, I appreciate your candour, and your admirable sentiments. However, since everyone else in town knows, or at least thinks they know the truth, you should as well. Mr. Bingley is generally considered to have five thousand pounds per year, and my nephew is rumoured to have ten." She watched for their reactions.

Their eyes grew wide, and looked to Aunt Gardiner, who did not seem surprised. Elizabeth regained her wit quickly. "Well, the wives of these men certainly will not have to be worried about starving in the hedgerows!"

They all laughed and Lady Matlock rose. "Miss Elizabeth, I would like to speak to you privately for a moment. Would you please join me in my study? I am sure that your aunt and sister will be fine on their own." She looked at her expectantly.

"Of course, Lady Matlock." Elizabeth was a little taken aback, but quickly regained her possession. "Aunt Gardiner, will you excuse us for a moment?"

"Certainly my dear." Mrs. Gardiner smiled, but looked at the Countess appraisingly.

They left the room, and entered Lady Matlock's personal study, a cosy room, and obviously well-used. "Miss Elizabeth, please do not be alarmed by my asking you here. I wanted to simply take the opportunity to tell you something of my nephew. He seems to have become attached to you very quickly, and ordinarily that would possibly alarm me if he were a younger man, however, I realize that he is quite old enough to know his own mind. That being said, I want you to know that his behaviour with you is singular, and it is a great delight to see. My nephew has a life of extraordinary privilege and is a very powerful man, but also carries the burden of enormous responsibility. He was thrust into the role at a very early age when his father died. That is the age when young men should be thinking of the next ball, not the yield of wool, or if his tenants' efforts would produce enough from the crops to feed both them and support the estate. William has never displayed a desire for society. He did his duty as was required by his station, but as often as not, he would prefer to hide in a corner, or stay at home with a book. What I saw in his face in your company was most extraordinary. Even his body was different, he held himself, when directly in your company, in a relaxed posture. What I am trying to tell you, my dear, is to be gentle with him. He truly is an innocent in opening his heart. He has been hurt terribly by people and events outside of his control, and his uncle and I have recognized for years that he needed to find someone who would care for him, and not his image. I think that he immediately recognized you as that person." She was relieved to see the young woman's concern.

"Thank you Lady Matlock. I have been developing my suspicions about some sort of pain in Mr. Darcy's past, and although we have only known each other a little over a week, I recognize that he is a man who needs to be cared for, because it seems that he is very much alone, and far too busy caring for everyone and everything except himself." She smiled. "I am honoured that he thinks that I am the person who might be the one he needs to be happy. I promise you, I will be gentle with him, as I know that he will be gentle with my rather innocent heart as well."

Lady Matlock smiled with relief and nodded. "Thank you my dear. I know that you have nothing to fear from him. He is the best of men." She gave Elizabeth's hand a squeeze and they rejoined the others. Mrs. Gardiner looked at her niece carefully and was glad to see that her talk with Lady Matlock was not one of censure or warning, as was evident by the warm smiles they held for each other when they entered the room. Soon they returned to Gracechurch Street, and prepared for the coming of the gentlemen for dinner, all armed with new information and questions.

28 YEARS EARLIER

"Philip?" Amanda Carrington looked in the door of her husband's study at his estate, Kingston Park, in Buckingham.

Smiling at the sound of his wife's voice, Philip Carrington looked up. "Yes, my dear? Come in." He loved his wife dearly. They had been married for nearly seven years, in perfect harmony, but for one very sad deficit. They could not have children. His bout with mumps at the late age of twenty was probably to blame. And as Mr. Carrington had no brothers, and most likely no heirs, Kingston Park would eventually go to some very distant cousin someday. The thought of it was heartbreaking.

Hesitating, Amanda entered and sat, not in the guest chair by his great desk, but instead in his lap. She wrapped her arms around him and buried her face in his neck. These were sure signs that she had something of weight to say.

"Philip, did you know that Cook has a niece who is, or was, in service?"

Knitting his brow, Carrington said, "No, but I imagine it is not a surprise. Did you say that she *was* in service?"

"Yes, she was serving as a chambermaid for the Markham family, in Surry."

"Oh. And she has lost her position? Are you asking if we should hire her? Those decisions are yours, dear."

"I know, but you see, her niece was very innocent, and when a young friend of the Markham's son came to visit a few months ago, she was . . ." Mrs. Carrington paused.

"I see, and now she is with child. What do you propose, Amanda?"

Amanda finally pulled her head from her husband's shoulder and looked at him with teary eyes. "The girl is only fifteen years old, Philip. If she survives the birth at all, she will have no way of caring for the baby. I propose that we offer to take him in as our own, and give him your name. We could find her a position with another family and hire a wet nurse. We would have a child, and you would have an heir." She looked at him pleadingly. "It would be such a blessing to save this little one, Philip. Please?"

Carrington gazed into his wife's eyes. "Are we sure that this is a gentleman's child?"

"Yes, Cook said that her niece would provide his name if we take him. She had never been with a man before, or since, and she remembers him well."

"And why has the girl not approached the man's family, or told her old employer who he was?"

"They know, and they said that it was her own fault for allowing him to impose himself on her, and dismissed her from their home."

"Let me think about this, Amanda, and speak to my attorney. If we can take the baby, and we can somehow make it my heir, then we will help this girl, but an illegitimate child cannot inherit." He brushed some hair from her eyes. "I know how desperately you want to be a mother, and I would love to be a father."

"Oh thank you, Philip! I love you!" Amanda showered his face with kisses.

Laughing, Carrington pushed her away, and held her face in his hands. "It seems that the decision has already been made!"

ROGERS TOOK his brush and carefully removed any lint that may have found its way onto Darcy's fine black coat. He had fussed over his Master's appearance that evening, from tying a spectacular knot in his cravat to making sure that his shoes held the perfect shine. He and the rest of the staff at Darcy House knew that Mr. Darcy had entered into a courtship with Miss Elizabeth Bennet and were relieved that their very real fears of gaining Miss Caroline Bingley as their Mistress could be safely put aside. They were impressed with the unmistakable improvement in the Darcy siblings' emotions since Miss Bennet entered their lives. The staff, at first quite concerned about the lady after enduring Mr. Darcy's unprecedented preparations for tea, were greatly relieved to find an amiable, pleasant, unpretentious young woman who spoke kindly to them and complimented their efforts. All of the staff hoped that Mr. Darcy's pursuit of this lady would prove successful.

"Well Rogers, will I do for a trip to the theatre?" Darcy asked, looking at his appearance critically.

"Very well, sir. You will make an excellent impression." Darcy caught the valet's eye in the mirror and nodded.

"Quite."

Darcy entered his carriage to collect Bingley before proceeding to Gracechurch Street. He had not seen Elizabeth since Wednesday and missed her intensely. He laughed to himself, a fortnight ago he did not know that she existed, and now he could not stand to be away from her for two days.

Elizabeth was dressed and watching for Darcy's carriage from her usual position in the window. She was missing him terribly and marvelled over how much she thought about him, and wondered if he missed her at all.

When the carriage finally arrived, Darcy exited the coach and caught sight of Elizabeth's lovely eyes watching him from their window, and again the warmth of homecoming stole over him. Before the gentlemen had a chance to enter the house, they were joined by their guests outside, and there was no chance for a private greeting. Elizabeth and Darcy were simply left to exchange heartfelt gazes across the distance of the carriage seats.

Jane welcomed Mr. Bingley's warm greeting and while enjoying his attentions, had formed no opinion about wishing for a future with him. For now, she simply resolved to know him better. Bingley had already decided that he certainly liked her very much, and he was serious when he told Darcy that he thought she was the woman he would marry. However, he also knew that Darcy was correct, he had been in love many times before, and this time, perhaps the most important time, he would take it slowly.

CAROLINE BINGLEY was infuriated. Her brother and the Hursts returned to town nearly three weeks earlier, and she still had not seen Mr. Darcy. She knew that her brother had been out with him several evenings, and paid calls to him at his home. She did not understand why he did not ask her to accompany him. Did he not wish her to marry his best friend? And tonight, she learned that Charles was attending the theatre with him. Why did he not ask Mr. Darcy to invite the rest of his family to share his box? She knew that Mr. Darcy would come to pick up Charles to take him to the theatre. Why did he not offer to transport the rest of his family? It was almost as if Charles and Mr. Darcy were trying to avoid them!

Caroline stood with Louisa and Hurst in the lobby of the theatre, dressed in her newest, finest burnt orange silk gown, accented by tiny yellow feathers in her hair. She paid particular attention to her appearance that evening because she intended to speak to Mr. Darcy without fail. It was the habit of the people of society to gather in the lobby before a performance, to see and be seen. The low murmur of conversation took on a heightened volume, and Caroline strained to see who had caused the disturbance.

Into the theatre walked Mr. Darcy, handsome as ever, and on his arm was a small woman, her head barely reaching the top of his shoulder, several dark curls dancing along her throat. She was looking up at him, an amused smile twisting her lips, and dancing eyes looking into his. If that sight had not been disturbing enough for Caroline, the vision of Mr. Darcy smiling warmly at this chit was nauseating. To make matters worse, she saw her own brother following closely behind with another unknown woman on his arm. She was smiling, but shyly, keeping her gaze down. Her brother was grinning like a fool. The older couple that followed them seemed to be enjoying the spectacle. The couples stopped to leave their coats, and the crowd watched as the ladies' appearance was revealed. The collective whispering from the women and sounds of appreciation from the men confirmed the opinions that Darcy and Bingley both seemed to share. They both stood momentarily open-mouthed in intense admiration of their particular lady before reclaiming their arms and, ignoring the entreaties of acquaintances, walked straight up the stairs to take their seats.

Darcy spent some time over the last days considering the seating arrangements for the theatre. He looked forward to spending several hours sitting in close company with Elizabeth in the dark. His blood fairly boiled in anticipation of drinking in her scent and perhaps, he hoped, holding her hand. His box was situated on the right side of the theatre, and he decided that the best arrangement would place him in the far left seat with Elizabeth to his right. With such an arrangement, he could pretend to watch the stage but instead look at her. Jane took the seat next to Elizabeth, with Bingley to her right. Mr. and Mrs. Gardiner sat behind Jane and Bingley. Darcy was happy to realize that with everyone else's chairs turned towards the stage, whatever liberties that Elizabeth would allow him would go undetected.

He had been floored when her gown of deep rose was revealed in the lobby. The cut and draping of the fabric accentuated her every curve. He felt himself become irrationally jealous of the silk that that hugged her form. When everyone was settled, Darcy leaned close to her and whispered warmly, "Miss Elizabeth, you are absolutely stunning! I see that your endeavours were successful, for the shade of your gown matches your lovely blush most becomingly."

Elizabeth gasped, first at his words then to see desire kindled in his eyes. "Mr. Darcy, I had intended to say how devastatingly handsome you were, and that you quite take my breath away, but since you have chosen to tease me, I will limit my comment to say that I think you look tolerable tonight." She pursed her lips and raised her brow.

"That is hardly kind, Miss Elizabeth! You have taunted me with the hope of your good opinion and then thrown it in my face. You are forcing me to demand satisfaction for such an insult!"

"And what would satisfy you, Mr. Darcy?" She flirted shamelessly.

All manner of responses came to mind, physical and verbal. Looking down into her face, he allowed his gaze to rest on her luscious mouth, and then travel back up to her laughing, challenging eyes. "Wait and see, Miss Bennet." He said roguishly, and taking her gloved hand in his, he bestowed a kiss.

The moment that Darcy kissed Elizabeth's hand was seen by at least half of the theatre. Opera glasses had been trained on his box from the moment the party entered, thoroughly examining the unknown women, Elizabeth in particular. Two pairs of glasses belonged to Caroline and Louisa, who were engaged in an earnest conversation, disparaging her appearance, and declaring that they would instantly accost their brother when he arrived home for an explanation. Caroline also planned a call on Georgiana to wheedle out any information that her future sister could give her. Mr. Darcy must be saved from this trollop!

The kiss was witnessed by Lord and Lady Matlock as well. They looked at each other, smiling. "Well, my dear," said Lord Matlock, "The cat is out of the bag now. If he could have just sat next to her they might have been able to continue this courtship quietly, but I am sure that there is bound to be a notice in the papers tomorrow, about a certain gentleman from Derbyshire."

Lady Matlock nodded. "I think that we should go over and publicly greet them during the first intermission, Henry. That will help quell the gossip, especially once her lack of connection is known."

"Excellent idea, my dear. I think that I should also begin devising a story to calm Catherine when she hears about Darcy's behaviour. She will give him no peace if she thinks that he will marry someone other than Anne."

"But you have already told her that he does not want Anne."

"Yes, and Anne has told me that she does not want Darcy."

"So what will you tell your sister?"

"I think that I will tell her that he was simply accompanying his friend to the theatre with some acquaintances, and assure her that he is not engaged. That is truthful enough, do you not think so?"

"It is your sister, Henry. I will not say a word."

"That is because you do not like her either!"

When the first act began, Elizabeth, feeling warm, removed her gloves and placed them on her knee. Darcy immediately acted upon the opportunity and reaching over with his right hand, gently brushed the back of his fingers across her hands which were clasped in her lap. He heard her sharp intake of breath when his warm skin touched hers, but she did not pull away. Becoming bolder he entwined their fingers and whispered closely in her ear. "You have beautiful hands, Miss Elizabeth. You should not cover them with gloves." He could feel the heat of her blush, and a few tendrils of her hair moved with the touch of his breath.

She looked up to him. "I think that I will leave the sight of my hands for you alone, sir."

Too soon the end of the first act arrived, and to the disappointment of some, the Darcy party remained in their places. However, those who decided to watch them expressed great interest when Lord and Lady Matlock made a visit to the box and greeted everyone warmly, particularly the young woman with Darcy. Speculation was fierce over the meaning of the gesture.

"Alex, is that not your friend from Cambridge, Mr. Darcy?" Amanda Carrington asked. "He seems to be attracting a great deal of attention tonight. I wonder if he is attached to the young lady by his side. Lord and Lady Matlock are greeting her most warmly."

Alexander Carrington took the opera glasses from his mother, and looked over to the Darcy box. He saw his friend wearing an uncharacteristic smile. He observed the young lady, who was laughing at something Lord Matlock said, and was struck by a sense of familiarity. He continued to peruse the occupants and looked upon Jane. His attraction to her was instantaneous. He needed to meet her. Noticing that she was standing next to Charles Bingley, and knowing that he never formed permanent attachments, he felt fairly confident that an introduction to this woman would not cause any lasting problems. He decided that at the next intermission he would go to greet his friend.

When the second act ended, the party agreed to leave the box and seek refreshment. Elizabeth and Darcy had immediately resumed their hand-holding after the first act, and were both giddy with the close contact. They walked out, arms entwined, smiling, until they began to be accosted by the curious. Elizabeth watched in fascination as a mask of hauteur descended over Darcy's face. His smile disappeared, his body stiffened, and wariness came into his eyes. He was distinctly uncomfortable. She was not sure how to account for his sudden change in behaviour and hoped that it was not because he was somehow ashamed to be with her and her relations in such a public setting.

"Mr. Darcy, are you well?"

"Do I appear ill?" He asked with an oddly detached voice.

"Something is wrong. The wonderful man who was caressing my hands so sweetly has disappeared, and a brooding statue has taken his place. Have I done something to disappoint you?"

Elizabeth's fear of failure snapped him out of his state. He looked at her apologetically. "Forgive me Miss Elizabeth, you have done nothing wrong. I am so used to distancing myself in social situations that it is quite automatic. I despise being in crowded places, and tonight in particular, I know that I am, we are, undergoing close observation. It makes me very uncomfortable and I feel isolated. I hope that you understand and can tolerate my behaviour."

"I can tolerate it more readily now that I know its cause." Then looking up at him with that gentle smile he first saw when they met she whispered, "Mr. Darcy, you are safe. You are not alone anymore."

Finally a small smile came to his lips. "You are quite right, Miss Elizabeth, and with your help, I will never be alone again." She blushed and looked down, but he felt the squeeze of her hand on his arm.

The moment was broken when he heard his name called, and sighing, he was relieved to see the face of his friend Alex Carrington. "Alex! What a surprise! Have you come to town with your parents?"

"Yes, I left Mother and Father in the box, but when Mother pointed you out to me, I had to come over and greet you." He smiled, and looking at Elizabeth, he glanced expectantly at his friend.

Smiling ruefully, Darcy knew what he was about. "Miss Elizabeth Bennet, may I present my friend Mr. Alexander Carrington? He and I attended Cambridge together, and he is the heir to Kingston Park in Buckingham. Alex, Miss Elizabeth's family estate is Longbourn, in Hertfordshire."

"It is an honour to meet you Miss Elizabeth." Elizabeth stared into the young man's eyes, suddenly fascinated and unable to respond. There was something so familiar about him. "Miss Elizabeth? Are you well?"

Shaken from her reverie, she looked up to see concern etched on Darcy's face. He did not at all like the way that his friend had captured his Elizabeth's attention. Elizabeth smiled at him and turned to Mr. Carrington. "Excuse me sir, I was momentarily distracted. I had the oddest feeling that I had met you before. Have you ever spent any time in Meryton?"

"You know, Miss Elizabeth, when I was spying on your box with my mother's opera glasses, the first thing that went through my mind was a feeling of familiarity. Strange is it not? But no, I have not spent any time in Meryton, although I have passed through that part of Hertfordshire on my travels to and from London. I take it that is where your father's estate is?"

"Yes it is."

"Are you staying with friends in town, then?" He said glancing over at Jane.

"My sister and I are staying with our aunt and uncle, sir. Would you care to be introduced?"

"Indeed I would, Miss Elizabeth, please lead the way!" Alex cast a huge grin at Darcy, who understanding now that his friend's objective was an introduction to Jane, relaxed.

The three made their way over to the rest of their party, and Darcy performed the introductions. Watching the man's obvious appreciation of Jane, Bingley began to feel a little possessive. He was about to say something to make it clear that Miss Bennet's attention was occupied when he heard Caroline calling his name and insisting on his attendance. Reluctantly he took his leave, but not without sending a significant look to Darcy, clearly implying that he was in charge of looking after his interests. Darcy shook his head and sighed.

Alex saw the golden opportunity given by Bingley's absence and pounced. "Miss Bennet, your sister tells me that you are from Hertfordshire. Will you be staying in town long?"

"I believe that I will remain until after Easter, Mr. Carrington." Jane tilted her head, fascinated by the handsome blonde man with the familiar eyes.

"That is excellent news!" He turned to Darcy. "My parents are throwing a ball next week. I am sure that you were sent an invitation, and if you have not discarded it yet, I would be happy to see you and the lovely Bennet sisters attend," noticing Bingley's return he added, "and Bingley as well, of course."

Not wanting to miss an opportunity to spend a night dancing with Elizabeth, Darcy looked for her opinion. She in turn looked at Jane and the Gardiners. Seeing approval everywhere, except a touch of reluctance from Bingley, she smiled and nodded at Darcy. "I think that we would all enjoy the evening, Alex. I do not remember seeing your invitation, but I imagine it remains with my correspondence. If I do not locate it, I will send you a note asking for the particulars."

"Excellent! Then we will see you next Thursday!" Then hearing the bell announcing the end of intermission, he bowed and took his leave.

Caroline had hovered on the edge of the conversation, waiting to greet Mr. Darcy and see the woman on his arm. The party made to return to the box, and there was only time for Bingley to notice her and perform a brief introduction. The ladies curtseyed, and Elizabeth and Caroline eyed each other, taking stock of their opponent. Darcy quickly apologized and they returned to their seats.

They remained in their box for the rest of the performance, Elizabeth and Darcy continuing to hold hands. Elizabeth at some point leaned over to Darcy and settled her head against his shoulder. He drank in her lavender scent, gently stroking her silky hair with his face and lips. Elizabeth allowed herself to be enveloped by his scent of sandalwood and soap, and when she turned her head, she could hear for the first time the strong, steady thrum of his heart.

Chapter 9

To Darcy's surprise, he did still have the invitation to the Carrington ball, and he sent the acceptance for the two couples immediately. The ball was set for the next Thursday, and Elizabeth was to travel to Kent on Saturday. He was determined to make the most of the next week.

Elizabeth knew that the ball would be a special night, almost the last time she would see Mr. Darcy until he arrived at Rosings, and she decided that she would wear one of her new purchases, a gown of ivory silk, embroidered with mauve thread, and finished with a matching sash and edging.

Since Elizabeth was not caught up in dress shopping, she was free to visit with Georgiana and Mr. Darcy while Jane went out with her aunt to the modiste. Mr. Bingley came to call on her several mornings, and the gentlemen were asked to stay for dinner several nights. It was now mid-March, and the spring bulbs were beginning to grow and bloom. Mr. Darcy had suggested a walk in Hyde Park to Elizabeth on Wednesday morning, and she gladly accepted. He sent the carriage for her, and almost upon her arrival, they set off for their stroll, arms entwined, revelling in the feel of each other and the intimacy that their walk provided.

"Miss Elizabeth, it occurred to me that I have not asked you to reserve any dances for me. I hope that I am not too late to request the first set?"

Elizabeth laughed, "Well sir, since I only know two other gentlemen who will be attending this ball, I think that you were quite assured in winning those dances. So yes, you may have them."

"And, may I be so bold as to request the supper set?" His eyes crinkled in a smile.

"Absolutely sir, I wish to be assured of a companionable dinner partner!" She tilted her head and pursed her lips.

"In that case, since you think me so pleasant, may I complete the evening and ask for the last as well?" His voice was teasing, but his look was determined.

"Mr. Darcy! Three dances! What will the other guests think of us?" She grinned at him.

"Is that a yes?" He stared at her intently.

Catching his seriousness, Elizabeth looked at him thoughtfully. "Yes, Mr. Darcy. My answer is yes." She did not mistake the relief that came over his face. "Mr. Darcy, do you often ask your partner to dance three sets?"

"Miss Elizabeth, I must tell you that in the past, I have avoided dancing, unless I was particularly acquainted with my partner, and never, ever, did I dance more than once with any of them. That is something that I have only ever wished to do with you." He stopped and taking her hand in his, raised it to his lips. He hoped that she understood the depth of his feelings.

Elizabeth hoped that he understood what he was implying. She reached up and brushed a wayward curl from his brow, smiled, and giving his arm a tug, they walked on.

"Miss Elizabeth, when is your birthday?"

Elizabeth knew why he was asking. He wanted to know when she would come of age. He was thinking of marriage, and was considering her father refusing consent. Her heart started pumping wildly and she tried to control the quaver in her voice. "My birthday is April 4th, Mr. Darcy." She watched as his eyes kindled, first in joy, then with something else, something she could not define, but intense, nonetheless.

"Truly, Miss Elizabeth? Then I shall have to bring you a particularly special gift when I come to Rosings."

Elizabeth looked at the ground. "The only gift that I will wish for is the return of your presence in my life, Mr. Darcy." She looked up at him. "I am afraid that I will miss you terribly when we part on Saturday."

"Elizabeth." He whispered. He wanted nothing more than to take her in his arms. Instead he took her hands and removed the gloves. He stroked them softly with his bare hands and raised first one, then the other to his lips, softly kissing the backs. Turning them, he trailed kisses from the palms to her wrists. Elizabeth stood mesmerized, emotions and sensations flowing through her that she had never experienced before and could hardly name. Finally, cradling both of her hands in his left; he raised his free hand to stroke her cheek with the back of his fingers, and stared deeply into her eyes. "I miss you every time that we say goodbye, though I know we will meet again soon. I miss you when you are across the room, and I can see you. I miss you when you sit beside me and I cannot touch you. The two weeks that will part us will be torture."

Speechless, Elizabeth tried to put everything she felt into her eyes. She stared at his lips, so soft and warm on her hands, and saw him looking down at her mouth. They moved towards each other, now tilting their heads slightly, leaning, almost touching. . .

The sound of approaching riders startled them out of their enchanted moment. Elizabeth turned her head away in disappointment and embarrassment. Darcy closed his eyes in frustration. Seeing the flush in her face, he turned his back to her and began taking deep breaths in an attempt to regain control.

Concerned, Elizabeth stepped up to him. "Mr. Darcy?"

"Give me a moment please, Miss Elizabeth."

She stood, confused, and watched him struggle. Finally he seemed to calm, and turned to face her.

"Did I do something. . ."

"Forgive me, I . . ."

They looked at each other and sighed.

"Perhaps it is for the best." Elizabeth said quietly.

Incredulous, he looked at her. "How can that possibly be true?"

"Sir, if what I think was about to happen did; I am afraid that parting from you Saturday would be even harder."

"I do not believe that I would have been able to let you go."

They sighed again and Darcy held out his arm, "Come, let us walk."

They walked in silence until Elizabeth looked at him. "When is your birthday?"

He smiled. "February 25th."

She knit her brow. "That was the day we met!"

"So it was." His smile grew. "It was the greatest birthday of my life."

Elizabeth fought her blush. "How old are you?"

He laughed. "Guess!"

Eyeing him carefully, she raised her brow and tilted her head. "Hmm. You graduated from Cambridge, and your sister said that you have been managing Pemberley for five years, so that would make you . . . seven and twenty?"

"Eight and twenty." He corrected.

"Ah, so you are old." She tried to look sympathetic.

"Too old?" He feigned sadness.

Smiling cheekily, she replied, "No, I like mature men." She placed her free hand on his arm and hugged it to her.

Darcy thrilled with the wave of affection that spread through him. He attempted to control his rising passion by switching to an unpleasant subject. "I received a letter from my Aunt Catherine. She saw a note in a gossip column about us."

"About us? What did it say?"

"A certain gentleman from Derbyshire was seen enjoying the company of a beautiful raven-haired siren at the theatre Friday night. It speculated if my elusive heart had finally been captured."

"Oh my! What did your aunt say?"

"She knows that the claim must be ridiculous because my Uncle had already told her that I was accompanying the companions of my friend. That satisfied her but she admonished me to be more careful."

"She will not be happy with me?"

"No. Remember I was surprised that my Aunt and Uncle accepted you so readily. I am afraid that Aunt Catherine will not be so kind. For that reason I think that we should keep our courtship to ourselves until I can be there with you. I do not want you to have to bear her alone."

"In that case, you should not be at my Uncle's house when we depart. I am travelling with Sir William Lucas and his daughter, Maria, Mrs. Collins' family. If they met you there, it will certainly be told to my cousin, Mr. Collins, who would undoubtedly tell your aunt."

"As much as I would want to spend every moment with you that I can, I agree. I doubt that your father has spoken of our attachment to anyone given his objections. Have you or your sister written to anyone about it?"

"I am not that close with my other sisters, and I know better than to tell Mama."

"Then it should be our secret until I arrive. Will you write to me?" He asked, hopefully.

"You know I cannot." She said, sadly.

"You could write to Georgiana." He suggested.

"And how do I explain a letter addressed to Darcy House?"

"You are finding too many excuses. You do not wish to communicate with me." He looked away.

She touched his face, and he looked back at her. "You know that I do. Perhaps I could get a message to you through Jane."

"And I could do the same?" He suggested hopefully.

"I will speak to her about it. She will not be pleased breaking the rules of propriety, but she may be willing if my aunt does not learn of it."

"I could not bear the separation without hearing from you." Elizabeth gripped his arm in support, and they silently continued their walk, simply enjoying the pleasure of being together.

THE GENTLEMEN arrived at Gracechurch Street early and had to wait for the ladies to finish their preparations before leaving for the ball. They planned their arrival on purpose. Both wanted to have their first sight of their particular lady in the relative privacy of the Gardiner home.

They were not disappointed. Jane appeared first, in a cream-coloured gown with a sash of sapphire blue, almost the exact shade of her eyes. She had borrowed a comb from her aunt with tiny blue stones that sparkled in her hair. Bingley was entranced, and was more convinced than ever that he was looking at seraphic beauty. He rushed to kiss her hand.

Darcy impatiently waited for Elizabeth's appearance. When she entered the room in her ivory gown, his eyes lit up with pleasure. This was the colour for his Elizabeth. The glow of her cheeks and the sparkle in her eyes set off the warmth of the dress. *Oh, to have Mother's rubies at this moment to place around her neck!* Instead, she wore a simple pendant of pearls, which he jealously noted lay just upon the swell of her breasts. There was no other word for it; he was undone.

As he stood, shifting uncomfortably from side to side trying to calm his arousal, he felt Mr. Gardiner's hand clasp his shoulder. He turned to see his understanding smile. "She is looking exceptionally lovely this evening, is she not, Mr. Darcy?" He nodded, transfixed. "I trust you to take good care of her, sir." Mr. Gardiner fixed him with a stern look, and raised his brows.

Darcy knew that he was being warned to behave. "Yes sir, I will see that she comes to no harm."

"Good, good, now go and enjoy your evening."

UPON ARRIVAL at the Carrington home, murmurs of speculation were voiced by the crowd when the butler announced their names. Darcy had donned his mask, and Elizabeth, now aware of its meaning, did her best to help him relax. She was nervous herself, being presented to a ballroom full of people from a station far above her own. She had the distinct advantage; however, of being unknown. Also, by arriving on Mr. Darcy's arm, she automatically received begrudging respect, if not outright envy, by the other ladies of the room. They approached the receiving line and Darcy introduced her to Mr. and Mrs. Carrington, and then moved on to their son.

"Darcy! I am so glad to see that you really came. It must be Miss Elizabeth's influence. I can think of little else that would entice you to attend our little ball." He smirked sardonically at his friend. Elizabeth was once again struck by the feeling of familiarity, and caught herself studying him.

"Alex, I am not as unsociable as you proclaim, but yes, I agree, the pleasure of dancing with Miss Elizabeth tonight was my greatest incentive to attend. It certainly was not for the speculation that I have been hearing since our names were announced." He indicated the gossiping groups staring shamelessly at them

"Ah, well Darcy. That is the burden you must bear for being so rich!" He turned to Elizabeth, "Miss Elizabeth, may I say that you are exceptionally lovely tonight? I think there would be whispers about you even if you were not on the arm of England's most eligible bachelor!" Elizabeth blushed and thanked him, and looked down, but not before seeing Mr. Darcy's uncomfortable expression. "I have my own burden to carry tonight, and that is one of host. So Miss Elizabeth, while I have the opportunity, may I ask you for a set? Before your card is completely full? I am sure that it will not be long." He was enjoying watching his friend squirm. He had never had the chance to watch him with a lady before, and intended to do all he could to see how attached he was. It was a game to him, and besides, he still felt that strange attraction to Elizabeth that he had felt at the theatre.

Elizabeth noted Mr. Darcy's set jaw, and knew that he was unhappy with her dancing with anyone else, but she also knew that she could not refuse without foregoing dancing with him the rest of the evening. "I am available for the second set, sir, and would be happy to help you fulfil your hosting duties by accepting your kind offer."

"Excellent!" Alex grinned at Darcy's discomfort. He then turned to greet Jane and Bingley. "Miss Bennet! I have just secured your sister for the second set; may I ask you for the third? I told your sister that she was exceptionally lovely, but I find you ethereally beautiful. What a joy it would be to dance with two lovely ladies tonight!" Bingley unhappily stood mute as his jaw worked.

Jane studied Alex's smiling face; it had a different expression than the flirting one he used on Elizabeth. He looked at her very sincerely. He was drawn to her in a way that he could not begin to describe, and she felt the same odd power coming over her. She blushed lightly, "Thank you sir, as I hope that you will enjoy dancing the second with my sister, I will leave you the third for myself."

Alex was thrilled. "Thank you, Miss Bennet, I look forward to it." He nodded at Bingley, and turned to the next guests in the receiving line.

Darcy secured Jane for the second set and Bingley secured Elizabeth for the third. They then stood together discussing what they would do to any other men who dared ask their particular sister for a dance that evening. Jane and Elizabeth took advantage of the gentleman's disgruntlement to take in the atmosphere and comment on the attention they had attracted upon entering the room. When the couples came back together, Darcy immediately gave Elizabeth his arm, and held her to him possessively. He was about to take her across the room to offer some refreshment when the unwelcome voice of Caroline Bingley sounded in his ear.

"Why Mr. Darcy! Charles! What a surprise to see you here! I had no idea that this was where you were going tonight, we could have come together!" Louisa and Mr. Hurst joined the group.

"Caroline, how did you get an invitation to this ball?" Charles was upset. He was there only because he was Darcy's friend, and had been standing with him when Carrington spoke of the ball. His sister had no such connection.

"Oh Charles, you know that I have friends all over London!" Caroline dismissed him, and turned her gaze on Darcy.

Resigning himself to the fact that his sister was there and bound to ruin the evening somehow, he made the introductions, "Caroline, Louisa, Hurst, do you remember our companions this evening? This is Miss Elizabeth Bennet, and her sister, Miss Jane Bennet." He turned to the sisters, "Miss Bennet, Miss Elizabeth, this is my sister Caroline Bingley, my sister Louisa Hurst, and her husband, Gilbert Hurst." Elizabeth and Jane curtseyed, while they noticed that Charles's sisters only nodded.

Caroline stared possessively where Elizabeth's hand securely grasped Darcy's arm, "Yes, I remember meeting you at the theatre, Miss Elizabeth." Then, looking her over, she took note of Elizabeth's blush. "My, what a lovely shade of pink for your gown. It matches your complexion so well."

Elizabeth, not one to be intimidated by a shrew smiled, "Actually, the shade is ivory, as I understand that shades of white are the proper colours to be worn at a ball. I noticed that you are fond of the colour orange Miss Bingley. Is that not the same gown that you wore to the theatre?"

Caroline coldly replied, "No, it is not."

Elizabeth smiled, "My mistake, the shade truly compliments your face, and the feathers are most becoming."

Caroline's face turned bright red, clashing spectacularly with her gown. "Thank you. You are most kind."

"Not at all, Miss Bingley." Elizabeth gave her a brilliant smile.

Just then the music began, and Darcy indicated that they should move on to the ballroom. He had watched the exchange with great amusement and had a difficult time not laughing. He leaned down to Elizabeth and whispered, "You are wicked, Miss Elizabeth." She grinned at him. "I believe that round one went to the Lady from Hertfordshire."

"Sir, I am not a pugilist." She replied, feigning affront.

"I would enjoy fighting with you!" He whispered roguishly. Elizabeth coloured immediately, and he laughed, "Ha! You do complement your gown!"

"Mr. Darcy!"

He was flirting shamelessly and he loved it. He had never allowed himself such freedom before, and he knew that he could only be this way with her. And, he reasoned, if he was going to be separated from her for two weeks, he was going to grab onto and enjoy every moment that he could.

ELIZABETH LOOKED across to Mr. Darcy as they awaited the opening set. His eyes were twinkling at her; and there was a slight smile on his face. She knew him well enough by now to be sure that he was only able to relax this way with her and it gave her such a feeling of contentment. The music began and the pattern started. They grasped hands, gently moving around each other, turning, gliding, and always maintaining eye contact. They did not speak. There was no need to break the moment. They were simply lost in each other, and were alone in their own world. They were the objects of intense interest and curiosity, and for once in his life, Darcy did not care.

He did care, however, when it was time for the second set. He stood across from Jane, his mask firmly in place, body stiff, and eyes on Elizabeth and Alex.

Something about the man attracted his Elizabeth, and he did not like it at all. He listened, trying to catch their conversation, but all he heard was their laughter. He knew that she was jousting with him, he recognized the expression on her face; and from what he could tell; Alex was matching her, wit for wit. It bothered him intensely, and he almost did not hear it when Jane spoke to him.

"Mr. Darcy, are you well?" Jane asked tentatively. She had not spoken directly to him very often. She found him to be very intimidating, and extremely complex. She could not begin to imagine a relationship with such a man.

Darcy, startled out of his reverie, saw Jane's concern. "I am sorry Miss Bennet. I was not attending. Yes, I am well."

Jane looked over to her sister. "I think that you are perhaps a little distracted?"

Darcy followed her glance. "Yes, I am afraid I am. Your sister is oddly attracted to my friend, and I do not understand why."

"Mr. Darcy, you have never had the opportunity to see Lizzy in a social situation like this before. I can assure you that she is certainly entertained and curious about your friend, but he is not at all attracting her."

Darcy looked at her seriously. "How can you tell, Miss Bennet?"

"Sir, you should know by now that Lizzy is always intrigued by understanding the foibles and inconsistencies of people, and takes great pleasure in observing characters in many situations. Mr. Carrington was baiting you in the reception line, Lizzy saw it, and she is simply curious to determine what he is about." Jane watched Darcy process what she said. "I admit that there is something about Mr. Carrington which is very intriguing to me as well. Lizzy and I spoke about it after we first met. He seems oddly familiar in a way, as if he reminds us of someone who we know very well. I think that is Lizzy's ultimate goal, to determine who that person is."

"So I should relax, is that what you are saying?" Darcy asked with a note of resignation in his voice.

"I know that you have absolutely nothing to fear, sir." Then, taking pity on him she smiled, "I have never seen my sister as happy as I have in these past weeks in your company."

"Truly Miss Bennet?" He gave her a brilliant smile, his dimples on display.

Jane's eyes grew wide, never having witnessed the phenomenon before, and suddenly understanding the faraway look in Elizabeth's eyes when she described Mr. Darcy's rare smile. She nodded, "Yes Mr. Darcy, you may trust me, and you have my approval and support."

"Thank you, Miss Bennet, I am grateful."

The set ended, and Darcy walked her over to Bingley, who was not at all upset with his friend dancing with her. Alex brought Elizabeth to Darcy, and complimented him on his brilliant luck at finding such a lovely partner. "I had planned to spend the night baiting you over finally falling under a lady's spell, but after a half-hour of lively debate with Miss Elizabeth, I can find no reason to fault you for securing this lady as fast as you could. I am jealous of your luck, Darcy, and I will quit the field." He bowed deeply, and moved to claim Jane for the next.

Darcy took her hand, and looked anxiously into her eyes. "Is everything well? He did not bother you?"

Elizabeth gave his hand a reassuring squeeze. "Of course, he was charming and so combative. I was attempting to understand of whom he reminded me."

"That was what your sister said you were doing." Elizabeth tilted her head. "Did she reassure you?" Looking at his shoes he spoke softly, "Yes." "Mr. Darcy." He lifted his eyes and shyly looked into hers. She entwined her fingers with his for a moment, and gently grasped his hand. "I promise you, there is nothing to fear."

"You must think me such a silly fool."

"As long as you are my fool, I do not mind." She smiled, squeezing his hand harder this time, and let go.

With Bingley dancing the next with Elizabeth, Darcy was free to relax and concentrate on watching Alex with Jane. His friend's behaviour with her was entirely different. There were no arguments or cunning smiles; he seemed everything gentle and solicitous towards her. And, he noted, she was responding. He wondered if she was attracted to him, or if she was just being kind. He could see no difference in her behaviour towards Alex and Bingley. If Bingley were to tell him tonight that he intended to propose, he would have to advise him to wait.

Darcy's were not the only eyes watching Jane and Alex dance. "Philip, what was the name of that girl who is dancing with Alex?" Amanda Carrington asked.

"Ben-something, Benning, no, that is not it. . ."

"Bennet!" Amanda looked at her husband, her eyes wide. "And the other girl, the one who came with Mr. Darcy, she is her sister." Their eyes met. "Is it possible . . .?" Turning, Amanda nervously addressed Darcy.

"Mr. Darcy." He tore his eyes from Elizabeth and looked down at Amanda. "The young lady dancing with Alex, is her name Bennet?"

"Yes, madam, Jane Bennet. My friend Bingley is dancing with her younger sister, Elizabeth."

Amanda took a breath. "I am familiar with the name. I wonder if these ladies are related. Where are they from?"

"Hertfordshire. Their father's estate, Longbourn, is located near the village of Meryton. Is this the same family?"

Ignoring the question, Amanda turned to look at her husband, who wore a similar stunned expression. "Philip?"

He came to his senses and looked at his wife then met Darcy's concerned gaze. "Am I correct in my suspicions that you are quite close to Miss Elizabeth?"

"We are very good friends." He said carefully. "Why do you ask?"

Seeing Darcy's concern, he moved quickly to reassure him. "Sir, please, I am not concerned with Miss Elizabeth or Miss Bennet's character or behaviour. They are lovely young ladies."

Darcy relaxed, "I never doubted either lady sir, but I cannot help but wonder at your questions."

"Mr. Darcy, this is not the proper setting for this conversation, and I would appreciate your advice. May I call on you tomorrow?"

"Mr. Carrington, I will be happy to help you with advice, however, Miss Elizabeth will be leaving town on Saturday, and I intend to spend as much time with her as possible before she departs. I will be happy to meet with you on Monday morning. Is eleven o'clock acceptable?"

"Yes, Mr. Darcy, I thank you. Please be assured there is nothing wrong with your or Mr. Bingley's relationship to either lady. Their presence simply made me realize my need for advice."

"Thank you for your reassurance, sir. I look forward to understanding this mystery on Monday." The gentleman bowed, and Darcy quickly moved to reclaim Elizabeth from Bingley before her next partner arrived.

Finally the supper dance began and Darcy had Elizabeth back. This time they laughed through the time together, both able to relax in each other's company, unlike how they had to behave when others were about. The four of them found seats together in the supper room, and were enjoying their meals when Caroline reappeared. She had been waiting for Darcy to ask her to dance. He had no such intention. He, at Bingley's urging, had spoken to Alex, and asked him how Caroline came to be invited. Alex looked at him with surprise, and said that she had sent a note, saying that as dear friends of himself and sister to another invited guest, Bingley, she asked that they be included. He said that he assumed it was with Darcy's approval. Darcy was infuriated. He had been letting the behaviour go for years, but now it was time to put a stop to it. He would let it quietly be known that Caroline Bingley was not to be invited to events based on her connection to the Darcy name. He would speak to Bingley about it privately.

Elizabeth and Jane were both asked to dance several more times during the evening, and each time, Darcy and Bingley stood guard at the edge of the dance floor, staring at their partners. Bingley was obligated to dance with each of his sisters, but Darcy steadfastly refused, no matter how many times Caroline sighed or stood close by him. She tried to strike up a conversation with him, criticizing Elizabeth's appearance, and asking him probing questions about her background. Darcy was happy to know that Caroline had been entirely unsuccessful in finding anything out about Elizabeth and Jane. He knew that she visited Georgiana during the week, and had asked pointedly about the ladies who attended the theatre with their brother, but Georgiana was able, with her newfound confidence, to withstand the onslaught and say that who Darcy associates with was none of her business. He was very pleased with her.

Finally the time for the final set arrived, and it was the new and very scandalous waltz. Darcy decided that he would risk the gossip and led Elizabeth out onto the floor.

"But sir, I have no idea what the steps are to this dance!" Elizabeth protested.

"I do, and that is all that matters. The gentleman leads. All you have to do is follow me. I am sure that you will have it down very quickly." He smiled encouragingly at her.

"How do you know it so well? I thought that you dislike dancing?" she asked suspiciously.

"Georgiana has a dance master. I was her partner. Sooner or later this will replace all of the quadrilles and country dances. She was taught it in anticipation of her coming out next year."

"Very well, but if I trip, I will place the blame entirely on you."

"If you trip, Miss Elizabeth, it will be my supreme pleasure to catch you." He smiled warmly into her worried eyes.

He told her how to place her hand on his shoulder, and he gently placed his on her waist. They both blushed with the intimate contact. He held her other hand in his, and with the beginning of the music, he showed her how to sway, and then took his first steps with her. He was correct, it was easy. She just followed him and soon she could move without thinking. It was glorious to be held so securely. The room spun by, and she was caught in his unyielding gaze. They both wished that it would never end, and were greatly disappointed when the music stopped and they were forced to part. Jane ran over to Elizabeth and told her how beautiful she looked, spinning around the room with her skirts floating around her. Bingley shook Darcy's hand and asked if he might have a private lesson with Georgiana's dance master when he next visited.

AFTER THE VERY late evening at the ball, Elizabeth had no expectation of seeing Darcy before the afternoon. She spent her time after rising packing her things for Kent, and gossiping with Jane and Aunt Gardiner. She asked Jane if she would be willing to help her communicate with Darcy while she was away by forwarding letters between them. Jane was not happy about being party to such a breach in propriety, but decided that it was fairly obvious they would likely be engaged soon, and at that time, such letters would be allowed. It was on that theory that she agreed to help. They agreed to enlist Mr. Bingley's aid as well, as either delivering Elizabeth's letters to Darcy, or bringing his letters to Jane. In that way, no servants would be involved.

The gentlemen arrived in the afternoon and were invited to stay for dinner. While taking a last walk in the park, Elizabeth told Darcy of their letter writing plans, and he enthusiastically approved it. When Bingley and Jane later met with them, he expressed his happiness to help with the scheme. During their walk, Darcy told Elizabeth how much he had enjoyed the ball with her, how wonderful it was to dance with her, and how much he had treasured the last three weeks. He wanted to tell her everything that was in his heart, but he knew that it would have to wait until he arrived in Kent. They spoke of so many things, trying to get in all of their conversation for the time that they would be parted, because even with communication by letters, it just would not be the same. When they returned to the house, Darcy held back in a corner of the entrance hall, and taking Elizabeth's ungloved hands in his, kissed them tenderly. They both wanted so much more.

Saturday morning Darcy arrived alone and early. He knew that he did not have a great amount of time or opportunity, and he shyly pulled a book of Shakespeare's sonnets out of his pocket. He had marked one that he said reminded him of her. When she opened the book to see the 17th sonnet, she saw that a letter was holding the place. She quickly closed the book and blushing, placed it in the bag she would keep in the carriage with her. At the same time she covertly drew out a letter that she had prepared for him, which he kissed before slipping into his coat. He wanted to hold her, kiss her, stroke her hair, and bury his face against her throat. She was desperate to lay her head on his chest and catch the sound of his heart beating, and feel his arms close around her. When it was finally time to part, he kissed her hands, touched her cheek, and with brightened eyes, turned his back on her and left. She watched as his carriage pulled away, and ran upstairs to cry.

An hour later the coach bearing Sir William Lucas and his daughter Maria arrived, and after a short repast, the three travellers were on their way. Elizabeth did not know that Darcy had returned on horseback and stood in the park across the street, watching until she pulled away.

Chapter 10

"Eliza!" Charlotte ran to greet the carriage as it pulled in front of Hunsford Parsonage, bypassing her father and sister.

Mr. Collins stood bobbing and wheezing, "Welcome to our humble abode!" He bowed to his father-in-law, acknowledged his sister, and made pointed remarks about the quality of his home to Elizabeth, not too subtly reminding her that all this could have been hers.

The guests settled into their rooms. Elizabeth duly admired the shelves in the closet of her bedchamber, and agreed wholeheartedly with Mr. Collins that it was a stroke of brilliance for Lady Catherine to suggest them while casting expressive eyes to Charlotte, who rolled hers. While Mr. Collins showed Sir William and Maria his gardens, Charlotte pulled Elizabeth into her private sitting room for a chat. She was dying to talk to her friend again.

"Oh Eliza, how I have missed you!" Charlotte took her hands and gave them a squeeze. "Now, tell me everything. You have been in London for some weeks. What have you done?"

Elizabeth smiled at the friend she thought that she had lost forever. She had been so angry with her for accepting Mr. Collins' offer and settling for a marriage of convenience. Over time, she realized that it was exactly the kind of marriage that Charlotte wanted and let her disappointment go.

"So much has happened, and I truly need to talk about it, but I am sorry to say I have to trust you not to say a word of it to Mr. Collins, or I will be unable to confide in you."

"This sounds most serious!"

"It is. It is the most serious matter."

"I am not comfortable keeping secrets from my husband." She looked sadly at her friend. They had shared so much together over the years, and she truly wanted to help her. "Is there a way that we can talk about it without giving me particulars? If I have no specific details, but just general conversation, I would not feel that I am deceiving him by not talking about something." She thought again, "And, if he does not ask me a specific question about a subject, I would not be deceiving him by not answering it entirely correctly either, would I?"

Elizabeth knew that Charlotte was trying to work out a way in her mind that she could still be her best friend. "Very well, I will talk, and if you think that I am giving you too much detail, you must tell me and I shall stop. But you must agree this goes no further than the two of us."

"Yes, I can abide by those conditions."

Taking a breath, Elizabeth told Charlotte that she met a gentleman, and that she had entered a courtship with him. She said that she seems to have the approval of his family and that she is hoping to meet another member and gain her approval as well, although the gentleman has his doubts of success.

"Why this is wonderful news! Why have I heard nothing of it? Surely your mother would have told mine, and she would write to me about it?"

"My mother does not know. I wrote to Jane to come to London, and help me during this time. Papa brought her and wished to meet him. Mr. . . . my friend invited all of us to dinner at his home, where we met his family. That night he asked Papa for his consent for our courtship and Papa accused him of terrible things. It was only after my friend refuted everything that Papa said that he finally agreed to the courtship. Papa spoke of changing his mind the next day, but my uncle talked him out of it."

Charlotte was shocked. "Is there something bad about this man, Eliza?"

"No! He is the best of men! He is kind, and generous, and intelligent, and has his own estate, and is so very, very lonely. I have made it my mission to make him smile." Elizabeth looked at her friend through teary eyes.

"But why does your father object to him so?" Charlotte asked, concerned.

"My friend thinks that he is reluctant to let me marry anyone at all, that he looks at me as his companion and expects me to stay at Longbourn." Charlotte nodded thoughtfully. "And, he thinks that Papa might be jealous that I would make a love match and be given all of the opportunities to experience the world that he never could."

"I do not know your young man, but he certainly has a point about your father not being willing to let you go. He is exceptionally close to you, and always seemed happier with you than with anyone else I have ever seen, including your mother and other men. Although I suspect that if a gentleman in Meryton offered for you, he would not object so strongly. As for jealousy with a love match, I honestly never thought that your father cared for such things, he seems, forgive me, too caught up with his own affairs to care about anyone else other than his own comforts. I wonder if he is capable of a love match." She saw Elizabeth's pensive expression. "I do, however agree that there may be some jealousy over your opportunities, particularly if it exposes you to things that you know he appreciates, books, conversation, challenges to the mind. Would your friend be able to provide such things for you?"

"Yes, he most definitely would; in fact, he already has, in a way." Elizabeth spoke softly, Charlotte had stated things that she knew were true, but had been unwilling to face.

"I take it that your friend is well-off?" She asked carefully.

"Yes, he is of the first circles."

"And you think that he loves you, despite the differences in your stations, your lack of dowry and wealth?"

Elizabeth spoke defiantly. "He has not spoken the word 'love' to me yet, but then we only met three weeks ago. If he had said it already, I would have mistrusted him. But yes, he has stated that he does not care for my rank or wealth. He wants to be wanted for himself, and that is how he feels about his future wife."

"Then what is the problem? You will be with a man who apparently cares deeply for you, even if he has not said the words yet. I imagine that they will come in time. And truly, we were meant to leave our families' homes and go out into the world. It is wrong of your father to want to selfishly keep you at home, and deny you your own life. I think that your decision is clear. If this man makes you an offer, and he is what you have hoped for, how could you say no?"

"I have been thinking the same things, but I needed to hear it confirmed. I have talked to Jane about it, but she is torn between her emotions for me and Papa. I needed to hear your impartial opinion."

"I am so glad that you value me in this way, Eliza. If you need to talk about this again, I feel very comfortable keeping this particular confidence between us."

Elizabeth retired thankfully to her bedchamber that evening after enduring the unending praises of her cousin to his father-in-law for producing his dear Charlotte, and his patroness for providing his living. He promised to introduce all of his guests to her after church in the morning. She admired Charlotte's fortitude to bear such a man as a husband, but realized that she entered the marriage with full knowledge of what the man was. His personality was unchanged from what she experienced for weeks last autumn. As angry as she was with her father now, she remained grateful that he did not force her to accept Mr. Collins' proposal.

Taking a candle and settling in the window seat, she looked out at the moonlit garden and at last examined the precious gift that Mr. Darcy had slipped to her that morning, the book of Shakespeare's sonnets, and opened to the 17th, the one he marked. *If I could write the beauty of your eyes . . .* She read it over and over. She thought of his eyes, deep, dark, expressing so many emotions. She had seen sadness, pain and loneliness, and now she was seeing hope, affection, and joy. She thought that she detected love, and something new that she could not name, but it made her feel so . . . oh what is the word? Wanting, needing something. Something only he could give. Desire? Passion? It was all so new. Taking a breath, she stroked the envelope that he gave her, and then broke the seal.

Dear

I wish to write your name, but I know that I cannot. You should know that it is constantly running through my mind. I think of your name, and I imagine your eyes, glowing, dancing, and enticing me to become the man that I hardly knew was inside of me. In these short weeks that we have known each other, I have lived a lifetime of emotions. I did not realize how I had cloistered myself from feeling anything, because to feel would make me vulnerable to hurt, and I have been hurt enough that I felt it was better to feel nothing. Now I know better. You have opened up my heart to feelings that I now treasure. I wish to speak of them to you. I wish to tell you my hopes and dreams and share with you my past. I know that you will listen to it all. I have never found anyone before who I can trust myself to, until you smiled on me. You were the greatest gift I could ever wish for.

Oh how I miss you! It is Friday night, and I am alone in my study. The house is silent and I can imagine your voice rising in song, floating through the hallways, filling the empty places of my soul with joy. You complete me. I will struggle through these weeks apart from you, but I will succeed because at the end I know that you will be there. Seeing you again will make this torture bearable.

I want to say so much more, but it will have to wait until I am in your blessed presence. I hope that you enjoy your visit with your friend, but is it too much to ask that you suffer and miss me, too? Just a little? I am selfish.

Please write to me. I will wait anxiously for any word and will treasure it.

With affection,

W

Elizabeth read the letter until she knew it by heart. She traced her fingers over the words. "He wishes me to call him William." She whispered. "Yes, William, you have your wish. I miss you very much."

DARCY STAYED in the park alone for a long time after Elizabeth's carriage departed. He considered following it, but he knew that once started he would never stop. He would have stayed with her the entire way. He sat on a bench; the chilly March wind had no effect on his reverie. There were children running about. Boys with kites, girls with their dolls, and he wondered what it would be like to be a father. In a way, he was one already. He had been Georgiana's guardian since she was ten years old, but he knew, as hard as he tried, he could not replace their father's memory, nor should he. He was not much older than she at the time his mother died, and as heart wrenching as that loss was, and as horribly lonely as his life became, he was grateful his father never remarried. He could not imagine trying to give his affection to another woman who came to take his mother's place.

He considered what Elizabeth had told him about Georgiana missing her father and how it related to Wickham. Was she trying to replace her father's affection with the attentions that she received from him? Did Wickham know that she was lonely and would unwittingly welcome what she thought was love? Did she feel as empty as he did? Darcy realized that as much as he loved his sister, and tried to show it, his inability to allow anyone to get close prevented him from being able to display the love he felt. He was so afraid of being hurt. The loss of his mother, the odd relationship with his father, the constant betrayal of his former friend Wickham, had all taken his already shy and reticent personality and made him unable to express himself in any way.

Until now. Until Elizabeth. Now he was feeling so many things that he never allowed himself to feel before. He knew attraction, affection, desire, passion, comfort, trust, friendship, and yes, he knew it now, love. He loved her. He knew now the moment that he fell in love. It was here in this park, when he impulsively pulled her into his arms and held her. He only knew her one day, and he had fallen instantly, completely, irrevocably in love with her. It was frightening and intoxicating. Every day was a new revelation, of her, of him. Now all he could think about was winning her hand and taking her home, to Pemberley, where they belonged. He began planning his proposal. It had to be perfect, he would write it down, yes, and practice it. He wanted everything to be wonderful for her.

He finally returned home and as tempted as he was, he did not read her letter but kept it in his breast pocket, next to his heart, and spent the rest of the day buried in his neglected work. After a pleasant dinner with Georgiana, he listened to her play. It was not until he finally retired that he settled into his favourite armchair in his sitting room, a glass of wine by his side, and broke the seal of her letter.

Dear

I miss you. I know that I am still here in London, and you left me only an hour ago, and you are still only a few miles away, but I can say without hesitation that at the moment you read this, I miss you, so very much.

Everything has happened between us so quickly. It overwhelms me when I think about it so I choose not to. Instead I will think about that which gives me pleasure, and that is you. Did you know that I dream about you? I have dreamed about you for years, but now I have a face to replace that murky vision that my mind created. Who was this mystery man? He was always tall and handsome, for what hero of a novel is not? But my dream man was kind, and caring, intelligent and sharing, respectful and silly. You are all of those things, and so many more. I am thrilled to see you slowly letting down your guard and showing me the hidden parts of you. I have a feeling that nobody else knows these special private places, and I am honoured for the opportunity.

Not very long ago I spent a day contemplating life, and how unlikely it was that I would ever meet someone who could bear my impertinence and coax me to reveal my true nature. I am afraid that I have been hiding behind my wit for a long time. I recognize your mask, now you know mine. Even my dear Jane does not truly know me, but I want to share it with you. The value that I feel for your friendship and affection is inestimable. How will I survive these weeks without you now that I know you are in the world? I miss you so much and I have not yet left. I have so much that I want to say, but I know that I must wait for two long, lonely weeks. I will bear it, for my reward will be your smile when we meet again.

May God bless you,

EB

Darcy thoughtfully folded her letter. He was smiling. She knew how to make him smile with her words whether she was in the room or not. He wondered about the dream man she had imagined and wondered about all of the things she had not said. He knew that she was speaking of the man she imagined marrying and all of the qualities she hoped for, her ideal. Because they were not engaged or even declared themselves in love, she could not be more explicit and tell him the details he dearly wished to know. He could only hope that from what she inferred, he was the man who measured up to her ideal. She certainly was his.

So she wore a mask as well. He suspected as much and wondered if she was lonely, too. She rarely spoke of her mother, and now he knew her father. Her family may be large and alive, but that did not mean she was at home there. He wondered if she had despaired of ever leaving. They had much to learn of each other. She wished to share herself with him, only him. An elated smile appeared on his lips, and he felt surer than ever that she loved him too.

"WERE THERE ANY difficulties with Miss Elizabeth's departure?" Bingley asked as he strolled with Jane through the park Sunday afternoon.

"No, the Lucas' arrived when we expected, and they stayed just long enough to eat and load Lizzy's trunks. I did not think of it before, but you should have been here. You could have met some more of your neighbours. Lucas Lodge is quite near to Netherfield."

"Well, I will be there in a fortnight. I suppose that I will be meeting a great number of your neighbours very soon."

"Oh, you will be leaving?" Jane's brow contracted. She had not really thought about losing his company so soon.

Bingley was pleased to see her concern. "Yes, I leave for Netherfield at the same time as Darcy departs for Rosings."

"Lizzy will be happy to see him. She was quite distraught after he left Saturday morning."

"Distraught? What happened, if I may ask?"

"He departed, and she ran upstairs. I could hear her crying, but she would not let me in." Jane was clearly upset. "They seem to have formed a very strong bond very quickly." She paused, "I noticed Mr. Darcy standing here in the park, watching the carriage when they departed. He must have returned and just waited."

"He did?" Bingley was surprised. He never would have imagined his friend doing something so romantic. "I suppose that he wanted one last glimpse of her. How do you feel about your sister and Darcy?"

"I do not know. I truly have never seen her so happy before, or so vulnerable." She bit her lip and asked pleadingly, "He is a good man, is he not?"

Bingley looked at her earnestly. "I realize that you know very little of both of us Miss Bennet, but I swear on all that I hold dear, Mr. Darcy is a good man, and if he gives his heart to Miss Elizabeth, he does it with the utmost sincerity."

"Thank you, sir. You words relieve my mind. Lizzy is suffering so. Our father's reaction to her courtship is so strange, and she cannot help but be torn by it." Jane was close to tears.

"Do you think that your father will object to anyone who wishes to court his daughters or is it just your sister?"

"I honestly never thought he would behave this way towards any of us, but his bond to Lizzy has always been very strong." She paused, looking shyly at him as a blush rose in her cheeks. "As for the rest of us, he did mention to me that he hoped I might meet someone soon."

Bingley smiled brilliantly at her. "Well that is an admirable sentiment; one that I hope is fulfilled for you, Miss Bennet!" He felt good enough to continue. "I enjoyed our dances together, I only regret not asking you to waltz!"

"Mr. Bingley! Such a scandalous dance!"

"Your sister seemed to enjoy it, and I distinctly remember you rushing to her side and exclaiming over her performance! Has your opinion changed?"

"That is not fair Mr. Bingley! You have caught me out!"

"Miss Bennet, I have asked to attend Miss Darcy's next dance lessons to specifically learn the waltz, perhaps you would like to join us? I am sure that Darcy and Miss Darcy would welcome you?" He looked at her hopefully.

Deciding it was high time for her to be bold like Lizzy, Jane delighted him, "Yes, Mr. Bingley, I would like that very much."

FORTITUDE, endurance, patience, a good imagination; all of these things are necessary to survive the exhausting droning of a Mr. Collins sermon. Elizabeth thought. *This is definitely a trial; thank heaven I only have to hear him four times. Poor Charlotte! This is her Sunday for life!* Elizabeth cast a sympathetic glance at her friend, who rolled her eyes at her then immediately resumed her look of reverence. Elizabeth stifled her laugh.

She looked over to where the formidable Lady Catherine sat with her daughter. Elizabeth was looking forward to meeting her and seeing just what sort of combatant she was. Mr. Darcy said that he thought she would be well matched with her. *No, I must try to behave. I want this woman to like me.* She then turned her attention to Miss de Bourgh. Her frailty was made more obvious by the direct comparison to her robust mother. Elizabeth wondered if the girl were truly ill, or simply cowed by her mother's behaviour.

When the service thankfully ended, Lady Catherine made her spectacular exit, closely followed by the fawning Mr. Collins. Charlotte indicated that they should go to meet the great Lady. Elizabeth was never one to be impressed by a title, so when she rose from her curtsy, she did not hesitate to look Lady Catherine in the eye. Lady Catherine did not like the lack of servility in the bold young girl, but it intrigued her nonetheless. She issued a perfunctory invitation to tea Tuesday afternoon and with a swish of her skirts, departed.

Monday morning Elizabeth walked the groves of Rosings, wrestling with her demons. Her father's behaviour confused and angered her. It was easier to not think about it when she was in London, when *He* was there. But now, alone in Kent, with nothing but her thoughts, she began to dwell on in incessantly. Why? Why had her father behaved in such a selfish, jealous manner? Had he always felt this way? Is it just because of the sudden nature of her courtship? Was he simply unprepared to see her attached and would soften with time or is their relationship irreparably damaged? She had written to her father after he left, telling him about tea with Lady Matlock, the theatre, the ball, the dinners, and she never received a reply. The letters from Longbourn were from her mother and Kitty. Jane heard from him, but no mention of William was made. Was she to be forced to choose? She wished that William was there already. She needed to talk to him. She was so emotional, and he so calm and rational. He would hear her out, and help her understand. Oh how she wished for his embrace! She wiped her tears and walked on. The next afternoon, after meeting Lady Catherine, she felt ready to write to him. She excused herself to her room, and put pen to paper.

Chapter 11

arcy regarded the man sitting opposite him in his study Monday morning. He was about the same age as his father would be if he were still alive. Fit, with signs of good humour in the deep laugh lines around his eyes, but he now wore an expression of extreme discomfort on his face.

"I would like to thank you again for giving me your time today, Mr. Darcy." Philip Carrington may have been nearly thirty years Darcy's elder, but he was, nonetheless, below him in consequence.

"It is no trouble at all, sir. You must understand my great curiosity in any mention of the Bennet family."

"Yes, I can well imagine." He hesitated, and decided to simply plunge in. "Mr. Darcy, I will move straight to the point. What I am about to tell you is a very closely held confidence, which even my son Alex does not know. I am relying on your renowned reputation of honour to keep it that way, until I feel it is time to reveal all to him."

"Sir, if you are asking if you can trust me, you can. Why you would wish to share something so important with a relative stranger instead of your own child is not my business, but I cannot help but be curious." Darcy's brow furrowed and he frowned.

"Mr. Darcy. You have a reputation of being a very private man, and as such, you have never shown your favour to any particular lady before. Your obvious attention to Miss Elizabeth Bennet has raised a great deal of speculation that there may be some attachment to this unknown young lady. You indicated a friendship with her at the ball. I realize that you were being careful about what you said in such a public forum, but am I correct in assuming that your intentions towards her are honourable?" Mr. Carrington looked anxious. "Sir, I assure you, I am not here to gain gossip to pass along the *ton*, and I only wish to verify the strength of your relationship, because if you are attached, you will be very interested in the story that I must tell you."

"I am not comfortable discussing my private life with anyone, but in this case I will make an exception. You seem to want to confide a very personal secret of your own to me, so I will trust you with mine. If I hear anything of it beyond this room, I will certainly know the source." Taking a breath he admitted, "Yes, I have entered a courtship with Miss Elizabeth Bennet, and I do intend to ask her to be my wife. Do you know any reason that I should not continue this relationship?" His eyes bore into Mr. Carrington's, and he tightly gripped the arms of his chair.

"Oh, no! I am delighted to know that you have found a woman who you feel would make you a good wife, and from what my son said about her after his dance, she will certainly challenge you with her wit and good humour, as well as her beauty, on a daily basis. No sir, I can be nothing but happy for you!" Darcy relaxed slightly. Carrington continued, "The reason that I ask about your relationship has to do with my son, and if you are to be husband to Miss Elizabeth, you need to know this, if not for your own sake, then for your friend, Mr. Bingley. You see, my son has shown great interest in Miss Jane Bennet, who is apparently not as challenging in wit as your Miss Elizabeth. He is very much attracted to both ladies, for a reason that he could not define to me."

Darcy sat up straighter, "That is interesting, both Misses Bennet mentioned something of the same nature, they felt that they recognized something about Alex, particularly his eyes and manner of speaking, and were both very curious about him."

Mr. Carrington sighed. "I was afraid of that." Finally gathering himself he looked at Darcy. "Mr. Darcy. Alex is not my natural son." Darcy's eyes opened wide in surprise. "Twenty-eight years ago, the niece of our cook was in service at the estate of the Markham family in Sussex. When she was," he paused, "*with,* he looked significantly at Darcy, who nodded, "the young university friend of their son, and soon found herself with child. When the information was told to the Mistress, and the father named, she was dismissed. Neither the Markham family or the child's father gave her a second thought. She came to her aunt for help, who in turn spoke to my wife, hoping to secure her a position in our household." He looked down. "My wife and I had been married for seven years, and we were unable to have our own child. Without an heir my estate would have gone to a very distant cousin. I have no living siblings. We both desperately wished to be parents, so when Amanda suggested that we take in the girl's child, who we knew was the issue of a gentleman, and give him or her my name, we jumped at the chance. The girl was only fifteen and did not survive the birth. The boy was healthy, and we did accept him. With no family to question us . . . we made him my heir, it was assumed that he was ours. Before the girl delivered, she signed a statement telling her story and naming the father. She was illiterate, but she trusted her aunt to read the statement and witness her mark. That statement is in the possession of my attorney."

Mr. Carrington looked at Darcy with tired eyes. "The gift of Alex was the greatest of our lives. My wife doted on him, and I did my best to instil in him a love of the estate, and a sense of responsibility for it. He seems to display all of our values, and other than a bit of a selfish streak and a tendency to seek solitude from time to time; he bears a very great resemblance to us."

Darcy was absorbing all of this information, to learn that his friend was illegitimate was enormous news indeed, why he even resembled his mother! Then he began piecing things together, and looking closely at Mr. Carrington, he asked, "Is Alex's natural father Mr. Thomas Bennet of Longbourn, Hertfordshire?"

"Yes, he is." The two men stared at each other.

At last Darcy broke the silence. "It is early in the day, sir, but could I offer you a glass of port?" Mr. Carrington nodded, and after Darcy poured the glasses and handed one to the man, he sat down and spoke thoughtfully, "I can understand now your concern over Alex's attraction to the Bennets. They are his sisters."

"So it would seem. He said that Mr. Bingley has a reputation of growing bored with ladies quickly, and that he would simply wait him out before approaching Miss Bennet. Do you know if they are more seriously attached? If they are, there is no need to reveal this secret to any of them, at least, no urgent need."

"Bingley does have a propensity to fall in and out of love easily, but it is not him growing bored so much as the discovery that the ladies are only interested in his fortune that is the problem, as well as his exceptionally open and friendly nature that seems to attract ladies in the first place." He took a sip of his drink. "Neither of the Bennet ladies are fortune hunters." He stared directly at Mr. Carrington. "I have great experience in spotting them, and I can assure you of that. They are both kind and wonderful women. My friend has told me that he intends to marry Miss Bennet, but has not declared himself to her in any way. His feelings for her are so strong that he has promised me that he will, for once, take the situation slowly, and be absolutely sure before he speaks to her."

"That could be a problem, no matter how good the news is for us ultimately. Alex may see his hesitation to declare himself as an opportunity to approach her."

"He did ask her for permission to call." Darcy mused, looking into his glass and thinking. Mr. Carrington grew alarmed. Noting his reaction Darcy explained, "She had no reason to refuse him; she has no attachment to Bingley."

"There must be something we can do without revealing the truth to Mr. Bingley." Mr. Carrington said urgently.

"Perhaps if I speak to him, to encourage him to further his suit with her it will move things along. If I mention Alex's interest it might move him to action. He did make note of Alex's attention and her response to it with some degree of jealousy at the ball."

"If you could do that, I would appreciate it, Mr. Darcy." Mr. Carrington seemed relieved. "Mr. Darcy, you said that you have entered a courtship with Miss Elizabeth?" Darcy nodded. "Then you have met Mr. Bennet?"

"Yes, I have. I can say that it was not a pleasant experience." Seeing Mr. Carrington's concern he continued, "Mr. Bennet is possibly the only father in England who would not welcome me as a potential suitor for his daughter's hand. He made it quite clear that I was not acceptable, and accused me of a great number of ridiculous ideas for seeking out Miss Elizabeth's favour. In the end he agreed to the courtship, but it was only after an argument. I sincerely doubt that he will give his consent to marriage. Fortunately, Miss Elizabeth will soon be of age, and that will not be necessary." Darcy glared at an imagined memory of Mr. Bennet striding around his library.

Mr. Carrington studied Darcy's darkened countenance in disbelief. "Why on earth would he reject you? I have heard the rumours of your income, sir, and I know enough of Pemberley and your reputation to assume that they are grossly underestimated. You are well-known as a good and honourable man; to what could he possibly object?"

"I have decided that Mr. Bennet is very selfish, and sees Miss Elizabeth as his companion, and would not wish to let her go to any man. He is also, I think, jealous of the opportunities that she will have as my wife. I understand that he is negligent of his estate and spends most of his time in his library alone, except for those times when he enjoys conversations with Miss Elizabeth, who she says, is the son he never had." Darcy met Mr. Carrington's gaze.

"I am glad that you have decided to fight for your lady, sir."

"I never had any other thought. Her father will not stop me."

"I wonder if he would be this way if he had a son."

"We will never know that." Darcy shook his head. "You mentioned yourself Alex's occasional selfishness and desire for solitude. Perhaps that trait is something he inherited. Fortunately, you and your wife have raised him to be a man of fine character. I do not think he would be the same man if he had been raised as Mr. Bennet's son."

"Thank you for that, Mr. Darcy." He looked at him. "Should I tell him?"

Darcy considered the question. "Mr. Carrington, I grew up as an only child for twelve years until my sister was born. During those years I wished desperately for a sibling. No matter how much I knew that I was loved, I wished for someone to share my family history. When my parents died, if I had not my sister, I would have been alone in the world. Alex has five half-sisters. He should know about it."

He nodded. "I will tell him, but perhaps I will wait until Miss Elizabeth is back from her trip. Then he could speak to both of his sisters. We could arrange a meeting?"

"That would mean informing the Bennet sisters as well, and I would like to do that in person, rather than by letter. With your permission, I will tell Miss Elizabeth when I see her in two weeks. She is staying with a cousin, actually the cousin who will inherit her father's estate, and he lives near my aunt's home where I will be visiting for Easter."

"Yes, Mr. Darcy, you have my permission. Also, if you could carry through with the conversation to Mr. Bingley about furthering his relationship with Miss Bennet, I would appreciate it. If you have any questions or concerns, you are welcome to contact me. We will be remaining in London for the Season." He stood and offered his hand, greatly relieved for having shared his story.

Taking it Darcy replied, "Thank you, sir, I will do that, and after I speak to Miss Elizabeth, I will write."

Carrington took his leave, and Darcy returned to his study, deep in thought. Alex was Elizabeth and Jane's brother. It was incredible! Could the lack of an heir explain Mr. Bennet's odd behaviour, or was it just something inherent? He tried to compare his friend to what he saw in his brief encounter with his natural father, and could recognize some familiar qualities. He wondered over the legal aspects of the situation. Alex was the legal heir of Kingston Park, but is he also the legal heir of Longbourn? That news would affect the lives of not only Elizabeth's family, but also the prospects of her cousin Mr. Collins. He decided to speak to his lawyer hypothetically about it. He knew that Elizabeth's quick mind would ask the same questions, and he wished to have answers ready for her when they came. He thought some more. Does the knowledge that Mr. Bennet was profligate in his youth and fathered and then abandoned a child change in any way his feelings for Elizabeth? He laughed. No. The sins of the father were not hers, and how many thousands of unclaimed children of gentlemen's habits were out in the world? Mr. Bennet's actions were distasteful, but sadly, not uncommon. Alex was a very fortunate man. Darcy's anger with Mr. Bennet was centred on his treatment of the child he did acknowledge.

He thought of his father's admonition to him not to engage in any such activity until he was married, and the reasons behind it. Darcy wondered how many children he might have unknowingly fathered without it. Following his father's dictum had been very difficult, but he was proud that he had. He was also undeniably happy that time in his life appeared to be coming to an end.

LATER THAT DAY, Darcy sat in his study, staring unseeing at the fire in the grate. Georgiana had just left after finally speaking to him about Wickham. Suddenly he stood and with quick strides began pacing the room. His anger with the man's actions against his sister, dormant for months, came raging back and his intense desire was to find and destroy Wickham. "How dare he impose himself on her! After what my father did for him! After he loved him and cared for him. Cared for him more than me!" He struck his fist on the window frame and finally came to rest, staring blindly out at the world beyond the glass. "My sister believed his lie because she was a child, lonely for attention, for the love of her father. The love that he so freely gave to her and denied me! Why?" Walking around his desk, he dropped into the chair and hung his head despondently, "Love that I could not replace, no matter how hard I tried."

Georgiana had steadfastly refused to let him take the blame for what happened. She said that she knew Wickham instigated it, but that she had naively and willingly complied with him, and that she was finally ready to accept that and use the experience to grow. She was grateful that her brother had found out the scheme in time to stop it, and that there were no consequences for her actions, but now that it was over, she refused to let her error rule her life. Darcy could hear Elizabeth's voice as Georgiana spoke. It was her strength and courage that had made this change in Georgiana. At that moment, he wanted to leap on his horse and ride to her side. He wanted to thank her for whatever she said to Georgiana, and he wanted to beg her to listen to him. Never had he wished to pour his heart out to someone before, and now that he knew there was someone who was willing to hear him, he was desperately unhappy that she was not there with him, where she belonged. Drawing out a sheet of paper, he began to write.

THURSDAY AFTERNOON, Bingley and Jane arrived at Darcy House for Georgiana's dance lesson. The instructor and the pianist were already there, and they met in the grand ballroom. "Do you often give balls, Mr. Darcy?"

Bingley laughed, "Miss Bennet, it is difficult enough to make the man attend someone else's ball let alone give one himself!"

Darcy could not help but smile at his friend. "I am afraid that Bingley is quite correct with his assessment, although I do know my obligations. I always have a small ball here and at Pemberley once a year, as well as a few dinner parties."

Jane looked at Georgiana, "I suppose that may increase next year when you come out?"

Georgiana made a face. "I do not want to think about it. Thank goodness I have another Season to prepare!"

"And hence, the dance lessons. Shall we?" Darcy wanted to complete the lesson quickly. There was only one person we wished to dance with, and she was not there, and there was enough resemblance in Jane's face and voice that he longed for Elizabeth even more.

After nearly two hours, Jane and Charles were thoroughly acquainted with the waltz, as well as the other dances Georgiana was learning, and were now beginning to show their mutual admiration of each other more openly. That gave

Darcy some relief, thinking of how he would speak to Bingley about his relationship with Miss Bennet.

Before they departed, Darcy drew Jane aside and quietly handed her a sealed letter. She looked into his sad face, and nodded. "I will send it to her in tomorrow's post, sir."

"Thank you." Turning to Bingley, he said, "I would appreciate it if you could stop by again sometime."

"Is there anything wrong?" Bingley was concerned over the serious tone of his friend's voice.

"No, not at all, it is a personal situation." He replied enigmatically. Although he did not quite understand the problem, Bingley realized Darcy could not speak of it in front of Jane, so he agreed to pay a call later in the week, shook his hand and they were on their way.

JANE WAS ENTERTAINING Mr. Bingley in the drawing room Friday morning when Mrs. Gardiner entered, carrying the newly arrived post. "Jane, you seem to have a very long letter from Lizzy. She must have a great deal of news from Kent!" Jane's eyes widened as she took the thick letter, and looked up at Bingley. He nodded, realizing that there was probably a letter for Darcy contained inside. "Thank you Aunt, I will read it later when Mr. Bingley has left." She put it into her reticule and looked at him worriedly, wondering how she would be able to pass him Lizzy's letter.

Bingley smiled at her and then declared, "It is a lovely mild spring day, Miss Bennet. Will you join me for a walk in the park before I depart?" Jane smiled in relief. "Yes, Mr. Bingley, just let me get my bonnet and shawl and we shall depart directly." Jane gathered her things, and the two of them set off on their excursion. She looked up at him and smiled. "That was some quick thinking, sir!"

"Well I must admit it was for my own benefit as well, Miss Bennet." He grinned down at her as she blushed. They took a seat on a bench and she opened the letter. Inside there was a note to Jane, and a second sealed letter, simply bearing the letter W.

"W?"

"William" smiled Bingley. Jane's mouth made an "O". He took the letter and placed it in the inside pocket of his coat. "I will be seeing him tonight at dinner. He will be very pleased to receive this."

DARCY FINALLY gave in to the invitation for dinner at the Hurst residence. He did want to avoid Caroline, but he could not cut off the relationship entirely, despite his anger with her constant unwanted attentions, and abuse of her connection to him. She was his best friend's sister after all.

He and Georgiana arrived, looking at each other with apprehension, and entered the overly ornate drawing room. "Mr. Darcy! Dear Miss Darcy!" Caroline flew over to greet them as if she were the hostess. She was so eager to attach herself to Darcy's arm that she nearly knocked Georgiana out of the way. "My, how well you both look! Do you not agree, Louisa?"

"Indeed they do, Caroline. Welcome to our home. We are pleased that you could join us tonight." She looked pointedly at her sister. She had told her countless times that Darcy would never be hers.

Caroline ignored her and smiled coquettishly at him. "Mr. Darcy, I was so sorry that we did not have an opportunity to dance at the Carrington ball." Darcy detached her hand from his arm and stepped away from her.

"Yes, well, you know that I rarely indulge in the practice." He attempted to hide his disgust with her behaviour, and stared into a corner of the room.

"You seemed to have been quite taken with Miss Elizabeth Bennet." Darcy's mask was firmly in place, and he looked at her blankly. "I know nothing of her. She and her sister seem to have appeared out of nowhere. Nobody could answer my queries."

"Why would they interest you, Miss Bingley?"

Unfazed by his evident irritation, she attempted to reattach herself to his arm, "I was just concerned that you were being taken advantage of, sir. Miss Elizabeth is pretty enough; in a common way, but what do you know of her? Who are her parents, and what are her connections?"

"It is none of your concern is it Miss Bingley? I can take care of myself without your assistance, in fact, I am quite happy to do so. Will you excuse me?" He stepped over to Bingley.

"I am sorry for her Darcy. I have been enduring her inquiries about the Bennets all week, and have thus far succeeded in fending her off."

"I just wish that she would give up this obsession with me."

"It is not you *per se*, it is Pemberley, you know."

"Yes, I know, that is what I realized very soon after we were first introduced. I am quite adept at spotting a fortune hunter." Seeing his pained expression he added, "Forgive me Bingley."

"No, I know what she is. I will speak to her again." He paused, "I was visiting Miss Bennet today when the post arrived." He laughed when he saw Darcy's eyes widen and his head snap up to face him. His expression of hope was palpable.

"Did anything in particular arrive?" His voice was strained.

"I will not torture you Darcy. I leave that to my relations." He reached into his pocket and pulled out the letter. Darcy ran his finger over the W and the undisguised love in his face made Bingley draw in his breath. Georgiana saw it and guessed what the letter was. Caroline saw it and did not realize the emotion he was feeling. Darcy carefully tucked the letter in his coat, and thanked Bingley. He managed to endure the rest of the evening by gently touching his pocket to hear the crinkle of the paper inside. She was with him.

He took the opportunity at the separation of the sexes after dinner to talk to Bingley about Jane. Mr. Hurst was already snoring in a corner of the room. "So, you are seeing quite a good deal of Miss Bennet, Bingley. How is the relationship progressing?"

Bingley smiled, "Quite nicely, thank you. I have taken your advice, and I am proceeding with deliberation."

Darcy grimaced; it was time to stop following his advice. "I noticed that she seemed to be responding quite favourably to your efforts when you visited. In fact, I believe that she was quite at home in your arms during the waltz." He raised his brow at him.

Bingley looked excited. "Do you really think so? She seems to enjoy my company, and she blushes quite a bit when I speak to her."

"Well if blushing is the trait that you are looking for in a woman who welcomes your attention, I can attest that her sister is quite adept at the practice. Miss Elizabeth and I even joke about her tendency to blush in my presence. I find it quite," he paused, "delicious." He smiled wickedly.

"Darcy! I never knew you had this roguish side to you!"

Darcy laughed. "Miss Elizabeth has inspired a great many sides to me that I never knew I possessed, and I am enjoying the discovery." Returning to his purpose he prodded him, "Perhaps Miss Bennet will do the same for you?"

"I think that she has already!" Bingley said enthusiastically. Then, furrowing his brow he looked at Darcy. "I say, Darcy, are you encouraging me to make my feelings for Miss Bennet more obvious?"

He smiled at how suggestible his friend was, "I believe I am, Bingley."

"What happened to being cautious?"

"Blame it on the rogue!" They laughed. "But seriously, I noticed Alex Carrington's interest in her, and I do not wish for you to lose out on Miss Bennet if she does not think that your intent is serious. Perhaps you might wish to state some level of your feelings to her."

"I think that is very sound advice. I will think about what I shall say when we next meet. Thank you for your concern." He looked at him brightly. "We may someday be brothers after all!"

Darcy smiled. "Yes, but not by your sister!"

At home, he settled into his favourite chair and opened her letter.

Dear W

Let me begin with this. I miss you. I miss you with a feeling that I can hardly explain to you, let alone to myself. I have spent this week wandering the groves of Rosings with so many thoughts filling my mind and I realize that the sole person in this world who I can speak to about them is you.

The troubles all revolve around my father and I keep asking myself "why?" My friend Charlotte Collins has been helpful, because she knows him and can see his behaviour impartially. She is a help. But it is not you. I need you. I will wait impatiently for you to come, and continue my musings on my own.

But what of my visit? Well, I have met your aunt. I truly believe that I could end this letter now because I think the statement stands for itself. I believe that she knows more about me than my own mother does. I have never known a woman with so few accomplishments so ready to criticize those of people she hardly knows! She is apparently the greatest authority on all things of the least interest to anyone else. I have tried to curb my impertinence, truly I have, but I just cannot resist the woman. In vexing me she is most proficient, which should please her to no end! Forgive me W, I do not mean to sound unkind, but you did warn me what I would be facing so you should not take offence with my agreement!

Your cousin Anne is a puzzle. She is sickly and frail, but is she so quiet just to avoid her mother or is it her true nature? I should like to speak to her outside of her mother's presence. Your aunt said that she would soon be engaged. I cannot imagine how she ever managed to meet a man. I wonder if she is strong enough to be married.

My cousin, Mr. Collins, is everything that I remembered. He is fawning and subservient to your aunt, ridiculously attentive to my friend and her family members and seems determined to show me all of the things I lost when I refused his hand. He does this in front of Charlotte, which infuriates me. As angry as I am with Papa, I am grateful he did not force my marriage to him, whatever his reasons.

Sir William departs Saturday for Hertfordshire. Charlotte's sister will stay another eight weeks. I will return by post coach after Easter, unless my uncle sends his carriage for me.

Now may I end by thanking you for your wonderful letter and book? They are with me constantly, and I know the letter by heart. Thank you for thinking so well of me. I feel the same of you. I would say so much more, but I wish to do that in person.

Come to me soon, please?

With affection,

EB

She misses me! She wants me to come to her! She needs me and wants to talk to me, only me, of her troubles! Darcy was ecstatic. It seemed that Elizabeth's feelings were as fervent as his. She certainly understood his aunt well. He chuckled, imagining the two of them together, antagonizing each other. He knew that it would end soon enough, once he proposes to her. *Should I tell her about Aunt Catherine's desire for me to marry Anne? She must be thinking that they will become engaged when he arrives, but surely she would not say his name to nonfamily members?* He decided that it would be best not to mention it and would tell her of it in person. Standing, he walked to his dressing room, and took out his mother's jewel box and found the ring he was searching for. It was a perfect diamond, surrounded by rubies. He thought of how and where he would propose to her, and imagined their first kiss. One thing was certain; she would *not* be travelling home by post coach.

Chapter 12

lizabeth came down for breakfast Saturday morning and found a very thick letter sitting by her place. It took all of her strength not to pick it up and run directly out of the house to read it. She was sure that Jane's letter included one from William. Charlotte expressed great curiosity over such a lengthy letter from Jane, but stopped after one glare from Elizabeth. She knew when to leave her be.

Elizabeth wrote a note for her family and gave it to Sir William to deliver. When he was finally on his way, she took her precious letter and walked out to the groves. She forced herself to read Jane's letter first and found herself exceptionally jealous to hear of her dance lesson at Darcy House. She was pleased to hear how miserable William seemed to be in her absence and was thrilled when Jane told of seeing him in the park watching her departure. She was happy learning of Jane and Bingley's increasing attraction but concerned to hear that Mr. Carrington had called. Elizabeth and Jane both felt oddly attracted to him. She decided to concentrate on of whom he reminded her to give her relief over her troubled thoughts of her father. She wondered which man she would prefer to see with Jane. Finally, she settled under an apple tree loaded with fragrant white blossoms, and opened the envelope marked only with an elaborate E.

My Dear E,

At this moment I am beside myself with emotion. My sister came to me and spoke of your talk with her, and how she finally came to understand why she behaved as she did with W. I will be forever grateful to you for both drawing her out and encouraging her to understand herself. She is beginning to mature. At the same time my anger for W has increased, as if it were possible, not simply for what he did to Georgiana, but how he gained my father's love and admiration over me. I have never spoken of this to anyone and I now know that you are the one person in the world who I can trust with this, my greatest pain. It seems that we both have fathers who we do not understand.

I also have learned something of a very private nature that concerns a mutual acquaintance of ours. It is very important that I speak of it to you, but I wish to do so in person. I know that I am being cryptic, but given the nature of our already clandestine communication, I cannot risk saying more. Please trust me.

Your beautiful letter resides in my coat pocket. It is with me always, and I read it whenever I miss you which is constantly. I need you E. I need you here, by my side. This is your place. Ten more days. How will I survive? Please write to me. It is my only hope. I miss you, my E.

Yours, with affection,
W

She was struck by the intensity of William's letter. His every expression said one thing. He wanted her. He said that he had never told anyone of his private pain. Only her. "Me. He must love me!" Elizabeth hugged herself with the realization. "Oh to be loved by such a man!" She wondered what had happened with his father and if Colonel Fitzwilliam would be able to shed some light on it, and what was this mysterious information that he wished to speak to her about?

She began to wander the groves, and finding a pathway she had not tried before, she found herself in a small clearing near a stream running high with the waters from a recent rainstorm. Her thoughts were full of William. She laughed out loud. "When did he suddenly change into William?" It seemed so comforting to think of him by that name. She imagined whispering endearments into his ear, and blushed at her boldness. It seemed that he could make her blush whether he was there or not.

Needing a distraction, she thought about Mr. Carrington and his attentions towards Jane. Elizabeth liked him. He had a certain familiarity about him that made her comfortable. She just could not put her finger on it. His eyes definitely reminded her of someone, the way that they looked at her with a mixture of amusement and challenge. He seemed to be very intelligent, and combative. And his sense of humour was very dry, in fact she thought, few people could catch the underlying joke in his sarcastic wit, it almost reminded her of . . . her father.

CHARLES BINGLEY and Alexander Carrington sat on chairs on either side of Jane Bennet attempting to remain civil. Bingley was in possession of a letter for Elizabeth from Darcy. Jane received one from her sister that morning. Bingley arrived to the distinctly unpleasant surprise of Carrington already there. He did not know that the man had already visited.

Mrs. Gardiner, recognizing the volatile situation, attempted to act as a calm mediator and aided the conversation. "How is Mr. Darcy? We have not seen him since Lizzy left."

"He is well, but he misses her very much. He is looking forward to leaving to see his aunt Saturday." Replied Bingley, while glaring at Carrington.

Mrs. Gardiner tried to distract him, "You will be leaving soon as well?"

"Yes, I leave Saturday for Hertfordshire."

Carrington took notice. "Really, Bingley? What takes you there?" He was pleased to hear that his competition was going to be well out of the way.

"I have leased an estate there. Darcy will join me in a few weeks to lend his opinion if I should purchase." Bingley said tersely.

"I am surprised that you wish to leave even before the height of the Season! You will miss out on so many of the ladies, you will disappoint them. You are really quite popular with them, you know!" Carrington gave him a brilliant smile and glanced at Jane for her reaction.

Seeing Jane's blush, Bingley defended himself, "I think that a smile and willingness to dance is not a mark against my character, sir."

"Forgive me, Bingley, I did not mean to offend." Carrington was pleased. Jane's blush and downcast eyes proved that he had made his point.

"None taken." Bingley bit out.

Carrington felt that his work was done, and soon took his leave, promising to come and visit Jane the next week, when Bingley would be conveniently absent.

Mrs. Gardiner showed him to the door. As soon as she left the room, Bingley leaned over to Jane. "Miss Bennet, while we have the opportunity, I have a message from Darcy for your sister."

Jane finally raised her eyes from the floor. "Oh, and I have one for him, as well." She quickly took the letter from her reticule and as they exchanged them, their hands brushed together. Jane blushed again, and Bingley, after quickly pocketing Elizabeth's note, reached out for Jane's hand and raised it to his lips.

"Miss Bennet, would you please take a walk with me? I would like the opportunity to refute the claims that Mr. Carrington implied about my character, and I am afraid that it would be difficult to do so in front of your aunt."

She agreed and rose to gather her bonnet and shawl. Soon they were walking silently in the park. Bingley finally drew up his courage and looked over to her. "Miss Bennet. I wish to clarify something that Carrington said."

"It is not necessary, sir."

"I think that it is." He led her to a bench and they sat down. "You see, I have been attracted to you from the first moment that I met you at Darcy's house. I found you to be the most enchantingly beautiful woman I have ever seen. The next morning I visited Darcy and told him so. He heard me out, and wished me well, but said something that I did not like to hear. He told me to go very slowly and be sure of myself. He did not wish you to be hurt if I were to behave as I usually do. You see, I have often fancied myself in love." He looked at her closely.

"Oh." She looked away.

"I have fancied myself in love, because I did not know what it was to feel myself in love. I now know the difference between a slight inclination and true feeling. Miss Bennet, I have great hopes for you as I have never felt the way I do now for any other woman." He looked at her earnestly.

Jane finally looked into his eyes, trying to see the truth in them. "What are you trying to tell me, sir?"

"Miss Bennet, I promised Darcy that I would take my time. I would be sure before I declared my feelings. I promised this despite my jealousy over his rapid relationship with your sister. You see, he has never given any attention to any woman before, so as he pointed out, he was completely aware of his feelings when he met Miss Elizabeth. I have been fooled so many times by ladies interested in my fortune or mien that I have been taken in." He hung his head at his weakness. Then looked back up, "But this time felt so different. I saw you and I saw the future. I just want to be sure that I know myself before I impose my feelings on you. I thought that our short separation would be good for us. I would have the opportunity to know if my feelings last when we are parted, and you would as well. I am correct am I not? I am not imagining that you have some feeling for me?" He looked at her hopefully.

"No, Mr. Bingley, you are not imagining it. And you are very correct, as is your friend. The separation would tell us if our feelings are worth pursuing further. We will certainly see each other soon, and perhaps even more conveniently than we do now."

"So you are willing to give us a chance, Miss Bennet? Will you trust me?"

Jane looked into his wide green eyes, and smiled gently, "Yes, Mr. Bingley. I will."

"Thank you so very much, Miss Bennet!" He took her hand and kissed it fervently. "What are your feelings for Mr. Carrington?"

"I have none, other than enjoying his company, and he truly reminds me of someone. Lizzy has been trying to puzzle it out as well. I am not attached to anyone Mr. Bingley, and I had no reasonable excuse to refuse his visits. I still do not, as much as I realize that it pains you to hear."

Bingley sighed. "I know, but at least you do not feel as strongly for him as you do me?"

She smiled and gave his arm a reassuring squeeze. "That is quite true, Mr. Bingley."

"So, Miss Bennet, will you do me a great favour? Will you promise me not to fall madly in love with him before you see me again in Hertfordshire?" He smiled shyly at her.

Jane laughed. "I think that I can easily make that promise to you, sir. I will await our reunion before I make any decisions about any man. Will that satisfy you?"

"It will have to do. I thank you."

"Shall we walk on, sir? It is a lovely day." She stood and tilted her head to him.

Grinning widely he jumped up and offered her his arm. "Lead on, Miss Bennet. Lead on!"

SURPRISED TO FIND herself actually welcoming Lady Catherine's command to play, Elizabeth settled herself at the pianoforte after dinner. She thought that by playing she would finally avoid the woman's unending examination of the minutia of her life, and hopefully drown out her strident voice for a while with a pleasant melody. Her thoughts wandered to the note she had received from William that morning. He told her that they would be arriving sometime Saturday afternoon, but could not say for sure when because his cousin was out of town on some military matter, and would not arrive until late Friday night. He hoped to visit her that evening if he could escape his aunt, if not, he would see her at church Sunday morning. She was full of nervous anticipation. Suddenly, the sound of Lady Catherine saying his name caught her undivided attention.

"Yes, it will be a very good thing to have Darcy and Fitzwilliam here. They visit me every Easter. Darcy especially will be welcome. We are expecting a very exciting announcement from him with this visit."

"Your Ladyship, what could it be? Has your nephew at last decided to marry?"

"Yes, Mr. Collins, that is it exactly!" Lady Catherine cast a satisfied look at the assembled audience, and then looked proudly at her daughter, huddled on a sofa under a heavy shawl. "Mr. Darcy will be coming here to propose marriage to my daughter. It was a fond wish of both of their mothers', decided when they were in their cradles. They are to be married and unite the great estates of Rosings and Pemberley. As you can see, Anne's health is robust, and she is now ready to assume her rightful place at Darcy's side. He recognizes this, and he is most excited to come and officially ask for her hand. They will be married by the end of the summer. I am most pleased, as is all of his family."

Elizabeth stopped playing and was now white. She felt sick. She felt betrayed. She needed to leave. Immediately. She rose from the pianoforte and murmured an excuse about a headache and rushed out of the room to the indignant cries of Lady Catherine and worried queries from Charlotte.

She ran back to the parsonage and up to her room where she threw herself on the bed. *Could it be true? Is he to marry his cousin? Has he led me on all of this time? But why did he not say anything? How could he write such beautiful letters and lie to me?* She wrestled with the endless questions. She cried until her pillows were soaked through, and refused to answer the door when Charlotte knocked. She just sat in a corner on the floor and hugged herself, hoping for him to come and tell her it was all wrong. But how could Lady Catherine declare such a thing so publicly if it were not true? *What should I do? Perhaps I should leave. I should catch the first post coach in the morning.* Elizabeth finally fell asleep early in the morning hours, with a vision of William kissing his cousin Anne torturing her soul. When she finally arose, she looked at her red eyes and haggard face, and ordered a bath.

Charlotte came to speak to her, but she was unable to share this pain. She considered running away, and avoiding him and the painful conversation where he would tell her that her father's theories had all been correct. He was using her. He did mean to take advantage of her and toss her aside. She was just a toy for a rich man. Elizabeth began sobbing again. She could not believe it. She would not believe that William would treat her so poorly. He was a good man, she knew it, she did. She hoped. Running away would be the coward's way out. Her courage rose while she tried to stop the continued rending of her heart. She would have to wait to speak to William. Nothing could be solved until she did. She spent the day wandering the groves, and hoping that all would be well, she could no longer imagine her life without him.

Chapter 13

$\mathcal{D}$arcy closed his eyes and let the rumble and rocking of the carriage lull him into a state of reflection. He remembered it as if it were yesterday. He had recently reached the age of two and twenty, and was seated in the study of Pemberley at a heavy oak table, spread with the results of his first independent foray into planning the spring planting. Alongside him were the estate's steward, Mr. Wickham, and his father, who was silently observing with an undisguised look of pride on his face. Darcy was meticulously laying out the details of his plans. He had been given this assignment by his father at Christmas, and was asked to use all of his skills learned from his time at Cambridge, his love of reading and research, and his lifetime of grooming to be the heir of Pemberley, to prepare his report. What he did not know was that his father would soon die.

It was not until the spring when he was twenty years old that he truly felt the expression of his father's love for him, and although it confused him, Darcy welcomed it with open arms. The lack of affection was not so bad when his mother was alive, she expressed enough love to take the place of a hundred fathers, but once she died, George Darcy changed. As an adult, Darcy recognized that he was essentially orphaned that day; however, at the time, he was too young to see that his father put an emotional wall around himself to contain his grief over the loss of his best friend and soul mate.

He did not see that every time George Darcy looked at his son, it brought forth memories of the lost life with his wife, leaving him incapable of performing his duties. Darcy also did not know that his father had another terrible secret that he kept close to his heart, one that ate away at his soul and further destroyed their relationship. Fortunately for George Darcy, when his wife died, his son was at the proper age to be sent away to school, and for the intensely shy boy, it was a very lonely time.

Darcy poured himself into excelling at school, and paid great attention to his duties as the future Master of Pemberley, anything to receive a bit of approval from his reticent father. He watched with frustration as the son of his father's steward, George Wickham, effortlessly received the unending support and affection of George Darcy which he neither deserved nor had earned. Darcy truly did not know that his father loved him dearly or that the guilt that his father felt for his love tore him apart.

A wheel stuck in a rut made the carriage suddenly jerk to the side, startling Darcy from his reverie. He shook his head and blinked, the scene outside of the carriage window was of fruit trees covered with the blossoms of spring. His yearly pilgrimage to Kent to spend yet another Easter with his cousin Richard at Rosings; always seemed to bring back the memories of that last spring with his father, nearly six years ago. He had by now come to the conclusion that his father had given him the assignment to design the planting for Pemberley that year to determine if his son had indeed learned enough to carry on after his demise.

Enough of the past, you are driving towards your future. Watching the scenery go by, he reviewed the letter Bingley brought him the day before. Elizabeth's note was short and to the point. She commanded him to make time pass faster so that she would see him sooner. He chuckled to himself; life with Elizabeth would be a joy.

Turning his mind to other subjects, he thought of the conversation that he held with Bingley, and was relieved to learn of the talk he had with Jane Bennet. It seemed that even if Alex Carrington chose to visit her in Bingley's absence, she was safe from him. She had all but told Bingley that her heart was his, if he knew himself well enough to ask for it.

As the carriage turned into the gate to his aunt's estate, he was full of anticipation. Darcy kicked his sleeping cousin's leg.

"Richard! Wake up, we have arrived!"

He moaned, and began whining, "Five more minutes, Darcy, I need all of the rest that I can get to survive this visit."

Darcy prodded him with his foot, his lips twitching. "You have been resting for the past two hours, and your snoring has been less than entertaining. Now put yourself to rights before our beloved aunt descends to drag you out of the coach herself."

Richard chuckled, "She would, too." He looked out the carriage window, "Darcy, look over here, who is that tiny man, and what on earth is he doing genuflecting to our carriage?"

"I wonder if that can be Mr. Collins? He does seem to be a bit of an odd-looking character. Elizabeth's description was correct." *Is this the man who dared offer marriage to my Elizabeth?* Darcy stared at the small man and was struck once again by the extraordinary bravery Elizabeth displayed in refusing him. He would be forever grateful that she did.

"I just hope that we do not have to spend too much time with him. If he is bowing to the carriage, imagine what he is like in person!" Richard laughed. "From what Miss Elizabeth has said, he is a toady of the highest order, just what Aunt Catherine would desire in a parson."

The carriage continued up the drive, passing through a grove of trees, one of the few parts of the estate allowed to stay in its relatively wild state. This was Darcy's favourite area. It was full of boyhood memories of tree-climbing and imaginative adventures played with his then young cousin, Richard. The carriage came to an unexpected halt and upon lowering the window; they saw that a small tree had fallen across the road. The carriage driver and postillion jumped off to move it aside, and at that moment Darcy's attention was suddenly drawn by a flash of colour in the grove. His heart started pumping wildly when he instantly recognized who it was.

Elizabeth. Dressed in a simple yellow muslin gown, she had a bonnet slung over her arm and her dark hair was pulled up with yellow and green ribbons, reminding him of his first sight of her at the theatre. A few stray curls had escaped their pins and were bouncing along her neck and touching her shoulder. A book was open in her hands and she was paying no attention at all to the carriage in the road. It was a shout of success from the men moving the tree that caused her to finally look up. Her gaze travelled from the tree, to the carriage, to the face of the beaming young man in the carriage window. Their eyes locked. Astonishment registered on her face. It was William. The wait was over. Darcy threw open the carriage door and leapt out, landing in a crouch, and quickly straightened.

"Where are you going?"

"It is Elizabeth!" Darcy cried. "She is here, I must go to her! I cannot wait to see her!" He turned and anxiously searched for her.

"Elizabeth," Richard said, suddenly understanding. He looked at his thoroughly discomposed cousin and thought that he had never seen him in such a state. *No, that is wrong. I have seen this before, at the theatre in February.* Richard called, "Aunt Catherine will want to know where you are, what should I say?"

"I do not care, tell her what you will." Darcy looked up at the carriage driver and ordered him to walk on, and turned back to the grove. *Where is she?* He ran to the spot where he had last seen her, and started calling, "Elizabeth? Please, Lizzy, please, where are you?"

Elizabeth saw Darcy jump from the carriage, and overwhelmed with emotion, she turned and ran from him, hiding behind an ancient oak tree. She peeked around the side, watching him frantically search for her. She finally calmed her breathing, and her wildly beating heart. *Yes, it truly is William.* She heard him pleading for her to come out, and then she heard the sound of her name fall from his lips. It was like magic, it sounded so natural, and it drew her out. She stepped from the shelter of the tree, almost directly behind him. "Here I am," she softly called.

Darcy spun around and found that he was standing face to face with the woman who had haunted his dreams and filled the lonely moments of his days for nearly two months. Breathing hard, his eyes drank in her lovely form, taking in every part of her from head to toe, finally rising to meet her gaze. He saw reflected in her eyes the same emotions that he was feeling, hope, joy, relief, and passion. But one other emotion was present, pain.

He took a few steps forward, until they stood only inches apart, so close that he could feel her ragged breath on his neck as she gazed up at him. "Why did you run from me?" Darcy lifted his hand and tenderly caressed her face. "Elizabeth," he breathed. She took a step closer and lifted a trembling hand to gently touch his cheek. He closed his eyes for a moment, and when he opened them, he saw that she was crying.

Her voice breaking, she turned away. "How could you?"

"What have I done?"

"You are engaged to Anne de Bourgh. Your aunt spoke of nothing else last night. She crowed how you were to finalize the engagement during this visit and that you would be married this summer." Facing him, her eyes full of hurt and anguish, she accused, "Papa was right about you! Why did you lead me on?"

Darcy felt as if she had slapped his face. How could she possibly believe her father's false pronouncements against him? Fighting through the storm of pain and anger that her accusation inspired, he realized exactly what she had said, and fixed her with a steady gaze, "I am *NOT* engaged to Anne. That is the fantasy of my aunt, but it has never been my or Anne's wish. I am not in any way bound to her. My aunt had dreams of joining our estates, and has declared for years that we would marry. It should be obvious to her by now that it would never happen. She never said it directly to me, so I could not deny it to her face. It is all in her head. It is not the truth. I am so very sorry that my aunt's words led you to doubt me or my intentions in any way."

Elizabeth's eyes flashed at him, "But I wrote to you of it. I told you of your aunt speaking about how your cousin would soon be married. Surely you knew that she referred to you? She must expect you to propose. I told you of this and you did not reassure me then. I could have been prepared to hear her talk. I could have been spared the anguish that I endured last night. Why William? Why did you not tell me? You could have told me before I left for Kent. You could have spoken of your aunt's imagined plans for you. We could have laughed about it." Her tears fell steadily, and she had to turn away.

Darcy hung his head in shame. He had hurt the single most important person in his life for no reason. He reached out and touched her shoulder. He was gladded when she did not pull away, but she still would not look at him. "Elizabeth, I have no good answer for you. I did not think that Aunt Catherine would speak of such things in front of anyone who was not family. It shames me to know that she did. But the pain that you felt then and now makes my proud self rejoice. Do you see how terrible I am? I am happy that you suffered because it tells me that you might care for me the way that I care for you." He gently turned her to face him.

Taking a deep breath, he took Elizabeth's hands in his and looked deeply into her eyes. "There is no possibility of me making a marriage of convenience to my cousin or any other woman when my heart belongs to you." Elizabeth's hope rose.

He looked down at their entwined fingers, seeking strength from the union of their hands and returned his gaze to her teary eyes. "Elizabeth, I have imagined this so many times. I planned my words, our location, everything, but now I find that I cannot possibly let this moment pass without telling you how ardently I love you and how desperately I need you. I cannot bear to spend another day without knowing you are mine and I am yours. I want to give myself to you, all of me. I do not ever wish to be parted from your side again. My life is empty without you. Please, can you love me? Please say yes. Please complete me. Please end this lonely existence that I have endured for so very long. Please Elizabeth, will you grant my wish, will you give me the honour of your hand in marriage?"

He appeared so vulnerable, and she knew that he had just laid his soul bare. She knew her answer weeks ago; when he first embraced her in the park, knowing then that he was the only man she could ever love. She lifted her hand to caress his brow, only to have it caught and held to his cheek.

She smiled up at him, feeling his grip tighten with each new word. "You do not have to beg me to love you. I knew when you first took me in your arms. That very moment I knew that was where I belonged. I was home. I knew that I wanted to spend every night for the rest of my life listening to your heartbeat. You have filled the emptiness of my life in a way that I only dreamed could happen. You are the best man I have ever known and I want to care for you, and love you, and tease you, and vex you, and kiss you, everyday for the rest of our lives. Yes William, I am honoured to give you my hand. I am overjoyed to call you mine!"

"My Elizabeth," he whispered, his voice shaking. His eyes bore into hers and then his gaze lowered to her lips. Her eyes followed the same path. They stood transfixed and slowly he raised his right hand and placed it gently under her chin, tipping it upwards, while she laid her hands on his chest. His left hand moved behind her head, and he lowered his mouth to hers. She closed her eyes and felt the growing warmth as the whisper of his breath sent a tingle of anticipation throughout her body. The first touch of his lips was feather-light and they both shivered. It was exactly as he had imagined it countless times, the dream, the fantasy of that first hesitant, tender, shattering touch of their lips. Trembling, he increased the pressure and stroked again and again. His right hand moved down her shoulder and to the small of her back, pulling her possessively against him. Elizabeth soon learned how to respond to his touch, and when she felt the trace of his tongue, she parted her lips and welcomed his entry. Their tongues met tentatively, tasting each other for the first time. Darcy held her tightly, and Elizabeth wrapped her arms around his waist, pressing her body to his. He groaned softly and pulled his mouth from hers, and brushed his lips gently over her cheeks, and down her neck, his warm breath creating the sensation of a thousand fingers dancing over her body.

Gliding his tongue beneath her ear he revelled in her gasp and low moan. "Oh how I love you!" He whispered, the warmth tickling her ear.

"William," She breathed. She opened her eyes to see his were closed, his dark lashes heightening the intense expression of bliss upon his face. They opened and gazed into hers, holding them, and he kissed her while moving his hands to stroke her back. Finally they drew apart, resting their foreheads together; eyes closed; arms around each other's waists. A sigh passed between them. They held each other, enveloped in relief and in their newly-realized joy.

Eventually, Darcy pulled away and looked down at Elizabeth. He took a steadying breath and spoke quietly. "I will of course ask your father for consent, but he was so against our courtship, I fear that he will not welcome my request. In six days, however, you will be of age; we will not require his consent to marry."

Elizabeth regarded him seriously. "We will need to procure a special license, regardless."

Smiling, he bit his lip and looked down while saying softly, "I already have one."

"What do you mean?" She demanded.

He looked back up into her insistent gaze. "I applied for one before I left London."

"You were feeling very confident, sir." She said, tilting her head.

Darcy's smile broadened. "I knew what I wished for."

"Arrogant!"

"Determined." He corrected.

"Conceited." She shot back.

"Hopeful." He wrapped his arms tightly around her waist.

"Selfish." She murmured, softening.

"In love." He whispered, drawing her against him.

"Oh." She rested her head against his chest.

"Marry me." He whispered into her ear.

"Yes." She whispered back.

Cupping her face with his hands, his lips met hers, softly stroking, over and over. His tongue again slipped into her mouth and gently touched hers. He slid his hands down her body and held her securely. Their mouths and tongues danced together, leaving them breathless and anticipating so much more. Finally drawing apart, Darcy ran his hands up and down her back, and he smiled into her slightly glazed eyes. "I love you Elizabeth. I cannot wait to give myself to you and bring you home."

"I love you William, I know that I have no home without you."

"I love hearing you say my name." He kissed her nose and she ran her fingers through his hair and stood on her toes to kiss his chin. Darcy laughed.

"What should we do now?"

"We could ask your cousin to marry us?" He suggested with a grin.

Elizabeth looked at him sceptically. "Although I share your suspicions that my father will not be happy with our engagement, I think that we should at least give him the benefit of the doubt and allow him the chance to say yes."

Darcy sighed, but agreed. "Yes, I suppose for the sake of family harmony, we should approach him. But remember, you will be of age, and his consent is not needed. We *will* marry," he promised, and looking from her eyes to her mouth, his lips captured hers, "as soon as possible." Finally moving apart to draw breath, Darcy hugged her tightly. "As much as I truly hate to say this, I think that I must go to the house. If I do not make an appearance soon, my aunt will be sending a party to search me out and drag me to her presence."

"Having met her, I have no doubt of that." Elizabeth said dryly.

"When may I see you again?" His soft brown eyes begged.

"I have been walking the paths of Rosings every morning." She smiled and stroked his cheek.

"Perfect!" He displayed his dazzling dimpled smile and began speaking as the confident man in charge. "I usually ride every morning, but now I will walk. Where and when shall we meet? I should have you know that we must keep this from my aunt's knowledge. As you became painfully aware, she is determined to have me marry Anne, and will not tolerate you getting in the way. She would certainly be difficult if she found out about us, and may make things difficult for your cousin as he is your host. He is dependent on her good will."

"Oh, is nothing ever simple?" Elizabeth bit her lip and sighed. "I will meet you at seven o'clock right here. It is not far from the gate to the parsonage, and it seems fairly secluded." Darcy covered her face with kisses, and with an enormous effort, let go.

Taking her hands in his he smiled into her sparkling hazel eyes. "Good evening, my Elizabeth. I love you." Smiling joyfully she gave his fingers a squeeze and rose up on her toes to bestow another peck on his chin.

"Good evening, my William. I am yours." Darcy laughed then watched her until she reached the gate to the parsonage. He took a deep breath, and turned his steps to Rosings.

Chapter 14

The sound of Darcy's boots echoed as he strode confidently into Rosings. He was ecstatic, and proud. He had just received the greatest honour of his life. The woman he loved had granted him permission to love her back. Forever. Nothing could dampen his happiness. Not even the strident, demanding tones of his aunt renting the otherwise deadened air of the household.

"Is that my nephew? Where has he been? Tell him to attend me at once!" Lady Catherine shrilled.

Darcy was hoping that he would be able to escape upstairs before greeting his aunt, but he knew that was very unlikely. She was ever vigilant. He sighed, and with great effort, he toned down his joyful expression to assume his usual sombre mask, and redirected his steps to his aunt's sitting room.

"Good afternoon, Aunt Catherine. Please forgive my delay." He bowed low to her and kissed the bejewelled fingers of her proffered hand.

"Where have you been, Darcy? Your cousin arrived here over an hour ago, and we have been waiting for you."

"When our carriage stopped to await the removal of a fallen tree, I felt an intense need to exercise my legs. It was rather cramped in the carriage after so long of a ride." He glanced up to the raised eyebrows of his cousin.

"I assume that you are quite recovered?" Her eyes swept over him and she pursed her lips disapprovingly.

"Yes, Aunt, the movement prevented any ill-effects. I look forward to walking the paths of Rosings a great deal during our visit, and my stroll today reminded me of the beauty of the estate." This time he caught Richard's knowing smirk.

He knew that he struck the correct note when he saw Lady Catherine begin to preen in delight of the compliment. "It is good that you appreciate the beauty of Rosings, Darcy. I hope that you will appreciate it for many years to come."

"I am sure that I will, Aunt. After all, it is where my family lives, and I have always known the importance of these bonds." He met her gaze, and then nodded his head with a smile towards his cousin Anne.

Lady Catherine lifted her head proudly. "It is proper that you do. Your parents would be most pleased."

"Now Aunt, I would like to change from these travelling clothes, if you will excuse me?" He looked at her inquiringly.

"Of course Darcy, you should have changed immediately instead of speaking to me." Turning to Richard, "And you Fitzwilliam, why have you not changed? This is not a battlefield! You should not be leaving your dust on my furnishings!"

"Yes Aunt, forgive me, I will change immediately." Richard looked at Darcy and they quickly quit the rooms and rapidly ascended the stairs. "How did you manage that? I have been listening to her rage at your absence for an hour, and you breeze in and get yourself dismissed in five minutes!" Richard was half-angry and half-envious.

"Ah, Cousin, have you not learned that the best path to our aunt's good mood is to compliment her?" Darcy smirked at him.

"I suppose that implying your interest in certain family members did not hurt either." Richard shot back.

"Did I do that? I did not realize. I will have to correct that notion very soon, I think." Darcy's jubilant smile returned.

They reached the door to Darcy's suite, and Richard opened it, pushing him in. He checked to be sure that his valet was not about, closed all of the doors and stood directly in front of him with his arms folded. "All right, out with it. You are going to burst if you do not tell me your news, or surely your face will be permanently disfigured from that ridiculous grin you are wearing. There must be something to cause all of this, and it must be something more than simply exchanging pleasantries with Miss Elizabeth." If possible, Darcy's grin grew larger. Richard had no memory of his cousin ever expressing such elation.

"I have the best possible news!" His eyes were shining with joy. "I am engaged to be married to the most wonderful woman in the world! Miss Elizabeth Bennet has accepted me!"

"You proposed already! That is fast work! Congratulations Darcy! I am floored with this news! I expected it sometime, but so soon?" He pumped Darcy's hand and slapped his back. His cousin radiated his happiness, and Richard gratefully shared in it. "What happened to the careful plans and the speech that you prepared? You bored me silly with it the whole way here, and you did not even get to use it!"

Darcy raised his brow. "I did not realize that you were bored Richard. I rather had the impression that you were amused at my expense."

"So I was, so I was. Well, tell me all." Richard dropped into a chair, propped his feet on a table and folded his arms.

As Darcy leaned on the mantle of the unlit fireplace, his smile disappeared. "When she ran away from me I panicked that I had lost her."

"She ran away?" Richard sat up as concern crossed his face.

"She was angry, and very hurt. Last night she dined here." He closed his eyes. "Aunt Catherine spoke of her happiness for our impending arrival, and of the expected engagement between Anne and me."

"Good Lord, Darcy. You let her come here without a warning? What a horrible way to learn of Aunt Catherine's delusion!"

Darcy shook his head and looked down at his boots. "It never occurred to me that she would speak of it to anyone outside of the family. I am just grateful that Elizabeth forgave me, after soundly thrashing me with her fury."

"Good for her!" Richard cheered, a wide grin appeared.

Darcy smiled and looked up at him. "Yes. Then I could not help myself. I had to know that she was mine. I proposed, she said yes, and I cannot wait to marry her!"

Richard cocked his head at him, "What about Aunt Catherine?"

"That is a problem." Darcy's smile again disappeared.

Looking thoughtfully at his subdued cousin he suggested, "Perhaps I should ask father for advice? I will send him a letter immediately."

Relieved knowing that he had the support of the rest of his family he regained his confidence. "That is an excellent idea, Richard. I will also go to Anne and tell her the news. I think that she will be happy for it. She never wanted to marry me or anyone, for that matter."

"Will you go to Miss Elizabeth's father?"

"I honestly do not know. Elizabeth wants me to go, but I know that he will not welcome me. I have learned something about him recently that may prove useful, however." He said, becoming lost in thought.

"What is that?" Richard asked, curiously..

Darcy startled and regarded Richard. "I wish to speak to Elizabeth about it first."

"When do you see her again?" He asked, a little smirk playing on his lips.

"Tomorrow morning, before breakfast." Darcy grinned.

He laughed. "Well, it seems that I have a letter to write. I will see you at dinner. Congratulations again, Cousin. I am quite envious of you. She is an exceptional woman." Richard slapped him on the back and shook his hand. As he left the room, his smile faded, feeling every bit of the envy he professed.

DARCY KNOCKED on the door to Anne's sitting room and entered when he heard her soft call. "Anne, it is a pleasure to see you. You look well."

Anne smiled. "Thank you William, you are kind. Please take a seat." She waved vaguely at the chairs, and pulled her shawl closer.

"I need to speak to you while I have the opportunity to see you alone. I want to tell you my news before your mother hears of it." Anne looked up at him curiously. "I am engaged to be married." He looked steadily into her face.

A look of profound relief spread over her wan features. "How wonderful, William! I cannot begin to tell you how pleased I am to hear this news!" Her cold frail hand grasped his strong warm one. "What is the lady's name?"

Darcy smiled and gave her hand a gentle squeeze. "You will be surprised, I think. She is Miss Elizabeth Bennet."

Anne's eyes widened. "You mean the lady who is staying at the parsonage?"

"Yes, we met in February, and have been courting for a month. I spotted her when our carriage pulled into the drive. I could not wait another moment to see her again. That was why I was late coming to the house."

"And that was when you proposed?" Anne smiled.

Darcy smiled in return. "Yes, I just could not wait any longer."

"I like her very much, William. She is very kind, and quite intelligent, and she is not intimidated by mother. I admire her confidence. I think that secretly, mother admires her as well."

"I told her that I would like to see her take on Aunt Catherine, though I suppose any admiration she had for Elizabeth will be gone when she hears our news." A look of apprehension replaced his smile.

"Yes, that is true. But neither of us wished for our union, William." She suddenly had a thought. "Now I understand what happened last night when Miss Elizabeth fled the drawing room, close to tears. She was playing the pianoforte when mother began speaking of our forthcoming engagement. Miss Elizabeth stopped playing and listened, and then she turned white and ran out, pleading a sudden headache. Oh, William, you did not warn her!"

Darcy hung his head. "No, I failed her. She told me about what happened, Anne. I have apologized, and she has accepted me, thankfully." Shaking his head he looked to her, "Our union was only your mother's wish. Uncle Henry supports my relationship with Elizabeth and Georgiana was thrilled that she may become her sister."

Anne grasped his hand. "When will you tell Mother?"

"Elizabeth will be of age on Friday. Her father, for his own odd reasons does not support the marriage. I think that after Friday we will make our announcement, and since I have a special license we can hold the ceremony anywhere, we may just go ahead and marry." His voice held a note of determination.

"A *fait accompli*?" Anne suggested as small smile played on her lips.

"Exactly."

"ELIZA!" Charlotte attempted to gain her friend's attention as she floated past on her way up the stairs to her bedchamber. She did not recognize Elizabeth at all. There was a glow to her face and a lustre in her eyes that could in no way be compared to the distraught woman who fled from Lady Catherine's parlour the night before. Charlotte entered the room and decidedly closed the door behind her. She wanted some answers. "Eliza . . ." She began.

"Oh Charlotte! He loves me!" Elizabeth woke out of her dream and flew across the room. She grabbed her friend's hands and gave them a tight squeeze. "He loves me and asked me to marry him!" She laughed and still holding Charlotte's hands, she spun them around, finally collapsing onto the bed in a dizzy, giggling heap. Neither Charlotte nor Elizabeth were prone to giggles, which made it all the more singular.

Charlotte shook Elizabeth's shoulders. "Who, Eliza? Who loves you? Who has proposed?"

"William." Elizabeth replied dreamily. "Fitzwilliam Darcy, the man I will marry." She laughed with delight.

"Fitzwilliam Darcy? Lady Catherine's nephew? He is the man who has been courting you?"

Finally coming to her senses, Elizabeth sat up and held her hands. "Yes, dear Charlotte. He is the wonderful man who has been courting me. He just arrived, and saw me from the carriage as it passed through the groves. He leapt out and ran after me." She smiled at the memory of his impetuous behaviour.

"But Lady Catherine said that he was to marry Miss de Bourgh!" She saw Elizabeth's beaming smile disappear. "No wonder you fled the room last night. Oh, Eliza!"

"Yes, you can well understand my distress. When William saw me I ran away, I was so hurt and afraid that it was true. Fortunately he assured me it was his aunt's desire alone. Lady Catherine refuses to listen to anyone who has told her otherwise, and keeps to her own plans." She shook her head. "I lashed out at him for not warning me. He apologized." She sighed, and then her smile returned, softly. "Then he begged me to love him and be his wife, and then he kissed me." She closed her eyes, reliving the memory.

Charlotte saw the joy in her friend's face and briefly entertained a feeling of jealousy, then she put that aside. Romance was a feeling that she simply did not possess. She touched Elizabeth's cheek, "I am so very happy for you."

THE NEXT MORNING, Darcy eagerly strode out of Rosings to meet Elizabeth. It was the first day of their engagement, and he could not wait to see her. He arrived early and leaned on a tree facing the parsonage, watching for her and remembering the dreams he had the night before, now even more vivid for having finally experienced her kiss. Soon, the sound of skirts rustling and the soft hum of her voice in song tickled the air. "Good morning, my love!" He called out joyfully.

Elizabeth, hearing his deep voice, searched for him then ran into his open arms. "Good morning, my William!"

Darcy encased her in his embrace, holding her tightly to him, resting his cheek on her bonnet, and drank in the lavender that perfumed her hair. She buried her face in his chest, allowing his scent to envelop her. They stood for some moments, until she lifted her face to his and they stared into each other's eyes. His heart was bursting from his chest, and he raised his hands to cup her face. Smiling, he met her lips in a fervent kiss, then dropped his hands to reclaim her body and bond her as closely to his as he could. Elizabeth stood on her toes and wrapped her arms around his neck, meeting his hungry mouth with equal passion. Darcy finally dragged his lips away and raked his ravenous eyes over her.

"Lizzy what you do to me!"

She caught her breath and laughed, "I love you, too!"

He laughed and smiled into her eyes, so delighted to be wanted and to be permitted to express his affection for her. "Come, let us walk. We have much to discuss." He took her hand, raised it to his lips; and then entwining their fingers they set off.

"Have you decided when you would like to marry?"

"Today seems perfect." His eyes twinkled mischievously.

"William!" She stopped dead.

He looked down at her flashing eyes and leaned to kiss her nose. "Very well, I will be serious. I was speaking with Anne last night and she thought that it might be best to simply marry when you are of age and present the news as unalterable fact."

"And bypass my father and your aunt's objections all together?" She said thoughtfully as they began walking again.

"Yes. I know that you would wish to have your family around you, and enjoy the large wedding that you have dreamed of . . ."

"Actually William, I have never really thought of the wedding. I was more concerned with whom I would marry and the life I would lead. The ceremony itself, the trappings at least, are unimportant to me."

"Truly? Because if it were up to me, if I could not be married in the chapel at Pemberley, I would like something as small as possible. You know how I hate being on display in front of a crowd."

"Well then perhaps it would be best to arrange something small on our own. If my mother were to be involved, the event would be enormous, especially once she heard of your ten thousand a year!"

He looked at her quizzically. "Where did you hear that figure?"

"Is it not common knowledge?" She asked impertinently.

"Come Lizzy, where did you hear it?"

"Lady Matlock told me, and told Jane that Mr. Bingley was worth five thousand. She did say that was the current rumour." She pursed her lips, her eyes twinkling.

"Hmm. It is inaccurate, you know, at least for me." He tilted his head at her, his own mouth twitching with a suppressed smile.

She laughed. "As long as the roof over our heads is sound, I really do not care, my love."

Darcy stopped and hugged her. "You are definitely not a fortune hunter."

"Do not tell me you are disappointed!"

"Not at all, my love." They found the shelter of a convenient tree and kissed for quite some time. "Ahem, now back to the subject at hand. . ." Darcy said after straightening his clothes and recovering his hat which had landed some ten yards away when Elizabeth tore it from his head. "Are we agreed to marry before you return to Hertfordshire?"

"Yes." She said softly.

"In London? Perhaps your Aunt and Uncle Gardiner could be there? Your uncle could sign the settlement papers, although you could do that yourself after Friday." He was all business and making his plans.

Elizabeth caught his mood and joined in. "I will write to them directly. They could make the arrangements for the church."

He nodded and continued his line of thought. "Eventually we will need to face your father. Perhaps we could simply invite your family to London for the wedding?"

"Or, we could go to Longbourn and ask his consent, and if he refuses we could simply walk to the Meryton church and marry immediately." Elizabeth bit her lip and peeked up at him.

Darcy stopped walking and drew her into his arms. "This is truly what you want is it not, Lizzy?"

She nodded. "I cannot believe he would say no, William, and I would always regret not giving him the chance to do the best thing for me. If he says no, I will not hesitate to take your hand and walk out of Longbourn to the church with you."

His eyes searched hers, seeking confirmation of her desire. She appeared anxious but determined. "Very well, my darling, it shall be as you say. We will stay here until Easter. I will bring you to your uncle's home, collect Jane, and take you to Longbourn. I will speak to your father. If he says no, we will proceed directly to the church. If he says yes, we will set the wedding for no longer than one week after our arrival. Agreed?"

"Agreed. Thank you, William." The smile on her lips did not reach her eyes. He could see the fear there, and knew that she was doing her best to hide it from him. Darcy looked around them. They had wandered down a track he remembered from childhood, and was obviously neglected by the Rosings gardener. It was overgrown and the trace of a path was barely visible. He smiled and taking her hand led her further along. "Where are you taking me, sir?" She asked with a small smile, allowing her curiosity to overtake her worry.

He looked back to where she followed slightly behind him. "To a place full of memories." The corners of his mouth lifted. He carefully moved the vines and branches that crossed the path out of the way until suddenly a bright patch of sunlight came into view. Exiting the growth Elizabeth gasped with delight to see a small pond with a roughly hewn bench perched by its side. Darcy led her over to it. "It appears to still be sound; would you care to sit here with me?" He looked at her hopefully.

"I would love to William." He helped her to sit and taking his place beside her untied the ribbons of her bonnet then carefully removed her gloves. His hat and gloves soon joined hers and he pulled her over to his side. She rested her head on his chest, and fell in love with his steady heartbeat. He wrapped his arms around her waist and entwined his fingers with hers. They sat staring at the clear water, watching some ducks paddling about and gathered strength for the battle to come.

His soft voice broke the peaceful moment. "I have dreamed of this, Elizabeth, sitting here with the woman I loved." He kissed her hair. "When I was a boy, perhaps ten years old, I escaped Rosings and went off wandering in this forest. Richard did not accompany us that year; he did not start coming until after my mother died." He paused for a moment, awash in the memory. "I found my way to this place and was disappointed to hear the sound of voices when I approached. I looked and was surprised to find my parents sitting here on this bench, embraced much as we are now." He looked down at Elizabeth's upturned face and leaned, softly caressing her lips. "I saw how deeply they loved each other. It was not so obviously on display at home in front of me." He looked as if he wanted to say more but did not. He closed his eyes as if blocking some great pain, then continued. "It was witnessing that exchange that made me determined to only marry for love. Of course, I knew my duties to honour our name, to increase the value of the estate, to marry and produce an heir, all of the common things of which you are no doubt aware, and believe me; those things were deeply and frequently impressed upon me. I imagine that at some point I resigned myself to following that dictate, fulfilling my duty, but deep down in my heart, I knew that I would rather live alone than marry without love, without the deepest love. The love that I saw displayed between my parents that spring day, here on this very bench." He stroked her cheek. "This is why I waited to marry. I was hoping for you." She was looking up at him, mesmerized. "So my love, I know that you fear facing your father, but you once told me that you wished to marry for love. Is that what you are doing by accepting me?"

"Yes, William." She reached up to touch his face, and he captured her hand to kiss her fingers.

"I have been so impressed with your bravery for rejecting Mr. Collins. You had no idea what your future would hold, but you chose to follow your heart, to listen to its whisper, to wait. I am so grateful that you did. Please do not be afraid, my love. Together we will face your father and unlike my parents, our love will be easily seen. If he cannot accept it, then it is his loss, not yours."

Elizabeth's eyes were moist with emotion. He was slowly opening up to her, it was only right that she do the same for him. "You call me brave. Most would call me very foolish and selfish. I could have secured both my and my family's future by sacrificing myself to Mr. Collins. If I had not met you, the truth is that upon my father's death . . ." She stopped, and looked down at her hands. "I do not know what may have become of us. Of me." Darcy embraced her tightly. Drawing away, she smiled slightly. "My parents do not have a loving marriage. I doubt that my father has kissed my mother for years, and he speaks only to ridicule her flighty behaviour. I sometimes wonder if her behaviour was caused by his." She bit her lip then took his hands back into her grasp. "It was watching my parents that made me determined to marry for love, just as you watching your parents did the same. I suppose in some way, our parents did us both a great favour by unwittingly displaying their true natures to their children."

Darcy looked down at their clasped hands. He was not ready to speak of his father yet, so as much as he wished to reply, he could not. Instead he gripped her hand tightly. Elizabeth could feel him holding back now. They had reversed positions.

"My father, whatever his motivation, whatever his true disposition, formed me by his instruction and by my observation of his behaviour. I do not know how he will respond to your approach, William; I can only hope that the man I once thought he was will prove to be the man he truly is."

"I hope so as well." He said softly. "I understand now your need to go and ask for his consent, even though his answer is not assured." He embraced her, so thankful that she waited to find him. "I just do not understand how he can profess to care for you but not allow you to secure your future through a marriage you desire." He stopped and closed his eyes. Darcy buried his face in her hair. She heard him whisper to himself. "No, not yet." He was struggling with the decision to tell her about her brother, and to share with her his own painful past. He then lifted his head and looked into her eyes. "Elizabeth." He said urgently, then crushed his lips to hers, stroking them, seeking reassurance from her response that he was no longer alone. Elizabeth felt his need and met his fervency with her own. He pulled her up onto his lap and they wrapped their arms around each other, exchanging kisses, learning how to express their passion. They pulled apart, breathing heavily. Elizabeth looked into his eyes, and saw them darken, burning with a fire that she now recognized as desire. He saw the same intensity in her face. Neither one of them wanted to stop, but they both knew that they must. With a groan of pure frustration he tucked her head onto his chest and kissed her hair, trying to regain control of his emotions and ardour. Elizabeth concentrated on his rapidly pounding heart, and as it slowed, she returned from the brink of total abandon. Eventually they sighed.

Darcy lifted her chin and kissed her gently. "We should return. The morning is advancing." His eyes told her that leaving was the last thing he wanted.

"Yes, we must breakfast and prepare for church." Her gaze answered his in every way.

He nodded and helped her off of his lap and onto her feet. He returned her bonnet and gloves and watched with affection as she adjusted them and smoothed her gown. They held hands and walked to the main path, and taking care to separate before they came into public view, returned to their respective homes, both dearly anticipating the day when their separation would forever end.

LATER THAT AFTERNOON, Darcy and Richard walked down to the parsonage to pay a call. Darcy informed Richard of their wedding plans, and he agreed that it was probably the best course of action, as unlikely as it was to be well-received by Mr. Bennet.

"What about Aunt Catherine?" He asked. "Have you decided when to tell her?"

"No, I will await your father's advice, but I will tell her before we leave."

They arrived at the parsonage and were announced. Lady Catherine had ignored the parsonage party at church that morning, so they had not yet been introduced. Elizabeth stepped up to do the honours and barely finished when her cousin interrupted.

Mr. Collins bowed to his toes. "My dear sirs, it is such an extraordinary honour to make the acquaintance of such illustrious relatives of my noble patroness Lady Catherine de Bourgh! The favour that you show on my humble dwelling cannot be compared to any other kind gesture given by such honoured visitors!" He took a deep breath as if to continue his incomprehensible babbling, and Richard, his eyes widening with increasing alarm, stopped him.

"We thank you for your kind words, sir." Turning to Elizabeth, he cried, "Miss Elizabeth! It is a distinct pleasure to see you again! It has been far too long!" He quickly grabbed her elbow and moving her away to some chairs near a window engaged her in a conversation full of laughter.

Darcy watched with increasing unhappiness. Not only had his cousin left him with Mr. Collins, he was stealing away the attention of *his* Elizabeth! He did not like the way Richard smiled and laughed with her at all. He was feeling exceptionally possessive. It was with a start that he heard Charlotte's quiet voice.

"May I offer you my sincere congratulations, Mr. Darcy? I have known Eliza since she was newborn and I have never seen her as happy as she was when she told me her news."

Darcy smiled to the sincere woman. "Thank you, Mrs. Collins. I have never felt such joy before myself." He relaxed a little, and while ignoring the endless effusions of Mr. Collins who took no notice of his missing audience, he spoke to Charlotte quietly. "Mrs. Collins, do you know Mr. Bennet?"

"I do, and Eliza has spoken to me of his objections." She responded, keeping her voice low.

"She wishes for me to apply for his consent. Do you think that he will give it? Will he see that I wish only to care for her and love her?"

"I am afraid, sir, that Mr. Bennet is not thinking of Eliza."

"Then you and I are in agreement, he will be implacable."

"I am afraid that you should be prepared for that situation, sir." Charlotte met his gaze sincerely.

He nodded. "Thank you Mrs. Collins. I will do as Lizzy asks, but I will prepare the way for our immediate marriage. Could you please give me the name of the parson and the direction of his parish in Meryton?"

Charlotte discreetly left the room and came back with the information. Darcy decided to write to the man and reserve the church for a wedding the morning after their expected arrival at Longbourn. He would not give the names of the couple.

Elizabeth finally escaped Richard and rescued Darcy from Mr. Collins by suggesting a stroll in the garden. Charlotte convinced her husband to stay inside with her and Maria, and Darcy and Richard accompanied Elizabeth outside. "We have received an invitation to dine at Rosings on Thursday."

"Aunt Catherine will be most displeased that she did not have the opportunity to introduce us." Darcy smiled when she sighed.

Richard watched the couple becoming lost in their gaze. "I think that she will have more to be displeased about soon enough!"

Chapter 15

ingley's coach entered Meryton not long after noon on Saturday. He had stopped at the Gardiner home before he left town to bid a very heart-wrenching farewell to Jane and was already wondering if he would be strong enough to survive the fortnight apart from her.

He was surprised at the attention that his carriage drew as it entered the village. It was well-made, but certainly nothing to the carriages that Darcy owned, and unlike his friend, he enjoyed smiling and waving to the curious townspeople who tried to catch a glimpse of him. It seemed that he was already recognized as the mysterious Mr. Bingley.

Caroline chose not to make the journey, which was fine with him. He was rather looking forward to coming home to a quiet atmosphere for a change. He was full of enthusiasm, and wanted to immerse himself in the responsibilities of the estate. The owner's steward was set to begin instructing him the next morning, beginning with a ride around the perimeter, and a thorough explanation of the crops and expected yields from each tenant.

There was one more duty to fulfil. Miss Bennet and the Gardiners had letters prepared for him to deliver to Longbourn. That much-appreciated favour would certainly earn him the approbation of the Bennet household; as they would not have to pay the postage for the letters delivered the normal way. It would also give him a convenient reintroduction to Mr. Bennet.

Sunday morning he of course attended church, and was instantly surrounded by the locals. He found that Sir William Lucas seemed to be the ringleader of the welcoming committee, and introduced him to the various heads of house that were present. When he bowed to Mr. Bennet, he informed him of the letters, and was invited to pay a call that afternoon.

"Mr. Bennet, I hope that your family is all well?" Bingley asked eagerly after they took their seats in Longbourn's library.

He is harmless enough and seems to be financially secure, if Jane likes him, then I will support the engagement. Mr. Bennet leaned back in his chair and folded his hands across his stomach. "Well enough, sir. I understand that you have some letters for me?"

"Yes sir, I called at the Gardiner's home before I left London, and they asked me to deliver these." He drew out the much wrinkled envelopes.

"Thank you for your trouble." Mr. Bennet cast an amused glance at the state of the missives. "I understand from my brother Gardiner and daughter that you have been a frequent and welcome visitor." He noted Bingley's delighted smile. "How was Jane when you saw her?"

Bingley's eyes instantly acquired a dreamy expression. "Miss Bennet was wonderful . . . ahem, I mean, she was very well, sir, very well. She was a little lonely without Miss Elizabeth now that she has left for Kent, but she is looking forward to being reunited with her in a fortnight." He straightened his shoulders and met the man's gaze.

Mr. Bennet's face reflected his sadness. "Yes, Lizzy is greatly missed by us all. Tell me, how well do you know Mr. Darcy?"

"I have known him nearly seven years, sir, a better man I could not name."

"What are his habits with the ladies?"

"That is an easy answer sir, there are none; he has never courted a woman before Miss Elizabeth, and he has not escorted any particular lady to an event more than once. He rarely dances, but when he does, it is never the first, and will only dance one time. He does not visit brothels or keep a mistress. He is the epitome of honour."

"A man with no vices? That is difficult to believe for one of such wealth." Mr. Bennet scoffed.

Bingley wrinkled his brow. "If Mr. Darcy has a vice, sir, it is a tendency to hide away and read. He is not fond of social situations. He prefers to spend his time at home alone or with close friends, and caring for his sister. He is most diligent with his estate duties, and he is going to help me make a beginning at estate management by guiding and advising me with Netherfield."

"A man without fault, then." Mr. Bennet almost sneered.

Even Bingley could hear the insult in his voice, and he rose to defend his friend. "No man is completely without faults, sir, but hopefully his are not the type that will cause harm to others. He is truly a very good man."

"Forgive me Mr. Bingley; I am concerned over his supposed fondness for my daughter, Elizabeth. I am just curious to learn the character of my daughter's admirer, it is what a good father does, you know."

Wondering at the reasons behind the man's suspicions of Darcy's motives, he cautiously agreed. "Of course, sir, I hope to find that out myself one day."

Bingley left the house without seeing the rest of the Bennet ladies, although he could certainly hear them. He wondered how his Jane had grown up to be so quiet and reserved when living in the midst of such noise, and suddenly realized that he had answered his own question.

By the end of his first week, Bingley was entirely overwhelmed by the endless duties and details required of the Master of an estate, and was grateful he was only leasing. Netherfield was a fraction of the size of Pemberley, and his admiration for Darcy was growing by the hour.

He was also missing Jane. Their decision to take this time of separation to test if his feelings for her were genuine was proving to be unnecessary. The gnawing emptiness that he felt in his heart was something that no other woman would be able to fill. He could not wait to see her again. When a letter arrived from Caroline stating that she had learned, who knows how, that Darcy would be coming to Netherfield in a week's time, and that she insisted that he come and escort her there immediately so that she could prepare the house for his visit, he was glad for the excuse to order his carriage and depart for London. *What will Caroline do when she learns who her new neighbours are?*

AFTER BINGLEY DEPARTED, Mr. Bennet sat staring at the closed door to his library deep in thought. He had spent time over the last month trying to find someone who had something negative to say about Darcy with no success. This visit from Bingley was just the latest proof that he was, in fact, a good man. That, which to any other father of a daughter involved in a courtship would ordinarily be most welcome, just made Mr. Bennet all the more agitated. How was he to convince Lizzy not to accept him if he had no proof of his unworthiness? He knew full well that his refusal to give consent would have no weight after her birthday and given her headstrong attitude, she would likely follow her own heart, and leave her home, and her father.

Suddenly a thought occurred to him. He remembered a conversation that he had with Jane. Yes! Darcy had a falling out with Wickham! Perhaps the story that Lizzy was told was incorrect, perhaps he caused the man some injury, and he did not hurt Darcy at all! Completely disregarding the fact that Wickham had attempted to seduce Elizabeth and was shown to leave numerous debts in Meryton, he left Longbourn to search out Colonel Forster and learn Wickham's location. He would write to him and request his help.

SEVERAL DAYS LATER, George Wickham stood looking with confusion at the letter in his hand. "Why would someone from Longbourn be writing to me?" Remembering his last visit, he unconsciously lowered his hand to protect his groin, before kicking himself for being a fool. He opened the letter and laughed. "So, Darcy is in love with the girl who kneed me. How rich! And her father disapproves! What a simpleton! To disapprove of Darcy! And he wants my help to break them apart." Wickham smiled. This could prove to be very profitable. He could demand money from the father for his assistance, and perhaps demand a great deal more from Darcy to desist. "Yes, this could be a very profitable enterprise." He was very disappointed when he did not succeed with Georgiana. *Well*, he thought, *I had succeeded, but not in marrying her.* He grinned and wondered if Darcy knew.

He wanted to hurt Darcy. All of those years, a lifetime of doting attention from Mr. Darcy, and suddenly it was taken away from him, just when the old man was ill, and he thought that a huge inheritance was in his future. Wickham even entertained the fantastic thought that Mr. Darcy would bypass his son and leave Pemberley to him. He was bitterly disappointed when he was left with one thousand pounds and the living as a parson. Darcy had to pay for that. The three thousand pounds that he wheedled out of him in exchange for the living was gone almost as soon as had it in his hands. That was when he set his sights on Georgiana, and Darcy arriving in time to prevent their marriage had left an even stronger desire for revenge in his jealous heart. Taking away Darcy's choice for wife; or better yet, making him pay for the ability to marry her was right up his alley.

IF ELIZABETH HAD any regret for becoming engaged to William at Rosings it was solely her lack of interest in anything other than him. She was afraid that she was proving to be a very poor houseguest to her friend Charlotte. She apologized for her lack of attention, and Charlotte good naturedly assured her that she was providing plenty of amusement by wandering around the house with a dreamy look in her eyes.

The engaged couple met every morning in the groves without fail, and once upon the most secluded paths, walked hand in hand, talking about anything and everything. Darcy told her of Lord Matlock's letter of congratulations on their engagement, and his recommendation to wait until the day of their departure to tell Lady Catherine the news. Darcy was admittedly pleased to delay the confrontation. He was delighted to instead spend their time in peaceful conversation. He could not wait to tell her all about Pemberley, and how eager he was to take her there. They discussed honeymoon plans, estate issues, and dreams of their future. Nothing was out of bounds, except they chose not to talk about the subject that pained them the most, their fathers.

Of course, they could not spend all of their time together. Darcy and Richard had estate duties to tend for Rosings and the two of them often arrived together to pay calls on the parsonage, at times that they were assured of Mr. Collins' absence.

By Thursday, they settled into a pleasant routine of visiting and were looking forward to spending the evening together, even if it was to be spent in the company of Lady Catherine. The parsonage party had not been invited back to Rosings since the Friday before, when Elizabeth ran out of the drawing room in tears. She was relieved that the Lady chose not to bring that subject up, but once they were seated at the table, she did not hesitate to indulge her favourite pastime of interrogating her guests. Darcy and Anne were seated on either side of her, with Elizabeth beside Anne, and Richard on her left. Charlotte was on Darcy's right, followed by Maria. Mr. Collins was next to Richard. Elizabeth was pleased with the seating because it gave her a chance to exchange glances and expressions with William as his aunt droned on. Lady Catherine returned to her inquisition of Elizabeth's accomplishments and lack of opportunities when she finally reached the end of her tolerance.

Turning towards her, Elizabeth asked with a sweet smile, "Lady Catherine, certainly by now you know all that could possibly be known about my upbringing. Would you please share with us your story?" Darcy's eyes widened and he looked across the table at her. She could feel Richard suppress a cough.

"What do you mean?" Lady Catherine demanded irritably.

"Well, surely you had the benefit of working with the masters, could you tell of your experiences and accomplishments? They must be too numerous to mention them all, but you could perhaps give us a flavour of them?" She smiled again.

Lady Catherine's mouth set in an angry line. "My accomplishments are not fodder for dinner conversation."

And mine are. Elizabeth thought. "Oh, I am sorry to hear that. I thought that we could discuss such things because you were so fond of examining me and my family. Perhaps instead you could tell us the story of your court presentation and first Season? I was never given this honour, and I know that Mr. Darcy's sister will be presented next year. I would enjoy hearing of the experience?" She raised her brows.

Lady Catherine's eyes narrowed with displeasure. Her coming out and first Season was a disappointment. She could only attract fortune hunters. No man was romantically inclined to her. Instead of suffering a second Season, she accepted the offer of the man with the largest estate, Louis de Bourgh. "I would not wish to bore this company by speaking of my own experiences, especially to people who would never be able to share them. It would be unseemly to discuss it."

"Forgive me, Lady Catherine, I meant no offense." Elizabeth stared unflinchingly into her eyes.

Meeting her gaze, Lady Catherine replied tersely, "Not at all, Miss Bennet, you can plead ignorance for your behaviour."

Elizabeth knew that she had won the argument, if for no other reason, Lady Catherine was now silent. She lifted her eyes and met William's. He was pressing his lips together, suppressing a smile. Richard's eyes were dancing merrily. He began a new subject about books, and the rest of the party soon joined in, much to the displeasure of his aunt, who was no longer the centre of attention.

After dinner, the gentlemen remained with the ladies, and Elizabeth was asked to play by Darcy. She settled herself at the pianoforte, and Richard, with a bit too much alacrity for Darcy's taste, took the seat beside her and offered to turn the pages. Darcy resigned himself to leaning on the instrument, and decided that it was an exceptionally good place to stand and gaze at his beloved. Richard bent to her and whispered, "I say, Miss Elizabeth that was an excellent demonstration of wit you gave us at dinner."

Elizabeth grinned, "I hope that I did not offend her too much, I was just weary of her unending determination to point out my inferiority."

"No, no, if she is offended, it is her own fault. I would guess that it has been quite some time since she was last so soundly put in her place." Richard laughed with delight at her triumphant smile. "Do you not agree, Darcy?"

Startled from his pleasant musings of kissing that smile, he nodded gravely. "Of course, I always knew that I would enjoy an evening watching Miss Elizabeth enter into verbal combat with our aunt."

"Why, thank you kind sir. I am thrilled to bring you pleasure." She batted her eyes at him coquettishly.

Darcy could not suppress his loud laugh at her silliness, and gave her his rare dimpled smile. *Oh how I love this woman!* Lady Catherine's strident demands broke through their happy exchange, and Elizabeth entertained them with several songs until the party finally departed for the evening.

THE NEXT MORNING, Darcy was waiting for her at their favourite tree, and as soon as she arrived he took her in his arms and kissed her with the fervency he wished to bestow upon her the night before. When they finally drew apart, he smiled down into her sparkling eyes, and kissed her nose. "Happy Birthday, my love!"

"Oh, I almost forgot! Thank you William!"

"How could you forget such an important day? I have been waiting for this since you first told me the date! Today you are a free woman!" He was jubilant. As of that day, nothing could stand in the way of their marrying, no matter what her father's feelings may be.

Elizabeth laughed at his obvious joy. "How shall we celebrate?"

"I do have that special license in my bedchamber, just waiting to be used." He said suggestively, running his hands up and down her back. She shook her head and smiled. He did not know how close she was to agreeing. "I know." He sighed, resigned that she would make him wait to speak to her father, and decided not to press her again. "Well, perhaps I could give you something else, then. Something to remind you of me when I am away, pining for your presence."

He reached into his pocket and drew something out in the palm of his hand. Looking deeply into her eyes, his expression changed to one of utmost tenderness. "I love you, Elizabeth. And I want to give you a symbol of my love, something that will always be with you." Gently he took her left hand in his and slipped the diamond and ruby ring onto her second finger. She gasped, looking from the ring to his brightened eyes. "This was my mother's ring, and her mother's before her. I want you to have it. You are my family now. I love you my darling, you are my heart, and I count the days until I can make you mine in every way." He lifted her hand to his mouth and gently kissed the ring. He then moved his lips to her third finger and looking into her teary eyes whispered, "The moment that I place a ring on this finger will be the happiest of my life."

She tried to speak, to thank him for the ring, for the honour, but had no opportunity. The words were just forming, "Will. . ." when his mouth descended upon hers, and she was lost in the overwhelming feeling of his body encompassing hers. His lips brushed over her face, down to her neck, his hands lovingly, possessively caressed her body. She felt the evidence of his ardour pressing into her belly, and she responded by pressing closer to him. Her fingers wound into his curls and her lips searched for bare skin to kiss as his mouth moved over and around her face.

"I want to love you, Lizzy." He breathed into her ear. She held his face in her hands and pulled him down to kiss his lips, demonstrating the passion she felt. Darcy rejoiced in the reassurance of her welcome. He tenderly kissed her, fighting his need. At that moment he knew that there was nothing to hold them back from marrying. They needed nothing but a church. *Please Elizabeth, please marry me today.* He begged in his mind.

Elizabeth brought her hands back down to wrap around his waist, and rested her head on his chest, *I want to marry you today.* Neither one of them had the courage to voice their thoughts. Darcy took her withdrawal as a sign that he needed to stop, and disappointed, he took a deep breath and accepted her decision, resting his cheek on top of her head until they calmed.

Pulling back, he smiled and kissed the tears of emotion from her face. She sniffed and smiled ruefully, "What are you grinning about, sir?"

"I was just wondering if you will be moved to tears at every joyful moment of our lives." He wrapped his arms back around her and whispered warmly in her ear, "I already know how accomplished you are at blushing." Elizabeth instantly turned crimson, and he laughed, embracing her and smiling widely. "Oh, I love your blushes!"

"Sir, you are driving me to retaliate!" She glared at him, flushing all the more.

"And what exactly will you do to me, my dear, almost-wife?" He grinned, squeezing her tightly and anticipating her answer.

Elizabeth bit her lip, and then tilted her head to the side. "I will speak to your sister to find out your secrets."

"Ha! She knows nothing!" He flashed his brilliant dimpled smile.

Her eyes narrowed, and she replied evenly. "But I am sure that the good colonel does."

"Lizzy . . ." His grin disappeared, his eyes suddenly pleading with her.

"Ah-ha!" She grinned in triumph. "What have you done, sir?"

"Nothing." He said quietly, pressing his lips together.

"Youthful transgressions? Embarrassing moments? Poorly chosen words? I plan to learn it all, sir." She prodded him mercilessly.

Darcy turned red. "Lizzy, please."

"William." She stroked his cheek, her voice soft.

"Yes." He said, shyly looking at the ground.

"I love your blushes, too."

JANE LOOKED THOUGHTFULLY at the man walking by her side. She certainly liked Mr. Carrington, she found him handsome and engaging. She enjoyed his company, and felt a certain familiar comfort, almost a kinship in his company. But after a week of separation from Mr. Bingley, she was sure of her affection for him. She enjoyed Mr. Carrington's company, yet she knew that the time had arrived when she must tell him that all she could offer was friendship. She began to formulate the words when suddenly her foot caught in an uneven spot of the pathway. As she cried out, Alex's strong arms reached for and caught her. Turning her around to face him, he drew her closer. "Are you all right, Miss Bennet?"

Jane, staring up at him in surprise, nodded silently. Alex, taking in her expression, allowed his gaze to drift to her mouth, and back to her eyes. He was overcome with the need to kiss her, to connect with her somehow. He felt so completely drawn to her. "Jane." He whispered, and began to lower his lips to hers.

"Miss Bennet!!" Bingley flew up the path. "Miss Bennet! Are you well? I saw you almost fall!"

Bingley rapidly caught up to the pair, noting with internal satisfaction the look of profound relief on Jane's face at his arrival. Carrington, annoyed at the interruption also noted Jane's relief, and instantly released and stepped away.

"Yes, Mr. Bingley, I am well, I suppose that I should know to lift my feet when I walk. Mr. Carrington was kind enough to stop my fall in time." Turning to him she bowed her head, "I thank you, sir."

"It was nothing, Miss Bennet." Then looking to Bingley, he said suspiciously, "I thought you had gone to Hertfordshire."

"So I did, but my sister Caroline decided that she wanted to come to Netherfield sooner, and begged me to return and escort her there. I thought that I must pay a call on Miss Bennet while I was in the neighbourhood, and offer to bring a letter to her family if she wished." He said this as he moved to stand protectively between Jane and Alex, his warning to the other man clear in his stance.

"How very kind of you, Mr. Bingley." She looked at him gratefully.

Alex was no fool. He saw when he was defeated, and decided to quit the field with his dignity intact. "Well then, since you are assured of companionship, I will take my leave. I have many appointments to attend today."

"Oh, must you leave so soon?" Jane asked, breathing a sigh of relief.

"I am afraid that I must." Then taking her hand in his, he kissed it before looking into her eyes once more, "It has been a pleasure Miss Bennet. I wish you well. Goodbye." He took a breath, and turning, walked down the path and out of the park.

Bingley and Jane stood looking at each other silently, and mortified she lowered her head and cast her eyes down, "Mr. Bingley, I, I do not know what to say. . ."

"Miss Bennet. . ."

"I, I assure you, sir, I was not trying to encourage. . ."

"Miss Bennet. . ."

"I, I, I truly did trip, and I was not wishing for him to. . ."

"Miss Bennet." Bingley gently placed his fingers under Jane's chin and raised her head. "Miss Bennet, I have no doubt in my mind that your clumsiness on the footpath was entirely accidental, and not at all contrived to gain Mr. Carrington's attentions." He smiled into her flustered face.

"You do not?" She whispered, mesmerized by his warm green eyes.

"No, Miss Bennet. I know that you are a lady of the highest honour, and besides, you made a promise to me, and I know that my trust was not misplaced." He now took her hands in his and stood, gently caressing them. "Miss Bennet, do you not wish to know what act of serendipity brought me to this little park today?"

"Yes I do wish to know, I thought that I would not see you for some time." She said softly.

"I found that I could not follow my own decision to stay away from you. I was determined to see if my feelings for you would change if we were to separate, and what I found was that my feelings grew. They grew so strong that I knew I must tell you of them as soon as possible. This morning at daybreak, I climbed into my carriage, and came straight here." He lifted her hand to his lips. "And now, are you willing to hear what I have to say, Miss Bennet?"

Jane could barely stand; her knees were shaking so badly. "Yes, Mr. Bingley, please tell me."

"Miss Bennet, I have realized that I no longer wish to be parted from you. I know for certain that what my heart told me the first time I saw you was true. You are the woman I have been searching for. I wish with all my heart to marry you, and with your help, build our family and establish our home together. I have no great estate, or old family name to give you. That is what we will begin together. Are you willing to enter this adventure with me, Jane? Will you be my wife and allow me to love you forever? Please, will you marry me?" Bingley looked deeply into her blushing face, hoping for her acceptance.

Jane drew a breath, and blinking back the tears, she raised his hand to her lips, and gently kissed it. "Yes, Mr. Bingley, yes, I will marry you and join you in our wonderful new life together. I love you very, very much."

"Jane." Charles kissed her hand, his eyes bright with tears. "Thank you, my love."

They entwined their arms and started to walk aimlessly around the park, whispering of their feelings and talking of their future. Charles decided to speak with his attorney while he was in town about the settlement, return to Netherfield the next morning with his sister, and speak to Mr. Bennet after Jane returned.

ALEX CARRINGTON was walking past his father's study when he heard his name called. "Yes, Father?"

"Please come in and close the door." Philip Carrington regarded his son's pensive face. "Is something bothering you?"

He smiled wryly. "It shows, does it?"

Philip returned his smile, and indicated the chair before his desk. "You never have been accomplished at hiding your feelings, Alex, despite your cunning wit."

Alex sighed and took the offered chair. "Do you remember meeting two ladies at our ball; the Bennet sisters? They came with Darcy and Bingley."

Cautiously, Philip nodded. "Yes, they were very lovely."

"Well I felt myself oddly attracted to them, in a way I could not define. I felt a desire for friendship with Miss Elizabeth, her humour and wit seemed similar to mine and I really enjoyed talking with her. But I did not feel the attraction in a romantic way. I was very happy for Darcy." He paused; "I did not feel the same about Miss Jane Bennet. She is so different from Miss Elizabeth, so quiet and gentle, and simply lovely, that what I felt for her, I thought was more of a romantic nature. I called on her several times, and although she never said or did anything to encourage me, she did seem to enjoy, almost seemed intrigued by my attentions. I thought that we were developing a comfortable relationship." He paused.

"And what happened?"

"I met her today and we went for a walk. We were enjoying our conversation, and then she tripped and I caught her in my arms. I looked into her eyes and felt the desire to kiss her." Alex's eyes took on a look of wonder at his reaction. Philip gripped the arms of his chair tightly, waiting. "And suddenly from nowhere Bingley appeared, running up the path, calling her name. I thought that he had left for Hertfordshire, but he said that he was there to see his sister." He laughed, "That was obviously not the case because he looked at my arms around Miss Bennet with such possession that I felt if he had a pistol he would have shot me on the spot. Of course, I immediately let go of her, but what struck me was the look of relief on her face when he came, and oddly the feeling I had was momentarily disappointment, but now I realize that it was relief as well. I think that I just want the same friendship with Miss Bennet as I did with her sister. It is so odd, the attraction. I do not understand it." He shook his head and stared down at his hands.

Philip closed his eyes, feeling his own relief. He opened them, and looked at his son's face. His brow was furrowed in confusion. "I think that I can help you to understand this. In fact, this is what I wished to speak to you about today. I am just pleased that nothing happened between you and Miss Bennet." He took a breath. "Alex I wish you to know that you are loved very much by both me and your mother. There has never been a child so wanted and anticipated than you. Your mother and I tried for seven years to have a child before we were blessed with you."

Alex smiled at his father. "I have always felt wanted and loved Father, I cannot have asked for greater parents."

Philip had tears in his eyes. "Thank you, Son." He closed his eyes then meeting his son's concerned gaze, he began. "I did not know if I would ever tell you this but the situation with Miss Bennet has forced me to reveal this truth to you."

"Miss Bennet? Why would my friendship with her have anything to do with a secret of yours?"

Philip drew a deep breath, and finally revealed the truth. "Alex, you are not my natural son."

He stared. "I do not understand, did Mother . . .?"

"NO! No Son, you are not a blood relation to either of us. You were, for lack of a better word, adopted. I gave you my name and made you my heir. Everyone assumes that you are our natural child, it was a well-done deception." He looked at his stunned son and continued quickly. "Your mother and I were unable to have our own child, and we both desperately wished to be parents, to give our love to a child, and make him the heir of Kingston Park. When we learned of a young girl who had been imposed upon by a gentleman, we offered to take the child whatever the sex, and raise him or her completely as our own."

"What happened to the girl, my mother?" He choked out; everything he had ever known of himself was suddenly irrevocably changed.

Philip quietly explained. "The girl was only fifteen and died in childbirth. Her name was Sarah Jones."

Alex nodded, his hands were shaking. "And who is my natural father?" He felt that he knew this answer.

Philip stared directly into his son's eyes. "Thomas Bennet, of Longbourn, Hertfordshire."

"Then Elizabeth and Jane Bennet are. . ."

"Your sisters."

"My God."

They sat in silence for quite some time. A thousand questions flew through Alex's mind. Who was he? Did he belong in this house? Should he confront Mr. Bennet? Should he relinquish the Carrington name? Horrified, he realized that he had almost tried to seduce his sister. His mind whirled with confusion, and ultimately he latched onto the only anchor he had. The people who had loved him and wanted him from the moment he was born. Alex looked at Philip, who had an expression of anguish on his face.

"Father." He saw the tears of relief in his eyes, and knew that he had reached the correct conclusion, for all of them. "Father, this news is a shock but you and Mother are my parents. You raised me, you loved me, and you have given me a wonderful life. I am the man I am because of you, and if you still wish it, I will proudly bear your name for the rest of my life."

"Thank you, Son. I love you." Philip said; his relief evident.

"And I love you, Father." Alex said sincerely.

Alex and Philip rose and embraced each other, both in tears. When the men separated they returned to their seats and quietly sat, trying to regain their equilibrium. "I assume that Mr. Bennet refused to acknowledge my birth?" Alex asked, his face showing his bitterness.

Philip nodded slowly. "He would not take responsibility for the pregnancy, and Miss Jones, who was a chamber maid, was dismissed from the home of the family she served when Mr. Bennet visited."

"She was cast out!" He said angrily.

"Yes, our cook at the time was her aunt. She went to your mother begging for her to hire the girl. Your mother immediately proposed saving you, and well, here we are."

"What would have become of me if you had not?" The question hung in the air between them. They both knew the answer. "What about Miss Elizabeth and Miss Bennet? I would like to know my sisters."

Philip nodded, understanding his desire. "Darcy will tell Miss Elizabeth. He wanted to speak to her in person."

"You told Darcy!" Alex exclaimed, shocked that his good friend knew his secret.

Philip rushed to explain, "I was concerned about you and Miss Bennet once I realized who they were. His obvious attachment to Miss Elizabeth made me turn to him. I asked him for advice. I knew that he was a good friend of yours, and his honourable reputation made me confident in his discretion. He is the one who told me that if he was an only child, he would be thrilled to learn that he had five half-sisters." Philip watched him anxiously.

"Five!" Alex's eyes grew wide.

"Darcy suggested that when he and Miss Elizabeth return from Kent, you could all meet and get to know one another. He also suggested that Bingley could invite you to Netherfield and perhaps meet the rest of your siblings, just as a friend of theirs, and not reveal your true relationship if you do not wish." Philip tried to read the emotions in his son's face.

Alex worked through the myriad of thoughts running through his mind, processing the astounding information he had received, and finally smiled, shaking his head. "You can always count on Darcy to think sensibly." He looked at his true father, relieved at last of his great secret. If possible, Alex loved him more now than he had when he entered the room. This man had saved him from a miserable existence, possibly as a servant if he had lived at all. "I think that I will go and kiss Mother. Will you excuse me, Father?" He shook his father's hand. "Thank you for my life."

Chapter 16

"**A**re you well, Elizabeth?" Darcy sat with his back against a tree in the secluded copse, his legs straight out, and his arms wrapped tightly around her. Elizabeth was curled against him, one hand on his chest, the other around his waist, her ear pressed to hear his steady heartbeat, reassuring her in the midst of the incredible storm of thoughts filling her mind. He had received a letter from Philip Carrington that morning, and he just told Elizabeth the story of her father and his son. "I am well, William, just terribly overwhelmed."

He gently kissed her. "I do not know what to say, darling. I can try to answer your questions."

Elizabeth gazed into the eyes of the man who had asked her to share his life. He loved her. He cared for her. He cared for his family, and he was a wonderful, honourable, gentleman. And now she had learned that there is a new man in her life. A brother. She never imagined gaining a brother in any way other than through the marriage of her sisters, and here she was, learning that she had a brother. A brother she wished for so many times. Not just to end the entailment on Longbourn and secure her home and future, but a brother to be her friend, her protector, to teach her how to behave with men, to, oh so many things. She could not be angry, learning that he lived. No, she was not angry with Alex. If anything she was curious, and grateful, and so happy that he was William's friend. That fact more than anything reassured her that he was a good man. No, none of this was Alex's fault, and she would gladly accept him into her life in whatever way he felt comfortable, whether it be as a friend, a sibling, or as an indifferent acquaintance. She would leave that to him.

But her father, she just could not think about him. Not yet. It was too fresh. This news on top of the torment that she was already enduring due to his actions against her courtship with William made her want to hide. She began to cry, and held onto William. Everything she had ever known or believed had changed ever since she met him, through no fault of hers or William's, but through the actions of one man. Her father. The man she no longer recognized, the man who was the foundation of everything in her life. Her family, her beliefs, even her sense of humour. Everything. That once strong foundation was now crumbling around her. She was so confused.

"Please talk to me, Lizzy." Darcy urged, wiping her tears.

She shook her head. "I do not know what to say, William. It is all too much. I need to think. I need time to think." Her voice cracked as her tears began to fall again.

Darcy had dreaded this conversation since the morning nearly four weeks earlier when he met Philip Carrington. He delayed it as long as he could, selfishly wishing to spend this precious time happily alone with Elizabeth. At Rosings the only challenge was keeping the engagement from his aunt. Here they were free from Mr. Bennet. Here they were free to open up to each other, talk, love, learn, and finally reveal their true selves to one another. He knew that when he told Elizabeth of yet another painful act by her father, that time of carefree joy would end, and would not return until some confrontation or conclusion had been reached.

Darcy stroked her cheek and wound a curl of hair around his finger. He had no idea what to say, but he tried. "All those years at Cambridge. Who knew that I would fall in love with my good friend's sister?" He smiled slightly.

She appreciated his effort and squeezed his hand. "Well, I have noticed that Alex and I are similar in our wit, so if you can bear his company, you should not have trouble with mine."

"No, no trouble at all." He kissed her hair and tried again. "Would you like me to tell you about Alex? His father is . . ." He stopped, wishing to take back the word. "Forgive me Elizabeth." He whispered.

She smiled at him. "There is no need for you to apologize, William. Mr. Carrington is Alex's father. Papa gave up that title when he refused to acknowledge the result of his behaviour." Darcy heard the bitter disappointment in her tone. "I just cannot quite grasp the truth that I have an elder brother, and that my father rejected him. Would he have married my mother, would I even have been born if he acknowledged him as his heir?" Elizabeth shook her head trying hard to understand what had become of all that she knew.

That was one possibility that had not occurred to Darcy, and the thought of the world without his Elizabeth was inconceivable. He pulled her to him, scooping her onto his lap, and she wrapped her arms around his neck. He immediately lowered his mouth to hers and said fervently, "Lizzy, please, please, do not even mention such a horrible thought!" His impulsive reaction to hold her close and reassure them both resulted in a very sudden awareness of her position on top of him. Lifting his mouth from hers and breathing raggedly, he stared into her eyes, his need and desire overtaking his senses at the same moment that he recognized the identical reaction in her.

Elizabeth stared into his eyes and saw her home. The safety and comfort she found in his arms calmed her. The unfaltering assurance of his love strengthened her. And the need to give him her love and receive his in return drove her to respond to his unspoken offer of passion. They needed each other.

Her hands found their way into his hair, pulling his head down. He revelled in the feeling of her mouth hovering over his, her moist lips delicately drawing his in. They kissed slowly, so very slowly, drinking from each other. The sensation of their warm breath and caressing faces sent their hearts pounding, while delicious fingers of pleasure overspread their bodies, making them moan. His hands began to roam, still holding her tightly with his arms, his left hand came to brush, tentatively, the side of her breast. He felt her gasp in his mouth, but she did not pull away. He gently touched her again, and becoming bolder began to draw circles on her softness. His right hand travelled down to the hem of her skirt and his fingertips glided slowly up the silk stockings encasing her legs, and higher to the bare skin of her thigh. "Oh Lizzy." He groaned, pulling his mouth from hers, he lovingly trailed kisses down her neck.

She tilted her head back and whispered, "William."

Encouraged by her response, he dragged his lips to her breasts, kissing and tenderly tasting the sweet valley that spilled from the edge of her gown. His left hand began gently squeezing while his right found its way to the warm, damp treasure between her legs. "Do you know how much I want you, my love, my Lizzy." He whispered heatedly, his mouth was back on her neck, suckling beneath her ear. He brought his hand down and caressed hers, before returning to continue its determined fondling of her breasts.

She felt him seeking her hands, willing them to touch his body. She tried to run her fingers under his cravat, but was foiled by the tightly knotted fabric. She replaced her fingers with her lips, nibbling his jaw and neck while he tasted hers. The feel of his hair brushing against her face and his fingers, now simultaneously stimulating her breast and her core, was driving her to a place unknown. She desperately ran her hands over his chest, seeking to touch him and bring him the same pleasure.

Elizabeth heard his loud groan as she shifted her position on top of the enormous bulge in his breeches. She brought her lips back to his hungry mouth, tenderness now surrendered to unbridled passion as their mouths joined, devouring each other. She slipped her left hand around his back, as her right came to rest upon his arousal. She began stroking it the same insistent way that he was stroking her. "Oh God, Lizzy!" He groaned desperately.

"William! Oh, William! The taut, straining pressure that she felt building above the spot where he was relentlessly caressing finally gave way and she felt waves of exquisite pleasure travel up her body as she arched against him.

Gasping, Elizabeth looked into Darcy's face and saw a mixture of joy at her bliss, and intense concentration as he tried to maintain his control. Instinctively she knew that he needed to be touched in the same way that he had caressed her. She kissed him and without thought, moved so that she could unbutton the fall of his breeches, releasing him. She looked deeply into his eyes and gently touched his straining arousal. His eyes begged her to touch him again. They both watched as Elizabeth's hand encircled his rigid manhood. Her thumb delicately spread the single clear drop of fluid poised at its apex. She looked up as Darcy shuddered violently. "Teach me how to please you." She whispered urgently. Their eyes met and he kissed her deeply. Then looking down, he placed his hand over hers and they moved them together. His eyes closed. Moaning uncontrollably he increased the pace. The motion, so familiar to him, was so much more intense with her touch. He showed her how to stroke him, and let go of her hand, giving her complete control. Very soon he felt the rising tide of his pleasure. He managed to pull out his handkerchief to capture his essence, his hips thrusting forcefully, his chest heaving.

"Lizzy!" He cried out at his moment of release and desperately kissed her. The sound of his cry was music to her ears. She had done this to him and he brought her the same joy.

Slowly, their breathing began to calm. Elizabeth remained firmly in his lap, tightly held in his arms. He buried his face in her hair, breathing in her scent. She rejoiced listening to the pounding of his heart. "I love you, William." She whispered.

"Oh Lizzy, I cannot begin to express how I love you." He murmured softly into her ear. Finally he had felt the touch of the woman he loved, and it was wonderful.

They sat quietly together, recovering for a few minutes. Then lifting his head, he looked into her eyes, "How can you ever forgive me?" His voice was husky and full of remorse.

Elizabeth immediately sat up and took his face into her hands to look at him directly in the eye. "Do not even *think* of being sorry for what just happened between us! It was natural. Neither of us forced the other to do anything and it was an expression of the love that we share for each other. We both needed each other at that moment. Do not *ever* apologize for loving me!"

"Lizzy." He kissed her. "Thank you for loving me so much." They held each other until he let out a long sigh. "I am fighting with a promise that I made to my father. I promised him that I would never love a woman until I married. He made me pledge to never take the chance of fathering a child that would have the Darcy blood, but would grow up without my knowledge."

She looked sharply up at him, understanding the irony. "Do you mean as Alex Carrington did?"

"Yes, but he was saved from a terrible life by the kindness of the Carrington's." He nuzzled his face in her hair

Elizabeth sat up and looked at him seriously, and rested her hands on his chest. "Your father was wise to ask you to abstain until marriage. You and I both know that there are countless children fathered by gentlemen in the world. Your father's request was remarkable, and what is even more remarkable is your willingness to adhere to it." Darcy looked at her with surprise. He did not realize that she knew of such things. "But this is not the same situation that he admonished you to avoid. We are engaged, even if we had lost ourselves completely, we are still to be married." The image of her father flashed through her mind. "This is not a tryst with a stranger." She touched his cheek gently and looked into his dark eyes, "But I must admit that I appreciate your father's request for my own selfish reasons."

"What are those, Lizzy?" He asked quietly.

"I will never have to compete with the ghosts of your past lovers. I know that all of our experiences loving each other will be secrets that we alone will know. Just like today. We expressed our love and desire for each other, perhaps a few weeks early, but I did not lose myself, and I will still give myself to you completely on our wedding night. I have no regrets, and you should not either." She kissed him softly, and he drew her back against his chest.

"I do not deserve you." He whispered, resting his chin on her head.

"Are you well?" She entwined her fingers with his, absorbing his strength.

"Yes." He grasped her hand.

"Are you happy?" She squeezed back.

He lifted his head and looked down into her eyes, astonished that she was so concerned for his well-being after all she had learned. "I did not know what happiness was until you smiled at me, my love." He kissed her nose and smiled slightly at her. "I am only interested in you. How are you?"

"I am well as long as I have you, William."

They adjusted their clothing and Elizabeth returned to sitting by his side. They resumed holding hands and she rested her head back on his chest. Darcy draped his arm around her shoulders. They held each other for a long time. Their act of passion had served to both bring them closer together, and to relieve the tension that their conversation created. They were both capable of thinking and speaking clearly now. Darcy kissed her temple as he voiced his thoughts. "I told Mr. Carrington that I would arrange a meeting between Alex, you, and Jane, so that he could ask about your family. I suggested that Bingley might invite him to Netherfield so that he could meet your other sisters, but just as a visitor, not to reveal who he is. I will have to write and inform him of the secret. He can be trusted with it. I know that he will be surprised, but I also know that he will be pleased as well."

Elizabeth grasped his hand. "Thank heaven nothing happened between Alex and Jane. I admit to wondering if he would be a good match for her."

Darcy raised his brows. "And what did you conclude?"

She smiled. "I thought that he would regret the attachment. She is much better suited to Mr. Bingley, they are very similar."

He smiled back. "I agree, and I admit to urging Bingley to declare himself sooner than he intended."

She raised a brow. "How fortunate that he is easily persuaded." Darcy had the grace to look abashed. Returning her thoughts to her brother she stroked his cheek. "A few days before you arrived, I finally realized of whom he reminded me. He resembles Papa. His eyes, his sense of humour, some mannerisms, it just struck me while I was walking, how odd that it has turned out to be true. Your ideas for meeting with him are very good, as are the plans to invite him to Netherfield."

Darcy appreciated her words. "I will write to his father and let him know that we will contact him when we return." He paused. "Alex is deeply grateful for the Carrington's love and the gift of the wonderful life he has. He is curious to meet your father socially, but has no desire to reveal who he is."

Elizabeth could not begin to imagine that meeting. Then struck by an idea she asked, "Is he the heir of Longbourn?" She wondered how many things would change if he were.

He smiled; pleased he had anticipated her question. "It is very complicated, but I spoke to my lawyer hypothetically about it. He believes that only if your father recognizes him as his son, and he takes the Bennet name might he be considered the heir. The problem there is that he would still be illegitimate and legally, he has no claim. If somehow he did . . . well, it would also mean relinquishing the Carrington name, and Alex has stated that he will not dishonour his true father in favour of the man who abandoned him."

"As it should be." Elizabeth added. "I think that I will like having such a good brother." She smiled at Darcy, "And such a very good husband." His eyes lit up. "I love you, William."

"I love you, so very much, Elizabeth." He closed his eyes and held her tightly. She had once again amazed him.

CAROLINE BINGLEY looked out of the carriage window at the village of Meryton with satisfaction. Finally her brother was doing his duty, and moving into Netherfield. They were putting away their repulsive ties to their father's occupation in trade, and becoming part of the landed gentry. At least they would as soon as her brother actually purchased an estate. From the look of the people outside of her window, Caroline would be assured of being the example of good breeding and fashion for all of the ladies for miles around. She preened in anticipation of the adulation she would receive and the condescension she would bestow upon the undeserving masses. Unconsciously, she was planning to treat these people the way that she was treated by those of the first circles, the set that she desperately wished to join.

Mr. Darcy will soon be here, and living in the same house he will have no other women to distract him. He will soon succumb to my charms, and Pemberley will be mine! She packed all of her most alluring, in her mind anyway, gowns and jewels, and was planning to spend some time going over the house, discovering the best places to accidentally find herself alone with him. She laughed to herself, by Michaelmas, she would be married!

Two days after their arrival, Bingley and Caroline were invited to a dinner hosted by Sir William Lucas. Caroline was pleased that her prediction came true, and that she was immediately the centre of attention. She was enjoying giving her sneering pronouncements of superiority to Mrs. Long, when another lady was introduced to her.

"Oh Miss Bingley, have you met your nearest neighbour? This is Mrs. Bennet, of Longbourn. Their estate directly borders Netherfield." Lady Lucas said.

Caroline inclined her head, and started to say something vaguely friendly when she was struck by the name. "Mrs. Bennet? Do you have two daughters, Elizabeth and Jane?" She asked suspiciously.

Mrs. Bennet beamed. "Why yes, Miss Bingley! My two eldest girls have been in town for some time! My eldest is currently staying with her aunt and uncle, and my second eldest Lizzy is now staying at Hunsford parsonage in Kent, visiting Lady Lucas' daughter Charlotte Collins. Have you met them?"

"Yes, Mrs. Bennet, I have. I saw them both at the theatre and at a ball." Caroline's alarm began to grow. Why had Charles taken Netherfield? Surely it could not be a coincidence that he has been seen out with Jane Bennet and is leasing the estate next to hers? Surely he does not mean to attach himself to such a family? And Mr. Darcy is he not in Kent? Is his aunt's house near this Mrs. Collins' home?

"Oh how wonderful for my girls to be among such wonderful company! I am hoping that their trip to town will put them in the way of some rich men. I hope to have them well married soon!" Mrs. Bennet effused happily.

"Do you know if either of your daughters is attached to any gentlemen yet?" She asked, afraid to hear the answer.

"No, I have not heard anything as yet, but they will be home in about a week, and I look forward to hearing all of their news. Especially my Jane, she is so beautiful, she is bound to have found a young man and has just not told me of it yet!" Mrs. Bennet was thrilled with the prospect.

"And your daughter Miss Elizabeth, you say she is in Kent?"

"Yes, she is staying at Hunsford Parsonage, which is attached to the estate of Rosings. Mr. Collins is our cousin, and his patroness is Lady Catherine de Bourgh." Mrs. Bennet sniffed in distaste of mentioning Mr. Collins. She still had not forgiven Elizabeth for rejecting him.

Caroline thought that she would faint. Mr. Darcy was at Rosings, and so was Elizabeth Bennet. When she returned to Netherfield that night, she attempted to interrogate her brother about the Bennet sisters. He knew that she would find out eventually who their neighbours were and put it all together, but he was not about to tell her of his or Darcy's engagements until the ladies returned and the men approached Mr. Bennet. Until then, he simply smiled and said that he had no idea the ladies lived nearby when he took the lease, and Mr. Darcy's business was not his. Caroline had no option but to wait for them to come to Hertfordshire, and plot her next move.

FRIDAY MORNING, Elizabeth was out walking a garden path on the grounds of Rosings alone. William was inside, dealing with the estate matters which were his true reasons for coming to see his aunt each year. She was thinking of her father. *He is not the man I thought he was.* She used to be so proud of him, but his behaviour towards her and now towards the son he always wanted but willingly rejected had changed her once-beloved perception of him. It was not so much learning that he had enjoyed the habits, no matter how distasteful, common to gentlemen. It was the idea that when confronted with the results of his actions, he did nothing to help the girl he ruined or the child she bore. It was the illegitimacy of the child that made him disposable, and it disgusted her. She thought that her father's reception of William when he asks for his blessing on their marriage will determine if the damage he already inflicted on their relationship could ever be repaired.

Her reverie was interrupted by a booming voice. "Miss Elizabeth! Fancy meeting you here! May I join you on your stroll?" Richard came striding to her, a grin brightening his face.

"Colonel! Of course! I will be glad to have your company." She smiled at him. "How do you escape the estate duties while William must toil alone?"

"Well, you see that is the advantage to being a second son and a soldier. I am useless with estate paperwork. Visiting tenants, examining fences, looking at drainage, I can do readily enough, but the rest of it, I leave to my able cousin. He can handle a problem with efficiency that I would undoubtedly botch with alacrity." He laughed.

"It is good that you know your strengths, Colonel." She grinned up at his twinkling blue eyes.

"I know my weaknesses as well, Miss Elizabeth." He said softly. Elizabeth blushed and looked away. *Darcy was right; making her blush is a pleasure!*

Richard was happy for Darcy, he truly was. If anyone deserved a love match in marriage it was he. The woman he found was exceptional, and he looked forward to them joining in a long and happy life together. But. If only it had been he who caught her eye at the theatre that night, how different his life would be right now. His envy was great, and he knew that Darcy had noticed it. The two walked on in silence for a few moments. For all of his jovial countenance, he was a man who was struggling with the nightmare of all that he had seen in battle. He knew that he was tired of trying to carry on alone.

Elizabeth was not at all comfortable with Richard's implied admiration, and decided to move the topic of conversation along. "Colonel, could you tell me about William's relationship with his father? He seems to hold him in high esteem, but I cannot help but feel that he suffered somehow with him."

Richard looked at her with surprise. In some ways he was a little disappointed. He was not sure what sort of a response he hoped for, anger or encouragement, but avoidance was unexpected. He studied her face etched with concern for his cousin and immediately knew her feelings were for him alone, but he would still hope that someday. . .

"Colonel?" She asked, not sure what to think about the myriad of emotions crossing his face.

"Forgive me, Miss Elizabeth, you asked a very difficult question." He pulled himself together. "My uncle, George Darcy, was a very good man, and his son is very much like him, honourable, loyal, dedicated, extremely complex, and they both bury things deep inside. Uncle George loved Darcy, but he had a very difficult time displaying it. It was not a huge problem when Aunt Anne was alive, she was a woman who exuded love, and Darcy, well, knowing the man, you can imagine how shy he was as a boy, always felt loved by his mother. When she died. . ." He paused, his mind drifting with the memory. He looked into Elizabeth's eyes, so full of worry for Darcy. Fighting his envy he continued, "I was fourteen when Aunt Anne died, so my perspective is probably a little naïve, but I remember that Uncle George just, I do not know, it was as if he had died, too. I only saw him smile at Georgiana and George Wickham. He rarely praised Darcy, and seemed relieved to send him off to school. Darcy worked so hard to make his father proud, but I watched over and over as Wickham received the attention. Darcy tried to be a friend to Wickham, but he would play cruel tricks on him, or cause trouble that Darcy would try to cover up to keep his friendship." Richard looked at her. "He was very lonely." Elizabeth had tears in her eyes. She wanted to find him that moment and hold him.

He looked away from her obvious emotion and went on, "And so it continued for eight years, until Darcy reached the age of twenty. About then I noticed a great change came over Uncle George. He suddenly gave all of his attention to Darcy. He praised him and talked, and laughed. It was as if he was trying to make up for all of the years that he neglected his son. I was busy with my assignments in the army, but I would receive letters from Darcy, describing his father. He enjoyed the attention, of course, but he did not understand it. After so many years of being so insecure, he just did not know if he could trust his father, and he was incapable of opening his heart completely to him. He was too afraid of being hurt again. That was probably a good thing because his father died two years after the great change began. Darcy, of course, was devastated. He had just found his father only to lose him again, but since he was so accustomed to not having him, he recovered fairly quickly."

"But Georgiana did not." Elizabeth murmured. "She always had her father's undivided attention."

Richard studied her. "I understand that you have spoken to her about this."

She met his gaze. "Yes, I have. It may have driven her actions with Mr. Wickham. Did Mr. Darcy's behaviour towards that man change?"

"Yes, he seemed less enamoured, but he never withdrew his support of him, he just did not demonstrate it very readily."

"I thank you, Colonel, you have given me insight to William that I needed. You are correct, he is very complex, and I have sensed, and he has written to me about, a deep pain. At least now I will be better prepared when he finally opens up to me." She smiled at him.

"He is so very fortunate to have found you, Miss Elizabeth. You are exactly who he needed." Richard looked into her eyes, his longing for the same kind of love was evident.

"I think that he is exactly who I needed, too." Richard smiled at her sadly. "Colonel, someday you will find the perfect woman for you, too." She reached out, and gave his arm a squeeze. He was grateful for the gesture.

"I hope so, Miss Elizabeth, but if you do not mind, allow me to bask in your and my cousin's happiness for a while. Please forgive me for imposing my feelings upon you." He took her hand and raised it to his lips. She nodded and smiled. At that moment, Darcy appeared.

He had been sitting in the study in front of a window with his work, delighted to see Elizabeth in the garden. He watched as Richard approached her, and saw the unmistakable sign that she had blushed, an action he knew so well. That disconcerted him. Then he watched as they seemed to be joined in a very earnest conversation, and saw them looking at each other so intently, that he could not contain his possessiveness any longer. He stood and strode out of the house, arriving in time to witness his cousin's kiss and her smile. He felt as if a knife went through his heart. In a very tightly controlled voice he said, "Elizabeth, what a pleasant surprise to see you here." His eyes bore into hers, searching for any sign of disappointment in his arrival.

Elizabeth knew that he was unhappy, and she smiled at him, she hoped reassuringly. "I felt a great need to escape my cousin this afternoon, William. I knew that you were working, but I could not resist walking amongst the spring flowers. The Colonel was good enough to accompany me."

Darcy's gaze immediately fell on Richard, who after a lifetime; knew how angry Darcy really was. Ordinarily he might feel a justified affront, since nothing had happened with Elizabeth, but he also knew the feelings that he held in his heart for her, and he did not blame his cousin's reaction at all. He was there to protect what was his.

"Yes Darcy, I was telling Miss Elizabeth some family secrets. She was an excellent audience, shocked in all of the right places!" He laughed.

Still not smiling, Darcy replied. "I thank you for entertaining my betrothed so well, Richard, and since you have enjoyed the pleasure of her company for some time, I am sure that you will excuse us if we take a little stroll together now." There was no mistaking the warning in his eyes.

Understanding it, Richard nodded. "Absolutely Cousin, I was thinking of saddling one of Aunt Catherine's nags and seeing if I can get it to move faster than a trot." Turning to Elizabeth, he bowed. "Miss Elizabeth, it has been a pleasure."

"Thank you, sir, for the walk, and the story." Elizabeth smiled at Richard, and slipped her hand onto Darcy's arm.

Richard left, and Darcy fixed his burning gaze upon Elizabeth. Without saying a word, they started walking until they left the garden and entered a thick growth of trees out of sight of the house. Elizabeth felt her anger growing over his behaviour, and when they stopped, she intended to tell him about it. When they arrived at a secluded clearing, he instantly wrapped his arms around her and pulled her possessively to him. She could feel him shaking. "I thought I had lost you." He confessed; his voice cracking.

"Why would you think such a thing?" Elizabeth pulled away to look up at him. His apparent intense insecurity and fear dissolved her immediate angry reaction to his possessive behaviour and replaced it with compassion. Her conversation with Richard about William's past flooded back into her mind

"I have seen his reaction to you, Elizabeth, I know Richard well. He admires you. I see his envy, and I know the thoughts that cross his mind when he looks at you." He kissed her forehead and stared into her eyes. "Please tell me what he said to you."

Elizabeth knew that her next words could change his relationship with his cousin forever, and chose them carefully. "He told me of your history with your father." Darcy continued to stare at her. She sighed; he knew she was holding back. "He told me that he wants the same love that you and I have." Darcy closed his eyes, he knew Richard had spoken of his feelings, and knew there must be more. "I told him that someday he would find that woman. That was when he kissed my hand."

"He said nothing more?" He asked quietly.

"No."

"Then he implied it somehow." Elizabeth was silent. She had no intention of coming between the two men. She had only seen him angry once before and did not know what to do. She wanted to reassure him, but she also wanted to shake him. He was acting so much the part of the jealous, lovesick, fool.

Suddenly Darcy pulled her against him and crushing his lips to hers, kissed her, thrusting his tongue into her mouth. His hands travelled over her body, cupping her behind and raising her up so that he could rub his arousal onto her. He pressed her against a tree and pushed his hips against her, as one hand massaged her breasts and the other pulled off her bonnet and buried itself in her hair, dislodging the pins. He pulled his mouth from hers and they both gasped for air. Understanding that he needed her touch and not her words to reassure him, Elizabeth unbuttoned his waist coat, and pulled his shirt from his trousers, finally slipping her hands underneath to touch the bare skin of his back and chest. He groaned and shuddered at her caress, and renewed his assault on her mouth. He knew that he was losing control. He knew that if they carried on much longer he would take her right then and there, and he also knew that she would let him. The realization that she would only do that for him is what finally gave him the strength to tear himself away, chest heaving, desire darkening his eyes. It was the hardest thing he had ever done. How could he not love Elizabeth, with her hair fallen down around her shoulders, and her swollen lips presenting the picture of a woman who needed to be loved, right then, by him? He put his hand on a tree and breathed hard, trying to regain control. Elizabeth watched and she knew that if she touched him again, he would instantly have her in his arms and he would not be able to stop. She was very tempted, but she held back. They both dealt with their unfulfilled arousal as best as they could.

Elizabeth started searching for her hairpins, and Darcy fixed his clothes. When he was finished he walked to her and stayed the hand that was starting to put up her hair. "Wait a moment, Lizzy. I have imagined you like this; please let me enjoy it for a moment." He lifted her dark tresses and combed his fingers through the soft hair. Finally with a sigh of regret, he stepped back and watched as she wound her hair into a simple knot and pinned it in place.

"How does it look? Am I presentable?" She asked; a small smile on her face.

He gently embraced her. "You look absolutely beautiful, my love."

"Thank you, William." She rested her head on his chest, listening to his still-pounding heart.

"Lizzy?" He said softly, his lips caressing her hair.

"Yes, dear?"

"I know that you told me to never apologize for loving you, but. . ."

"But?"

"I behaved like a possessive, selfish beast to you, and I do apologize. I do not know what came over me. I was thinking of my needs, not yours. I know that I should not be concerned about losing you to someone else, but. . ."

"Were you jealous, William?"

"I saw that he made you blush." He said very quietly.

"And that made you jealous?" She embraced him tightly.

"I only want your blushes to be for me."

Hearing the emotion in his voice, Elizabeth lifted her head from where it lay on his chest and examined his face. He looked so shy and so vulnerable. She knew exactly what he was feeling. It was the same pain she experienced when she thought he was engaged to his cousin Anne. She realized that he finally had completely given her his heart, and he was terrified of losing her and being hurt.

"William, do not be afraid, my heart, body and soul belong only to you. You will never lose me, my love." She caressed his face.

"How did you know that I am afraid?" He whispered as he buried his face in her hair.

"I feel the same way."

They silently agreed to start walking and eventually found a large rock near a stream and sat next to it. There they reclined, arms wrapped around each other, Elizabeth told him about her conversation with Richard, and Darcy whispered to her the complete story of his relationship with his father. Richard had the basic facts correct, but he could in no way understand or describe the pain and torment that Darcy confessed to her. When he finally finished purging his heart, they were both emotionally spent. They sat, tightly embraced, his head resting on top of hers, she with her face in his shoulder. They had reached a level of trust and connection that neither one of them could have ever imagined. When they drew apart and wiped each other's wet faces, they knew that no matter what ever happened in the future, they would face it together.

They emerged from the trees back into the garden, when suddenly; they came upon a grim-faced Richard. "She knows."

Chapter 17

*D*arcy's first impulse upon seeing his cousin was to throw him down on the ground and beat him to a pulp. How dare he impose himself upon Elizabeth? He had observed Richard's reaction to her from the beginning, feeling possessive of her from the first moment he met her, and no matter how dismissively Elizabeth treated his approach, Darcy knew how serious Richard's feelings for her must be if he were to dare say anything to her at all. He knew that his cousin was not a man who easily or ever fell in love.

Richard watched as Darcy thought over his next move, seeing the clenching and unclenching of his fist, and steeled himself for the blow. It was with no small amount of relief that he heard Darcy ask, "What do you mean, she knows?"

He stopped his pacing and stood in front of the couple. "Aunt Catherine. Somehow she learned of your engagement. She is in a state of affront that I have never before witnessed, and is demanding your immediate attendance. I think that it is best that we go face her now. I know that you planned to tell her before we left, in a calmer situation, but what is done is done. I will stand by you." He met Elizabeth's gaze and then look intently with grim resolution at Darcy.

Darcy stared into his cousin's eyes, deciding if he should reject his oldest friend's offer. He was completely confident in Elizabeth's love. He just needed to decide if he could ever trust his cousin again. Nothing had happened, he thought, and both he and Elizabeth had made it very clear to Richard that nothing ever would. He closed his eyes. Is this worth the loss of his friend, his cousin? Letting out a long breath, he reached out and shook his hand while looking him in the eye.

"Thank you, Richard; you do not know what your support means to me."

"It is the least that I can do." Richard said gratefully, now ashamed of his unchanged feelings for Elizabeth, and fully appreciating the forgiveness that Darcy just silently extended to him.

Both men turned to look down at her ashen face. Darcy took her hands in his, "Darling, perhaps it would be best if you return to the parsonage. I will come to you when this is over."

Elizabeth saw his worry, and felt a wave of anger come over her. Her eyes flashed and her countenance regained its colour. "No, William. I will not run away from your aunt. We have the support of every other member of your family. She is the only one who does not hope for you a marriage of love and happiness. Her own selfishness is what is driving her, not concern for her daughter's well-being. No. I will not let you go in and face her fury alone. We will do this together."

Darcy gazed upon her defiant, determined face, and felt the strength of her conviction flowing through him. He smiled and took her hand, kissing it. "Of course, Elizabeth. I was a fool to think that you could possibly be left behind. Come. Let us go see our aunt."

Darcy and Richard entered the sitting room first, blocking Lady Catherine's view of Elizabeth. "Darcy, come here. I have been the recipient of a report of the most alarming nature, that you are engaged to be married to that bold, upstart girl, Elizabeth Bennet! I cannot believe such a lie to be true, and I demand that you refute it this instant!"

"Where did you hear such a report?" Darcy asked.

She sniffed, her chin in the air, distaste dripped from every word. "My parson, Mr. Collins claims that he heard some talk among his staff about a ring that Miss Bennet was wearing, and the speculation was that you gave it to her." She glared at him.

"Is that what you do, believe the gossip of servants?" Darcy said coolly, raising his eyebrow.

"You know that I abhor gossip of every kind, but this sort of rumour will affect not only your reputation, but Anne's. I demand that you answer me. Are you engaged to her?" The woman's anger was palpable.

Struck by his aunt's sudden concern for anyone other than herself, he responded, "What if I am? What business is it of yours?" He could feel the gentle pressure of Elizabeth's hand on his back, and he moved his right hand behind him.

"It is my business as nearly your closest relation, and the mother of your betrothed. You are to marry my daughter!"

As he observed her approaching apoplexy, Darcy felt Elizabeth's fingers entwine with his. It quelled his anger and gave him the ability to address the infuriated woman with equanimity. "I do not recall entering an engagement with Anne, Aunt Catherine. In fact, I seem to remember stating several times that I do not wish to enter into marriage with my cousin, and she has made similar statements about me." Turning to Anne, who was sitting nearby, "Is that not correct, Cousin Anne?" He looked at her inquiringly.

Anne, who was enjoying this thoroughly, inclined her head, "Yes Cousin William that is correct. I have never wished to marry you, or anyone."

Darcy turned to face Lady Catherine again and smiled slightly, feeling Elizabeth now covering their clasped hands with her free one. "So you see, Aunt, whether or not these rumours are true does not matter. If I am engaged to Miss Bennet it will have no bearing on my relationship with my cousin. You need not worry that I have hurt her in any way."

Lady Catherine sat, mouth agape, staring at Darcy, and then demanded, "This is not to be bourn! You must marry Anne!"

Darcy looked at Anne, who was gaping at her mother incredulously. He decided that it was time to end the conversation. "No, Aunt Catherine, I am not in any way bound to my cousin, and that is fortunate because then I would not have the great joy of being engaged to Miss Elizabeth." He turned and held out his hand to Elizabeth, who stepped forward and took it, and then wrapping her hand around his arm, smiled up at him.

"No!!" Lady Catherine screamed. "No, this cannot be true! How can you bring this lowborn, arrogant, conceited, impertinent girl into the family? Your friends will laugh at you; she will not be accepted! You will live a life of seclusion and be dismissed by society! She will be the ruin of Pemberley and our families' name. And what of Georgiana? She will be shunned before she comes out. This woman will be the ruin of you!" Her face was bright red, her eyes bulging with fury.

"No, Aunt, Elizabeth will be the making of me." He lifted her hand to his lips and kissed it, smiling down into her glowing face. "And for your information, she has already been accepted by Lord and Lady Matlock, who have decided to give their assistance introducing her to society. I have no fear that when my friends meet her, they will be as charmed as I, and I will enjoy seeing their envy. If they are foolish enough to reject her, then they were never friends of mine. I have little use for the society of fools. I am truly blessed to have such an extraordinary woman agree to be my wife." He never turned his gaze away from Elizabeth.

"Fitzwilliam, tell me this is not true! Tell me that your parents do not support this union!" Lady Catherine turned to Richard, pleading.

He looked upon his cousin feeling envious, proud, and protective. He turned and addressed his aunt with a smirk, "Yes, Aunt Catherine, it is quite true. They have dined with her, and met her family. They even publicly acknowledged her at the theatre. My brother and I are also very happy to give our approval to the match and gladly welcome Elizabeth into the family, and I know that Georgiana is ecstatic to gain such a sister."

Desperate, Lady Catherine turned her ire on Elizabeth. "You, girl! How can you aspire to leave the ranks in which you were born? You dare to join the first circles? You will be laughed at, alone; surely you see this is a mistake!"

Elizabeth unflinchingly addressed her. "Lady Catherine, Mr. Darcy is a gentleman, and I am a gentleman's daughter, as far as that goes, I believe we are equal. As for your claim that we will not be accepted and I must spend my life alone," She looked up into Darcy's smiling eyes, "I can think of no happier future than to spend my life in the sole company my husband and our children. If that is my punishment for daring to marry him, I accept it with open arms." She could feel him struggle not to pull her into his embrace.

Lady Catherine knew she had lost. But she did have one more card to play. "Well, if you are determined to ruin yourself you will do it outside of my sight. I demand that you leave this house immediately! If you enter into this union, you will never be welcomed at Rosings again!"

"NO!" The unexpectedly forceful sound of Anne de Bourgh's voice shocked the room into silence. She stood slowly and walked over to her mother. "You forget, Mama, that by my father's will, when I reached the age of five and twenty, *I* became the Mistress of Rosings. *I* shall decide who is and is not welcome within these walls. Cousin William and his betrothed, Miss Bennet, will always have a place here, as well as Cousin Richard. I have let you continue as the figurehead to this home long enough, Mama. If you do not like my decision, we can have the dowager's house prepared for you quite quickly, I am sure." Then turning back to Darcy and Elizabeth, she said, "I congratulate you and wish you both joy. I hope that your marriage will be full of the love and happiness you both deserve." Seeing Darcy and Richard's astonishment she further explained, "There was no entailment. Father was free to leave Rosings to his daughter and as I am not married, I am free to leave it as I wish." Looking to Richard, she said, "You should know, Cousin, that my will leaves Rosings to you." She turned to view her mother's blank face. "That should satisfy you, Mama. Rosings will remain in the Fitzwilliam family."

Richard was stunned. "Thank you, Anne; I do not know what to say."

She smiled. "Your brother has Matlock, William has Pemberley, I have no wish to marry, and if I did, I could not bear a child. I know that my time is coming, and I knew that Rosings should go to you. Now, follow your good cousin's example and find a bride to bring here and make it a home again. It has been quiet for too long." She gave his hand a squeeze. Richard still could not quite grasp the enormity of her gift. He stared at Darcy, who had a growing smile spreading across his face. Elizabeth embraced her and whispered, "I hope that you can come and visit us at Pemberley."

"I would like that, Miss Elizabeth. We shall see." She smiled at her sadly, and then leaned against her, suddenly exhausted by the exertion of the argument. With Richard's help, she walked upstairs to her bedchamber.

Darcy and Elizabeth faced the silenced Lady Catherine. "Aunt Catherine, we planned to leave here on Monday, but I think that it will be best for all concerned that we depart tomorrow. I will arrange to have our luggage prepared, and we will leave you in peace."

Lady Catherine just nodded. "Whatever you wish, nephew." She said nothing more.

Darcy and Elizabeth left the room and they walked back outside to the sunshine. Elizabeth did not hesitate to wrap her arms around him. "Thank you, William, thank you for defending me to your aunt."

He smiled down at her. "How could I not? You are the single most important person in my life. I could never fail you, my love. And please allow me to thank you for speaking with such conviction of your feelings for me." He softly kissed her lips. "Do you think there will be a problem with you arriving early at your uncle's house tomorrow? Should we send an express to alert them?"

"No, it should be fine. I am glad to be going earlier; it will give us more time in town to arrange to meet Mr. Carrington." She looked at him, then down at the ground.

"I think that you are not looking forward to returning to Longbourn." He gently touched her face.

Sighing, she shook her head. "I think that you are far too perceptive, Mr. Darcy."

"We have survived one irate relative, what is another?" He suggested, as a small smile played on his mouth.

"That is what I am afraid to find out." She said apprehensively.

Darcy hugged her tightly. "Whatever it is darling, we shall face it together."

EARLY SATURDAY MORNING, Darcy's coach stopped at the parsonage to collect Elizabeth. While she gave Charlotte a tearful hug of farewell, Darcy took Mr. Collins aside and told him in no uncertain terms that he was not to spread any rumours of the engagement to Longbourn or Lucas Lodge under threat of losing favour with the Mistress of Rosings, Lady Anne de Bourgh. In wide-eyed obeisance, Mr. Collins readily agreed to remain silent. Darcy wanted the announcement to come on his and Elizabeth's terms.

They departed Kent, and after some conversation, the three travellers lapsed into silence and Richard, feeling very much unwanted, soon fell asleep. Elizabeth sat alone facing the front of the carriage, while the men sat opposite. Darcy glanced over at his sleeping cousin then meeting Elizabeth's gaze, carefully rose and sat next to her, drawing her into his embrace.

"Forgive me my love, I know this is breaking every rule of propriety, but I recall you once saying that rules were meant to be bent from time to time." He kissed her, his mouth lingering over hers, then moving to her ear, whispered, "And I could not bear to be so near and not hold you." He glanced again at Richard then lifting her chin, he softly kissed her. Elizabeth nestled into his chest and sighed. "Could we just stay like this forever?"

"Lizzy, hiding is very unlike you." He whispered into her hair. "Please tell me what is wrong." He kissed her forehead. "Are you nervous to see your father?" He felt her head nod. "The decision is yours, my love. We do not have to go, but I think that you need to face him, and know if he will accept the decision you have made. You will never be able to move on with your own life if you cannot put the past hurt behind you." He kissed her again. "You taught me that." He felt her arms squeeze him, and she looked up into his face.

"I do not know him anymore."

"Perhaps he has come to his senses with time."

She smiled and stroked his nose with her finger. "I have never thought of you as an optimist, sir."

Darcy laughed. "Caught out!"

She snuggled back into the comfort of his embrace and closed her eyes. He was soon aware of her soft steady breathing. He rejoiced knowing that she felt safe enough to sleep in his arms, and eventually dropped off as well. Richard awoke to the sight of the embraced couple's sleeping faces, and watched them thoughtfully, while wondering about his own future.

They were received in Gracechurch Street with great surprise, and seeing the frown on Mr. Gardiner's face, Darcy requested an immediate conference in his study. "Mr. Darcy, I realize that you have entered a courtship with my niece, and I do appreciate your safely bringing her to London, however, I do not appreciate the breech in propriety that you have displayed. It is not proper for an unmarried woman to ride unchaperoned with two unmarried men."

"Yes sir and I beg your forgiveness, but perhaps you will grant us your dispensation when I tell you that Miss Elizabeth and I are engaged, and my cousin was acting as chaperone."

"You are engaged!" Mr. Gardiner said, surprise and delight replacing his frown.

"Yes, sir. We hope to receive your blessing?" Darcy smiled at him.

"Of course! I can think of no finer man for our Lizzy! When did this happen?" Mr. Gardiner took his hand and shook it vigorously.

"A fortnight ago, exactly." He grinned at the man's suddenly improved mood.

"Well that is quite an accomplishment, keeping such a secret for so long. I do not think even Jane knows of it." He settled into the chair behind his desk.

"Actually sir, she does. Elizabeth threatened her not to tell." His grin widened. Seeing Mr. Gardiner indicate a chair, he sat down and rested his elbows on his knees.

Mr. Gardiner laughed. "Well what are your plans? I must tell you my brother Bennet remains unmoved in his opinion of you."

Darcy sighed, and sat back in the chair. "As you know sir, Elizabeth is of age. I told her the decision is hers. We could marry immediately or I am willing to speak with her father. She is determined to give him a last chance. We will travel to Hertfordshire on Tuesday as originally planned. On Wednesday morning I will speak with Mr. Bennet. If he continues in his stance, we will immediately proceed to the church. I have the license and have already contacted the parson and he is prepared to perform a wedding for an unknown couple that morning. Afterwards we will return to London for a short time before going to Pemberley and our honeymoon in the Lake District."

"You seem to have put a great deal of thought into this, sir." He regarded the younger man. "And what would you do if by some miracle he does agree?"

"We have agreed to marry the following Wednesday, but will delay our plans no more than one week." Darcy said with a determined look on his face.

"I think that is for the best, sir." Mr. Gardiner stood and placed his hand on Darcy's shoulder. "I know that you are a good man, and I have no doubt of Lizzy's well being in your care. You will always be welcome in this house."

Darcy nodded. "I truly thank you for your support. Please know that your family will be welcome at Pemberley." He looked up to Mr. Gardiner. "Sir, do you know why Mr. Bennet feels the way he does? From what Elizabeth tells me, he is supportive of Miss Bennet and my friend Bingley's attachment. So it cannot be a desire to keep all of his daughters at home. Why is he so determined to keep Elizabeth with him?" Darcy allowed his confusion and pain to show, very briefly, but long enough for Mr. Gardiner to see how deeply affected the younger man was.

"Mr. Darcy, if I knew, I would tell you. I asked Thomas about it when he was here, and he used the same pitiful excuses that he presented to you, that he feared you taking advantage of Lizzy and casting her aside. I have spoken to Jane, and she thinks that he would be lonely without her. Either reason is weak. I have no answer for you. I do however have no fear of you prevailing when you speak to him." He smiled slightly. "I can see where you could be quite intimidating if you so choose."

Darcy looked up from staring at his hands, and smiled slightly. "I will take that as a compliment, sir." Then making a decision, he said. "Sir, on Monday, I am going to invite both Misses Bennet to my home. They will likely be there for most of the day. They will be meeting with a previously unknown relation." Seeing Mr. Gardiner's confusion, he explained, "Mr. Gardiner, you have earned my trust. I wish to share this information with you. But you must know that only Elizabeth, Miss Bennet, Mr. Bingley, Alex Carrington and his parents know the truth. If it is spread beyond us, it will be at the direction of the Carrington's. May I trust you, sir?" Mr. Gardiner nodded, intrigued, and returned to his seat.

Darcy told him the story of Alex Carrington. When he finished, Mr. Gardiner sat quietly. "How has this affected Lizzy's opinion of her father?"

"She says that he is not the man she thought he was."

"And it must not help to have added this to his ridiculous stance to your courtship." He looked at Darcy, "Which makes her willingness to ask his blessing even more remarkable."

Darcy nodded gravely. "Yes, I realize that, sir. She is a most loyal and forgiving woman."

Mr. Gardiner sighed. His respect for his brother-in-law was rapidly diminishing. He regarded Darcy closely. "What is your opinion in all this? What would you have done in my brother's place?"

An expression of great concentration came over his face. "Sir, I have never been in a situation that could possibly have precipitated such an occurrence, however; I do have acquaintances who have knowingly fathered illegitimate children. Some acknowledge them, some provide for them, some find homes for them, and some, sadly ignore them. I do not know what I would have done exactly, but I believe at the very least I would have assured the child of a future, and safety. I suppose it is something you cannot answer until you face it yourself."

Mr. Gardiner nodded his head in agreement, thankful that he never had to face such a situation. "So what is your opinion of Lizzy's father? Will you use this against him?"

Darcy studied Mr. Gardiner, he was perhaps fifteen years older than himself, but talking with him was not unlike talking with his father. "I have decided that I will only address the issues that are between us now. What he did in the past is not my concern; at least it is only my concern as far as it affects Elizabeth. I will not use it against him. That would mean exposing Alex Carrington to him, and that is not my choice to make."

"I think that your reasoning is sound." He laughed softly. "He has given you plenty to work with already." Darcy shook his head in resigned agreement. Mr. Gardiner stood. "Well sir, let us go and rejoin the ladies and your cousin." The men regretfully declined the offer to stay for dinner, and after managing to only kiss Elizabeth's hand, they departed for Matlock House where they told their surprised relatives their experiences at Rosings. Lord Matlock knew of Anne's will, but saw no reason to inform Richard of it. She was young, and could marry, which would make the ownership of Rosings her husband's concern. He was now delighted to know that his son's future would be secure. Georgiana was overjoyed to know that Elizabeth would soon be her sister.

Darcy returned alone to his home, leaving Georgiana with the Matlocks as he would again be leaving town soon. He took the time to review the settlement papers he had directed his solicitor to prepare and decided to bring them for Mr. Gardiner to sign on Sunday after Easter services. He sent a letter to Bingley telling him of their plans, and a note to the Carrington's inviting them to visit on Monday. Finally, exhausted, he walked upstairs to his silent bedchamber feeling exceptionally lonely. He walked to the door of the mistress' chambers, and hesitating a moment, entered. The room was as feminine as his was masculine. Before leaving for Kent he directed his housekeeper to clean and air out the long abandoned rooms. He wandered around them, touching the furniture then sat on the bed, imagining Elizabeth's laughter filling the air, her sweet form looking up to him from the bed, and her arms, welcoming him into her loving embrace. That was where his valet found him the next morning.

Elizabeth and Jane reunited, both dying to share the news of their engagements. Jane was properly impressed with Darcy leaping from the carriage to propose and utterly horrified by Lady Catherine's behaviour. In her turn, Jane told of Alex Carrington almost kissing her and Bingley's sudden appearance and proposal. When she finished, Elizabeth took her hands and told her that Alex was their brother. Jane was stunned, but then she began to put together all of the thoughts that she had about him and realized that she felt the connection all along. She agreed with Elizabeth that she would like to meet with him at Darcy's house on Monday. They spoke long into the night about their father.

Easter saw the families attending services at their separate churches, but Darcy came to Elizabeth for dinner. He drew Mrs. Gardiner aside and asked her to do a great favour for him. She nodded happily in agreement and promised to begin taking care of it Monday. Once again Darcy was denied anything more than a kiss to Elizabeth's hand before departing. He determined that he must get her alone the next day.

"GOOD MORNING, DARCY." Alex said as he shook his friend's hand. "Thank you for arranging this for us."

Alex and Mr. Carrington arrived a bit earlier than expected, much to Darcy's disappointment. He was missing Elizabeth terribly. He had become so accustomed to seeing her every morning that he was rapidly finding himself incapable of concentrating on anything but the memory of her kiss, and God help him, the tender touch of her hand caressing him . . . He sighed. Guiltily, he hoped that she would arrive first so that he could corner her somewhere for a moment or twenty and calm the voracious appetite she unleashed inside him. But, she did not, and he must instead concentrate on his guests.

Darcy nodded, "It is my pleasure, Alex, Mr. Carrington. Let's await the ladies in my study? I sent my carriage to collect them and they should arrive shortly." The men entered the room and were seated. "I know that Elizabeth was going to speak to Jane about this last night, Alex, so there will be no surprises to anyone this morning."

Alex noted the use of the ladies' Christian names and cocked his head at him. "I understand that you have been courting Miss Elizabeth?"

Darcy smiled. Alex was always very quick. "Yes, I was."

"Was?"

"I never expected to say this to you Alex, but it seems," he paused, his lips twitching, "we are to be brothers."

Alex and his father looked at each other in surprise and burst out laughing. "Congratulations! I have not been a brother long enough to feel properly possessive over my sister, but knowing you, I trust she will be well cared for." Darcy smiled. "Of course," he added, "you will have to answer to me if I hear otherwise." He said, attempting a look of intimidation.

The men's laughter was interrupted by the announcement of Elizabeth and Jane's arrival. They met them in the drawing room, and Darcy instantly went to Elizabeth and kissed her hand. "You are so lovely this morning, Lizzy." He whispered.

She smiled and whispered softly back, "I miss my morning kisses, William." His look of longing assured her of his shared desire. Before they could lose themselves, they redirected their attention to the rest of the room. Darcy invited everyone to be seated.

After an awkward silence, Alex began. "I understand that you are to be married to Darcy, Miss Elizabeth. May I extend my heartfelt congratulations?"

"Thank you, sir, I do appreciate it. I have never been so happy." She smiled at Darcy. "You should also know that Jane is engaged to Mr. Bingley." Alex and Jane looked at each other, both blushing.

He met her eye. "Congratulations to you as well, Miss Bennet. Mr. Bingley is a fine man."

"Thank you Mr. Carrington." Jane whispered.

Elizabeth then broke the uncomfortable moment. "I think that we need to make a change in the way that we address each other. My brother would not call me Miss Elizabeth." She raised her brow and smiled at him.

Alex smiled. "What do you prefer?"

"My family calls me Lizzy." She suggested. Alex caught sight of Darcy slowly shaking his head negatively. Apparently, *he* was the only young man to have that distinction. Elizabeth did not miss the exchange and smiled to herself.

Alex laughed at his friend's behaviour. "Perhaps I could call you Elizabeth?"

"That would be fine." She pursed her lips and met Darcy's intense stare.

"And I am Jane." She added, confused, missing the exchange.

"Then I shall be Alex to both of you." He grinned.

"Well, good, now that is established, I imagine that you have questions for us?" Elizabeth encouraged him.

Alex looked at the faces of his sisters and said very sincerely, "First, I want to thank you for being so receptive to me. I remember the shock that I felt when I learned this news, and I imagine that it was equally overwhelming to you."

Elizabeth glanced at Darcy, and took his hand. "Yes I am afraid it was very emotional." Darcy met her gaze and squeezed back. She looked back at Alex's serious face. "I want you to know Jane and I agreed that you should be part of our lives, to whatever extent you wish. You are already friends with William, and you certainly did not create this situation. But it is before us, and I think that instead of concentrating on the cause, we should rejoice in the fact that we have found each other."

Jane nodded in agreement. "Yes, Alex, we have already enjoyed each other's company, and I think that we were developing a friendship before we learned this news."

"Elizabeth, Jane, thank you. I am astounded with your generosity. I will be honoured to be your friend and I hope someday, a welcome family member. I am delighted to know that I have such kind sisters."

Elizabeth grinned, "Well sir, you have three others, would you care to hear about them?"

Alex glanced at his smiling father, shaking his head in disbelief. "Yes, tell me all."

She gestured to Jane. "Jane is three and twenty, I am one and twenty, our next sister is Mary, who is nineteen, then there is Kitty, who is seventeen, and finally Lydia, who is fifteen."

Still amazed, Alex asked, "Are they like the two of you?"

Elizabeth and Jane exchanged glances. "Go ahead and tell him Lizzy, he will find out soon enough!"

She laughed. "No Alex, I am afraid that all of your sisters have very distinct personalities. You have had the opportunity to see that Jane and I are dissimilar, but reasonably sensible." She sighed. "Mary is rather moralistic. She enjoys quoting sermons, playing the pianoforte, and singing. Kitty is a follower, and although older, she follows Lydia's bold lead in their mutual desire to wed a man in a red coat. They are all three rather silly."

Alex laughed at the descriptions. "Well, they are quite young yet. How did you two become so sensible?"

The sisters laughed. "We had the advantage of our Aunt and Uncle Gardiner's guidance before they started having children and our father's attention before he seemed to withdraw from his family and into his library." Elizabeth's voice died away.

The subject had finally been broached and the tension in the room was thick. Alex looked at his apprehensive sisters. "Please tell me about Mr. Bennet."

Elizabeth, by agreement with Jane, answered. "If you had asked me that question two months ago, I would have told you without hesitation that he was a good man. Papa has a very sharp wit, which is beyond my mother, and which he uses regularly to combat her nervous and annoying behaviour. He has a dilatory attitude towards Longbourn, only doing what is necessary to keep it running and providing an income. He does not extend himself if not needed and prefers to spend his time in his library. He has essentially lost interest in his family, and that lack of attention is evident in our younger sisters' behaviour."

"Forgive me, but the picture you paint is not complimentary."

The sisters sighed and looked at each other. "No, you are correct, it is not. But, you see, he gave me so much attention. He educated me, he challenged me, I learned so much from him and I am the person I am now because of him. I have not always admired him, I have often wished better of him, but I am grateful for what he has given me. He always had my respect, at least he used to . . ." She looked up at Alex then turned her eyes to Darcy who gripped her hand tightly.

Philip spoke. "I understand that he is not supportive of your engagement?"

"He does not know of it yet, sir, but when William approached him about our courtship he threw out terrible accusations about his motivation for selecting me, a woman with no fortune, no connections, and he told me, little beauty." The raw pain of her father's words had caused was clear. "He said that William would only want me . . ." She choked back a sob. "I do not understand why! Excuse me." She stood and ran from the room.

Jane rose to chase after her, but Darcy was up first and out the door. The remaining guests sat in silence until Alex spoke quietly. "Does your father support your engagement, Jane?"

"Mr. Bingley has not approached Papa yet, but he has written to me and my uncle, and he seems happy for our attachment."

"Do you know why he is so against Miss Elizabeth and Darcy?" Philip asked, not understanding the man.

Jane thought. "I believe that he does not wish her to leave home. You see, Papa was so attentive to the two of us. I suppose to me because I was his first child." She glanced briefly at Alex. "But then, as we grew older, and Mama kept having girls, he just lost interest in his children. I think that he saw in Lizzy a reflection of himself, his wit and intelligence, and he seemed to centre all of his attention upon her. I suppose that he does not wish to be alone, and wants to keep her with him."

"No matter what his motivation, he has no business denying Elizabeth her life and security." Alex said with some anger. The men continued discussing the

Bennet family with Jane, but found that listening to her was far different from listening to Elizabeth. Jane seemed to want to create a picture of everything being well, where Elizabeth's description appeared to be much closer to the truth.

Darcy led Elizabeth into the nearby music room and closed the door. "Oh William, I am so sorry. I did not mean to cry." She buried her face in his chest and sobbed. He held her close and rubbed her back until she calmed.

"What can I do for you, my love?"

"Just hold me." She sniffed. "There is nothing to say, we know nothing until we go to Longbourn."

"You are correct." He was at a loss. He hated seeing her cry, and wanted to find a way to comfort her. Then, he remembered that humour always seemed to bring her away from her sadness. "May I tell you something? I was secretly plotting a way to get you alone while you visited today, and although I would not choose you running away in tears, I must say that it has suited my purpose quite well." He smiled down at her.

She looked up, a small smile on her lips, "And what exactly is this purpose, sir?"

"Let me show you," he whispered softly in her ear. He ran his hands along her back and down to her behind and easily lifted her so that his arousal was snugly pressed against her. Elizabeth's fingers wound into his hair. He began rhythmically rubbing against her while running his tongue over her lips, and parting, they kissed deeply. "Oh Lizzy, I want you so much!" Elizabeth could hear the desperation in his voice. He began kissing her neck, and if it had not been for the sound of knocking on the door, he may have allowed his torrid daydreams to come true. Instead, they tore very reluctantly from each other and tried to regain their composure. Resting his head on hers, Darcy called out, a little harshly, "Yes?"

They heard Jane's muffled voice. "It is Jane, Mr. Darcy. Is Lizzy well?"

They sighed, and Elizabeth looked apologetically at him. She called out, "I am well, Jane. We will be right with you."

They stood embracing tightly, wishing for privacy, but knowing they must quickly return to the others. Darcy attempted to distract himself from the woman in his arms. "How did Jane take the news? She seems very calm."

"Jane always seems calm." Elizabeth said, not without some noticeable exasperation. "She wants to see the good in everyone at all times. She will work to justify Papa's behaviour." She laughed. "I sincerely doubt that she and Mr. Bingley will ever disagree about any subject."

Darcy laughed. "Then you were correct in your assessment, they are well suited." He looked down into her smiling eyes, and could not resist the urge to kiss her again. Soon they were tightly embraced, rapidly falling back into their shared need for each other. He pulled his mouth from hers, bending to kiss her shoulder. "Lizzy." He whispered. Elizabeth ran her hands down his chest and gently caressed his very evident arousal. "Oh God, Lizzy!" He moaned.

She instantly withdrew her hand. "Forgive me! I thought that you liked me touching you there."

"No, no." He took her hand and placed it back where it was. "I do like you touching me there." He pulled her back to him. "I crave you touching me, Lizzy; I dream of you touching me, there and so many other places." He whispered, "And I dream of touching you." He waited, his face buried in her hair, waited to see if she would be offended with his confession.

It was with relief that he heard her soft voice, so quiet that he could barely understand. "I have those dreams of you, William."

"You do?" He asked hopefully, and feeling her nod, promised, "Soon darling, soon."

The two gave in to several more minutes of passion before Elizabeth checked her appearance and returned to the company. Darcy followed a few minutes later. Jane was concerned over her flushed face. Alex and Mr. Carrington exchanged knowing glances after seeing her countenance and obviously swollen lips. Darcy met their amused smiles with a defiant glance and suggested they discuss the pending trip to Hertfordshire. It was agreed that Alex would travel with Darcy, Elizabeth and Jane on Tuesday. He was given a thorough warning about Caroline Bingley, and her fortune hunting tendencies. After they left, Darcy wished to show Elizabeth the mistress' chambers and led the way upstairs. "Please tell me if there is anything you wish to change, Elizabeth. These rooms have not been in use for many years."

Elizabeth and Jane looked at the splendour around them and tried to remain nonchalant about it. "Oh, I think that the rooms will be perfectly adequate, sir."

Darcy was momentarily surprised at her lack of enthusiasm when he caught her exchanging glances of astonishment with Jane. Smiling to himself and seeking to discompose her, he took her hand and led her to the door to his bedchamber. "I am pleased to hear of your satisfaction. Perhaps you can lend me your suggestions for this room." He pulled her inside and stood behind her. His arms wrapped around her waist, his broad back blocking Jane's view. Elizabeth stood perfectly still, staring at the massive bed in his decidedly masculine room. She felt his arousal pressing on her back. His warm breath tickled her ear and he was delighted when she took his hands and slid them down from her waist to her thighs. "Do you have any ideas for this room, Lizzy?"

"Oh, yes." She sighed longingly.

"Shall you sleep with me here every night?" He whispered, nuzzling her ear.

"Wherever you are, I will be beside you." She pressed her body back against his.

"I love you, Elizabeth."

ALEX AND PHILIP had walked to Darcy's townhouse; it was not terribly far from their home. Philip regarded his pensive son. "You have two very lovely sisters."

Alex, drawn from his reverie, smiled at his father. "Yes, I do. I am interested to meet the others, even if they are silly by Elizabeth's description."

Philip laughed, and then asked, "And how do you feel about meeting Mr. Bennet?"

"I do not know. I have not decided how I feel about him. Jane and Elizabeth have given me much to think about."

"Yes, I have been thinking a great deal as well." Philip weighed what he was about to say, and decided to continue. "Alex, am I correct in assuming that you have not taken a vow of celibacy?"

Surprised, Alex looked at him. "No, Father."

"And may I ask, when you were twenty, or one and twenty, did you visit courtesans, or perhaps other ladies? I know that you have not kept a mistress, you did not have the funds for it." He smiled slightly and tilted his head.

"Yes Father, I did occasionally visit the houses for gentlemen at Cambridge and London. Why do you ask?"

"What would you have done if you found that you had impregnated one of these women, if you knew for certain that it was to be your issue? Would you have immediately declared the child your heir?" Philip looked at his son seriously.

Alex walked along in silence, watching the ground before him and considered the question. "No, I would not have done that. But, I think, if I knew without a doubt that the child was mine, I would have tried to look after him in some way, perhaps provided funds for his upbringing, kept an eye on his progress." He looked at Philip. "What are you trying to tell me, Father?"

"I am trying to tell you that there are many ways to look at what Mr. Bennet did." He took a breath. "He was probably just barely of age when he learned the news of the maid's pregnancy. And yes, it would have been wonderful if he had, obviously not married the girl, but perhaps had done as you say, provided for you somehow. He did not, and thank God we had the chance to adopt you. What I am trying to tell you Son, is that the man, very young at the time, living with who knows what charges from his own father, behaved in a way that is not unusual, and not too far off from what you might have done. If he had behaved as you think you would, and we had not had the opportunity to take you in, you may have still lived the life of a servant or tradesman. Upon realizing that he would only have daughters with Mrs. Bennet, he might have chosen at that time to acknowledge you as his heir. We will never know. But it gives you something to think about when you go to meet him.

"Are you saying that I should not be angry with him? That I should excuse him? After all, he did not make any attempt to provide for me, so my future was very much unknown, and he played no part in it, even if it had been destined to be that of a servant." Alex looked at him, astonished with his counsel.

"I will not tell you how you should feel, Alex. But I think that instead of going to Hertfordshire with an attitude of anger or with a desire to confront the man, I think that you should instead just go and observe. It is up to you if you wish to ever reveal your identity to him. I doubt that Elizabeth or Jane will tell him. They seem simply grateful to have you as their brother. I ask only that you consider all possibilities."

Alex stopped walking and faced Philip. "But what of his behaviour towards his family? And especially towards Elizabeth and Darcy?" Philip stopped as well, and placed a hand on Alex's shoulder. "That has nothing to do with you, Alex. His behaviour now may in fact have something to do with not having a son, we cannot know. Your only concern should be if you wish to know and reveal yourself to the man."

"You have given me much think about, Father." The men began walking. "I am grateful for what chance has brought me."

Chapter 18

T he servant closed the door and Bingley broke open the message from Darcy. They would arrive by noon the next day. The time to speak to Mr. Bennet had come. He agreed with Darcy, he wished to have his private conversation to ask Mr. Bennet's consent to marry Jane before the storm of Darcy and Elizabeth's arrival distracted and upset the household. He decided to visit Longbourn in the morning and remain there to greet Jane when she arrived. He missed her terribly.

He also needed to speak to Caroline. Exiting his study, he found her in the sitting room, talking to the newly arrived Hursts. "Caroline, I just received a letter from Darcy. He and Alex Carrington will be arriving tomorrow. Please have two rooms prepared for them."

"I did not realize that Mr. Carrington was coming as well. How long will he be staying?" She was unhappy. Mr. Carrington would undoubtedly distract Mr. Darcy's attention from her.

"I am not sure. I think that it will be a short visit. He has some business in the area, and I offered him a place to stay while he completes it."

"And Mr. Darcy, does he say how long he will stay?"

"No, he does not." Bingley saw the displeasure in her eyes. "Caroline, I wish to take this opportunity to remind you, Darcy is coming here as my friend. Not as your suitor. He has made it clear that he is not seeking a wife." He thought to himself, *Because he has found one.*

"I have no idea what you are implying, Charles!"

"You know full well that I am implying nothing. I am stating a fact. Stop pursuing Darcy. I do not wish my friend to be uncomfortable visiting me." He considered telling her that he would be marrying Jane soon, but decided to wait until he spoke to Mr. Bennet. He certainly would not inform her about Darcy and Elizabeth; that was their secret to tell.

The next morning Bingley dressed carefully, rehearsed his speech, mounted his horse, and rode to Longbourn. Before he knew it, he was admitted to Mr. Bennet's library.

DARCY'S CARRIAGE rumbled into Longbourn's courtyard. The emotions of the four occupants were diverse. Jane spotted the beaming Bingley standing next to her father, and her heart leapt with joy. Darcy looked at Mr. Bennet stone faced. His day of reckoning would be tomorrow, for today, his position was to maintain a civil attitude. Elizabeth looked at her father with hope and anguish. *This may be the last time that she ever comes to see him.* Alex observed the oddly familiar countenance of the man who abandoned him and wondered if he was committing an error by coming.

Mr. Bennet watched the arrival of the carriage with a mixture of anxiety and relief. Jane had written to him the week before, telling him of Mr. Darcy's offer to transport his daughters home, as he was coming to Netherfield to visit Bingley. Mr. Bennet hesitated only briefly in granting his permission. With both of his daughters in the coach, he did not feel there was a breach in propriety, and he could not overlook the significant savings he would enjoy by not sending his own coach or paying the fare for the post. What bothered him now was observing that there was a second young man in the carriage. As a man who disliked extending himself in any manner, he decided that confrontation on this point was not worth his effort. Instead, he focused on the pleasure of seeing his daughters again after six weeks of separation. He was happy to bring joy to Jane by giving his consent to Bingley, and hoped that he would find a way to convince Elizabeth to give up Darcy. He would attempt civility with the man, for now.

BINGLEY IMMEDIATELY RAN to the coach and greeted the men as they descended. He hovered and soon took Jane's hand to help her exit, whispering their good news to her in the process. Darcy then took his place and waited for Elizabeth. They grasped hands, trying to gain strength from each other.

When she came to rest on the ground, he kissed her hand and whispered, "I love you, Elizabeth."

She smiled and mouthed, "I love you, William."

"Welcome home, Lizzy." Mr. Bennet said, trying not to stare at her hand clutching Darcy's arm. "I hope that your travels are finished for quite a long time, you have been missed."

"Thank you, Papa; it is good to see my family again." Elizabeth made a point of not agreeing and looked to William. "Of course you remember Mr. Darcy?"

Mr. Bennet finally looked into Darcy's expressionless face and nodded. "Yes, I remember him. I thank you for bringing my daughters safely home. I see that you have not grown weary of my Lizzy's company, sir."

Darcy met his gaze, noting the possession he indicated when speaking of Elizabeth. "No sir. No man with any intelligence could ever grow tired of such a treasure. *I* never will."

Elizabeth smiled up at him. "Thank you, William."

He looked down, smiling only for her. "It is my pleasure, Elizabeth."

Mr. Bennet grimaced, hearing their familiar address. Then noticing Alex standing quietly nearby, he looked at Elizabeth questioningly. "Papa, may I introduce you to Mr. Alex Carrington? Mr. Carrington is a very good friend of Mr. Darcy's and he has become a much favoured friend of mine and Jane's. It was his family's ball that we attended in London." Then turning to Alex, she said, "Mr. Carrington, may I present my father, Mr. Thomas Bennet." She gave him an encouraging smile.

Alex first looked into the warm eyes of his sister, glanced at Darcy, who nodded his encouragement, then turned to bow to his birth father. "Mr. Bennet, it is an honour to meet you. Please forgive my intrusion into your home. I have business in the area and Mr. Bingley was kind enough to extend an invitation to Netherfield, and Darcy was equally willing to provide transportation."

Mr. Bennet's face displayed his confusion. Something about this young man struck him as familiar. He nodded slowly. "You are most welcome, sir."

The party then turned to enter the house, Jane and Bingley leading the way. Mr. Bennet was hoping to speak with Elizabeth alone, but it was obvious that she had no intention of letting Darcy's arm go. He resigned himself to walking alongside Alex.

"What part of the country are you from, Mr. Carrington?"

"My family home is in Buckingham, sir. The estate is called Kingston Park. I have passed through this part of Hertfordshire many times on my travels to and from London, but this is my first time actually staying here."

Trying to understand the discomfort he felt, he asked. "How long do you expect to stay?"

"Not too long. I am just here to meet some people, and then I will return to London." Alex was scrutinizing Mr. Bennet as closely as his birth father was observing him. He could see himself in the man's face, his build, even in his voice.

"Well then, I hope that your business is concluded satisfactorily." Mr. Bennet saw what he swore was a younger version of himself, and was at a loss as to why.

"As do I, sir."

By this time they had all entered the drawing room where Mrs. Bennet and the other girls were waiting. As Elizabeth performed the introductions, Mrs. Bennet saw the obvious closeness between her second daughter and the elegant, handsome man beside her. Happily she began wondering if he would marry her. She then turned her attention to the other handsome young man, and thought that he would do very nicely for one of her other daughters. When she turned to encourage him to take a seat, she was surprised to see that the girls were all looking at him curiously. Trying to understand her daughters' unusual behaviour, she examined Alex, and was suddenly struck by the thought that she was viewing a younger incarnation of her husband. Before she had a chance to say anything, Mr. Bennet called everyone's attention, and announced the engagement of Jane to Charles.

Pandemonium broke out, and Mrs. Bennet was instantly in the full throes of exclaiming her joy, and immediately forgot about the resemblance between Alex and Mr. Bennet. She invited the three gentlemen to stay for dinner to celebrate, and upon their agreement, scurried off to the kitchens.

The gentlemen decided to leave for Netherfield and settle in. Elizabeth and Jane walked out with them to the carriage, and it was with great difficulty that Darcy did not pull Elizabeth into his arms. He settled for a kiss on the hand, and heartfelt looks; and they were gone. When Elizabeth and Jane came downstairs after changing from their travelling clothes, Mrs. Bennet immediately dragged Jane away to express her happiness and Elizabeth found herself being summoned to her father's presence.

Closing the library door, she took her accustomed chair in front of his desk. For the first time in her life, she was not comfortable there. Knowledge of his behaviour, both as a young man and presently, had opened her eyes.

"Well Lizzy, it is good to have you home at last." Mr. Bennet began, looking at her closely. "You must tell me of your travels."

Elizabeth was feeling very defiant. "I believe that I wrote of them quite extensively, did you not receive my letters? I never heard from you, so I hope that they were not lost."

He answered slowly, "No, they were not lost. I read them all with great interest. I had no news to report, so I did not write to you."

"You had time to write to Jane, Papa."

"Yes, I did. I thought that she would share her letters with you."

"She did, but I was hoping for a more personal response from you, given your awareness of my courtship with Mr. Darcy. I would have appreciated your support."

"You are certainly aware that my approval for this courtship was given reluctantly."

"I am aware of it, and I have yet to understand the reasons behind your disapproval. Mr. Darcy is the best of men. He is kind, intelligent, generous, and respectful. He is everything a gentleman should be, and my esteem and regard for him continues to grow."

"I do not agree with you, Lizzy. I have allowed this little adventure of yours to continue, but I know that in time he will move on to a more suitable candidate for his wife."

His insult was as painful as a slap would have been. How could he think so poorly of his own daughter? She glared, "If I am so unsuitable, why would he introduce me to his family?"

"It is a rich man's game. They can do whatever they wish to achieve their ends."

"What exactly are you implying, Papa?" Her offense at his words was making it difficult for her to continue the conversation.

"As I have stated before, I think that he wishes to take advantage of you. Fortunately, you are now home and safe from his machinations. I will keep you well protected, and he will quickly grow tired of the difficulties and return to his women in London. His attempt at seducing a country girl will be over, and he will laugh about it with his friends."

"Well protected? Safe from him? You know nothing of this man and that is your own fault!" Elizabeth stared at him in disbelief. "If Mr. Darcy had wished to take advantage of me, he had plenty of opportunity over the course of our courtship, and always treated me with respect. How can you say such lies with a straight face?"

"You are old enough, Lizzy, to know the true ways of men."

Unable to stand any more, she rose from her seat. "Yes, Papa, I certainly have recently learned the ways of some men, and they disappoint me completely." She walked out of the room. It had taken every bit of her self-restraint not to throw Alex's existence in his face. It was only her respect for her brother that kept her from hurling that truth at her father.

Mr. Bennet watched her go. "She will thank me for this someday." He said to the empty room, but even to his own ears the words sounded ridiculous. His desire to keep Lizzy close to home was warring with his growing guilt and disgust with his own behaviour. He saw the hypocrisy of supporting Jane and denying Elizabeth. By now he was fully aware of just what a great man of consequence Darcy was. He knew his honourable character. He knew that he was infinitely more important and wealthy than Mr. Bingley, and he was in no doubt of Lizzy's affection for him. Her astonishing defiant attitude made that perfectly clear. He was completely cognizant that she would, now that she was of age, exercise her own desire and marry Darcy with or without his consent. His eyes closed. If he chose to take it, there was one last chance to be redeemed in her eyes. He was sure that eventually Darcy would come to ask for his consent. The question remained, could he put his pride aside, admit he was wrong, and receive the man as he should have months ago, or would he let his selfish desires and disappointment over his life drive Lizzy away forever? He did not know.

ELIZABETH WAS FURIOUS both with her father and herself, and stormed out the front door and into the garden. What was she thinking, coming back home? She should have remained in London and married, then simply sent a note to Longbourn proclaiming the news. Now she was here and would have to suffer through whatever her father's plans were to protect her. And, because of her, William would have to come to dinner and pretend that all was well, and then face her father in the morning!

"What a fool I am!" She declared as she paced through the trees. "I hoped that the man I thought my father was would welcome us back; instead I found nothing but disappointment. Our relationship has changed forever." She mourned the man she once proudly called Father.

She continued her walk and could not help but feel resentment towards Jane and Mr. Bingley. Why were they permitted happiness in marriage, and she and William were not? Dinner that night should have been a celebration for both couples; instead it would be an uncomfortable trial to be endured. And Jane, she would continue as ever, seeing the world in rosy hues, and not admit that anything could possibly be wrong. Elizabeth's frustration grew.

When she returned to the house, her mother pulled her into the empty drawing room. "Lizzy! Tell me of Mr. Darcy! Am I correct in what I saw? Are you attached to him?" She eagerly grasped Elizabeth's hands.

Ordinarily Elizabeth would prefer to keep such information to herself, but her mother's knowing of her attachment would make things harder for her father. Smiling, she squeezed her mother's hands. "Yes, Mama, Mr. Darcy asked Papa for permission for us to court almost two months ago. We are very close to an understanding."

"Oh Lord Bless me! Could I have two daughters married?" Mrs. Bennet exclaimed. "Tell me of him, Lizzy! Where does he live?"

Hoping that William would understand and bear the effusions that he would receive upon his arrival, she braced herself and said with a smile, "Mr. Darcy has a large estate in Derbyshire, and owns a townhouse in London. He has a younger sister who is not yet out, and his parents have both passed, so he is Master of both homes." Seeing her mother's eyes widen, she hurriedly added, "He is very kind and gentlemanly, and I hold him in great esteem."

Mrs. Bennet asked the inevitable question. "Do you know his income, Lizzy?" Elizabeth felt herself cringing a little. "It is rumoured at ten thousand a year, but that is not why I . . ." Her attempt to temper the news of Darcy's income with the statement of her affections was interrupted by her mother's screech. "Ten thousand a year!! Oh my, oh my, I shall faint dead away! Where are my salts? Is it true? Oh Lizzy, can it be true?"

"Yes Mama, but Mr. Darcy does not like people talking about such things in front of him." Then with a flash of brilliance, she added, "It may drive him away if you do, so please, do not talk about these things in his presence."

"Oh no! I would not think of it! I could not live with myself if I drove him away! Oh Lizzy! I knew that if you went to town you would find someone suitable! Mr. Collins is nothing to this! Just wait until I tell Lady Lucas!"

Elizabeth heard the danger. "Please Mama, until everything is settled, you must not tell anyone. When the time is right, I will let you know, and then you can inform the neighbourhood."

Mrs. Bennet did not like that at all and glared at Elizabeth for spoiling her plans. Then, thinking of her remaining daughters, she asked. "Tell me about Mr. Carrington. Is he married?"

Kicking herself for not thinking of this sooner, Elizabeth hurriedly replied, "No, Mama, he is not married, but he is close to an attachment to a lady in town. He will not welcome any suggestion of a friendship with my sisters, so it is best not to offend him by promoting it."

Her disappointment was unhidden. "Oh, what a shame, such a handsome man, he reminds me of your father when we were courting." Elizabeth's eyes widened. "But I would not wish to offend any friend of Mr. Darcy's, so I will not suggest anything. He is certainly welcome to visit with us tonight." She ended, sniffing.

Elizabeth breathed a sigh of relief. "Thank you Mama, I am sure that Mr. Darcy will appreciate you welcoming his friend." She had not considered Alex's resemblance to her father as a young man and its impression on her mother. She hoped that her mother would not mention it again. Now that she knew he was not a candidate to marry one of her daughters, Elizabeth knew that she would not pay him any more attention than absolutely necessary.

The gentlemen returned for dinner, and Elizabeth made a point of meeting the carriage. She drew Alex and Darcy aside before entering the house. "Alex, you should know, my mother was asking me about your marital status," Alex rolled his eyes, "I informed her that you were close to an attachment to a lady in London and would not welcome any suggestions from her regarding my sisters. I apologize for the deceit, but under the circumstances. . ."

He smiled at her. "No, I appreciate it; you have saved all of us a great deal of misery. I thank you. Perhaps I can ask Bingley to mention the news to his sister. I made the mistake of answering her questions about my father's estate." Then noticing Darcy's fixed stare at Elizabeth, he said, "I think that I will go ahead inside and talk to my other sisters." He left, grinning.

Immediately Darcy took Elizabeth's hand and led her to the garden, away from view, and held her tightly. "I can see the pain in your face, Elizabeth, please tell me what has happened. I did not wish to leave you, and I can see that my misgivings were correct." Elizabeth told him of her conversation with her father, and Darcy's mouth set in a grim line. She confessed to him her regret in wishing to come to Longbourn at all, and berated herself for ever believing in her father. Darcy kissed her, "Elizabeth, you were right to come here, as painful as it is proving to be. You would have never forgiven yourself for not making the attempt to come to terms with him. None of us know the reasons behind his behaviour, but we will get through dinner tonight. He surely will not behave badly in front of his family and guests, and tomorrow, I will speak to him. After that it is up to him what part he will play in our future. You and I will have done all that we can." He embraced her, lending his strength.

Listening to his heart she asked quietly, "Am I worth this, William? Would you be happier with some woman who does not bring with her all of this trouble?"

"You are worth the world to me, Lizzy. I cannot imagine spending my life without you by my side." He captured her lips and they shared a reassuring kiss.

"I suppose that we must go in." She said softly as they drew apart, and smiled at his resigned nod. "I did gain one huge ally for you today."

"And who might that be? I appreciate anyone who welcomes me."

"You may live to regret those words. I told Mama that we are courting. I told her of Pemberley and the house in town, and," She paused dramatically, "I told her that you have ten thousand a year!" Darcy groaned. "But take heart, sir, I also told her that you are much offended when anyone speaks of these things in front of you, and she agreed that we must not chase you away before our engagement is secured!" She laughed gleefully.

Darcy grinned. "That was a very well executed plan, my dear! I thank you for it!" He kissed her nose and hugged her to him. "I love you, dearest, loveliest, Elizabeth!"

They turned and entered the house, and were immediately called to dinner. Mrs. Bennet arranged the seating so that the two couples were together, and Alex found himself seated to the left of Mr. Bennet. The elder man stared pensively down the table to Elizabeth and Darcy. The two were obviously in love. The glances, the slight touches, the small smiles, and soft laughter made the situation clear, and it was painful for him to see. He was roused from his musings by the young man beside him.

"Mr. Bennet, could you tell me about your estate? From what I have observed, it is of a fair size."

"No, it is not terribly large, enough to provide for our family and tenants, but little else." He refocused his mind on the confusing man.

"If you use the latest farming techniques, you would increase your yield substantially. It has proven to be true with my father's estate."

"I do not like change."

That is obvious by your objection to Darcy and Elizabeth's marriage. Wishing to learn more of his own history, he asked, "Has your family held Longbourn long? My own father's estate had an entailment on it, which was broken with my coming."

Startled and unhappy to be reminded of his lack of an heir, he said shortly, "Yes, Longbourn has been in the Bennet family for generations. Unfortunately, it will be no more after my demise. A distant cousin will inherit."

"I am sorry to hear that, sir."

"As am I." His attention returned to Darcy and Elizabeth, talking with Charles and Jane. Mr. Bennet sighed and turned to Alex. "Have you known Mr. Darcy long Mr. Carrington?"

"Yes, sir. I was a year behind him at Cambridge." He paused looking at him, "He is a very good man."

"So I have heard."

Alex regarded him. "You are not losing a daughter, sir. You are gaining a son."

Mr. Bennet sighed again and said, almost to himself, "I have always wanted a son."

Alex opened his mouth as if to say something, then shook his head and looked away. Mr. Bennet did not notice that he never spoke again.

The rest of the evening went as Elizabeth expected. Her father, not wishing to pretend civility with Darcy any more than necessary did not encourage the separation of the sexes after the meal. Instead, he bid the group a good evening and retired to his library. After their initial interest in Alex, their mother's whispered news that he was unavailable encouraged Lydia and Kitty to ignore the men completely for the rest of the evening, and instead they entertained themselves in their usual exuberant fashion. Mary, who cared little for any man, retired to another room, and the sound of the pianoforte could be heard in the distance. Mrs. Bennet fawned over Bingley, and paid even greater attention to Darcy's needs and wants. Alex was, as Elizabeth expected, only tolerated. Darcy and Alex observed with astonishment the behaviour of the younger sisters and Mrs. Bennet, and regularly caught Elizabeth blushing in embarrassment, sent her small smiles of encouragement and understanding.

Darcy could not help but wonder what his opinion of her might have been had they met the previous autumn with her family present. He hoped that he would have seen her for the treasure she was and been able to separate her from their behaviour. He smiled to himself, yes, Elizabeth's beauty and charm would have outshined them all, and he would have undoubtedly approached her immediately, just as he had done at the theatre.

WITH GREAT RELUCTANCE, Darcy left Elizabeth at Longbourn. Her father reappeared upon hearing the gentleman ready to depart and gave them no opportunity to kiss goodnight. The gentlemen boarded the carriage and returned to Netherfield where they were immediately welcomed by Caroline, who insisted that they join her and the Hursts in the music room. She was unhappy that Darcy stayed in his suite after arriving in the afternoon, and had managed to avoid her completely before leaving for dinner. She did have the opportunity to enjoy Alex's company, and was pleased to learn about him being the only child of a man with an estate of six thousand a year. It was not Pemberley, but it had possibilities. Darcy was in no mood to bear Caroline, and suggested that Bingley announce his engagement to his family. Charles, not realizing what unhappiness he was about to unleash, joyfully agreed.

"Caroline, Louisa, Hurst, I have an announcement to make!" Charles stood and beamed at his family.

"Well, for heaven's sake, what is it, Charles?" Louisa cried. "You look as if you are about to burst!"

"I am, I am!" He laughed. "I have been given the great honour of Jane Bennet's acceptance of my hand, and today, her father gave me his consent! I am to be married!"

His two sisters stared. Gilbert Hurst rose unsteadily to his feet and walked over to him, hand extended. "Congratulations, Bingley. She is a damn fine looking girl." He glanced with amusement at his wife and sister, and settled himself down to watch the fireworks.

Darcy and Alex exchanged glances and congratulated Bingley with enthusiasm. Bingley's smile was huge, and he accepted his friends' words with joy. Finally, he turned to his silent sisters. "Well, Caroline, Louisa, what do you say?"

"What do we say?" Caroline screeched. "Are you out of your mind? Have you met this woman's family? They are our inferiors! Our father did not work to amass his fortune for you to waste it on this country nobody! How can you consider such a thing? Could you not simply fall out of love with her like you do all of the rest and find someone suitable?"

Bingley, shocked and hurt, turned to Louisa. "Do you feel the same way?"

"Charles, I have met her twice, and she seems nice enough, but you know that you were to marry a woman with a fortune to improve the family name and add to its value."

"I was to marry a gentleman's daughter and purchase an estate." Charles said defensively.

"That is exactly what you are doing, Charles." Darcy stepped in. "Miss Bennet is a gentleman's daughter, and as much as your sisters dislike the fact, she is several steps above themselves in social consequence by her birth. She may not have a large dowry, but in terms of connections, they have nothing of which to complain. When you purchase an estate, you will have fulfilled the rest of your father's desires for your generation. It will be up to your children to continue the advancement."

Bingley looked at him gratefully. "Thank you, Darcy. I could not have stated it clearer. Besides, I would marry Jane Bennet regardless of her status. I know that she is the perfect woman to have by my side."

"She is a wonderful woman, Bingley, you are a fortunate man." Alex slapped his back

"Mr. Darcy, surely you cannot support this! You would never lower yourself to such a woman!" Caroline ran to his side and clutched his arm.

Darcy quickly detached her hand from his sleeve. "I am a gentleman, if I were to marry one of the Misses Bennet, I would be marrying a gentleman's daughter, she would be my equal. I would only be lowering myself if I were to marry someone like you." Caroline gasped. It was harsh but he had tolerated her behaviour for too many years. He addressed Bingley, "Of course, if I were in love with the lady, her status would be meaningless. Like your brother, I share his desire to marry for affection. He is simply fortunate to fall in love with exactly the woman who his father charged him to find. Well done, Bingley!"

"Thank you!" Bingley's confidence was renewed by his friend's support. Then looking to Caroline he said, "We have not as yet set a wedding date, Caroline, but when we do, we would be happy to have your involvement in the celebration plans. Tomorrow we will speak of your living arrangements after the wedding, so that you will have time to prepare your own home." Charles had been thinking long about this. He was tired of Caroline overspending her allowance, and ordering his life. His marriage would be the perfect time to make the break from his sister. If she did not marry, she would have to establish her own household in any case, and there certainly were no suitors knocking on her door.

Caroline looked at her brother in disbelief. She never thought that she would be displaced upon his marriage. She looked at Louisa, who nodded to her, agreeing with Charles. She looked to Alex, who did not meet her eyes. She then looked at Darcy, who met her gaze with no expression. There was no sign of hope there. Finally, she swallowed, "I will be interested in hearing what you have to say tomorrow, Charles." Then mustering all of the dignity she could, she and Louisa left the room.

The men waited a few moments in silence and it was Hurst who spoke first, "Good for you, Charles."

Chapter 19

*D*arcy arose at dawn Wednesday morning after a fitful night. He wished desperately that he could have spoken to Elizabeth before leaving Longbourn, but it was not to be. He wanted to hold her and reassure her that all would be well. He then looked at the rumpled bed and wondered if this was the last time that he would spend his night alone. Deciding that he needed some exercise before arriving at Longbourn, he dressed in his riding clothes and went downstairs to have some coffee before leaving. To his surprise, he found Alex in the breakfast room.

"Good Morning, Alex, you are up early!"

"Good Morning, Darcy, I can imagine what awakened you."

"Yes, it is a momentous day. I have mixed feelings about it, though by my reception, I have a feeling that I may be a married man in a few hours." He smiled.

Alex smiled back. "As painful as it will likely be to my sister, I do hope that your feeling is correct." He paused, "I have decided to return to London this morning."

"You have seen all that you wish?"

"Yes. My three younger sisters are, as Elizabeth warned me, silly and vacant, nothing to herself or Jane. I have no need to further the acquaintance, perhaps when they are older, but for now, no. Mr. Bennet, well, after listening to him for an evening, I felt an uncomfortable familiarity in character which I will endeavour to repair. I always felt a little selfish at times, but seeing how my birth father's behaviour has hurt my sister through his selfishness, I know that I must change. I will emulate my true father as much as possible." He looked thoughtfully into the distance.

"Shall I give a message to Elizabeth and Jane from you?" Darcy asked, pleased and interested to watch his friend's self-realization.

"Yes, thank them for allowing me this opportunity to see what my blood heritage is, and tell them that I truly do wish to continue the relationship with them, and be a part of their lives." He smiled, "It is good to know that I will not be alone in the world when my parents are no more."

"I will be proud to have you as part of my family, Alex. You will always be welcome at Pemberley."

"And you and Elizabeth will always be welcomed at Kingston Park." The two men shook hands. "I am sorry to be missing your wedding, Darcy, but I do not belong here." Alex was glad to have followed his father's advice to simply come and observe; now he could leave quietly, and probably never return.

Struck by a thought, Alex looked at Darcy. "Would you prefer that I stay? I am incensed with Mr. Bennet's behaviour towards you and Elizabeth, and to be honest with you, I would not even consider approaching the man for his consent, and admire your willingness to do so. However, I know you will not be remotely intimidated by whatever he will throw at you, and that you will not need someone to hold your hand while you face him. I do feel more of a brother to you than I do Elizabeth. I have known you years where in all honesty, I have only seen her on three occasions. It would be presumptuous of me to assume the role of protective brother at this point in our relationship, especially when I have chosen not to reveal who I am to Mr. Bennet. I will however be honoured to stand by you if my support will aid you in any way."

Darcy listened to Alex's statement of commitment to their friendship and was deeply gratified. "Alex, I cannot begin to tell you how much I appreciate your offer of support. You are correct though, I do not at all fear facing Mr. Bennet. This is not your fight, your purpose for coming here was to meet and assess the man, and see where your blood lies. If you feel that you have seen all you need, then I do not begrudge your desire to leave." Darcy held out his hand and the friends shook once more. "How will you return to London?"

"I will rent a horse at the post stop in town."

"I will accompany you there." Darcy finished his coffee and returned the cup to the sideboard. They walked from the house to the stables, and set out; followed by a groom who would lead back Alex's mount. He and Darcy said their farewells, and soon he was off to town.

Darcy then rode out over the fields of Netherfield, trying to relax his mind by looking over Bingley's estate. It was not bad; certainly nothing that a little influx of capital could not mend. He looked at the fences, and rode past the tenant homes. He was about to turn back when he spied a familiar figure in a yellow gown wandering pensively down a nearby lane.

"Elizabeth!" He called out, turning his horse towards her. She stopped at the sound of his voice, and spotted him riding to her.

"William!" She cried with delight. He reigned in the animal and jumped down, picking her up in his arms and spinning her about.

"Oh darling how I have missed you! I woke up regretting not speaking to you last night and wishing that I could see you this morning." He began covering her face in kisses.

Laughing, she pulled his head away from her and smiled into his beaming face. "I escaped the house hoping that I might find you."

He held her tight. "It seems wishes do come true." He kissed her sweet lips. "I love you, Lizzy."

"I love you, my William." She said, softly stroking his face.

"How was your night? Did your father give you any more trouble?" He asked, calming but not letting go.

"No, I have not seen him since you departed. I rose up with the birds and have been walking ever since. I have been anticipating what this day will bring." She looked at him uncertainly.

"I have been up early as well. I went with Alex to the post station to rent a horse. He has decided that there is nothing for him here, and is returning home, with much insight into his own character."

"He did not think much of Papa, did he?"

Darcy met her eyes and stroked her cheek. "No, he did not. Nor of your younger sisters, I am afraid. He said maybe when they are older. . ."

"No, I doubt that they will be much changed then, either." She shook her head sadly.

"He did say that he wishes to be close to you and Jane. He welcomes us to Kingston Park, and I extended our welcome to Pemberley." He smiled, trying to cheer her.

Elizabeth returned his smile. "Thank you; that was kind of you."

"He is my friend; it was something that I would do in any case."

Elizabeth stared at the ground. "Are you going to speak to Papa today?" He lifted her chin and looked into her eyes. "You know that I am." He kissed her. "If he reacts as I think he will, what do you wish to do?"

She took a deep breath. "If he refuses, when you leave the library, Jane and I will invite my mother and sisters to come for a walk to town. We will go straight to the church. I will not extend this any longer. I wish to be your wife. Today." She looked defiantly at him.

"Well, that seems a wonderful plan of action, my dear." He whispered into her ear. "I cannot wait to be your husband." He felt the heat of her blush on his cheek. They walked towards Longbourn, and before they came too near, he kissed her and mounted his horse. "I will go and change now. I will be there to speak to your father in two hours."

"And *I* will be ready to leave after you do." She watched as he rode away. Then straightening her shoulders returned to the house to pack.

DARCY washed up and dressed, and spoke to Bingley when they were alone in the breakfast room. He told him of Alex's departure, and then gave him his thoughts on Netherfield, since he doubted he would have another chance anytime soon. Finally, he told him of his and Elizabeth's plan for the day. Bingley said that he would accompany him to Longbourn, and stand up with him at the wedding. Darcy was grateful for his friend's support. Bingley also offered to host the couple that night if their departure for London was delayed unexpectedly. Although the last place that Darcy wished to spend his wedding night was Netherfield, he accepted the invitation. It was agreed that no word of the day's plans would be spoken to Bingley's family, so when they left together, all that Caroline knew was that they were going visiting.

Mr. Bennet looked out of the library window to see the two men arrive. He knew they would come. He had not decided yet how he would receive Darcy. It was not until he saw the man striding determinedly into his home that his possessive anger overtook him and he decided to fight his attempt to take Lizzy away. He knew how fruitless it was, but that hopelessness just made him more irrationally angry. He heard the expected knock on the door, and saw Darcy enter the room. He closed it behind him, and stood before the desk: tall, serious, with an aura of great strength.

"Mr. Bennet. I have come to tell you that almost three weeks ago I asked for your daughter Miss Elizabeth's hand in marriage. I was honoured and delighted to receive her acceptance." Mr. Bennet sat straight up, anger crossing his face. "I now respectfully request that you fulfil your daughter's desire to become my wife, and ask for your consent and blessing on our union." Darcy stood with his unreadable mask firmly in place, and watched the father of his beloved struggle for words.

He glared. "Mr. Darcy. I am surprised that you would come here with such a request. I believe that I made it quite clear to you that I do not favour you as my daughter's husband."

Darcy regarded him coolly. "If that is so sir, then you should not have allowed me to court her. By allowing me that privilege, your consent was implied. You should not be surprised with the natural conclusion to the courtship."

"It was my error to allow it at all." He said bitterly.

"Nonetheless, you did, and I have won Miss Elizabeth's heart, as she has won mine. I assure you sir, I want nothing but the best for her, and I will love and care for her all the days of her life." His eyes bore into Mr. Bennet, daring him to dispute his words.

Mr. Bennet laughed shortly. "You have won her heart! I doubt that she sees past your wealth!"

With difficulty, Darcy controlled his growing anger. "I believe that your daughter has stated quite clearly that she has no interest in marrying for anything less than love, mutual respect, and esteem. Why would you think that she has suddenly changed her mind? Miss Elizabeth is not mercenary. I have seen enough of that type of woman to be able to know the difference."

Mr. Bennet ignored the truth of his statement. "Come now, Mr. Darcy. Any woman could be dazzled by your riches." Then he stated with conviction, "I will not allow my daughter to leave her home to go to a man who will abuse her."

"Abuse her!" Darcy was instantly incensed. "How did you form such an idea? What do you know of my character to make such an allegation!"

Mr. Bennet pointed an accusing finger at him. "You only want her to make your heir, and you will continue to see your mistresses and prostitutes, as all rich men do. I warned her of this. You want a simple country girl who you can control." He missed the dangerous light brewing in Darcy's dark eyes.

"Sir, I will not even address such a ridiculous statement! You are grasping at straws for no good reason. You should be ashamed of yourself!"

"You have no business coming into my home and taking my daughter away from me!!" Mr. Bennet shouted, leaping to his feet, finally letting all of his feelings be heard. "She is mine! I raised her! I made her who she is! She was meant to stay by my side always! She will be perfectly happy here. She has no need of your riches, your books, your friends, your connections. I will provide all that she needs. My other daughters will leave me, but Lizzy was always meant to stay here. I always planned it that way! I have made sure that no man would ever want her by educating her! Then you come along, and claim that you like that in her. You lie! You will grow bored with her, and she will languish in your house, a slave to your desires when she knows that she would have been happier here. You will not take her away from me!" Mr. Bennet glared at him, pounding his fists on the desk.

Darcy stared at the man in disbelief. "Do you care nothing for your daughter's happiness? How can you treat her like a possession?"

Mr. Bennet smirked. "I am her father; she will do as I say. When she marries, I will choose the man, one who will keep her near."

"Elizabeth once told me that you would support her decision to determine her own happiness. That you would never force her to accept a marriage that she despised. Is it that she has found a man who is her equal in intelligence? That there is no reason to object to me? That unlike the fool Collins who you knew she would reject, you know I am worthy of her and she of me?" Darcy was absolutely furious with him. His anger was the greatest he had ever experienced. His hands clenched into fists, he made a valiant effort to control his urge to pick up Mr. Bennet and shake the smirk off his face. "I refuse to believe these arguments that you put before me. Something else is driving you. What is it? Are you so afraid of losing your companion that you would force her to live her life unfulfilled to meet your own selfish desires? Are you jealous that she will have the love and companionship that you never had? Are you afraid to live with your own wife?" Then, coming to a sudden realization, Darcy's mouth opened and his eyes narrowed, "No, it is because *she* is the son you did not have. Daughters leave home, but sons stay. You raised her as your son and companion and now she is leaving you." In his fury he considered throwing the truth of Alex in his face, but remembered in time that he would not expose his friend.

Mr. Bennet made no answer; he was too numb to speak. A sick feeling spread over him as the reality of what had just happened finally permeated his consciousness, and the truth of Darcy's charge struck him to the bone.

Darcy cast one more look of absolute disdain at Elizabeth's father. "Mr. Bennet, Elizabeth is of age. If you will not give your consent, I will leave the decision to her." He pulled open the door and strode from the room.

Mr. Bennet stood staring out the open door. A servant entered and caught sight of the master's face and almost threw the morning's post on his desk before fleeing the room, closing the door behind him. Mr. Bennet was aware of the loud noises of the ladies calling out to each other but paid them no heed. He was desperately seeking a way to stop the loss of Lizzy from his life, and the weight of his mistake was hitting him with a crushing force. He looked down at his desk and snatched up the missive postmarked from Brighton. Surely this must be from Wickham. A last glimmer of possibility raised his foolish hope that he had been correct all along. At last he would have something to prove to Lizzy that Darcy was unworthy. Eagerly he broke the seal and began to read.

Brighton
April 11, 1811

Dear Mr. Bennet,
I was surprised to receive your letter, but will be pleased to help in your endeavour to end the attraction between Miss Elizabeth and Mr. Darcy. Since you do not wish her to marry I would be happy to provide my services to keep her satisfied and act as a proper gentleman friend to keep her company. I will be glad to lend you my services for a small fee. May I suggest three thousand pounds? Surely that is a sum worthy of

Mr. Bennet dropped the letter in disgust. He was disgusted with the obvious cad who was the writer, and disgusted with himself for contacting him in the first place. He looked out the window in time to see his entire family, with the company of the gentlemen; disappear down the lane towards Meryton.

DARCY LEFT the room, his face red with fury, and his first sight was of Elizabeth; her eyes flashing with anger. No words were necessary. She went into the drawing room, and nodding to Jane, turned to her mother.

"Mama, please get your things, we are taking a walk. Lydia, Kitty, Mary, get your things. We are all going together."

A cacophony of questions erupted from the four ladies. Elizabeth was in no humour to tolerate it. She was about to physically push them out of the door when Darcy's deep authoritative voice stopped the din. "Ladies, we will be leaving in five minutes if you wish to witness this important event, I suggest that you prepare immediately. We will not wait past that time." He turned to Elizabeth, and taking her hand, left the room. Jane and Bingley followed. Darcy's words sufficiently raised the ladies' curiosity and they ran for their bonnets. Soon they were all walking swiftly towards the Meryton church.

Darcy's face was set in a grim line, still furious with Mr. Bennet. Elizabeth was in an equal mood. They were both much better walkers than the rest of the group and were far ahead of them when the anger that compelled their rapid movement finally began to dissipate. Darcy slowed, and Elizabeth began to laugh.

He looked down at her. "Elizabeth if there is anything amusing in what we just experienced, please share it with me. I need the relief."

She smiled. "No sir, absolutely nothing is humorous in what my father said. I was just struck that I must remember never to try to walk with you when you are in an angry state. I fear that my legs cannot keep up with your colossal stride."

Darcy's lips twitched. "Do you mean that my steps are too long for you?"

She shook her head. "Only when you are preoccupied. I am a bit smaller than you, if you have not noticed."

He tilted his head, "So we are not well matched?"

"Did I say that?" She asked; her eyes wide in feigned astonishment.

"I believe that you did." He said with equally feigned seriousness.

She raised her brow. "That can be taken several ways, sir."

"Such as?" He bit back a smile.

"Either I am shorter than you, or perhaps we should not be approaching this church." Elizabeth pursed her lips, fighting her smile.

Darcy stopped, placed his hands on her waist and lifting her to his eye level, kissed her. "There, you are no longer shorter than I, and we are perfectly matched."

They could hear Mrs. Bennet's screech far behind them. Elizabeth grinned. "Oh dear, I believe that you have compromised me, sir. We will be forced to marry."

Darcy kissed her again, "It is the honourable thing to do. I will make this sacrifice," he said, setting her down and bowed with his hand over his heart.

"How gallant!" She said, batting her eyes. Darcy laughed. He could not believe how quickly she restored his humour.

"Now this is the proper mood in which to approach a wedding." He held out his arm. "Shall we, my love?"

Elizabeth beamed up at him. "By all means!"

The rest of the party approached, and they all caught the jubilant mood of the couple. Mrs. Bennet grabbed hold of Darcy's arm. "Mr. Darcy, Mr. Darcy, you just compromised Lizzy! Oh, where is Mr. Bennet! He must make you marry her! What shall we do?" She fluttered her handkerchief in distress.

"Mrs. Bennet, you are correct, I have compromised Miss Elizabeth, and I accept my fate. I shall marry her. Immediately." He smiled at his soon-to-be mother-in-law, and opening the church door, ushered her in.

"Pardon? Oh, but you are not engaged! You have not spoken to Mr. Bennet. You need a license. Oh, but the wedding clothes!" She was close to apoplexy.

"Mama," Elizabeth placed a calming hand on her arm. "Mr. Darcy and I have been engaged for almost three weeks, and he has spoken to Papa. He has refused consent, but I have decided to marry him. He is a good man, and I love him."

Fanny Bennet looked at Elizabeth with an intensity she had never seen before. "Are you sure about this Elizabeth? Are you sure that he loves you and is not just infatuated? That will fade so quickly, child. Will he wish for your company when you are no longer in the bloom of youth? Will he listen to you? Will he still want you if you do not give him a son?"

Elizabeth took her mother's hand, and gave it a squeeze. "Yes Mama, I love him for the man that he is and he feels the same for me. We are well matched in every way. Do not fear for me."

"Then may God bless you both." Mrs. Bennet kissed her cheek and in a second the silly nervous woman returned. "Oh dear, what will I do? We have no celebration planned, and your dress! Oh and where are your flowers?!"

Lydia and Kitty, realizing that they were about to see a wedding, pulled Mrs. Bennet to sit in a pew. Mary ran to the pianoforte and began to play. Bingley returned from summoning the parson and his clerk, and took his place with Jane at the altar. Elizabeth, still a little overcome by her mother's moment of clarity, looked up into Darcy's smiling eyes and taking his arm, walked down the aisle.

The parson called the small gathering to order and began the service. Nobody heard the door to the church open or saw Mr. Bennet slip inside. He stood in stunned silence as he saw his dear Lizzy being married. Reverend Morris asked the question, "Who gives this woman?"

Before anyone could speak, Mr. Bennet strode down the aisle calling out "I do" as he walked. He reached Elizabeth and looked into his daughter's teary face and whispered. "Please forgive me, Lizzy." Taking her hand, he placed it in Darcy's. He looked into Darcy's protective gaze and begged, "Take care of her." Mr. Bennet stepped back and away, to take his place by his wife.

Darcy gripped her hand tightly, and looked into her eyes. All they saw was their love for each other. They felt the weight of the words as they took their vows and slipping the ring upon her finger, raised her hand to his lips. After a blur of words and prayers they were finally pronounced married and the spell was broken. They signed the registry and ran out of the church. Darcy lifted his beaming, beautiful bride up and spun her around, laughing with joy. The lifetime of loneliness was over forever.

Chapter 20

*D*arcy set Elizabeth down and ignoring the curious stares of passersby, enveloped her in his arms and kissed her smiling mouth. "I love you, my dear Elizabeth. My wife." He spoke joyfully in her ear. He wore the ecstatic, dimpled grin that he seemed to only display for her, and so quickly sent her heart pounding.

Elizabeth took his face in her hands, pulling it down to her, "I love you my sweet husband. I cannot wait for you to take me home." She covered his face in kisses, making him laugh with her enthusiasm.

By this time the rest of the wedding party had joined them, the sisters surprised and delighted with the happy couple's behaviour. Jane threw her arms around Elizabeth, "Oh Lizzy! I am so happy for you! He is such a wonderful man!"

Elizabeth, eyes shining with delight hugged her back, all bitterness forgotten. "I am blessed to have found such a man who loves me and I love in return. I cannot wait to begin our lives together." She held Jane from her a little, and wiped her sister's happy tears, "My only regret will be leaving you, dear Jane. You must write to me, and you and Charles must visit us often!"

"Oh Lizzy, I do not even know when we will marry!" Jane cried and wiped Elizabeth's tear-stained cheek.

"Well, you just saw how easy it was for us, there is nothing to hold you back."

Jane shook her head while gripping Elizabeth's hands tightly. "Lizzy, you know Mama will never let that happen! Besides, I have always wanted a big wedding, where you did not."

"And my dreams came true!" Elizabeth laughed and turned to see Mrs. Bennet by her side.

"Lizzy! How could you marry like this! My poor nerves! There is no celebration planned!"

Elizabeth took her mother's hand and led her over to Darcy, who was being slapped on the back by Bingley. "William, I know that we wish to leave for London right away, and we cannot stay for dinner tonight. Perhaps we could stop here on the way to Pemberley, and Mama could invite the neighbours for a little celebration for us then?"

Darcy studied her, she really wanted the chance to say goodbye to her family in a proper manner, and he could not deny it, even if it meant spending time with her father. "We will come on Monday, and if Bingley will allow us to stay at Netherfield," He looked over to his nodding friend, "we will stay until Wednesday morning, when we will depart for Pemberley. Will that be sufficient time for you to prepare a celebration for us, Mrs. Bennet?" He looked to his new mother-in-law.

Mrs. Bennet stared at Darcy in awe. "Oh yes, sir! That is plenty of time to prepare! I will send the invitations today and have everything ready when you arrive."

"Excellent. Does this make you happy, my dear?" He smiled lovingly into Elizabeth's eyes.

"Yes, William, thank you." She took his hand and he raised hers to his lips.

The group turned and walked to Longbourn. Mr. Bennet lagged behind, still unable to speak to them. When they arrived, they saw that Darcy's carriage was there. He had told a servant to go to Netherfield and alert his driver to bring the coach over and load Elizabeth's things while they were at the church. All that was needed now was to say their farewells. She said goodbye to her mother, who tried to tell her of the wedding night and was duly ignored, and hugged her sisters. She especially hugged Jane. "This is not goodbye; we will be back very soon." She whispered in her ear. Jane nodded, too overcome for words.

Bingley stood with Darcy, watching the proceedings. "Well, that came off much better than I feared."

"Yes, I would have preferred Mr. Bennet's consent yesterday, but it seems we were given it in the end." Darcy looked at the man standing alone.

"Perhaps you should speak to him." Bingley suggested gently.

Darcy grimaced. Despite Mr. Bennet's appearance at the wedding, he could not easily forget the words that the man flung at him. He walked over to Elizabeth, and taking her hand, he said softly, "Let us farewell your father and be on our way, my love." She read his expression, and knew what he was feeling. The last thing that he wanted to do was pretend civility with her father, but he would do it for her if she wished. She caressed his face, and he stayed her hand on his cheek, turning to kiss her palm. Then taking his arm, she nodded, and they approached Mr. Bennet.

"Papa, we are ready to leave now. We wish to spend our wedding night in London."

"That is understandable." Mr. Bennet said quietly.

"Mr. Bennet, we will return on Monday, so that you will have time for a proper farewell. We will be travelling to Pemberley and taking a wedding trip to the Lake District. We will of course return to the area for Jane and Bingley's wedding." Darcy made a great effort to voice this speech, and Elizabeth could feel the tension in his arm.

Mr. Bennet made an even greater effort to look Darcy in the eye and address him. "I thank you, Mr. Darcy for giving me the opportunity to see my daughter again. I also wish to apologize to you for my harsh words and behaviour. You have done nothing but act in an honourable and gentlemanly manner towards Lizzy, and I have been a selfish fool who attempted to destroy this chance of happiness and security for my favourite child. I am grateful that I failed in my attempt." He appeared to speak sincerely and with contrition, but could no longer meet his stare.

Darcy had no desire to forgive the man, but to follow the tenets of his church, he knew that he must. "I forgive you sir. But, I must say that nothing would have stopped me from making Elizabeth my wife once she agreed to have me." He looked down at her teary face. "I think that the person who you must apply to for forgiveness is Mrs. Darcy."

Mr. Bennet turned to her, forcing himself to meet her critical gaze. "Can you forgive me, Lizzy? I am afraid that the glow you had in your eyes for me is dimmed forever, but I hope that someday you will be able to love me again."

Elizabeth drew herself up. "I never stopped loving you, Papa. That is why you hurt me so terribly. If I did not love you so much, I would not have been so pained. I could not understand why the man I so admired and respected would do such a thing as deny me the good man I loved. I will forgive you, Papa, but it will take time for me to forget."

Mr. Bennet nodded. "I understand, and thank you." Then he kissed her cheek and bowed to Darcy. "Have a safe journey, and I look forward to seeing you soon. Your mother will be planning a grand celebration for you." He stepped away, and stood next to Mrs. Bennet. Darcy looked down at Elizabeth and they both let out the breath they had been holding. He then handed her into the carriage. Waving from the door, they heard the calls of good luck from their family, and were off.

DARCY SETTLED BACK into the carriage seat; reached for Elizabeth and pulled her to his side. She snuggled into him, wrapping her arms around his waist and resting her head on his chest. He rested his cheek in her hair, having immediately removed her bonnet when they entered the coach, quickly followed by their gloves. They sat in contented silence, absorbing the reality of their marriage, and the frantic activity that led to it that morning. Elizabeth relished the strong, steady beat of his heart, and that more than anything allowed her to relax. It was not long before the tension and uncertainty that had prevented sleep for the past few nights dissipated, and she felt herself drifting off, safe in the comfort of his arms. Darcy soon followed.

When the carriage stopped to rest the horses, Darcy's valet, who was riding on top of the coach, knocked on the door when the couple did not appear. Hearing no response, he opened it to the sight of the soundly sleeping couple. Unsure of what to do, he decided to simply leave them be. He was aware of his master's agitation over the past few days, and was loathe disturbing them. Instead he purchased an assortment of food and wine, and quietly left the basket on the seat opposite them in case they awoke during the rest of the journey.

The purchase was not necessary. Darcy awoke only when the sounds of London and the slower movement of the carriage permeated his consciousness. He opened his eyes with a start, at first confused. He immediately saw Elizabeth's pink cheek resting on his chest, and a feeling of wholeness that he had never before experienced came over him. He caressed her tenderly, and was delighted to see her lips form a smile, and hear her whisper, "William."

Looking out of the window, he recognized their location. He bent and softly kissed her. "Elizabeth, wake up, my love, we are almost home."

Her eyes fluttered open and she blinked, straight into his warm gaze. "Home? Already? But, we just left!"

He chuckled. "That was nearly four hours ago, Lizzy. We apparently needed to catch up on our sleep."

She slowly sat up and stretched. "I cannot remember ever taking such a long nap before, at least, not when I was not ill." She looked at him and smiled. "Now we will be entirely unable to sleep tonight, we are too well rested."

Darcy pulled her back into his embrace. "I do not have any fear of us not finding a pleasant way to occupy our time." He murmured into her ear, while nibbling on her neck. He delighted in feeling the heat of her blush.

The reality of the approaching wedding night and what that entailed suddenly struck her, and she dealt with her unexpected onslaught of nerves with denial. "Mr. Darcy! I cannot begin to imagine what you are implying!"

"Yes you can." He whispered gently, holding her tighter.

"You are quite mistaken!" She declared, finally turning to face him.

"Then why is your face red?" He asked triumphantly, smiling as it became even redder.

"Oh, you take delight in vexing me!" She was suddenly horrified at sounding like her mother.

Darcy laughed and let her go, adjusting his clothing and retrieving her bonnet and gloves. The carriage soon pulled up to the townhouse, and watchful servants, warned of their possible arrival, immediately ran to open the door and retrieved the luggage. Darcy handed her out and taking her arm, led her into the house, grinning from ear to ear. "Welcome home, Mrs. Darcy!" Elizabeth, recovered from her fit of nerves, beamed back up at him.

Mr. Franklin and Mrs. Harris were there to greet them, along with the rest of the staff. If they were surprised with the sudden nature of the wedding, they contained their views. Elizabeth had already won the hearts of the staff with her kindness, and her obviously excellent influence on the Master and Miss Darcy. The staff could not help but notice the joyful expressions on the couple's faces, and were glad for it.

They were both quite hungry, and gratefully took tea which was laid out in the drawing room. Dinner was to be in two hours, so they soon found their way to their bedchambers to bathe and change. Darcy opened her door. "Will an hour be long enough, Elizabeth? Shall I come for you then?"

"I think that will be fine, William." She smiled up at him, and tried to hide the quaver in her voice. He kissed her hand and departed through the adjoining door to his rooms.

Elizabeth turned to be greeted by a young girl. "Good afternoon, Mrs. Darcy. Your bags are nearly unpacked, and your new things have been delivered, although I understand that there is more to come. Would you like to bathe now? The water is ready." The girl was very nervous, and was trying her best to please the new Mistress. All of the staff was nervous, not having a Mistress in the house for so many years.

Elizabeth was a little confused by the girl's speech. "First, please tell me your name." She smiled at her encouragingly.

"Pardon me, Mrs. Darcy! My name is Rosie." The girl turned crimson with her error.

"That is a beautiful name, Rosie." Elizabeth smiled again. "Yes, I would like to bathe and change out of these clothes, but you said something that I did not understand. I am not aware of any new purchases."

"Oh, I could not say, Mrs. Darcy, I only know that they began arriving yesterday morning, and they have been coming steadily since. There are gowns, and undergarments, and night clothes, and outerwear, and well, everything that should be in a trousseau." Rosie led the way into the dressing room and Elizabeth's eyes grew wide, seeing all of the beautiful things.

"Well, this is certainly a wonderful surprise!" She thought, *This must be William's doing, but how?* She looked forward to asking him.

Rosie may have been nervous, but she was very efficient. She had Elizabeth bathed, her hair washed, dried and pinned; and dressed just as Darcy's knock came on the dressing room door. "Come in!" She sang out.

Darcy opened the door cautiously. Upon seeing her smiling face he pulled it fully open, and grinning himself, stepped in. "You are beautiful, Elizabeth!" His look of open admiration made his eyes shine.

Rosie quickly looked between her two beaming employers and smiling, exited the room. Elizabeth stood and walked into his open arms. "Thank you William, you look rather handsome yourself." He laughed, kissing her nose. She pulled back a little, "I have a bit of a mystery to solve." He bit his lip, trying to look innocent. "I seem to have acquired a new wardrobe, and I am told that there is more to come?" She looked at him with her brows raised. "How did this happen? And do not try to claim ignorance, sir."

He gave her a squeeze. "I am thrilled to see you surprised, dearest. I will own to it. I spoke to your aunt before we left town, and asked that she purchase, or at least begin purchasing, some new things for you. She was under instructions to have all of the bills sent to me. I knew that her modiste had your measurements from the new gown that was made for your theatre visit, so she was able to order you the perfect gowns. I know that you will need much more, and will have to visit some different dressmakers, but this at least will give you a start. Are you truly pleased? I was not presuming too much? I assumed that your aunt was well-acquainted with your tastes, and I felt terrible that you would be starting your married life without new things." He looked at her eagerly, hoping that he had done well.

Elizabeth laughed, and kissed his chin. "My goodness, sir, I do not recall ever hearing you speak so quickly!" He laughed. "Yes, I am truly delighted, and gratified that you thought of such things. I am sure that Georgiana will enjoy visiting dressmakers with me, since you have stated clearly that you do not."

"If it means spending time with you, my love, I will gladly make the sacrifice." He ran his hands down her back.

"Oh no, I would rather make my purchases, then see your reaction when I make my entrance!" She hugged him tightly. "Thank you."

They heard the dinner bell ring and proceeded downstairs. Mrs. Harris had ordered a simple meal. Remembering her wedding night she realized that nothing much would be eaten. The newlyweds were grateful for her decision. They simply wanted to be together, rejoicing in their new freedom to talk and touch, and revel in their solitude. When they finished, they walked to the music room, where Elizabeth played for him. He came and sat beside her, and soon they were entwined, exchanging the kisses they had been denied for days.

They pulled slightly apart, and Darcy tucked her head to his chest. He tried to control his voice, but could not help the slight crack in it when he asked, "Lizzy, are you feeling tired?"

Elizabeth took a breath. This was the moment that they had been building towards. It was time to become his wife. She gazed into his passionate eyes. The desire there was unhidden. "Yes, I would like to retire. Shall we go upstairs?"

He nodded and rose, taking her hand to assist her. Keeping it tightly in his grasp, he led her to the bedchamber door. There they stood. He looked down to their clasped hands and ran his thumb over the circle of gold on her finger. Lifting his eyes, he gazed into hers and slowly lifted her left hand to his lips, first kissing the ring then turning her hand to kiss the palm and her wrist. She closed her eyes slowly then opened them, and following his lead, lifted his left hand to her mouth, kissing his palm, and rubbing her cheek upon it. Darcy traced her lips with his finger and whispered, his voice shaking slightly. "Shall I come for you in half an hour?" Unable to speak she nodded, and entered her rooms.

ELIZABETH EXAMINED herself in the mirror; her new nightdress was very revealing. She shook her head, knowing that her aunt had chosen it for that very reason. She decided not to wear the robe. The half hour had passed, and there was no sign of William. She heard the nervousness in his voice; she knew that he was as anxious as she was. Their passionate encounter at Rosings relieved her initial trepidation, but that had been spontaneous. This night was the farthest thing from it. They both knew exactly what was supposed to happen, and she was grateful for her aunt's honesty with her. After waiting another ten minutes, she took a long last look at herself, then smiling, she took a breath and opened the door to his bedchamber. The room was lit only by a few candles and the softly glowing fire. She spotted him, dressed only in his breeches and shirt. He was barefoot, and stood leaning on the window frame, staring out at the darkness.

Elizabeth entered the room. He did not see her. She cleared her throat. He did not hear her. "William." Nothing. Finally, Elizabeth picked up a book from a nearby table and dropped it onto the floor with a loud thud. Startled, he turned, and caught sight of the barely covered Elizabeth, her hair flowing around her shoulders, her eyes dancing, and a very amused smile on her face.

He sucked in his breath. "Oh Lizzy, you are so beautiful!"

"I was wondering if you would ever notice me." She crossed the room and placed her hands on his chest. Darcy's heart was pounding, watching her breasts and hips sway with each step. When she touched him, running her hands over his well-muscled body, he shuddered. "What captured your thoughts, my love?"

He touched her hair. "Are you not nervous?"

"No, I know that I should be, but I feel so comfortable with you, I am not at all worried." Then she placed a kiss over his heart. "What concerns you, William?" He placed his hands lightly on her waist, and looked into her eyes. "I am afraid that my inexperience may be a disadvantage for you. I am so afraid of hurting you."

Elizabeth looked at his dear face. He was so nervous, and she truly was not. His anxiety had served to calm hers. She trusted him completely, and she decided it was entirely up to her to put him at ease. She smiled and immediately started unbuttoning his breeches. Darcy watched her hands. "What are you doing?"

"I think that it is high time that you acquired some experience, Mr. Darcy." She grinned at him and pulled his shirt free. Darcy looked down at her, a slow smile spreading over his face. "Sir, I am more inexperienced than you, but I think that even I know that this will be much more enjoyable with your assistance."

She slipped her hands over his skin. He jumped, closed his eyes and groaned. "Lizzy, that feels so. . ." His voice trailed off. Suddenly he opened his eyes, and seeing the desire in hers, he quickly tore off his shirt.

"Mmmm. That is much better." She purred, delighted to see his chest and arms. She was not entirely ignorant of the male form. She had been to museums and saw the marble statues and paintings, and she did have access to her father's library, but none of that was comparable to the warm, hard beauty of his finely toned body. She ran her hands over him, delighting in the feel of his soft, smooth skin, and then up to touch his deliciously bare neck. "Oh, I wish I were taller!"

Darcy burst out laughing, all nervousness decidedly gone. *How does she have this power to change my moods so quickly?* It was his turn to touch now. He ran his fingers through her hair, spreading it out like wings, delighting in the softness and sweet scent released by his ministrations. "I have dreamed of seeing you like this, my love." His eyes moved down to her lips, and he drew her to him, first kissing her softly, then deepening the pressure, he stroked them repeatedly. Feeling her breathing increase he pulled back, placing his fingers beneath the straps of her gown. "May I see you now?"

"Yes, please," she whispered. He untied the belt of the nightdress and pulled the straps over her shoulders, watching as the gown slipped silently into a puddle of silk at her feet. He took her hands in his, and stepped back, his eyes travelling slowly down and back up her rapidly blushing form. "I always wondered what happened when you blush, Lizzy. Now I know that it is not only your cheeks." This only made her blush more, and he laughed, reaching out to touch her breasts for the first time. "Oh darling, you are so soft." He moaned.

"I think that it is only fair that I see all of you, too." Trying to regain her composure she finished unbuttoning his breeches and slid them down over his hips, exposing his arousal, and dropped them to the floor. "Ah, that is better. Now we are on even ground." She whispered, stroking its thick and heavy length and revelling once again in the odd combination of his soft skin and hardened flesh.

He shuddered and knew that he could not allow her to touch him for long and still be able to achieve the purpose of this first union. He pulled her to him and they stood, kissing deeply, both of them allowing their hands to travel unceasingly over the other's form, learning every curve, until breathless, they pulled apart.

Without a word, Darcy drew back the covers to the bed, and helped her in. He willed himself to walk around to the other side and climbed in next to her, immediately pulling her back into his embrace, so that his body encompassed hers. They took their time, despite the desperate screaming urgings of their bodies. They both knew that they wanted this to be special. Darcy began by cupping her small face in his large warm hands, "I am overjoyed that I waited for you, Lizzy." He whispered, his eyes speaking his emotions as his lips descended to take possession of hers. Elizabeth's hands came up to hold his face, and they exchanged the tender, lingering strokes marking their first journey to passion. They took turns tasting each other. He indulged his desire to run his tongue from her delicate earlobe to her breasts; she suckled the neck that had been hidden from view for far too long. His hands ran over her breasts over and over, making her moan and writhe. She discovered that he responded to the barest touch of her fingertips, stimulating his body so that he jumped and groaned as she traced her way over his smooth chest, sides and bottom.

Darcy kissed his way down from where he suckled her breasts, to her flat belly, and to her thighs, pausing to brush his nose and mouth over the thatch of curls, and lovingly partaking of her sweet essence. She moaned softly, begging for more while shying away at the same time, her fingers wrapped in his hair. Trembling with anticipation, he nuzzled his way back to her lips, brushing his mouth, hair, and hands over her body, and gently urged her legs apart, to settle himself in between. He held her face in his hands, and they kissed, their tongues dancing, as she grew used to his weight. When he felt her relax, he whispered, "Look at me Lizzy." Opening her eyes she saw nothing but love looking back at her. "Are you ready for me, my love?" He asked softly, leaning to kiss her again when she nodded and watched as he swallowed and drew a deep breath. As one hand moved between her legs, she felt his fingers gently stroke her moist folds, then taking himself in his hand; he eased into her. Her eyes opened with surprise at the first feel of him, and his closed in relief. He paused, and forcing himself to hold back, he slowly and steadily continued to push, moaning, as the warmth and her tight clasp almost overwhelmed him. Finally he felt her barrier. He looked at her closed eyes, and panting, begged her to look at him. She did, and with a shaking voice he said, "I promise I will try not to . . ."

She put her hand to his lips. "I love you, William. You will not hurt me." He stared deeply into her eyes, took a breath, and entered her fully. She gasped for a moment, but felt no pain. When he opened his eyes to anxiously see her face, he was overjoyed to see her smile.

"You are well?" He asked, disbelieving.

"You seem disappointed!" She laughed, all of her anxiety forever banished.

Relief and joy flooded through him. "No, my love, I am thrilled!" The extraordinary pleasure he was feeling, being encased within the body of the woman he loved, sent his heart pounding and his desire for completion instantly replaced all of his fears.

They both relaxed, and he began to move within her, steadily increasing his pace, in a movement that he had no need to be taught. She instinctively opened wider for him, and moved with him. They rocked together, smiling, staring into each other's eyes, and then finally kissing deeply as he thrust faster and faster. The straining taut feeling that she experienced when he touched her before began rising in her again, and this time she knew what it meant. She relaxed and let the exquisite feeling rush over her, and felt the exhilaration of her body embracing his inside of her. She moaned his name over and over, her completion finally allowing him to find his. He gasped and shook and called her name, declaring his love for her, ultimately collapsing in a trembling heap, then kissing her with utter abandon. They lay together, joined; then slowly, he withdrew and pulled her close to him, her head resting on his chest. She revelled in the pounding of his heart.

After lying quietly for a few minutes, he kissed her hair. "Are you well, darling?" He whispered. Elizabeth turned so that she could see him, and caressed his face, "Yes, it was . . . so wonderful, William. I love you."

A sense of male pride flowed through him, "You cannot begin to know how happy that makes me feel, Lizzy." Combing his fingers through her hair he laughed and suddenly declared, "I guess that we are not so inexperienced now!"

Elizabeth was delighted in his silliness. "No we are not, but I would suggest that we follow the old adage, practice makes perfect."

"Is it lesson time, my love?" He asked hopefully.

Elizabeth laughed. "It seems that you were right, we need not worry about being unable to fall asleep tonight!"

Darcy's low growl of warning made her squeal with delight as she found herself tumbled over and pinned under his body. "Sleep is the last thing that you will experience tonight, my good wife." Elizabeth looked up into William's eyes and saw a different man. Gone was the cautious bridegroom. Here for the first time, she was viewing her lover, a man alive with confidence and passion. There was a fire burning in his gaze as he moved to her side and raked his eyes over her body. His gaze followed the path of his open hand, stroking her firmly from her neck, down over her breasts, across her belly to her thighs. It was a movement indicating possession and adoration. He stroked his hand back up to her face. His desire so evident, that she burned to feel him take her again. He leaned down and hovered over her mouth then kissed her deeply, his tongue exploring. He pulled away and looked into her eyes. "Mine," was all he said before reclaiming her mouth, entwining his fingers in her hair and holding her head in his grasp. Elizabeth brought her hands around him, and caressed his broad back, pulling him against her, and kissed him, suckling his tongue and revelling in his groan. "Lizzy." He moaned heatedly in her ear.

"Are you mine, Will?" She spoke as he scraped his teeth over her neck.

"Yes, Lizzy, every bit of me is yours, yours alone." His mouth descended to lave her breasts and massage them with his hands while she ran her fingers through the hair that brushed her face. She felt his potent manhood pushing against her thigh as his mouth returned to devour hers again.

She pulled away long enough to beg, "Please love me William," before he immediately reclaimed his prize.

Unspeaking he rose from her, lifted her legs and wrapped them around his waist while looking deeply into her eyes, then without hesitation, plunged completely into her and thrust with the vigour and relentless motion he had imagined time and again, a motion she had unknowingly craved. He felt his need for release building and with joy felt her body again embracing his, and drank in the incoherent moans she uttered as she pulled his head down for a desperate kiss. At last he reached his moment of release and held her tightly to him, gasping, filling her with his essence. He rolled to his side, taking her with him where they remained entwined, unwilling to separate. Darcy's cheek rested on her hair, and she could feel his lips press against her temple just as he felt her kiss upon his chest. They said not a word, but fell asleep safe in each other's arms. Home.

Chapter 21

Once the carriage containing Elizabeth and Darcy departed, Bingley observed with a combination of amusement and horror the reactions of the various members of the Bennet household. Mrs. Bennet was overcome with joy for having married off her least favourite daughter to a man she now knew was one of the most eligible in the country. She demanded that Jane tell her everything of their courtship, and insisted that she describe his home to her in detail. She burst into Mr. Bennet's library, where he had silently retreated, and chastised him for not telling her of the courtship. While this occurred, Lydia and Kitty were giggling over the suddenness of the ceremony, and discussing if their sister had needed to be so quickly married. That in turn horrified Jane, who assured them, not necessarily successfully, that it was decidedly not the case. Lydia flipped her hair at Jane and declared that even if it was not true, she certainly would not say no to such a handsome man, even if he did not smile and talk. Mary jumped on the theme and began preaching of the need to guard a young lady's virtue, and was happy that at least Elizabeth had the sense to marry right away. Jane was mortified, and ran into the garden, where Bingley had the supreme pleasure of comforting her, and assuring her that the behaviour of her family meant nothing to him, since he was marrying her, and not her sisters. He, of course, stayed for dinner. Mr. Bennet ate alone in his library, and said not a word to anyone the remainder of the day.

Upon returning to Netherfield, Bingley dismounted, handed the reins to his and Darcy's horses to the stable boy, and with an uncharacteristically serious look on his face, entered the house.

"Charles, where have you been? We waited dinner for you. And where is Mr. Darcy?" Caroline asked when he came into the music room. She and the Hursts were gathered there playing cards.

"I have been at Longbourn all day, Caroline, where I suspect I will be spending most of my days from now on, with my betrothed." He poured himself some wine and walked to look out of the window. Caroline wrinkled her nose in distaste. "As for Darcy, he has departed. I suspect he has been in London for some hours by now."

"London?" Caroline and Louisa looked at each other. Neither of them had noticed his removal from the house. "Why would he leave for London? He only just arrived yesterday. Has something happened?"

Bingley laughed to himself. *Yes indeed, something has happened!* He turned away from the window and regarded his sister. Even though he had assured her for quite some time that she would never win Darcy, this news would be a blow. "Yes, Caroline. This morning, Darcy and Miss Elizabeth Bennet were married. I stood up with him at the church. They have gone to London to begin their honeymoon."

"NO!!" Caroline stood with her hand on her chest. Louisa stood with her and stared at her brother. "But they were not even engaged! I have heard nothing of this! Did he court her? How could this happen? Was she compromised?" Caroline voiced each thought as it flew through her mind. "This cannot be! His family must disapprove, they must!" Then growing increasingly agitated she howled, "He was mine! Pemberley was mine! I am the rightful mistress, not that, that, that, impertinent, country chit!"

"Caroline, calm down!" Louisa held her sister. "This is certainly a shock, but you know full well that he was never going to marry you. You have refused to accept this, but now you must!"

Caroline pulled away from her and stormed up to Bingley, who was regarding her with trepidation. He was never good with displays of anger from anyone. "How did this happen? When did they meet? How did she fool him? Why did you not stop the wedding? Why was it so sudden?" She demanded, her hands grasped his lapels and she shook him.

"Caroline! Enough!" Louisa pulled her away and made her sit on the sofa, where she glared at her brother and breathed erratically. Louisa looked up to him; he was staring in disbelief at his sister. He had never seen her so disturbed before. "Charles." She gained his attention. "Perhaps if you just tell us what happened, Caroline will understand and calm." Louisa was the eldest sister, and she had cared for both of her younger siblings. She knew their characters and how to handle them. Caroline needed details, and Bingley needed to be directed.

"Of course, Louisa." He looked up as Hurst, an amused smile on his face, brought him some more wine and gave a glass of sherry to Caroline. "Darcy met Elizabeth in February at the theatre performance where we saw him with his cousin, Colonel Fitzwilliam. He was actually on his way out the door to introduce himself to her when I was speaking to him." Caroline groaned. If they had arrived sooner, she could have prevented this ever happening. Bingley continued. "He began paying calls, and invited her family to dinner to meet Georgiana and his family. I was invited that night as well, which is when I met Jane." He paused, smiling at the memory of his first sight of her.

"You were invited to dinner?" Caroline said, suddenly remembering the night that he said Darcy was inviting family over. "That was why he did not ask us to dinner that night." She said putting the pieces together.

"Yes, he asked Mr. Bennet for permission to court her that night." He left out the tension of the evening. "They spent the next few weeks seeing each other, then Elizabeth left for Kent, to visit Mrs. Collins, Sir William Lucas' daughter. Mr. Collins has the living at Hunsford, which is attached to Rosings, Darcy's aunt's home."

"Mr. Darcy just came from visiting there, did he not?" Caroline whispered.

"Yes, that was where he and Elizabeth were engaged." He saw Caroline's pained expression. "His aunt apparently did not object, and she was already accepted by Lord and Lady Matlock. They decided that they would marry as soon as they arrived here. They did not want a fuss, and saw no point in a long engagement. Darcy spoke to Mr. Bennet this morning and since he had the license, we all walked straight to the church, and well, now they are very happily married."

Caroline said nothing. She just sat staring. Louisa grasped her hand. "It was surely a love match, then, was it not, Charles?"

"Oh most definitely. I have never seen Darcy so happy. He smiles and laughs. Georgiana is thrilled with her new sister." Bingley spoke happily, not realizing how his words pained Caroline.

"Well, Caroline, Louisa, it seems that your objections to your brother's choice should be quite significantly lessened." Hurst grinned. They looked at him without understanding. "By Darcy marrying Miss Bennet's sister, her connections have vastly improved!" He laughed, watching the truth register on their faces.

"He never wanted me." Caroline finally said.

"You never wanted him." Louisa told her. "You just wanted what he had and represented." Caroline just looked at her blankly. "I suspect that he wanted someone who truly loved him."

"But we were taught to marry for connection and money!" Caroline cried out.

"I heard the same lessons you did, Caroline," Bingley tried to help her understand, "but I decided to marry for love. I am happy that nobody tried to persuade me otherwise, or I might have listened to those lessons and foolishly given Jane up."

Caroline soon left for her rooms. She decided to ask Charles to lend her his carriage and return to London, and throw herself into the Season; surely her friends would be willing to escort her. She hoped to catch a man before she was forced to establish her own home, and secretly, and foolishly, she hoped that Darcy would realize his mistake and turn to her for comfort, she wondered if it was not too late.

"I WONDER IF I could be as strong as Darcy?" Bingley said to his horse as he rode towards Longbourn the next day. "Could I have continued with my courtship of Jane if I were faced with Mr. Bennet's anger? Could I have stood and taken his abuse as Darcy did when he asked for his consent and could I have defended her and won her as Darcy did Elizabeth?" Deep down in his heart, he knew that he would have run away. Perhaps that was what Mr. Bennet had been counting on, he might have hoped Darcy would think Elizabeth was not worth the trouble.

Bingley was standing outside of the library door with Elizabeth when Darcy went in. He heard every word of the conversation and watched the increasing fury on her face, and physically held her back from storming into the room. He saw Elizabeth's, and heard Darcy's passion. He did not think that he had that in him and was grateful that he did not have to find out.

Bingley entered Longbourn to find it strangely quiet. Mrs. Bennet and the girls were out paying calls and spreading the word of Elizabeth's marriage. Jane welcomed him, and taking his hand asked, "Could we go for a walk this morning?" Seeing her strained face, he immediately agreed.

They walked down the lane and when they were out of sight of the house, he stopped and raised his hand and touched her face. "What is troubling you, Jane?"

She bit her lip and sighed. "Papa. He has not spoken a word since Lizzy left. I am worried about him."

"If you had heard what he said to Darcy, perhaps you would not be so concerned about his well-being, but instead be happy that he is suffering." It was harsh, but he meant it.

"Charles! That was cruel! He surely feels terrible about losing his daughter!" Her blue eyes showed an unusual flash of anger.

"So you supported his plans to prevent your sister from marrying?" He prodded, questioning her choice.

Obviously torn, she wrung her hands. "No, of course not! I just do not wish him to be unhappy!"

"You cannot have it both ways, Jane. Someone will be unhappy in this. Either your father or Elizabeth and Darcy." He looked very seriously into her eyes. "Jane, I know that you love both your sister and your father, and you look for the good in everyone, but sometimes you just have to accept that the people who you love can be weak, and make terrible decisions. If they realize their mistakes, then it is up to us to love them more." He thought of Caroline. She might come out of her disappointment a stronger woman. He hoped.

"Then there is nothing that I can do but wait and see what my father does when they return." She unhappily looked down.

"I am afraid that it is up to the three of them. I know that it is difficult to be caught in the middle of a family conflict, and trying to play mediator, but I have faith in you." He smiled at her, tipping her chin up so that she met his gaze.

"You do?" She stood mesmerized by his large green eyes.

"I have the utmost faith that you wish nothing more than to make people happy. You certainly make me happy, Jane." His gaze moved to her mouth.

Jane licked her lips nervously. "You make me happy, too, Charles."

"Good, because that is my plan." He softly kissed her. It was a gentle and tender meeting, but very soon was followed by another and another, until breathless, they drew apart. Bingley encased her in a warm embrace, thrilled that he finally kissed her. She was trembling like a leaf. "Now, my dear Jane, shall we discuss *our* wedding day?" He moved away and looked down at her, grinning.

All thoughts of her father were gone. Now the only subject she wished to discuss with Lizzy was what happened on her wedding night.

THE HAPPY COUPLE spent the next several days as newlyweds should. They did absolutely nothing but make love, eat, tease, and talk. They discovered the joy of openness and the comfort of being in the company of their soul mate. Neither one had ever experienced such a feeling of solace and absolute love.

On Sunday they emerged from the townhouse to attend church in the morning, much to the great interest of their fellow parishioners. The announcement of the marriage of Fitzwilliam Darcy to Elizabeth Bennet was the sensation of the Season, first because he was amongst the most eligible and hunted bachelors in the country, and second, because nobody knew his bride. She had been seen with him twice, and other than learning her name, very little information was available. It was a poorly kept secret that Lady Catherine de Bourgh had long declared that he would marry her daughter, but she remained unexpectedly silent on the marriage. It was further known that Lord and Lady Matlock had publicly acknowledged Miss Bennet at the theatre, so it was surmised that she was of good breeding and was accepted by the family. That made the members of the *ton* even more desperate for a good look at her, and to invite the couple to their affairs. There were a great many unhappy mothers and daughters who wanted to see just what this girl had that they did not to ensnare such an elusive man. Darcy's desk was piled high with invitations that he decidedly ignored.

Sunday evening they were invited to dinner at Matlock House. Elizabeth donned one of her lovely new gowns, and Rosie was finishing her hair when Darcy knocked on the door frame and entered the room. Elizabeth stood, and the deep red of her gown matched perfectly the lovely blush that was gracing her cheeks. It seemed that the look of desire in Darcy's eyes, and the reminder of what would follow, was all that was needed to make her respond. Rosie rapidly retreated from the room, and Darcy came to her and looked appreciatively down from her face to her bare neck, "You are stunning, Elizabeth. How could I be so fortunate to have won such a beautiful woman?" He then began to caress her throat with his lips.

Elizabeth attempted to maintain control. "William! You must stop! We must attend this dinner!"

His muffled voice rose from behind her ear. "I have plenty to nibble on here in my arms." Feeling her trembling in response to his ministrations, he began tenderly caressing her, knowing that his touch was weakening her resolve.

"William." She pleaded, now turning her head to kiss his hungry mouth. He pulled her closer and she felt how much he wanted her. She was rapidly losing her commitment to attend the dinner.

"I love you." His warm breath tickled her ear. Her moan only encouraged him, and feeling the bliss of her body melting into his arms, he began gently working at the buttons of her dress.

His soft tugging finally brought her back to the moment, and she pulled herself together. "William! We must stop!"

He sighed in frustration, he knew that she was correct, but he really did not care. "I will stop, but only because it is family that we are going to see. If it was some silly dinner party. . ."

Elizabeth took his hand and kissing it, finished his thought, "Then we would be in our bed by now." They both sighed.

Darcy drew from his pocket a velvet box. "This is for you. My mother left this for me to give to my wife, and I have often imagined you wearing it."

Elizabeth opened the box and gasped. Inside was a lovely ruby necklace, simple, but very elegant. Darcy lifted it out, and standing behind her, placed it around her neck and hooked the clasp. He then ran his hands over her shoulders and kissed her neck. "It is perfect for you." He whispered, wrapping his arms around her waist, and looking at their reflection in the mirror.

"I do not know what to say, William. Thank you." She touched the jewels with wonder in her eyes.

"The look on your face is all I needed." He turned her around and kissed her deeply. His hands again ran over her body, caressing her seductively. She wrapped her arms around him, and gloried in the evidence of his desire pressing insistently into her belly. She could feel his hands lifting the fabric of her gown, and soon the sensation of his fingers running up her legs to her bare bottom made her moan with anticipation. Darcy pulled his lips from hers and growled into her ear. "Let me love you, Lizzy." His husky voice heightened the growing need that she felt for him.

Helplessly she nodded as he captured her mouth again, and lifted her to sit on the edge of the bed. Her passion-drugged eyes watched as he opened his breeches and released his straining pride. Laying her back, he lifted her gown, grasped her hips, and swiftly entered her, thrusting with the unwavering rhythm of his deep desire. Elizabeth held onto his hands and wrapped her legs around his waist, allowing him to drive in further. The entire time, they never tore their eyes from each other. It was not until they reached their moment of release that they finally closed, as waves of sheer pleasure encompassed their bodies. When their shudders died away, Darcy leaned to kiss her gently. "Thank you, my love."

Elizabeth caressed his face and smiled. "Thank you for convincing me." He laughed softly, and withdrawing, found a towel to remove the evidence of their love from her, and helping her to rise, embraced her tightly.

After smoothing their wrinkled clothes they left their rooms and boarded the carriage. Matlock House was not far and they were soon there. Darcy observed the unusual number of carriages in front of the home with a frown. "I wonder if someone nearby is having an affair tonight." He looked at the other homes on the street. Only Matlock House was brightly lit. With a sinking feeling he closed his eyes.

"What is wrong, William?"

"I am afraid that this is not going to be a simple family dinner, after all, Elizabeth." He took her hand and kissed it. "I have a feeling that my aunt has decided to introduce us to the *ton* tonight."

Elizabeth gasped. "Oh no, William, I am not ready for this."

He laughed hollowly. "Neither am I. And I have been doing this for years." Then seeing the very real fear in her eyes, he straightened. "We will endure this together, my love. You know by now how I hate being on display, so I beg your forgiveness now if I seem to retreat into myself. I am hopeful that with you by my side I will be better behaved than is my wont." She did not look at all reassured. He saw this and hurriedly added, "I have every faith in the world that you will be magnificent. You are beautiful tonight, and every time that I have seen you in company, you have always been captivating and much admired. I have no doubt of your absolute success." Caressing her worried brow he promised, "I will not leave you alone."

Relaxing a little with his reassurance, she caressed his face in return. "I promise that you will not be left alone either. At least you know that you are finally safe from matchmaking mamas and their conniving daughters!" She laughed at his brightened countenance.

"You always know how to make me feel better, Lizzy." He captured her lips in a fervent kiss.

Their fears for the evening were rapidly confirmed upon entering the house. They could hear the distant hum of many voices upstairs. Darcy looked at the old family butler, "Are we the last to arrive?" Upon receiving the confirmation, he and Elizabeth exchanged resigned glances, and holding hands, ascended the staircase. They heard the footman announce, "Mr. and Mrs. Fitzwilliam Darcy." A little thrill passed through both of them, hearing that for the first time, and despite their trepidation, they turned to each other and grinned. They stepped into the room, still smiling at each other, and all conversation ceased as they were observed with great interest. Their happy glowing faces told the story to everyone. It was a love match.

The mothers and their daughters worked to find fault in Elizabeth, and failed utterly. She was beautiful, her gown, although perhaps not of the finest modiste in town, fit well, the colour was lovely with her glowing complexion, and the rubies matched it perfectly. The men looked with great appreciation at her voluptuous figure and enticing lips and eyes. Darcy could not help but note their reactions, and stood with great pride with her on his arm, waiting for the approach of Lord and Lady Matlock.

"Elizabeth, Darcy! It is so wonderful to see you! Congratulations!" Lady Matlock immediately gave Elizabeth a kiss on the cheek.

Surprised, Elizabeth thanked her. "Lady Matlock, this is such a surprise, we were expecting a family dinner, not a public reception. It is so kind of you to arrange this for us."

She smiled. "I apologize, Elizabeth. I knew that if I told my nephew that I planned to introduce you to society tonight, he would not have come. But since you are leaving for Pemberley tomorrow, it is very important that you be seen now. Not just for your sake, but for Georgiana's as well. You must be acknowledged and accepted in the first circles. I have every faith that you will do very well tonight. You look lovely, my dear." Noting Elizabeth's blush she added. "You must know that your wedding has been the talk of the town. Everyone wants to know who captured Darcy's heart."

Elizabeth tilted her head and raised her brow. That was a statement guaranteed to raise her courage. "Well, I suppose that I will simply have to let them know me, will I not?"

"I knew that I was right about you, Elizabeth! Please call me Aunt Elaine."

"Thank you, I will." She looked up at Darcy, who was receiving a similar greeting from his uncle. He smiled seeing her confidence, and drawing from it, he relaxed. He was happy to hear of his aunt's full acceptance of her.

Lord Matlock turned and gave her a kiss on her hand. "Mrs. Darcy, how well that sounds! It has been a long time since my sister held that title. I am proud to see that such an outstanding woman has followed her. Welcome to the family, my dear." He added, "And following my dear wife's lead, I ask that you call me Uncle Henry."

Elizabeth beamed. "Thank you sir, I am delighted to join the Darcys and the Fitzwilliams. I am afraid that I am still not quite familiar with my new name, it still surprises me to hear it!" They all laughed.

Richard arrived with Georgiana on his arm. Darcy was delighted to see her. "William! I have missed you so much!" She kissed his cheek then turned to hug Elizabeth. "Oh Elizabeth! At last I have a sister!" She kissed her and exclaimed. "You look so beautiful! Are those mother's rubies, William?"

"Yes Georgie, they are. I could not wait to give them to Elizabeth." He smiled at her enthusiasm.

"They look lovely on you, Elizabeth!"

"Thank you Georgiana, I hope that you do not mind me wearing them."

"Oh no, Mother left me several things, but these jewels were always meant for William's wife."

"Georgie, I am surprised to see you invited to this party." Darcy said, looking to his aunt.

"I know that she is not out, Darcy. But she wanted to see you and greet Elizabeth. You will not see her again for quite some time. She will not be staying for dinner." Lady Matlock assured him.

"I am glad that I will not, William, all of these people are far too intimidating." Georgiana looked around the room nervously.

"I am afraid that next year, you will not have a choice." He looked to Elizabeth, "Fortunately, we both have someone to help us through these social obligations now." He smiled at her and kissed her hand.

She gave his arm a squeeze. "I will do my best, William, but tonight, I am afraid that I am just as nervous as Georgiana!"

"Congratulations Mrs. Darcy, welcome to the family!" Richard took her hand and bestowed a kiss. "We are looking forward to hearing the story of your wedding!"

Elizabeth looked at Darcy. They had not discussed just what their story would be. "Thank you Colonel, we will be happy to entertain you all with the details, but perhaps we will save that for your first visit to Pemberley." She looked at him pointedly.

He raised his brows and looked to Darcy, who stared at him just as fiercely. He smirked. "Well, I am sure that I and your children will enjoy hearing it over the years. I have a feeling that it will prove to be fascinating." He laughed at them exchanging glances. "Mrs. Darcy, now that we are family, I would like you to call me Richard."

She smiled. "Of course, and you must call me. . ." She looked at Darcy, who had a slight smile on his lips and a very warm glow in his eyes, "Elizabeth."

Richard looked between them. He knew that some sort of hidden communication had taken place, but had no idea what it was. Whatever it was, the newlyweds were now completely lost in their own world, gazing at each other. "I will be happy to do that, Elizabeth." Seeing no response he continued. "I say Darcy; married life does seem to agree with you!" Darcy did not take his eyes from hers and his smile widened to expose the hidden dimples. "It certainly does, Cousin."

Lady Matlock apologized for the absence of her eldest son Mark and his wife Laura. He was overseeing the spring planting at Matlock this year and had left London early. She then began ushering them around the room, making introductions. Elizabeth held her own, performing with an excellent combination of poise and humour to all. Even the ladies who were disappointed in their loss of Darcy gave her grudging respect. She was not accepted by all, but that would have been a miracle. Darcy could not have been more pleased. He did not speak often, allowing her to take the point. They exchanged smiles and glances frequently, and when they could, they removed themselves to corners away from people to laugh and compare notes. It was not until dinner was announced that they were forced to separate. Elizabeth and Darcy were on opposite sides of the table, seated close enough to see but not speak to one another. They both felt the distance keenly. Darcy realized her loss immediately, feeling his protective mask, which he had managed to keep off for most of the evening, coming over him. Elizabeth, much better in social situations and bearing the curious questions of her table mates with aplomb, watched him struggle, and wished so much to be able to sit beside him and hold his hand. The dinner itself was interminable. After nearly three hours, the ladies and gentlemen separated. During all of this time, Elizabeth and Darcy had watched each other, trying to think of ways to escape.

Darcy was sequestered with the gentlemen and was finding their conversation increasingly distasteful. It seemed that their greatest desire was to discuss his marital encounters with Elizabeth, and comment on her beauty. They were not even subtle about it. They knew he never had a mistress, and had not ever seen him visiting the brothels. They noticed that he was a silent listener during certain conversations at the clubs, but he never participated in them. Now they were relentless in their questioning and suggestions. His opinion of society, already rather poor, was declining rapidly. All he wanted to do was find his wife and go home.

Elizabeth was not faring much better. It seemed now that she was married, she was privy to conversations she never knew existed before. The ladies were all interested in her wedding night, and rushed to tell her their own experiences and reassure her that it would soon quiet down when her husband took up with a mistress and left her alone. They assured her that she would only have to tolerate his attentions until he had his heir. She tried to change the subject, but they simply would not let it go. Lady Matlock finally rescued her and brought her over to some more well-behaved women, who spoke of music and travel, but the evening, already stressful, had been ruined by the innuendo of the so-called quality. She hoped the men would return soon.

Elizabeth was standing with a group of women with her back to the door when she felt a large warm hand encompass hers, and a soft whisper in her ear. "Please Lizzy, tell me that you are weary and wish to go home." She gave the hand a firm squeeze, and turned. There was Darcy, a look of pleading in his deep, brown eyes.

She smiled, "I have been wishing for you to say that for hours." The look of relief in his face made her laugh. Together they sought out their hosts, and said farewell.

"You cannot leave so early!" Lady Matlock cried.

"Aunt, it is past midnight and we are travelling today. We must go. Remember, we did not know what this evening was going to be. If we had been told, we would have planned our trip differently. As it is, we must go."

Elizabeth turned to her. "It has been a lovely evening, and we thank you for the invitation, but truly we must be off. You will be bringing Georgiana to Matlock soon?"

Lady Matlock considered her for a moment and smiled at the young woman's determination to support her husband, "Yes, we will be there in about six weeks or so. We will write to you at Pemberley and let you know our plans. Then you can decide if you wish to come to retrieve her, or we will be happy to bring her to you, the estates are not far apart."

"That will be fine, Aunt Elaine." She nudged William.

"Yes, Aunt, thank you for looking after her, and now, goodnight." He bowed, shook his uncle's hand, nodded at Richard, who to his displeasure kissed Elizabeth's cheek, and they departed. When they finally entered the carriage, they both let out long breaths of relief.

"I can see why you have such a tremendous dislike of socializing, William. Are all dinner parties like that?"

"No, actually, that was one of the better experiences, I am sorry to say." He reached over and pulled her to him, and started nibbling on her neck. "I missed you tonight. I could see you, but I could not touch you, and it was torture."

"Mmm. All I wanted to do was to find a way to come to your side." She snuggled into his embrace.

"You certainly made a good impression on the men. All they wished to speak to me about was your comely beauty." He began running his hands over her arms and lifted her onto his lap.

"And what did you say?" She asked, now suckling his neck and stroking his chest.

"I told no secrets, my love." He whispered.

"I told none of you either." She whispered back.

"Do ladies speak of such things?" He asked with surprise.

She shook her head in disbelief. "Apparently they do, since I certainly had an earful of very unwanted advice and reassurance."

"Reassurance? Of what?"

"That you would end your attentions to me soon and find a mistress. Especially once I produce your heir."

"Lizzy! I hope that you did not listen to such rubbish!" He was truly upset. "You know that I would never do anything. . ."

"I know, my love, I know." She kissed him deeply. The carriage arrived at their home, and they swiftly went up the stairs and straight into Darcy's bedchamber.

ACROSS TOWN, George Wickham read a wedding announcement.

Mr. Fitzwilliam Darcy, son of the late Mr. George and Lady Anne Darcy, of Pemberley, Derbyshire and London is pleased to announce his marriage to Miss Elizabeth Bennet, daughter of Mr. and Mrs. Thomas Bennet, of Longbourn, Hertfordshire.

Thoughtfully, he folded his newspaper. It was time to formulate a new plan.

Chapter 22

"Mr. and Mrs. Darcy! Welcome to Netherfield!" Bingley proclaimed, happily bounding down the stairs as Darcy and Elizabeth exited their carriage.

They exchanged amused glances. "I told you!" He whispered in her ear. "Now you owe me my prize." He brushed his hand over her behind.

"William!" She whispered, her eyes flashing. "Remind me never to bet with you on the behaviour of your friends again!" She darted her hand out and quickly pinched his backside. He grinned in delight.

Bingley reached them and grabbed Darcy's hand, wringing it. "Darcy it is so good to see you smiling. Marriage suits you!" He turned to Elizabeth. "And Mrs. Darcy! You are radiant!" He took her hand and kissed it.

They both laughed as they entered the house. "Bingley if this is the reception that you give to visitors; you will be inundated with houseguests."

"Would you like to go up to your rooms or are you hungry?" He asked eagerly.

Darcy glanced around the hallway. "I am surprised that Miss Bingley is not here acting hostess."

"Ah, well, she decided to return to town and finish the Season. Louisa and Hurst are still here, though." Bingley's smile faded.

Concerned, Elizabeth asked, "Is something wrong, Charles?"

"No, no, my sister did not respond well to the news of your wedding, I am afraid."

"Oh, I. . ." She looked at Darcy who just had a small smile on his face.

"It is quite all right. Really." Bingley smiled at her. "It was something that she needed to learn sometime." He glanced up at Darcy who nodded.

Louisa entered the hallway. She decided that it was best to maintain a relationship with the couple. "Mr. and Mrs. Darcy, may I wish you joy?"

Elizabeth regarded her cautiously, but sensing sincerity, she smiled. "Thank you Mrs. Hurst, we are very happy."

Darcy, with a longer history of her incivilities to overcome, simply smiled slightly and nodded. "Thank you."

Charles cleared his throat. "Well, from what I understand, the grand celebration with the neighbours will be tomorrow night. Tonight we are invited for a family dinner. Jane will be coming here for a visit, and then we will all go to Longbourn. That will give you time to rest from your journey."

Darcy turned to Elizabeth, "Perhaps we *should* go and rest for awhile, we had little sleep after the party last night, and then you will be refreshed for Jane's arrival. I am sure that you have much to discuss." He gave her hand a squeeze.

"Yes, I think that is a good idea, William." She gave him a small smile.

"Shall I show you to your rooms?" Louisa offered.

"You go ahead, dear. I would like a word with Bingley first." Darcy kissed her hand. "I will not be long."

Elizabeth left with Louisa and Darcy followed Bingley to his study. They closed the door and settled into the leather chairs in front of the desk. "Tell me the situation at Longbourn."

"Well, Mr. Bennet has barely spoken since the wedding. For the first four days he took all of his meals in his library. He finally rejoined the family on Sunday to farewell Miss Lydia."

"Miss Lydia? Where is she?"

"She was invited to join her friend Mrs. Forster, the wife of Colonel Forster of the militia regiment that was stationed here all winter. They removed to Brighton. Mrs. Bennet said she would doubtless find a husband there since Jane and Elizabeth were so successful on their trip to London."

Darcy grimaced. "She is quite young, is she not?

"Fifteen I believe, but she is well-chaperoned."

Darcy thought of Georgiana. "If she is determined a chaperone will not matter. She impressed me as . . ."

"A bit out of control?"

"Young, pretty, fearless, a bad combination. I wonder what Elizabeth's reaction will be." He said thoughtfully.

"Jane thought that she would be unhappy."

"Which means that she will be incensed. Mr. Bennet. . ."

Bingley interrupted. "He has been fairly listless. I think that he just wanted peace. I think that the combination of Mrs. Bennet's and Miss Lydia's complaints drove his decision."

"Yes, I can understand that. Elizabeth told me that the reason she came to London in February was to escape her mother." He looked at Bingley. "Perhaps that is something that you should keep in mind if you decide to purchase this estate."

"You mean the proximity to my mother-in-law?" His lips twitched.

"Precisely." He stared at him pointedly.

"Derbyshire seems pleasant." Bingley smiled at his friend.

Darcy laughed. "I will see what is available. When is the wedding?"

"We are set for June 12th. Does that interfere with your travel plans?"

Darcy frowned. "It may. We may need to delay our trip to the Lake District until after your wedding."

"I am sorry Darcy." He said sincerely.

"No, I will speak to Elizabeth about it." His mind was elsewhere. "I believe that I will go join her now."

"I will show you to your rooms." Bingley jumped up and led the way upstairs. He showed him a door. "This is yours, and Elizabeth is the next door down. Of course, they do connect inside."

Darcy looked at the door, and then at Bingley, "Thank you Charles, but we really only need one room." He smiled broadly and disappeared inside. Bingley stood grinning at the closed door

Elizabeth had just settled into a bath when Darcy knocked. Rosie opened the door, and seeing his wife in the water, he dismissed her. Elizabeth smiled at him, watching him quickly disrobe. "What are you doing, sir?"

"I intend to share your bath." His coat, waistcoat, and cravat were gone, and he was pulling off his shirt.

"You will not fit in here with me!"

He sat on a nearby chair and pulled off his boots and stockings. "I beg to differ. I will fit quite nicely." He unbuttoned his breeches and was quickly undressed. Elizabeth eyed him appreciatively.

"Stand up please, sweetheart." He held out his hands to help her. She stood, soap running down her body. He stepped into the warm water and kissed her, and settling into the water, reached for her and reached for her. Settling onto his lap, she wrapped her arms around his neck. "See my love, we fit very well." Darcy held her, caressing her wet body, and they joined in a very passionate kiss. "Let me show you how well we fit together." He lifted her hips.

"What are you doing?" She asked breathlessly.

He grinned. "I have been thinking about this." He entered her and urged her to slowly lower herself.

"Ohhhh." She moaned.

"Yessss" He groaned back.

He dropped his head onto her shoulder and closed his eyes. They stayed clinging tightly for several minutes and then Elizabeth began to move very deliberately, learning what felt best. Her eyes closed as she became lost in her own world while water sloshed around them. Darcy watched the expression on her face, and ran his hands over her. She discovered the tempo she needed and moaning softly, she found her release. With him still embedded deep inside of her, she relaxed in his arms and opened her eyes to encounter his warm smile.

"What happened?"

He laughed. "You do not know yet?"

She started laughing too. "But you did not. . ."

He kissed her again. "I will, darling. Let us finish bathing first." Elizabeth stepped out of the tub to his protests and putting on her robe, knelt beside him, delighting in washing his body. She had some difficulty pouring water over his head, but she was determined and soon he declared himself clean. Darcy could not stop smiling as she carefully dried him off, and finally took the towel from her hands and tossing it aside, lifted her up and carried her to the bed.

Untying the belt of her robe he opened it and drew his hand over her warm skin. Elizabeth held out her arms for him. "Come."

"Oh Lizzy, I love you." He fell into her embrace and entered her, thrusting deeply and leading to a frenzied intense release that left them both gasping. With a sigh he cuddled her, and pulled the comforter over them. "I think that we should always bathe that way." He whispered; his voice still hoarse from the effort.

Elizabeth kissed his pounding heart and ran her fingers through his damp curls. "Only if we acquire a larger bathtub. That was a very snug fit!"

"*Very* snug." He smiled wickedly. "Just wait until you see our new bathtub at Pemberley."

She raised her brow. "And when was this bathtub purchased, Mr. Darcy?"

"I ordered it March 2nd."

"The day that you asked to court me?"

"The very day, my love." He replied, a little self-satisfied smirk on his face.

She shook her head, smiling. "Have you always been a romantic, William?

"I have never been inspired before. I was waiting for you."

"So sweet!" She kissed him soundly.

His eyes twinkled. "Like honey?"

"Like wine, mellow and warm."

"Mmmm. I like that. Thank you." He kissed her and they dozed.

Finally she turned and raised her head from his chest. "What did Charles tell you about Longbourn?" His arms wrapped around her and he told her of his conversation. He was correct, she was very unhappy about Lydia. "What were they thinking?" She sighed. "They were not, that is the problem."

He tilted his head and regarded her closely. "I remember you saying that your mother can be rather persuasive."

"Relentless is the word." She said dryly.

"Perhaps your father was not able to fend her off as usual."

She looked at him with surprise. "Because we married?"

"Perhaps because he realized his mistakes." He said thoughtfully.

"So he creates another one instead?"

Darcy smiled, running his fingers through her hair. "Let us hope for the best."

"Once again, you are playing at optimism, sir." She looked at him sternly.

He grinned. "Are you saying that you are a bad influence on me?"

She raised her brows. "Is this my fault?"

"Of course it is. You made me happy, which gave me hope, which in turn brings me an optimistic outlook." He pursed his lips, his eyes warm.

"There must be a flaw in that logic, somewhere. I will not be the cause of disappointed hopes when things go wrong."

His brows rose. "You would prefer me to be silent and taciturn?"

She stared into his eyes. "You *are* silent and taciturn, sir."

"Not like I was, and definitely not with you." He held her face in his hands and regarded her seriously.

"True." She kissed him. "I like you exactly the way you are."

His serious expression remained, "But I am trying to be a better man for you."

"I know you are, William, you have changed since we first met, and I appreciate it." They kissed, sharing their ardour. Eventually they forced themselves from their cosy nest, and readied to meet their family.

As expected, Jane's visit brought with it a rosy picture of Longbourn, which Elizabeth wisely chose to disregard, leaving the assessment of the situation to her own eyes. The family dinner would have been pleasant had it not been for the pervading tension felt between the two couples and Mr. Bennet. Other than a bow and brief greeting, the man remained silent. Elizabeth found herself actually welcoming her mother's effusions. Her father quickly left for his library after the meal, and Elizabeth finally allowed herself to relax, her hand firmly clasped in William's. Although the situation with her father was painful, she could not regret spending this short time drinking in the atmosphere of her family home. She expected the wedding celebration to be a far more pleasant experience. The addition of their friends and neighbours, as well as the expected duty to distract and relax her reticent husband, would keep her well-occupied.

"EXCUSE ME, Miss Darcy?" Georgiana and Lady Matlock turned at the sound of the warm voice. She looked up into the face of the most handsome man she had ever seen, and instantly blushed.

"Yes?" She said nervously.

"I thought that was you! It has been some time, I am afraid, and I can tell by the look on your face that you do not recognize me. I am Alex Carrington." Alex smiled down into her wide blue eyes, and felt a jump in his chest when she realized who he was and smiled widely at him.

"Mr. Carrington! I am so sorry that I did not immediately know you! It *has* been some time. But, I thought that you were in Hertfordshire? Did you not travel there with William and Elizabeth last week?"

"I was, but I finished my business early and returned to town." He looked at Lady Matlock, who was regarding him with suspicion. "May I ask the name of your companion?" He tried a disarming smile, which did not work.

"Oh, forgive me!" She turned to her aunt. "Mr. Carrington, this is my aunt, Lady Matlock. I am staying with her while William and Elizabeth take their honeymoon trip. Aunt, this is Mr. Alex Carrington, one of William's friends from Cambridge, and a friend of Elizabeth's and her sister Jane."

Alex bowed to the Lady, "It is a pleasure to meet you, madam."

Lady Matlock relaxed slightly. "Good afternoon, Mr. Carrington. It is always good to meet one of William's friends. I am surprised that you are so well acquainted with his wife and her sister."

"We were introduced at the theatre. I believe that you were in attendance that night. We then discovered some mutual acquaintances. I invited both ladies to the ball that my parents held some weeks ago." He turned back to Georgiana. "I am sorry that your brother did not ask you to attend, Miss Darcy."

"I am not yet out, sir." She said shyly, blushing again.

"Oh, forgive me; I was sure that you were. I remember Darcy talking about it last summer, and I thought that it was to happen this Season. Well, then you have much to look forward to!" Alex was embarrassed. She was younger than he thought, maybe too young? He tried to hide his disappointment, he found her absolutely lovely.

"I am not looking forward to it at all, sir." She confessed, but thought maybe it would not be too bad if men like he wished to dance with her.

"Well, you will have the help of your new sister when you do, and from what I have observed of Elizabeth, she will guide you with ease. She is a very confident woman."

"She certainly is." Lady Matlock decided that she liked this young man. He was not pushing himself on Georgiana, but he was clearly interested. "What is your estate, sir?"

Alex was ready for the questions. "Kingston Park, in Buckingham."

She nodded and went right to the point. "And who is to inherit?"

"I am; your ladyship. I am an only child." He hated being valued for his possessions, but knew the social processes well in the first circles.

She nodded again, "And what brings you into a lady's millinery shop this morning, sir?"

Confused by the change in topic, he recovered quickly and smiled, "I wished to buy a gift for my mother."

Lady Matlock liked that answer very much. "Well sir, I believe that any lady of quality would enjoy the selection on display in that corner." She directed his attention to some elegant hairpieces.

"Thank you, I will be sure to examine them." He turned to Georgiana. "Of course, I would appreciate a lady's opinion. Could you tell me which one you prefer, Miss Darcy?"

Georgiana blushed and chose a simple piece with long blue feathers. "This is lovely, Miss Darcy, I shall not look any further. Thank you for your assistance." He smiled at her, and looked to Lady Matlock, who nodded.

"It was my pleasure, sir." She whispered, entranced by his warm smile and twinkling eyes.

"Come Georgiana, we must be on our way. Mr. Carrington, it was a pleasure to meet you." She looked at him appraisingly. "Your mother's name is . . . ?"

"Mrs. Philip Carrington, we live in Grosvenor Square." He felt a rising appreciation for what was happening.

She looked him square in the eye. "Please tell her to send her card around to Matlock House. I receive visitors on Tuesday morning."

He smiled. "Yes, your ladyship. She will be honoured to pay a call."

They bid their farewells, and he watched Georgiana as she looked back at him through the glass. His heart was still pounding, and he was utterly bewitched by her eyes. Darcy's sister had grown up, and he found himself wanting to know everything about her. He wondered if he had just encountered his future wife. Then he laughed to himself, *Well why not? I am already Darcy's brother!*

"ELIZABETH?" Darcy tried again. She just was not talking to him. They had left Netherfield an hour before. She did not talk to him all night, and he learned that indeed, they did need two beds because he spent the last night decidedly alone. He allowed the pressure of the wedding celebration to take over his good sense and magnify his own intense emotions, resulting in an impulsive, disappointing reaction. He deserved her ire and kicked himself yet again. He wished so much that he had insisted on talking about it last night, before it became the silent impasse they now faced. He did not know what to do.

She stared out of the window. She was sick of men. She was sick of being a possession of men. Her father thought of her as his companion and sought to deny her a future to keep him company, and then last night during the wedding reception, when John Lucas called her Lizzy and talked about all of the adventures they had as children and the dances they attended when they were older, William became a jealous fool.

Elizabeth could not forgive his behaviour as easily as she did when he reacted to Richard's advances; this was just not the same situation, at least in her mind. Granted, part of it was her fault. She saw that he was becoming very quiet, and did not end the conversation sooner, but that did not signify when he pulled John into a corner and threatened him to stay away from *HIS* wife. She was mortified. Fortunately it was the end of the evening and John took the rebuke with grace. They soon left for Netherfield and nobody really noticed anything was wrong, except her father who was watching them closely all night. He appeared as if he wanted to say something to her, but did not.

She watched the scenery go by, and her anger faded, knowing that she needed to let this go. William was so hurt when she closed the door on his face. She heard him pacing in the next room all night, and she simply lay there, missing him. She was disappointed with herself and her own petulant reaction, as well as her failure to read his growing distress and respond to it. She tried to see his reflection in the glass. He was staring at her, as he always did. He was twisting his gloves in his hands. And his eyes were so sad. *What did Papa want to say?* He would probably tell her to let it go. A man's heart is very fragile, and William is deeply in love with her, and any threat, real or perceived would make him act like a possessive fool. She sighed and agreed with her fantasy father, she should never have rejected him last night. They should have talked about it. She turned around and looked at him.

"I am sorry, Elizabeth." He immediately spoke, still twisting his gloves. "I do not know what came over me."

She rescued the mangled leather and took his hands in hers, and could see the relief crossing his face. "I am sorry, too, William. I should never have let him go on about our past."

"It is just the thought of you with anyone else just makes me . . ." He searched for a word that would describe the way his heart twisted hearing her laugh about dancing with the man, "absolutely insane."

"And I would feel the same way hearing about you doing anything with another woman." She smiled at him, stroking his face. "What upset me is the highhanded way that you dealt with your jealousy. I felt nothing more than your possession. I was not sure if it was your pride that was hurt, knowing that I ever danced with another man, or if you were afraid that I still liked him."

"Probably a little of both." He admitted.

She tried to reassure him. "I liked him because he was a nice man, and a playmate from childhood, nothing more. I never saw anything else in our friendship. I cannot speak for him, but I can say that he never tried to court me."

"But he was away at school, probably now that he is home, he would have tried." He began to imagine the worst.

"Well, we will never know that will we? I seem to recall marrying someone not too long ago." She smiled into his brightening face.

"That is correct! You did!" He smiled and kissed her cheek. "You married me!"

"Yes, so maybe you would do well to remember that the next time that you feel irrationally jealous, and behave accordingly. Perhaps you should talk to me about it first before you. . ."

"Act like an overbearing fool? I am sorry. Please forgive me?"

"I do, darling, if you will forgive me for letting it go on as long as I did, and for acting like a spoiled child last night by not talking to you about it. I never wish to spend another night without you by my side, especially for such a silly reason."

Caressing her cheek, he nodded, "Agreed, dear. I do love you so much, Lizzy."

"I love you my sweet William." She snuggled gratefully into his embrace, and soon the carriage lulled them to recapture the sleep they had missed.

Chapter 23

"When should we arrive?" Elizabeth asked, nestling against Darcy's chest and preventing him from reading his book.

He looked at her, and smiled wryly while he closed it. "Late this afternoon, perhaps around four o'clock." He stroked her back. "You know Lizzy, you remind me of a cat I once knew."

She smiled, "Because I purr?"

"Well you do make lovely noises at certain moments, but I meant that every time I try to read, you are in my lap."

"Do you object, sir? I could move."

"I will bear with it, my love." He started tickling her belly until she squealed and batted his hand away. He laughed, and speaking seriously, caressed her hair, "You have not said anything about your father since we left Longbourn."

She sat up and leaned her head against the back of the carriage seat. "I do not know what to say. He looked terribly lonesome, and when he talked, he seemed to be trying too hard."

"I think that we all felt that to some extent. It was hard to think of civil conversation after the accusations he threw at me. It took a great deal for me to publicly forgive him of that, and I remain highly offended for his behaviour towards me, but more so for his behaviour towards you. For someone who claims to love you so much, he certainly failed to prove it." He entwined his fingers with hers.

She sighed, looking down at their hands. "Yes, I know. I think that he wanted to apologize for it, but the problem is that this was not a single incident. He must have felt this way for years, and now he must realize his error in behaviour."

"Perhaps it will be easier to communicate through letters for a while, without the pressure of actually being in each other's company." He raised their hands to his lips and tenderly kissed hers. "I know how much you love him, Elizabeth. Until he spoke to you about our courtship, I heard nothing but admiration and regard in your description of him. I hate for that to end. Even when I felt completely neglected by my own father, I loved him, and I would not have given up that relationship for anything. Maybe that is why I tried so hard to please him." He shook his head. "My relationship with your father is short and painful, but you have a lifetime with him. If he shows signs of accepting our marriage and attempting to be a part of our lives, we should allow him in. I admit, I will take a great deal of convincing, and I doubt that I will ever be close to him, but I know that you will regret it if you do not try."

"I suppose only time will tell. I believe that I am as offended on your behalf as you are on mine, but I truly do appreciate your willingness to try." She gave him a small smile, and he returned it while gently caressing her face. "I will write to him when we arrive, and see if he responds."

"That will be a good start." They sat silently embraced for a while, then he looked down at her pensive face. "What did Jane ask you about in the garden? She was crimson when you came back into the house."

Elizabeth smiled up at him; the devil was in her eyes. "She was asking for advice."

He raised his brow. "About what, may I ask?"

She laughed. "Her wedding night!"

Darcy grinned broadly. "And what did you tell her?"

"I am certainly not going to tell you!"

He stared down at her with his brows raised. "Why not? You probably talked about me. Do I not have a right to know?"

"No sir, you do not. Besides, you will just tell Charles about it, and do not claim otherwise!" She accused, poking a finger in his chest.

"Maybe." He tilted his head and looked at her, and whispered warmly in her ear. "What did you say?"

"I said it was wonderful and she had nothing to worry about." She whispered back.

He smiled happily. "Thank you." She giggled. "Was she convinced?"

"Her face was red, was it not?"

They stopped to eat and rest the horses, and they both settled down to read for several hours, Elizabeth curled next to him, he with his arm around her. Finally, the carriage made a turn into a smooth drive. A man in uniform was standing outside of a small house, and waved at the coach while moving to open the heavy iron gate. "Welcome to Pemberley, Elizabeth." He turned to her and smiled.

She sat up, her eyes wide, taking in the surroundings. "Where is the house, William? All I see are trees."

"I am afraid that is all you will see for some time, my love; we have quite a way to go. We will have a good view of the house after we climb the hill, and I asked the driver to pause there." He moved to wrap his arm around her and eagerly pointed out the sights, and watched for her reaction. When the carriage did stop and she saw the magnificent house below, her gasp made his chest swell. "Do you like it, darling? Are you happy this will be our home?"

Elizabeth stared out of the carriage window. She was wholly unprepared for the majesty of what lay before her. "Oh William, I have tried to imagine it from your descriptions, but I never came close to creating such a vision in my mind! It is so very lovely!" She turned to him, her eyes bright. "I cannot believe that you chose me to come live in such a glorious place." She returned to the window, a sudden overwhelming sense of peace coming over her.

He gently placed his fingers under her chin and turned her head back to him. "This place has needed you for a very long time, Elizabeth. Now it will be a home again." He kissed her deeply. They stared into each other's eyes, both feeling something changing between them. He rapped the ceiling and the carriage moved on, winding down the drive, until it finally came to a rest in the courtyard where the assembled staff waited.

"Oh dear, how will I ever remember their names?" She whispered, looking at them. "Is this the entire staff?" Her eyes swept over them and then she looked at William. All of these people were dependent on her husband's good will. He glanced at the eager curious faces in the crowd.

"No, not quite, but it is a good many of them." He gave her hand a squeeze. "I will introduce you to our housekeeper, if you know her, you will be fine."

The coach door opened, and Darcy descended. He turned and handed her out, smiling warmly at her, and tucked her trembling hand in his arm. They walked up to an older woman who was looking at Darcy with teary eyes while simultaneously assessing Elizabeth.

Darcy stopped and smiled at the crowd. "Please join me in welcoming the new Mistress of Pemberley, Mrs. Elizabeth Darcy." He scooped her up in his arms and carried her up the steps to the cheers of the servants.

Elizabeth hid her face in his shoulder, blushing brightly. "William!" He laughed with joy.

They entered the beautiful house, and he introduced her to Mrs. Reynolds. Elizabeth insisted that he set her down, and she addressed her. "I am very pleased to meet you, Mrs. Reynolds. Mr. Darcy has spoken very highly of you, as has Mrs. Harris at Darcy House. I am looking forward to spending time with you learning my duties as Mistress. I hope that I can count on your help to make Pemberley the home of which our family will be proud."

Mrs. Reynolds regarded the small woman in front of her. She was not what she expected. This seemed to be a very sincere, straightforward woman, who had only the best interests of her family in mind. The letters she received from Mrs. Harris gave her hope that Mr. Darcy had chosen well. She was deeply relieved that he had not chosen a lady of society like that Miss Bingley who was always hanging on to him. When the marriage took place, she was concerned about its sudden nature, and worried that he had been compromised. But the glow in his eyes and the smile that she had not witnessed since he was a child was testament enough. He loved this woman. She made her decision. If Mr. Darcy loved her, she would do everything possible to make her the best Mistress Pemberley ever had. "Yes, Mrs. Darcy. It will be a pleasure to guide you through everything. I am delighted to see the Master finally settled."

"As am I, Mrs. Reynolds." He smiled, then bending down to take his protesting Elizabeth back into his arms, he carried her up the stairs.

"RICHARD, do you know Darcy's travel plans?" Lord Matlock asked. He was sitting at his desk, absent-mindedly turning a ribbon-tied bundle in his hands. Richard leaned on the doorframe to his father's study. "I imagine they are at Pemberley by now. I think that they were to stay there some weeks before going to the cottage, why?" His father shrugged. "It is not important. I simply need to send him a letter, and wish to be sure of his being home when it arrives."

"Well, if you were to send it now, it would be fine."

"Hmm." Lord Matlock continued playing with the envelope.

"Father? Is something wrong?" Richard regarded him with concern.

Startled, Lord Matlock looked up. "What was that, Son? Something wrong, no, no, not exactly." He sighed. "I have a duty to perform, that I wish I did not. I do not wish to spoil. . ." He stopped. Shaking his head, he gave Richard a grim smile.

"Father. . ." Richard came to sit on the edge of a chair in front of the desk. He leaned forward with his elbows on his knees. "Something is wrong." He fixed his piercing gaze on him. "What is it?"

Lord Matlock drew himself up. "I am sorry; it is an issue between Darcy and his father. I can say no more at this time." He took the parcel and placed it in a drawer of his desk and decidedly locked it. Then, looking back at his son, he said. "Richard, how did Anne appear to you when you were visiting Rosings?"

"Anne?" He asked, surprised by the sudden change of topic. "The same as usual, I suppose, although after her confrontation with Aunt Catherine, she seemed very tired."

"I received a note from Catherine this morning. It seems that Anne's health is deteriorating rapidly." Lord Matlock looked grim. "It is feared that she may not have long to live." He stared into his son's eyes, and saw all manner of emotion playing in them. "You now know that you shall inherit Rosings. I think that you should be prepared to leave the army soon."

"Father, I do not think that we should presume anything. Anne has had setbacks before and come back from them." He spoke quickly; thousands of thoughts were flying through his mind.

"Yes, but you should be prepared. I know that you cannot speak of it, but I have heard the rumours of the army deploying more troops to the continent. If you feel that you are likely to go soon, I would prefer you to resign your commission and stay here."

"And wait like a vulture for Anne to die?" He said with disgust.

"I would not put it that way, Son. But I would prefer that to seeing you sent to possibly your own demise needlessly when your future is soon to be secured, safely, here at home." Lord Matlock looked at his son beseechingly. "Please keep this in mind over the coming weeks. I will gladly support you in the meantime if it guarantees your safety."

Overwhelmed, Richard stood and shook his father's hand. "I will do that, sir, and thank you."

DARCY AND ELIZABETH reluctantly agreed that they must delay their honeymoon trip to the Lake District due to the timing of Jane and Bingley's wedding. They had no desire to rush their journey. Instead, he told his steward, Mr. Regar, that he was to be considered not at home for one week, and then he would return to his duties, supervising the planting and the shearing of the sheep. He steadfastly refused to enter his study and forced himself to ignore the growing pile of paperwork on his desk. Likewise, Elizabeth was not to begin the lessons on her duties as Mistress until he returned to work. This time was to be their own.

They spent their week in glorious solitude. Taking long walks, Darcy showed her his favourite path by the lake, and the flower gardens designed by the past Mistresses of Pemberley. He took great delight in presenting her with a gentle mare, and enhanced her rather poor equestrian education. He was excited to see that other than some wariness, she took to riding like a duck to water. He thought with anticipation of all the remote parts of the estate where they could go and enjoy each other's particular company once she was a little more proficient.

There simply were not enough hours in the day to do everything. And he did want to do everything. He was like an excited boy dragging her everywhere to show her parts of the house he loved, trees he had fallen from, views he admired, and the locations of special memories. All the while, Elizabeth held his hand and laughed at him with her sparkling eyes and made him feel, oh, so very alive. He loved Pemberley, but for so many years it had also been a place of such loneliness.

Now next to him was his best friend, the companion, the confidant he had always wished for. He began to see Elizabeth in a different light, now more than simply the bewitching, challenging, fascinating woman who so instantly captivated him. Here at his, their, home, with her by his side, he saw his future and the partner he needed.

Throughout the week, Elizabeth carefully observed everything around her. William took her on a ride in a curricle one day, and showed her a portion of the pastures and farmland, and some of the tenants' homes. She was impressed with the obvious pride the residents had in their homes, and the obvious care that William took in assuring their comfort. She asked, jokingly, if he was a good landlord, and he met her smiling eyes very seriously, and told her that if his tenants give him their hard work and rent for Pemberley's benefit, was it not right that he should ensure that they lived in comfortable circumstances?

He went on to describe how his mother used to visit the homes of the tenants, and that while he could not personally spare the time, he always made sure that if they were in need during an illness or some other crisis, his steward would provide what was required to help them. Elizabeth smiled, admiring him. He told her that without these people, Pemberley would not be the great estate it was. She told him that she would like to take up his mother's work again and was overwhelmed with the pride she saw in his eyes for her. Being at Pemberley, she was now seeing where his life truly was, and was gaining a sense of him she could not have known until she saw him there. She already loved him dearly, but it was growing beyond the giddiness and joy of their first few months and into a feeling of steadfastness and respect. She wished to be by his side in everything.

On their last day of their self-imposed solitude, they packed a picnic and mounted their horses. Darcy led the way to a meadow, already colourful with the wildflowers of spring. There they lay barefoot on a blanket overlooking a breathtaking view of the valley. Elizabeth sat with her legs stretched in front of her and Darcy lay with his head on her lap, clad only in his shirt and breeches and looking up to her smiling face.

Elizabeth idly ran her fingers through his hair. "Are you happy, William?"

He reached up and pulled the single pink ribbon from her hair, and watched as the wind began to blow her loosened locks gently around her "Oh yes, Lizzy. I am so very happy." His smile was warm and relaxed. "Are you happy, my love?"

She moved so that she lay alongside him and touched her nose to his. "Not even in my most optimistic imaginings could I have created the dream of you or this magical place." She kissed him gently. "Not so long before we met, I had almost resigned myself to a life of loneliness and disappointment. I cannot express to you what your love has done to and for me."

"Lizzy, I feel the same way about you. I had nearly given up the hope of marrying anyone at all, until you smiled at me." He twisted his fingers in a long curl. "Come here." He whispered and drew her close. With his right hand gently stroking her face, he began kissing her mouth with soft caresses; tenderly tracing her lips with his tongue.

He drew back and gazed down at her flushed face. She reached up and affectionately touched his cheek. "I have seen now how you love this place William; surely if you had not met me you would have married another. You would wish your own child to someday continue what you and your forefathers began."

He turned his face to kiss her palm and sighed. "I would hope that somehow, someway, we would have met, my love. I truly believe we were destined for each other." She smiled at his confidence, stroking back the hair that fell across his face as he bent towards her. His eyes closed. "I set myself a deadline. I gave myself until thirty to fall in love, and then . . ." He opened his eyes and looked deeply into hers, then unable to continue, he pulled her up into his embrace and began kissing her with the fervency that his intense emotion demanded.

She returned his kisses, and held him to her. She realized that he would have sacrificed his happiness for Pemberley, and it made her proud and sad at the same time. "Your uncle would not have let you give up, William." She whispered.

He laughed softly. "I hope not, but I am overjoyed that I never will have to find out." He began pulling the pins from her hair, and she watched his face as he concentrated on his work.

"What are you doing, sir?" She raised her brow and smiled. He kissed her and smiled back, saying nothing. Finally her long curls were free, and he ran his fingers through her hair, watching the play of sunlight make it glow and shine.

Elizabeth ran her hands over his back and began tugging his shirt from his breeches. He was soon awash with the sensation of her small sweet hands moving over his chest. "I love when you touch me like that." He moaned.

"I know." She whispered back.

He rolled her onto her back and bent over her, lifting her skirt and petticoat, while she worked to unbutton his breeches. Their kisses rapidly escalated from gentle caresses to a frantic exchange, and soon their bodies joined in a frenzied expression of their love.

Darcy rolled to his side, bringing Elizabeth with him. Neither was capable of speaking, breathing at a normal rate was the goal. After some time to recover, Darcy opened his eyes to see Elizabeth nose to nose with him and smiling.

He drew back a little. "I realize that I could lay here thinking that the satisfied grin on your face is entirely due to me, but I think that I know better." He brushed her hair from her face and rested his head on his hand. "So tell me, Mrs. Darcy, what precisely is on your mind?"

Elizabeth laughed, loving how good it felt to make him happy. "I was just thinking, Mr. Darcy, for such a serious and taciturn man, when you decide to relax, you are quite invigorating."

He chuckled. "Do you mean that I excite you, my dear?"

"Most definitely." She nodded her head enthusiastically.

"And you enjoy the exercise?" He asked, grinning.

She lifted her chin. "I find it exceedingly pleasurable."

Darcy combed his fingers through her hair and spoke softly, "I am so very pleased."

Enjoying his touch, she murmured, "Mmmm. William?"

"Yes, my love?" He said, watching the flow of the tresses through his fingers and swearing to himself that he would never tolerate his wife wearing a white cap.

"Would you care to be pleased again?" His fingers ceased their ministrations and his eyes lit up. His dazzling smile as he reached for her answered the question.

THE NEXT MORNING, the newlyweds reluctantly rose from their bed, and resigned themselves to returning to reality. They enjoyed breakfast together and unhappily separated. Darcy went to his study, and Elizabeth went to the capable hands of Mrs. Reynolds. They sadly knew that they would be apart for hours.

The enormous pile of correspondence awaiting his attention forced a loud groan from Darcy. He picked up a letter and let it drop back onto his desk. "I suppose the honeymoon is truly over now."

Never one to shirk responsibility, he resolutely sat down, determined to at least sort through everything. Nothing caught his eye until he saw a parcel from Uncle Henry. Curious, he set everything else aside. Breaking it open, he found a single sheet enveloping another letter.

May 15, 1811
Matlock House
London

Dear Darcy,
I hope that your honeymoon was everything you hoped for. Elizabeth is an exceptional woman and we are delighted that you found each other.
Your father left this letter to be delivered to you upon your marriage. I know its contents, and will be happy to discuss it with you if you wish.
Affectionately yours,
Uncle Henry

He picked up the thick letter, and regarded it with knit brows. He examined his father's old seal, and taking a breath, broke it.

April 24, 1803
Pemberley, Derbyshire

Dear Fitzwilliam,
I must begin this letter by telling you how very proud I am of you and how very much I love you. I have watched you grow, learning with such intensity your duties as the future Master of Pemberley. Your dedication to your duty and family is more than any father could hope for.
If you are reading this letter, you have recently married, and I have finally, thankfully, joined my dear Anne in peace. I hope with all of my heart that you have married for love, and that your wife returns it to you. Your uncle has promised me to look after you, and guide you away from a marriage of convenience. You were born with your mother's loving heart and I wish you a wife who will give you the joy that your dear mother gave me for fourteen wonderful years.
I have recently learned from my doctor that I am dying. That is no surprise because in truth, I have been dying since Anne left us. You have borne the brunt of my despair, Son, and for this I sincerely apologize. Where your mother gave you the ability to love deeply, I gave you your devotion to duty, family, and honour. Son, believe me, I saw how you threw yourself into your studies, and how you mastered all of the requirements to oversee Pemberley and its dependents. I saw it all. I know that you sought my approval and appreciation, but that I rarely showed

it to you. Believe me when I say you always had it. I was proud of every accomplishment, and loved you dearly. Now I shall finally tell you why I could not bring myself to express my feelings to you. I am ashamed that I do not have the courage to say this to you now, when I am alive and you could question me, but I just do not have the strength to bear your pain and anger. I cannot stand to hurt you again, my only son.

Two and twenty years ago, before I met your mother, I was a typical young man of the first circles. My father was alive, and I had no responsibility. I enjoyed the society and the favours of women. I thought nothing of it. I can see you now Son, staring at this letter in disbelief, thinking me a hypocrite after my charge that you remain celibate until marriage.

After the harvest that year, at the annual celebration, I was well in my cups and a pretty young girl offered herself to me. It is not an excuse, it is simply what happened. I make no excuses. I later learned that the young lady was to be married to my father's steward, Mr. Wickham. I was stunned to learn soon after the wedding that she was with child. I believed that child, George Wickham, to be mine.

I watched the boy grow, thinking that but for the circumstances of his birth, he would be my heir. I became his godfather so that I could watch over him. I married your mother, and soon you were born. I was so proud the day that your mother gave me the gift of you.

I harboured the hope that he was not my son and looked for differences between the two of you. You were both tall and dark, like me, like Wickham, so I could determine nothing from that. Where you had your mother's sweetness and the Darcy mannerisms, he showed no resemblance. He was wild and uncontrollable; his behaviour was always cruel and selfish. I saw what he did to you, Son, and did nothing to correct him. I saw that you were a lonely boy seeking a friend, and he was jealous. I tried to make up for the presumed loss of his birthright by giving him my attention, a gentleman's education, and you now know that I provided for his future in my will. The one thing I never gave him was my love, I could not. My guilt, his behaviour, and my hope that he was not mine prevented it.

I was so happy that I had you as my heir. You proved consistently that you were the better man, and I felt guilty for feeling that way when the man I thought was my first son, the one who I thought was deprived of his birthright by my failure to acknowledge him, was proving to be so unworthy.

Then, a month ago, Wickham and I were reminiscing about our courtships. Wickham revealed to me that he had to marry his wife, that they had indulged in a tryst, and that she was with child. I learned that she was already with child the night of the harvest ball. I realized that I was not George Wickham's father. Thank God I never moved to acknowledge him. For twenty years, I have deprived you of the father you deserved while wallowing in self-pity. I hope that you will forgive me, Son. Now you may understand why I begged you to remain celibate until marriage. I did not want you to live the torture that I have. I vow to spend the rest of my days giving you my undivided attention and love. It may be too late, but I will try. I want you to know that I have always loved you, and you were the only one I ever called Son.

Please forgive me, Fitzwilliam. My confused, selfish, irrational behaviour deprived both of us a relationship that I know we both needed and desired. I pray that your children will have the joy of knowing their father as dearly as I wish you had known me. I wish you a long, happy life with your wonderful wife. I know that if you love her, your mother and I would have as well.

Your loving father,

George Darcy

When Elizabeth entered the study several hours later, she found Darcy leaning on the window frame staring unseeing at the view. She asked what was wrong, and he silently handed her the letter. Finishing it, she embraced him. After a long time, he gently pushed her away and asked her to leave him to his thoughts. He would see her when he was ready to sleep. Although she was unhappy with his withdrawal, she respected his request and with a whispered declaration of her love, left the room.

DARCY SAT ALONE in his study, the pages of his father's letter fallen from his grasp, and now scattered on the floor at his feet. He understood so many things now, but knowing the reasons did not make it any easier to bear. Suddenly he was a young boy again, feeling so alone, and unable to understand why his father did not seem to love him.

The touch of Elizabeth's soft hand wiping the tears from his face finally brought him back to the present. She had recovered the scattered sheets, and folded them together. She gently kissed his cheek, and bringing her face close to his smiled softly into his eyes. "Come, my love." Wordlessly, he responded to the slight tug of her hand on his. He rose and they quietly ascended the stairs to their bedchamber.

When Elizabeth closed the door behind them, he clutched her to him tightly. His body wracked with silent sobs, releasing the pain of the past while holding tightly to his future. He realized then that he should not have pushed her away, and was grateful that she came to him. When he finally calmed, Elizabeth helped him to undress and soon they were naked, lying in each other's arms. Darcy started to kiss her, and pulling away, she smiled and placed her hand over his mouth.

"What is wrong?"

"Absolutely nothing. I want you to lay back and relax." She stroked his face and ran her fingers through his hair.

"I need you, Lizzy," he plead.

"I know." She pressed him back onto the pillows, and lay on top of him. Automatically, his arms came around her. She gently kissed his lips, and very slowly touched her tongue with his, allowing them to dance together until she heard him groan. She then dragged her mouth, her lips slightly parted, over his face, her warm breath making his skin tingle. She moved on and languorously nibbled his neck below his ear, and made her way to his shoulders.

"What are you doing?" He moaned.

"Loving you." She whispered.

She now added her gliding fingertips to the trace of her lips and mouth as she worked her way down his chest. When she reached his nipples, she drew them into her mouth while bringing his aroused manhood to rest in the warm valley between her breasts. She gently rocked her chest, allowing him to glide smoothly between her softness. She ran her fingers, barely touching, down his sides, and he dropped his head back, "Oh God, Lizzy. . ."

She moved on, now brushing her face over his arousal, her fingers stroking, feather light, his thighs, his calves, and finally suckling his toes.

Darcy was in such a state of heightened arousal he could barely register a coherent thought. His hands were balled into fists at his sides. His body was reacting with tremors and quaking under her gentle assault. When she slowly worked her way back up and took him into her burning mouth he nearly sat upright. She mimicked the movement of his thrusting with her mouth, her tongue never ceasing its torturous pleasure around and over him. Finally, she pulled away and lay completely on top of his body and allowed him to wrap his arms around her again. Their mouths met in a passionate, hungry kiss. Darcy rolled her over and without hesitation entered her fully. Their bodies rocked together, moving in a steady, unhurried rhythm, both moaning, both straining to be as close together as possible. Elizabeth reached her peak and the arching of her back and the call of his name pushed him finally to his shuddering release.

Their bodies remained entwined, as slowly they regained their equilibrium. He softly kissed her swollen lips, and gazing into her eyes, moved a fallen lock of hair from her face, "I shall always love you, Elizabeth Darcy."

She caressed his cheek, "And you shall always be my love, William Darcy. You will never be alone again." They turned, spooning in a lover's embrace.

"Thank you." He whispered, so overwhelmed that she wanted him, and so thankful that she loved him. He held onto his anchor and slept.

Chapter 24

lizabeth awoke to the sensation of a large hand caressing her hair. She opened her eyes and was met with the gaze of her husband, a look of sadness in his soft brown eyes. She touched his hair, entwining her fingers in his curls. "Good morning, love." She whispered.

"Good morning, my Lizzy." He whispered back.

She touched his face. "What are you thinking about?"

"The past." He said, looking down and pressing his lips together.

She wrapped her arms around him. "Would you like to talk about it?"

"Not yet." He buried his face in her hair, allowing the scent to surround him. "I think that I will go for a ride this morning."

"Shall I go with you?"

He laughed lightly. "You are learning my love, but for the ride I need today, I am afraid that you are not quite prepared."

She looked up at him. "You are not going to do anything foolish are you, William? You will not risk yourself to ride away from the devil that is on your mind, will you?" She was concerned. She had heard stories from Richard of his wild rides when he was upset with something, occasionally causing injury.

He hugged her tightly to him. "I promise I will come back to you in one piece. Then we will talk." He kissed her. "I just need to . . ." He sighed. "I cannot put it into words yet."

"I think that I understand. I often have taken a long walk to just put things in perspective." She touched his lips. "I think that I will do that this morning while you ride."

Now *he* was concerned. "You will not go too far, will you? You do not really know the estate very well yet."

She smiled. "I will keep to the path by the lake. Will that be safe enough for you?"

He relaxed. "Yes, now I will not worry as much. Perhaps you should take a footman with you."

"William, I spent how many years wandering around Hertfordshire alone? Surely I am safe on our own land?"

"I am just afraid."

"Of what?"

"Losing you."

Elizabeth kissed him and they held each other tightly. "You are stuck with me, William. You will just have to live with that fact." He sighed as she ran her fingers down his sides. "Perhaps we can enjoy that enormous bathtub when we return. I think that we will both need it!"

He pulled away and smiled at her. "You always make me feel better, Lizzy."

AFTER A QUICK BREAKFAST, Darcy left to take his ride. Elizabeth dressed and went downstairs, and was met by Mrs. Reynolds. "Oh, Mrs. Darcy, the post just came. You have several letters. I left them on your desk."

"Thank you, Mrs. Reynolds. I am going to take a walk on the lake path if anyone is looking for me." She left to collect her letters. There were three, one each from Jane, Mr. Bennet, and Lydia.

She set off on the long path. Finding a convenient bench, she sat down to read her letters. Jane's was full of news on their wedding plans. She seemed to think that Charles would have preferred to follow Elizabeth and Darcy's route to matrimony. She laughed. Her father's letter was short, but at least he was civil. He was trying hard to make amends, and his note was full of questions about her life. She was still trying to understand him, and was trying to find a new relationship with him. Lydia's letter was fascinating. She was her usual outrageous self, but then she wrote something that made Elizabeth sit up with surprise.

You will never believe it! I was looking in a ribbon shop and behind me I heard a voice saying my name. I turned around, and who could it be but Mr. Wickham! Well, he was as handsome as ever, and I smiled and said hello. Lizzy, he looked me up and down like he wanted to eat me! He even said that he thought that I was as sweet as ever, and that he missed me after he left Meryton. We went for a walk, and he kept telling me how pretty I was, and of course, I liked it, but you know, I have been getting rather close with Mr. Denny during my visit here, and I started to feel that maybe I should not be walking with Mr. Wickham. Then he said that he heard that you had married Mr. Darcy, and he asked me all kinds of questions about you. He does not seem to like Mr. Darcy very much, at all. I do not know why, he is nice when you can get him to talk, and if you like him, it is all that matters, he is rich after all. Anyway, he said that he would like to visit you soon and wish you joy, which does not make sense if he dislikes Mr. Darcy, does it? Then he pulled me behind a building and pressed me against the wall and started kissing me! I liked being kissed, but then I remembered that he did the same thing to you! That makes him a cad does it not? And Mr. Denny would not like it at all, so I told him to stop it, but he just pressed on me harder. So then I remembered what you did to him, Lizzy! I kicked my knee up onto him, and he screamed with pain! He rolled on the ground! Oh what a joke! Mr. Denny happened to walk by and saw him on the ground and asked me what happened. Of course I told him, and he got so angry at Mr. Wickham! He went to his colonel, and I think that he has been released from the militia!

Mr. Denny asked me to marry him the next day. I shall be Mrs. Denny! Does that not sound well? I cannot wait to tell Mama! But I will wait until I get home for Jane's wedding. So do not tell her! I want to see the look on her face!

Elizabeth sat with her mouth agape. So much information in one letter! Lydia engaged to Mr. Denny, well that is a good match. She will have her man in a red coat, and he was not a bad man, they had spent many months together in Meryton, so they had time to know one another. He would do well to tame her wild sister. But the news of Mr. Wickham was incredible! She thought of Lydia kicking him in the groin and laughed, she must be sure to teach that to her daughters someday!

Rereading the letter, she began to wonder, why would Mr. Wickham be so interested in her marrying William? And would he really come here to wish us well? For what purpose? After the shock of George Darcy's letter, and reopening all the old wounds, she could not begin to imagine what William's reaction would be. Whatever Wickham's reasons, they would not be performed out of kindness or a desire for reconciliation.

She folded her letters and slipped them under the sash of her gown. Taking off her bonnet, she hooked it over her arm and started down the path by the lake, soon disappearing into the trees. She walked for almost a half hour, and had reached the area where one side of the path was forested, and the other opened onto a deep ravine, containing the stream which flowed from the now distant lake. The woods were silent except for the occasional bird call, when she heard the crack of a twig. She looked around and was confronted with the leering face of George Wickham.

"Good morning, Mrs. Darcy, I have come to deliver my sincere congratulations."

When Elizabeth tried to scream, he grabbed her, stuffing her mouth with a handkerchief. He then pushed her onto the ground, quickly binding her wrists, and remembering too well the power of her knees, he bound her ankles together. Elizabeth struggled and twisted, trying to work the handkerchief out. Wickham saw it and struck her across the face with his palm, then took another length of cloth and tied it firmly around her mouth.

Finally he sat back on his heels, still on top of her. He looked into her terrified eyes and laughed. "Now I believe that we must continue that conversation we were having in Meryton, Mrs. Darcy." He leaned down and licked her cheek, while roughly squeezing her breasts. "You did not listen to me; you went and married my old friend Darcy." She struggled. "Did you know that your Papa wrote to me asking for my help in breaking your attachment? I missed out on a potentially profitable exercise when you married. I was vastly disappointed. Perhaps this situation is even better." He whispered hotly in her ear. "Let us see how much you are worth to him."

He began rubbing his arousal over her and kissing her neck. He stank of sweat and alcohol. "I was determined to find you after I met your sweet sister Lydia in Brighton. We had a very intimate conversation as well." Raising her skirt, he grinned at the revelation, and stroked her thighs. "A pity that your legs are bound. Well, no matter, we will get to know each other much better later. I must pay you back for the blow you delivered to me," he promised as he fingered her core, his eyes dark with lust. "I enjoyed watching your tryst with Darcy in the meadow. I never knew he had it in him." He licked his finger. "But soon you will enjoy the feel of a *real* man."

Picking up her writhing body and throwing her over his shoulder like a sack, he walked to where his horse was tethered and threw her up on the saddle, then climbing on behind he kicked the horse into motion.

Elizabeth knew that if she did not escape soon, he would surely take her somewhere and violate her or worse. She wriggled and twisted. He cursed at her to stay still, the horse bucking at the unusual movement on its back. Wickham raised his fist to strike her when, with an enormous effort, she kicked the horse so it reared up. Falling off she rolled down a slope and suddenly into nothingness, her scream silenced by the gag.

Calming the horse, he jumped off, and looked over the edge of the cliff. He saw Elizabeth's still body lying far below, partially hidden by some brush. Blood was on her face. He stood staring down at her, not once did the thought of going to her aid cross his mind.

Wickham's plan after securing Elizabeth was to take her on horseback to an abandoned barn located outside of Lambton. Waiting there was an enclosed carriage. He would place her inside, knocking her out if necessary, and drive the carriage himself to a small cabin he knew on the way to London. There he intended to take out his long festering revenge upon Darcy by repeatedly taking his pleasure with his wife. He would send a ransom note to Darcy from there, and continue to London, disappearing with her into the bowels of the city, and employing an unsuspecting waif to collect his fee at the appointed place and time. Only upon receiving his payment would he release his captive, and disappear forever.

That was his plan, but now with Elizabeth dead, he knew it was only a matter of time before her body was found, and he must adjust his plans to collect his reward and depart the area as soon as possible. He was disappointed that he would not enjoy Elizabeth's favours, but he rejoiced knowing how deeply he will have hurt Darcy, and he wanted his old friend to know it was *he* who was responsible. He knew this would be his last chance to ever hurt and profit from him again. Taking one last look at her broken body, he smiled, ran back to his horse, and rode off.

DARCY RETURNED to the house after his intense ride feeling exhausted, and a little better. He was ready to hold Elizabeth and talk now, and upon hearing that she was still on her walk, he glanced at the clock. It was nearly noon. Spotting Mrs. Reynolds, he asked if she knew when Mrs. Darcy had left, and learning that it was nearly four hours earlier, he became concerned and immediately returned to the stable to saddle a fresh horse and set off on the lake path to look for her. Elizabeth was a good walker, but four hours was quite unusual.

He started down the familiar path and was soon into the quiet of the trees. Searching the path and the forest on either side, he heard and saw nothing, until a yellow object appeared on the ground far ahead of him. He kicked the horse to move faster, and arriving, felt a fear rising in him that he had never known before. On the ground were Elizabeth's bonnet and the scattered pages of her letters.

He jumped down and picked them up, holding the bonnet to his face to catch the scent of lavender from her hair. Panicking, he called out, "Elizabeth! *Lizzy!* Where are you?"

Hearing nothing he looked around, desperate for a sign of her. Studying the earth he saw the evidence of a struggle in the disturbed soil. Looking further, he could see the imprints of boots, which led him to the signs of a horse's hoof prints.

Darcy stood paralyzed with fear. Wherever she was, and whoever took her, it was on horseback. "Lizzy!" He cried out in terror. Who could have done this? *Why?* What he did know was that he could not bear life without her.

Blankly he stared down at the crumpled letters in his hand. Suddenly, a name caught his eye. "Wickham?" Lydia's letter said that Wickham had been removed from the militia, that he was asking questions about Elizabeth and himself, and that he wished to "visit" them.

Closing his eyes, he tried to control his rage. "Wickham! He has come to try and destroy my life again!" Darcy ran back to his horse and rode like a madman back to the stables. He alerted the staff that Mrs. Darcy was kidnapped by George Wickham. Instantly the stable hands and grooms saddled horses to begin searching the woods. Word was sent to Lambton to alert the constable, and to search there. Darcy turned his horse around and returned to look for her at the only place he could, the woods. He tried to think of the places Wickham liked to hide during his boyhood.

They went through the trees and the brush, calling her name. The number of riders grew steadily as word spread. Elizabeth had already become much-liked and the concern for the new Mistress of Pemberley was high, especially when it was known that George Wickham was involved. The memory of his misdeeds at Pemberley and in Lambton was still fresh. The search continued unceasingly until nightfall, when Mr. Regar forced Darcy to abandon it until daylight. Darcy wanted to stay out. Elizabeth needed him. She was alone and she needed him. He could feel her calling out to him.

When he could no longer see through the moonless night, he entered the house. Mrs. Reynolds tried to encourage him to eat, but he refused, he doubted his Lizzy was eating, so neither would he. He went up to his rooms and removed the filthy clothes, but did no more, only walking aimlessly until finally settling in her dressing room, surrounded by her things, her scent. Clutching the robe she had worn the night before, he held it to his face and prayed.

AT DAWN, Darcy was awakened from a fitful sleep on the floor of the dressing room by Rogers. "Mr. Darcy, a message has arrived, to be delivered personally to you."

Darcy jumped up, instantly awake. "Who is it? Did you hold him?"

"Yes sir, he was not permitted to leave. He is waiting in your study."

Darcy flew down the stairs and into the room, his face a thundercloud of anger. The young man took one look at the Master of the estate and shrank back in fear.

"Sir, I was asked to bring you this." His shaking hand held out the missive. Darcy grabbed it from him and ripped it open.

Darcy,

I was in the neighbourhood, and thought that I would wish you joy for your wedding. Mrs. Darcy is lovely. I am enjoying getting to know her quite intimately. But perhaps you would enjoy her company, as well? I will be happy to send her back to you for a suitable reward. Leave a bank note for thirty thousand pounds under the rock by the chestnut tree in Lambton. You know that rock, do you not, old friend? I will expect it there by noon.

George Wickham

"Wickham!" Darcy spat out and read the note again. Wickham was clearly intimating that he had violated Elizabeth. He attempted to block that vision from his mind and turned to the young man. "Who gave this to you? Where was he?"

"A . . . a man sir, I did not know him, he offered me a guinea to deliver the note to the Master of Pemberley at dawn, sir. We were outside the Lambton Inn." He swallowed. "He was tall and dark like you, sir."

It was Wickham for certain. "Did you see where he went?" The boy shook his head. He had told all that he knew.

Mr. Regar stepped up to Darcy. "What does he want, sir?"

"Money. What else would Wickham want? Money and revenge." Darcy said, disgusted. It was not lost on him that Wickham demanded the same amount as Georgiana's dowry. He walked over to his desk and pulled out his bankbook. He wrote out the draft, sealed it in a folded page, and handed it to Mr. Regar. "This is to be placed under the rock by the chestnut tree in Lambton by noon. Obviously I cannot be there, but I want men all over the town, watching for who retrieves it and where he goes. I will be waiting in the Lambton Inn."

"Sir, you are not going to pay him off?" Mr. Regar had noted the amount written on the draft.

Darcy's eyes blazed. "I would sign over Pemberley to recover Elizabeth." He looked at his concerned steward, and calmed slightly, "I have altered my name on the draft, it will not be cashed, but I doubt that Wickham in his greed would notice it. He can only cash such a large draft in London. I will send an express to my bank and alert them to watch for it. He will never get anything from me." He sat down and quickly wrote the note. "What is important now is to find Elizabeth." He sat back, thinking. "Wickham must be working alone on this. He is foolish to have us come into Lambton, where he would be recognized and easily trapped. I wonder if something in his plan has gone wrong." He wondered if that something had to do with Elizabeth.

By noon, the Pemberley party had infiltrated Lambton. The constable and the magistrate were alerted, and Darcy anxiously took his post at the inn. Mr. Regar placed the letter under the rock as instructed and walked away. Soon a small boy was seen removing it, and he was followed through several winding alleys, and to a crumbling barn on the edge of town. Darcy was alerted when the chase was on and soon arrived at the building. They looked into the carriage standing near the door. He and several of his men entered and spotted the boy leaving a small room in the back corner. One man grabbed the boy and took him outside before he could make a sound. Darcy and the other men walked quietly to the closed door, listened, and then glancing at them, he burst inside. Wickham was just opening the envelope, and dropped it in surprise.

"Darcy!" He cried out.

"Wickham! Where is my wife?" Darcy growled, his eyes scanning the room.

"Not here, obviously."

Darcy was across the room in a second. His hands closed over Wickham's throat and shook him. "*Where* is she?"

"Killing me will not get you any closer to her!" He choked out.

Darcy removed his hands and turning away, tried to calm his anger. "Wickham, you are not getting my money. If you do not wish to hang for your crimes, tell me where my wife is!"

Foolishly, Wickham decided to bait him. "She is resting comfortably, I assure you, as she is quite worn out." Seeing Darcy's panicked expression he added, "It was a pleasure to know another of the Darcy women so intimately." He grinned.

In one movement, Darcy swung, and hit him in the ribs. Everyone in the room heard the crack. "Now, do I need to hit you again or will you talk?" Wickham had bent over, crumpling against the wall.

"Give me safe passage out of Derbyshire and I will send word back as to her location."

Darcy advanced and dragging Wickham up from his position on the floor threw him against the wall. Darcy's eyes were black with fury; he grabbed Wickham's head by his hair and slammed it back.

"Speak, you cur!" He demanded.

"All right, all right, she is in the woods." He said, gasping for air.

"We have searched the woods. *Where?*"

"Do you remember the cliff on the lake path?" Darcy nodded, his eyes narrowing. "She lies at the bottom of it." Wickham sneered.

"Is she alive?" He said very quietly, attempting to control his rage and growing terror.

"I think not." Wickham said, staring defiantly into Darcy's eyes, seeking to enjoy his pain. His eyes opened wide at the sight of Darcy's fist landing squarely on his jaw, breaking it. It was followed by his boot, firmly kicked in his groin.

"That was from Elizabeth." He turned and flew out of the barn, leaving the other men to deal with Wickham. He knew exactly the spot that Wickham described. Jumping on his horse he rode as a man possessed back to Pemberley, finally arriving back on the lake path. He reached the cliff and stood there for a moment, suddenly awash in the memory of when he fell over it as a boy. Wickham pushed him over, supposedly in jest, only later he realized that it was an attempt to inflict a grave injury. Darcy had fortunately landed in a large bush, and received only bruises and scratches. He prayed that Elizabeth had the same fate. Peering over the edge, he spotted her curled in a ball on the bank of the rushing stream.

"Lizzy!" There was no movement. His heart pounding, he searched for a pathway, and finding one, started down, frustrated by his slow progress.

Upon reaching her, he saw that her eyes were closed. Blood and tears were dried on her face and matted her hair. Trembling, he knelt down beside her and tenderly touched her cheek. It was warm. He let out the breath he had been holding, and said a prayer of thanks. He pulled out his knife, cutting the binding on her hands and feet, and then carefully removed the gag and handkerchief from her mouth.

"Lizzy, Lizzy, my love, it is William." He gently cradled her head in his lap, stroking her cheek and hair as he kissed her parched lips. "Sweetheart, please wake up, please." He felt her move slightly, and then joyfully, he saw her eyes slowly open.

"William." She whispered; her throat dry. Tears began pouring down her face, and she reached up to touch him with a shaking hand.

He had a flask of brandy in his pocket and supporting her head, he gave her a sip. She coughed and sputtered, but the liquor had the wanted effect. She tried to sit up, but he stopped her.

"Are you in pain, my love? We must not move you if you have broken any bones." He held her hand tightly.

"I am sore and tired, but I do not feel anything too painful. I think I landed in some brush and then rolled here." She whispered. Then smiling slightly, she said, "I did not have much choice as you can see."

Relieved with her attempt at humour, he gathered her up in his arms and held her in his lap, rocking her. "Oh darling, I have been searching everywhere for you. I found your bonnet and Lydia's letter, and I knew that it was Wickham. I am so sorry!" He buried his face in her neck and Elizabeth felt his tears as his shoulders shook. She held him, releasing her own flood of tears. It was a horrific experience for her, but she knew all along that she was alive. He had suffered the pain of not knowing anything.

"Did I not say that I would never leave you alone?" She held his face and kissed him. He nodded, staring into her eyes. "I love you, William."

"I love you, Lizzy. If you had died, I would have just laid down here beside you and stayed forever." Lifting her, he rose to his feet, "It is time we returned home."

Through her tears, she smiled at him. "Yes, I believe that we were to take a bath together, were we not?" He laughed softly, and rested his wet cheek to hers.

"A bath with you would be heavenly, my love." He kissed her again, and hugged his precious wife to his chest.

He carried her up the hillside and carefully setting her on the horse, they were soon on their way to the house. She leaned heavily on against him, and he clutched her waist securely with his left arm, while holding the reins in his right hand. The men had received word by then from Lambton to start searching by a cliff on the lake path, and were just heading towards them when Darcy's horse was spotted. Cheers were raised by all, and Elizabeth smiled at their joy. Darcy carried her straight up to their rooms, ordering a bath to be prepared, and asked to send for the doctor.

"I do not need the doctor, William, truly, I am fine." She leaned against him with her arms wrapped tightly around his waist.

"I need you to see the doctor. Please darling, for my peace of mind, if nothing else."

"For you, I will do anything." She rested against his chest and sought the comfort of his heartbeat.

"Thank you, darling." Darcy whispered, kissing her hair.

Rosie came in, announcing that the bath was ready, and that a meal was on its way. Darcy dismissed her, and unbuttoning Elizabeth's dress himself, carried her in to the bath and slowly lowered her down. She winced when the water touched the raw skin on her wrists from the binding. Darcy winced seeing her beautiful body covered in bruises and scratches from the struggle with Wickham and the fall. He lovingly washed her, and carefully rinsed the dirt and blood from her hair. "Will you not join me?" She asked beseechingly.

He soon lowered himself into the warm water. They sat, back to front; arms entwined, and closed their eyes, feeling safe once again. A knock at the door awakened them from their silent communion. "Sir?" Rogers' voice came. "The doctor has arrived. I have left you a robe outside of the door."

"Thank you; send him up in fifteen minutes."

"Yes sir."

They rose and Darcy gently dried her, towelling her hair. He pulled it back with a ribbon, and helped her to dress in the nightgown and robe that Rosie had left. Darcy slipped on his robe, and after settling her in their bed, left to dress. He quickly reappeared in breeches and a shirt.

The doctor was announced. He had been apprised of the situation, and was not sure what he would find. He was surprised and relieved to see Mrs. Darcy, sitting up on the bed, obviously battered, but alert. "Mrs. Darcy, I am Doctor Howard. I understand that you have had a difficult experience."

"Doctor, I am pleased to meet you, though I would rather it be under better circumstances." Elizabeth smiled slightly at him.

"My wife assures me that she is well, but I thought that it would be best to confirm it with you, sir." Darcy fixed his gaze on the doctor.

The doctor observed his obviously haggard appearance and determined to interview him next. "Well sir, if you will leave the room, I will begin my examination." He started towards the bed with his bag.

"I will stay." Darcy stated.

"Sir, I respectfully suggest. . ." Then seeing Darcy's stubborn face, he sighed. "Very well, sir. This is not a day for arguments." Darcy moved to the window and stared out at the lake. He did not actually want to see the doctor examining Elizabeth, but he did not wish to leave her either. He listened as he heard the rustle of her clothing, and heard the doctor's quiet questions as he treated the wounds. All seemed well, but then the doctor asked, "Did he strike you, Mrs. Darcy?" Darcy stiffened. Glancing at him, she said, "No, not really, it was mostly grabbing and pushing." She said softly, not meeting his gaze.

The doctor nodded, noting the bruise across her cheek, and looking to Darcy, he asked one other question, very softly. "Did he violate you?" Elizabeth saw Darcy clutch the window frame, and hang his head.

"No, he did not." She could see him let out his breath.

The doctor noted it as well, and saw the truth in her eyes. He nodded. "Thank heaven for that." He said softly, and then clearing his throat, he spoke louder. "It seems that your injuries, in the grand scheme of things, are fairly minor. The bruising will last a few weeks, but the scratches should heal quickly. I imagine that you are suffering a headache judging by the bruise and cut on your temple. I have powders which will relieve the pain." She nodded. "The abrasions on your wrists will heal soon. I will leave a salve for you to put on if they pain you, but simply keeping leaving them bandaged should be sufficient. I would say that you are thankfully quite well, Mrs. Darcy, and have nothing to worry about." He patted her shoulder. "I recommend a great deal of rest." She nodded, blinking back her tears.

Darcy finally felt able to turn around and came to her side. "Are you sure, Doctor?" He said, anxiously taking her hand.

"Absolutely." He looked at him. "Mr. Darcy, may I have a word with you?" They left the room. "First show me your hands."

"They are fine, sir."

"Nonsense. I examined Wickham. You broke his jaw and his ribs, and I believe punctured a lung, and I sincerely doubt that he will ever be able to father a child." Darcy could not help but smile with satisfaction. Both men knew that Wickham's fate likely lay at the end of a noose or on a ship to Australia. "Ahem. So show me your hands." The doctor looked. Darcy's right hand was swollen and bruised. "I recommend that you soak that in salt water." Darcy started to protest. "If you do not agree to do so, I will tell Mrs. Darcy. Do you want her to know?" He regarded him with twitching lips.

Knowing Elizabeth's reaction, he smiled slightly. "No. I will do as you order."

"Fine." Then seriously he said, "Mrs. Darcy said that she was not violated, sir. But I think that it would be foolish to think that she was not threatened in some way. I sincerely believe that she is putting on a brave face to spare your feelings. If you can encourage her to talk about it, no matter how painful it is for you to hear, it will help her." He patted Darcy's shoulder. "My prescription for rest applies to you as well, sir." The two men exchanged glances. "Now, I hope that the next time I am called here, it is for a more joyful event." Darcy looked up, surprised. "Well Son, get to work on it!" He laughed softly and left the room. Darcy smiled and wiped his eyes.

He started to return to the bedchamber, when he caught sight of Elizabeth through the open door. She was hugging herself, rocking back and forth, staring, with a look of abject terror on her face. He drew in his breath, and made a noise. Instantly he saw a look of serenity come over her features. The doctor was correct. She was hiding her feelings to protect him. "Oh, Lizzy." He whispered.

Entering the room he sat on the bed and wrapped his arms around her. She sat stiffly in his embrace. He did not speak or let go. After an eternity, he felt her body relax, and she was wracked with sobs. He kept holding her until she was spent, only kissing her forehead while waiting for her to speak. Finally she did.

"I was so afraid." Her voice broke. "I woke and did not know where I was. I was waiting for him to return, imagining what he would do to me, and when he did not, I kept waiting for an animal to find me. I tried to crawl but found I could only roll. I felt so helpless. I thought that I could hear you calling me. I could not move or scream. All I could do was call for you to find me in my mind." She sobbed again, and held him tighter. "He touched me." She whispered.

"Lizzy." He kissed her all over her face. "I love you." He kept kissing her. "I could hear you calling to me. I would not stop looking for you, ever." He was trying hard to remove the image of Wickham touching her from his mind, and desperately trying to think of the right things to say.

"William, he touched me but he did not. . ."

"Thank God." He kissed her again. "Lizzy, if you thought that I was jealous and possessive before, you have not seen the extent of my feelings. I make no more apologies."

"I will have no complaints."

He gave her a hug, "I did manage a bit of revenge for you."

Sniffing, Elizabeth hid her face in his neck. "What did you do?"

He caressed her hair and spoke softly in her ear. "I broke his ribs when he insulted you, and I broke his jaw. He made a reference to . . . touching you, and I remembered your technique of silencing him."

"You kneed him?" She asked, her voice muffled.

He gently kissed her cheek. "Well, I used my boot, actually. The doctor feels that he will never be a father."

Elizabeth pulled away from her hiding place with a tiny smile on her face. "Really?"

He nodded; the corners of his mouth lifting. "The doctor did suggest, however, that I begin work on that particular title." His smile grew slightly.

"That is an admirable idea." She kissed him and added quietly, "Not today."

Darcy kissed her nose and wiped her eyes, then settling her safely in his embrace under the covers, he closed his eyes, "No, not today, but soon."

Chapter 25

"*S*uch a lovely garden, perhaps a little too formal and fussy, but it is a pleasure to view." Kathleen Miller turned to look at her charge. Anne de Bourgh lay still, finally finding the peace of sleep after moving fretfully for hours. Her former companion, Mrs. Jenkinson, realized that she would soon die and when she had the opportunity to take a position as companion to another young lady, she quit her position at Rosings and departed. Kathleen, the daughter of a gentleman with a very small estate left to her older brother, had no dowry. Upon coming of age four years previously with no prospects for marriage, she was urged to find her life as a lady's companion. She seemed to have made it a specialty to care for the dying. It was not a conscious decision; it simply worked out that way. She thought that her next position should be as a governess before she gained the reputation as an "angel of death."

She was pretty, with dark brown hair, and wide, sparkling hazel eyes that were often crinkled in laughter. She found that humour aided in both easing the way for dying charges to pass peacefully, and for her to tolerate the atmosphere of sadness that permeated every home where she lived. Possessing a great amount of time to entertain herself sitting by bedsides, she was increasingly well-read, and was always ready to enjoy well-informed conversation when she had the rare opportunity.

The sound of a carriage coming up the drive led her back to the window. Kathleen watched with interest as an older gentleman and a younger man dressed in an officer's uniform exited. She was told by Lady Catherine that her brother, Lord Matlock and his son, Colonel Fitzwilliam, the heir of Rosings, were coming to visit Lady Anne for a few days.

Her cynical side wondered if the colonel was more likely coming to view the estate than to see his cousin, and if he would actually set foot into the sickroom. She heard the sounds of servants bringing in the trunks to the bedchambers across the hall. About a half hour later she heard a firm knock on the door. She rose and opened it to the most glorious example of masculinity that she had ever seen. She blushed and her eyes instantly dropped to the floor.

Richard stood, stunned, as one of the loveliest women he had ever encountered stood in blushing agitation before him. She looked so very familiar. "Excuse me; I have come to visit my cousin. Is Miss de Bourgh awake?"

Willing herself to breathe, Kathleen raised her eyes to his. She found the deep blue eyes searching her face. *What are you looking for?* She wondered. "Yes, sir, I mean, no, sir, she is asleep at the moment but you could come and sit with her. She does not rest for very long."

Richard smiled warmly at her, "Thank you, I will. Seeing Anne was the reason for my visit." He stepped into the room and walked to the bed. He gently took Anne's hand in his and stroked her forehead, then sitting in the chair by the bedside he tried to form a coherent sentence for the woman who had sent his heart thumping wildly. "Are you my cousin's new companion? My aunt wrote that Mrs. Jenkinson left her."

"Yes sir, my name is Kathleen Miller; I have been here eight days." She finally felt the blush fading and was able to smile. The blush immediately returned when she saw his face light up at the sound of her name.

"Forgive me, Miss Miller. I have entirely forgotten my manners." He gently lay down Anne's hand and rose to bow. "I am Colonel Richard Fitzwilliam."

"I am pleased to make your acquaintance, sir." She said softly.

Richard's mind was working quickly. *Talk you fool! You are not Darcy! You know how to speak to a pretty girl!* Taking a breath, he resumed his seat and grip of Anne's hand, the warmth giving him a steady comfort in this not unfamiliar territory. "Please be seated Miss Miller, or would you like to take advantage of my presence by leaving for a time?" He hoped she would stay.

She wanted to stay. "Oh thank you sir, but I am quite comfortable." She sat on the chair on the opposite side of the bed.

Relaxing and pleased, he began, "Well Miss Miller, has my cousin been a difficult charge? She has always had a rather biting humour, doubtless inherited from her overwhelming mother?" He grinned at her.

Kathleen's eyes grew wide, and she quickly stifled a laugh with her hand. "Colonel Fitzwilliam, you should not speak so of your aunt." She admonished, her eyes dancing.

Richard was delighted to detect a sense of humour and shrugged. "I only speak the truth Miss Miller; in fact, I have barely scratched the surface."

She pursed her lips together. "It is always best to speak the truth; however in this case, it may be wise to not do so within hearing of your aunt."

He laughed. "Not if you do not wish to hear a lecture on proper behaviour for several hours." He smiled at her. "I see that you have quickly taken my aunt's measure."

She shrugged. "It is there for anyone to see, sir, as you intimated, she is not reticent."

"Indeed." Then, becoming sombre, he said softly, "Seriously Miss Miller how is my cousin?"

"I would be far better if you were not gripping my hand quite so tightly, Richard." Arose the weak, but still very cognizant voice of Anne.

"Anne!" Richard cried. He kissed her cheek. "How are you feeling?"

"I have been better." She said dryly. A tiny smile played on her lips. "What brings you here? Are you not desperately needed to risk your life on some foreign shore?"

"You have always been eager to see me shot, Anne." Richard grinned at her.

"Ever since you hid my favourite doll in a tree. Fortunately my *good* cousin recovered it for me." She raised a brow.

"I was a boy! Will you never let me escape your censure for a misdeed committed twenty years ago?" He whined.

"Perhaps I would if you were not as likely to do the same thing again. You will never grow up, no matter how much braid decorates your shoulder."

Richard laughed. "You are correct. I remain unrepentant." He looked at her pale face and his smile died a little. "I wished to come while I had the opportunity.

I will be delivering Georgiana to Darcy next week. Mother and Father decided to stay in town, and since Darcy and Elizabeth will be in Hertfordshire for her sister's wedding, we agreed to meet half way. I will deliver her to them at Charles Bingley's estate."

"Oh, please give Cousin Darcy and Elizabeth my love, Richard. I am so happy for them. I so enjoyed meeting Elizabeth and listening to her take on Mama." She looked at Kathleen. "You remind me of her, Katie. You have similar dispositions, and even resemble each other a bit. She grew up on a small estate like your father's, but hers is entailed away. Mr. Collins will inherit it."

"The parson?" Kathleen asked, surprised.

"Yes, my cousin Darcy married Mr. Collin's cousin. It was a love match." She laughed and looked at Richard. "A very obvious love match, they never left each other alone."

Richard blushed slightly, remembering how much he wished Elizabeth would favour him instead. "Yes, and Darcy is quite possessive of her." He then looked into Kathleen's eyes. "It is wonderful to see such a match. They both were determined to marry for love."

"I think that is a most admirable goal, especially if finances are not an issue." She returned his gaze.

At that moment the door opened and Lord Matlock entered. "Richard, there you are, your aunt's steward wished to speak to you. Mr. Lawrence is waiting in the study." He then turned and saw his niece. "Anne! How are you? Your aunt sends her love, as does Georgiana." He kissed her cheek.

"I am doing as well as I can, Uncle."

Richard rose to leave. "Father, this is Miss Miller, Anne's new companion. Miss Miller, this is my father, Lord Matlock." His father looked at his son with surprise. Ordinarily he would not introduce him to a servant.

He looked at the small woman, and nodded his head. "I am happy to see that my niece has a companion to cheer her, Miss Miller."

"Thank you, sir." She whispered.

"If you will excuse me, I will take my leave. Anne, I will return later." Richard bowed to his cousin, and catching Kathleen's eye, nodded to her.

Lord Matlock followed him out. He observed the dreamy countenance of his usually imperturbable son. "What was that about, Richard?"

"What?" He asked defensively. "Is it not polite to make introductions to unknown people when in a room?"

"To a servant?"

"She is not a servant. She is a gentleman's daughter and a companion. She has nothing to be ashamed of." He heatedly replied.

Lord Matlock's lips twitched. "My mistake, Son. Forgive me." They walked quietly for a moment. "Perhaps you should consult your Cousin Darcy for advice on courting impoverished gentlemen's daughters."

"Father!" Richard cried and reddened as Lord Matlock laughed.

THE NEXT MORNING, Richard was up early and decided to take a walk around the park, now looking at it with the eyes of an owner instead of a reluctant visitor. Lady Catherine had been oddly silent. He was not sure if she was upset with Anne's health or his presence as the heir. He hated that he spent the day before immersed in estate matters with his father and Mr. Lawrence. He knew that it was wise to be fully aware of the status of things when the inevitable day arrived that Anne died, but it still made him feel greedy, waiting like an avaricious man, rubbing his hands together with anticipation. As he walked he found himself near the parsonage and thought of the man who lived there. He was exactly the picture of the man he himself was trying not to be. Mr. Collins made no secret of his eager anticipation of becoming the Master of Longbourn. Seeing the small man leaving the front door of his home and walking into the village, Richard decided to pay a call on his wife.

"Mrs. Collins, how very good it is to meet you again! I see that you have lost all of your company?" Richard said after he was asked to be seated by the always serene lady.

"Yes, Colonel, my sister departed just a few weeks ago. I miss her very much, and of course, I miss the company of my friend, Mrs. Darcy." She smiled at him.

"Ah, so you know of their nuptials? I imagine that your family sent you a report?"

"Indeed, it was quite the talk of Hertfordshire, first that it happened, but more the way it all took place set tongues wagging. I am afraid that your cousin made quite a display of affection to my friend in front of the church." She raised a brow, and pursed her lips, hiding her smile.

"Did he now? Well, that is one story I will have to hear. In fact, I will hopefully hear it quite soon. I am taking Miss Darcy to Hertfordshire in a few days to meet her brother and new sister, and they will take her the rest of the way back to Pemberley. One of the reasons I stopped today was to see if you would like me to deliver a letter to Elizabeth, or perhaps your own family?"

"Thank you, that is very kind of you. I will have the letters ready for you tomorrow morning. When do you depart?"

"My father and I expect to leave by nine o'clock. I will just have the carriage stop here on our way out of the gate."

"That will be fine. I am anxious to write to Eliza in any case, after her horrifying experience. I hope that she is recovering."

Richard startled. "Forgive me, Mrs. Collins, but did you say that Elizabeth suffered a horrifying experience? What happened and when? Is she well?"

"Oh, I am so sorry Colonel; I assumed that you knew. You are so close to your cousin, Mr. Darcy. I hate to be the bearer of such news." Charlotte bit her lip, not knowing what to do.

"I imagine that my Cousin may have desired to tell me news of such a painful nature in person. But Mrs. Collins, I would truly appreciate knowing what it is, if you feel able to tell me?"

Charlotte let out a breath and nodded her head. "Perhaps it would be easier if you simply read Eliza's letter. She did not tell her sister Jane yet. That I do know. I believe that she would wish to tell her in person. If you will excuse me a moment, I will get the letter for you." She left the room and soon returned.

Richard opened it, and read. His face betrayed the emotions that he felt. Elizabeth held little back in her description, it was obviously terrifying. "Wickham!" Richard muttered. He dropped the letter and started pacing the room, incensed. He wanted to find the cur and kill him. He was happy to hear that Darcy had soundly beaten him, but he wanted to do more. He could not even begin to imagine the suffering that both of them endured. Finally he sat back down. Charlotte had observed his agitation with calm concern, it was fascinating to see his mind working as he paced, and feel the power of his feelings radiating from him.

Turning to her, he said in a barely controlled voice, "Thank you for sharing that letter with me, Mrs. Collins. I agree. My cousin would have wished to tell me this in person. He knows that I would want to question him on every detail, and that cannot be accomplished in a page. I am, however, grateful for knowing this before I see him. It will make starting the conversation much easier." He let out a breath, and looking up at her, he asked, "How do you think Elizabeth will be?"

"She will try to put a happy face on it and hide her feelings from those she loves. I doubt that she will tell many about the incident." She said thoughtfully, "I think, however, that she will be able to talk to her husband about it. They have shared many painful memories with each other already. Their marriage is very unusual and strong."

"The advantage of a love match." Richard said, musing to himself.

"Indeed." Charlotte agreed, thinking of her own marriage of convenience.

Richard soon took his leave, thanking Charlotte again for her kindness, and walked back towards Rosings, his mind dwelling on the news. He would speak to his father about it on their long carriage ride home. His mind was so occupied that he did not notice he was about to walk directly into Kathleen, who was taking a short break from her duties to enjoy the sunshine while Anne slept.

"Colonel! Please, watch yourself!" She cried, quickly sidestepping the marching soldier.

"Miss Miller! Forgive me! My mind was very much engaged, and I did not see you!" He said, completely embarrassed at his inattention.

She laughed. "That is quite all right, sir. I should have known that a man travelling at such a rate should be avoided at all costs!"

He smiled. "Do you truly feel that I am a man to be avoided, Miss Miller?"

She blushed and looked down. "No, not at all, I. . ."

"Forgive me, Miss Miller, I do not wish to discompose you." He enjoyed her blush. "May I ask; how is my cousin faring today?"

Recovering, she looked back into his concerned blue eyes. "She is very weak sir, I am afraid that she will not be with us for long."

"Are you certain?" Kathleen noted his pain with compassion. "I have experience with death, but that is on the battlefield, so it looks quite different from this slow wasting that Anne has dealt with for years. I see that she is weaker, but I cannot see any particular signs."

"I have been the companion for a number of dying ladies over the last four years, sir, and yes there are certain subtle signs that I have learned to observe. I would truly not expect her to be with us more than a month longer." She touched her hand to his arm for a moment, and withdrew. "I am sorry to give you such news, but I find that it is best to be prepared for the inevitable."

Richard closed his eyes with her touch, and said, almost to himself, "I have seen enough of death." He then opened them to see Kathleen's understanding gaze. "I imagine that you have as well, Miss Miller."

She nodded. "That I have, sir."

"What will you do when my cousin passes?" He asked, both for her sake and his own.

"I do not know. I hope that perhaps Lady Catherine would wish for a companion, but I also thought that it would be nice to perhaps be a governess instead, and work with young, healthy children for a change." She looked at him sadly.

"You are weary of your life?" He asked gently, watching her face, thinking how much this lady would understand the secret pain that every soldier who had seen war knows.

She laughed slightly, "It is the life I have been dealt, sir. I have no choice."

"Until very recently I thought the same thing of myself. You never know when chance will come and change everything." He looked deeply into her eyes.

She caught her breath and returned his steady gaze. "I suppose that I will just have to wait for good fortune to smile on me, then."

"Perhaps we should return to the house now, Miss Miller." He offered her his arm, and hesitating a moment, she took it. "I will be departing tomorrow with my father, and travelling to Hertfordshire. I will soon return and stay here with my aunt. I think that she would like the support of family about her at this time." He paused, then making a decision he continued, "I hope to spend time talking with you on my next visit, Miss Miller." He smiled, his face showing the hope that he felt.

"I would be happy to discuss any topic you would find interesting, Colonel." She replied, returning his smile.

"Excellent! I look forward to it!" He gave her a heart-stopping smile. He led her into the house and left to meet with his father. He spent the afternoon visiting with Anne, sharing stories of their childhoods, sometimes with Kathleen in the room, laughing along with them. The next morning they departed, promising a relieved Lady Catherine that he would return soon, and stopped to collect the letters for Hertfordshire. Lord Matlock saw the thoughtful expression on his son's face, and wondered what it could mean.

THE SECOND DAY after he brought Elizabeth home, Darcy reluctantly, but determinedly, left her side for two hours while she slept. He saw her drink the doctor's powders and knew she would be peaceful for the time that he would be gone. The magistrate and constable asked him to provide his testimony about the event; they had agreed to Darcy's demand that they wait to interview Elizabeth later in the week when she was a little stronger. He and the constable offered to come to Pemberley, but Darcy declined. He wished to go to them, and see for himself the reality of Wickham in custody where he would remain until the travelling judge next came to Derbyshire, which could be months away. Darcy wanted to be assured of the devil's spawn's exact location, and to deliver a message.

He stood, staring at him from the doorway, and spat out his name. "Wickham!"

Wickham's mouth was bandaged shut; he was lying on a cot, coughing, his hideously bruised and swollen face expressing the pain he felt with every gasping breath. He lifted his fevered eyes to Darcy, and a hint of the old defiance registered. He could not speak, but his eyes searched Darcy's face, seeking the signs of the devastating pain he was sure his old enemy must be feeling. Darcy stared at him, his expression unreadable.

Suddenly he strode into the room, silently delighting in Wickham's involuntary flinch at his approach. Darcy stopped, his eyes running over him, and then a smile, a huge, undeniably joyous smile, spread over his tired, sombre face.

He bent close to Wickham's ear and whispered, "Elizabeth lives."

Moving back he regarded the broken man, his eyes wide with shock. Wickham saw the truth shining from Darcy's face, and with that his downfall was complete.

Darcy watched as the last vestiges of bravado drained from his enemy's soul. He nodded, satisfied, and left the room. His mission completed, he returned to the place where he belonged, home to his Elizabeth.

ELIZABETH WRESTLED with her decision to tell her father what happened with Wickham. In the past, any event of significance in her life was unhesitatingly shared with him, and now she was unsure if their relationship had been so irreparably damaged that she could ever trust him again. It was Darcy who encouraged her to tell him. After a fortnight of recovery from their day of hell, after each of them awoke night after night screaming in terror, to be comforted and returned to security by the other, and after receiving the news with unexpressed relief that Wickham had died of pneumonia in prison, Darcy felt the years of burden that Wickham had placed on his relationship with his father fade.

Darcy told her that she had been given the gift that his father denied him. She had the gift of time to re-establish their relationship during his lifetime. It would never be the same, but they could try to reach a comfortable place where she could accept the flawed man that he was, and he could accept that his daughter was always meant to leave home to create her own life.

So she wrote and let go of the resentment she held for him. She told him what she remembered of the incident, the physical threats and abuse, and the intense, unrelenting fear that gripped her while it happened, and as she prayed to be found. She then poured out her heart to tell him of her deep and continually growing love for William.

Several days later, Mr. Bennet put down Elizabeth's letter. The emotions that he was feeling overwhelmed him and he found himself crying for the first time since the death of his mother many years before.

Mr. Bennet's shame for his years of selfish behaviour grew with each sentence of her letter. His involvement with Wickham filled him with guilt and he prayed that his letter was not the impetus for Wickham's attack. "My God, what have I done?" He flogged himself for contacting the man, for telling him of their attachment. He suddenly realized that his actions, meant to keep Lizzy by his side, had in reality almost ended her life. He was ashamed and disgusted and knew that he was not worthy of the title Father. Trying to comfort himself, he thought that he had no true idea of just how vile a man Wickham was. He thought perhaps he was a rake, and at the time he had deluded himself to believe that Wickham was truly the injured party by Darcy's hands. But the more he tried to justify his behaviour, the closer he came to the truth. If he had not contacted Wickham, if he had not raised the man's expectations to gain a reward for separating his most bitter enemy from his beloved, as well as the satisfaction of the accomplishment, Wickham would never have attempted such a deed. Or would he?

Mr. Bennet shook his head. He had no idea how deep the animosity ran between the two men. He had no knowledge of their history, their youth, of

Georgiana, of his relationship with his godfather. All he could do was stare at his daughter's letter and berate himself, and decide that he would beg for Lizzy and Darcy's mercy when he saw them. He knew that if they ever learned of his betrayal, he would never see her again; Darcy would guarantee that without a doubt. Lizzy wrote in the letter that it was her husband who encouraged her to tell him this story.

Mr. Bennet thought about the man, and the way he had responded to Darcy's arguments against their marriage and one question resounded in his mind. "Are you afraid to live with your own wife?"

"No, and it is time that I begin again, not just with Lizzy, but with Fanny." Darcy had shown his mercy by allowing Elizabeth to continue her contact with him. Mr. Bennet would show his appreciation by proving he had listened to Darcy's words.

It was time to stop regretting what he lost and enjoy what he had. He walked out of the library, and finding his wife, he wrapped his arms around her and kissed her soundly on the mouth. "Well, well, well, Mrs. Bennet. I understand we have a wedding to plan. I want to hear all of the details." He sat down in front of her, folded his arms and looked up enquiringly.

Mrs. Bennet was stunned. He had not spoken in weeks, and had not kissed her in years. "Are you well, Mr. Bennet?" She asked cautiously.

"Never better, Fanny. Now tell me how we shall fete our lovely daughter and our future son." He looked at her encouragingly.

She slowly started talking, and realizing that her husband was actually paying attention to her, she was able to speak in a restrained, genteel manner, without all of the usual effusions and nervous declarations. Fanny Bennet did not understand what was happening, but after so many years of starving for his acknowledgement, she did not have the will to reject his seemingly sincere attempts at reconciliation. To the surprise of both spouses, they found themselves enjoying each other's company, and for the first time in many years, they extended that company into the night.

"CHARLES!" Jane cried.

"Mmmm?" His muffled voice spoke as he busily nibbled on her neck.

"Charles, look, what are they doing?"

Charles finally tore himself away from Jane and looked hazily into her eyes, wide with wonder and staring beyond the secluded copse in the garden of Longbourn where they stood hidden. He turned his head to look in the direction where she was gazing, and saw in the distance a couple engaged in a warm embrace.

"Well, it appears that they are doing the same thing we are, my dear." He said, resuming his former occupation.

"But that is my parents!" She said, shocked. "They have not so much as held hands in years!"

Wishing to draw her attention back to him, he said, "Do you not wish us to be so engaged at their age, my love?"

"Well of course, but. . ."

"Then why question the actions of your father wishing to court your mother again? I think that it is charming, and I also think that if I were your father, I would be quite unhappy to be observed doing it." He then decidedly captured her lips with his.

Still not to be distracted, she pulled away from him, "What will Lizzy say?"

Frustrated, Charles put his hands on either side of her head and stared directly into her eyes. "Lizzy will say nothing because her husband will be quite successful at capturing her attention, as I will do with you." He then kissed her soundly and ran his hands over her body. Suddenly, observing her parents' activities lost all attraction, and she melted into his embrace.

Chapter 26

early four weeks after the terrible day, Darcy and Elizabeth journeyed to Hertfordshire. Gradually with the passage of time, and the fading of the visible evidence of Wickham's attack on Elizabeth's body, they started to relax again and fell into what would prove to be the routine of their days at Pemberley for all of their life together. Both of them were early risers, preferring not to waste a moment of sunshine to sleep. Neither understood the sense of the hours kept by people in London, arising by noon, dinner at midnight, or staying out until nearly dawn. What was the point of living in the dark? No, Darcy and Elizabeth both wanted to experience the world around them, and that meant living in the full light of day.

Each day they would rise, dress quickly, perhaps have a cup of tea or coffee, and then they were off to spend time alone together, sometimes walking, sometimes riding. Elizabeth's skills on her horse were steadily improving and Darcy had many excursions planned for the future. When they returned, they would bathe and dress, eat their breakfast, and then, reluctantly, they would part to tend to their individual duties. At first, this was very difficult as neither one wanted to be out of the other's sight, the pain of that terrible day was too fresh. But reality intruded. Darcy had to be out on the estate, and Elizabeth had to be inside with Mrs. Reynolds.

They made an unspoken agreement that if they were both working inside the house they would do so in Darcy's study. He added a new desk alongside his, just for her use. He frequently sought her opinion or just her willing ear to discuss problems of the estate, and she likewise came to him for help with her household experiences and the needs of their tenants. If she had no business to attend, she would curl up on the leather chair next to his desk and read, just so they would remain near to each other. They took all meals together, unless there was some pressing business on the grounds that he would need to address. She was still unwilling to walk anywhere further than the gardens immediately adjacent to the house alone, but just in case, Darcy had quietly directed the staff to always watch for her when she was outside. Someone was to know where she was at all times, inside or out of the house. The staff would have done it without his direction, so shaken were they by what had happened. At one time Elizabeth might have bristled at such scrutiny, thinking it a sign of control over her freedom, but now she saw it for what it was, an expression of his deep love for her. And of course, throughout the day and night, they often and spontaneously displayed their love for each other.

They spent their evenings reading, playing music, walking, talking, laughing, and simply enjoying this private time together, before Georgiana would join them, before the inevitable guests would arrive. Their bond, so powerful almost from the very beginning of their relationship, had formed a strength that defied any foe to break.

The day before departing for Hertfordshire, the steps of their morning walk led them for the first time down the lake path. Their route for that morning had not been discussed, but upon finding themselves walking amongst those trees, their eyes met and the grip of their clasped hands tightened. The tension was fully felt by both and they only succeeded in continuing with the presence of the other. They arrived at the location that would be indelibly impressed in their minds, where Elizabeth was attacked. She turned and wrapped her arms tightly around William and stared at the soil, still visibly disturbed from her struggle weeks ago. She relived the feel of Wickham touching her. She could smell him and could hear the cruel tone of his voice. Darcy embraced her, kissing her head, remembering the sight of her abandoned bonnet, and feeling again the terror that gripped him as he searched desperately for her.

"I love you, Lizzy." He whispered.

She reached up to him, wiping his eyes. "I love you, Will." He gently brushed her cheek with his lips, kissing her tears away.

Darcy let go and walked over to a tree. Using his knife he cut off several young leafy branches and creating a makeshift broom, he began brushing the soil, rearranging the path so the traces of the struggle disappeared and the disturbed area now appeared no different from the rest. He reclaimed her hand and they walked on.

Soon they reached the cliff and the spot where Elizabeth fell over. She took the cut branches from him and tossed them down into the ravine. The soft sound of their fall carried back to them. Holding each other, they looked down at the peacefully flowing stream, and watched as a doe and her fawn appeared to take a drink.

"They are beautiful." Elizabeth said softly.

"Yes." Darcy kissed her hair. "This place is beautiful." His gaze met hers. "This is where my heart started beating again, when I found you."

Elizabeth smiled and touched his face. "Thank you, William. You have replaced the memory of terror with the joy of waking in your arms. I will not be afraid to come here now." He smiled slightly, and lowered his face to hers, first kissing her brow, then gently kissing her lips, and then together they created a new memory for that place.

ON THE SECOND DAY of the journey to Hertfordshire, Elizabeth decided to bring up the topic that had been forgotten that awful day. She sat beside him, their fingers entwined as they were almost always touching, a book open and ignored on her lap. He was similarly occupied, ignoring his book and lost in thought.

"William, we have never spoken of your father's letter." She began, squeezing his hand and studying his face.

"No, but I have come to peace with it. I have forgiven my father."

"How did you come to such a place?"

Darcy rested his chin on her head and said thoughtfully, "Your uncle once asked me what I would have done if I had fathered an illegitimate child, and my answer was surprisingly similar to what my father actually did do, except he carried with it a self-imposed burden of guilt that he was denying his heir his legacy. Thankfully he did not act on that guilt and recognize Wickham mistakenly as his son, and with time it was proven that he was not, but he could not allow himself to openly love me while he felt that he was rejecting his true heir." He paused, kissing her hair, "I could stand over my father's grave and shout of how his behaviour hurt my life, but what would that serve? It is done. For better or worse his actions formed my character, and my experiences by his and Wickham's hands created the person I was the day that I sat down in that theatre and lifted my eyes to yours. This past is done. Wickham's death has released me, and my father, from the grip of guilt and regret." He lifted his head and gently turned her face to his. "I choose life, Elizabeth, I choose you."

Elizabeth gazed at him, speechless and utterly overwhelmed. Her eyes soon filled with tears that spilled unheeded down her cheeks. Darcy smiled at her slightly, his own eyes brimming. He pulled out his handkerchief and gently wiped her face.

She took the cloth from his hand and dried his tears. "For a man who speaks so seldom, when you do, you simply take my breath away." She set the cloth down, and touched his face with her hands, delicately tracing his cheek. "I love you, too." Winding her fingers in his hair, she pulled his head down to hers, their lips meeting in a gentle exchange, expressing the depth of their passion.

"You know Lizzy, my goal in confessing my love to you was not to make you cry."

"Well then, sir, you have failed completely." Elizabeth softly replied, trying to stem the flow of her tears.

He looked at her seriously. "That cannot be. I will not fail you."

"You are bound to fail sometime, sir."

"That is not acceptable."

"In anyone or just yourself?"

"I suppose in both." He admitted.

She gently admonished him. "That sounds like the boy who was desperately seeking his father's approval, not the man who has chosen to live his future and let go of the past."

"I am trying so hard to change, Lizzy." He closed his eyes while shaking his head.

"You *have* changed. I doubt your sister will recognize you."

"Really? What is different?" He looked into her eyes.

She stroked his brow. "You smile."

He put his head down shyly. "Sometimes my face hurts. I have been smiling so much around you, Lizzy."

She laughed. "You are not used to such exercise?"

He twisted a long curl around his finger. "No, I suppose not, but with such an example of joy before me how can I not smile?"

"You are trying to change the subject, sir. We are talking about you." She raised her brow.

He hugged her to him. "Sometimes you are too intelligent."

"You would prefer a vapid and foolish wife?"

"Did I say that?"

"I believe that you did. Shall I step aside so that you may replace me with one of the pretty ladies of the *ton* who so wished to decorate your arm and spend your money?"

"Do not even suggest such a ridiculous thing!"

"Then let us return to the subject at hand." She tilted her head

"Which was?"

"Your smile." She tapped his lips with her finger.

Shaking his head he kissed the finger. "You are relentless, Madam."

"And you are avoiding the subject, sir!"

He sighed. "What do you want of me?"

Lifting her chin she smirked. "I want you to admit that you prefer to smile."

"That is easily done." He laughed.

Her chin still raised she continued, "And that people who smile also accept imperfection in themselves and others."

"Ah, now I see where you are going with this. You think that I demand too much of myself." He pursed his lips.

She stroked his nose. "Nobody is perfect, Mr. Darcy."

He held her tighter. "But everything must be perfect for you."

She pulled away and looked back up at him. "Now who is being ridiculous? If you have decided to stop brooding over the past, you must follow my philosophy to remember the past only as it gives you pleasure."

He regarded her seriously. "I am afraid that I cannot let it go so easily, but I wish to concentrate on the future."

Tilting her head she asked, "And embrace imperfection?"

He pulled her back to him. "I would prefer to embrace you."

"Mr. Darcy!" She admonished as her face rested on his chest.

"I will try." He whispered.

"That is all that I ask." She whispered back.

"Now may I kiss you?" He dragged his lips down her neck.

"So you are ready to embrace the future? If that is the case, I believe that Dr. Howard gave you a charge." She smiled up at him with a gleam in her eye.

He laughed. "And what was that, my love?"

"I believe it had something to do with fatherhood."

His eyes twinkled at hers. "Ah, yes, I do believe he did mention something of that sort. What do you propose, Mrs. Darcy?"

She raised her brows. "I think that it is high time that you act on it."

"I seem to recall doing something of the kind last night, or was it so forgettable, that my lovely wife missed the event entirely?"

She waved her hand, "No, no, I recall it all precisely. But you see; I have been researching the topic."

"You have?" He laughed.

She nodded her head vigorously, "Indeed! Most diligently! And there are a great many theories and suggestions for achieving the goal. I think that we should, as prospective parents, pursue this wise advice."

"And what is the advice, my sweet Lizzy?" He pulled her close to him, running his hands over her breasts while suckling her neck.

"Frequency, Mr. Darcy!" She declared with enthusiasm. "And position, why did you know that the Kama Sutra describes any number of positions for lovemaking? Some particularly designed to encourage pregnancy?"

He stared at her. "How on earth do *you* know about the Kama Sutra?"

"Why Mr. Darcy, am I not a great reader?" She batted her eyes, and began unbuttoning his breeches.

"Yes." He said suspiciously, looking down to watch her busy hands.

"And are you not proud of your library, the work of many generations?" She continued, gently freeing his decidedly erect member from its confines, and stroked the warm silky skin the way he taught her.

"Ohh, yess." He closed his eyes and swallowed hard, even while lifting her skirts to her waist.

"Then do you not think that such a fine example of literature would be located within the vast collection that is the Pemberley library?" She rose to straddle his lap.

His eyes still closed, he brought his hands up under her skirts to caress her bare bottom and his voice cracked with anticipation. "I thought that was well hidden."

"It was, sir, but you left me alone far too long one day, and well, you know, I am quite determined to discover your secrets." She whispered, and bringing her lips to his, she held his head in one hand and guided him into her with the other. "Mmmm. Will, my riding lessons are nothing like this!" She moaned, moving faster.

He opened his eyes and looked into her beautiful face. "I have not taught you to jump fences yet, my love."

The carriage rolled on, and the happy couple paid no heed to the volume of their voices. The carriage driver turned his head to glance back at the footmen positioned directly above their seat, and grinned at their wide smiles, displayed as they listened to the Master and Mistress work to create the next generation.

"I SIMPLY cannot understand what has happened, Louisa!" Caroline Bingley declared as she sat heavily on her bed at Netherfield and watched as the servants rushed to unpack her things.

"Well, perhaps your friends did not know that you were in town." Louisa offered weakly.

"How could they not? I sent my card around to everybody telling them that I had returned, and on every one of them I noted my connection to Mr. Darcy! That has always gained my entry into the most exclusive events!" She stared angrily at a maid who was hurrying to leave the room.

"I cannot imagine what went wrong, then." Actually, Louisa could. Charles told her that Darcy had wearied of Caroline using his name, and assuming a closer relationship than what truly existed. Now that he was married he was able to cut off his connection to anyone without any question. He made a point of letting his closest friends know that they were not to invite Caroline Bingley to their events based solely on her supposed connection to him, because one did not exist. Of course, Louisa was not hurrying to tell her sister that.

Caroline's eyes lit up with wonder. "Louisa, do you suppose that the *ton* has rejected Mr. Darcy because of his marriage to that chit, Elizabeth Bennet?"

Louisa's eyes grew wide, sensing danger. "Caroline! May I remind you that Jane Bennet is very soon to marry Charles and disparaging remarks about Mrs. Darcy reflect poorly on your own sister?"

"No, no, that is it exactly! Oh Louisa, I must tell him the damage that Elizabeth Bennet has done to his reputation! He will see the danger of destroying his sister's welcome into society, and he will immediately seek to divorce her to save his family's name!" Caroline's eyes were gleaming with the prospect of her plan's success. "And then, once she is gone, he will have to work hard to restore his name to its greatness! You know how proud he is of his heritage, he will not hesitate to instantly remarry, and find a proper wife to be Mistress of Pemberley, and to display her at all of the finest gatherings!" She laughed at the prospect.

"Caroline. . ."

"I will find him alone and tell him this news, and when he stands there, infuriated at his mistake, I will graciously offer myself to help him through this time of need!" She turned to her sister, her eyes wide with avarice and anticipation. "Yes, and then I will not have to find my own home! I will have Pemberley and Darcy House! Surely Charles will not force me to continue looking for accommodations when I am engaged to Mr. Darcy!"

"Caroline! You will not be engaged to Mr. Darcy! If he had wished to marry you, he could have done that any time in the years that he has known you! And you know that he cannot divorce, and with the grounds you suggest it would not be granted without an Act of Parliament, and his future children would be considered illegitimate. That is certainly something that he would never entertain! You must let go of this ridiculous delusion!" She put her hands on her sister's shoulders, shaking her. "What has come over you, Caroline? Surely you know that nothing will take Mr. Darcy from his wife. Is this all about Charles asking you to find your own home?"

Caroline looked up at her sister, the maniacal light dimming in her eyes. "Louisa, if nobody will ask me to their balls, I cannot find a husband, and if I cannot marry, I will spend my life as a spinster aunt. I do not wish to live alone." Finally the truth was out.

Louisa sat down and wrapped her arms around her. "Caroline, have you ever thought about why people would invite you to their balls and dinners in the past?"

Caroline looked at her. "Because they liked me!"

"I think it was because of your freely claiming a connection to Mr. Darcy. Those people wanted you at their parties because they thought that it would get them closer to him." Louisa looked seriously into her sister's confused eyes. "They were doing the same thing that you were doing, using him. He knew this Caroline, and he never liked it. Not from you, not from the *ton*, not from anyone. The first woman who did not look at him with greed in her eyes was Elizabeth Bennet. That is why he married her. She saw him as a man, not a means to wealth and recognition."

"But is that not why you married?" Caroline asked, trying to justify herself.

Louisa sighed. "Yes, it was. I made a marriage of convenience, not love. Gilbert and I have grown to have affection for each other, but it certainly is not what the Darcy's have, or I suspect, what Charles will have with Jane. You still have time to change yourself, and hopefully attract someone who will love you, and not your dowry. Do you think that you can do that?"

"I do not know. I do not know if I have the ability to change even if I decided to, and I certainly do not know how." Caroline, for the first time in a very long time, began to cry.

"I think that our new sister will help you, if you let her. Perhaps you should simply start by behaving civilly to Mrs. Darcy when she arrives. Watch and see her and Mr. Darcy's reaction to you. That should tell you if you are on the right path." She handed her a handkerchief and kissed her forehead. She rose and left the room, closing the door behind her. When she was alone in the hallway, she let out a breath.

Inside the room, Caroline sat, her tears stopped. "Can I change? Do I want to?"

Chapter 27

*U*pon arriving at Netherfield, Darcy and Elizabeth went to their bedchambers to change from their travel clothes and then descended to the sitting room to greet the household. "Lizzy!" Jane flew across the room into her sister's arms. Darcy stood, abandoned, and smiled at their enthusiasm.

"I did not know that you were here or I would have seen you before going upstairs!" Elizabeth exclaimed. "You look beautiful, Jane! Is everything ready?"

"Oh Lizzy, there is so much left to do. I am so glad that you are here. I especially need to talk to you about Mama and Papa." Jane was gripping her hands, staring eagerly into her eyes.

"What is it, Jane? From your behaviour, it seems to be good news?" Elizabeth felt cautiously optimistic.

"It is wonderful news!" She smiled, and noticing Darcy she looked at him and blushed. "Forgive me, William, I did not mean to ignore you."

Darcy bowed to her, smiling. "Not at all, Jane, I just thought it best to stand out of the way of the sisterly effusions."

"She is your sister, as well, sir." Elizabeth noted, smiling up to his amused face.

"So she is, and soon my best friend will be my brother." He looked at them both, and taking Jane's hand, he bestowed a kiss. "I am very happy to see you again, Jane. I see that you are bursting to speak to my wife, so I will graciously leave you alone." He bowed and walked across the room to speak to Bingley.

Jane immediately dragged Elizabeth to a sofa and sat down. "Lizzy, Mama and Papa are courting!"

"Excuse me, Jane, but they are doing *what*?" Elizabeth stared at her in disbelief.

"It is the strangest thing. It happened the day that your letter arrived. Papa still was not talking to anyone, all those weeks after you married. But he watched for the post every day, looking for a letter from you. Well, when the letter came he shut himself in the library, and I could hear him. He was in tears. What did you write? Whatever it was it certainly changed him. He left the library and went in search of Mama, and then he kissed her, and made her tell him all about the wedding plans! Can you imagine? He wanted to hear every detail. Then every day after that he has been spending time walking in the garden with her, and talking together, and Charles and I even came upon them embracing one evening!" Jane was incredulous, telling her own story. "What was in your letter, Lizzy? It has to be something that you wrote that made him change!"

Elizabeth listened to Jane, her eyes growing wider with each new bit of information. "I simply told him of an event that took place at Pemberley, and then told him how much I love William." She knew that her letter detailed what happened with Wickham. Was that what drove her father's epiphany?

"What happened at Pemberley, Lizzy?" Jane asked eagerly, sure it was something wonderful.

This was not the time for that particular story. "I will tell you later, maybe we can take a walk together?"

"Oh, of course." She said, disappointed. "Did you hear of Lydia's news?"

"Yes, she wrote to me that she was engaged to Lieutenant Denny. How did Mama react?"

"She was thrilled, naturally. She ran about the house saying, 'Three daughters married!' for the longest time!" Jane grinned. "I suppose that we will have to find husbands for Kitty and Mary now!"

"Well, if Lydia can find one, the other two should have no trouble at all." She laughed. "How is Mama responding to the new Thomas Bennet?"

"You will not recognize her, Lizzy. She is so calm. I think that she acted so oddly before just to get Papa's attention."

"And instead it just drove him further away." Elizabeth said, thoughtfully, wondering if the opposite was the real truth.

"You will see yourself, soon enough. We will have dinner here tonight, but I hope that you will come to Longbourn tomorrow to help me with the wedding preparations and visit. Aunt and Uncle Gardiner and the children arrive tomorrow, and we will be having dinner all together."

"I look forward to everything that you have planned, Jane. I am sure that William and Charles will be able to keep each other occupied while we fuss over the wedding." She looked up, and as expected, Darcy was seated speaking to Bingley, but his gaze was centred on her. She blushed, and he smiled.

Further conversation was ended by the entrance of the Hursts and Caroline. After exchanging greetings, Caroline seated herself near Darcy. It seemed that she had made her decision.

Louisa looked sadly over to her sister, and turned to Jane and Elizabeth who were next to her. "Mrs. Darcy, I must tell you now, my sister Caroline may try to come between you and Mr. Darcy. She seems to think that if she convinces him that you have ruined his standing in society he will divorce you and marry her instead." Elizabeth looked at her in disbelief. "She has recently discovered that her old practice of using his name to gain entry into balls is no longer effective."

"Of course not. William told everyone after the Carrington ball that they were not to extend their invitations to her based on a supposed connection to him. He was highly offended when she wrote to the Carrington's to be invited to their ball. But to try to break up our marriage? Is she delusional, Mrs. Hurst?"

"I do not think so, merely desperate. She does not take kindly to Charles telling her to form her own household upon his marriage."

"Perhaps she could continue to live with us." Jane said weakly.

"No, Jane, do not give in to her. Do not let her see you as vulnerable. You and Charles must stand together on this. Believe me, William and I have learned that it takes both of us to overcome adversity. You should talk to Charles before Miss Bingley does any damage to your relationship. Perhaps his steward could find her a suitable home if she has not already."

Louisa nodded. "That is an excellent suggestion, and I will speak to Gilbert about his secretary finding somewhere for her, the sooner that she is established, the better."

DARCY WAS APPALLED when Elizabeth told him of Caroline's hopes while they prepared for the night. "Is she out of her senses?" He asked as he joined her in the bed. "How can she possibly think that I would leave you to go to her? I never gave her so much as a hint of encouragement. Even when we were first introduced, I saw her as artificial and conniving. I just do not understand why she would continually attempt to pursue a man who was so obviously disinterested. Surely there must be someone in London who wants her dowry, if not her!"

"Mrs. Hurst said that she tried to talk her into changing her ways, and that a divorce between us is out of the question, but I suppose that her instincts are too much ingrained. You represent everything that she has always dreamed of attaining." Elizabeth hugged him tightly.

"You do not think that she would do anything drastic, do you?" Darcy said, wondering at just how desperate Caroline was.

"Such as?"

Now he regretted mentioning it. "Oh, never mind, I was just wondering out loud." He knew it was too late.

"William." Elizabeth sat up and looked at him sternly. "What are you not saying?"

He closed his eyes and sighed. "I am sorry, darling. I am probably being overly dramatic, but after what happened. . . I thought maybe she would try to hurt you, somehow." He opened his eyes cautiously.

Elizabeth continued staring, but understanding him, she stroked his cheek. "I think that you are assuming that she is insane. I think that she is merely angry."

"Angry people do insane things." He drew her back down to his embrace.

CAROLINE MADE no move that evening. She decided to observe instead. What she saw made her realize how difficult her plans to come between Elizabeth and Darcy would be. She watched how, when separated, their gazes were always on each other, and when they sat near, they were always touching. She gave a passing thought to preventing Charles and Jane from marrying by telling her of his past amorous affairs, but she surprisingly found that she did not have the heart to hurt her own brother.

She was considering what to do when she retired that night. The Darcys had gone upstairs an hour earlier, and when she passed their door, she heard an odd thumping noise. She stopped, curious, and heard what sounded like moaning. Alone in the hallway, she pressed her ear to the door and heard the muffled sounds of the couple calling out each other's names and declarations of love. She blushed, realizing what was occurring, and suddenly a burning desire to see the act came over her. Caroline looked quickly down the hallway and seeing it still empty, she tried the handle of the door. To her surprise and anticipation, it turned. Quietly she opened the door and slipped into the sitting room for the suite. She crept to the open bedroom door, and looked in. The light of a single candle provided the feeble illumination, but it was enough. The naked forms of the lovers were moving together on the bed. Elizabeth's legs were wrapped around Darcy's waist, and he was bending over her, his bare bottom moving with a constant rhythm as his powerful thrusts moved not only her body, but the bed so that it hit regularly against the wall. The room was filled with the sounds of the thumping bed, the creaking mattress, the slap of flesh, and the whispered words of the lovers. Caroline stood fascinated, watching them touch and stroke and kiss, and felt a deep desire building within herself. She was taken aback when Elizabeth cried out, clutching Darcy tightly, and thrilled when she saw that he continued his relentless motion. When he roared out his moment of pleasure, and collapsed on top of her, Caroline felt a distinct ache that she had never felt before. As she watched them, she had unknowingly walked into the room, inexorably drawn closer and closer, feeling the heat, and breathing in the scent of their union. When they finished, she was only a few a feet from the bed, staring at their sweat-slicked bodies, breathing heavily, and wanting to be the woman to lie beneath that man. It was when Darcy rolled off of Elizabeth and pulled her into his embrace that Caroline was discovered. Darcy's back was to her, but Elizabeth had just settled her head on his chest when she opened her eyes to look straight into Caroline's.

"MISS BINGLEY!!"

Darcy spun around and stared in disbelief at the voyeur. Caroline screamed, and with her hand to her mouth ran from the room. Darcy turned back to Elizabeth. "Was she watching us?!" Infuriated, he got up and stormed into the dressing room, pulling on his breeches and a shirt.

"Where are you going?" Elizabeth asked, rushing to pull on her nightdress and robe.

"To see Bingley. Either she goes or we do." He pulled on his boots and stepped into the empty hallway.

He proceeded to Bingley's door and pounded on it with his fist. The door soon opened and a half-dressed and confused Master of the house came to face the enraged countenance of his guest. "Darcy! What is wrong?"

Darcy pushed him into the room and slammed the door behind him. He told the horrified Bingley precisely what was wrong. "If it had been a man, Bingley, I would be within my rights to call him out! As it is, I demand that either your sister be sent away from here at first light, or Elizabeth and I will stay at the Meryton Inn or Longbourn until you are wed. I have tolerated your sister's behaviour for years, but this is the limit of my endurance. How she could have ever imagined that I would marry her is beyond me, and now with this latest display, I doubt that she would be acceptable by any honourable man!"

Bingley, a look of deep disgust on his usually buoyant face wholeheartedly agreed. He had hoped that Caroline would accept Darcy's marriage and finally seek out her own future elsewhere. That was not to be. He agreed with Darcy that she would be sent away to London in the morning and determined that he would send a letter to their relatives in Scarborough, asking them to take her in. She would get no further help from him, financially or physically. She would have to live on the interest of her dowry. It saddened him, but the break had to be made.

Darcy returned to his bedchamber to find Elizabeth absent. He noticed the breeze blowing the curtains, and looked out onto the balcony. There she stood, staring at the quiet garden. She looked up when he approached her, and held out her hand. He took and kissed it, then wrapped her in his embrace.

"What happened?" She asked.

"Bingley will send her away tomorrow." He said, hugging her tightly.

"It seems that you were correct to be concerned. I was wondering if she would have done anything else besides simply watch us." Elizabeth nestled her head on his chest.

"I do not even wish to think about it. Hopefully this is the final time that we will be under the same roof." He kissed her head. "And, we will be sure to always lock the door when we retire from now on." Elizabeth started to laugh softly. "What is so amusing, Lizzy?"

"I find myself jealous of her." He leaned back, looking at her with confusion. "She has had a view of you that I never will." Elizabeth smiled at him.

Finally understanding her he relaxed and smiling, whispered suggestively, "There is a mirror in your dressing room, my love."

"WHAT IS ON YOUR MIND, DARCY?" Bingley asked. The two friends were out riding the next morning. Caroline had her trunks packed and was dispatched to London at sunrise, with strict instructions on her expected behaviour. Bingley had also written to an aunt in Scarborough, asking if she will take in her now homeless niece. By silent agreement, the two men decided not to speak of the mortifying incident again. Elizabeth took a carriage over to Longbourn just after breakfast and they would not meet again until dinner time that evening. Despite the news of Mr. Bennet's dramatic change, Darcy was in no hurry to spend an extended visit with him. When Bingley suggested looking over the estate, he eagerly agreed. He also wanted to talk to his friend.

"My God, Darcy." Bingley said, numbly. His open, always happy face was creased with lines of distress. He felt shock, anger, and watching his friend's countenance, intense pain. "How are you faring? How is Elizabeth?"

Darcy hated talking about himself, his privacy was one of his most-guarded possessions, which made the experience with Caroline all the more infuriating, but he knew now, from sharing his past with Elizabeth, the relief that would come from talking about this particular event with Bingley. "We are better, I think. The nightmares for both of us are less frequent, and more easily stopped." He sighed. "I am afraid that Elizabeth has yet to feel comfortable walking alone for long periods, but I do admit to not encouraging her, either. I imagine with time we will both regain our confidence." He smiled grimly, "Perhaps she will put my nerves to the test while she is here in the familiar environment of Hertfordshire. I will not like it one bit, but knowing her, she will do it anyway."

"I will have the port ready for you as you await her return, Darcy." Bingley offered, regaining his humour a bit.

Darcy laughed softly. "Thank you, old friend."

They rode further, looking over the fields, and seeing the first hint of green as the seeds began to sprout. "What do you plan to do?" Darcy regarded his friend seriously. "Do you wish to purchase Netherfield?"

"I have not made a decision yet." He looked at Darcy, and then smiled crookedly. "My future in-laws have greatly enhanced their disposition of late."

Darcy laughed. "Ah, so the prospect of living next to Mrs. Bennet has improved?"

"A bit." He smiled. "My lease runs through Michaelmas. I may see if I can extend it to the New Year. At least then I would see what the hunting is like here in the autumn. It would also give me a feel for how invasive my relatives will be, and of course, I will be able to learn what Jane's opinion is. Perhaps she would prefer to live closer to her sister, instead." He looked to Darcy.

"Well, if you think about it, with the entailment, Jane's family will not be in Longbourn for many years longer. Not that I am wishing an early demise for Mr. Bennet, but it is a consideration." Darcy said, thoughtfully. "If you like, I will make inquiries about properties in the vicinity of Pemberley."

"I would appreciate it." They rode along silently for some time, enjoying the companionship. "Darcy?" Bingley said cautiously, breaking the silence. "How was your wedding night?"

Darcy sent him a punishing glare. "Surely you do not expect me to tell you that?"

"I mean . . . how did you . . . handle . . . you know . . . the first time for a lady . . . oh, I am putting this badly." He was bright red.

Darcy was amused, but he was not going to tell Bingley that. "Yes, you are."

"I have experience, but I have never been. . ."

"The first?"

"Yes."

"I would say just be slow and gentle." He looked at his frustrated friend, and decided to pity him. "Elizabeth and I laughed much of the way through it. It relaxed us quite considerably." He smiled at him.

"Laughed? I never would have thought of that." He looked hopeful. "That I can do!" He said, gaining confidence.

Darcy grinned. "Then have at it, Bingley!"

ELIZABETH LOOKED at the house where she had lived for nearly all of her years with mixed feelings. Jane's effusions over the change in her parents were difficult to believe. She still harboured a great deal of disappointment over her father's behaviour, but time and distance had helped, as had the strong, unending love and support of her husband. The carriage stopped and the moment that she descended, she was surrounded by women.

"Lizzy!" Lydia cried. "Oh, what a beautiful carriage! Do you think that Mr. Darcy would buy one for me and Mr. Denny? Did you bring me any presents? Will you take me to town to buy my wedding clothes?"

"NO! She is going to take *me* to town! Are you not, Lizzy? Lydia found her husband, and you and Jane have yours, it is my turn. You must take me there! It is still the Season! You can take me to balls and parties!"

"Girls, girls, leave your sister alone!" Mrs. Bennet walked up, far calmer than Elizabeth remembered her ever being. "Welcome home, Lizzy. My, this is a beautiful carriage, and this gown, is this one that your Aunt Gardiner purchased for you? She wrote to me about the trousseau that Mr. Darcy asked her to purchase for you."

Elizabeth ignored her two younger sisters and looked at her mother with undisguised astonishment. There was no fluttering handkerchief, or any call for smelling salts, just a simple, sincere, controlled excitement. It was astounding. She pulled herself together, and for the first time in years she found herself speaking to her mother like a sensible person. "Yes, Mama, this is one of the gowns that Aunt Gardiner purchased. I hope to select the rest of my new things soon, but will wait for my sister Georgiana to accompany me."

"How nice. Will you see her soon?" Mrs. Bennet took her arm and walked her into the house. Jane was standing at the door, watching the scene with a broad smile.

Elizabeth sent her a look of amazement then addressed her mother. "We expect Colonel Fitzwilliam to escort her here tomorrow. We will be taking her back to Pemberley with us after the wedding."

"We look forward to meeting her." Mrs. Bennet smiled. "Now, I know that your father is very anxious to see you. Why do you not go and speak to him, then you may join the rest of us to work on the wedding decorations. We expect the Gardiners to arrive by noon. When may we expect your dear husband and Mr. Bingley?"

"They will be here for dinner, Mama." She looked at Jane, who smiled at Charles' name.

"Very good, now off you go." Mrs. Bennet gave her a pat on the arm and gracefully departed to the kitchens.

"Jane, what has happened to her? Are you putting laudanum in her tea?" Elizabeth whispered hurriedly.

Jane laughed. "No, I think that she is the happy recipient of attention. It is extraordinary is it not?"

"I do not have words to describe it!" Elizabeth said, still amazed.

The sound of a door opening caught their attention. Mr. Bennet stepped out into the hallway. He stood looking at Elizabeth for a moment, then walked forward and without hesitation, wrapped his arms around her. "Lizzy." Suddenly they both started to cry. Jane turned and shooed Lydia and Kitty away to give them privacy. They held each other tightly, sobbing out all of the pain. After some time, Mr. Bennet lifted his favourite daughter's face from his shoulder, and looked into her eyes. "Come, let us sit down and talk." She nodded, and they went into the library and closed the door.

Instead of taking his customary seat behind his desk, he led her to a small sofa by the window where they sat down. He kept his arm around her, and she kept her face buried in his shoulder, as she did when she was a little girl. He took a deep breath. "Are you well, Lizzy? Your letter about what happened was devastating. Thank God your outstanding husband Mr. Darcy was able to find you, and deal with that reprehensible man."

At her father's reference to Wickham, Elizabeth was suddenly struck by a memory of that day. She was awash with Wickham's voice and the feel of his hot, rancid breath on her face. "Papa," She said shakily, still hidden in his shoulder, "When he was . . ." She hesitated, she could not say aloud what she was able to write in her letter. "When he . . . was with me, he said some things, taunting me. I know that his claim of . . .of . . . hurting Lydia was false because I had just read her letter telling me of her experience, so when he said that you wrote to him to ask that he help you to separate me from William, I knew that was false as well." She waited. Hearing nothing, she asked. "It was false, was it not, Papa?"

Mr. Bennet sat with his eyes closed, clutching his precious daughter to him, his face expressing the anguish of his twisting heart. His dreaded fear had come true, she knew his betrayal. He could not tell her the truth and lose her all over again. He could not. If Darcy learned the truth, he knew their separation would be forever. He was grateful she remained pressed to his shoulder so he could say, "Yes, Lizzy."

"I *knew* it was a lie. Everything he said to William was a lie as well. He was seeking to cause as much pain as possible." She concluded, relieved to know her father was not the cause of their terror.

Mr. Bennet felt his chest constrict with pain. The guilty knowledge of his actions would hang over him until the day he died. "Let us not speak of him anymore, Lizzy." He kissed her head, and tried to keep the quaver from his voice. "Now tell me, are you well?"

"I am much better, Papa. I could not have recovered so well if it were not for William's love for me. He is the best of men." She sniffed. "I am glad to hear that you recognize how good he is now."

Mr. Bennet closed his eyes. "I am ashamed, Lizzy, ashamed of myself for wanting to keep you from such a good husband; and ashamed of my behaviour and unpardonable words to Mr. Darcy. But most of all ashamed that my selfishness almost lost me the love of one of the dearest persons in my life, my daughter, Lizzy." He kissed her forehead. "Can you forgive a very foolish man?"

She looked up into his pained face. "Yes, Papa, if you are willing to recognize your errors, I am willing to forgive them. You will have to speak to William as well, because I will not speak for him. He was very highly offended by your accusations. But he is a very good man, Papa. I love him dearly."

"I will speak to him. I must, you see, thank him." He looked at her. "Not only must I thank him for saving you, but I must also thank him for saving my marriage."

"How did he do that? I could not help but see the incredible change in Mama, but what does William have to do with it?"

"The day that he asked for my consent, the day that he took you away from me forever, I threw some irrational, ridiculous, rash accusations at him, and he responded with anger and very pointed and correct statements. He asked me if I was afraid to live with my wife. I thought long and hard about that question. I decided that I never really gave my marriage a chance. When I did not have a son, I gave up entirely, and ignored your mother, and hid myself in this room, only to appear to make remarks on her silly behaviour which took away her confidence and only made her sillier. After I received your letter I saw how strong your relationship with your husband was. I realized what I had wasted. Instead of wishing to keep my favourite child near to me, I should have been concentrating on loving my wife. That day I vowed to begin again. As you can see, it has had a marked affect on your mother. I wish that I had done this years ago. How different my daughters might be today."

"Oh, Papa!" Elizabeth hugged him tightly. "I have missed you so much! I am so happy that you have decided to stop hiding yourself away in this room. Thank you for giving all of your family a chance to know the wonderful man that only I have known for so long. I love you, Papa."

"And I love you, Lizzy." They sat and hugged for a long time, and then wiping his eyes, Mr. Bennet drew himself up. "I think that Jane will need you. You should go to her aid. Your mother is much improved, but she remains a very silly woman."

Elizabeth laughed and rose. "I will endeavour to rescue my sister. Thank you, Papa." She kissed his forehead and left.

When the door closed behind her, Mr. Bennet closed his eyes and sighed. He had harboured a deep fear that somehow she would find out that he had contacted Wickham, and he was shaken to the core to hear her speak of it. He could not regret lying of his involvement, not now, not when he was finally re-establishing contact with her, not when he had made such great progress with his wife, not now that he was truly a changed and he hoped, better man. He would never forgive himself, and he would never forget what his actions began. That would be his penance. He knew that his relationship with Elizabeth had changed forever, that she would never look at him the same way again, but he was grateful for the chance to try and regain some of the respect she once had for him. And he was grateful for the exceptional man she had married.

BY THE TIME Bingley and Darcy arrived at Longbourn for dinner, Elizabeth had reached the end of her rope. Her mother was most definitely improved, but her younger sisters were not. Lydia and Kitty fought continually over Jane's wedding clothes, which she was trying very hard to pack. Mary had sequestered herself with the pianoforte, and that would not have been a bad thing if she had not insisted on singing. Elizabeth, who at one time missed the noise of her busy family, suddenly discovered that she was longing for the peace of Pemberley. She secretly thanked heaven that Darcy had not met her family before they were married. He surely would have run away as quickly as his horse could carry him.

So, she did as she had from the age of eight. She grabbed her bonnet and left the house to walk. She did tell Jane that she was going; thankfully, because when Darcy arrived to find no Elizabeth anywhere to be found he was ready to mount a full search. Elizabeth had told the wide-eyed Jane the tale of Wickham privately that morning so she understood Darcy's panic. She assured him that Elizabeth would be fine, and judging by the time, she should be home very soon. Bingley tried to appease him with the promised glass of port, and even Mr. Bennet came to offer his library to him, and distract him with a book. He declined all and instead remained outside of the house and paced.

Elizabeth could see him from the gate when she came into the garden near the house. She was struck by the intensely worried expression on his face, and felt absolutely terrible for it. She would have been back much sooner if she had not been waylaid by Mrs. Lucas. She approached him silently. He was striding back and forth, not even looking up anymore, the empty yard just made him panic more. Elizabeth positioned herself at the spot where he was making his turn, and waited for him to next arrive. He paced up and his downcast eyes spotted a gown. He stopped and looked up into the concerned eyes of his wife.

"Lizzy!" He grabbed her and held her tightly to him. "Please do not frighten me like this again!" Holding her allowed all of his suppressed fear to rise to the surface, and he expressed it in anger. Tightly grasping her shoulders, he pushed her away. His eyes burned into hers and he commanded, "You are never to go out walking alone again!"

"William!"

"I forbid it!" He declared. "You will walk with me, a companion, or a footman." His eyes searched her face, his jaw shaking with agitation. "I will not endure this torture again!" He let go of her and strode away, resting his hand on the corner of the house, trying to check his barely controlled emotions.

Elizabeth knew that he was acting out of fear. She walked to him and touched his shoulder. He closed his eyes tightly and hung his head, but did not turn towards her. "He is dead, William, he cannot hurt us again."

He took a great breath. "But what if there is someone else? What if you fall? What if you were lost?" His voice had lost some of the anger, but the pain was still very much present. "Perhaps you have recovered from it Elizabeth, but I have not. I am afraid that a lifetime will not be long enough. I am not exaggerating when I say that I could not bear this life without you." Finally he turned and stared into her eyes. "Do you understand?" This was not the pleading of a weak man, but a statement of fact by a man who knew exactly his heart and mind.

"William." Her soft voice held calm authority, and its effect was the wash of reassurance that he needed. She reached out and took his hands in hers.

He let out a deep breath and looked down into her eyes. "Yes, Lizzy?"

"Do you not think that it was a good thing that I was not frightened to walk alone for so far?"

"I suppose." He admitted grudgingly.

"I promise I will not stay out past my planned time again. I will always tell someone exactly where I will be and when possible, I will not go alone. But, sometimes I need that time to myself, as I did today." She smiled gently. "And, I would always prefer to take my walks with only you." She reached up and caressed his brightening face. "Believe me, darling, I do understand your fear. I have the same feelings about you every time you leave my side. But we cannot let it bury us."

He sighed and nodded his head, then leaned down and kissed her. "Thank you, my love."

Mr. Bennet was watching them from the library window, wondering how he could have ever considered keeping them apart.

They entered the house and were met immediately by Bingley and Jane. "You see, Darcy, all is well." He smiled reassuringly at him.

"Thank you for your support Bingley." Darcy was in no mood to joke about it, and he doubted that he ever would be. Elizabeth knew how upset he was and felt extremely guilty for the suffering he experienced, even if it was in his own mind.

Mr. Bennet was standing quietly nearby. "Mr. Darcy." He stopped glaring at Bingley and looked up with surprise. "Would you please join me in the library?"

Darcy glanced at Elizabeth and saw her nod and smile with encouragement. He met Mr. Bennet's eyes. "Certainly, sir."

They entered the room and again Mr. Bennet did not sit behind his desk. He took one of the two chairs before it and indicated the other to Darcy. "First sir, may I express my sincere appreciation and gratitude for your defence, rescue, and care for my daughter during the incident at your estate." He took a breath. "And now, may I please apologize to you for the inexcusable behaviour I displayed on every occasion we have ever met?" He then looked straight into Darcy's expressionless face. "Finally, I wish to thank you for changing my life. Without your words, I would have lost not only my favourite daughter's affection forever, but I would have missed the opportunity to begin anew with my wife, and hopefully, my other children." He humbled himself before him.

Outside of the library door, Jane and Bingley left to join the rest of the family in the drawing room while Elizabeth lingered. She waited nearly half an hour before it opened and Darcy appeared. He saw her anxious face and giving her a small smile, took her hand to kiss. "You father and I have come to a meeting of minds. I have invited him to visit Pemberley."

She touched his face. "Thank you, William."

Chapter 28

$\mathcal{U}$pon returning to Netherfield, they were informed that Colonel Fitzwilliam was awaiting them in the library and that Miss Darcy had retired to her rooms. Exchanging concerned glances, Darcy, Elizabeth and Charles entered the room. Richard was standing, staring out of the window. "Richard! We were not expecting you until tomorrow! What brings you here tonight?"

Richard searched their faces, and without a word, he strode across the room and wrapped his arms tightly around a very surprised Elizabeth. He closed his eyes as he held her to him. "Are you well, Elizabeth?" He asked urgently. Darcy stared at his cousin, his intense possessiveness driving him forward. Just as he was about to tear him away from her, Richard stepped back. "I heard what happened to you at Pemberley. I am so sorry, Elizabeth." He looked up at Darcy and reaching out for his hand, grasped it, "The terror you must have experienced, Darcy."

Elizabeth, caught for the fourth time that day with a reminder of the event, was not quite as able to suppress her feelings. This time, the tears began to fall. She took a great gasp of air, and tried to hold back a sob. Darcy, always alert for her emotions, was there in a heartbeat. He enfolded her into his embrace, and rested his head in her hair.

"You are safe, sweetheart." After a few moments, Elizabeth pulled herself together and looked up at Darcy's soft eyes. He kissed her gently and wiped her face. "Are you better now?"

"Oh William, I am trying so hard to appear well, and be strong and behave as my old self again, but I am just like you. I do not think I will ever completely recover." She reached up to touch his cheek. "I am so sorry for frightening you when I walked today; it was thoughtless of me to even risk worrying you. I was just trying to find a way to feel the way I did before . . ." Her voice trailed into a whisper and her tears slowly tracked down her cheek. Darcy knew full well that her calm and placating reaction that afternoon when she found him so panicked with her absence was her way of reassuring him. She was being strong when he was weak. He thought of how many times he needed to do the exact same thing for her over the past month when he had to leave her to work on Pemberley. How many times did he return home to find her sitting on the steps of the house, hugging herself, waiting . . .?

He held her to him, ignoring the presence of the other two men. "I do understand Lizzy, I do. I know how you are trying to prove to yourself and everyone else that you, we, are well, and that what happened had no effect on us, but I think that we both need to acknowledge that we are changed forever, and must start again as the new people we are." He kissed her head. "We have much to overcome, but if we keep talking to each other, together we will be well. I think that we have come a long way already."

She nodded and suddenly remembered that they were not alone. She blushed and looked at the two men. "Forgive me, I am so embarrassed." Finally pulling back from William a little, she took Richard's outstretched hand. "I guess that it will just take time." She smiled at the unhappy man. "You did nothing wrong, Richard." Bingley came over and patted her shoulder.

Elizabeth and Darcy continued their embrace. She smiled ruefully at the three men who were staring cautiously at her. "Enough!" She laughed, wiping the tears from her face. "I am not a specimen under glass!" The remark helped everyone to relax.

Taking a relieved breath, Darcy gave her a squeeze, and looked to his cousin. "Yes, Richard, it was an indescribable nightmare, but Wickham's death has helped us to realize that it will never happen again."

"Wickham is dead?" Richard asked with surprise.

"Yes, he died of pneumonia in prison about a fortnight later." Darcy looked at him, "How did you hear of this? I planned to tell you tomorrow."

"I was at Rosings last week, and paid a call on Mrs. Collins. I asked if she wished me to bring a letter to Elizabeth, and she said yes, and that she hoped you were recovered from your horrible experience. Naturally I had to ask what happened, and she showed me your letter. She expected that you would not tell many people about it, but I was sure that Darcy would rather tell me the story in person, so please do not be upset with her."

Elizabeth smiled. "I am not. I trust her judgment, and I know that she would not share this with anyone but you. I look forward to reading her letter. I have only told her, Papa, and Jane about it. In a way, I am glad that you have heard it already. I have no wish to again relive it, although, I think that I may have to tell one more person." She looked at Darcy, who nodded. "Georgiana."

He held her tightly and kissed her hair. Then looking at his cousin, he said, "We will talk later, Richard." He nodded, understanding Darcy's desire to spare Elizabeth from the conversation. "Have you any news of Anne?"

Richard's face became grim. "Miss Miller said that she is fading rapidly, it is a matter of weeks now, if that long."

"Miss Miller?" Elizabeth asked, exchanging glances of surprise with Darcy at the sudden blush that spread over Richard's face.

"Oh, um, yes, Miss Kathleen Miller is Anne's new companion. She replaced Mrs. Jenkinson. It is a blessing; really, she has much experience with death, and helping the person pass comfortably." He chanced a look at Darcy's raised brows. "She is a lovely young lady."

Elizabeth and Darcy smiled at each other. "Well I look forward to meeting her." Elizabeth said gently.

"She reminds me of you, Elizabeth; even Anne told me that you were similar." He said, brightening.

Darcy's brows creased. He was very aware of Richard's attraction to Elizabeth. Although he would be pleased if he had found someone, he hoped that she was not a mirror image of his wife.

"How are we alike?" Elizabeth was curious how others saw her.

He spoke eagerly, "Well you both love to laugh, and are well-read, and she is very kind, and she grew up on a small estate with no dowry, but unlike you, she did not find a Darcy to marry, so when she came of age, she was encouraged to go and become a lady's companion to support herself."

Elizabeth was thoughtful. "So she is essentially living the life that I might have had." She looked up at Darcy, who immediately kissed her.

"I would have found you, Lizzy."

She stroked his face. "I hope so, my love."

Richard watched the interaction between the two with a wistful expression on his face. "I will be leaving first thing in the morning. I wanted to bring Georgiana to you, and," he paused, looking at the embraced couple, "I just wanted to be sure that both of you were truly well." He blinked the emotion from his eyes and turned to Bingley. "I am sorry that I will be missing your wedding, but I hope that you understand that I must return to London and Rosings. Please extend my wishes for joy to your beautiful bride.

"I am disappointed to be losing your company, Colonel, you would have added greatly to the festivities. I will be sure to tell Jane of your congratulations. You will always be welcome in our home as a great friend of our family." Bingley shook his hand sincerely.

"Thank you, sir. I hope to someday extend the same invitation to you." Richard smiled.

Darcy looked at his cousin, concern crossing his brow, "What are your plans, Richard? When do you leave for Kent? Are your parents going with you?"

"I was hoping to depart in two days' time." Richard cleared his throat. "I have something that I need to take care of in London before leaving." He looked at Darcy. "I have decided to give up my commission."

Darcy let go of Elizabeth and embraced him. "Thank God. I was hoping that you would make this decision. You survived Richard, you lived through it. I am proud of what you accomplished, and sorry that you had to experience it at all." They drew apart and Richard turned to shake his hand. They both were emotional. Darcy knew the horrors that his cousin had experienced. He was the one confidant outside of fellow soldiers that Richard had.

Elizabeth hugged him tightly, and whispered in his ear so nobody else would hear; "Perhaps now you might find a new future with Miss Miller?" He looked down at her smiling lips, surprised, and a blush spread over his face.

Bingley looked on, "Are you well, Colonel? Your face is red."

Elizabeth laughed, and Richard started to chuckle as well. "You are far too perceptive, Elizabeth!" She turned and wrapped her arms back around Darcy, who held her possessively and was regarding her with a quizzical brow. "I will go up and greet Georgiana if she is still awake, and then I think that I will retire." She looked at the three men, "I am sure that you gentlemen will be quite able to entertain yourselves." Elizabeth kissed Darcy, and he reluctantly let her go from his embrace. "Goodnight, gentlemen." She smiled as she left the room.

Darcy watched her go and turned to meet the smiles of his two closest friends. His mouth curled slightly and he walked past them. "Shall we be seated, gentlemen? I have a feeling this will be a long evening."

Richard laughed and Bingley went to fill glasses with port. "Will you come to Rosings, Darcy?"

He frowned. "I want to. I would like to see Anne. I am; however, unsure of our welcome from Aunt Catherine. She has enough to contend with now. I was wondering if seeing Elizabeth, the woman who I chose over Anne, would be too much for her, and likely be cruel. We have not communicated since our departure from Rosings. I have every intention of eventually healing the breach, but the events with Wickham in all honesty kept me from thinking of little else but Elizabeth. I do not know what to do. Do you have any opinion?"

Richard rubbed his face, lost in thought.

Bingley handed them their glasses and sat down. "May I say something, Darcy, as an impartial observer?" Seeing his nod he continued. "I imagine that seeing Elizabeth would be very painful for your aunt, a reminder of the life she hoped for her daughter, or if nothing else, the marriage she hoped for her daughter, regardless of the reasons behind it. But, in the long run, she may eventually come to appreciate your willingness to be there, if only for a brief visit, at this difficult time. That is what she will remember. After all, Elizabeth is not going away, and eventually she will have to face the fact that she is your wife. Perhaps Elizabeth, in her own way, may be of comfort to her."

"I think you make an excellent point Bingley." Richard regarded his cousin. "How about this; after the wedding, go to London. Surely there is something that you need to take care of in town, shopping for Elizabeth, business concerns, and when I arrive at Rosings, I will send you word of the situation. London would not be out of the way for you, and you would be well situated for travel in either direction."

Darcy nodded. "Yes, that is what we shall do then. Send us a note to Darcy House, and we will proceed from there."

"Good, I think that Father and Mother will be pleased with your decision." He glanced at Bingley then rose to go close and lock the library door. "Now Darcy, I want to hear of Wickham." He placed a hand on his cousin's shoulder, and then went to settle himself back in his chair. Darcy drew breath, and again that day, told the story. Hours later, after Richard had debriefed him in a way that only a military man could; the men walked upstairs to their rooms. Darcy quietly moved about, trying not to disturb Elizabeth, and was filled with undeniable relief to find her open arms waiting for him when he slipped into bed.

THE NEXT MORNING, as Darcy and Elizabeth went down towards the breakfast room, Georgiana heard them in the hallway and came dashing out, immediately accosting her brother. "William!" She threw her arms around him, smiling from ear to ear. "Oh how I have missed you!" Then before he could say anything, she attacked Elizabeth. "Oh, Elizabeth! I have missed you, too! Finally I have my sister! I have so much to tell you!" She grabbed Elizabeth's hand and dragged her away into the drawing room, while Elizabeth turned her head, staring with bemusement at the men.

Darcy and Bingley stood in awe. "What happened?" Bingley asked him.

"I do not know; she must have been saving that up for her arrival. She is happier this morning than I have seen her in months, but this level of enthusiasm is quite singular." He looked at Bingley. "I suggest that we simply enjoy it, and see where it leads." Bingley nodded, and they followed the ladies into the room.

Georgiana wished to take Elizabeth to her room and talk to her all about the weddings, her impressions of Pemberley, and about a certain young man. Unfortunately, her brother and his friend were there.

"Georgiana, I know that you desperately wish to talk to Elizabeth, but perhaps it could be delayed until at least after breakfast?" Darcy suggested.

"Oh, bother!" Georgiana cried. Elizabeth tried to hide her smile behind her hand, and Darcy looked on with astonishment.

"Young lady, you have obviously spent entirely too much time at Matlock House with your cousin. Fortunately he has departed already, and you will be back under stricter guidance." He admonished. "Now, shall we return to the breakfast room?" He held out his arm for Elizabeth. She rose and took it, smiling at his stern face.

"Miss Darcy?" Bingley was trying hard not to smile, and held out his arm for her.

The rest of the guests soon arrived, and Georgiana had no chance to talk to Elizabeth until they boarded the carriage to ride to Longbourn. Alex had been invited to the wedding and was expected to arrive sometime that morning, and the men wished to be there to greet him. Louisa stayed behind to look after preparations for the wedding breakfast the next day.

ELIZABETH SAW that the noise of Longbourn was becoming too much for Georgiana and suggested that they take a walk. Both ladies were happy for the opportunity. Elizabeth knew that she needed to tell Georgiana about the encounter with Wickham before they reached Pemberley, as everyone there certainly knew the story. She steeled herself for the conversation, knowing that she had to remain in control of her emotions in front of Georgiana. She held back the most frightening details, but it was still enough to send the young girl into tears and hugging her new sister tightly. "Elizabeth, I can hardly imagine how frightened you and William were."

Elizabeth pulled away and squeezed her hands. "It was terrifying, but we managed it together, and continue to support each other daily. I do not know how I could have survived this without the love we have for each other."

Georgiana nodded, remaining silent for several moments, and then making a decision, she drew up her courage. "Elizabeth, I need to ask you something."

"Yes, Georgiana? You know that you can talk to me about anything." Elizabeth smiled at her.

"Aunt Elaine talked to me about . . . what happens when you marry, on the wedding night. She said that since I will be coming out, it was time for me to hear of these things." She looked at her, afraid of her reaction.

Elizabeth smiled. "That was a very good idea of hers. My Aunt Gardiner began speaking of those things with me at about the same age as you are now, and I appreciated it more than I can say. Did she tell you something that you need clarified?" She held her hand, encouraging her to talk.

"No, not exactly." She said, and closed her eyes. "I think that I might have experienced that situation already." She said softly.

"What do you mean, Georgiana?" Elizabeth gripped her hand.

"With Mr. Wickham." She hung her head, her eyes still closed.

Elizabeth controlled her emotions. "What exactly happened, Georgiana?" She stared at her earnestly.

"It was at Ramsgate." She looked at Elizabeth's worried face and then down at her twisting hands. "We were walking along the beach one morning, very early.

Mrs. Younge said that it would be fine for us to walk without her, she seemed to encourage it." She paused then took a deep breath. "There was an area where great piles of rock formed a kind of secluded room, and he led me there. We sat down together in the sand, and he told me wonderful, sweet things, how pretty I was, and how I made him feel. He kissed me, and it felt so good. He put his arms around me, and it was so warm. He just kept touching me and kissing me, and he asked me to kiss him back and touch him because it would make him happy. I did.

Then somehow we were lying next to each other and kissing some more. I felt him fumbling a little with his hands, but I was so overwhelmed with the feeling of his kisses that I did not think too much about it. I felt a breeze around my legs, but I could not see them, because he was lying so close that I could not move. I said that I was cold, and he said that he would warm me, and the next thing I knew, he was laying on top of me, and I felt something hard poking at me over and over. He was grunting, and moving, and I asked what was wrong, and he said that he was in pain, and only my kisses would make him feel better. So I put my arms around his neck and kissed him more. I did not wish to disappoint him. I felt that hard object poking into my leg, and then he groaned so loud, and I felt something wet. He was shaking, and I asked if he was still in pain, and he said no, he was better. He said that some seaweed was on my leg, and he took his handkerchief and wiped it off. Then he straightened his clothes and told me I was beautiful and he could not wait to marry me. We walked back up to the cottage, and he said he would see me the next morning, and maybe we could kiss the same way again. That did not happen because William arrived that afternoon." She paused, looking at the astonished countenance of her sister. "After Aunt Elaine talked to me, I started thinking about what happened. Did Mr. Wickham and I, did we, am I . . ."

Elizabeth pulled herself together and looked into her wide innocent eyes. "No, Georgiana, Mr. Wickham did not violate you, but he certainly tried." She squeezed her hand. "Did you ever feel that hard object enter you? Did you feel any pain at all?"

She shook her head. "No, it was on my leg. That was where the wetness was, too."

"Thank God." Elizabeth held her hand and looked straight into her eyes. "You did not experience what happens between a man and his wife. Mr. Wickham tried, but thankfully, failed." She closed her eyes. How naïve she was! And how could she have allowed him to touch her, let alone raise her skirts! Did nobody ever speak to her before, of maidenly comportment if nothing else? She knew that William would have, in his own awkward way. But coming from a man, a very shy man at that, it was obviously ineffective, but surely her governess or her aunt, or even that school she attended . . . she looked back into her questioning eyes and squeezed her hand, how alone this girl was without a mother or sister to guide her. Wickham was obviously a master at seduction to have convinced her to follow him so easily. "You may talk to me about this anytime, Georgiana, but your brother must never ever know about it." She could not begin to imagine William's reaction, his guilt and subsequent rage would be terrible to behold.

"That was not love, was it Elizabeth?" Georgiana said quietly, watching carefully Elizabeth's emotional face.

"No, that was the farthest thing from it." She held her hand tightly.

Georgiana listened. She saw how changed William was, and how he was smiling and so relaxed around Elizabeth. It had to be the result of their love. "Elizabeth? How do you know if you are in love?"

She regarded her new sister with caution, afraid to hear what else she was to reveal. "Why do you ask, Georgiana?"

Georgiana looked at her, biting her lip. "I have been receiving some attentions from a man, and after what happened with Mr. Wickham, I am afraid that I do not trust my judgment."

"What kind of attentions?" Elizabeth asked, fearing the worst, and wondering how the Colonel and her aunt and uncle could have missed them.

"Oh, nothing overt, I assure you, he just. . ." She smiled; a faraway look in her eyes. "He comes to church and always seems to find me; and smile, and sometimes I see him outside of Matlock House, gazing at the windows, and we did meet once at the milliner's, and Aunt Elaine invited his mother to come and call."

Relieved that this was not what she feared, she asked, "What did your aunt think of him?"

"She told him that I was not yet out, but she seemed to like him. I was not there when his mother called, but Aunt Elaine said that Mrs. Carrington was a very kind lady."

"Mrs. Carrington? Is this young man Alex Carrington?" Elizabeth asked, stunned.

"Yes! When he saw us in the milliner's shop, he had to reintroduce himself to me. I had not seen him for so long. But he said that he had just come from seeing you here." Her eyes were bright with excitement. "He is ever so handsome!"

"He is also ever so much older than you, Georgiana." Elizabeth said pointedly, while wondering what exactly her new brother was thinking. He would be inheriting a sizable estate, and was very eligible. Why would he be interested in such a young girl? He did not strike her as mercenary, and he certainly would not be a friend of William's if he were not honourable.

Georgiana sighed. "I know. I will not be out for another nine months, or at least, that is when I will be presented at court. It seems silly to have to wait so long."

"Georgiana, did we not have a talk about behaving as an adult?" Elizabeth's mind was working rapidly. She needed to reign in this enthusiasm before Alex himself arrived at Netherfield and she had a chance to speak to William.

"You mean; I should not be mooning over Mr. Carrington, Elizabeth?" She looked at the ground. "But, how should I be feeling? He does seem to make an effort to gain my attention."

"Yes, and he should know better. I will have a talk with your brother, and he will be speaking to Mr. Carrington about his behaviour as well. It is not at all proper, and even if it is done in innocence, as I sincerely hope it is, it must be stopped until you are out, and he has sought your brother's consent." What on earth is this about?

"What does love feel like, Elizabeth? How do I know that what I am feeling is love or just infatuation?"

Elizabeth sighed, wondering how to answer such a question. "Georgiana, there is no one description for love. I think that the definition for every person is as different as they are. What I can tell you is that for me, it is a feeling of regard, esteem, trust, safety, wholeness, desire, happiness, and joy that I feel with and for your brother, a feeling that is with me always. Add to that the desire to care for him, see to his needs and fulfil his dreams, and the deep wish to share these things and experiences together. It is very complex." She looked at the young girl's furrowed brow. She was obviously reviewing her every encounter with Alex, and measuring him to Elizabeth's ideal. "Do your feelings for him, whatever they are at this point, extend beyond the transitory moments when you are in his presence?" She asked her gently.

"I think about him when he is not there. Is that what you mean?" Georgiana studied her, trying to understand.

"Yes and no." Trying to describe such a deep and powerful emotion was difficult. "Do you feel that he is necessary for you to . . ." She struggled for the words. Breathe? No, that is too dramatic, no matter how true it was. Finally settling on something, she said, "To feel complete?"

"I do not know. I do not know what that means."

"Then you are not ready for this kind of love, Georgiana. You are very young. Do not be in a hurry. If Mr. Carrington is truly interested in you, he will wait. But there are nine long months before you are out, and I sincerely doubt that your brother will allow any man to court you before you finish your first Season, so that means that you must wait just over a year before anything can come of this. Please do not overwhelm yourself with thoughts of a man who may not be waiting for you a year from now. There is no need to be hurt. There is plenty of time."

SINCE THE ENCOUNTER at the millinery shop, Alex found himself spending an inordinate amount of time in the vicinity of Matlock House. He would find excuses to walk or ride past, sometimes stopping to stare up at the windows, hoping for a glimpse of a blonde head. He followed the family one Sunday morning, and since then, he attended their church, always making a point of greeting the party and taking hope from the blush that overspread Georgiana's face. He noticed that she began seeking him out in the crowded pews, and the expression of content that came over her face once her eyes found his. She was so young. He knew that, and sometimes he thought he was the greatest fool for engaging in this pursuit. It would be a very long wait before she was out, and there was still Darcy to contend with.

He was greatly surprised and pleased to receive an invitation to Jane and Bingley's wedding. He was grateful that Bingley did not hold his past attention to Jane against him. It felt good to be so accepted as part of a larger family. He dearly loved his parents, but he did admit to some sense of loneliness being an only child. He decided to accept the invitation to stay at Netherfield, and wondered if Miss Darcy would be there, and if he should speak to her brother. His mother did pay a call to Lady Matlock some weeks earlier, and though she was quite nervous about it, she said that she survived the experience unscathed. The Lady was curious, and took care to mention that her niece would not be coming out for nearly a year. Amanda took the news as she knew it was meant to be conveyed, to warn her son both of Miss Darcy's age and unavailability for quite some time, and to perhaps rethink his interest.

Since he was only to be at Netherfield one night, he decided to ride and pack his things for the two days in several saddlebags to be pressed into presentable clothing by the servants. In a matter of hours, he arrived to the warm welcome of his host.

"Alex! Welcome to Netherfield!" Bingley exclaimed as he strode across the foyer. "We are so pleased that you could accept our invitation." He reached out and wrung his soon-to-be brother's hand.

"I was very gratified to receive it, Bingley. How is your fair bride?" He smiled at the man's irrepressible joy.

"She is lovely as always. Of course, she is also knee-deep in wedding preparations! Thankfully she now has Elizabeth and Miss Darcy to aid her." He grinned.

"Ah, Miss Darcy is here!" His heart jumped. "I thought that your aunt and uncle were to take her to Matlock, Darcy?" He said as he shook his friend's hand.

"That was the original plan, however, we have a family illness to attend, and they were unable to leave London. My cousin delivered her here yesterday before returning to town this morning." He looked grave.

"An illness? Nothing too serious, I hope?"

"My cousin Anne."

"Oh, I am so sorry." Alex knew of Anne de Bourgh's ill health. "Is there hope?"

Darcy shook his head. "Not this time, I am afraid. We may still go to Kent. I am waiting for word from my Uncle Matlock on what course we will take." He sighed. "In the meantime, I think that you will enjoy your time here much better than the last trip."

"Really? The last trip was for your wedding, almost, anyway." He grinned.

"You will be pleasantly surprised with Mr. Bennet." He smiled at him.

"Truly? Has he changed?" Alex glanced at Bingley.

"Dramatically."

"I would certainly like to hear about this." Alex was curious; perhaps he might have a relationship with his birth father after all.

DARCY WAS PACING. Elizabeth and Georgiana were to return from Longbourn in time for tea, and they should arrive soon. He needed to talk to his wife, his conversation with Alex concerned him greatly. After the gentlemen had joined Hurst for a few rounds at the billiards table, Alex took Darcy aside and asked that they have a private conversation. The two men entered the library, and settled into some chairs near the unlit fireplace.

"Well, Alex, what can I do for you? I think that I have told you all that I can about Mr. Bennet. You will just have to assess him for yourself and proceed from there." Darcy smiled slightly at his friend.

"No, this is not about Mr. Bennet." He took a breath and plunged in. "It is about Miss Darcy."

"Georgiana?" Darcy sat up straight and leaned forward, concern etched his face. "What exactly are you talking about, Alex?"

Swallowing, he began. "I think that I am developing a tender regard for Miss Darcy." He flinched when he saw the rapid change in Darcy's expression.

"And how exactly has this come to pass? She is not yet out!" He demanded.

He rushed to give him his explanation. "Nothing sinister, I assure you, Darcy! I merely encountered her in a shop one day when she was out with your aunt, and reintroduced myself to her. I found her lovely and charming, and since then, I have endeavoured to attend the same church service as she, and to greet her when we meet. Truly, nothing more than that, I would never do anything to harm her! Your aunt asked me to tell my mother to call on her, and she did."

Darcy's face was red with anger. "She did? And what was the result of this meeting? Are you engaged?" He snarled.

"Darcy! How can you say such a thing! My mother tells me that your aunt was very direct, and said that Georgiana was not out, was very young, and that it would be at least a year before she was available to be courted." He was trying hard to appease his very unhappy friend.

Relieved that his aunt had shown some sense, but angry that she had not bothered to inform him of any of this, he sat back a little in the chair. He regarded the very flustered face of his friend. "So, what is it that you want, Alex? My aunt is quite correct. Georgiana will not be available for courtship for a year. She is eleven years your junior. Perhaps you should reconsider this, because I assure you, she will not be allowed any early opportunities to be with you." He thought of Wickham. No, there was no chance at all for that circumstance to ever be repeated.

"I realize the age difference, Darcy, but there is something about her, a gentleness, a sweetness, and she is so very well educated that she would surely never be the same as the women of the *ton* who only think of the newest dress or piece of gossip. I want a woman who will keep me on my toes." He smiled. "I think that under the influence of Elizabeth, she will, in a year's time, be quite remarkable. I think that I am willing to wait. I just want to tell you of my interest now, before every other young man arrives to beat down your door." He took a breath, he had said his piece, and waited.

Darcy sat staring at him. He had no doubt at all that what he said was true, under Elizabeth's guidance; Georgiana would be an entirely different person in a year's time. "Alex, I had been hoping to avoid conversations with likely suitors for quite some time. I know you and your circumstances, and there is nothing wanting. I cannot reject you out of hand for anything except perhaps your age." He paused, weighing his words. "I will tell you this. I do not want you approaching her without a family member present, and no overt displays of interest may be made to her until she is out. At that time, if you are still interested, I will invite you to whatever affairs we hold for her, and will be sure that you are on her dance card. I will attend to her reaction to you very closely. You are a good man Alex, but you will have to wait."

He nodded. It was more than he expected, and could not argue with Darcy in any way, if anything he was grateful. "Thank you, Darcy. I will adhere to your conditions. I will behave in a completely gentlemanly manner whenever I am in her presence, and will not speak to her during this visit without someone else being present."

Darcy stood. He held out his hand and Alex gratefully took it. "If you are patient, perhaps we will become closer brothers than we already are. I make no promises." Alex nodded, and they left the room. Darcy departed to wait for Elizabeth outside and Alex went to his rooms.

The coach arrived, and Georgiana went upstairs to her bedchamber. Elizabeth met Darcy and was ready to follow her example. The exhausting conversation with

Georgiana about Wickham and Alex had left her drained. All she could think about was an intense desire to lie down, preferably in her husband's arms.

"Lizzy." Darcy kissed her hand. "Please, could you take a walk with me? I need to talk with you."

She saw the distress in his face, and put her own exhaustion aside. But she did have a request. "I need to talk with you as well, William, but could we perhaps find a comfortable place to sit and have our discussion? I am afraid that I just have not the strength for a long walk."

Immediately, Darcy's concern centred on her. "Are you not well? Perhaps we should just go to our chambers?"

"I am just tired, William, but I think that we would have more privacy outdoors. Come, I think that I know where we can go." She smiled up at his worried face, and took his hand. They walked out into the garden, and found a comfortable grassy area beneath a tree. Darcy settled his back against the trunk, and pulled Elizabeth to him, so that she rested her head on his chest. "Now, I will close my eyes, but I promise I am listening." She kissed his chin, and nestled into his embrace. "Please tell me what is troubling you."

He continued to examine her peaceful face. Elizabeth's hand stole up to stroke his cheek. "Please stop worrying and talk to me before I do fall asleep." He smiled, and taking the hand that rested on his face, he kissed the palm. He then told her of his conversation with Alex. Relieved, Elizabeth told him of Georgiana's feelings for him. They agreed that she was in no way ready for a serious relationship. Elizabeth agreed with his decisions on how to proceed. They would just have to sit back and watch carefully, and wait until next year.

Chapter 29

he morning of the Bingley wedding dawned with sunshine and a soft breeze. Elizabeth stood by the open window in their bedchamber breathing in the fresh air and did not hear the silent approach of her naked husband. "Good morning, my love." He whispered into her ear, while sliding his hands around her waist. "You crept out of bed so quietly; I did not realize that you had left until I began to feel cold."

She looked back up at him, smiling. "How could you possibly feel cold on such a warm day?"

"You know that I cannot sleep without you by my side. You have quite ruined me. And yes, I was cold, but I know how you might warm me." His deep voice whispered suggestively, as his lips began trailing a path down the back of her neck.

Her eyes closed, "What do you have in mind, William?"

Saying nothing, his hands began exploring her body over the gossamer fabric of her robe, and he turned her slowly around to face him. His eyes were dark with desire, and his lips burned against hers. He stroked her mouth softly at first; and deepening the pressure he pulled her against him, leaving her breathless and in no doubt of his wishes, his every touch enflamed her.

"I thought you were cold." She whispered weakly as she clung to him. His lips descended to stroke her throat and her legs nearly buckled in response. Darcy held her tighter, enjoying her trembling with his touch, and hungrily reclaimed her mouth. One hand rose to caress her breast, while the other fell to slip inside the robe and stroke her. The wetness he felt spreading over his fingers filled him with a possessive pride. *She is wet like this for me!* The certain knowledge of his wife's desire made him almost painfully swollen.

His lips finally tore from hers to whisper heatedly, "Touch me." She smiled against his rough cheek.

"Where?"

He pulled slightly away and looked deeply into her sparkling eyes. "Everywhere."

They held the gaze for a moment, then applying her hands and her lips, she began caressing his face, his shoulders, his chest, moving languorously lower and lower, his eyes closed, and he lost himself in her touch. The feel of her sweet hands on his rock hard arousal brought forth a low moan. She felt his body quake as one hand grasped him and stroked, while the other cupped and fondled the surrounding curls.

"Oh Lizzy, please, please taste me." He begged, his voice rasping in her ear.

Elizabeth's eyes met his and she smiled, "Yes, darling."

He watched as she slowly dragged her fingertips down his hips and settled on her knees before him, feeling her own possession. This was her Will at his most vulnerable. She gently traced over his engorged length. Darcy entwined his fingers through her hair, panting with the anticipation of the extraordinary pleasure of her soft lips encasing him. His moan was long and he had to hold onto her shoulders for support. Loving his incoherent whispers, she suckled his rigid manhood, one hand at its base while the other firmly held onto his tight buttocks. His fingers wound into her long curls, stilling her movement, and he began slowly thrusting into her mouth, watching with fascination as her lips took in more of him. Beginning to tense, and not wishing to spend so soon, he removed himself and helped her to rise. He held her face in his hands and kissed her deeply, wordlessly expressing his appreciation.

Darcy drew away and whispered, "Come back to bed, my love."

He untied the belt of her robe and slipped it from her shoulders, then taking her hand; he led her to the bed, lovingly scooped her up and laid her amongst the tousled linen, then remained looking down at her. "Will?" His expression was one she did not know, but one she hoped she would witness every day for the rest of her life. Climbing in he gathered her in his arms, pulling her to lie atop him. One hand gently caressed her back while the other held her head.

"So beautiful." He whispered. Elizabeth brought her mouth to his, sensing his desire to take their lovemaking very slowly. She hovered above then gave him the barest hint of a brush across his mouth. "Ohhhh." She gently took his lip between her teeth and nipped lightly. "Lizzzzzy." She nuzzled her face into his neck and sensuously glided her lips over the skin, feeling him quiver as he moaned.

"What do you wish of me, my William?" She whispered in his ear as she continued her gentle ministrations with her mouth and fingers.

"You will think me a beast if I tell you." He whispered. She raised her head and met his shy, but hopeful face.

"I trust you."

He responded by kissing her deeply then rolling so he was on top. He kissed her again, and looked once more for her permission. Seeing her smile, he rose from her, and asked her to lie on her belly, and then encouraged her onto her knees. She looked back to where he kneeled behind her. "Will?" His gaze was pleading, and she nodded. He rose behind her and they joined, and he thrust slowly; fulfilling the long-held fantasy of watching himself move in and out of her. His hands held her hips, and her gasp of surprised at his entry and movement enticed him to rapidly increase his pace, sending Elizabeth almost instantly to find her passion. Her cries urging him on sent him into a vigorous, powerful movement demanding her to concentrate on remaining upright as he finally found the intense release that the slow seduction gifted him. Elizabeth's legs gave way and they collapsed together on the bed, both of them gasping.

He quickly rolled off of her and immediately pulled her to his chest. "I have wanted to do that for so long, Lizzy. Did I hurt you?"

She laughed and kissed him. "Did I sound like I was in pain? No, darling, you surprised me, that is all."

Smiling, he embraced her. "Well, you are the one who was talking about positions, and this one always intrigued me."

"And why is that?" Her eyes twinkled up at him, and she pushed a stray curl from his damp brow.

"Can you not imagine the possibilities, my love? And the locations?" He grinned at her; the devil danced in his eyes.

"Mr. Darcy! I never would have imagined there was such an adventurous rake living inside of you!" She laughed while taking his face in her hands.

"I did buy that book, did I not?" He captured her lips and caressed her body. "I knew it would come in handy someday."

"Perhaps you should give one to Charles and Jane as a wedding gift." Elizabeth suggested, kissing his nose.

"Hmm. Now that is something they would appreciate more than candlesticks!" They laughed, and cuddled, dozing, until they reluctantly rose. Darcy held her tightly to him. "Thank you so much for marrying me, Lizzy."

She embraced him as tightly as she could. "I could only give myself to you, Will."

JANE'S WEDDING was everything that Elizabeth's was not. There were flowers, new gowns, many people, and an elaborate wedding breakfast. Darcy stood up with Bingley and endeavoured to ignore the crowd of people, and only attained relief when his eyes found Elizabeth's where she was standing with Jane. Together, they held each other's gaze and relived the recitation of their own vows.

The wedding party and guests left for Netherfield for the wedding breakfast. Mrs. Bennet had originally planned to hold it at Longbourn, but with the unexpectedly gracious offer by Mrs. Hurst, who was now acting as hostess at Caroline's removal, to give her full access to the far grander home, she could not say no to the change in plans.

Mr. Bennet stood watching his wife with twitching lips. Mrs. Bennet was attempting to contain her effusions, and he could see her continually stopping herself from waving her handkerchief. He noticed he had been joined by someone, and looked up to see Darcy standing nearby, his eyes glued to Elizabeth who was laughing with Jane and Mrs. Gardiner.

"Well, Mr. Darcy, I imagine that you are considering yourself quite pleased that you missed such a display for your own nuptials." He gave him a wry smile.

Darcy turned his gaze to take in his father-in-law. "Sir, the story of my wedding will be one that I can imagine my children will repeat with relish. You are correct, though, a wedding breakfast was never something that I looked forward to; the only memory of importance is the one where Elizabeth said 'I will' to me."

"I am grateful that you did not give up on her, after my behaviour." He said, gravely.

"I never would have given up on her, sir." Darcy said, his eyes returning to their home. At that moment, Elizabeth looked up to him, and seeing his stare and his proximity to her father, she blushed and joined them.

"And what are you gentlemen talking about?" She asked, looping her arm with William's.

"We were discussing the story of our wedding, and what we will tell our children." He took her hand and brought it to his lips, loving the flush of her cheeks.

"Hmm. I think that we need to determine what story we will be telling your family first. We have some time before the need to entertain children will arise."

"So true, and we may be seeing them soon." The sound of Lydia and Kitty laughing and carrying on drew his attention, and he frowned. Elizabeth looked at him and sighed. "I apologize William; they are a bit lively today."

"Forgive me, Elizabeth, but they seem a bit lively every day." Noting her cringing at his words, he squeezed her hand. "When does Lydia marry?"

They looked at Mr. Bennet. "Her wedding is set for the end of September. A good, long engagement."

"I imagine Lydia is unhappy with that." Elizabeth noted.

"She is, but Lieutenant Denny's duties will keep him busy until then, he is scheduled for an extended leave in October. It was a pleasant surprise to see him arrive here this morning in time for the wedding." He nodded to a corner of the ballroom where Denny was talking with his soon-to-be brother, Bingley, then closed his eyes at a high pitched squeal. "Perhaps when she is gone, Kitty will settle down."

"Well, Papa, perhaps with the additional attention from you, she and Mary will both improve."

"To be like you?" Asked Mr. Bennet, disbelieving.

"That would require a miracle, sir." Darcy quietly said. Mr. Bennet looked up, unsure of his meaning. "Nobody could ever be compared to Elizabeth."

She smiled. "You are far too kind, sir."

He smiled back. "I know."

"Mr. Darcy!"

"Yes, my love?" His warm gaze offset his twitching lips. Elizabeth admonished him. "It is not gentlemanly to deliver a compliment then take it back a moment later."

"Are you saying that I am not behaving as a gentleman?" He frowned at her.

"That is precisely what I am saying, sir." She frowned back.

Mr. Bennet looked on in admiration. His daughter had truly found her perfect match, and he now found that he took even more pleasure from seeing her share herself with the man she loved than he would have if she were to stay at Longbourn with him. He could not wait to see how this pair faced parenthood together and hoped that he would be there to witness their joy someday.

Darcy kept a close watch on Georgiana and Alex. True to his word, Alex only spoke to her when another family member was present. Georgiana was completely confused over her feelings for him since her conversation with Elizabeth, and found herself frequently seeking her sister's eyes when she was standing with him. Darcy and Elizabeth both noticed that Alex drew many looks of curiosity. He did not seem to be singled out for his resemblance to Mr. Bennet, but rather for his unmarried and wealthy status. Mrs. Bennet, knowing already of his supposed attachment to a woman in London did not spare him a second glance. Mr. Bennet was concentrating most of his attention on Elizabeth and Darcy, and therefore only paid scant attention to the young man.

Mrs. Bennet and Mrs. Hurst discovered that they worked well together, and put on a beautiful display of foods for the breakfast. Darcy was quite hungry and filled his plate with the tempting delicacies, while Elizabeth seemed to be disinterested.

"Are you not hungry, Lizzy?" Mrs. Gardiner asked.

Elizabeth sat at the table, toying with the food on her plate, and gave her a small smile. "No, not really."

"She has not been hungry for weeks." Darcy said softly, looking at her with concern. "She has been very sleepy, as well."

Leaning towards him she whispered, "I think that is your fault." She gave his arm a squeeze. He smiled. Darcy thought that she was still recovering from that day. She cried so easily, and sometimes seemed so sad. Mrs. Gardiner had other ideas. When the meal ended, she took Elizabeth into a corner of the room and started asking her questions.

When she left, Darcy was approached by Denny and Bingley who made the introductions.

"Mr. Darcy, it is a pleasure to meet you. I am happy for the opportunity before my own wedding day."

Darcy bowed and smiled slightly, still very much the reticent man when meeting new people. "I am pleased to meet you as well. I seem to be acquiring new brothers at a rapid pace. Please call me Darcy, sir."

Denny smiled, he was a very affable man. "Thank you, sir, and please call me Denny." He looked Darcy up and down. "It seems that I have received some incorrect information about you."

Darcy's brow furrowed. "I do not understand you."

"You are acquainted with George Wickham?"

"I was; he is deceased." Darcy's lips pressed together and he searched the room for Elizabeth but did not see her.

Denny's brows rose. "I did not know of that. After how he treated my Lydia, I cannot say that I regret him at all. Well it seems his plans never came to fruition in any case."

Bingley and Darcy exchanged glances. "What plans were those?"

"Before he was discharged from the militia, actually several weeks before, I would say, he received a letter from someone asking for his help to prevent your marriage. Obviously that was unsuccessful, as I see you and Mrs. Darcy before me, and quite happy as I have observed. Congratulations, sir, she is a wonderful woman. I enjoyed meeting her while I was stationed in Meryton." He smiled, oblivious to what emotions he had stirred.

Darcy controlled the tension he was feeling and asked quietly, "Do you happen to know who sent this letter to Wickham?"

Denny shook his head. "No, I do not. He was simply gloating about it, and was actually thinking it would be his ticket out of the militia and into a gentleman's existence. Nobody who heard him believed it, but he seemed quite sure that he would somehow profit greatly from the letter writer, and I believe from you somehow." Finally he noticed Darcy's dark countenance, "I hope that he did not have the opportunity to act on this?"

Bingley jumped in. "No, no. Wickham, from what I have heard, died several weeks ago, and as you said, Darcy and Elizabeth are obviously happily married."

Denny waited for Darcy to respond, but he was far away. He was trying to determine who would have contacted Wickham. Realizing that he should remove himself and that he probably should have said nothing, the soldier made his excuses and returned to Lydia. Bingley grasped Darcy's shoulder. "There is nothing you can do about this now, Darcy. Let it go."

Darcy stared at him incredulously, and was about to tell him that was impossible in no uncertain terms when Elizabeth approached, simply glowing with happiness. Her elation naturally drew him straight to her side.

"What is it, Elizabeth?" He could not help but smile into her dancing eyes.

"I am simply very happy, William." She took his hand and held it tightly. Aunt Gardiner told her of her suspicions that she may be with child. By their calculation, she would only be four weeks or so along, far too soon to make an announcement, and far too soon to begin worrying her husband. Her aunt recommended waiting to give him the news when she felt the baby begin to move, if it truly existed, in another eight weeks.

"Please tell me, Lizzy." He begged.

"Can I not be full of joy on the day that my dearest sister weds your best friend?" She teased. Darcy looked at her suspiciously. "Come, let us go and speak to the happy couple. I know that we must be leaving for London soon, unless you would like to proceed directly to Rosings?"

Still trying to read her face, Darcy stared at her for several moments more. He shook his head and kissed her hand, silently admitting defeat for the moment. "I have not heard anything from Rosings, and do not want to go where we may not be wanted. I think that we will stay with the initial plan and go to London for a few days, then decide from there." He smiled slightly. "If nothing else, you and Georgiana can go shopping for the rest of your trousseau."

Elizabeth shook her head, "Ah sir, you have found a way to avoid the dress shops at last!" He grinned, relaxing again. The two approached Jane and Bingley, who were staring at each other with undisguised longing.

Darcy smiled at the sight and grasping his friend's shoulder spoke quietly in his ear. "So, have you settled on a plan for tonight?"

Bingley startled. "I thought that you do not speak of such things!"

"I do not speak of my own situation. I never said anything of yours!" He grinned. "Besides, you did ask me for advice."

Bingley looked at the floor. "Yes, I did, and I think that I will follow it." He looked over to Jane, who was tearfully embracing Elizabeth.

"Oh Jane, we are two old married women now!" Elizabeth hugged her tightly. "I know that you will have a wonderful life with Charles, he is a very good man."

"I know he is, Lizzy. I am so happy." Jane tried to find a dry bit of handkerchief to wipe her eyes.

"William was going to invite you to come visit us in a few months. I hope that you can come. Aunt and Uncle Gardiner will be visiting in July when they take their tour of Derbyshire, and it will be so good to see the both of you as well." She gave her a squeeze. "I cannot wait to show you Pemberley! It is breathtaking!"

"I am so happy to hear you say that, my love." Darcy's voice sounded in her ear. "I am afraid that it is time for us to depart. Let us farewell your family and be on our way."

Soon Darcy handed Georgiana into the coach. He turned to see Alex looking thoughtfully at her face in the window. The men's eyes met, and a look of agreement passed between them. Mr. Bennet stepped up and shook his hand, wishing them a safe journey. Darcy now saw the source of so much of his Elizabeth's wit. He watched the son and unwitting father standing side by side, with the same wistful expression on their faces.

Finally Elizabeth finished saying goodbye to everyone and Darcy handed her into the carriage. After one more wave, he climbed in and took the seat by her side. The coach began to move and without hesitation or regard for his sister's presence, he pulled her into his arms. She rested her head on his shoulder and together, they rested their hands on her waist. Her thoughts were with the life that may be growing within her, and his began to wonder over Denny's revelation. So few people knew of his attachment to Elizabeth at the time, who had objected? He thought, Mr. Bennet, obviously, and he had met Wickham, but he also knew that the man had tried to seduce Elizabeth, so he certainly would not have contacted him to try and entice her away. Darcy thought many things of Mr. Bennet, but he was not that low, was he? He shook his head. Who else? Aunt Catherine, but no, there was no time. They were married only days after she was told of their engagement.

The vision of Caroline watching him love Elizabeth came to his mind, and he shuddered with revulsion. Yes, that is someone who would certainly stoop to such an act, but again, she did not know Wickham, or know of the engagement. Again his thoughts returned to Mr. Bennet. He was angry, and desperate. Darcy looked down at Elizabeth's peaceful form, now cuddled against his chest, sleeping. He glanced over to Georgiana who was lost in a book. Was Bingley correct, should he let it go? Was Denny correct, Wickham was lying about the letter? He certainly did form a plan to extract money from him, but was it truly a letter that was meant to separate them that instigated it? What if it *was* Mr. Bennet who began this? He certainly would not have predicted the horrific events that followed. Darcy tightened his embrace of Elizabeth. He vowed that if he learned for certain that Mr. Bennet had instigated their pain, the man would never see her again, no matter what improvements he made to himself. But he did not know. And likely never would without a direct confrontation with her father. He gently brushed a curl from her face. For now, he would be forced to remain silent, but would forever be watchful.

INSTEAD OF LEAVING for Rosings quickly as he had planned, Richard and his parents were delayed in London for several extra days. It seemed that resigning his commission took longer than expected. They departed the day after the Bingley wedding. The carriage arrived at Rosings and Richard pulled uncomfortably at his new civilian clothes. "I suppose those will take some getting used to, Son." Lord Matlock smiled at him.

"But they look very well on you, Richard." Lady Matlock declared.

"It is the blasted cravat that bothers me the most." He said, giving the fabric a frustrated glare. "That is the one great feature of a uniform, no neck cloth, just a good black stock!" They all laughed.

The family's frivolity was silenced as they passed the church. The tolling of the bell from the tower was heard. It was the passing bell, alerting the village of an imminent death. Silently they counted the peals, six, a woman. There was a pause, and as the carriage continued up the drive, they counted the following peals, twenty-seven. It must be for Anne.

Inside of the house they were greeted by the housekeeper, Mrs. Withers, who informed them that Lady Catherine had taken to her bed. The physician was concerned about her and had prescribed laudanum to calm her agitation over

Anne. Lord and Lady Matlock said that they would go to visit her first. They entered the room to find an unfamiliar woman sitting by her bedside. She did not appear to be a servant.

"Good afternoon. Are you Lord and Lady Matlock?" The plain-faced woman asked after she rose to her feet.

"Yes, and you are?" Lord Matlock addressed the woman, but was looking at the peaceful countenance of his sister.

"I am Mrs. Collins, the pastor's wife. I thought that I might be of assistance here until the family arrived." Charlotte stepped away from the bed. "Yesterday Lady Catherine was hysterical, shaking Lady Anne when she fell into a deep state of unconsciousness. The physician was fortunately here, and prescribed laudanum to calm her. Miss Miller sent me a note asking if I could come and sit with her, as she was busy with Lady Anne." She looked at the still form of the previously formidable woman, now appearing very small and old. "The doctor wished to be notified when you arrived, to decide if you would like to awaken her now, or wait until Lady Anne passes. You may have heard the bell tolling as you arrived." She looked at the sombre face of the brother, noting the similarities to his sister, but also seeing the evidence of a life of laughter in the deep furrows around his eyes and mouth, something that Lady Catherine de Bourgh never achieved.

"Mrs. Collins, I am deeply grateful for you taking the time to be here for our family." He turned to his wife, looking lost.

Lady Matlock gave his hand a squeeze. "Yes, Mrs. Collins, we are thankful for your help. From what you say, our niece is near her end?"

"The physician and Miss Miller believe that it will not be long." She said softly.

Lady Matlock took charge. "I believe that Catherine would want to be awake when she passes. Perhaps she will be calmer with us here. We should send for the physician, and discuss how best to rouse her. I will speak to Mrs. Withers about it. What should we tell Darcy? Should they come?"

Charlotte's demeanour changed. "Are Mr. and Mrs. Darcy coming?"

Lady Matlock noted the sudden brightening of the solemn woman. "Do you know them?"

"Yes, I grew up with Eliza, Mrs. Darcy. Longbourn is next to my father's home, and she stayed at the parsonage when she visited here at Easter. My husband is her cousin." She smiled, remembering, "I was the first person she told of her engagement to Mr. Darcy. She was walking on air."

Lord and Lady Matlock both smiled at the image. Focusing on something joyful for a moment brought relief to the room. "Yes, I believe that she still is. They attended her sister's wedding, and they intended to leave for London immediately afterwards."

"Yes, Jane and Mr. Bingley's wedding. I wish that I could have gone, but it seems that I was needed here." She looked down at Lady Catherine.

"Thank you again, Mrs. Collins. I think that you can safely return to your own home now. I will be sure to tell Elizabeth that we met."

"If you need anything else, please do not hesitate to send for me." Charlotte curtseyed, gathered up her sewing, and left the room.

WHILE HIS PARENTS attended to Lady Catherine, Richard went up the stairs towards Anne's bedchamber. When he reached the top, he heard a door open, and Kathleen stepped into the hallway. She looked up to see Richard. Their eyes locked, and both of them felt their hearts start to pound. Richard walked, seemingly taking years to reach her, and when he finally did, he looked down into her blushing face, wanting to kiss her hand, and her soft lips.

"Miss Miller, I am pleased to see you." He spoke, trying to put so much more meaning into his voice.

"Colonel Fitzwilliam, I am happy to see you have arrived safely." Kathleen met his gaze, and took a sharp breath, seeing his ardour.

"Ah, Miss Miller, I am Colonel no longer. I am now merely the Honourable Richard Fitzwilliam." He smiled. "I have resigned my commission. It is time for younger men to fight the battles. I am ready to settle down."

"That is wonderful news!" Kathleen said, hoping in a small part of her heart that maybe, just maybe, he might want to settle down with her. "I am sure that the army will feel your loss, though, sir."

"Ha! I think the men I was training will be dancing a jig in relief of my absence!" He laughed, loving her blushes. Then, seeing the obvious exhaustion in her face, he returned his thoughts to the most pressing concerns. "Miss Miller, you look very tired, I know that this has been difficult, how is my cousin?"

"She is no longer responsive, sir. It will be soon. I was just going to refresh myself before going back to her." She smiled slightly. "I will return very soon. Perhaps you could keep her company until I do?"

He wanted to stay and talk with her, but he knew that this was not the time for courting. He nodded. "Yes, I will be happy to watch over Anne until your return." He bowed, and taking a breath, entered the darkened bedchamber. Closing the door behind him, he saw a young maid sitting by the bed. He dismissed her, and smiled at her grateful expression.

He took the chair and took Anne's hand, and told her that she was loved and could go whenever she was ready. Kathleen returned unnoticed then, and listened to his soft words, tearing up at his tenderness. She pulled herself together and walked to stand beside him. They watched as Anne took a breath, then a long pause, another breath, and then nothing. They waited, staring, for several minutes, and then Kathleen checked her heart and placed her ear near her mouth. She was gone.

Richard stood with tears tracing down his face and let go of her hand. Without thinking, they together began to recite the 23rd psalm, and when finished, Richard reached out and wrapped his arms around Kathleen, and held her tightly to him. She rested her head on his shoulder. Without saying a word, they knew that all three of them had found their home.

Chapter 30

*I*t was with great relief that Darcy paused in the doorway of Elizabeth's dressing room and saw her standing before the mirror in a pale pink gown. The bombazine that she had worn for the past six weeks to honour Anne was gone. The black fabric seemed to depress her spirit. She seemed so sad and tired. He hoped that the brightening of her mood would come with the new wardrobe. She was happy to wear mourning for Anne; it was the only gesture she could make for the woman who so kindly welcomed her into the family. Lord Matlock suggested that only Darcy come for the funeral. As women, Elizabeth and Georgiana could not attend, and Lady Catherine was not strong enough to see Darcy's wife yet. The ladies stayed in London, and he made the day trip to Rosings.

"You look beautiful, Lizzy." He walked into the room and kissed her.

Elizabeth smiled up at him. "Thank you William. It feels so good to wear a happy colour again. I imagine Georgiana is overjoyed dressing this morning."

He slipped his arms around her and held her tightly. "I hated your beauty being hidden away."

"Thank you, William." She whispered

"For what, my love?" He asked, kissing her nose.

"You are the only one who has ever thought of me as beautiful." Her eyes were bright. "I was always told that I had great wit, but no beauty, at least, next to Jane."

"Then whoever said that was blind." He could not seem to break through the strange sadness that came upon her suddenly and just as suddenly disappeared, and hoped that the arrival of the Gardiners that afternoon would help both of them. He planned to seek Mr. Gardiner's advice.

Elizabeth did feel a little better than she had. Her appetite had returned. The smell of certain foods no longer seemed to bother her and she was not so sleepy. She knew that William was very concerned. She just was not ready to talk about it yet. After her overwhelming conversation with her aunt at Jane's wedding, she was so disappointed when her courses began several days later. It was intensely painful, and much heavier than usual, and she had a feeling that when she spoke to her aunt, she would learn the truth of what she felt in her heart. She had miscarried. The only thing that she was grateful for was the knowledge that she had not told her husband of her suspicions.

He was blissfully ignorant of what did not happen, although she thought, smiling to herself, he certainly was confused when she suddenly began to experience her monthly courses for the first time in their nearly three month marriage, and she had to explain to him that this was something that would occur regularly. She tried to reassure him that they rarely left her bedridden and in such pain. Eventually, she knew that he would puzzle out the truth, but she was not ready to bring up the subject. Not yet. She barely acknowledged it herself. They took their customary morning walk, and returned to the house for breakfast.

"Oh Elizabeth is it not wonderful to wear colour again!" Georgiana said as she spun around the room.

Elizabeth laughed at her exuberance. "It certainly is Georgiana. I wish that women were as fortunate as men, and could simply wear a black armband or ribbons." She looked over to Darcy, who was nodding his head emphatically and laughed again.

Darcy opened the letter that was sitting by his place setting and began to read. "This is from Richard." He smiled. "He has proposed to Miss Miller." Darcy looked up, and seeing Elizabeth's happy face, he grinned. "It seems that he just could not explain her continued presence at Rosings now that Aunt Catherine has decided to move to the townhouse in London. He felt that he would make the great sacrifice of ending his bachelorhood and marry the girl." He laughed. "He plans to emulate us, Lizzy. He will procure a license, and just pull her into the church at Hunsford and marry her with no great fuss. In fact, he may have done it by now. He was accompanying Aunt Catherine to London to see her to the townhouse, and planned to arrange the marriage settlement while there."

"What do his parents have to say about it?" Elizabeth asked, her eyes dancing.

Darcy consulted the letter. "He has not spoken with them yet. He does say that if his marriage can even approach the joy that he knows we share he will be a lucky man." His gaze met Elizabeth's and they were lost in each other until Georgiana spoke.

"Will we meet Miss Miller soon, William?" Georgiana had become accustomed by now to her brother and Elizabeth frequently forgetting about her presence, and had learned to simply start talking and eventually they would refocus on her.

"I am afraid that it may be some time, Georgie. We will be entertaining the Gardiners, then the Bingleys, and then we must travel to Hertfordshire for Lydia's wedding."

"Why do we not invite them for Christmas?" Elizabeth asked. "I remember Aunt Gardiner telling me how Pemberley was always opened for visitors then, but Mrs. Reynolds said that the tradition ended. Could we begin again? Perhaps have a ball? I think that I should be confident enough by then with my duties, and it will give me some practice for entertaining during Georgiana's Season."

"Oh yes William! Please? We could invite all of our family. I would love to have a ball and see Pemberley decorated properly for Christmas again!" Georgiana said with enthusiasm.

Darcy could not help but smile at the two dearest people in his life, so full of excitement. It was wonderful to see Elizabeth feeling joy. "As much as I truly dislike the ordeal of a ball. . ." He paused, watching their anticipation, "I think that it is time to reinstate the Christmas tradition." The ladies both jumped up and kissed his cheeks, hugging him. Darcy pretended to fight them off, but loved the attention. "Enough!" He laughed. "I am going to finish some work before our guests arrive." He stood and lovingly kissed Elizabeth, and shaking his head, grinning, left the room.

Georgiana set off for her lessons with Mrs. Annesley, and Elizabeth rose to meet with Mrs. Reynolds. She wished to make sure that all was prepared for the

Gardiner's arrival, and set to work deciding the menus for the week. Once they arrived, she wanted no domestic worries to prevent her from enjoying their company. Her confidence in her duties as Mistress was growing steadily. Her mother had many faults, but she did give the Bennet girls a thorough grounding in what was involved with managing a household. Pemberley was nearly ten times the size of Longbourn, but the same principals applied. Mrs. Reynolds was vastly pleased with her new Mistress. And Elizabeth had earned her respect very quickly. Not simply for her domestic skills, but for the life and happiness that she brought back to the estate. She had changed Darcy and Georgiana. Darcy was still the quiet, reserved, sombre man he ever was, but in the presence of his wife, he allowed himself to express his happiness in laughter and open affection. It was glorious to see. Georgiana seemed to be gaining confidence in herself, and was not as shy. Mrs. Darcy was kind and amiable, but she was also a force to be reckoned with, and had earned the unending loyalty of the staff by displaying her fortitude when surviving the attack by Wickham.

"There, Mrs. Reynolds, I think that settles the menus for the whole week. Is there anything else that we need to address?" Elizabeth handed the sheaf of papers to her and looked at her inquiringly.

"There is one other subject that has been concerning me, Mrs. Darcy." Mrs. Reynolds said quietly.

"Yes? Please tell me." Elizabeth smiled encouragingly, wondering at the unusual hesitation.

"I noticed some changes in you, madam. For some time I suspected that perhaps you might be with child, but I understand from Rosie that is not possible." She looked at Elizabeth, whose smiling face had disappeared, and was replaced by one of sadness. "Mrs. Darcy, were you with child?" She asked gently.

Elizabeth looked down and nodded. "It was not long. I hardly believed it myself, but my aunt told me the signs to watch for, and they were all there, until. . ." She could not go on and buried her face in her hands.

Mrs. Reynolds embraced Elizabeth, and she finally stopped denying the truth and cried. It was at that moment that Darcy came into the room, having finished speaking with Mr. Regar and hoping to see Elizabeth before returning to answer correspondence. Seeing his wife sobbing in his housekeeper's arms, he immediately came forward, and knelt by the chair.

"Lizzy, what is wrong?" He begged, staring from her to Mrs. Reynolds.

"I think that Mrs. Darcy needs to talk with you, sir." Mrs. Reynolds gently pushed Elizabeth away from her, and was immediately replaced by Darcy. She quietly left the room, turning to look at the embraced couple before closing the door behind her.

"Lizzy?" Darcy had gathered her in his arms and carried her to a large wing chair by a window, and settled her in his lap. "Darling, please tell me what is wrong. You have been so sad for so long, and I have been at a loss as to what has made you this way. Please do not shut me out." He held her tightly, kissing her head and stroking her back. Elizabeth's sobs faded but she kept her face buried in his shoulder. He could barely hear her soft, broken voice.

"I am so sorry, William. It seems that my sadness and need for more sleep and less food was for a reason. I was with child." She ended in a whisper.

Darcy at first did not hear her say "was" and began to rejoice. Then the truth hit him. "You are no longer with child?" He asked softly, embracing her. He felt her head shake. "This explains your courses." He left it at that and kissed her.

"Should I have told you my suspicions?" She asked in a small voice.

He took a deep breath and let it out slowly. "Some part of me says yes, and the rest is grateful that you did not." He was saddened by the loss, but he knew that he would have been devastated if he had known of the pregnancy.

"I listened to my aunt's advice to not say anything until I felt movement. I never did. Somehow, it did not feel real to me. I know that I had symptoms, my eating and sleepiness you noticed, and there were other things that only I could feel, but . . ." She paused, thinking. "I suppose that I did not allow myself to become attached to the idea of being a mother until I was sure, until I could share it with you."

"Perhaps that will help both of us. Since neither of us truly knew. . ." He was at a loss.

Elizabeth turned in his embrace. She saw sadness but mostly she saw his concern for her. She stroked his face and he leaned into her touch, closing his eyes. They both were well aware that miscarriage was common; childbirth often carried risk, and death for the baby or mother not unusual.

She kissed him, and his eyes opened, staring deeply into hers. "We will try again, my love."

"When you are well, in body and spirit. I shall await your call." He ran his fingers through the curls at her neck.

"Do you wish to know next time? As soon as I suspect?"

"As soon as you are convinced, I wish you to tell me, whenever it occurs. I wish us to face all things together."

She snuggled into his chest, pressing her ear to hear his steady heartbeat. "So it shall be." She wrapped her arms around him, safe in his embrace, and so glad that he knew.

THE GARDINER'S CARRIAGE rolled into Pemberley and the astonishment on the faces of the occupants would undoubtedly make its owner proud. Even Mrs. Gardiner, who had seen the estate once before in the winter, was awed by the stunning natural beauty that the grounds and house displayed. Darcy, Elizabeth, and Georgiana were all waiting outside of the house to greet them.

Mrs. Gardiner's eyes swept up and down her niece's form, and she saw no visible signs of the pregnancy, but when her gaze rested on her face she saw beneath the smile evidence of tears in her red, puffy eyes. She quickly glanced at Darcy, and saw the same sadness on his face. She had a sinking feeling that she knew what was behind it, but would wait to ask. Instead, she drew Elizabeth into a particularly loving embrace. "You look lovely my dear, you bring even more beauty to this extraordinary estate."

Darcy was standing by, watching them, and took Elizabeth's hand. "I could not agree with you more."

They whisked their guests into the house, and up to their rooms with the agreement to meet again in an hour for tea. Elizabeth laughingly volunteered to guide them to the proper room, as she assured them, they would surely be lost otherwise.

"Well, Aunt, tell me the news from Longbourn! I have had no letters of late." Elizabeth was seated next to her aunt, pouring out the tea.

"You have had no letters because I have been charged to bring them with me. They are in my luggage; I will bring them to you once it is all unpacked." She smiled at Elizabeth's eagerness. "But as to the news, let me see. Well, your father and mother's antics continue to surprise and confound your sisters and the neighbourhood in general. They have taken to strolling down the lanes after dinner, and have been seen stealing an occasional kiss in the process." She smiled at Elizabeth's wide eyes. "There is even some mention of them going to London for a short visit to take in the theatre, perhaps after Lydia's wedding."

"That would be an enormous sacrifice of Father's to do such a thing." Elizabeth shook her head, and looked at Darcy. "He despises London, too many people, too much noise. He likes a very controlled, quiet atmosphere."

"In that we have something in common. I like London for the occasional cultural performance, but would much prefer to spend my life right here with you."

The Gardiners exchanged smiling glances. "Well, Lizzy, I think that you will be pleased to hear this bit of news, your father has decided to send Kitty to a finishing school, hoping to remove Lydia's influence from her behaviour. He wished to send Mary as well, but she has no desire to go. I have a feeling that she will be the child that will stay at home with her parents forever, just when they are hoping to rid themselves of all their children and be alone!" Mr. Gardiner laughed.

"Kitty to school! That is extraordinary! I wonder who my sister will be when she comes away from it." She looked to Georgiana. "What did you think of school? I never attended, so I cannot even imagine what she will encounter there."

Georgiana, still shy in company, saw her sister's encouraging smile and drew breath. "I did not enjoy school at all, Elizabeth. I liked my friends, of course, and being with other girls, but sometimes they can be so mean, especially the ones from titled families. The daughters of peers are quite cruel sometimes. They were very much concerned with class. I am afraid that your sister may be in for a difficult time if she is not sent to the best school for her." She looked at Darcy.

"Yes, as much as the Darcy name is admired for being very old and wealthy, we are not titled. I will be happy to advise your father on which school to choose, as we certainly reviewed a great many of them when finding the best for Georgiana. I think that you did learn a great deal from the experience, but as I hated being sent away as a child, I can certainly understand your lack of enthusiasm. In that, dear sister, we are very much alike." He smiled at her.

"I think that Papa would appreciate your help, William, thank you." Elizabeth was encouraged by his willingness to communicate with her father, at least on Kitty's behalf. The distance between them was great, and likely would remain forever, but at least he was willing to behave civilly with him.

"Now, as to Lydia, she returned to Brighton, of course, to be near her Lieutenant Denny. She remains with the Forsters, and I understand that she is becoming very impatient waiting for her wedding day. I have an uncomfortable feeling that she may simply demand a trip to Gretna Green from the man!"

Elizabeth stared at her aunt in astonishment. "She would not! Elope? When a wedding is already being planned?"

"Lizzy, you know how impetuous your sister is, especially now when she has completed all of her shopping for her wedding clothes, she has nothing left to look forward to but the wedding, and almost two months of waiting will be impossible for her. Perhaps it would be a blessing for all that she has her way in this."

Elizabeth closed her eyes, ashamed at the truth of her aunt's words. "Let us hope that Mr. Denny has the good sense and willpower to outlast my youngest sister." She looked up to Darcy, who had his lips pressed together tightly. He would not discuss his true feelings about Elizabeth's sisters in front of anyone but her, and alone. "Now, tell me some happy news, are Jane and Charles well?"

"Oh yes, they are as happy as larks, both always smiling, never a complaint. Jane is always calm and serene, and Charles is exuberant and laughing. It is quite extraordinary. Of course, it is early days in the marriage; it is difficult to believe that one of them might not eventually find something to frown about."

"You have been friends with Charles for years, William, have you ever seen him unhappy?" Elizabeth smiled up at him. Darcy started; the mention of Denny took him back to their conversation at Bingley's wedding. He refocused on his amused wife.

"Yes, I know that is difficult to believe, but it has happened, however, it is generally associated with the actions of his sisters more than anything."

"That I can believe!" Georgiana exclaimed, and quickly clapped her hand to her mouth. "Oh, I am so sorry!"

"Never apologize for speaking the truth, Georgiana, but perhaps, be sure of your companions before you do!" Elizabeth laughed, and the rest joined in.

IT WAS NOT UNTIL the next day when Mrs. Gardiner found a few minutes alone with Elizabeth, and they had the chance to quickly discuss her symptoms. The aunt sadly confirmed what the niece suspected. She had miscarried. Elizabeth felt that she had no tears left to cry, but she managed to find them anyway, and let down the happy mask she had been wearing. Mrs. Gardiner held her and related her own experiences, and it helped Elizabeth to know that she was not alone. Before they could speak further, Georgiana joined them, and seeing Elizabeth's teary face, grew concerned.

"Elizabeth are you well? Has something happened?" She asked anxiously.

Elizabeth had no intention of telling her about the miscarriage, so she quickly created an excuse. "I am quite well, Georgiana, I assure you. My aunt and I were talking about some family history, and it just made me a little sentimental, that is all." She looked up to her aunt for help.

"Yes, Georgiana, I do not know if you have discerned this about your sister yet, but she is very soft-hearted. She hides it well, but she is quite easily moved." She smiled at them both.

"Oh, I know how soft-hearted she is. I have seen it when she thinks nobody is looking."

"What do you mean, Georgiana?" Elizabeth asked.

"I have seen you when you are alone with William. I see the way that you smile at him, almost like a little game. He is in a dark mood, and you just keep smiling a little more and a little more, until he just cannot resist you and smiles back!" She laughed and looked at the now blushing countenance of her sister. "It is very sweet!"

"Your brother is very sweet, Georgiana." She said softly.

"RICHARD!" I did not expect to see you! What brings you to town?" Lord Matlock rose from behind his desk and came to shake his son's hand.

"I accompanied Aunt Catherine, and I have some business to address while I am here." He took a seat. "I have applied for a marriage license, and spoke to my solicitor about a settlement. Upon my return to Rosings, I intend to marry Kathleen."

Lord Matlock sat back, considering his son. "You just became engaged days ago, what is the rush?"

"Life is short, Father. I have seen enough of it to know that truth for certain, and Kathleen, who was compelled to become a companion to survive, has seen more than enough herself. Neither of us ever really expected the chance to marry for love. I had the burden of being the second son, and she had the reality of no dowry or connections. We both faced the prospect of having to marry for necessity, if at all. I have been given this gift by Anne to be my own man, and she charged me to bring happiness back to Rosings. I think that it will honour her memory more than anything else I could ever do to marry a woman who I truly love and respect and fill that cold, tired estate with life." Richard fixed his piercing blue eyes on his father, almost defiantly.

A slow smile began to spread over Lord Matlock's face. "Son, I am proud of you. I have been proud of you since you were a little rascal running about and poking me in the leg with your wooden sword." The two men both grinned at the memory. "I want you to be happy, and if you and Miss Miller see no need to delay, than I do not either. You are hardly a babe, and she is certainly not a blushing lass in her first Season."

He chuckled. "No, at thirty, you could hardly call me a stuttering youth; I certainly know my own mind. And Kathleen, well, I do not believe that she ever had a Season, but at five and twenty, she certainly has the wisdom of her years, and I appreciate that so much more than I would some little girl."

"I have a feeling that you have not informed her of your plan, Son." Lord Matlock's eyes twinkled at him.

Richard pursed his lips, failing at hiding his smile. "No, I intend to return to Rosings, and grab her hand to drag her down to that idiot Collins and marry her as soon as I arrive."

"Do you think that she will appreciate that? She might have had dreams of a grand affair for her nuptials. Believe me Son, a wife has a very long memory for the misdeeds of a husband, and she will find a way to extract her vengeance if she is crossed." He raised his brow, and knocked lightly on his desk for emphasis.

Richard laughed. "She is a feisty lady when you get her dander up. But no, I do not think she will mind. I told her the story of Darcy's wedding, and she was very thoroughly impressed with it. I think that she admires Elizabeth greatly and cannot wait to meet her."

"I think that they shall be great friends, Richard. They are similar, although, I would say that Miss Miller is not quite as confident and bold as Elizabeth." He smiled, remembering the arch of Elizabeth's brow when she challenged him.

"I look forward to seeing them together." Richard smiled. He had never lost his deep admiration for Elizabeth, but he was grateful that he had found Kathleen before he allowed himself to act upon it, to the detriment of his relationship with Darcy. He was happy with his choice. Kathleen was very well suited for him, even more so than Elizabeth, and he was happy that he recognized it so quickly.

"Well then, Son, perhaps you should mention this to your mother. I imagine that you will be returning to Rosings soon?"

"Yes. I left a note for Collins that I wanted to purchase a license to marry, and to keep quiet about it. I will return tomorrow morning and plan to marry her by noon." He was determined, but very happy.

Lord Matlock rose, and shook his son's hand. "Let us go and see your mother. I do not wish to miss her reaction." They left, grinning, to go and face the Lady.

Chapter 31

"*Jane.*" Bingley was ready to broach the subject of moving north. They had just finally rid themselves of the Bennets who came to dine with them again that week, and despite the astonishing improvement in Mrs. Bennet, and the mellowing of Mr. Bennet, their company was not something that he had counted on as a daily occurrence after he wed. "I have been giving it some thought, when the lease for Netherfield is up, I will not renew."

"You will purchase it?" Jane asked, looking up from her sewing.

"No." He stood and paced a bit. "I would like to look elsewhere." He shot her a glance. "I was thinking of Derbyshire, perhaps."

"Near Pemberley?"

Eagerly, Bingley sat next to her. "Yes! Darcy sent me the particulars of several estates within a reasonable distance. I thought that we could look at them when we go to visit."

"We would be leaving Mama and Papa." She said quietly, thinking that would be good.

Bingley worried that she was upset. "But you will be close to Elizabeth again."

She looked at his anxious face. "Charles are you under the impression that I am against this idea?"

He searched her eyes. "You are not?"

"No, I am quite ready to live in peace, without the constant intrusion of my family."

He grabbed her hands and kissed them. "Oh Jane, thank you!"

"I did not realize that you felt the same way I do."

"Perhaps I was afraid of upsetting you." He looked at her cautiously, regretting his effusions.

"Perhaps we should speak our minds instead of trying to pretend all is well to maintain peace." Jane was amazed at the sudden revelation.

"Do you think that Darcy and Elizabeth have this problem?" He shook his head, and hugged her. "No. I doubt that there is a single subject that is left unsaid between the two of them."

Jane's arms tightened around him. "Their marriage seems so . . ." She paused, afraid to voice the thought.

"Different from ours?" Bingley asked, finally saying what was on his mind.

"Yes." She said softly. "You have noticed it as well?"

"Yes. It seems so intense. But they are two very intense people. We are . . ."

"Peace loving?" She suggested tentatively.

He smiled. "I suppose so. I was always the peacemaker between my sisters. I suspect that you had the same role with your family."

Jane smiled back. "Yes, you can imagine, no you do not have to imagine it, you have lived it. My family can be rather . . ."

"Exuberant?"

"Yes." She blushed. "Although it is quieter without Lydia and Lizzy there."

"And which sister had the greater share in the disruption of the peace?"

"Oh Lydia by far! Lizzy would say her piece and disappear into the woods!" They laughed and she said quietly, "I miss her so much."

"Then a move will be just what we need. You will be closer to your sister. I will be closer to my friend and brother, and we both will be farther from Caroline." His smile faded.

"You received a letter from your aunt this morning, I noticed." Jane gave him a squeeze of support.

Bingley laughed hollowly. "My aunt tells me that Caroline is driving her loyal servants to beg for removal. She is making everyone insane from her demands. She still has not accepted Darcy's marriage to Elizabeth. She speaks of him constantly, and wrote to me only yesterday begging me to speak to him on her behalf. She wishes to return to London. How can I impose myself on him, after all they have been through, to bring him this added burden?" He shook his head hopelessly.

"You cannot." He looked at Jane with surprise. She never took sides. "Caroline's bed is what she made for herself; it is not up to you to rescue her from her mistakes anymore." She looked at him seriously.

"Jane, what has come over you?" He held her face in his hands. "This is not the attitude of a peacemaker!"

"No, Charles, it is not. But it is the attitude of a person who wishes to see peace come to the people who most deserve it. We deserve it, Lizzy and William deserve it. Caroline has done nothing to earn it, and until she does," here she took a deep breath and said what she thought in her deepest moments, "she can stew in her own pudding!"

Bingley stared at his wife, a huge grin spreading over his face, and kissed her. "My goodness woman, such a mouth you have!"

THE GARDINERS were only to stay at Pemberley for five days, and several of those days were taken up with visiting old friends in Lambton. On the fourth morning, when Elizabeth accompanied her aunt on a call, the gentlemen left for the lake and indulged in a bit of fishing.

"So William, tell me, how do you like married life?" Mr. Gardiner's eyes twinkled, looking at the younger man.

"I truly cannot imagine how I lived so long alone, sir. I have no idea how I managed to get through the day without having Elizabeth by my side." He smiled; his expression blissful.

Mr. Gardiner laughed. "I am delighted to hear it, sir. After the rough start the two of you had, I think that you deserve some days of joy."

Darcy's smile fell off of his face. "Yes, however, it seems that we are still experiencing some difficulties." He looked over to his companion. "I imagine that you have heard of Elizabeth's miscarriage?"

Mr. Gardiner walked over to Darcy and clasped his shoulder. "I am so sorry, Son."

"I did not know she was with child." He looked up at Mr. Gardiner. "I planned to talk with you when you came. She had been so sad, and tired, and her eating. . ." He stared at the water.

Mr. Gardiner sighed. "Yes, those are some of the signs. My wife suspected it and advised her not to say anything until she felt the quickening. She did not wish to raise your hopes too soon. It seems that she was right. Please do not be upset with Lizzy. She did not believe it was really true from what I understand.

"I am not upset with her." He said softly. "But she has been carrying this secret for . . ." He looked at Mr. Gardiner. "Since Bingley's wedding?" He nodded. Darcy sighed. "I wish she had told me, but I understand why she did not."

"We lost two before we had our first, and now we have four. That is why Madeline told Elizabeth to wait to speak to you. I am grateful that she waited each time with me, I am afraid that I am very much a worrier." He smiled slightly, trying to reassure him.

Darcy was staring, watching his line bob on the water. "But you do have four beautiful children."

"Yes, we do." He said quietly.

"Thank you, sir." Darcy was unsure of what to do. He naturally was looking forward to fatherhood, but it had not been in the forefront of his mind. He was so thrilled with being a husband, and wanted to enjoy this time with Elizabeth before beginning their family. The two of them had certainly joked about it, played with the idea as a good excuse for increasing their lovemaking, but with the knowledge that he was almost a father; his emotions were difficult to understand. Now he wished more than anything that it had happened. Mr. Gardiner's reassurance that there would be children in the future helped a great deal to soothe him. Now he needed a way to care for his wife.

Elizabeth enjoyed her visit to Lambton with her aunt, but was a little overwhelmed by the deference shown to her at every turn as Mrs. Darcy. They walked down the main street, looking in the shop windows as yet another person mumbled a greeting and backed away from her. "Aunt, I do not think that I will ever become used to this. How much different it would have been visiting your friends this summer if I was still plain Elizabeth Bennet. How can I convince people that I am no more important than they are?"

Mrs. Gardiner smiled at her. "Lizzy, you have yet to realize that you are *not* plain Elizabeth Bennet. You are the Mistress of Pemberley, and a very important figure in this area. The livelihoods of a great deal of the population depend on your estate, and your husband, and I might add, you."

"Me? What do I have to do with it?" She asked curiously. "I may sit in William's study with him while he works, and he does ask for my opinions and talks over his worries with me, but I would hardly say that the future of Pemberley lies in my hands." She smiled at the thought.

"It does not lie in your hands, my dear; it lies in your marriage." Mrs. Gardiner said gently. Confused, Elizabeth looked at her. "My friends have told me of the great joy that filled the district when it was learned that Mr. Darcy had married. They look forward with great anticipation the birth of your children, because with that the estate will be secured for another of their generation as well as yours. They will be secure in the knowledge that the good Darcy family will continue at Pemberley, and that it will be operated in the same reliable fashion as it is today. If

Mr. Darcy had never married, as some speculated he would not, and an heir was not begat, the fear amongst the populace as to who would inherit would have been quite real."

"I never realized how much was involved in my simply saying "I will" to William." Elizabeth felt the loss of their first child deeply, but was, she felt, handling the sadness with an attitude of acceptance and optimism. But now, with her aunt's words, she felt completely overwhelmed with the pressure to produce an heir, and the far-reaching importance of her success. She was suddenly afraid of failing William again.

Mrs. Gardiner sensed her deepening mood. "Lizzy, I am sorry if I have made you feel as if you carried the world on your shoulders. When the time is right, you will have your family. You know how long your uncle and I waited. You must relax. It will come."

The next morning the three Darcys gathered in front of the house to farewell the Gardiners, who were continuing on their journey to the Lake District. Darcy regarded their leaving with longing. He still had not taken Elizabeth on their honeymoon, and with the harvest fast approaching, he would not be able to leave Pemberley anytime soon. He looked over to his wife, who was tearfully embracing her aunt. Elizabeth was not yet recovered and he held firm in his promise to wait for her to tell him when she was ready to begin again. He could sense a new reticence about her.

As Elizabeth embraced her aunt and their conversation played over and over in her head, her fear began to slowly overtake her, and for the first time, she felt unable to talk about a problem with William. She decided that she would work this out alone.

AFTER ANNE'S DEATH, Kathleen stayed on as companion to Lady Catherine, helping her to recover from the shock. With time, the woman returned to herself, perhaps almost defiantly more formidable than she was before. She flatly refused Richard's offer to let her stay at Rosings, much to his relief, and decided to spend the remainder of her days in town. She also decided she had no need for a companion; so, when she prepared to leave for London, Kathleen knew that she now must leave Rosings, and had begun to pack her belongings. Throughout this time Richard had courted her most assiduously. They already felt a deep connection with each other, having both witnessed far too many tragedies, but they also shared an intense desire to laugh. They were well matched. Richard's proposal was straightforward.

"Miss Miller." said he as they walked in the groves the day before he left to accompany Lady Catherine to London.

"Yes, Mr. Fitzwilliam?"

He shook his head and grinned. "I cannot quite get used to being called Mr. Fitzwilliam. Too many years in the army, I suppose. I was Colonel, Major, Captain, Lieutenant, and before that well, I will not mention what my friends called me." He laughed.

"Well sir, I have not known you long enough to become mired in your many titles." Her eyes sparkled up at him as she smiled.

"Ha!" He grinned. Then becoming serious, he said, "Miss Miller, I understand that you are considering leaving Rosings when Lady Catherine departs for London tomorrow. I do not understand why. Where will you go?"

"I will stay with my brother until I can find a new position." She looked away, not wishing him to see her distress.

"There is no need for you to leave Miss Miller." He said softly, touching her arm.

"I can hardly stay in your home without a lady to care for, sir." She said sadly, speaking the truth of the matter.

He turned, and glanced back at the imposing building. "My home. It is difficult to think of this place as home." He returned his gaze to her face. "It is not a home without a family, and one man does not constitute a family."

"What does it require, sir?" She asked, her voice shaking, then looking away.

He placed his fingers under her chin and lifted her face so he could look in her eyes. "To begin with, it requires a woman to join the man. The man needs a wife. This man needs you." She gasped. "Miss Miller, we have come to know each other. I know I have opened myself to you more than any other woman, perhaps more than almost any friend I have ever known, I deeply value your friendship, and I have come to find that I am lost without your company." He stood directly in front of her, taking her hands in his, and looked down into her tear-brightened eyes. "Miss Miller, Kathleen, my Katie, I find myself in the extraordinary position of being a man who is very much in love with a woman who takes my breath away and sets my heart and mind singing with joy. I want to share this place with you, and fill it with our hopes, our dreams, our children, and our love. Would you please do me the great honour of becoming my wife?"

Kathleen looked up into his piercing blue eyes; there was not a trace of hesitancy in his countenance. He was a commander, waiting for an answer. She drew herself up and pulling her shoulders back, addressed him straight on. "Yes, Mr. Fitzwilliam, Richard, or whatever name you choose for me to use, I will be honoured, pleased, and thrilled to accept you as my husband, because I find myself quite unquestionably in love with you, and cannot possibly imagine my life without you."

Richard threw his head back and laughed. He grinned down at her and raised her hand to his lips. "Thank you my Katie-love, and I think we will begin with Richard, until you devise a name of your own for me." She laughed at him, and then gasped as he swept her up and twirled her around. He set her down on the ground and wrapped his arms around her, then bringing his face nose to nose with her he looked deeply into her eyes. "I will enjoy very much spending the rest of my life loving you." He then brought his mouth down to hers in a hungry, passionate kiss. She met him with the same degree of fervour. Neither of them felt a need at that moment for gentleness, there was too much pent-up energy between them. They kissed, their tongues meeting and wrestling with each other, and he proceeded to drag his lips down her neck as she ran her fingers through his golden hair. He held her tightly to him, and she could feel how much he wanted her. She did not shy away but pressed herself closer. They stayed in the strong embrace, knowing they must stop before they lost complete control. He whispered hoarsely in her ear. "Promise me you will not leave before I return from London." He felt her head nod. "Say it, Katie. Promise me you will be here waiting for me." He pulled back and looked at her, the blue eyes demanding her answer.

"I promise Richard, I will wait for you." She said matching his gaze.

He nodded. "Good. I will not be long."

That was four days previously, and she expected him back sometime that day. She knew that she could not stay under his roof, despite the engagement. It was not proper for either of them, no matter how much they both wanted it. So, she slowly began packing up her meagre belongings and hoped he would understand. The sound of a carriage arriving brought her to the window, and she saw his handsome form emerge. He ran up the steps into the house and it was mere moments before she heard his firm knock on her chamber door.

"Katie!" He beamed at her, and advanced into the room, quickly sweeping her into his arms while she laughed. He kissed her ardently, and finally pulled back to see her beaming back at him. "I missed you, my girl!" He let go and his eyes swept the room, taking in the state of her packing. "What is this?" He asked, turning to her with a frown.

"Richard, I missed you too, but you knew that I must leave here upon your return. I promised to wait for you, but you know I must go." She took his hand in hers, imploring him to understand.

"No." He said flatly. "You must stay. This is our home."

"Richard, we are not married. It is not possible."

"Ah, but if we were married, it would be, would it not?" He raised his brows, his eyes challenging her.

"Well, yes, of course, but we are only just engaged."

"Come." He took a look around, spotted a bonnet, and stuck it on her head. He took the ribbons and tied a clumsy bow and looking her over, nodded his head. "Beautiful." He kissed her, and taking her hand, pulled her out the door.

"Richard! Where are we going?"

"You will see." He grinned at her.

They rapidly left the house and passed through the gardens. He paused for a moment, quickly picked a bunch of flowers, and presented them to her. Nodding again at her appearance, he took her hand and continued their journey.

"Richard!" She cried, trying to slow his unfaltering stride, "What are you doing?" He just turned and grinned at her.

Finally they arrived at the parsonage, where he knocked on the door. "Mr. Collins, please." They entered and found the man in his study. "Are you ready, sir?" Richard addressed him.

"Yes, Mr. Fitzwilliam, all is ready, I will just ask Mrs. Collins to join us, sir." The little man bobbed in his excitement. He had been warned quite severely to desist in his fawning attentions or he would soon find himself without a position.

"Fine, we will proceed to the church." Richard turned, pulling Kathleen with him.

"The church?" Kathleen said as they left the house. She finally stopped dead and refused to move another step. "Richard Fitzwilliam, you will tell me exactly what is happening this instant!" She glared at him, her hands on her hips, the flowers upside down, slapping against her thigh, and dropping petals at an alarming rate on the ground.

"My dear, if you keep that up, you will be carrying stems at your wedding." Richard righted the unfortunate blooms.

"My wedding?" The shock was clear on her face.

"Of course, how else was I to keep you from leaving Rosings? We are getting married today." He looked to see the Collins' joining them. "Now, as a matter of fact." He grinned.

She stared at him, mouth agape. "It would have been pleasant to have received some sort of warning, perhaps a chance to prepare?"

"Nonsense. You have a bonnet, you have flowers, your dress is most becoming, and most importantly, you have a very willing and eager groom. What is life without some surprise! Come my love, come and marry me." He smiled, his joy radiating from his face. He held out his hand to her.

She sighed and shook her head. "What am I doing with a madman like you?"

"Loving me, just as I will love you, all the days of our lives." He spoke very softly. He kissed her hand with the utmost tenderness. "Now, Miss Miller, shall we proceed to the church?"

She looked at him with affection and touched his cheek. "Yes, Mr. Fitzwilliam, let us be wed." Within a half hour the two were married, Rosings had a new Mistress, and Richard had a wedding story to rival Darcy's.

THREE WEEKS after the Gardiner's departure Darcy came upon Elizabeth in the music room, alone, playing a rather melancholy piece. He came and sat beside her on the bench. She smiled, but it did not reach her eyes. He knew that she was physically recovered from the miscarriage; however, she had given him no signal that she was ready to begin again. He was determined to honour her silent request for distance, but it was so difficult when he loved and needed her so much.

"How are you today, dear?" He asked softly, watching her fingers glide over the keys.

"I am well." She could not meet his gaze. Darcy reached out and touched her fingers, stopping their progress.

He entwined their fingers together and gently turning her to face him, stroked her cheek. "Talk to me, Lizzy. Please." His soft eyes looked into hers.

She blinked back the welling tears. How could she tell him her fear? How could she tell him that he had married the wrong woman? That she could not give him his heir? She was sure that this first miscarriage was just a warning of things to come. In her grief, her fear of failing him again was haunting her every thought. She was afraid to begin again, because she knew he would be disappointed. Pemberley was too important to be hurt by her weak body.

One large tear rolled down her cheek. It broke Darcy's heart to see it. He wiped it away with his thumb and leaned in to kiss her. "I love you so much, Lizzy." Their lips met tenderly. The soft caress made her breath catch, and he felt her respond for the first time in weeks. It was like water to a parched man, and he acted as any starving man would when presented with a feast, he wrapped his arms around her and pulled her to him. He looked down into her eyes, caressed her face, and lowered his mouth. They kissed, again and again. His tongue explored her mouth and to his joy, she responded in kind, holding him tightly, kissing him with the ardour that he held for her, when suddenly she stiffened and pulled away.

Darcy, intensely aroused, stared at her, confusion spread over his face; she had never withdrawn from him before. He leaned in to recapture her lips and she turned her face away from him, and looked down. "Lizzy?"

Elizabeth broke away from his embrace and stood. "I am sorry, William, I, I, I forgot a letter that I have to write. Please excuse me." She glanced up at his face and pained by the expression he wore, quit the room. Darcy was left alone on the piano bench, his ardour dying as his heart ached from her rejection. He did not understand; he must have pushed her too soon. He determined to not approach her again and would wait for her to welcome him. His shoulders slumped; he retired to his study, and pretended to work. In his pain and confusion, Darcy withdrew into himself and once again donned the protective mask of indifference that he thought had been abandoned forever.

"HOW ARE YOU SON?" Philip asked Alex. They were astride their horses, observing their tenants tending the fields at Kingston Park. Alex startled from his reverie and met his father's concerned, but understanding, face.

He smiled slightly. "I am well, Father."

"You seem to be lost in thought, is there anything you would like to discuss, perhaps it will help you to work out what troubles you?"

Sighing, he shook his head. "I suppose it would be a waste of time to deny it, so yes, I will admit that I could use your advice."

Philip nodded and guided his horse to a nearby fence and dismounted. Tying the reins to a post he leaned on the rail and watched as Alex mirrored his moves. He waited for his son to begin.

"I spoke to Darcy." He glanced over to his father. "I told him of my interest in Miss Darcy."

"And what was his response?"

He laughed. "At first, I was sure had he been armed, he would have run me through, but he did eventually calm, and listened." He looked down. "He said he had no objection other than our difference in ages and of course her not yet being out. He indicated her not being available for another year." Alex's eyes met Philip's.

"Ah, so the question is, are you truly ready to put your life on hold, to have the chance of pursing a girl who may not have the slightest interest in you a year from now? I am assuming that Darcy, as reluctant as he is to introduce his sister to society is also reluctant to settle her future on you. He will want her to at least see who else is available to her and let her make the decision."

Alex nodded. "Yes on both of those counts." He picked a long blade of grass and bit it. "I realize that it could be a foolish mistake to pin my hopes on her, but I sense something, I just know she will be extraordinary, especially under Elizabeth's influence."

Philip regarded his son. Like Darcy, he was waiting for a love match, and Darcy was fortunate enough to find his. He placed his hand on Alex's shoulder. "The Season is over. You can stay here on the estate with no need to socialize with anyone other than our neighbours, spend the autumn hunting and working with me, and not return to town until February. You will not be exposed to women who you have not already met and obviously rejected, and you will be safe from temptation before Miss Darcy's presentation. I know it seems a long wait, but it will be over before you know it." Alex looked at him doubtfully. "Or, you could just give her up now, save yourself the misery and get on with selecting a bride from elsewhere." He met his gaze. "Is she worth the wait?"

Alex stared into his father's eyes, but what he saw was a girl, with the lovely form of a woman, tall, with blonde curls and brilliant blue eyes, smiling shyly at him. He smiled and refocusing on his father he drew a deep breath. "Yes, she is."

Philip smiled; he knew the answer before his son did. "Well then, during this wait I suggest that you begin learning about her."

"How? I doubt that I will be in her company anytime soon, she is at Pemberley, and I do not foresee a convenient invitation coming my way." He thought of Darcy's face during their interview, no, an invitation was *not* forthcoming.

Philip laughed. "No indeed, but I do recall you have a sister living in that very place. A sister who you professed a desire to know better, and a sister who is in no doubt aware of your application to Darcy, as well as Miss Darcy's feelings, whatever they are, for you. I suggest you begin a friendly correspondence with her." He looked at him significantly. "Perhaps send a note to Darcy as well."

Alex's face expressed his approval of the idea, but on the last item he smiled. "You do not think he would be jealous of my writing to my sister, do you?"

"Ha! I think Darcy capable of being jealous of the ribbons his wife wears in her hair!" They both laughed, and Alex agreed, he would write to his friend first. He was relieved to make a decision. February did not seem quite so far away now.

AFTER ESCAPING from the music room, Elizabeth found herself blindly running through the hallways of Pemberley. She was completely overwhelmed. For the last three weeks she had been dealing with not only her grief with the loss of their first child, but the all-encompassing fear of failure that now ruled nearly her every thought. William had been so wonderful; he was as loving and attentive as he had been after Wickham's attack. The difference this time was that she was also fighting herself, and in a way that she could not easily communicate to him. And now she had rejected him. "Oh how can I hurt him?" She whispered, finally finding her way into the conservatory and sitting on a bench. She knew that he had not meant to push; he was trying to comfort her and was carried away. She sighed. "And I hurt him." She would never forget the look of confused pain on his face as she ran from the room. She knew that she needed to go to him, hold him, but she still had no ability to tell him what was wrong. She hoped that he would stop asking until she could understand herself.

Darcy sat in his study, staring blankly at the papers in front of him. "All I wanted to do was love her." He said softly. He closed his eyes, seeing her face, so full of fear. "She is afraid of me." That thought chilled him to the bone. He was trying so hard to understand what she was experiencing. Grief, surely, he felt it himself, and he believed that they were of comfort to each other. No doubt her grief was greater, she had known of the pregnancy for weeks where he only learned of it after it ended. Perhaps that was the problem; she was more attached to the possible child than she cared to admit. Perhaps she did believe that it was real. He understood her reluctance to begin again, and he knew that he had been carried away by his own natural ardour, but for her to run away . . . It made his insecure nature rise back to the surface. "What have I done?"

He knew what he needed to do, and started to rise from his desk when a knock came to the door. Thinking it was Elizabeth he rushed to open it, only to be disappointed with the sight of Mrs. Reynolds. His obviously distressed countenance struck her immediately. "Sir, is there anything the matter?"

"No, Mrs. Reynolds." He stepped back, his face again unreadable. "May I help you with anything?" She stood and looked at the man she had known since he was four years old, a man who was in many ways a son to her. She knew him so well. "I was seeking Mrs. Darcy."

"Oh." He looked away. "I was just going to seek her myself."

Mrs. Reynolds decided that the master needed some gentle help, he reminded her very much of his father. "I noticed that she is quite sad, sir." She watched his face. "You should know that recovering from such an event takes time."

Relieved at receiving some explanation, he looked up at her. "I suspected as much, a long time?" His eyes searched hers.

"It is different for every woman. Each carries her grief uniquely." She went on to explain that a woman's body goes through great changes when it is preparing for a child, and that it would take time to return to its normal state. She also said that Elizabeth was likely grieving for the life that did not come.

Darcy listened very closely and dismissed her. He understood the explanation, and it made perfect sense. He also felt his own grief, but none of this explained the look of panic and fear that he saw in Elizabeth's eyes when he approached. To have the one person he loved above everyone fear him was deeply disturbing, but he could not begin to repair the damage if she would not speak of it. He stepped out into the hallway to see Elizabeth approaching him. He stood, trying to read her expression, and not knowing how to respond.

She took the decision away when she reached him and grasping his hands, looked up into his eyes. "I am so sorry, William." Instantly his arms were around her and he pulled her tightly against him.

Burying his face in her hair he replied. "I am sorry for pushing you too soon, Lizzy. I just love you so much." He kissed her softly. "I understand your need to heal, but . . ." He stopped. He would not press her again. He would wait for her to speak. Embracing her he whispered. "I will wait for you my love, as long as I may still hold you, I can wait."

"Thank you, dear." She whispered. She knew that she owed him an explanation. "Will?" He closed his eyes. She only called him that name during their most intimate moments; she still loved him. His hold tightened. "Please bear with me, I am so . . ." She paused, searching for a word and failing. "You see, I cannot even express to myself what is wrong . . . I am struggling . . . I do not understand . . . I . . ."

"Shh, darling, shh." Darcy drew back and held her face in his hands. "I do not understand either, but I seem to worry you when I ask questions." His eyes searched hers seeing so many emotions, her confusion seemed to rule them all, but fear was still evident. "I will not press you to explain, just please do not be afraid to talk to me, about anything." He gave her a small smile. "Remember you are married to a man who excels at not speaking."

She nodded. He drew a breath and whispered, "Do you wish me not to . . . touch you anymore?"

She saw his fear now, and stroked his brow. "I always wish for your touch,

Will, but I am not yet ready . . ."

His fingers pressed her lips, and he nodded. "You will tell me if I press you too much, no more running away, please."

She tried to smile. "I promise." They held each other and hoped the other would be well.

Chapter 32

ime passed, as it must. It was neither fast nor slow, but simply a progression of days. Very gradually Elizabeth began to feel closer to her old self again; or at least as close to herself as she had felt in the past months, first enduring the nightmare of Wickham, and then the pregnancy, she barely knew who she was anymore. She had not recovered from one event only to find herself completely immersed in another. She was able to take walks again without too much fear, keeping her promise to William and always telling Mrs. Reynolds where she would go and returning on time. She did not have to worry so much about upsetting him now; he had been away from her almost constantly, overseeing the harvest. They did not even have time to take their morning walks together anymore. He was out the door and on his way as soon as he inhaled his breakfast, and in the evening he was so exhausted, it was all he could do to stay awake after supper. It had been six weeks now since the miscarriage. She had grieved as much as she could. She knew the ache would always be there, but she also sensed that the worst of it was over and had almost come to terms with her fear of failing again. Almost. The fear of disappointing William, the overwhelming feeling that she was incapable of bearing him his heir was still there, lurking beneath the surface, but she thought that maybe she was ready to begin again.

In all of this time, they had not once made love. She had been so lost, so very sad, so terribly afraid, that she shied away from him and did not even realize she was doing it. She had known of his devotion and importance to Pemberley, but it took this event to drive home her importance as well, and it frightened her. William had given up trying to talk to her. And now that she was waking from the fog, he was so far away. She needed him, she missed him, and she was afraid that she had lost him.

Darcy *was* lost. She was his anchor and he missed her constantly. He desperately wanted to restore the mind and soul of his dearest friend and companion, and reclaim the extraordinary woman he married, and he admitted to himself, he needed his *wife* back. It took every bit of his strength not to take her in his arms and love her. It was torture to lie next to her, to wake up, finding their bodies spooned together, his face always tucked in the crook of her neck, his arms holding her close, and her hands entwined with his. Always. He would wake first and gently kiss her, watching a soft smile cross her lips and hear her whisper his name. That was his salvation. That told him she did still love him. But then she would wake, the look of fear would appear in her eyes, and the wall would descend between them. He did not understand, but was so afraid to ask her again, fearing that it would push her farther away. He was grateful for the small liberties she did grant him. She still held him, still allowed his kiss, still would lean against him, giving him the comfort and reassurance he deeply needed, and he hoped the closeness somehow reassured her as well. He thought of spilling his own feelings out for her to hear, but then decided that might make her feel worse, again driving her away. He was relieved when the harvest began and made sure he was away all day and too exhausted at night to even contemplate making love to her.

It was all for naught, he would have gladly come to her in a heartbeat if she only gave him the slightest welcome. He missed her so much, but for his own sake, he erected a wall of protection around himself and became blind to her slow improvement.

Georgiana was not oblivious to the couple's tension, no matter how much they tried to hide it from her. They did not appear to be angry with each other, something else was at the bottom of the problem and they seemed no closer to resolving it now than they were over a month ago when she first sensed something was wrong. Elizabeth's despondency resembled her own behaviour after Ramsgate, and her brother seemed numb, reminding her of seeing her father when he was unaware of her presence. She was deeply worried, they were together, yet also distant, but she saw that when they thought one was not observing, each would gaze upon the other with equal yearning and unmistakable love. Whatever the chasm was seemed to be growing deeper, and Georgiana, who finally had the family she needed and wanted for so long, was determined to overcome her own reticence and speak.

"William? May I speak to you?" She was waiting at the stables for his return from the fields.

Darcy's face, tired and preoccupied, turned to his sister. He stared at her blankly for a moment, and then blinking, he asked quietly, "What is it, Georgie?"

Taking his hand, she led him down the path towards the house, and finding a bench pulled him to sit next to her. "I know that you will say this is not my concern, but since I live here, and I love both of you . . . I want you to tell me what has happened between you and Elizabeth, and what you intend to do about it." She drew a breath and cast her eyes down.

Darcy stared at her in amazement. "Georgiana, what has come over you?" She had never spoken so directly to him before. He wondered if this was Elizabeth's influence beginning to take hold. Inwardly he smiled at the thought. He touched her hand. "I appreciate your worry, but you are correct, it is not your place to interfere."

She raised her chin in defiance. "I disagree, William. The two of you used to laugh and have such fascinating conversations, I could barely keep up with your banter, and I could hardly understand it half of the time, now it is so silent, it is as if Elizabeth never came to live at Pemberley. You used to always be touching or stealing kisses, and were always together. Now it is as if you are avoiding each other, and both seem so sad. I see the way you look at her, with such longing, but did you know that she looks at you the same way?"

Darcy's eyes desperately searched her face. "She does?"

"Yes!" Georgiana stood up, frustrated. "Yes! She has the same wistful, miserable expression that you wear all of the time, but as soon as you turn your head she hides it. What has happened? Why do you not talk this out? It is obvious that you both wish to reconcile. Why don't you just get on with it?"

His mind was whirling. He would not doubt his sister's observations. Perhaps they were both so busy protecting themselves that they failed to see they were ready to talk. He looked up at his waiting sister. "I cannot tell you what happened." She gifted him with an unmistakable Darcy glare. He sighed. "Trust me Georgie." She nodded her head unhappily, and sat back down beside him. "I hardly know why we are in the situation that we are now. But you are correct. I do wish to reconcile, very much." He took her hand in his and gave her the first genuine smile she had seen in over a month. "I count on you to help me."

"Anything Brother, I will be glad to help." She breathed a sigh of relief. Darcy kissed her cheek and they rose from the bench, already he was formulating his plan to win his wife back.

He began by writing to Bingley, and telling him that they would be unable to host him until the second week of September. He then wrote to the caretaker of the cottage, and told him to have it readied for their visit, and gave very detailed instructions for its preparation. He finally wrote to his uncle who had recently returned to Matlock, and asked if they could host Georgiana for three weeks. He went about his plans with that same intense attention to detail that a general would use in a military campaign. He was determined to restore the joyful, vivacious, delightful woman he had married. With his activity, he felt himself emerging from his retreat, coming alive again to be strong for her, finally realizing *that* was what she needed.

The day arrived when he would set his plan in motion. He told Georgiana that he was taking Elizabeth on a surprise honeymoon trip to the Lake District and had her things quietly packed, prepared to depart when her uncle's carriage arrived in the morning. It took every bit of her strength not to breathe a word of the plan to Elizabeth, who could not understand why her sister kept breaking out into uncontrolled giggles. The couple went for their newly re-established morning stroll, and the moment that they left the house, a carriage pulled up to the door and was loaded with their surreptitiously packed luggage. When they returned, Darcy led her to the breakfast room, where they sat and ate.

"William." Elizabeth said, watching her husband butter a piece of toast, but noticing an unusual tremble in his hands. "Is there something on your mind?"

He smiled and looked towards her but did not meet her eye. "On my mind, my love? What makes you ask that?"

"You seem particularly animated this morning."

He pressed his lips together, suppressing a smile. "Really?" Georgiana giggled and he kicked her leg under the table. "How so?"

Elizabeth's gaze moved between the siblings, becoming more suspicious as the time passed. "You are both behaving like guilty children. What have you done?" She demanded.

"Done? Why nothing, nothing at all." Darcy smiled.

"No, nothing, Elizabeth." Georgiana giggled again.

She sighed. "Fine, if you prefer to behave childishly I will. . ."

Darcy interrupted. "Lizzy, shall we take a carriage ride today?"

She was completely thrown by the change of subject. "A carriage ride? But do you not have work to do with the harvest?"

"No, my work is finished for now. I thought that since we have not seen much of each other of late, you might enjoy a ride with me. You have seen very little of the surrounding area." He stared into her eyes, determined to give nothing away.

"Well, yes, I would enjoy that very much, but. . ."

"Splendid!" Darcy interrupted again. "Shall we say, let us meet in the foyer in fifteen minutes?" He jumped up and left the room, leaving his completely befuddled Elizabeth watching as he disappeared.

"You should go and prepare yourself, Elizabeth; you know how William behaves when he is late." She smiled sweetly.

Elizabeth's eyes narrowed. "Georgiana, what is he up to?"

"Really Elizabeth it is simply a carriage ride. Now go!" Georgiana had advanced upon her and dragged her from the chair.

Elizabeth admitted defeat and went upstairs to take care of necessities. She could hear Darcy rattling around in his dressing room, but he did not approach her. She appeared on time in the foyer to find her widely grinning husband waiting.

"Are you ready, my love?" He was bouncing on his heels.

"I suppose I must be." She looked at him suspiciously, wondering what had happened to the man she married, something had changed.

He turned and kissed Georgiana's cheek. "Now you behave yourself while we are gone, dear."

"I could say the same of you!" She smiled at him and sent a look of delight to her sister. He laughed and grabbing Elizabeth's hand pulled her outside and quickly into the carriage, which immediately began to move.

"William, I could not help but notice Rosie and Rogers and a vast amount of luggage in a second carriage. Please tell me what we are doing?" She demanded, brooking no more foolishness.

He pulled her gently into his embrace and kissed her lips, very softly, allowing their mouths to linger and their senses to drink in the warmth of their mingled breath, and whispered into her ear. "My dearest wife, I am absconding with you to a beautiful cottage on a lake. I think we have earned ourselves a honeymoon." He looked into her eyes, his soft and warm, and full of his love for her. She stared into his and she finally let her fear go. This was her husband and he loved her, whatever life brought them they would face together. She touched his cheek and nodded.

"Yes it is time to begin again." Darcy held her tightly and sighed with relief.

THE TRIP TO THE COTTAGE would take two days. After leaving Pemberley, the couple settled into a comfortable embrace, talking about everything but the subject that most concerned them both. Darcy was undecided about what to do that first night. If things between them were as they had been, he would not hesitate to take her to bed and love her most thoroughly at the inn; however, things being as they were, he wondered if he should wait until they had the privacy of the cottage to start over. He kept a quiet watch on Elizabeth all day, trying to measure her mood, and finally decided that he would leave it in her hands. If she gave him even the slightest signal of readiness, he would gladly acquiesce to her desires.

For her part, Elizabeth could feel the intense desire radiating from William. Every look, every sigh, even the way that he held her to him, made the purpose of this trip quite clear. He wanted her. It was extraordinarily satisfying to have such an incredibly handsome and powerful man want her so palpably. The wonderful discovery was that she felt the return of her equally intense appetite for him as well. She closed her eyes and considered the night. Should they wait until arriving at the cottage? If this had truly been their honeymoon trip, as was originally planned, would they have been capable of waiting so long? She smiled and inwardly laughed. No, they would not have been able to keep their hands off each other, despite their mutual lack of experience. She decided to pretend that they were truly just leaving the church, freshly wed, and began to behave accordingly.

She glanced up at William from her position nestled against his chest. She saw that he was staring out the window, deep in thought. Taking a breath, she thought, *Now, Lizzy, what did you imagine touching first on this man?* She decided to start with the spot that always garnered his attention. He loved to feel her touch his chest. Her hand was already resting on his stomach, so it was no great accomplishment to begin gently unbuttoning his waistcoat. He did not seem to be aware of her movements. Succeeding with her task, she considered the best method to claim his bare skin. His cravat was definitely in the way, and she knew from experience that she would likely strangle him if she tried to untie it without his help, so approaching from above was not an option. She looked down at his waist and realized that the only way to achieve her goal was to unbutton his trousers, but how to do it without his notice? Looking up to him, she found to her delight that he had closed his eyes, and was resting his head on the back of the seat. What she did not realize was that Darcy was well aware of her quiet movements, as he had been watching her most carefully. Inwardly he was rejoicing in her instigating their play, and chose to simply let her take the lead.

Elizabeth carefully loosened the buttons at the top of his trousers, accidentally brushing her hand over the fall, and feeling the unmistakable presence of a very full erection. She quickly drew her hand away and looked back up at him. He did not react. She then began to slowly tug his shirt upwards. When it seemed to become stuck, William fortunately moved slightly in his sleep, and she was able to completely remove the shirt tail from its tucked position. Smiling with her success, she then slid her hands underneath, and finally up to touch his warm, smooth skin, gliding her fingers along him in the way that he desperately craved.

Unable to hold back any longer he let out a low moan. "Oh Lizzy, how I have missed you!" Darcy's eyes, darkened with desire, bore into hers and he pulled her up to his lap. Lowering his mouth, their lips met with deep hunger and longing. They did absolutely nothing but kiss and caress each other until their jaws ached. When they finally pulled apart, Darcy held her tightly to him and buried his face in her hair. "Please Elizabeth, may I love you tonight?"

"Yes, William. I need you, and have missed you so much." They both sighed, and spent the remaining hour of that day's journey wrapped in their embrace.

UPON THEIR ARRIVAL at the inn, Darcy burst into a frenzy of activity. The carriage containing the luggage had arrived ahead of them and their servants had already prepared the rooms. Darcy gave them precise orders. A meal was to be delivered and left in the sitting room, a bath was to be prepared in the Mistress's chambers, and they were otherwise to leave them alone until morning. This information was given within moments of descending from the carriage, and Elizabeth hardly noticed that he had left her side as she was occupied admiring the scenery and the appearance of mountains in the distance. She felt the change in temperature. It was much cooler there than Derbyshire, and she shivered a little.

Darcy returned just in time to see her rub her arms, and offered her his large warm hand. "Shall we, my love?" He looked down at her, so many emotions playing across his face.

She nodded and smiled shyly up at him, stroking his cheek. "Yes please, William."

They entered the inn and Rogers led them straight to their rooms. Elizabeth walked into the sitting room, then into the far bedroom and stood, looking out of the window. It was not until she heard the soft click of the lock turning in the door that she looked around to see her husband standing before her, staring unblinking down into her face, practically shaking with desire. "Lizzy." Was all he said before he pulled her against him and crushed his mouth down to hers. His kisses were matched in fervour with those from his wife. His hands were all over her, stroking, caressing, and ultimately cupping her bottom and raising her off of the floor so that he could rub his erection into the warmth that he knew was waiting for him. Elizabeth's hands began to tug at his clothes. Deftly her small fingers made short work of the buttons, and for once, successfully untied his neck cloth. His clothing began forming a neglected heap on the floor, leaving his warm, bare chest anticipating her strokes. He began to wrestle with the hopelessly small buttons on her dress, until with a growl of frustration, he spun her around and ripped the back of her dress apart, showering them with a cascade of white shell. Her squeal of surprise only made him more intent to expose her body. He ripped off her corset, her chemise, her petticoat and soon left her standing trembling before him in nothing but her silk stockings and garters, a sight that made him harder, if possible. Elizabeth pulled open his trousers and small clothes and dropped them to the ground, so he too stood before her, in all of his masculine glory.

He pulled her back against him, and kissed her, rubbed her, felt her, revelled in her luscious, voluptuous body. Elizabeth grabbed his behind and held him firmly against her, joyously reacquainting herself with the feel of his engorged manhood stabbing into her belly. Darcy scooped her up and dropped her on the bed, her body bouncing slightly before he dove on top of her. She barely had time to draw breath before he began laving her breasts, running his tongue up and around, sucking in the nipples, moaning the entire time, telling her exactly what he thought of her body and what he wanted to do next. And he was as good as his word. As soon as he satisfied his hunger for her breasts, his ravenous mouth ate its way down to her mound. He spread her legs apart and plunged between them, first rubbing his lips and nose over her, drinking in the scent and spreading the wetness over his face, then licking, shuddering with the longed-for taste of his wife's essence. He worked hard, satisfying another craving, hearing his Elizabeth's moans. They were soft at first, and grew harsher and rasping until he felt her fingers, deeply entwined in his curls, grab his head and drive it deeper into her as she shook violently with her passion. Only then did he relent and climb back up her body, and with the utmost joy entered her, thrusting with precision and power. He watched her face, watched her breasts roll with each of his strokes, and loved the feeling of passion he achieved taking this woman once again. *Oh, how he loved her!*

Elizabeth tried to keep up with him, but she realized very quickly that this act was his alone; he needed to prove his desire for her. He needed to touch and love her in the ways that he had been imagining throughout the long, long, wait for her to welcome him again. She held onto him and revelled in everything that he had to give. His thrusting returned her to the peak, and her moans turned into the calls for him to love her harder, faster, deeper. He wanted it to go on forever, but his moment was fast approaching, and with a great roar of satisfaction, he felt his own release arrive, lasting longer and more powerfully than ever before. He collapsed upon her, kissing her desperately, telling her of his love and passion for her, and held her against him, promising his love for her would never die.

The two spent lovers lay clasped in each other's arms for some time, regaining their breath and their composure. It was Elizabeth who finally broke the silence that had descended between them. "Will?" She whispered, running her hands over his chest.

"Mmm. Yes, my dearest, loveliest, Elizabeth?" Darcy murmured contentedly.

"What do you suppose we will find to do with our time once we reach the cottage?" She lifted her head from its preferred position over his thumping heart and looked at him, grinning. Darcy rejoiced, smiling into her dancing, mischievous eyes. His Lizzy was back.

"I think, my love, we are far too long out of practice, and we must work to refine our lovemaking techniques."

Elizabeth laughed. "Yes, we must become most proficient in our study."

"Lizzy, references to my Aunt Catherine will not encourage proficiency, particularly in this field." Darcy looked at her seriously. Elizabeth began tracing her hands down his sides, eliciting a groan which was only heightened when her clever fingers wrapped around his growing sticky manhood. "But you will not object to proficiency in this area, will you my love?"

He growled, and reached his hand to stroke between her legs. "Not if you do not object to proficiency in *this* area, my love."

She moaned. "Teach me again, William."

A GREAT DEAL OF SLEEP was lost that night, and upon rising the next morning, the couple stared in awe at the havoc their reunion has wreaked upon the room. A very proud Darcy escorted his deeply blushing wife past the curious gazes of the inn's other guests, and had his man provide the innkeeper with a bonus for their trouble. The two climbed into their carriage and looked at each other silently for a moment, then burst into laughter. They settled into a comfortable embrace and soon the rocking of the carriage lulled them to regain the sleep they neglected during the night.

Elizabeth awakened many hours later to the soft trace of Darcy's fingers as he brushed the hair from her face. "Good afternoon, Elizabeth." He said smiling down at her.

She stretched and yawned, and smiled back at him. "Good afternoon, William." She sat up and looked out of the window and gasped. The scenery was stunning. All around them were snow-capped mountains, and before them was a beautiful lake nestled in a great green valley. It was breathtaking. "Where are we?" She whispered.

"This is Cumbria." he said, pointing, "And that is Windermere." He indicated the sparkling lake. "Our cottage has a beautiful view of the lake, and there are many walking trails and scenic vistas. And the waterfalls, Lizzy, I cannot wait to show them to you!" He kissed her cheek and hugged her tightly.

"When were you last here?" She tipped her head back to see his eyes shining.

"Last summer. I brought Georgiana here after Ramsgate. I hoped it would help her, but she was not able to enjoy it then." He said sadly.

"I think that you are wrong. When I have spoken to her about our plans to visit here, she described it with great fondness, and said that it was a place that brought her peace when she felt troubled." She studied his face. "I think that your idea to bring her here was very effective, she just could not express it to you then."

He kissed her. "How do you always know how to make me feel better, darling?" She just smiled. She was very much aware of how deeply she had hurt him by her withdrawal, how much he must have been starving for some sort of sign from her that all would be well. She knew better than anyone his insecurity and how she failed to reassure him. And here he was telling her that she made him happy. What a fool she had been! In her defence, she could only say that she hardly realized what she was doing at the time.

Before long they reached the cottage and she laughed. "What is it?" He asked, watching her.

"I realize that I should know better by now, William, but when you said "cottage" I envisioned something in the way of a building with four or five rooms." She looked at the imposing stone structure before her. "This is as large as Longbourn! I wonder what your definition of a hunter's blind would be? Perhaps a six room apartment with a butler and cook?"

He grinned at her. "Are you calling me overindulged, my lady?"

"No, I am calling you under experienced, sir." She smiled, stroking his nose.

He shook his head. "I think that I know the difference between each of the dwellings you described. It is not my fault that some ancient ancestor dubbed this place a cottage."

She raised her brow. "You simply continue the tradition of the improper description?"

He nodded. "Precisely, my dear wife. You know how deeply ingrained is my desire to always uphold duty, honour, and tradition for the Darcy name."

"Except when choosing your wife."

"Especially when choosing my wife."

She looked at him, surprised. "How did choosing me satisfy all of your requirements of being an exemplary member of the Darcy family?"

"I chose the very best." He kissed her. "That alone meets all of the requirements, and honours our name." He looked sincerely into her eyes.

"Thank you, William." She said, very softly.

THE TWO SOON SETTLED into the beautiful home and spent the next two weeks in blissful solitude. The outside world could not intrude upon them. He showed her the views, and took her sailing on the lake. They climbed rocks and enjoyed long walks and rides. They made love spontaneously and passionately, even indulging a few of his favourite fantasies in the process. Through it all though, he kept a careful watch on her, looking for evidence of sadness, or worse, the fear that seemed to lurk in her. After trying and failing so many times, he had not the courage anymore to ask her about it, and his not knowing made him dread that he was the cause of her anxiety. He tried very hard to tell himself that it was his foolish imagination, and was pleased that he could honestly say that she seemed to be returning to her vibrant, happy self.

Elizabeth had finally come to terms with their loss, and knew that she needed to put away her fear of failure. After finally allowing William to care for her, and reassure her of his love, she was able to embrace their future whatever it brought, with open arms, and was determined to never let anything come between them again.

Elizabeth discovered her favourite feature of the house was an enormous wing back chair placed before the fireplace in the library. Darcy explained that the exceptionally wide chair was custom made to fit a particularly large ancestor. She loved it because she found that they could sit cuddled next to each other with their feet stretched out before them in the evening and read, or talk, or kiss, or simply stare in companionable silence at the crackling flames. Darcy determined that as soon as they arrived home he would have four such chairs made; one for each library and master's bedchamber in their homes. He envisioned spending many nights cuddled with his dearest Elizabeth in these chairs, and if he let the dream continue, he could imagine the presence of their children and the sound of their voices as they climbed over them, begging for a story. Someday.

AS THE TIME approached for them to leave their little utopia and return to their real lives, Darcy's insecurity over Elizabeth rose to the surface. He was concerned that upon returning to Pemberley there would also be the return of the sad, frightened woman he hoped had been left behind. He finally found the strength to talk to her about his fears and reaching for her hand, asked, "Could we share one more walk together before we leave tomorrow?"

She stroked his cheek. "Yes, shall we go now?" He nodded, and they set off. He did not speak, but led her to a hill which afforded a view of the house and lake, and settling himself on the ground beneath a tree, leaned back and held his hands out for her. She rested between his legs, and he wrapped his arms around her, nestling his face in her fragrant hair.

"Elizabeth?" He said softly.

"Yes, William?" She could not see his face, but his hands tightened their grip on her arms.

"Is everything well between us now?"

She turned in his embrace and looked closely at him. "What is wrong?"

He became silent. Elizabeth turned and held him, and he rested his head on her shoulder, returning the embrace. She stroked his head and waited.

"You know that I love you, do you not?" He whispered.

"Yes, of course I do, and I hope you know that I love you, as well." She kissed him, holding him tighter; he was so obviously in pain.

"Yes, I know." And suddenly it flowed from him, "I am so afraid of losing you. I am so afraid to be alone." He buried his face deeper into her neck. His muffled voice rose from her. "I am so afraid that my dream of fatherhood would end your life." She could feel his wet cheek on her skin. "I am so afraid that I would be the cause of your . . . my selfish desires . . . I would rather remain forever celibate than risk losing you, Elizabeth."

"William!" Elizabeth was overwhelmed. "Darling what has put these thoughts in your mind?" She tried to look at his face, but he would not relinquish his position, cradled in her arms.

"You seemed so afraid of me after . . . after . . . we lost . . . as if you knew that my actions would hurt you." He took a deep breath, and asked the question that had burdened his heart. "Why did you push me away, Elizabeth? Why would you not speak to me? Did I frighten you? Did you hate me?"

By now, Elizabeth was crying. "No! Stop thinking that!" She felt so guilty for not speaking before, and knew she must bare all. "I was afraid, yes, but I was afraid of failing again. I was afraid of losing another child. I could not stand the thought of hurting you again, and I know how important it is for Pemberley to have an heir." He tried to protest that an heir was not important, but she silenced him with her fingers pressed to his lips, knowing the truth. "I was never concerned that our loving each other would risk my life." She kissed his head. "I have never ever been afraid of you, and I will never regret loving you or becoming your wife in every way. I needed time to recover from what occurred, William. I was overwhelmed with so many things, and so very, very sad, but I realized when you pulled me into the carriage to come here, all I needed to recover was you. Please forgive me for not telling you what I was feeling. I was so caught up in my own pain that I failed to realize I was pushing you away. When I began to feel better, I did not know how to begin again, we were so far apart. I never meant to hurt you."

There was a long pause, and she knew he was thinking through what she said. Finally she heard his deep soft voice. "When you first told me that you had miscarried, I was of course disappointed and saddened, but I thought that we both understood that miscarriage is not uncommon, and that we would work through this together. I felt that we, you, I, understood that we would be well, and when you were ready, we would try again. I even spoke to your uncle about this, and he told me of his experience with the loss of a child. We have weathered so much together, Lizzy, I thought that we would be well, but something changed, you were as different as night and day. It was as if you changed from an understandable grief to an overwhelming fear, almost instantly." He kept his head on her shoulder. "Did something happen? Did I do something to make you withdraw?

Elizabeth sighed and stroked his hair. "Oh William, no it was not you. It, well, it was some words that my aunt said that I took far too much to heart."

"What was that?" He began to feel an unreasonable anger towards the woman.

She felt him tense. "She told me of the importance to the people of Pemberley, the tenants, the local businesses, the other landowners, everyone, that you have an heir, and that the stability of Pemberley is assured. She pointed out to me the importance of our marriage, and how so many people are counting on its success. I am afraid that I took her truthful words and allowed them to overwhelm me. I felt that I was a failure, and that this loss was proof of my unworthiness to be your wife. I was afraid to try to become with child again because I convinced myself that I would lose that baby, too. I was sure that the loss was my fault, and I could not bear to fail you or Pemberley again."

"Oh Lizzy." He whispered. "I wish I had known the burden that you placed on yourself." He tightened his grip around her. "Yes, I will admit, an heir is important, but if it does not come from our union, I will be sure to have it come from Georgiana's. I do not want you to ever feel that you have failed me. We have not even been married for five months! You are very young, and there is plenty of time. I am so sorry for not understanding the depth of your despair."

"Thank you William." She needed to address something else that he said. "So you do not fear losing me in childbirth anymore? I assure you, I am a strong country girl, not one of those pampered ladies of London. My mother had five babies in seven years. I think that the odds are highly in my favour to do very well." She managed to pry his face out of its nest and looked into his reddened eyes. "And, sir, I have no doubt in my mind that when my time comes, I will be provided with an overabundance of excellent care from my adoring husband." She smiled gently at him. "Do not fear for me, my love." He stared into her eyes, he would always fear for her, just as she would for him. They both knew that without saying the words. She stroked his face, and said softly. "My courses began this morning." With their abstinence, there was no possibility that she could have been with child, but the event was still significant to her.

"Oh." He said, not knowing if he should be happy or sad.

She continued her caress. "You do not know how to react."

"You must think you have married a silly fool." He whispered.

"If I have, than you have as well."

"You feel the same confusion?"

"Yes." She confessed.

They sat quietly, absorbing all that was said between them. Darcy then took her face in his hands and softly kissed her lips. "I should not have given up asking you of your feelings, perhaps if I had voiced my own grief it would have helped you to share yours. Men are not supposed to express such feelings." He looked down, then back up to her face, knowing that he had always shared his feelings with her in the past, but failed to do so this time. "I think that what we have learned from this experience is not to let our fears overtake us. Please do not ever be afraid to talk to me. The sooner we talk about something, the better."

"Before it overtakes us and becomes a wedge, driving us apart." She nodded her head and kissed him. "I am too used to my parents' marriage of silence. I should have opened up to you. I am so sorry that I did not. I am afraid that I have felt so numb and I was trying to handle my emotions alone, but instead by keeping silent I made a difficult situation so much worse. I should know very well by now that we are strongest when we face things together. I have missed you, desperately. Please forgive me, Will." She kissed him again.

"Only if you forgive me for not speaking. I could not bear to lose you, Lizzy, in any way. I need you. I thought I knew that before, but the time that we spent growing further apart just drove that point home. I could not bear this life without you." He gazed into her eyes, still cupping her face in his hands.

"I promise you will not have to. You will never be alone."

"I hold you to that, Madam."

Chapter 33

arcy and Elizabeth arrived home and arose the next morning only to look at each other sadly. "Back to our lives." Darcy sighed. "I dread the pile of correspondence that awaits me."

"I am sure that Mrs. Reynolds awaits me with eagerness as well."

"Will you keep me company when you finish with her? I am afraid that I have been too much with you these past weeks, and cannot possibly work without you near." He took her hands and kissed her nose.

Elizabeth laughed. "Well, if the continued operation of Pemberley depends upon my presence by your side, of course I will join you."

Darcy hugged her. "Thank you my love."

Several hours later, Elizabeth and Darcy were sitting at work in his study, when a footman knocked and was bid enter. "Sir, two carriages have been spotted entering at the gate."

"Thank you." Grimacing, Darcy looked up at Elizabeth.

"Two carriages?" She asked.

"It seems that Uncle Henry has decided to honour us with a visit."

"But even if he and your aunt have come with Georgiana, why would two carriages be needed? There cannot be that much luggage?" She began thinking of the possibility of a much extended visit with their relatives.

"Perhaps my cousin Mark and his wife Laura have joined them. You have not met the Viscount as yet."

"I think that I should alert Mrs. Reynolds." A footman was called and asked to have the housekeeper join them at the front entrance.

Very soon the two carriages rolled into the courtyard and Lord Matlock descended first. He took one look at the apprehensive couple and laughed. "I know, I know, we are descending upon you like locusts!"

Darcy shook his head. "I would not quite use that description, Uncle."

"Nonetheless, I am sure that your good wife would, and feels that you are now under siege." He smiled at Elizabeth as he handed down Lady Matlock.

"If I did not know better, I would say that you are testing my reaction to your sudden arrival, sir." Elizabeth challenged him. The party was soon joined by Georgiana and the surprising arrival of Richard and Kathleen in the second carriage.

"You are quite clever, Mrs. Darcy." Lord Matlock grinned.

"And you are quite transparent, sir." She smiled back, her eyes dancing.

"Ha!" Lord Matlock laughed his appreciation, and looked around to see Richard and Darcy both smiling at Elizabeth.

Kathleen watched Elizabeth with admiration. She was handling the unexpected onslaught of guests with calm. Kathleen knew that if this was her home, she would be in a panic. She was gaining a little more confidence in her role as Mistress of

Rosings, but she was in no way prepared for her new position. She hoped that talking to Elizabeth might help.

"If you will excuse me a moment?" Elizabeth turned to address the waiting Mrs. Reynolds, then looked back. "Oh, and how long will you be inspecting me, sir?"

"Two nights, my dear." He said chortling. Elizabeth bowed her head, "Thank you, sir." She met Mrs. Reynolds's eye and said quietly, "It seems that we have some unexpected guests."

"So it does, Mrs. Darcy. I might say that his behaviour was not entirely unanticipated."

Elizabeth looked at her with surprise. "You suspected something of this sort?"

"Yes, Madam." She sighed.

Elizabeth shook her head, feeling the woman's exasperation. "You are a treasure, Mrs. Reynolds, I bow to your superior experience and will be grateful for your assistance."

She smiled and nodded. "I will have the rooms prepared immediately."

"Please have tea sent to the yellow drawing room."

"Yes, Mrs. Darcy." The two women exchanged resigned glances. Elizabeth returned her attention to her unexpected guests and found that Georgiana had already led the ladies inside.

Lord Matlock grinned at her and declared, "You look absolutely blooming Elizabeth! Did my nephew show you a properly pleasant time on your delayed honeymoon?"

"Indeed he did, sir, I have never come away from a trip feeling more satisfied." Elizabeth grinned mischievously at him, and glanced up at Darcy.

His eyes opened wide and he cleared his throat before taking her hand and facing his grinning uncle and cousin. "Yes, the view and activities were most invigorating." His lips twitched and he tried hard not to look too pleased with himself.

Richard slapped him on the shoulder. "Excellent man, excellent! I am pleased to hear that you were well occupied." He turned to Elizabeth, and bending, kissed her cheek. "I am delighted to see you, Elizabeth."

"Thank you, Richard. I look forward to at last meeting your bride." Darcy placed his hand on her waist and brought her possessively back to his side.

Richard shook his head at his cousin's behaviour and smiled. "Indeed you will. She has gone inside with Georgie and Mother. Shall we join them?"

They proceeded into the house and heard the sound of running feet. "Oh it is so good to be home!" Georgiana burst upon them. "What did you think of the cottage, Elizabeth? Is it not everything I told you? What did you do? What did you see?" She was filled with joy and excitement, already recognizing the restoration of her brother and sister.

"Georgie." Darcy's quiet voice spoke and she instantly calmed. "Could we at least enjoy a simple greeting before the inquisition begins?"

Blushing, Georgiana gave her brother a hug and kissed his cheek. "I am sorry William. I was just so excited to have arrived." She then whispered, "Is all well now?" Feeling his nod, she turned to Elizabeth. "I hope that you had a very pleasant journey, Elizabeth."

"Most satisfying from what I have heard." Richard quipped. Darcy sighed, and Elizabeth smiled and squeezed his hand. He looked down at her dancing eyes and smiled back, unable to resist a quick kiss.

Upon entering the sitting room, Lady Matlock and Kathleen rose. "William, Elizabeth, it is good to see you." She looked over to her son, her brows raised.

"I was about to do it, Mother." He went to the small woman's side and took her hand. "Kathleen, may I introduce to you my cousin, Fitzwilliam Darcy, and his lovely bride, Elizabeth. Mr. and Mrs. Darcy, may I present Kathleen Fitzwilliam, my wife." He said it with great pride, and looked at her with unmistakable affection.

"Mrs. Fitzwilliam, it is a great pleasure to meet you, Richard has spoken and written to us about you. Meeting you today is a wonderful surprise." Elizabeth smiled warmly at the obviously nervous woman.

Darcy observed Kathleen intently. She was slightly taller, and less womanly than Elizabeth, her hair not quite as dark, her eyes pretty but not the dancing orbs of his lover's, and her face, though obviously strained, was not the expressive canvas he lived to gaze upon. He relaxed. She was similar but not the twin of Elizabeth he had feared.

"Indeed it is a pleasure, Mrs. Fitzwilliam. I am delighted to meet the woman who so thoroughly captured my cousin's heart. I am sorry that I missed making your acquaintance at Rosings when I came for our Cousin Anne's funeral, but I understand that you were quite occupied tending our aunt. May we wish you joy on your wedding?" Darcy bowed over her hand.

"Thank you, Mr. and Mrs. Darcy. I have been anticipating this meeting for some time. We hoped to come with Georgiana to Pemberley when it was time to return her, but . . ." Her nervousness overtook her, and she looked to Richard for help. She was very intimidated meeting Elizabeth, she had heard her husband and his family speak nothing but high praise of her, and she was very afraid of failing in front of her.

Before Richard had an opportunity to say anything, Elizabeth saw her unease and stepped forward, taking her arm and leading her to a sofa. "Now that we have the formal introductions out of the way, I want you to call me Elizabeth and my husband William. We are family now! I understand that you are just like me, Mrs. Fitzwilliam, you grew up on a small estate?"

Kathleen looked at the warm, smiling woman next to her and breathed a sigh of relief. No matter how much everyone reassured her, she had built an image in her mind of a person who was as formidable as Lady Catherine, but Elizabeth, although exuding confidence, was also glowing with good humour and kindness. "Please call me Kathleen." Elizabeth nodded. "Yes, I did grow up on a small estate. My only sibling, my brother, inherited it."

"My situation was different, our home is entailed away."

"Yes, I know Mr. Collins."

"Oh, I am sorry for that!" Elizabeth laughed. "I should not say that, forgive me. He is my cousin and my best friend's wife."

"Yes! Mrs. Collins, Charlotte, has spoken very fondly of you." She smiled, now having some common ground.

"She is my dearest friend besides my sister, Jane. If you and Richard can stay longer, you will meet my sister. She and her husband will be arriving in four days."

"I am not sure. We were expecting to stay with you for two days and continue our journey home. I will have to see what Richard wants to do." She looked over to her husband fondly. Elizabeth caught her gaze.

"He is a very good man. I am so happy that he found love." She smiled at the surprised look on Kathleen's face. She laughed. "I married for love myself. I have heard that the story of your wedding rivals mine!" They both laughed. "How are you settling into Rosings? The house is similar in size to Pemberley, and I know how completely overwhelmed I felt when I first arrived here as Mistress." She smiled at her encouragingly.

"I think that overwhelmed does not even touch how frightening it was, and still is. Suddenly the staff was coming to me for answers, and I have no experience at all with operating a household. I am afraid that I have been quite a failure."

"I am sure that is quite wrong. Do you not have a housekeeper? Surely she can teach you what is required. I sincerely doubt that Lady Catherine was that involved in the daily operation of the household."

"You know the lady well."

"We have had some conversations."

"So I have heard." The ladies looked at each other, lips twitching, and burst into laughter. From there they sat and discussed the trials of suddenly becoming Mistress of a mansion. Lady Matlock and Georgiana watched them with great enjoyment.

Darcy and Richard both looked up from their conversation with Lord Matlock at the sound of their wives' gaiety and grinned. "I knew they would like each other." Richard said.

Smiling, Darcy declared, "I think, gentlemen, that we have just witnessed the birth of a friendship."

THAT AFTERNOON, Lord Matlock asked if he could have a few moments with Darcy. They entered his study and Lord Matlock closed the door behind him.

"Please take a seat, Uncle. Would you care for some brandy?"

"No, thank you." He regarded his nephew closely. He was struggling to find the words to begin the conversation. It was Darcy who guessed the subject of his distress. "I read father's letter."

Lord Matlock sighed. "Am I so easily read?"

"No, but we have not had the opportunity to discuss it. Much has happened in the intervening time."

"So it has. We were devastated to hear of Wickham's attack." Seeing Darcy's surprise he smiled slightly. "Certainly you did not expect Richard to keep that to himself, did you?" Darcy shook his head. He should have known better. "Elizabeth seems well." He stated quietly.

"Yes, it took some time, but we recovered." He paused, deciding. "Then we lost our first baby." He said sadly, telling the news for the first time.

Lord Matlock looked at him, concern and grief in his expression. "When did this occur? Georgiana said nothing of it."

"We did not tell her." He paused. "It was at the end of July. We . . . lost our way for a time. Our honeymoon was planned to help us start over again." Then smiling slightly, he said, "It has been a great success, I think."

His uncle smiled and came over to clasp his shoulder. "Darcy, I can honestly say that I have never seen a couple more in love than the two of you, and that includes your own parents."

Darcy's face brightened. "I imagine that we are quite the oddity."

"Revel in it, Son. Make the world jealous!" Lord Matlock grinned.

"Yes sir, with pleasure." Darcy smiled and easily imagined Elizabeth standing by his side just then.

He let out a breath, "Now, as to your father. . ."

Darcy interrupted. "Sir, I have determined there is nothing to be done, so I will not dwell upon it. I cannot excuse or understand my father's behaviour or his reaction to the situation."

Lord Matlock seemed surprised. "This comes from Elizabeth's influence?"

"I imagine in a way it does." He smiled, realizing the power his wife held over him.

"Do you have any questions?"

Darcy spoke the one thought that had been nagging at him. "I always thought of Father as a sensible man. Surely he must have calculated that Wickham was born less than nine months after he had . . . the encounter with his mother. Why did he immediately jump to the conclusion that he was the father?"

Lord Matlock shook his head ruefully. "I asked him the same question. He simply could not imagine that Wickham's mother had been with another man. He just assumed the baby came early. He was so ready to assume the worst."

"He had never been confronted with the consequences of his habits before." Darcy said thoughtfully.

"That is very true. Few men are. I do know that he did not renew such activity until he married my sister."

"I am glad that I waited for my Elizabeth." Darcy said softly.

He again felt his uncle's hand on his shoulder and looked up. "What the two of you have endured in such a short time would have broken any other couple. I do not know if my own marriage would have survived it. Perhaps now, after years of building our trust and learning of each other, but when we started out, we did not love with the strength you and Elizabeth seemed to have found so quickly. Watching the two of you weather these storms has helped us to accept your choice. We hoped for a love match, but we did not expect you to marry so far below yourself, however we abided by your father's desires, and are glad that we did. Your aunt and I had a marriage of convenience, and fortunately it grew into love. Your own parents were the same way."

Darcy was surprised. "They were? But I was under the impression that they were deeply in love."

"They were, but it was not that way from the beginning. Their marriage was as much a business transaction as mine was. They were fortunate, very fortunate, to find quickly that they were perfect for each other. Nonetheless, your father always expected you to follow that same path and choose your bride in the normal, dispassionate way that all other members of our circle did. It was not until he learned of the truth of Wickham's paternity that he changed his attitude, although he had always regretted the way he treated you."

"But if he knew the value of a love match from his own marriage, why would he not always wish that for me?" He leaned on his desk, his arms folded, staring with confusion at his uncle.

Lord Matlock moved to lean against the desk by his side. "Son, there are so many rules governing the way society behaves. You know that. I know it was pounded into you as thoroughly as I told my sons. He could not go against them. You are a far stronger man than either one of us."

Darcy's brow furrowed. "How so?"

"You have married with your heart, and because of it, you showed society that you can live without them. Instead of shunning you, I have it on good authority that you are being actively sought out because your favour is deemed as a rare commodity." The men glanced back at his desk, piled high with invitations for Elizabeth to sort through. "It takes a rare and brave man to be willing to risk the ill favour of his entire world for something as seemingly silly as love."

Darcy nodded his head, understanding now, but still surprised. "In all honesty, I do not think I could have done such a thing for anyone but Elizabeth. I do find it hard to believe that she will be universally accepted by the *ton*, but I am happy to know that despite her status, she has been accepted by you."

A soft knock at the door prevented the Earl's reply. Upon Darcy's call, it opened and Elizabeth peeked in. "Excuse me gentlemen, but tea is ready, would you care to join us?" She came into the room, and to her surprise, Darcy took her hand and kissed it. She smiled up at him. "What was that for?"

Darcy looked to his uncle. "Sir, would you excuse us for a moment?"

He chuckled. "I was just on my way." He bowed and walked out, then returned to pull the door closed behind him, grinning to see Elizabeth already firmly encased in Darcy's arms.

"NO!!!" Richard sat straight up, drenched in sweat, his heart pounding, his eyes wild, staring around the unfamiliar dark chamber. Kathleen's hand touched his arm and he almost leapt away from her.

"Richard." She said softly. Over the short weeks since their marriage, she had come to know his frequent nightmares and was gradually learning how to comfort him. And though she truly regretted Lady Anne's passing, she could not regret anything that would have ended her husband's chances to ever return to the battlefield.

Richard took a deep breath and closed his eyes. He rubbed his hands over his face, and then looked down at Kathleen, who sat up next to him, now embracing his waist. "I did it again."

She nodded. "Do you remember it at all? Perhaps if you talk it out, the memory will be less powerful and leave you to rest."

He shook his head. There were so many horrific images, men dead, other men blown apart yet writhing in agony, green fields stained red with blood, blood from men in both uniforms. Sometimes it was the image of children, alone and crying for a parent who was missing. Sometimes it was the image of a guillotine doing its work and the frenzy of the crowds. Sometimes it was the moans and empty rattle of a cot aboard the returning ship, a cot that moments before carried a living wounded man, and now bore more waste. Tonight it was Wickham upon Elizabeth; it must be seeing her that brought this dream on. "It is all the same Katie, all violence, blood, death. I hate being so weak." He stared down at his still-trembling hands.

Kathleen squeezed him. "You are not weak Richard. You survived countless engagements, and led your men to safety time and again."

"Not all of them." He said bitterly.

"No, and you know full well that you cannot take responsibility for that." She reached up and pushed his hair away from his face, then lightly traced an old scar on his arm.

He relaxed with her touch. "Well that is one mark not earned from the French." At her raised brow he wrapped his arms around her and settled back onto the pillows, pulling her tightly to him. "That scar is courtesy of my esteemed cousin."

"Mr. Darcy?" Kathleen said with surprise. Pleased to see his tension reduced, she encouraged him to talk. "What happened?"

Richard regarded her. "I think you may call him William." He smiled at her pursed lips, she very much felt herself still a lady's companion, not the Mistress of Rosings. "My brother Mark and I were visiting here. Darcy was showing off his lately acquired fencing skills. He was thirteen mind you, not the master swordsman he is now, and I was facing him. Well, my brother decided to bait him, calling out insults to his skill, which naturally already outfoxed by his older cousin, set him on edge. He lost his concentration for a moment, and unfortunately my arm was in the way. I bled profusely, which infuriated his housekeeper and both of our fathers. I think all three of us received a sound thrashing." He looked across the room, reflecting on it.

"Why would your fathers be so angry? It was accidental, was it not?" Kathleen was indignant on his behalf.

Richard chuckled at her angry face and kissed her. "Oh of course, Darcy would never hurt someone intentionally. I have only known that to happen once." He thought of his cousin's reaction to Wickham's attack on Elizabeth, but even there, he was trying to protect her, although she was not present. His cousin's passion for her was demonstrated again and again.

"Then why?" Kathleen persisted.

"They were afraid. Neither father wished to see their son injured. By reminding us of that so well, we learned not to unnecessarily provoke, and to maintain control when we were."

"It seems that advice would serve you well in later years." She held him tightly. "That is something that helped you to survive."

He smiled at her. "I never thought of that. Perhaps."

"Do you feel guilty for surviving relatively unscathed, and now living in our grand home? Were your dreams this often before you resigned your commission?"

"I had them, but no, not as often. I do not know." His voice grew soft.

She stroked back the hair that fell across his face. "Perhaps you feel safe now and can finally express the pain you have kept hidden away for so long."

"I do feel safe now Katie. I have you. I do love you, you know?" He looked at her sincerely.

"I know, and I love you, Richard." The two settled back down under the covers, and soon found themselves reaffirming their declarations.

In another part of the house, a second couple lay embraced, relaxing in the glow of passion their own activities inspired. Darcy kissed the head that rested on his chest. "Thank you, Lizzy." She lifted her head and smiled into his warm eyes.

"And what have I done to garner your gratitude?"

He caressed her face. "You have tolerated the arrival of my family with grace and good humour."

She laughed. "It is not difficult to be kind to such happy people, William."

"The Fitzwilliams generally are a jovial lot. Humour often allows my uncle to achieve goals in the House of Lords where a less-skilled man would fail, and I know it served Richard well in earning the loyalty of his troops."

"I wish they would stay longer. I would like to introduce Kathleen to Jane and Charles."

"What do you think of her?" Darcy asked innocently. He had continued his observation of Richard's wife, and noticed more small similarities to Elizabeth. Her smile and good humour featured most prominently in his mind.

"I like her. I think that she needs a friend, she is so nervous about being the Mistress of Rosings. She seems almost desperate for advice." She kissed his chest and absentmindedly stroked his skin as she talked. Darcy closed his eyes, enjoying her touch. "I will definitely be writing to her, and Charlotte, to encourage their friendship." She paused and added in a very soft voice, "If I was more insecure, I would have guessed that you felt strongly about her as well."

He took instant notice of those careful words and sat up, bringing Elizabeth with him. "Lizzy?" He put his fingers under her chin and lifted her head so that she would meet his concerned eyes. "Are you worried that I am attracted to Kathleen?"

"You seem to look at her quite frequently." Elizabeth looked down.

Darcy closed his eyes and embraced her. "Oh sweetheart, I am sorry if I seemed odd. No, I am not attracted to her, I just . . . this is going to sound silly, but I was looking to see if there was a resemblance to you in her."

Relieved, Elizabeth let out the breath she had been holding and looked up. "Why would you wish to do that?"

He laughed slightly. "Because I am a jealous fool. I know how attracted Richard was to you, and I remembered him comparing Kathleen to you when we saw him at Netherfield. I was afraid that he had purposely tried to marry your twin because he was unsuccessful at winning you."

"Oh Will, you are a silly jealous fool." She reached up and caressed his blushing cheek. He turned and kissed her hand. "And what have you concluded?"

"She does have similar qualities to you in appearance, but she does not have your confidence, your knowledge, your wit, your strength . . ."

"In other words, she is her own person, and comparisons between the two of us are useless to make." She gently kissed his lips.

"I think Richard still has feelings for you." He said a little defensively.

"Perhaps he does. But he has found his bride, they seem happy together, and I am not at all interested in him other than as our cousin and friend, so what is the point of trying to see if I compare to Kathleen?"

He sighed. "I just, oh Lizzy, I am a fool."

She hugged him, he was hopeless. She simply had to accept that he would be jealous of any man who ever entered her world, and that she would spend her life reassuring him. She smiled into his chest. *That was not such a bad duty.*

"Will, I want you to know; I am just as jealous as you." His soft chuckle rumbled in her ear, he loved hearing that. She felt his arms hold her tighter, and his lips came to find hers. After a long satisfying kiss they looked into each other's eyes and smiled.

THE FAMILY GATHERED for tea the next afternoon and Lady Matlock approached Darcy. "I am very pleased with the improvement in Georgiana. She is gaining confidence in herself. She is not as shy and even attempted an argument with your uncle."

"Did she?" He said with surprise and looked across the room at his sister where she sat with Elizabeth and Kathleen. "On what subject, may I ask?"

Lady Matlock smiled. "On the acceptable age difference between young ladies and their suitors."

Darcy's brows went up. "I understand that you spoke to Alex Carrington and his mother."

"I did, and I apologize for not speaking to you of it. I wanted to assess his mother, and inform her that Georgiana was not yet out."

"When I learned of it, I was quite unhappy with you, but perhaps that was simply from receiving the shocking news of Alex's intentions towards my little sister."

"She will always be a baby to you, as will any daughters you ever have." She looked knowingly at him.

"Yes."

"Your uncle told me." She touched his arm. "I am sorry"

He nodded, not willing to talk about it again. "I told Alex to keep his distance until Georgie comes out."

"I liked him, and yes he is older, but I think Georgiana needs that. With Elizabeth's help, she will be magnificent at her presentation."

"Of that, I have no doubt." He caught her eye. Elizabeth excused herself from the others and joined them. Darcy held out his hand and their fingers intertwined.

"I have tried to convince your cousin to stay longer, but he insists he must away to Rosings. Some silly excuse about the harvest, I believe." Her eyes twinkled up at him.

"Yes, he is quite the gentleman farmer now, is he not?" Darcy laughed, and raised her hand to his lips.

"Are you two disparaging me?" Richard was up and joined them. "I am quite dedicated to my new position, you know."

Darcy cocked a brow. "Yes, quite, and what exactly are your tenants harvesting, Cousin?"

Richard puffed out his chest importantly. "Some sort of edible plant, I would assume!"

"Well with that outstanding knowledge, Pemberley will soon be put to shame by Rosings." Darcy shook his head and met Elizabeth's grin with one of his own.

Richard looked between the two of them, "Give me time, Cousin, and I shall overtake you!"

Darcy looked at him speculatively, "Is this a challenge, Richard? Has the gauntlet been thrown?"

He was about to respond when Kathleen called out, "Richard! Please do not gamble away our home. I have just redecorated!"

Shaking his head, he bowed to his wife. "Yes, my love." He smiled at Elizabeth. "Tell me Mrs. Darcy, have you also learned the secret to ruining your husband's fun?"

"No sir, I create it!" She declared and looping her hand onto Darcy's arm, smiled into his beaming face.

Richard shook his head and looked with wonder at Darcy. He barely recognized this new man. He leaned to her and spoke softly, "Elizabeth, please let me take this opportunity to thank you for being so kind to Kathleen. She was very anxious to meet you. In truth, she is hoping to find in you a friend."

"Well I cannot imagine why she would be anything but my friend. We have so much in common and she is a very sweet lady. If you would stay longer, we could really come to know each other so much better than we will if we are only able to talk through letters." She touched his arm. "Please stay."

He drew a breath, and glancing at Darcy, shook his head, "No, we truly must return to Rosings, but I promise we will come early for Christmas. Will that satisfy you?"

She smiled. "I suppose it must.

"Now then, may I steal your husband for a while?

"Only if I may steal your wife!" She grinned.

He laughed. "Done!"

The men departed for the library and when settled before the fireplace with glasses of wine, Darcy nodded at him, "Well Richard, what can I do for you?"

"This is probably not necessary from what I have observed, but Georgiana was quite worried about you and Elizabeth. She said that something was terribly wrong. You were not talking as you once were, but did not seem angry either. She said when confronted, you told her it was not her concern."

Darcy bristled, "That is true, what makes you think it is yours?"

Richard knew him too well to be put off by his scowl. "Come on, Darcy, if there is a problem, you know you can trust me."

"Yes, I know, but not this time." Richard kept staring at him and he sighed. "I must say I am surprised that you father has not told you already." Seeing Richard's expectant expression, he relented. "Elizabeth miscarried at the end of July. She withdrew from me, and I did not know what was wrong. Instead of sharing our pain and fears with each other, we kept them to ourselves and thought everything would resolve itself on its own. Georgie's demand that I repair the problem forced me to action, hence the honeymoon, which led to our reconciliation and communication." He tried to say it all dispassionately, but he could not hide the emotion in his eyes and voice.

Richard's face reflected his sorrow. "I had no idea. I am so sorry. Is everything well now? How much more must you both endure?"

Darcy gave a short laugh, and then said softly, "We are well. I think we are even stronger than before, and I pray we will always be this way." He drew a deep breath and let it out. "Enough of this. Tell me, how do you like marriage? Kathleen seems very happy, if a little nervous."

"I think we are both nervous. Marriage, Rosings, there are so many changes and new things to learn and understand. I envy you Darcy. Despite all you have experienced, what I see between you and Elizabeth is exceptional."

"You know as well as I do how extraordinary circumstances force maturation at an accelerated rate. You learned it in battle; I did the same when my father died. Elizabeth and I have experienced more in the last seven months than some couples face in a lifetime. We could either collapse or become the couple you see now. You will hopefully take the slower path as our parents did. I wish our experience on no one."

Richard nodded. There was nothing he could add to that statement. He instead changed the subject. "How do you like Kathleen? I noticed you watching her."

"Ha! So did Elizabeth!" He smiled. "*She* was jealous."

"No, really?" He grinned. "*Do* you like her?"

Darcy saw his cousin's need for his approval. "I do Richard, I truly do. Neither of us wished for a lady of the *ton*. We both found exactly what we needed in the countryside."

"Yes." He said softly. Looking up to his cousin he confessed. "I am having nightmares again."

Concern crossed Darcy's face and he leaned forward. "Frequently?"

"Every few days. It is worsening, I think."

"You always had them upon returning from battle, could it be that being safe at Rosings, with Kathleen, you are able to dream of those painful things?"

He shook his head. "That was Katie's theory, but I do not wish to dream of it!"

"It is the same dreams as before?" Darcy was the only one with whom Richard had ever shared this.

"Essentially." Richard knew better than to tell him of his dreams of Elizabeth.

Darcy sat back and steepled his hands under his chin. "I know that after Wickham, Elizabeth and I both had terrible dreams each night. Gradually they faded away. Only when I am particularly worried do they return."

Richard nodded and asked intuitively, "Did they during your separation?"

He laughed slightly and nodded. "Yes, for both of us."

"Perhaps it will be better then. Perhaps I just need to become accustomed to being safe. They always seemed to fade away towards the end of my leave." He closed his eyes and said almost to himself, "If Katie was not there, I do not know what I would do."

Darcy smiled. "Now that is good to hear." Richard looked up, seeing the relief that his subtle declaration of devotion brought. Darcy studied him for a moment. "Richard, I understand why you are leaving tomorrow. I hope someday you will be able to stay as you used to."

"Thank you." He paused. "I do love Katie, and I am overjoyed she is my wife."

"You should be." Darcy smiled and prodded him, "You should be grateful she would have you." Richard smiled at the jab. Then becoming serious again, Darcy looked him directly in the eye. "You may love my Elizabeth as your cousin, but nothing more. Do you understand?" There was not a hint of humour in his voice.

Richard took no offence with the quiet warning. "I do, and I do believe that is all I need."

"Oh believe it Cousin that is all you will ever have!" Darcy was still deadly serious, but this was delivered with a smile. The cousins were back on even ground.

Early the next morning, the two carriages departed, one to Matlock, the other to Rosings. Married or not, Darcy was relieved to see his cousin go. What he did not know was Richard felt the same relief.

Chapter 34

*J*ane and Bingley arrived and Elizabeth was amused to see the size of her sister's eyes when she stepped out of the coach. They flew into each other's arms. "Lizzy! Oh how I have missed you!" She looked up at the mansion. "This is Pemberley. I cannot begin to say how beautiful it is. Your letters were detailed, but oh my, Mama would go distracted if she were here!"

"Well thank heaven that she is not!" Elizabeth laughed. "We will see them soon enough. Come, let us go inside, you must want to change out of those travel clothes." She turned to lead Jane into the house, leaving the neglected Charles standing with the smiling Darcy. "Oh, and Charles, it is wonderful to see you, too." Elizabeth smiled back at him.

"Clearly, I am not the favoured guest, here." Bingley laughed.

"Do not fear Bingley, *I* am pleased to have your company." Darcy shook his hand and the men followed the ladies indoors.

Soon they were gathered together in a parlour, enjoying the great variety of refreshments laid before them. "I was looking forward to seeing Georgiana, Lizzy. Is she not at home?"

"She is sitting for her portrait right now. She will join us very soon, I expect." She looked at William and said teasingly, "I will be the next victim of the artist's brush I fear. William insists on having my likeness put on canvas."

"Indeed I do, unfortunately, the artist I wish to employ has another commission to fulfil before he can create Elizabeth's painting, so we will have to wait another month or so before he can begin."

"Is this someone different from who is painting Georgiana?" Jane asked.

"Yes, I have thought quite long about it, and I have chosen an artist who I feel will be able to capture Elizabeth's beauty to the best advantage." His intent stare did not waver from his now blushing wife. "However, Georgiana's master will paint several miniatures for me while he is here."

Still blushing, Elizabeth returned his steady look. "Yes, you see, he wishes to fill the halls with my image, so that he knows that I am watching him at every turn." She smiled. "I have agreed on the condition that I receive a similar gift of his handsome face to keep near."

Bingley laughed, "Well, that is only fair! Now, tell us about this honeymoon you two finally took."

The two happily regaled them with the tale of their trip, and Darcy offered the cottage to the Bingleys to enjoy if they ever had the inclination. That brought them around to speaking of moving into the area, and they decided on a schedule for visiting the various estates that Darcy felt were suitable for Bingley to purchase, both in way of price, and in his ability to run profitably. Georgiana at last joined them, exhausted from the tedium of sitting still for the artist.

"How much longer?" Elizabeth asked sympathetically, handing her a reinvigorating cup of tea.

"He said one more day should be all he needs with me actually present. He will be able to take care of the finishing touches in his studio. I admit that I will be vastly pleased when the ordeal is over. I think Mrs. Annesley will be, too!" They laughed. "I suppose it is required to have a portrait painted for my coming out, I only wish it did not take so terribly long!"

Elizabeth smiled ruefully at her. "I am not looking forward to my experience. You have much more patience than I for sitting still. I am afraid that sitting for hours on end with an artist will have me imagining all sorts of terrible mishaps that might befall the man so that I might escape his unwavering gaze." Everyone laughed but Darcy, who was suddenly struck by her words.

"You will not be sitting alone, my dear. I shall keep you company." He said determinedly.

"You will? Why would you do that? Surely you have better things to occupy your time?" She noted the change in his expression, but could not read it.

"I will bring my work into the room and sit with you while you pose, Elizabeth." There was a tone of finality in his voice. He saw her questioning brow and added, "I do not wish for you to be left in a room with a strange man staring at you all day, my love."

"I will be glad for your company, William." She softly replied.

Georgiana whispered loudly to Jane, "This is when they start staring at each other with great affection. I have learned that if I just start talking, eventually they will remember I am present and awaken from it." She giggled. Elizabeth and Darcy both blushed, but smiled at each other, admitting their guilt.

Bingley laughed. "I say, you two are almost as bad as Mr. and Mrs. Bennet!" He met Jane's widened eyes. "Well, no, they do not display their affection quite so readily, but it is fascinating to watch, nonetheless."

Thus began a discussion of the inhabitants of Longbourn. Kitty had departed for her new school, chosen after Darcy wrote to Mr. Bennet and recommended several establishments that were more suited to a gentleman's daughter not of the first circles. She would receive an excellent education, but it would be a more comfortable atmosphere. With Kitty out of the house, Mary was beginning to show signs of coming into her own at last. She was the only child, and enjoyed the attention of both parents. Mrs. Bennet was determined to marry her off, and had begun with forcing her to begin dressing in a more becoming manner.

Amazed, Elizabeth asked, "Is it working, do you think, Jane?"

"Well it has not been long, but I admit to being curious to see her upon our return." She smiled. "We certainly tried for years to encourage her to change her appearance and habits, Lizzy; perhaps she was not ready until now." Elizabeth nodded. Maybe there was hope for the middle sister after all.

"How is Lydia faring? I have not had a word from her in weeks."

"Oh, she is driving Mrs. Forster to distraction! She complains constantly that she wants to be married right away. So far Papa has managed to discourage her, and kept her happy by sending a little money each week so she can add to her trousseau. Poor Mr. Denny. I wonder if he is rethinking his commitment." The ladies shook their heads, and Darcy raised his brows to Bingley, who rolled his eyes.

"And what of your family, Charles? How is your sister, Mrs. Hurst?" Elizabeth had come to a tolerable acceptance of his eldest sister; she at least had not obviously tried to come between her and William.

"Well, Louisa and Hurst spent the summer at his parent's estate in Surrey. They seem to have enjoyed themselves quite well. From what I understand, Hurst has cut his drinking significantly, and is returning to the man I knew when my sister was first being courted."

"That is wonderful news! What could have affected such a significant change?" Elizabeth was very curious to know.

"I believe that it is the absence of my sister Caroline from Louisa's life, I am sorry to admit. She was seemingly poisoning their relationship. Hurst took to drink to avoid her. With her gone, they are finding each other. It was always a marriage of convenience for both of them, but they were well suited, and always fond of each other. Not passionate, but fond." He paused, considering the couple. "It is good to see them happy in their situation."

It was as strong a declaration of contentment that had ever been spoken of the Hursts, and the group took a moment to consider it.

Georgiana innocently asked, "How is Miss Bingley? She was absent from your wedding, I never heard why. Is she well?"

The sudden stillness of the room told Georgiana that something significant had happened with Miss Bingley, and she doubted that she would be told what it was any time soon. Bingley cleared his throat and sent an uncomfortable look at Darcy, who had a thundercloud gathering on his brow, remembering his last sight of Caroline running from his bedchamber after watching him loving Elizabeth.

"Ah, Caroline." He cleared his throat again. "She is in Scarborough with an aunt currently. She will be there for some time." He looked at Darcy. Despite Jane's declaration that he could not impose his troubles with Caroline upon Darcy, Bingley knew that he needed his friend's counsel. He needed to talk to someone besides himself about it, but it would have to wait until the men were very much alone.

DARCY AND BINGLEY went for a ride the next afternoon. They stopped on top of a hill, looking out upon the great sweep of land before them. "I can understand your pride for this, Darcy."

"We will soon find you your estate, Bingley. We have several very good possibilities to view."

"Yes." He sighed.

Darcy looked at his friend's miserable face. "Out with it."

"Caroline." Bingley said, glancing quickly at him.

Darcy closed his eyes. "What is wrong?"

"She keeps writing to me, asking me to beg you to allow her to apologize, to regain your favour. She has been completely cut from society in London. Even amongst the new money crowd. It seems even her dowry will not buy her favour in town."

"And this is *my* fault?" Darcy was indignant. "I am supposed to rescue her reputation? I did not create this, Bingley. She used me, my name, declared to society that I was hers, and I will not even mention that incident at Netherfield."

"I do not know what to do, she is my sister!"

"I thought that you made a break from her, told her to establish her own home and live off of her income?"

"I did."

Fighting an urge to shake some sense into him, Darcy cried, "She has used you for years. Do you not see this? She has created her situation, not you." He sighed and looked at his friend. "What are you asking of me?"

He took a breath. "Would you lift the ban of her using your name to enter social situations?"

Incredulous, he stared at Bingley. "Absolutely not! Her behaviour would reflect upon my and Elizabeth's reputations, Georgiana's reputation, imply a relationship that does not exist, and create rumours about the viability of my marriage. No Charles. No." He glared. "You are the head of your family. Act like it!"

Nodding, resigned, he said, "There seems to be no hope for her in London."

"Then she will have to find her life elsewhere." Darcy felt no remorse at all for his decision. Caroline had long ago lost his good opinion. "She is staying with an aunt of yours?"

"Yes, my aunt Rachel."

"Have you written, asking of your sister's behaviour? Is she improved?"

"I have heard from her, and . . ." He sighed. "No, she is unrepentant. She is angry and blames her misfortune on . . ." He did not wish to say it.

Darcy's eyes bore into him. "On what?"

"Elizabeth."

Incensed, Darcy reacted, "And you come to me asking for my forgiveness? To welcome her into society and I imagine into my home? No. If I was against it before, I am adamant now. No. Never. And if she comes to visit you, we will not be calling until she is gone. I am sure that you understand." Darcy's horse was dancing under the violent gestures of its rider. It took some skill to calm him.

Bingley watched the activity and met his friend's burning gaze and nodded.

Darcy regarded him. "What drove you to make such a request of me?"

"It seems that my aunt wishes her gone as well." He laughed hollowly. "I thought that if she could return to London, she could live alone, and leave us in peace."

"Perhaps she will live alone quite comfortably in Scarborough. I am sorry, Bingley, you know that I would do most anything for you, but not this."

"I understand. At least I can say that I spoke to you." He looked at his stony face. "Forgive me for imposing on you, Darcy."

"Of course. I know that you are simply doing what you feel you must." He turned his mount. "Come, let us go and find our lovely wives." He galloped off and Bingley smiled. He had not lost his best friend, and secretly he was relieved at his decision. Caroline would have to make her way on her own. He laughed softly to himself and thought, *she can stew in her own pudding* as Jane said.

THEY HAD JUST SAT DOWN to dinner that evening when a footman entered the dining room. "Sir, an express has just arrived addressed to Mrs. Darcy and Mrs. Bingley."

Elizabeth and Jane looked at each other. Darcy took the missive and saw that it was from Longbourn. He was hoping that it was not bad news and hesitating, handed it to Elizabeth. "Perhaps you should read this now; otherwise we will all be staring at it throughout the meal."

She took the envelope and broke it open. Her eyes grew wide as she read, her hand coming up to her mouth. Jane was beside herself watching, and four pairs of eyes bore into her.

"Lizzy! What is it? Has something happened?"

Elizabeth looked up, shaking her head. "I do not believe it. I am not entirely surprised, but I do not believe it." She suddenly remembered the other occupants of the room. "There is no need for us to travel to Hertfordshire next week, William. Lydia is married."

"Pardon?" Jane asked, grabbing the letter from her sister.

"Apparently Colonel and Mrs. Forster found that they could not bear Lydia's complaints and behaviour any longer, and the Colonel personally went to the church and bought a wedding license for them. He gave Lieutenant Denny an early leave, and saw them wed five days ago." She looked helplessly at Darcy. "They are honeymooning in London, and will travel to Hertfordshire, then on to his family's home in Essex before returning to the married officers' quarters in Brighton. They expect to remove to their winter post in Berks in late October. Lieutenant Denny is seeking a permanent assignment somewhere, he hopes in London with the regulars."

Jane dropped the letter onto the table. "Oh Mama must be devastated!" She looked at her husband. "You saw how excited she was to have another wedding, and to have the breakfast at Longbourn."

"What does your father have to say about this?" Darcy asked his still incredulous wife.

"He is glad that it is over, and is surprised that she lasted this long. He was expecting at any time to receive a letter that they had eloped. In his opinion, this was the far better outcome." She said sadly while looking at the letter, "I suppose that Papa will never change completely."

"We can still go and visit your family, Elizabeth." He offered gently, taking her hand in his.

She squeezed his fingers and knew that his making the offer to go was a great gift, and she appreciated it more than she could say. "No, William. If they come here for Christmas, I think that will be enough of my father's presence for you to have to bear for some time. I will write that we will stay home." She looked at Jane. "I know that probably disappoints you, Jane, but perhaps you can extend your stay here since there is no reason to rush back to Hertfordshire."

Bingley immediately jumped in, "I would like to stay here longer, Jane. We have many estates to view, and perhaps we could settle on one, and complete the negotiations in person instead of by post. That would be much better I think."

"Yes Lizzy. I would like to stay." Jane smiled at her sister. "I need the relief from Mama and Papa!"

"Good! That is settled!" Bingley turned to Darcy. "Perhaps we can get some sport in as well?"

Elizabeth grimaced at Georgiana and turned to Jane. "Oh dear, men and their sport, thank you for staying Jane, and rescuing us from those conversations!" The ladies laughed and began planning their activities for the weeks to come.

"OH, HOW LOVELY!" Jane exclaimed as the Darcy carriage approached Lyndon Hall. She turned to her husband who was watching her eagerly. "Charles it is perfect!"

Bingley took her hand and kissed it. "We have not entered yet, Jane, it may prove disappointing once we do."

Elizabeth leaned forward across the coach and touched her sister's knee. "What I think Charles is trying to say is to keep your effusions to yourself until a price has been negotiated." She smiled as the look of dawning understanding crossed her sister's face.

Darcy took Elizabeth's hand and squeezed. "I think I should have you present during my negotiations for next year's wool production. I have a feeling you would drive a hard bargain."

Elizabeth laughed. "Well, I imagine my presence would be quite unsettling to all of those men. They would be offended to have a woman in their midst, and they might not notice what they are signing."

"Hmm, perhaps I would be the one unsettled." He brushed his lips over her hand and enjoyed her blush.

The two couples had spent the past week visiting properties around Derbyshire for the Bingleys to purchase. There were four that Darcy deemed suitable to both Bingley's resources and meeting the required income generating potential. Lyndon Hall was, he felt, the best and therefore the last one to be viewed. It was located approximately thirty miles from Pemberley House, but if taking into account the acreage, Lyndon Hall was actually within seven miles of the nearest Darcy-owned land. As they travelled, Elizabeth kept looking at him expectantly, and he would just smile and shake his head. Finally after hours of travel, he nodded, and laughed at her stunned expression upon his confirmation that they had finally passed the outer boundary of Pemberley. The enormity of his estate was indelibly impressed upon her, and he saw that slight trace of fear in her expression that he immediately acted to dispel.

"It is just sheep and pasture out here, sweetheart, please do not let it overwhelm you." She drew breath and nodded, reassured by his steady gaze and warm caress of her hands.

They disembarked from the carriage and were soon met by the estate's steward, Mr. Douglass. He explained the history of the home, the former owner had died a bachelor, with no entailment and no heirs who wished to live in Derbyshire. They also had no desire to see the estate, and had ordered that the property be sold complete, including the contents, as soon as possible. For a man who was coming to landownership for the first time, it presented an ideal situation, and Darcy's research proved that the income could certainly be enough to match, and with proper management, exceed what Bingley currently drew on the interest from his father's savings, funds which would be significantly depleted upon purchasing the estate. It was essentially the size of Netherfield, but with the savings from not needing to furnish the rooms, Bingley could purchase additional land nearby which was available. The profits from the estate, combined with the income from his continued interests in trade would raise his income to at least seven thousand pounds.

Elizabeth and Jane set off to investigate the house, while the men spoke with the steward. The furniture was dated, but in good condition. The wall coverings needed to be replaced, and some minor repairs were necessary, but those were superficial things, as the house was sound. The gentlemen rejoined the ladies and the couples separated. Elizabeth watched her sister from afar, smiling as she valiantly tried to suppress her excitement. Darcy's lifted brow caught her eye and she smiled up at him. "It seems to me that Jane's choice is made."

"That is a good thing as Bingley just negotiated a price."

She shook her head. "You knew he would take this place all along?"

Darcy shrugged. "I had a fairly good idea."

"What would Charles do without your subtle guidance?" She asked as she gently stroked his cheek.

Darcy blushed slightly. "I am sure he would do quite well."

Elizabeth laughed and squeezed his hand. He gazed at her, she was restored to her happy self again, and he was overjoyed to share her vibrancy. Since returning from their honeymoon, the two had become practically inseparable. Only estate business or entertaining their guests drew them apart. They walked through the secluded gardens adjacent to the house, arm in arm in a comfortable silence. "I am so pleased that we will be present for the tenants' harvest celebration, Lizzy. It is the one event each year where I really should appear, and I am delighted to have you by my side this time."

She grinned. "Do you join in the frivolity? I know the harvest celebrations in Hertfordshire are always rather raucous."

He kissed her cheek. "I doubt that you would believe my participating in anything remotely frivolous, my love."

She smiled, thinking that indeed, he would likely be very uncomfortable, but there to do his duty. "Perhaps this year it will be a happier occasion for you."

He caressed the hand resting on his arm. "I know it will. I shall dance for the first time."

"Really? With whom?" She teased.

He placed his arms around her waist and pulled her against him. "If you think that I will dance with anyone but you, my dear, you are sadly mistaken."

She raised her brow. "Not even one with Jane?"

He sighed. "One with Jane and you shall have one with Bingley. I refuse to relinquish you to any other man." She blushed and looked up to his loving gaze.

"Thank you. I would not wish for any other arrangement." Darcy caressed her face and gently raised her chin. She watched as his eyes closed and her breath caught as his lips lowered to capture hers. Her own eyes closed and she felt the racing of her heart as his beat against hers. His hand left her face and moved to the back of her head, as his other pulled her waist so they were pressed tightly together. She felt his tongue lightly trace her parted lips, and sighed as it entered and began tasting her own. The kiss escalated from softly caressing to an ardent exchange. His hands roamed her back, and he pulled away to kiss her neck.

His husky voice whispered, "Lizzy, could we not go and explore the park?" His lips then found their target, the sensitive spot on her throat that gave him the pleasure of her moan.

Her arms tight around his waist, she whispered, "Do we have time?"

His eyes opened and met hers, they were warm with desire. "They cannot leave without us." She laughed. Darcy firmly grasped her hand, and scanned the garden. Spotting a copse of trees he glanced down at her flushed face and leaned to kiss her. "Come."

They soon arrived at the chosen spot. It was perfect, the surrounding trees formed a private room, and the dappled sunlight through the leaves warmed the long, soft grass. Darcy removed his topcoat and laid it on the ground. Elizabeth added her shawl, and he aided her to lie upon their makeshift bed. They knew their tryst must be quickly achieved, but that did not stop them from savouring each other's bodies. He carefully lowered himself on top of her and they lay, she enjoying the comfort of his weight, he the softness of her form. His hands caressed her face. "I could not go another moment without loving you, Lizzy." Before she could reply, his lips were upon hers and she was lost in the sensation of his kiss. She ran her hands through his hair, and down his broad back, pressing his bottom firmly to place him between her parted legs. He moved to again suckle her neck and she moaned.

"Oh Will, please. . ."

He breathed into her ear. "Tell me what you want, Lizzy."

She clutched him and her voice begged, "Slow, please go slow." He smiled, and propping himself on an elbow, opened his breeches while she gathered up her skirts. He gently pushed her back, kissed her tenderly, and slowly entered her in one long, delicious stroke. "Ohhhhhh." They moaned together.

Completely joined, they held each other and took a moment to lose themselves in the pleasure of their intimate embrace. Darcy raised his head from where it lay against her curls and began to bestow lingering, increasingly hungry kisses as his hips began driving rhythmically into her. Her hips rose and met his with equal desire, and their clandestine, passionate, devoted lovemaking soon resulted in Elizabeth's back arching up into his thrusting body, her muscles milking him of every precious drop of the essence that now flooded her. He gasped her name as the blackness of total, joyful oblivion overtook his senses when his final stroke pushed him as deeply inside of her as he could go. They remained in their lover's clasp, softly kissing, their hands buried in each other's hair, until their hearts and breathing calmed.

With regret, they separated and then carefully rose to adjust their appearance. Elizabeth gasped and blushed. When he looked at her with questioning eyes she lifted her skirt, so he could see the evidence of their love slowly running down her thigh and catching in her stocking.

He stared and swallowed. It was all he could do not to throw her onto the ground and love her again. "Do you mind? Shall we go inside so you can refresh yourself?"

Shaking her head, she lowered her skirt, "There is no hurry. I like the feel of you upon me, it marks me as yours." He swallowed again, such words only made him want her more. She gently caressed the growing bulge in his breeches.

"Lizzy. . ."

Taking his hand she began to lead him back into the sunlight. She took one step but was brought instantly to a dead stop. He remained where he was. She turned to look at him. "Will?"

His searing gaze burned into her and instantly her heart started pounding. With one strong tug she found herself encircled in his arms of iron. He stared down at her, his breath ragged. His eyes travelled down her face, her throat, her heaving chest, then back up to her mouth. She watched as he slowly licked his lips, like an animal about to devour his prey and feeling his erection pressing urgently against her, stood in trembling anticipation of his passion.

"Do you remember all of those mornings at Rosings Lizzy, when we met at that one particular tree at dawn?" She nodded mutely. He pushed her backwards until she felt the jolt of her back contacting the solid oak tree behind her. Fascinated, she watched as his hands hovered over her body, following, but not touching her curves, the heat from his near touch escalated her trembling to shivers. Her breathing now was in short pants, as his became harsher, his burning eyes raking over her. She watched as he again released his throbbing arousal, and then lifted her skirts. He pressed his mouth to her ear. "Do you know how hard it was for me not to take you against that tree like you are right now?" He lifted her up to his eye level, and kissed her deeply. She wrapped her arms around his neck, and he lifted her bottom with his hands, placing her legs so they encircled his waist. He broke the kiss. "Did you want me then, Lizzy?" He thrust himself into her, and then ground his hips, spearing her against the tree. "Did you? Tell me Lizzy. I wanted you constantly." He began pounding into her.

She closed her eyes. "Oh . . . yes. . . I . . . wanted you. I . . . ached . . . every time you . . . touched me."

"Do you still ache for me?" His voice rasped. Her head dropped onto his shoulder, and she gave herself completely over to him. "Always, Will." She moaned.

"Look at me." He demanded. She lifted her head and stared into his face. "I love you." He watched as her lips began to respond and saw instead her eyes close as she fell over the brink. Smiling with satisfaction, he crushed his lips to hers as his seed again pumped into her and groaned with his release. The tree held her firmly as his body shook against hers. Finally letting her down, she stood on shaking legs and they pressed their foreheads together, holding hands and breathing hard. Elizabeth's skirts fell back down around her. "Did I frighten you?" Darcy's soft voice was back, the rake retreated.

She touched his face and he opened his eyes, looking at her shyly. Yes, her gentle lover was back.

"No Will, you surprise, but never frighten me." He smiled. "Was that a dream of yours?" He nodded and looked down. She caressed him again. "I love making your dreams come true."

He kissed her hand. "Thank you, my love. If you have any I would be happy to . . ." She giggled. He blushed and cleared his throat. Once again they righted their clothes and hair. Darcy held out his hand. "We should return, I think." She just smiled and together they returned to the garden and settled on a bench, leaning against each other and regaining their composure. Soon they were joined by the beaming Bingleys.

"Well Darcy, I believe I am about to join the ranks of the landed gentry." Bingley was practically jumping up and down with his excitement; it would not be until the carriage ride home that he would remember the flush on his friend's face or the red marks on Elizabeth's neck.

Darcy stood and held out his hand. "I am delighted to see your happiness, and witness the fulfilment of your father's wishes. Congratulations, Bingley!"

Elizabeth and Jane embraced. "When will you move here?"

"With the redecorating and repairs that must be completed, Mr. Douglass thinks that we may relocate here by Christmas." Jane was beaming.

"Oh how wonderful! You can come and stay with us at Pemberley for Christmas, then move in afterwards. We already planned to invite Mama and Papa, and William's family."

Jane looked to Charles who was listening. "I am not sure, what of your sisters?"

Bingley met Darcy's gaze and grimaced slightly. "I believe that the Hursts will be visiting with his family, and I am sure that Caroline will remain in Scarborough." Darcy nodded. "Pemberley will be full of guests and as it is not our home, I will not feel obligated to invite my sisters."

Relief crossed all four faces. After a quick meal provided by the skeleton staff on the estate and a much needed chance to freshen themselves before the trip, they entered the coach and made the journey home, this time taking note of the landmarks between the estates that would become familiar friends for years to come.

Eventually, Elizabeth fell asleep in Darcy's arms, and he soon joined her. Bingley and Jane could not help but study the pair opposite them and looked at each other. Bingley asked, "Do you think that they . . ?"

Jane blushed at the suggestion. "Outside?" She whispered.

He laughed. "It is a wonder they are not yet expecting a baby!" He smiled, but stopped when he saw Jane's face. "Jane?"

She sighed. "They were. Lizzy told me yesterday. Neither of them wishes to discuss it further. It seemed to have been a very difficult time, but she will not say anything more."

Bingley sighed, again looking at the sleeping couple. "No wonder they are so close." He took Jane's hand and kissed it. "I have found myself sometimes feeling jealous of them, not their experiences, but their depth of feeling." She looked up to his warm green eyes. "I would not be averse to learning from them. Indeed, I would not be averse to repeating any of the behaviours we have seen Darcy and Elizabeth display." He stroked her hand. "Are you?" Deeply blushing and staring at her feet, she shook her head. Bingley smiled. He now had her permission, but knew to go slowly.

Chapter 35

fter returning from their morning walk, Darcy was approached by his steward with a question, and Elizabeth was told the post had arrived. She wandered into Darcy's study to see if there was anything for her and found a letter from Longbourn waiting. She sat reading it in the chair before the fireplace. Darcy entered and settled behind his desk, watching her expression as he looked over his correspondence.

She sighed and met his eyes. "Papa is disappointed that we will not be making the trip. He regrets that Mrs. Denny's impatience to wed has changed our plans."

Darcy bit back the first words that came to mind, something along the lines of not regretting the missed trip at all, and instead asked, "Are you disappointed?"

She leaned into a corner of the chair and regarded him. "Yes and no. I miss my family and the neighbours, but in all honesty, I really only want to be home, and experience peace for a good long while."

Darcy smiled and held out his arms. She rose and came to his side and he pulled her onto his lap, where she settled her head in the crook of his neck. "I feel the same way." He murmured into her ear. His gaze fell to the letter she still held in her hands. He looked at Mr. Bennet's handwriting, and saw his mention of the Dennys. The memory of his conversation with Denny at Bingley's wedding came to mind and he wondered if his supposition could be true. Unconsciously, his musings made him clutch Elizabeth.

She raised her head and looked at his pensive face. "What is wrong, William?"

He startled. "Oh, nothing."

She shook her head. "No. That is not acceptable. We talk now. Tell me." She met his gaze and was not going to back down.

"Elizabeth . . ." He began to try to distract her but knew the mistake they made not immediately talking before. "Very well then, this may be painful, and I hope ridiculous, but at Bingley's wedding, Denny said Wickham had intimated that he received a letter from someone petitioning him to separate us. He apparently felt it would be profitable, and hoped that it would also help him to win enough funds from the letter writer and me to make him able to quit the militia and live the life of a gentleman." He looked into her widening eyes. "Denny said that everyone who heard this felt it was just Wickham spouting off nonsense as usual, but of course, I was aware of his attempt to extort funds from me . . ." He stopped. Elizabeth's eyes were now full of tears and indescribable pain. "Lizzy?" He took her hands in his. "What is it?" He asked urgently.

"It cannot be true! He said it was not true!"

"What cannot be true? Lizzy?"

"When Wickham . . . spoke to me . . . during . . ." He nodded, letting her pass over the description. "He said that Papa wrote to him, asking him to come and separate us. He said that it would have been very profitable, and that our marriage ended that possibility, and he then said that he looked forward to seeing how much I was worth to you." Darcy stared at her, he *had* been correct. "I did not remember his words until the day I went to Longbourn and saw Papa for the first time. I asked him then if it was true. I thought it was a lie because everything that Wickham said to me had proved to be false, and you said that his words to you were false as well. When Papa denied writing to him, I accepted his word." She sobbed, "Oh, William!"

Darcy's face darkened, and if it were not for the presence of his wife on his lap he would have jumped to his feet and begun pacing at a furious rate. Instead he clutched her to him and said fiercely, "Never, Elizabeth. Never will that man darken my threshold and never, ever will he see us again!" His grip tightened, his eyes were black with rage. "What he did is unforgivable. I was willing, for your sake, to come to a civil understanding with him, to tolerate his occasional company, and to accept your desire to reconcile, but I cannot do that now. His actions began a nightmare that we have only just begun to put aside. I will not ever allow him near us again!" His arms crushed her to him. "He is as guilty as Wickham."

Elizabeth's body shook with her sobs. Darcy's anger was terrible to behold, and she could not in any way blame him for it. "William . . . please." She managed to choke out.

His face pressed against her cheek holding his precious wife, he barely heard her, but her weak voice somehow broke through his anger. His voice shook. "What is it Elizabeth?"

"I cannot breathe."

Darcy, realizing his tremendous grip on her body and arms, instantly let go. His fury was immediately replaced with his contrition and concern. "I am so sorry, Lizzy; I did not realize I was holding you so tightly." He was dismayed to see the obvious mark of his hands on her bare skin, and began rubbing her arms, bringing back the circulation. "Oh darling, I am so sorry. Does it hurt? How can I help you?" He looked into her eyes, begging for her forgiveness and reassurance.

Elizabeth stared at him, suddenly struck by what he said. "William, did you hear yourself?"

Busily rubbing her arms, he looked at her with confusion. "What did I say?"

"You said that when you were holding me so tightly, you did not realize you were hurting me."

"That is true, I did not; I just needed to know you were safe, that I would not have to let you go."

"Do you not see, William? You were doing the same thing that Papa was doing. He did not want to let me go. He was holding on tightly and searching for a way to keep me near. He did not mean to hurt me. I do not believe he ever knew what Wickham was, or had any idea that he would attempt what he did upon us."

"Lizzy . . ."

"Nothing can change what happened, Will. You said the same thing yourself about your own father's behaviour. We can spend our lives dwelling on the offenses of others upon ourselves, remaining bitter and angry, or move on. I am not asking you to forgive him, or even like him, but perhaps you can accept that what Wickham did was not sanctioned by my father."

"I do not know if I can. I might have been sitting here alone at this moment, because Wickham had succeeded." His eyes grew bright.

"But you are not." She said softly and touched his cheek.

"No." He ran his fingers through her hair. "Please do not ask the impossible of me." His hand fell to caress her face. "Can you forgive him?"

She shook her head. "I do not know. But I imagine that he is punishing himself daily with the knowledge of what his actions have wrought." She kissed him tenderly. "I wonder if Wickham would have found a way to terrorize us even without Papa's letter. He seemed to indicate that his plans were thwarted when he learned of our wedding. What he did here was something that he formulated entirely on his own. Wickham seemed to come to you regularly either to demand money or in the case of Georgiana, hurt your family. Do you truly think he would have stopped after your confrontation at Ramsgate?"

Darcy wound his fingers in her curls, and watched her expressive eyes. "No. In all honesty, I was half-expecting him to try to blackmail me when her presentation approached to remain silent on the affair. I expected him to claim that he had ruined Georgiana and would tell all of society about it to destroy her chances of a good marriage." He took her hand and kissed it. "Thank God she at least was spared that."

Elizabeth considered telling him what had happened with Wickham and Georgiana, but decided against it. Instead she caressed his hair. "So what do we do now? You are my husband; I will follow whatever you decide."

He looked into her sincere eyes and a small rueful smile played on his lips. He saw her confusion. "Mrs. Darcy. When have you ever docilely followed anything that I decided?"

Surprised at his unexpected levity she regarded him closely. "William?"

He gave a resigned laugh. "Surely you know that I am putty in your hands, my dear wife. So you should tell me. What will we do now?"

Smiling she kissed him. "Do you know how much I love you?"

He kissed her back. "Yes, almost as much as I love you."

They held each other and sat quietly in their embrace, thinking over the situation. Elizabeth lifted her head from where it lay on his shoulder. "We were not going to see my family again until Christmas. That is over three months from now. Perhaps time and distance will be to our benefit. Perhaps we should simply continue as we have. After all, Papa was nowhere near earning your approbation now in any case. All that has changed is that perhaps we know what may have inspired Wickham, but in truth, only that man is culpable for what occurred."

"I doubt that I will ever accept your father, Lizzy, and if I had known of this news when you were attacked, I would have permanently cut off your relationship with him at that time." His face and steady voice told her the absolute certainty of his words, and she knew that he would never have relented.

"I understand, and I accept your decision. Perhaps then it is good that our knowledge of the truth was delayed."

"Perhaps." They sighed. "How are your arms?" He looked at the skin, still reddened but thankfully not bruised. "I am so very sorry, Lizzy. I did not mean to hurt you. I do not wish you to fear me causing you pain, I . . ."

"Shhh." She touched his lips. "Stop. I know that you wished me no harm." She raised and kissed the hand that was stroking her arm. "You are the best of men."

He shook his head, and stared at her arms. "You caught me on a good day."

Elizabeth laughed. "Mr. Darcy! Twice in one serious conversation you manage to surprise me! What has become of my taciturn, unendingly serious husband?"

He sighed and smiled. "I am afraid that I am the victim of a pair of bewitching eyes."

THE WEEKS WENT BY and the Harvest Dance was held. Georgiana was, of course, not permitted to dance, but she found great enjoyment in playing with the children. Elizabeth was presented officially to the tenants and their families, although she already had met many of them through her weekly visits to the needy and at church. The dance was even more raucous than the ones she remembered in Hertfordshire, and her glowing smile and infectious laughter made the Mistress of Pemberley a much admired lady to Pemberley's population. The story of her kidnapping was well known, and the people did not hide their curiosity to see her in person. Elizabeth took it all in stride, but Darcy naturally was extremely protective and never strayed farther than an arm's length from her the entire evening. He did, however; find that he rather enjoyed a country dance.

A few days before Bingley and Jane were to return to Hertfordshire, the two couples were invited to the nearby estate of the Drake's, to meet and dine with the principal landowners of Derbyshire.

Nathaniel and Julia Drake were an older couple, closer to their sixth decade than not, both quite short, quite round, and quite insatiably curious about their neighbours. They had been dying to invite the Darcys for dinner for some time, but as it was known that the couple had their own problems as well their obvious desire to be left to their own newlywed activities, they refrained from issuing an invitation. However, when Pemberley held its harvest celebrations, and word of the glorious Mrs. Darcy's admired attendance as well as the elusive Mr. Darcy's unprecedented dancing reached their ears, nothing could stop the delightful scheming and planning to hold a dinner to welcome the couple to the world of wedded bliss, and of course to the equally exciting world of Derbyshire gossip. The fact that Mrs. Darcy's sister and her husband, soon-to-be new neighbours, were in residence as well, was an added bonus.

An impeccably attired Darcy appeared in Elizabeth's dressing room as Rosie put the finishing touches on her hair. His eyes raked over her form, dressed in a very enticing gown of ivory silk, her bosom well-displayed, and her figure flawless. "Why do you do this to me, Lizzy?" He moaned when Rosie retreated down the servant's steps.

"What exactly have I done?" She rose, knowing full well the effect she had on him, but a quick glance to the front of his breeches left no lingering doubt. She walked over and gave him a light kiss.

He shook his head. "No, I am not going to be tempted. We must behave." He seemed to be trying to convince himself.

Elizabeth could not resist, and caressed the bulge, eliciting a low groan. "Hmm. Too bad, I was feeling quite like misbehaving." She winked at him and turned away but not in time to escape his hand.

"You, my dear, are a tease." He said as he pulled her tightly against him.

"Mmmm, and I intend to torture you all night." She looked up at him, and tenderly traced her tongue along his parted lips.

"Ohhh." His low moan told her that she struck the mark. He grabbed her face in his hands and stared into her eyes. "Two can play that game, madam." He crushed his mouth to hers.

Breathless, she pulled away. "En garde!!" He laughed and let go.

Despite their distraction, the Darcys were the ones awaiting the Bingley's arrival in the foyer, but it seemed their delay was clothing related. Bingley began to compliment Elizabeth's appearance, and was distracted by her very swollen lips; he cast a quick glance at his friend, whose mouth was equally affected, and meeting his raised brow, bit down his smile and finished his statement. Darcy equally admired Jane, who wondered at her sister's heightened colour. Georgiana wished them a pleasant evening, and smiling, watched as her brother gallantly helped Elizabeth into the carriage, fortunately missing the slight caress of her bottom as she stepped up. Darcy took his place next to her and was met by pursed lips.

"Touché" she whispered as he grinned.

"I say, Darcy, I cannot remember ever seeing you so delighted to attend a dinner party before." Bingley noted, watching their interaction. He had not yet been brave enough to be so publicly affectionate with Jane.

"Ah, well, you have never attended such an event with me since I married, Bingley." He took Elizabeth's hand and kissed her gloved fingers.

"Thank you, William." She smiled.

"It is my deepest pleasure, my love." He replied.

Jane blushed, watching their open affection, and feeling no small amount of jealousy interrupted their exchange. "How far is it to the Drake's home?"

Darcy straightened. "Not too far, I would say it is about six miles, just the other side of Lambton. It is not a very large estate, probably about the size of Longbourn. Despite that fact, Mr. Drake and his wife are quite comfortably ensconced as the resident busybodies of Derbyshire. I tell you this as a fair warning. They will wish to discover every secret of yours before the night is over." His pointed gaze swept the faces in the carriage.

His warning intrigued Elizabeth. Darcy rarely stated such opinions. "How do they go about their discovery?"

"It is hard to describe, they will simply cajole you to talk, and before you know it . . ."

Bingley finished, "All of your dirty laundry and that of your closest friends is flapping in the breeze."

"Precisely."

"Oh dear." Jane looked at Elizabeth.

The carriage soon arrived at the brightly lit house. Many others were there, and various groups of people were milling about, shaking out skirts or greeting friends before ascending the stairs to the entrance. The Darcy party joined the throng, and Elizabeth and the Bingleys were introduced to the neighbours Darcy had known all of his life. Upon entering the hallway, Elizabeth spotted the two merry round people welcoming their guests and raised a gloved hand to suppress a laugh.

"What is it?" Darcy asked, smiling into her dancing eyes.

"Forgive me William, but I cannot help but think that the Drakes are very appropriately named." He looked to his hosts who both had walked over to shake hands with some friends and noted their distinct duck-like waddle. He bit his lips.

"Stop that sir!" He met her gaze, a question in his eyes. "Biting your lips is my duty." She whispered.

He blushed. "Touché, madam."

They finally gained a position before the Drakes. "Mr. Darcy! We have been waiting so many months to meet your bride, and at last she is here. Welcome to Derbyshire, Mrs. Darcy. I say, we had begun to despair that young Darcy here would ever find a girl to wed. Well, it just proves that he who waits wins the prize! You are quite remarkable, my dear! We have heard such intriguing stories! I am sure that if only a few of them are true we will be entertained for hours!" Mrs. Drake paused to draw breath, and before Elizabeth could remark on anything, Mr. Drake jumped in.

"Darcy you sly dog, hiding away such a beauty in that stone mansion of yours, for shame sir!"

Darcy smiled slightly. "Thank you for your concern, sir."

"Silent as ever, I see. Well, hopefully your bride will have more to say?" Mrs. Drake looked hopefully at Elizabeth.

"I assure you Mrs. Drake, I will be happy to entertain your questions." She smiled, and Darcy shook his head.

"Excellent!" The Drakes exchanged looks of delight.

"Mrs. Drake, may I present my sister Jane Bingley, and her husband, Charles Bingley? They will soon be moving to Derbyshire." The Drakes' attention was fully on the Bingleys and Elizabeth and Darcy made a quick escape into the drawing room.

"You realize that they will be hounding us for the rest of the evening." Darcy whispered.

She met his grimace with an arched brow. "Do you fear my skills at verbal discourse, sir?"

"No, my love, not at all, I have simply known them for so long, and have managed to avoid their machinations thus far. I was hoping to continue the tradition."

She was curious. "What machinations were those?"

He coloured and cleared his throat. "They have a daughter."

"Oh." She looked at him. "Is she married?"

"No."

"Is she here tonight?"

Darcy glanced about the room and spotting her, stopped. "Yes, as are many other daughters who . . ."

"Set their caps for you?" He nodded, embarrassed and worried. She looked into his dark warm eyes, and setting aside her own jealousy declared, "I care not, William. I won you."

"Touché." Their gaze held, and the other occupants of the room disappeared. The arrival of Jane and Bingley broke their silent lovemaking.

"Well that was exhausting!" Bingley declared, startling Darcy. He smiled at his blinking friend. "I have a feeling that Mrs. Drake is now somehow in possession of knowledge of my income, my family's history, and my hat size. You were not far from the mark in your description of their relentless curiosity."

They laughed. "How did you fare Jane?" Elizabeth asked, taking her hand.

Jane shook her head. "Oh Lizzy, I thought mother was a whirlwind of gossip, but she is nothing to Mrs. Drake!"

Darcy took them around the room, making introductions. Elizabeth held his arm, performing with her excellent humour and wit. She seemed far more comfortable here with their country neighbours than the inquisition she received at her one dinner party in London at Matlock House. Although many of these people were only residents of Derbyshire in the off-season, they also seemed more relaxed here. All were eager to make the acquaintance of the new Mistress of Pemberley, and all were dying to hear the details of her storied kidnapping, the telling of which had been expounded upon in the drawing rooms of the district for months. Darcy kept his essentially silent but very obvious vigil, and stepped in when necessary to dissuade the more pointed inquiries. In the end, the only information their new neighbours learned was that Darcy and Elizabeth were together a force to be reckoned with, and would not allow anyone to violate their privacy.

Mrs. Drake did not believe in place cards, so when dinner was announced, Darcy was delighted to find that Elizabeth was free to sit next to him. Upon taking their seats she smiled, and without taking her eyes from his, she surreptitiously entwined their legs. He gave no indication of noticing, but he also did not refrain from continually dropping his hand to his lap and caressing her thigh while attending with assumed interest the conversation of his other dinner partners. During one such caress, Elizabeth's hand found his, and briefly their fingers grasped. Their eyes met; their gaze so brief but so open that Mrs. Drake, who had been watching them, nearly gasped.

Upon the separation of the sexes, the ladies descended upon Elizabeth and Jane, alternately questioning and welcoming them into their society. New blood is always fascinating, and they wished to assess their new neighbours. For the most part, the women were curious and kind, although it was clear which ladies either had the disappointed unmarried daughters, or were very unhappy that a man of Darcy's status had married someone outside of the *ton*. She felt the intense gazes on her body, and correctly assumed they had effectively destroyed the theories on a forced marriage. She could hear the whispers in speculation of her and Jane surely being fortune hunters. Not all of the women participated in the catty comments she was pleased to realize, and they did have a pleasant conversation with a quiet woman, Mrs. Sarah Hill, who had hidden away in a corner. Elizabeth then noticed a small group of young ladies, standing together and openly staring at her. She whispered to Jane. "I think that I have just discovered some of my unknown competition."

"What do you mean?"

"William indicated that the Drakes wished him to choose their daughter, and many of the other landowners of the area had the same wish for their daughters."

"Oh Lizzy, he was not even safe from matchmaking mamas in his own district!"

"I suppose that is to be expected, who would know him better than the families he grew up around? I imagine you will find something similar when you travel to Scarborough with Charles." She met her sister's suddenly disconcerted gaze and laughed at her innocence. "You never thought Charles was a sought-after commodity before?"

"In all honesty, no." She looked at the door to the room, willing her husband to reappear.

Elizabeth grasped her arm. "Well, as I told William, I do not care about meeting these ladies, as I have won him. They may regret him, but he is mine. You should feel the same way about Charles." Jane nodded, her brow still wrinkled in thought. At that moment one of the young ladies approached them.

"Mrs. Darcy, I have not had an opportunity to greet you. I am Penelope Drake." She curtseyed.

"Miss Drake, it is a pleasure to meet you. This is my sister, Jane Bingley." They exchanged courtesies. "Your parents are most wonderful hosts; I have enjoyed meeting everyone tonight, and feel quite welcome in my new neighbourhood."

Penelope inclined her head. "Yes, they have been quite anxious to meet you, especially after the story of the incident at your estate came out. I imagine Mr. Darcy was quite mortified to have such an event happen at Pemberley. He has always been the epitome of excellent behaviour and I am sure he was quite disappointed to have such happenings blacken his reputation." She regarded the arched brows of her adversary. "I wonder if he regrets the circumstances that led to its occurrence."

Elizabeth regarded the woman with cold civility. She was daring to suggest that William made a mistake in choosing her. "I believe Mr. Darcy was more concerned with my well-being than mortification, Miss Drake." She looked her up and down, noticing her uncanny resemblance to a shorter version of Miss Bingley. "And as I am sure his reputation in Derbyshire can prove; he is a man who considers very carefully before making decisions that would affect his family and estate. He is the best of men."

Penelope had no choice but to agree with such a statement, and sending a cold look she excused herself from the sisters. Jane's eyes met Elizabeth's. "Did she actually try to imply that marrying you has ruined William's reputation?"

"She did." Elizabeth regarded the woman, who was now whispering furiously with the other single ladies. She turned back to Jane and smiled. "I never realized what a feeling of power I would enjoy being William's wife." Seeing Jane's confusion she elaborated. "No matter what our background Jane, we have married for love, we were chosen specifically by our husbands for our own qualities, we were not weighed as worthy for material reasons. With that knowledge, no disappointed ladies, or their mothers, will ever have power over us. Let the ladies of the *ton* dare to object to us. We know that we are secure and will enjoy happiness of which they will only dream."

Jane smiled. "Thank you, Lizzy. I shall not let any of them intimidate me."

In another part of the house the gentlemen were gathered in the panelled confines of Mr. Drake's library. The room rapidly filled with the low rumble of masculine voices and laughter. Darcy refused the offered cigar, keeping only to a small glass of cognac, and Bingley raised a surprised brow while drawing on his. Darcy smiled at his silent question. "It has been made clear to me that the taste is offensive." Bingley looked at him with confusion for a moment then his eyes opened wide with understanding. He took the cigar from his mouth and stared at it with regret, then to the laughter of his friend, deposited it in a nearby tray.

"I am glad to be soon departing Pemberley. You set the bar far too high, Darcy. How am I to impress my wife with my meagre offerings when all she sees is you and Elizabeth together?"

Darcy smirked. "Do you really expect an answer to that?"

"No, no, I am just making noise." Bingley laughed.

Three men approached the friends. "Darcy! I have been charged by my wife to learn every detail of yours." Frederick Hill declared.

Darcy shook the proffered hand and raised his brow. "Surely your wife is capable of speaking to mine on her own, Hill."

Hill turned to his companions. "I told you he would not say anything."

Henry Fairchild laughed. "I did not doubt you." He grinned and turned to Darcy. "Congratulations, Darcy. You had best be prepared for a trial when you return to town. The *ton* was vastly unhappy that you spirited your bride away from the Season."

Darcy bowed. "We have received a great number of invitations but have no intention of returning until late January." His curiosity got the best of him and he wished to confirm his uncle's theory. "I suppose my choice has received some criticism?"

Robert Hitchins laughed and looked to Bingley. "It seems your friend is curious!" Bingley grinned. "You married Mrs. Darcy's sister, I understand?"

The men shook hands. "Indeed I did. The greatest honour of my life was to win her hand."

Hitchins grinned. "Well we all say that at the beginning of the marriage, but with time, the bloom will fall away, especially after a few babes are born." Fairchild nodded in agreement, while Hill frowned.

"And our wives are more than pleased to send us to our own devices!" Fairchild smiled while Hitchins gave him a knowing smirk.

Seeing Darcy and Bingley not joining in their frivolity, and deciding it was due to the newness of their marriages, Hitchins returned to the previous subject. "So Darcy, you were wondering at your wife's reception in London? To be honest with you, I think it will go well. That little dinner the Matlocks put on went a long way to encouraging her acceptance. It seems all the right people were there to spread the good word of her. It was very well done on their part. Of course, that does not shut up the caterwauling of the disappointed ladies and mothers. *Those* ladies are waiting for your arrival with some amount of glee. You had best be prepared." He looked at him significantly.

Darcy found much of Hitchins' conversation distasteful, but he did appreciate the warning, although it was nothing more than he expected. "Thank you, although, I imagine there is bound to be someone unhappy when any man marries."

"Especially you!" Fairchild laughed. "Oh my, the gnashing of teeth I heard from my wife's sitting room when the ladies came to call!" He smiled and tilted his head. "Quite brave of you, really, taking on a simple country girl. The rumour around White's was there was a babe on the way, but of course, everyone there knew better than to claim that of you. Nonetheless, a betting book was formed for a due date. Seeing your wife tonight effectively ends that speculation!" Darcy was not at all amused, and it took a great deal of concentration to keep his face calm.

Several other men raised their voices in argument, attracting the attention of Fairchild and Hitchins, who drifted away, leaving Hill behind. "I am sorry gentlemen, their behaviour was abominable. Just because their marriages are cold does not mean that all of ours are."

"Thank you." Darcy sighed. "They have not changed since we were all at Eton together. We were never close. The only time I see them is at dinners such as tonight or occasionally at the club." He looked at Bingley who was still staring after them with distaste, and returned his gaze to Hill. "How is your wife, I do not believe we saw her earlier?"

Hill smiled. "She is well, she hates these dinners, but you know we have to go. I hope she is faring well in the lioness' den now, although, I imagine she is safe now that there are your wives there to investigate."

Bingley's eyes opened wide, he had not thought of what Jane might be experiencing. Darcy had not stopped thinking of Elizabeth, but was also sure that she could take care of herself. Nonetheless, when Drake indicated that they return to the ladies, Darcy was first out of the door with their host.

Upon entering the room Darcy went to her side. His gaze asked if she was well. She squeezed his arm and he relaxed. Before long the four took their leave, with the assurance of many upcoming invitations to the other homes in the area, and the promise of an invitation to Pemberley and Lyndon Hall in the future. Upon arriving at home, Elizabeth and Darcy dismissed their servants and went about readying each other for bed, soon finding themselves tightly entwined, recovering from the pleasure of their slowly simmering passion.

Bingley and Jane were similarly engaged. Each of them had their eyes opened to new ideas that night. Jane realized that Charles probably was pursued quite strongly by some ladies. After all, if her own mother's reaction to her finding a man of five thousand a year was any indication, surely there were many such ladies who hoped to secure him. Although she was his wife, it was the first time she had felt the gnawing sting of competition, and fully appreciated his sacrifice in choosing her, instead of a lady with a fortune. Bingley's ears were ringing with the obvious declarations of the other men they had met, who had not so subtly indicated their betrayal of their wives. The fact that their marriages were ones of convenience was not lost on him, and it made him value the choice he had made all the more. On the way back in the carriage, both of them watched the open expressions of affection that Elizabeth and Darcy made to each other with nothing more than their gaze and entwined fingers. Bingley moved his hand to cover Jane's and soon held it in his clasp. When they arrived back at Pemberley, neither couple expressed a desire for anything other than a wish to retire. Charles followed Jane into her bedchamber and dismissed her maid and his valet.

"What are you doing, Charles?" Jane asked with confusion.

He smiled and began undressing her. "I am going to love you Jane, and I am going to leave you breathless and wanting more." She gasped at his declaration.

"Charles!" Was the last word from her mouth before his lips claimed hers. It was many hours before either one of them said anything intelligible again.

Charles and Jane departed for Hertfordshire with a new glow, amid promises to write, and assurances of their arrival for Christmas in mid-December. The Darcys settled down to enjoy the rest of the autumn, and the remaining days of sunshine before the rain and snow descended upon them. The shades of Pemberley found peace at last.

Chapter 36

eorgiana went in search of Elizabeth, who disappeared soon after breakfast. She looked in her bedchamber, the library, the music room, and finally after thinking about it for a while, she entered the gallery. There she found her sister, sitting across from the portrait of her brother.

"Elizabeth?" Georgiana said cautiously.

"Do you need me Georgiana?" Elizabeth looked away from William's face and smiled; her eyes suspiciously red and bright.

Georgiana sat down next to her and looked up to the portrait. It was very well done, and captured the gentle smile that she often saw him give to Elizabeth. "He will be home soon." She said reassuringly and put her arm around her sister's shoulder.

"I know." She said softly and glanced up at his sweet brown eyes. "I miss him."

Georgiana sighed and clasped her hands together. "I know. I miss him, too. It was always hard when he would leave home. I would just become used to him coming back and he would be gone again. I think he was always happy to arrive here, but then he always seemed in a hurry to leave."

Elizabeth wiped her eyes with her handkerchief and turned to Georgiana. "Did he travel a great deal when you were younger?"

"When I was in school he was touring the continent. I remember the summer he left. If I did not have a portrait of him, I would have forgotten what he looked like."

"I cannot imagine forgetting his face." She returned her gaze to his eyes.

Georgiana watched the expression of love on Elizabeth's face and felt her own hidden heartache. "Elizabeth, I cannot remember what Mr. Carrington looks like."

She glanced at Georgiana and forced her thoughts away from her absent husband. "Do you wish to remember him Georgiana? I have not heard you mention his name in six months."

She looked down at her hands. "That is because I knew William would not let me see him until I came out. I thought it was best not to think about how much I liked him too often, so I would not miss him."

Elizabeth took her hand. "And did that work for you?"

Georgiana shook her head. "No, not at all." She looked sadly at Elizabeth. "Do you know if he is well?"

Elizabeth smiled. Sitting on the bench nearby was a large stack of letters. She was answering her correspondence with William, as she would have done if he were home. "As a matter of fact Georgiana, I received a letter from him yesterday."

"He wrote to you?" Georgiana's eyes grew wide. "How is he? Did he ask about me?" Elizabeth smiled and gave her the letter. With trembling hands, she opened it, tracing the words formed by his pen strokes.

December 1, 1811
Kingston Hall
Buckingham

Dear Elizabeth,
I was delighted to receive your letter. My parents and I would be honoured to spend Christmas at Pemberley with the Darcys; unfortunately we are already committed to spend the season with my mother's family. If it were my decision, I would prefer to be with you, and to see Miss Darcy again. I hope that she is well. Could you please let me know when she will be presented at court? I realize that it is months away, but as I promised Darcy to not declare myself until she is out, I would at least like to know when I may finally see her again. Does she ever mention me? I look forward to seeing you all in London. May I wish you a very happy Christmas.
Sincerely yours,
Alex Carrington

"Oh Elizabeth!" Georgiana was beaming.

"Do you feel better now? It seems that he has remained true to you. We need to become serious about your coming out. It is only three and a half months away."

"You are being presented at court, too, Elizabeth." Georgiana reminded her, grinning.

"Yes, but fortunately, I am married and I do not have to worry about enduring the Season." She looked back at the portrait and sighed.

"Do not remind me please." Georgiana's smile disappeared.

"Have you forgotten already that you will have a dance partner you favour?"

Georgiana brightened again. "I wish that he could come for Christmas." She was suddenly struck by a thought. "Why did you invite him? If William wanted us to be separated until I am out, why would he be invited here?"

Elizabeth decided it was not time to tell Georgiana her relationship to Alex; she would leave that tale to him. Instead, she smiled. "We decided that if he wanted to come it would tell us of his continued interest in you. We will miss his company."

Georgiana's regret was clearly displayed. "I know that I will. This will be my first ball, at least one where I can actually dance and not have to go upstairs after greeting the guests." Elizabeth looked back at Darcy's portrait, remembering the last time they danced at the harvest celebration. She sighed again, missing him so much. Georgiana saw that she was losing Elizabeth. "Come, we have much work to do. Let us go to the attic and pull out the Christmas decorations. We will have a houseful of guests soon."

Elizabeth appreciated her gesture. "All right, Georgiana. Let us go." She gathered up her letters, lovingly caressing the first, and taking one last look at William whispered, "I will return soon, my love."

"THREE MORE DAYS Angel, three more days." Bingley whispered.
"Could we not leave today?" She whispered back.

Bingley chuckled. "I imagine Darcy and Elizabeth would not mind, but we are not quite finished packing yet."

"Leave it behind!" She declared in a fervent whisper, then closed her eyes and held a handkerchief to her mouth, feeling nauseas once again. Charles, now accustomed to the worrisome behaviour squeezed her hand. When she opened her eyes, it was not his gaze that she saw, but her father's questioning eyes, regarding her from across the aisle in the Meryton church. She gave him a weak smile and sat a little straighter. She and Charles were fairly convinced that she was with child, but after the Darcy's loss, she was not going to make any announcement before she felt the quickening. She wrote to Aunt Gardiner when she first felt oddly, wishing for her counsel rather than her mother's. She also took the opportunity to bring up Lizzy's experience, and her aunt was able to tell her the details that her sister refused to relate. It was Georgiana who told her of the couple's despondency, although she remained ignorant as to the cause. Jane of course told all of it to Charles, and together, they wondered if such an event could so disable a strong marriage, what would be the affect on a weak one? They failed to take into account the importance of intense affection in the marriage as both a reason for the pain and the catalyst for the recovery.

Jane was ready to make the move to Derbyshire. Most of their possessions had left for Lyndon Hall that morning, and she watched the wagons depart with envy. Mrs. Bennet was becoming increasingly upset as their moving day approached and made her unhappiness quite clear to her daughter. She liked having her eldest daughter living in the grandest house for miles. She liked dining and visiting there several times a week, she liked telling her friends about it as well. It also gave her a sense of security, that she had somewhere to go if the worst happened. Not that her sister Phillips or the neighbours would refuse her, but to have a daughter well-situated and nearby was of great comfort. So her insecurity gave Jane the heretofore unknown ability to be aggravated and even more shocking, especially to her husband, the ability to express her irritation in a most Lydia-like way.

"Lord, but I am anxious to leave here!" Jane said, then clapped her hand to her mouth and stared wide-eyed at her husband. "Oh my!"

He stared back at her, then remembering the signs of pregnancy that her uncle had sent him relaxed, and smiled at her. "Perhaps we could leave tomorrow?"

DARCY GRATEFULLY RETURNED to his bedchamber after supper and immediately crossed the room, picked up the miniature portrait of Elizabeth to give her a kiss, and gently traced his fingers across her painted cheek. He sighed. He missed her so much it hurt. It had been two weeks since he last held her and his arms ached with emptiness. Embracing his pillow was no replacement for his wife. He thought back to his first night in that lonely room, and how overjoyed he had been to find a love letter from her laying across his pillow, placed by Rogers at her instruction. He kept the letter in his pocket at all times.

The travel to Rosings took almost four days. Richard's plea for his help could not be ignored. His steward had died, and had no immediate replacement, leaving

Rosings in great disarray. Richard had been learning quickly, but he was no Darcy. He desperately needed help. Darcy spoke to Mr. Regar, and he offered one of his assistants, his nephew Mr. Barnes, as qualified to take over as steward. He and Darcy set off together to help Richard put the estate back in order.

Elizabeth tried hard to convince Darcy to allow her to join him, but with Christmas approaching, bringing its corresponding onslaught of guests, he knew that she was needed at Pemberley. He regretted the decision almost the moment he made it, and as the miles between them increased, he vowed he would never be separated from her like this again.

Upon arriving at Rosings, he found that rents were not collected, tenant homes were in need of repair for winter, and the added burden that the housekeeper was very ill, leaving the still-learning Kathleen at her wits' end. He shook his grateful cousin's hand and dove into the work. The faster he finished, the sooner he could go home.

Darcy changed into his nightshirt and readied for another sleepless night in his cold and lonely bed. He settled under the covers, and looking at Elizabeth once again, he drew out the letter that had arrived late that afternoon. It was all he could do not to open it immediately, but he exercised restraint. He wished to savour his Lizzy's words in the privacy of his chambers. He held the envelope to his nose, catching the scent of the lavender water she sprinkled over the paper and sighed, smiling for the first time in days, and broke the seal.

November 30, 1811
Pemberley

My Dearest William,
It has been so long since I have written you a letter. I will not count the message you received upon your arrival at Rosings; that was a love note, and not posted. It does not qualify as a true letter, which is something sent with a desire to please and received with one hopes, surprise and joy. There was no need to write before, as you are always by my side, but now that you are not, I find that I am lost. I cannot walk the halls of our home without thinking that at any moment you will appear and I am devastated when the sound of an opening door or footsteps are not followed by your handsome figure.

It is so quiet here without you. I can just imagine you staring at that, but it is true. Certainly Georgiana plays her music, and the servants bustle about, but you see, I rather grew used to the constant pounding of my heart, anticipating your touch, and now it is so quiet that the normal sounds of the house are deafening in their insignificance. I need your whispers, your laugh, your stubborn arguments, oh Will, I need your voice.

I wish to be in your arms, my love. I want to feel your soft, warm lips wandering over my face and down my body. Your tender, yet demanding kisses make my skin tingle and I want to feel your mouth envelop my breasts and then your tongue as you continue lower to taste and bring me to the indescribable heaven you have shown me. I wish to feel your beautiful hands, your caress, all over me. Oh my love, I will never have enough of your touch; you make me feel so very wanted.

My darling, I miss everything about you; not just your dear voice and sweet hands, but your scent, your beautiful loving gaze, and your ultimate gift of your body. The feel of your body overwhelming mine with its weight and strength, entering and infusing me with your passion and seed completes me in every sense of the word. You made me a woman. You made me experience the heights of joy. Your give me the hope of a family, and most of all you give me your very essence, you share with me your soul, and that my love, I treasure. I can only hope that you feel a tenth the satisfaction with my endeavours. I cannot wait for you to come home to me darling, please come home and let me love you. I want to love you, my Will, my husband, my lover, my dearest friend. Come home.

Yours alone,
Elizabeth

"Lizzy." Darcy whispered, tracing the letters of her name with his finger. "I want to come home, this instant. I want to hold you and never let go again. Soon, darling, very soon I will leave this place and return to where I belong. I promise you my love." He blinked back the emotion that he let no other person see, and read her letter again and again.

RICHARD EMBRACED KATHLEEN, enjoying the lassitude he felt after their lovemaking. He had been making a very concerted effort to ignore the feelings he had for Elizabeth and replace them with the love he knew he had for the woman in his arms. He needed Kathleen, so much, especially now when he was utterly overwhelmed with the still unfamiliar duties as the Master of a large estate, and the troubles that Darcy had thankfully come to sort out. He was grateful his cousin had come without his wife, although Kathleen was very disappointed. He settled back on his pillow and closed his eyes, ready to hopefully find dreamless sleep when he was forced back to consciousness by the sound of his wife's voice.

"Your cousin is very unhappy."

His eyes opened wide and looked down at the pensive face lying on his chest. "Forgive me, my dear, but I cannot help but marvel at the subject you choose to discuss after such a moment. I fear that I have failed to distract you properly."

Kathleen tugged on the thatch of blond hair blooming on her husband's chest, to his pained protest. "Do stop thinking of yourself for a moment, Richard!" She looked at him. "Have you finished with your need for William's help yet? Can you and Mr. Barnes now carry on without him?"

"Perhaps." Finally seeing how serious she was, he sat up and gave her his full attention. "What concerns you?"

"William does not smile, and barely speaks."

Richard laughed. "That is not unusual. In fact, that is his normal state, my dear. I have known him all my life. He is not a joyful person."

"I realize that I have only seen him once before and briefly at that, but I must disagree with you. The man I met at Pemberley and the one here now are entirely different. At Pemberley he smiled, laughed, was even I would say playful in a very modest way, but now . . .

"He misses Elizabeth." Richard said softly. "I can certainly understand that." Kathleen looked at him sharply, and he fortunately saw it. "I would miss you deeply if we were parted, my love."

Satisfied, Kathleen returned to the subject. "Is it not time to send him home?"

Richard laughed. "He will go when he feels he has done everything he can for us, and no sooner. He is very stubborn that way. No matter how much he is suffering."

"That is ridiculous. You must push him away."

"And how exactly do you propose I accomplish that?" He smiled at her, raising his brow.

"You say that you know him so well, think of something." She challenged him.

Richard wrapped his arms around her and thought. "He received a letter from Elizabeth today."

"Yes, I did as well."

"What did she say?"

"She did not wish to burden him, but she needs him at home." She paused, wondering over the hidden meaning of Elizabeth's words. "She said that she is feeling unwell, and is not sure if her melancholy is due to his absence or perhaps something else . . . more significant." She stared directly at her husband.

He was completely in the dark. "What do you mean?"

Kathleen rolled her eyes and sighed. "She may be with child again."

Richard's eyes opened wide. "Really?" The thought of Elizabeth pregnant with Darcy's child brought an unexpected feeling of contentment. He knew the joy this news would bring to them. He looked down into Kathleen's face and smiled. "Then we must send him home. Tomorrow I will convince him his work is completed and the next day we will push him into his carriage and on his way!"

"Now that is the soldier I married, a man of action!" She smiled at him approvingly.

"Speaking of action, Katie. . ." He grabbed his squealing wife and rolled back on top of her. "Let us see if I can sufficiently distract you this time." After another most satisfying encounter, Richard spooned his body to hers and relaxed. He awoke in the morning to the great realization that he had enjoyed a rare night of peace.

GEORGIANA AND ELIZABETH spent the better part of the day going through the Christmas decorations that had sat neglected since Mr. Darcy died. The mice had found some, but most things were in excellent condition, having been packed away so carefully. They found a box of masks and entertained themselves trying them on. Elizabeth found her sadness lifting with Georgiana's enthusiasm. Servants carried the boxes downstairs and everything was laid out in the ballroom. Mrs. Reynolds took one look at the filthy ladies and like a mother hen ordered them to their rooms to bathe.

"Imagine what the Master would say if he saw the two of you!" She clucked.

"I think that he would scold us while trying hard to hide his laughter. What do you think Elizabeth?" Georgiana smiled over to her sister who had suddenly become very pale.

"Oh, I think he would be quite amused." She said, her voice drifting away to a whisper. "Please excuse me." She ran out of the room and into a small washroom nearby. Georgiana and Mrs. Reynolds rushed after her, and could hear the sound of Elizabeth's retching through the door.

"Elizabeth!" Georgiana cried. "Mrs. Reynolds! We must help!"

"As soon as it is over, we will dear." Mrs. Reynolds' mind was whirling. Could this be what she hoped?

Elizabeth opened the door and looked at the faces of the two waiting women, Georgiana's concerned and Mrs. Reynolds' questioning. She smiled weakly to her sister, and looking directly at her housekeeper, nodded her head. Mrs. Reynolds clapped her hand to her mouth and tried to contain herself. "Let us get you up to a bath Mrs. Darcy, and then I will send up some herbal tea to settle your stomach."

Georgiana's face was full of worry, and she wrapped her arm around her sister's waist. "I will help you, Elizabeth."

"Thank you Georgiana." She said gratefully. She did not wish to even think that it was true. It could only be a few weeks along, but she had almost instantly known that her body was changing. Oh how she wished William was home!

"WELL DARCY, THAT SHOULD put Rosings back on firm ground." Richard declared as he watched Mr. Barnes enter the last of the rent payments into the ledger. "You can be on your way home now." He grinned at him.

"Believe me Richard, there is no place I would rather be, but are you sure that you have a good grasp of everything now?" He smiled slightly. "I do not wish to return anytime soon."

"I think that I will choose not to take offense at that Cousin, although that statement surely disparages my hospitality and insults my dear wife."

"I would never insult your wife, Richard, only you." His humour had returned slightly with the receipt of Elizabeth's letter.

"Hmm." Richard eyed him. "I think that Barnes and I will be well rid of you." Seeing the stubborn set of his cousin's jaw, and knowing his opinion that all would fall apart if he left too early; he played his trump card. "How is Elizabeth?" Darcy started; they had, by silent agreement, only spoken of her when Kathleen was present. "I saw you received a letter from her yesterday." He said innocently.

"She is well." He said quietly. He was not about to recite the torrid contents of the letter to Richard. He had savoured her words so many times that night he could easily repeat them. His imagination was suddenly fully engaged in acting out the suggestions contained in her prose

"Kathleen received a letter from her as well." He said bringing his cousin's drifting attention back. "She mentioned feeling decidedly unwell."

Darcy immediately focused completely on Richard. "What do you mean, unwell? Is she ill? What is wrong?" He demanded.

"She mentions feeling sad, but blames that on your absence, perhaps her desire to stay in bed and lack of appetite are due to that as well." Richard watched Darcy with growing amusement.

"She is in bed?" He leaped to his feet. "Could it be true?" He spoke to himself, pacing rapidly. He turned to Richard. "I must leave for home."

"But what about Rosings?" He contained his smile.

"Rosings is fine. Mr. Barnes is a good steward, and you know what to do." He said dismissively, his mind racing.

"You would leave me now? At my time of need?" Richard's voice took on a plaintive whine.

"Hang your need, Richard! Elizabeth needs me!" He declared.

"I think you should stay at least another week, Darcy." He said solemnly.

Darcy snarled in his face. "Just try to stop me from going!" He strode from the room and flew up the stairs calling out orders to have his carriage readied instantly and sending Rogers into a panicked frenzy of packing.

Richard and Kathleen stood on the steps of Rosings and waved farewell to the speeding coach less than an hour later. She slipped her hand into the crook of his arm. "What on earth did you say to him?"

He smiled and looked down into her curious eyes. "All I had to do was suggest that Elizabeth needed him."

DARCY STAYED OVERNIGHT in London, giving Rogers the opportunity to repack all of his master's clothes and Darcy a chance to pick up some special Christmas gifts he had ordered for his wife and sister. The next day he left again. The going was very slow, winter rains made the roads slippery and sticky, the ruts broke more than one carriage wheel for many unfortunate travellers. It grew worse as they travelled farther north, now fighting through snow squalls and deep drifts. The usual three day journey from London became four. By the time he reached Pemberley, Darcy completely destroyed the pair of leather gloves he had been twisting in his anxiety the entire trip.

He jumped down from the carriage and ran straight into the house, disregarding the servants trying to take his coat. "Where is Mrs. Darcy?" He demanded.

"She is in the ballroom, sir." A footman stuttered.

He started down the hallway and hearing the sound of Elizabeth's laughter, broke into a run. He came to a skidding stop in the doorway to see the enchanting sight of his wife with a wreath of holly in her hair, laughing heartily at Georgiana. *Now* he was home.

"Lizzy," was all he said. She turned, her eyes immediately locked onto his, and they both flew into each other's arms, kissing with such passion that Georgiana and the servants immediately left the room, closing the door behind them.

Simultaneous cries of "I love you" echoed off of the walls. Darcy tore his coat off and pulled Elizabeth back into his arms, kissing every bit of exposed skin his lips could reach. They drew away from each other, panting, and his eyes swept the room, searching for some soft surface to lie upon. Failing that he growled, "Come" scooped her up and carried her out and straight to their bedchamber. They no sooner arrived before he dropped her onto the bed and unbuttoned the fall of his breeches. She had pulled up her skirts and in a second he thrust into her and in minutes the torrid, passionate act was over, leaving the two staring up at the canopy, gasping for breath.

Elizabeth turned her head and met his eye. She grasped his hand and smiled, her eyes dancing with her happiness. "Well, Mr. Darcy, may I assume by your enthusiastic display that you missed me?"

Darcy grinned. "Why yes, Mrs. Darcy, I believe I did." They looked at each other and began to laugh, the tears of joy flowed down their faces, and they held each other tightly, shaking with happiness and relief at their reunion.

He propped himself upon his elbow and looked down into his wife's happy face. "I will never make that mistake again, Lizzy. I do not care to ever spend another night without you by my side."

She ran her fingers lovingly through his curls. "I tried to convince you that I should accompany you, as you may recall, dear sir."

"And I was a stubborn fool for not listening to you." He reached over, playing with a tendril of her hair.

She raised her brow, "You are admitting to making a mistake?"

"I am." He smiled. His eyes were full of love for her.

"My goodness, sir! What has become of you! I was under the distinct impression that you were a man without fault!"

"There is no fault in making a mistake, only in not admitting it." He instructed.

"But only when caught." She added seriously.

"Well, I did not say when I would admit the mistake." His smile widened.

"Only that you should." She nodded while biting her lip.

"Precisely."

"I missed you desperately, William." She whispered, her eyes filled with tears of emotion.

"And I you." He caressed her face, his eyes bright as well. "I am afraid that you must sit for another portrait, my love. I think that I kissed yours too many times."

"If I could have reached your lips in the gallery, your portrait would be in a similar state."

He smiled. "You looked upon my portrait?"

"I sat and answered my correspondence with you every day." She admitted, the tears flowing freely now.

"Oh Lizzy." They lay quietly, holding each other, so happy to be whole again. "Lizzy." He began cautiously. "Kathleen received a letter from you . . ."

"Yes." She gave his hand a tight squeeze.

"Yes?" He said, his hope rising.

"Yes. I think. I feel. Yes."

"When?" He whispered.

"August." She whispered back.

"So long!" He said mournfully.

"It will be at least another two months before I will feel anything, so let us not tell anyone yet. Only Mrs. Reynolds knows for sure. I just placed some hints in Kathleen's letter. I hoped it might bring you home sooner." She grinned. "As I see by the evidence before me, it was most effective!"

"Minx!" He said fondly. "I will contain my joy until you tell me I can shout to the world."

"I know it will be difficult, but . . ."

"It would be prudent. Yes, I know." He kissed her hand. "I love you Lizzy."

"I love you Will." She sighed, and gratefully rested her head over his beating heart.

Chapter 37

he next week was spent preparing Pemberley for Christmas. Cuttings of laurel, holly and rosemary were festooned over doorways, colourful ribbons and garlands of pine were wound on the banisters. The Yule log was prepared, and mistletoe was everywhere. The scent of Christmas was in the air as sugar plums, gingerbread and ginger nuts were made to give to those who came to view the estate. Elizabeth, Georgiana, and Mrs. Reynolds worked together to prepare for their guests. When a footman approached Elizabeth and informed her of a carriage's arrival, she asked him to inform Mr. Darcy, who was catching up on his own work. The women went to the front door in time to see Jane emerging from the carriage on Bingley's arm. Elizabeth ran out of the door and promptly slipped on the icy steps, landing in a heap at their feet.

"Lizzy!" Jane cried out and rushed over to her.

"My goodness Elizabeth, are you well?" Bingley came immediately to her side and easily lifted her to her feet. Jane started brushing the snow from her.

"Oh Jane, stop, I am fine, really!" Elizabeth laughed. "Come; let us move inside where it is warm."

By this time, Darcy had arrived at the door and seeing Elizabeth with a wet gown and limping, immediately became alarmed. "Lizzy, what happened?" He removed her from Jane's grasp and looked her over.

"I am fine; I just slipped on the steps, and took a little tumble. I am fine, truly." She smiled reassuringly at him.

He shook his head. "No more, Elizabeth. You will not greet any more carriages. You will wait in the foyer and the visitors will come to you. I will not allow the risk of another fall." He held her hand and looked seriously into her eyes. "Agreed?"

She stared at him for a moment. He had become the greatest mother hen and protector imaginable after learning of his Lizzy's pregnancy. Elizabeth had no intention of making him change, no matter how annoying it may become. She squeezed his hand. "Agreed, William."

He let out a breath, relieved she had not argued with him, and finally turned to greet their surprised guests. "Bingley, Jane, we were not expecting you for several days, did you decide to leave early to take advantage of the good weather?"

Bingley coloured. "Please forgive our early appearance, we, ah, well . . ."

Elizabeth was watching Jane. "You wished to escape Mama?" Jane's eyes met hers and the silent confirmation of the sisters took place. Elizabeth smiled and hugged her. "I understand."

Mrs. Reynolds had their rooms ready in no time and the couple was happy to go relax in warm baths and rest until they all met in the dining room. Amid the conversation and exchange of news, Darcy watched in fascination as Jane heaped enormous quantities of food onto her plate and devoured it while Bingley watched

Elizabeth barely nibble on a roll. The two friends looked at each other. Darcy raised his brows in question. Bingley glanced at Jane and a bright smile appeared as he nodded. Darcy smiled. Bingley then glanced at Elizabeth and tilted his head, and Darcy's grin widened as he nodded. The two men sat smiling like fools for a moment before Elizabeth noticed them and stopped speaking to Jane in mid-sentence. Her eyes went to Jane's and widened. Jane nodded and smiled, then noticing her sister's poor appetite, she asked silently and Elizabeth grinned.

By this time Georgiana was completely confused by all of the silent smiling and burst out, "What are you talking about? I must have my share!"

They started laughing. "Oh Georgiana, please do not tell me you are turning into Aunt Catherine!" Elizabeth cried. That sufficiently distracted their sister and the two couples secretly rejoiced in the others' good news.

SEVERAL DAYS LATER two carriages arrived from Matlock. Elizabeth and Darcy awaited them in the foyer with a contingent of servants. "Elizabeth!" Lord Matlock entered the house and went straight to his niece, taking her hands in his. "You are glowing! Has my nephew taken you on another satisfying trip?" He laughed at his own joke.

Elizabeth shook her head and kissed his cheek. "How long have you been working on that Uncle Henry?"

"Ha! You know me too well already!" He let go and vigorously shook Darcy's hand. "I have been looking forward to this Christmas Darcy, I feel like a boy!"

Darcy smiled and turned to Elizabeth. "I apologize in advance for the Fitzwilliam family, my love."

Elizabeth laughed and embraced Lady Matlock. "I count on you to help me reign in your mens' enthusiasm, Aunt Elaine."

"Oh no, my dear, I gave that up years ago." She smiled and turned to the couple standing nearby. "Elizabeth, this is my eldest son Mark and his wife, Laura." Before she could continue the introduction, Darcy took Elizabeth's hand and spoke. "Mark, Laura, this is my wife, Elizabeth." He looked upon her with great affection and smiled at his cousins.

Mark, an older, but oddly younger-looking version of Richard, gazed upon the joyous expression of his cousin with awe. "I am delighted to meet you at last Elizabeth. I have heard tales of you and the miraculous transformation that you have wrought upon Darcy, but I refused to believe it until this moment. Who knew the man could smile!"

Elizabeth's eyes danced. "Oh sir, I assure you, the achievement of that smile has been the result of a great deal of practice."

"From a very willing student." Darcy raised her hand to his lips.

"Most satisfying!" Lord Matlock called out.

Mark's eyes met Laura's. "If I was not witnessing this I would not believe it."

His wife smiled slightly at him. "Well we have certainly heard enough of it. Did you really doubt your brother's praises?" Darcy's brows furrowed for a moment, but it was unnoticed by everyone except Elizabeth. Laura curtseyed to her. "I am happy to meet you at last, Elizabeth. It seems we were destined to miss each other constantly this year."

"I am pleased to meet you as well, Laura. Perhaps you can give me more insight into these men we have married while you are here." She smiled warmly.

Laura nodded. She, the daughter of a peer, and very much raised to be conscious of her position in society, had been reluctant to accept Darcy's choice of wife. She wished Aunt Catherine had made the trip. She was sure *that* Lady would share her opinions without hesitation. Nevertheless, the efforts of her Fitzwilliam relatives allowed her to at least be open to meeting Elizabeth. Seeing the woman in person, and the extraordinary behaviour of Darcy, was enough to make her curious, and be willing to consider tolerating her. "Of course, I would be happy to share secrets with you."

Before the party could move to a sitting room, the sound of a third carriage was heard. Into the house came Richard and Kathleen, obviously cold and tired from the journey, but beaming to have arrived at such a good time. The cacophony of greetings echoed around the hallways as the family members embraced. Darcy and Elizabeth stood out of the way until Richard extricated himself from them, and holding Kathleen's hand tightly, approached his hosts. "I suppose we should greet the two of you, as you are putting up with all of us!" He grinned, then let go of Kathleen to shake Darcy's hand. "I hope you have something stronger than tea waiting!"

Darcy laughed and clapped his shoulder. "I believe I may have something, Cousin." Elizabeth and Kathleen greeted each other with happiness and embraced, then turned to the men. Darcy bent and kissed Kathleen's hand and wished her well, and Richard stood before Elizabeth. He gave her a quick embrace and closing his eyes, kissed her cheek, and then stepped back.

"You are looking lovely, Elizabeth." She smiled warmly at him and took the hand that was brushing hers. "Thank you Richard, I am so happy that you and Kathleen have arrived safely. We shall be a very merry party indeed." She then looked up into Darcy's dark eyes, and squeezed his hand. The party set off to their rooms and eventually all met again in one of the larger sitting rooms.

The reunion of the Fitzwilliam family over the following days was a sight to behold. It amused Elizabeth to no end seeing the two brothers working together to abuse their much taller cousin, who recruited Bingley to his side. They behaved as little boys and instantly took to challenging each other at their old games of fencing, riding, and billiards. Lord Matlock looked on with great enjoyment, and acted as judge and mediator between the inevitable arguments. The wives and Georgiana shook their heads at their antics, and spent a great deal of time commiserating with each other over the trials of marriage to such exuberant men. Elizabeth had to smile at the thought of anyone calling William exuberant, but here, at his home, amongst the safety of his family, he allowed himself to let his guard down.

Perhaps it was the season or the great number of guests, but whatever the reason, Elizabeth did not suffer as greatly with this pregnancy as she had with the first. With William home she no longer felt sadness. The smell of certain foods still bothered her, but she kept some peppermint nearby when she sat at the table and it helped. She was not at all hungry and was losing weight, a condition noticed by her husband and sisters, but at least the nausea had stopped. She could not complain of her physical well-being.

When the Bennet carriage crested the hill and the first sight of Pemberley appeared through the trees, the occupants sounded a collective gasp. "Oh, Mr. Bennet!" Mrs. Bennet's eyes were wide with amazement. She stared at the imposing home until it disappeared from view again, and then turned to her husband, her mouth agape. "I knew that Mr. Darcy was rich, but I could not even begin to imagine this!" Signs of the old Fanny Bennet made their ominous reappearance. Fortunately the new Thomas Bennet recognized it.

"Mrs. Bennet, please take care. Lizzy has made it quite clear that her husband does not in any way appreciate loud effusions about his wealth. I think that it would be most unwise to embarrass him or Lizzy by behaving in anything other than a refined and genteel manner." He looked to Mary and Kitty. "That advice should be applied to you ladies as well."

"Really Papa, you act as if we are ruffians!" Kitty said, pasting a look of indifference to the estate on her face.

"Yes, Papa, certainly we know how to behave with decorum." Mary claimed, while nervously adjusting her bonnet.

Mr. Bennet sighed. At least Lydia was not able to make the journey with them. Her husband's duties kept him at his post. He regarded his daughters and wife. Their excitement was palpable. He hoped they would try to behave well. He had not seen Elizabeth and Darcy since June. His relationship with his daughter was improving slowly through letters, but with Darcy, it remained coldly polite. He was not sure if it would ever grow beyond that.

The carriage pulled up to the door, and a footman directed them inside where Darcy and Elizabeth waited. The three ladies entered with open mouths and wide eyes, and were practically bowled over by the rush of servants who descended upon them to take their coats.

Mr. Bennet walked directly to them and bowed. "Thank you for inviting us to your home, Mr. Darcy."

He nodded and said without expression, "We are pleased to have you and the ladies with us."

Mr. Bennet looked at Elizabeth, cocking his head a little, and the light of comprehension came across his face. "It is wonderful to see you, Lizzy." She embraced him and he whispered, "Are congratulations in order?" She looked at him in surprise. "You are not saying anything, yet?" She shook her head, and he nodded, smiling slightly.

Darcy wondered at the odd exchange between father and daughter. Elizabeth greeted her mother and sisters, and suggested that they refresh themselves in their rooms before joining the rest of the guests. Mrs. Bennet, mindful of her husband's admonition contained her effusions over the décor and bit her tongue. Elizabeth led them to their rooms and returned to the parlour where everyone else had gathered before dinner.

Darcy came over to her immediately. "Are they settling in?" He asked, squeezing her hand.

"Yes, I imagine they will join us in a half hour or so." She smiled slightly

"What did your father say to you? You looked surprised." He was concerned about any emotion that Mr. Bennet evoked from Elizabeth.

"Apparently experiencing five pregnancies with Mama has made him very perceptive." She looked at him, raising her brows.

"He can tell?" Darcy stood back and looked closely at Elizabeth. Her jaw line was softened, her skin glowed, and she did look different. Why had he not seen it before? The corners of his mouth lifted. "I suppose there is something to be said for experience."

"Lizzy!" Jane grasped her hand. "How are Mama and Papa? Was their trip difficult? I was so worried that the weather would prevent their travel."

"They seem fine, Jane. They will join us soon."

"Elizabeth." Lord Matlock came over to her. "I understand that your father has arrived. Before he comes in, please tell me how you are getting on with him." He looked at her with concern. Everyone else in the room stopped talking and turned their attention towards them. They all knew what Mr. Bennet had said about Darcy, and how he tried to interfere in their courtship and marriage, no one but Elizabeth and Darcy knew of his letter to Wickham.

"We are improving slowly, I would say. We have not seen each other since June, but we have been corresponding regularly. I do not believe that we will ever regain the relationship that we once had, but perhaps that would have changed upon my marriage in any case. I do not know. All I ask from you all is to treat him with civility, and give him a chance. I have no desire to spend this joyful time of year with a roomful of tension." She looked at them all pleadingly.

Richard stood. "If that is your desire, then the protective nature of the Fitzwilliam men will stand down." He looked to his father and brother, who nodded.

"I have already promised to behave." Darcy kissed her hand.

"And you know that I would not hurt a fly!" Bingley added. That broke the seriousness of the moment and the family returned to their conversations.

Soon the Bennets arrived and after they were introduced to everyone, they all moved into the dining room. Lady Matlock sat at Elizabeth's right, across from Mrs. Bennet. "It is so good to see Pemberley decorated for Christmas again, Elizabeth. Darcy tells me that you will open the house for visitors tomorrow?"

"Yes, we have put out word that the estate will accept visitors from the hours of ten o'clock until two o'clock Christmas Eve. We will allow them to wait in the foyer, and small groups will be shown the public rooms, ending in the ballroom, where refreshments will be available. We have small gifts for the children who come. We also have hired musicians to play there. After this experience, I may plan a more elaborate celebration next year. Perhaps we will have sleigh rides, or winter games. We will see." She smiled at her.

"My goodness, Lizzy! Such elaborate plans! The ball is only three days away; you have taken on a great weight!" Mrs. Bennet was amazed at how Elizabeth could possibly consider such events following so closely upon each other.

"Mama, I have hardly accomplished all of this alone. Georgiana has been a great help, and of course, Mrs. Reynolds and our staff have been indispensable." Georgiana looked towards her with gratitude. "I need the practice, since we will have a coming out ball to plan for very soon!" She teased her.

"Oh, please do not remind me!" Georgiana groaned.

"When is your presentation, Georgiana?" Lady Matlock asked.

"Well, *Elizabeth* and I are to be presented on February 25th, and my ball will be the next day." She smiled wickedly back at Elizabeth.

Elizabeth shook her head. "At least that is an auspicious day to be tortured." Seeing her mother's confusion she added, "That was the day that I met William, and is also his birthday. I take it as a good sign that all will be well, and I will not trip over my train!" The ladies laughed.

Kitty and Mary had been sitting in silence for the entire meal, both quite in awe of their sister's magnificent home. Kitty was the first to pluck up the courage to speak. "Many of the girls at school will be presented at court this spring."

Georgiana spoke before Elizabeth had a chance. "How do you like your school, Kitty?"

She smiled. Elizabeth had written to her about Georgiana, and she was hoping to become friends with her new sister. "Oh, I like it very much. I am not rich as some of them are, but I think I fit in well with most of them. I have made many friends there."

"And what are you learning, my dear?" Lady Matlock addressed her.

Kitty's eyes grew wide with alarm, but seeing the kindness on her face relaxed a little. "We are learning the proper way to conduct ourselves in a parlour amongst gentlemen and how to host a tea." The ladies laughed.

"Practical teachings, so it would seem!" Lady Matlock declared. "That is better than what you learned, Georgiana. I must say, you certainly came away from the experience with great knowledge of sewing, but little of use elsewhere."

"Perhaps because her school was meant for those who would always have servants to do the work, the teaching of such things was unnecessary." Mary quietly said.

The ladies all looked at Mary in silence. Elizabeth knew that Mary regretted not going to school with Kitty, and was feeling jealous of the opportunity the two girls experienced. "That is quite possible, Mary; however, I would not disparage Georgiana's school. I am aware that her time there was meant to concentrate on her musical skills, in which she excels." Elizabeth looked to her newest sister and smiled. "I know for a fact how talented she is, as she plays and sings all day. My sister Mary is quite skilled with her playing as well, perhaps the two of you could play something together one evening." She looked at Georgiana with a raised brow, encouraging her to step up and make friends with Mary.

Georgiana knew that Elizabeth was pushing her forward in a new social situation and she would not let her down. "Oh yes, Mary, I would love to hear you play! Elizabeth has spoken of your talent!" She then saw Kitty look disappointed, and knowing that music was not her forte glanced at Elizabeth for help.

"I think that Kitty would enjoy helping you choose what to wear for the ball, Georgiana, I am afraid that I will not have the time I hoped to find to look through your things."

Smiling Georgiana turned to her. "Would you like that Kitty? And you Mary, I would appreciate your help as well. Perhaps there is something of mine you might like to borrow for the evening?" She was rewarded by huge smiles from both girls, and nods of approval from Elizabeth and Lady Matlock.

Jane leaned towards Elizabeth. "I never thought I would see the day when Kitty wanted to speak about pouring tea and Mary wanted to talk about fashion!" They laughed.

Mrs. Bennet nodded. "You see, it is all going as I planned, soon you girls will be able to introduce your sisters to their husbands, and my work will be done!"

Elizabeth rolled her eyes at Jane and sighed. "Yes, Mama." Some things would never change.

At the other end of the table, the gentlemen were caught up in discourse over horses, a subject that Mr. Bennet did not entertain often. He sat and quietly listened to the conversation, looking up when he heard Darcy's voice, watching his solemn face, and listening to his opinion and knowledge. When the subject came around to estate affairs, he listened even more closely. Every man at that table either had an estate or would eventually. The pride that they showed in their lands was obvious, and the care that they put into them now and for future generations was humbling. He saw how he had failed his family by not placing more interest in his own land, even if he would have to let it go to Mr. Collins someday.

Darcy kept a close watch on Mr. Bennet, noticing his silence. He would not worry for him. Everyone at that table knew what he had done, although if they knew of the letter he wrote to Wickham, the man would have done well not to enter the house at all. Darcy remained angry and had forgiven him as much as he was able. His only concern was how Mr. Bennet's behaviour affected Elizabeth; he would honour her request to give it time, and would accept her word that she would never expect anything more from him.

He looked up at one point, seeing her too far away at the other end of the table. She was watching him. She tilted her head a little, and gave him a gentle smile. Darcy could not help himself, the corners of his mouth lifted slightly. She nodded her head, and smiled a little wider. Knowing her game, he laughed softly and his smile grew. Finally she nodded again, giving him her full, radiant, glowing smile, her eyes shining with love. He responded with his own dazzling display of dimples. *Oh how he loved her!*

Neither of them noticed that the table had become silent, as everyone there saw the gentle challenge played out by their hosts. As their smiles grew, so too did those of their guests. When they reached their pinnacle, a collective "ahhhh" travelled around the table. Elizabeth and Darcy were so lost in each other that they never noticed it. It took Richard's voice to break the mood.

"Well, now you all know exactly what I witnessed at the theatre the day that they first spotted each other. At the time I thought it was cupid's arrow, now, I think that they just cannot help themselves." He smiled, and raising his glass declared with great emotion and greater effort, "To our hosts, may they live a long and happy life together!" Everyone laughed and raised their glasses. Richard closed his eyes and opened them to the sight of Kathleen's smile.

Bingley stood. "While we are making toasts," He looked over to Jane and grinned, "I would like to make one to my wife Jane, who is expecting our first child." He lifted his glass. "To my dear wife, who grows more beautiful with each day." Everyone drank, and the room was suddenly filled with the excited inquiries about the baby. She would be due sometime in late May, which would most likely prevent her from being presented at court until the next year. Elizabeth looked to Darcy, who raised his brows, silently asking if she wanted to announce their news, and she shook her head. They would wait. He nodded, disappointed, but still knowing that it was for the best.

ELIZABETH HAD NO IDEA how exhausting it would be to have the house opened to the general public for only four hours Christmas Eve. They had hundreds of visitors; people from all over Derbyshire came to see the great house.

It had not been opened in such a way for seventeen years. They were anxious to catch a glimpse of the occupants as well. As Mistress, Elizabeth greeted the people from her station in the music room. Darcy was excused from the exercise, but he did come in to check on her whenever he saw a lull in the crowd. Georgiana and Jane sat with her, keeping her company. It was by uniform agreement that the remaining Bennets and Fitzwilliams would keep themselves busy elsewhere during the event. If the murmurings of the crowd could be properly discerned, the tour was a great success. Mrs. Darcy was pronounced to be beautiful and gracious, the treats were gobbled happily, and every child left with an apple and a few coins. After church services that evening, Elizabeth gratefully collapsed into Darcy's waiting arms. He held her and told her how proud he was of her, and she fell instantly asleep.

ON CHRISTMAS DAY, gifts were exchanged and delight was exclaimed by all. Darcy shyly handed Elizabeth a beautifully wrapped box. She opened it to find a lovely gold locket with a cameo in yellow on the cover. He whispered, "She reminded me of you." She looked up into his shining eyes and tenderly caressed his face. "Open it." He encouraged her. She did and smiled, her eyes now brightened with tears. Inside was a miniature of his face, and encased behind glass on the front cover was a lock of his hair. "Now I shall always be with you." He placed the locket around her neck, carefully adjusting its position, and looked into her eyes.

"I love you." She whispered as they exchanged a gentle kiss.

It was Georgiana's giggle that brought them back. Elizabeth opened her eyes and blushed, remembering where they were. Her eye caught her father's who was looking at her, his face a mixture of emotion she could not read. She looked back at William, and said, "I have a gift for you as well." She handed him a small box.

"What could it be?" He untied the ribbon, carefully placed it in his pocket, and then opened the box to find a handsome pocket watch.

"Open it." She urged. He raised his brow, and looked at her suspiciously after seeing her warm smile. Upon opening the cover he found a perfect circle of porcelain painted with a miniature version of her face from the full-sized portrait that now hung in the gallery. "It seems sir, great minds think alike." He laughed. "Well, you said that you needed a new likeness of me!"

She helped him to attach the new watch to the chain in his pocket. He held the old one thoughtfully, "I will save this watch for our eldest son." The two smiled at each other. "Thank you my love, I will treasure this always. Now you will never leave my side." He kissed her, so very happy.

After enjoying a hearty Christmas dinner, the party settled down to play games, the ladies played music, the men rose and sang for them, and the house was filled with joy as it had not felt in years, not since the loss of Anne Darcy. They enjoyed a beautiful Christmas tea, and all exhausted from the day, retired early.

THE NEXT MORNING saw the arrival of Boxing Day, and the monetary gifts for the servants were handed out, along with a small gift of appreciation from Mrs. Darcy. She was acquainted enough with the staff now to be able to choose a personal item for each that suited them, whether it was chocolate, a shawl, or a good pair of socks. Her attention to detail only raised their esteem.

While Darcy was entertaining the other men in the billiards room, Mr. Bennet asked Elizabeth if she could show him the library. She brought him in, and looked as he closed the door behind him. His eyes travelled the enormous room; the shelves were floor to ceiling, a spiral staircase led to yet another level of books contained on the wide balcony which surrounded the perimeter of the room. A brass rail was installed along the top shelves, and attached was a strong ladder, for reaching the most hidden resources, a past time that Elizabeth enjoyed often. He sighed, enveloping himself in the scent of parchment and leather. His eye was caught by the imposing chair by the fireplace. "My goodness, Lizzy. You could be swallowed up in a chair like that."

She smiled at him and lovingly caressed it. "William had this made after our honeymoon at the cottage. It is similar to a chair that we enjoyed together there. We spend a great deal of time reading together here and in its twin in our bedchamber." She smiled at it fondly, and looked up to see her father staring at her with tears in his eyes.

"What is it, Papa?" She asked with concern.

"Lizzy, please let me apologize once more for my behaviour towards you and your husband. You endured my selfish behaviour for a lifetime, and I am forever grateful that you and Mr. Darcy would even consider welcoming me into your home. It is an honour. I cannot begin to express my appreciation."

"Papa, please sit down." Elizabeth indicated the chair opposite her, and she sat down in the honeymoon chair, feeling surrounded and supported by William's presence. She drew a breath. "Papa, both William and I have experienced painful actions on the part of our fathers, actions that our fathers performed in their desire to mistakenly protect their own pride or self-interest, and to assuage their guilt over their own behaviour." She looked into his pained eyes. "William's suffering lasted almost his entire life. He had only two brief years with his father where he truly received his undeniable and open affection, and then he died. He did not learn the reasons for his father's behaviour until we married, and he was given a letter explaining his actions. William has, through much thought and time been able to forgive his father and let go of his resentment. He had recommended that I do the same for you, now, while you are still here with me and we have the opportunity to reclaim our relationship. He pointed out that my affection for you was untainted until I showed that I was going to leave home. Our rift, although intense and very painful, is of short duration, and he hoped that our years of loving respect and affection might eventually repair the damage that your behaviour evoked. I hope for that as well. I think that we have made a good effort to re-establish our relationship, and although its nature is forever changed, and likely would have been upon my marriage to any man, I think that we can safely say that it is time to put the past aside, and move on."

Mr. Bennet listened, then asked, "You say that Mr. Darcy *had* recommended this course to you? Has he changed his mind?"

Elizabeth grimaced. "We have become aware that you wrote to Wickham requesting that he come and attempt to separate me from William for a fee. If William had learned of this immediately after the incident, you would never have seen me again." She paused, and saw the truth of his guilt all over his face. She closed her eyes with its confirmation, and gathering herself together, continued. "As it was, we did not learn of this until October when purely by coincidence, we shared conversations that we had with others. At the time, William's anger was of such a level that I doubted he knew what he was doing. If the circumstances had been different, and you were present in our home, I believe he would have called you out. It was terrible to behold. I will not share with you the conversation that we had at the time, but I will tell you, it is a gift that you are permitted here now." She watched him suffering, and softened. "But as I said, we have determined that it is time to put the past aside."

Mr. Bennet looked into the lovely eyes of his daughter, so wise beyond her years, so full of the intelligence he valued and so confident in the love for and from her husband. "Yes, Lizzy, I am ready to leave the past behind. I thank you for the kindness and love that you extend to me. I want you to know that I never offered a payment to Wickham, although it was foolish of me to expect him to come to Longbourn for no compensation, and I did not know how vile the man was, or in any way anticipated what he would do to you." He blinked back a tear. "How does Mr. Darcy feel about me? Something must have changed from his fury if I am now sleeping under his roof and not lying in a field with his bullet in my chest."

Elizabeth smiled slightly. "He remains quite angry with you, and is in doubt of his ability to ever accept you. His relationship with you has not the years of love and affection behind it that ours does. His only experience with you has been heated and painful. I am afraid that you are starting from the beginning with him. He will treat you in the way he feels you treat me. If he sees love and respect towards me, he will give you civility. From this point, it is up to the two of you."

Mr. Bennet nodded. "It seems that I am the suitor now."

Elizabeth smiled. "That is quite an apt description, Papa." He rose and held out his arms and kissed her brow. Elizabeth stood and accepted his embrace.

"Thank you, Lizzy." He held her back and looked at her. "You will be a wonderful mother."

She laughed. "I have a long wait ahead of me."

"When are you due?"

"August, and we are not making an announcement until I feel the quickening, which probably will be in February." She tilted her head. "How did you know?"

"Ah, I have seen your mother in this condition many times, my dear, I know that look quite well." He grimaced.

"I notice that Mama continues to improve in her disposition and behaviour. I can almost say that it is a pleasure to have her here. What have you done?"

"Something that I should have done a long time ago, I have given her the attention she deserves. It is not her fault we never had a son. And it is my fault that I let our marriage languish as it did. I am rather enjoying this second courtship we are having. Now if we could just marry off your other sisters . . . will there be any rich men to put in their way at this ball of yours tomorrow?"

"Papa! You sound like Mama!" Elizabeth scolded him.

After their emotional conversation, Elizabeth left the library to tend to her duties. Mr. Bennet was tempted to behave in his normal fashion, and hole up in that magnificent room, contemplate what she said, and simply hide from the world. But this time he knew that he must instead face judgment. Despite

Elizabeth's statement that Mr. Darcy wished to put the past behind them, it was clear that his son-in-law had not in any way forgiven him, and in fact was tolerating his presence at Pemberley as a concession to his wife. He knew that the only possibility of Mr. Darcy ever accepting him on any level would come after he was able to express his anger. Mr. Bennet decided that he must allow him to do so, and left the library, walking down the hall to accept his fate.

In the billiards room, the men were gathered around the table. Mark was thoroughly routing Bingley and they were all in good spirits. At the end of the match they moved to depart, laughing and joking as they exited the room, each falling silent at the sight of Mr. Bennet standing outside of the door, his eyes fixed on Darcy. It was apparent that a confrontation was about to occur, and as much as the other men wished to stay and support Darcy, and listen in, they continued on their way. Mr. Bennet stepped forward. "Mr. Darcy, I have just concluded a lengthy conversation with Elizabeth, and I would like to hear your opinion of the matter, if you could give me some moments of your time."

Darcy's face was impassive, but his eyes blazed instantly with his deep anger towards the man. He knew exactly what Elizabeth would say to her father. She had discussed it with him before he arrived. He nodded and stepped back, allowing Mr. Bennet to pass before him, and closed the door with a snap. "What do you wish to discuss, Mr. Bennet?"

"Sir, my daughter has informed me that you are aware of the letter that I wrote to Wickham. She further informed me you made it clear that had you known of this at the time of the incident here at Pemberley, you would have ended our relationship permanently, and I would have never seen her again. She indicated that time had allowed you to soften your stance, and that you are willing to put the past behind you." He paused, assessing the cold countenance of the man before him. "It is my opinion that your stance has not in any way softened, but that you have acquiesced to this course solely out of your love for Elizabeth. I am in no doubt that if you had your way, I would at this moment be lying dead next to Wickham. Am I correct, sir?"

Darcy stared directly into his eyes, and unblinkingly said, "You are."

"Mr. Darcy. We are alone. Say and do what you must." He drew a deep breath, stood straight, and waited.

The tension in Darcy's body radiated from him. It took all of his strength not to leap across the room and throttle the man before him. Instead he closed his eyes and gathered his thoughts. He then opened his new pocket watch, gazed at the image of Elizabeth it contained, and returned his gaze to Mr. Bennet. "Sir. The *ONLY* reason you are allowed at Pemberley is because Elizabeth wished for it. That woman is my life, without her . . ." He stopped and shook his head. "No, you do not deserve to know my feelings for her." He closed his eyes and attempted to contain his fury. "Sir, I do not respect you, forgive you, or like you. In all honesty, I wish to cut off all contact with you and never see you again, but my wife, my precious wife . . .," his voice softened and he gazed again upon her portrait, ". . . has asked me to tolerate you and treat you with civility."

He paused, looking into the beautiful sparkling eyes; and the memory of that horrible day and the sight of her bound and unmoving flashed before him. His anger rose and his voice again became harsh. "Your actions began . . . How could you, sir? How could you approach that cur? Do not tell me you could not have known what he was! He had attempted to harm Elizabeth months before we ever met! You *KNEW* what he was, and yet you petitioned him to be what . . . her companion? Her suitor? What were you thinking?! Did you think that Wickham would wish for a platonic friendship? Wickham would come only for money, revenge, or his own pleasure. *YOU* sir, are not unfamiliar with that practice!"

Darcy began pacing, valiantly trying to regain control of his emotions, and failed. He spun around and stopped to face her father. "How could you profess to love Elizabeth and subject her to that? I reject your claim of not knowing his truth. Perhaps it makes you feel better, perhaps it helps Elizabeth to accept that the man she loves as her father made a mistake, but I will never allow sentiment to cloud my opinion of you, sir. Never." His enraged black eyes bore into Mr. Bennet, who remained standing, but only barely so. Darcy regained control of his breathing, and the volume of his voice lowered. His tone lost its heat, but was now even more frightening with its cold delivery. "I tolerate you for my Elizabeth. Never expect more from me." He looked again at her portrait and silently apologized, but knew that he needed to purge this from him. He felt completely drained, as if an enormous cancer had been cut from his body.

Mr. Bennet swallowed, feeling whipped from the assault of words, and fully aware that a lesser man would have beaten him soundly. "Mr. Darcy, I realize there is nothing I can say to excuse my behaviour, and I do not deserve your mercy. Shall I remove my family from your home?"

Darcy stared at him, it was clear the man was tenuously holding on to his composure. The devastation and guilt that he saw displayed served both to justify his beliefs and disgust him with their truth. He looked again to Elizabeth's face, and feeling her love, calmed. "No sir. You may stay. I will not separate Elizabeth from her family."

"Thank you." Mr. Bennet bowed and gratefully left the room. As he left he saw Elizabeth standing outside of the door, where she had listened to all. Her eyes were fixed on her husband. She walked past her father and entered, closing the door behind her. She stood unnoticed before William, who was still staring down at her portrait, and startled him with her embrace. He was still trembling with the expression of his fury.

He clutched her tightly. "Forgive me Elizabeth. I needed to confront him." He kissed her forehead. "Do you understand?"

She pulled back and studied his pained face. "I do understand, William. I have been trying to move past it, and forgive him. He is my father. I *had* to try. You had no such requirement, and you are not blinded by affection. You could see clearly where I could not. You have no need for my forgiveness, you have done nothing wrong. Your feelings are just." She gently caressed his hair, still looking up into his now brown eyes. "I heard everything that you said, and am hurt to know that it was all so very true. I realize now that you needed to confront him before you could ever consider moving beyond this pain."

He nodded and rested his face in her hair, drawing strength from her embrace. "You know me so well, my love. Thank you for understanding and allowing me to have and express my feelings. I do feel relieved of a great burden now." He kissed her. "I love you."

She stroked his face. "That, my Will, is obvious. I love you."

ALTHOUGH THE OTHER GENTLEMEN of Pemberley would have wished to speak to Darcy about his conversation with Mr. Bennet, it was abundantly clear that the issue would remain private. It was Bingley who had directed Elizabeth to the billiards room, and he worriedly watched the couple when they returned to the company. Darcy and Elizabeth remained inseparable for the remainder of the day, only parting upon the division of the sexes after dinner. When Darcy stiffly offered Mr. Bennet a drink and he quietly accepted; the men knew that a silent truce had been offered and signed.

That night, after the much-needed release achieved from making love, they lay tightly entwined and Elizabeth told William about her conversation with her father. He held her and listened, proud of her for presenting her feelings without hesitation. She had learned not to shy away from difficult conversations just to preserve the appearance of peace. He reluctantly accepted her desire to continue the attempt at reconciliation. Confronting the man himself had finally given him the ability to choose to move on. He realized that only Elizabeth could have such power over him to even consider such a decision.

"So, my love, it seems that I am to be courted by your father, now?" Resigned, he laughed softly and kissed her hair. "Will he bring me flowers?"

"William!" She pinched his bottom, then rubbed it tenderly after his cry, and hugged him tighter. "Perhaps you could show him some special books in your library, as a peace offering."

He was unwilling. "I think perhaps he is the one who should be making such gestures."

"Maybe you could let him call you by your name?" She suggested tentatively.

"I do not know if we are on such terms yet, Lizzy. I think that I need to be courted a bit more first." He kissed her nose, but his face was very serious.

She stroked his brow, feeling his tension. "You want him to work for it."

"I do. I think I have made enough concessions. Do you mind?"

"No, not at all, I told him it was between the two of you now. I will not interfere for either side." She smiled.

Darcy relaxed, knowing she would not push him. The corners of his mouth lifted. "Perhaps a fencing exercise would settle it."

"You would skewer him, I am afraid."

"Target practice?"

"He would likely shoot his foot by mistake."

Darcy thought. "A horse race!"

Elizabeth laughed. "And he would break his neck and Mr. Collins would throw Mama from Longbourn and send her to live here! No sir, no! Please, no!"

Darcy laughed quietly. "I agree, please, no!" He hugged his wife and caressed her belly. He sighed. "Well, I suppose we will simply have to give civility a try."

Elizabeth looked up into his soft brown eyes. "You are always a gentleman."

"Always for you, my love." They snuggled down into the pillows and slept.

Chapter 38

*T*he morning of the ball Elizabeth was walking alone through the house, mentally checking off all of the items that had to be addressed before their guests arrived in, she glanced at her watch and sighed, ten hours. Her eyes closed, she had never been so nervous in her life. The house was bustling with servants going about their duties, and she felt as if everything was happening around her in a blur. The sound of men's voices and the eerie sound of steel on steel caught her attention, and she found herself standing before the partially open door to William's fencing room. She had been there many times before, enjoying watching her husband go through his training exercises, and occasionally practicing with Mr. Regar's son. This time when she peeked in the door, all of the male guests except her father were present, and there was William, but this time, he was shirtless, as was his opponent, Richard. None of the men noticed her. As a woman, she knew that she had no business seeing men in such a state of undress, but she could not tear her eyes away from her husband. His beautifully toned body glistened with perspiration, and moved with grace and finesse; his eyes were wholly focused on Richard. The expression on his face, his intense gaze, his skilled movements, made Elizabeth's breath catch, and the only thing she could think about at that moment was how much she wanted him to overpower her the way he was thoroughly outwitting his cousin.

She trembled and felt warm in her desire for him. "Oh, what a man I have married!"

Out of the corner of his eye, Richard spotted her leaning against the doorway, one hand on her heart, the other clutching tightly the fabric of her skirt. The look of desire in her face threw him completely and Darcy's next parry caught him unprepared. He suddenly found himself with empty hands and saw his foil landing with a soft clang across the room. He looked up to Darcy's widely grinning face amid the catcalls from Bingley and the sounds of consolation from his father and brother.

Darcy came over to shake his hand. "What happened there Richard, it was as if you forgot we were fencing?" Richard glanced at the doorway, and before he could reply, Darcy's eyes followed Richard's direction and he saw Elizabeth standing there, still entranced, and clearly to every man there, quite undone. Darcy at first smiled at her, then thinking for a moment looked sharply at Richard, who caught his gaze and hurriedly turned away to pull on his shirt. Bingley threw Darcy his own shirt, which he quickly put on and strode over to his wife.

"Elizabeth, what are you doing here?" He whispered, taking her hand and leading her into the hall.

She came out of her appreciative haze and blinked. "I was just walking by and heard you . . . Oh William, you are so very handsome!"

He blushed, and taking her hand he led her into an unoccupied sitting room and closed the door. "Elizabeth, do you have any idea how fetching you looked, standing in the doorway watching me?" He kissed her. "If we had been alone, and I saw you with such desire in your eyes, I am afraid that we would be quite occupied at this moment."

She wrapped her arms around him, not at all put off by the now wet shirt clinging to his very warm body. "Could we not be occupied now? I believe that we are quite alone." Looking up at him, she lifted a hand to pull his head down to her lips, and kissed him passionately.

"Lizzy, are you seducing me?" He groaned. Her hands moved to unbutton his equally damp breeches, and soon slipped inside to pull out his own blade.

She pushed him against a wall and seeing a very thick book, dropped it on the floor and stood upon it. She pulled his sodden shirt over his head and rubbed her hands over his chest. He was still taller than she, but at least now she could reach his lips. She said nothing as she began kissing him with the wantonness of a harlot. Her hands were all over him and he moaned. "You *are* seducing me!" His breath was coming in rapid gasps, and he felt one of her hands wrap firmly around his stiffened organ. He grasped her to him, and kissed her deeply. "Lizzy, oh, God, Lizzy, what do you want of me?".

"I want you to enjoy yourself." She whispered then kicking the book aside she slid down to her knees and began suckling him, moving her head in a steady motion, swirling her tongue around him ceaselessly, all the while running her hands over him with the sensuous light touch that always left him breathless and wanting more. His hands clenched into tight fists and he moaned and struggled to stay upright, the wall behind him his only salvation. Staring down to her beautiful face, he watched her soft lips taking him in and out, and saw her hair come loose from its binding, spilling over her shoulders. Moving faster and faster, she felt him begin to tense, then slowed, making the excruciating tension last until with a cry, he let go and spilled into her mouth. He watched with hazy eyes as his beloved swallowed his essence, and then slowly withdrew, still gently licking off every drop.

She stood to wrap her arms around his boneless body, holding him until he could breathe calmly again. Darcy kissed her head and she looked up and smiled at him. "Did you enjoy yourself, my love?"

"Oh, Lord, yes, Lizzy." He moaned, and kissed her very swollen lips. He touched them gently. "What did I do to inspire that? Please tell me so that I can repeat it!"

Elizabeth laughed softly and kissed him again. "I do not know. I have seen you fence, but never without your shirt before, you were just so beautiful . . . I suppose I just wanted to show you my appreciation."

He chuckled, and took a deep breath. "Anytime you wish to express your appreciation, my love, please, do not hesitate." He looked into her dancing eyes, and said very seriously, "*Any*time."

She laughed, and took his hand. "I will keep that in mind, Will." She leaned down and picked up his discarded shirt as he readjusted his breeches.

After slipping it back on they held hands and kissed. "I think that you deserve a proper thank you."

She kissed him as they walked to the door, "After the ball."

He stopped to caress her face as she repinned her hair. "If we are awake."

She laughed. "Shall we say when we wake tomorrow?"

He nodded and they kissed one more time and stepped out of the room. Elizabeth returned to her duties, seeking out Mrs. Reynolds. Darcy went upstairs to wash and change into clean clothes. On the way he ran across Mark and Bingley, who pulled him aside to demand where he had gone. He grinned and said nothing, and started on his way back up the steps.

Mark called after him, "I should let you know, Darcy, the walls of the sitting room are not quite as thick as those of the bedchambers." Darcy stopped for a moment, turned red, and without turning back continued on his way up the stairs, feeling not as embarrassed as he let on.

AFTER DARCY DISAPPEARED from the fencing room with Elizabeth, Richard stood in a corner fixing his clothes and listening to the soft laughter of the other men at the expense of their relative and friend. He wished he could join in, but he was overcome by the look of absolute desire on Elizabeth's face, and the undeniable love she felt for Darcy that was clear as day. He bent his head, wrestling again with the overwhelming feelings he had for her. He had worked so hard over the past months since he was last at Pemberley, concentrating on Kathleen. He sighed. Kathleen. He loved her. He knew it, and he knew that he needed her desperately. What was wrong with him? Why could he not give his entire heart to the woman he had pledged to care for all the days of his life, and who had solemnly declared the same of him? He saw that look Darcy gave him. His cousin knew exactly what he was thinking when he stared at Elizabeth. But was not every other man in the room thinking the same? Would all of them not give their eye teeth to have their wives stare at them in such a wanton manner?

He looked at them. No, Laura would not, and what he had seen of Jane, she would not. His mother? He did not wish to think about. Kathleen. No, not *that* look. He had never seen that expression on her face. Maybe that was the problem, he simply wished for the intense love that Darcy had. Sighing, he walked out of the room, ignoring the other men. Passing the door to the sitting room, he paused for a moment, hearing Darcy's soft moans. He closed his eyes and sped past on his way upstairs to change from his perspiration-soaked clothes. He did not notice his father following him.

He was in his dressing room rubbing a wet washcloth over himself when his father walked in and closed the door. He took a seat in the barbering chair and watched his son silently dry then dress.

"It seems all those years in the army served you well, Son. You have no need for a valet."

"I still have not learned to tie a cravat well."

Lord Matlock stood and walked over to his son, standing before him and tying the neck cloth, adjusting the knot carefully, and then smoothing it down. When finished he looked into his eyes. "Something is eating at you Richard, and has been for some time. What is it?"

It was useless to deny it; his father was as tenacious as a bulldog and would not be easily put off. Richard leaned against the wall, his arms crossed in front of him, and Lord Matlock returned to the chair. "I do not know what is wrong; I feel . . . overwhelmed, lost, I cannot put it into words." He sighed and began pacing. "I am wholly unprepared to be Master of Rosings. I was not raised as Mark was, to take over Matlock. I feel so useless." He closed his eyes. "I had to beg for Darcy's help to save me from the disaster I created when my steward died. If it was not for him and Barnes, God knows what misery my tenants would be suffering, and my income would be nonexistent. If it were not for them, my taxes would not have been paid . . . I am useless!" Lord Matlock said nothing, sensing there was more to come. "Then I am haunted by dreams of death and violence. I try to sleep but wake screaming in terror. Poor Kathleen must suffer through the ranting of a weak man every night. A weak failure is what she has married." He paused. "I love her Father, I do, but I cannot seem to give her . . ." He looked up. "Do you see the way Darcy and Elizabeth are? Do you feel the strength of their bond? Did you see the way she looked at him in the fencing room? Have you ever witnessed such behaviour with any other couple? Is my marriage normal or is theirs? I do not have that intensity that they do. God knows I am trying, but it is not there, and all I can think about is what would have happened if Elizabeth had looked at me that night in the theatre instead of Darcy. Would I be the one she would look at with such love?" He wiped his hands over his face.

Lord Matlock watched the emotion in his son, and spoke quietly. "Are you in love with Elizabeth?"

"No! No, of course not, she is my cousin's wife!" He turned away, closing his eyes and resting his hands on a table for support.

"Before she was his wife, you knew her. What did you feel then?"

Richard looked back at his father, his eyes begging him not to force him to say it. His father's relentless gaze made him face his truth. "I loved her. I fell in love with her the night that she came to dinner at Darcy House." He hung his head; he had finally said the words out loud.

Lord Matlock nodded; he and his wife had suspected this for some time. "How do you feel about her now?"

Richard looked up and said bitterly, "I am endeavouring to feel nothing."

"Perhaps that is your mistake." Richard stared at him. "Has Darcy addressed this with you? Surely he is not blind to your feelings."

Richard nodded. "Yes, he has told me I may love her as my cousin and his wife, but not to dare attempt anything more, not that I would."

"For such a possessive and insecure man as Darcy, that is an extraordinary position for him to take on the subject."

"Darcy? Insecure?" He was incredulous.

Lord Matlock laughed. "He is the most insecure man I know, even more so than you." Richard remained confused. "He lost his mother, he never had his father, he was given the burden of Pemberley when he was still a boy, tried to be a father to Georgiana, failed her in his mind with Wickham, finds Elizabeth, fears losing her to her father's plans, almost loses *her* to Wickham, finally *does* lose her for weeks due to his fear of speaking to her, because he feared he would lose her if he did! No wonder he clings to her like she is his only surety in life and is ready to defend and protect her at the slightest provocation. If he is truly aware of your infatuation, it is a wonder that you ever considered fencing with him today. It is fortunate his foil was not in his hand when he saw you staring at her."

"ALL of us were staring at her!" Richard cried, overwhelmed by his father's description of his best friend. "Do not tell me you were not drawn to her!"

His father nodded, admitting his own attraction. "Yes, but you are the only one he sees as a threat. Why do you think he puts up with you, knowing all that he does?"

Richard sank against the table. "I do not know."

"First, because he loves you. Second, because he is sure, without any doubt, that Elizabeth loves him, without any hesitation, and will not be tempted away by you or any other man. Third, he sees what all of us see. Kathleen is a very good woman and loves you, and you Son, *DO* love her. You both have a great deal of learning and growing to do. No, you were not raised to be Master of an estate, that was my error, but even Darcy, who was, struggled for years after his father died. It will come. I will help, your new steward will help, and your brother and Darcy will help. You are not alone. Kathleen is just as lost as you. Support each other. This is your opportunity to learn and grow together. Through this experience you will find the deep love that I know you wish for, and envy of your cousin. They seem to have found it instantly, perhaps they were both ready for it when it came, but I have watched, and through each of their trials they have grown stronger. You and Kathleen have had only one trial as yet. You are taking the slower path as I did with your mother. If you give it your full attention, you will be rewarded in the end."

Richard had listened closely, and then said softly. "Then what is my mistake with Elizabeth?"

"If you truly did fall in love with her, not lust, not infatuation, that feeling will never leave you. Darcy has given you his extraordinary permission to love her, not as a husband, but as a friend. I think that your struggle to deny all feeling for her is what is behind your inability to suppress the memory of the violence you have witnessed in the past. I am willing to wager that when you stop denying that you have any feeling at all for her, you will be able to let her go to reside in a part of your heart where you may freely, and without guilt, care for her. Then you will be able to be the husband you truly wish to be for the woman you truly do love. I have a feeling that those conflicted dreams will fade as your marriage strengthens. Kathleen deserves no less from you."

"That is easier said than done, Father."

"No it is not, you simply have to decide to do it." He rose and clasped his shoulder. "You can and will succeed."

Richard drew a deep breath and nodded. "Thank you, Father; I needed to talk about this."

"Anytime, Son." The men embraced, both close to tears. "Ahem, well, it should be about time for some sort of a meal, I think, let us return to our wives before they start fretting over their frocks for tonight."

ELIZABETH STOOD holding William's hand and touched the spectacular diamond necklace he presented to her that afternoon, and then straightened, watching the door for their first guests to enter their home. She peeked up at him. His face was relaxed, but his eyes were watching every move of the bustling servants. She felt him squeeze her hand and saw his eyes turn to her and smile. "Are you ready?"

She took a breath and smiled back. "I think so." He kissed her hand and returned to his vigilant watch over his staff.

Elizabeth thought back to earlier that afternoon when William swept into the ballroom, took her hand, excused her from Mrs. Reynolds and pulled her up to their bedchamber where he insisted that she eat and rest. She smiled remembering his Master of Pemberley voice and face as he informed her that his wife and child would not be permitted to attend the ball without full bellies or without a nap. After eating he led her to the enormous upholstered honeymoon chair in their bedroom and taking a blanket, settled in next to her, wrapped her in his embrace, and to her great surprise, coaxed her to sleep, not waking until his soft kisses roused her with plenty of time to bathe and dress. It was exactly the calm she needed before the stress of her first ball.

The residents of Pemberley made their way down the stairs, everyone exclaiming over the ladies' lovely gowns and their handsome escorts. Soon their neighbours arrived, twenty carriages bringing almost one hundred guests. When the last were greeted and welcomed, Elizabeth, her confidence now fully restored, looked up to her now retreating husband and gave his arm a hug. It was her turn now to relax him.

"I believe, Mr. Darcy, it is time for us to begin the dance."

He groaned. "You know I am doing this solely for the privilege of dancing with you, do you not?"

"I do, but you know you cannot monopolize me as you did at the harvest dance?"

His face fell. "No?" She shook her head. "Which may I have?"

She kissed his cheek. "Definitely the first, supper and last." She smiled at his pout.

"That is all?"

She caressed his hand and laughed. "Come, my love."

Darcy endeavoured to ignore the crowd and instead concentrated on his wife whose face was glowing, taking in the atmosphere. She nudged him and laughed, pointing out Mrs. Drake and her mother having already found their other half in the milling guests. With a subtle wave from Darcy, the musicians began and the couples moved to the centre of the room to take their places for the first dance.

The ball progressed. Elizabeth was very pleased to see William ask Mary and Kitty to dance, as well as Georgiana and each of the other wives of their party. Her mother declined his request, blushing crimson and claiming she was too old. Darcy was inwardly relieved. He kept a close watch on Elizabeth's partners, and her reaction to them. When he saw her on the arm of Hitchins, he had to stop himself from snatching her away from his leering smile. He oddly felt relief when Richard bowed formally to her and led her back to the floor, but the momentary relief ended and he watched the pair very intently.

Richard knew Darcy was watching. He asked Elizabeth to dance on purpose, to see if he could touch her without feeling desire. Elizabeth smiled and took his hand. "I was hoping you would ask me to dance, Richard."

Startled he looked at her. "You were?"

"Yes, we have not had much opportunity to talk since you came. I was beginning to feel as if you were avoiding me."

He forced a laugh. "That is ridiculous, why would I wish to avoid you?"

Elizabeth tilted her head at him. "I wish that I knew." His eyes were drawn to hers, and they went through the next movements without speaking.

Darcy was more disturbed by his cousin's staring than his speaking, and feeling a deep need to assert his territory, began to step towards them when he felt a hand on his shoulder. "Let it go, Darcy."

He turned to see his uncle. "I have let it go, time and again. I have spoken to him twice. I will tolerate no more."

"Do you trust Elizabeth so little?"

He returned to his uncle and stared. "How can you say such a thing?"

He shrugged. "I wished to gain your attention and keep you from making a spectacle of yourself." Darcy searched his face in disbelief. "She is in no danger, not from Richard. We had a very good talk today. Give him a chance, give him time."

"Time for what?"

"To let her go."

"He never had her!" He whispered furiously

"*That* is what he must let go." Lord Matlock said firmly.

Darcy sighed. "And I am to just stand by and let him stare at her like this?"

"No, I suggest that you ask Kathleen to dance." He smiled.

Darcy shook his head. "I cannot pretend infatuation with her. I will not upset Elizabeth.

"Of course not. I do not suggest that you do. Perhaps though, he should see his wife dancing with the man who inspires such open affection in Elizabeth. Make *him* jealous for a change." He raised his brows. "Hmmm?"

Darcy sighed and nodded. At the beginning of the next dance he offered his hand to Kathleen and led her to the floor. Elizabeth's eye caught his. To anyone else he wore his usual sombre expression. To her, she saw how unhappy he was and sent him a gentle smile. She knew his upset was with Richard. His eyes brightened with her look, and he was able to give his attention to Kathleen. Richard saw his wife dancing and smiling up at Darcy, and Elizabeth felt his grip tighten on her hand. She smiled and considered reassuring him that Kathleen was quite safe from William, but decided it would do Richard good to feel some jealousy. Instead she began talking about Rosings and enjoyed listening to him trying to pay attention to the conversation as his head continually swivelled to watch his wife. When the dance ended, he bowed and took Elizabeth directly to the spot where Darcy brought Kathleen, and quickly reclaimed her hand.

"I believe the next set is ours, my love." He smiled and kissed her hand.

"And I do believe; I finally have the next with you, Elizabeth." Darcy took her hand and raised it to his lips.

"Yes, you do indeed, William." She touched his face, ignoring the whispers of the people standing nearby, and took her place at her husband's side.

MR. BENNET SPENT THE BALL observing the people around him; he stood to the side, a drink in his hand, first taking in the excited faces of Kitty and Mary, and their new friend Georgiana. Each of the girls had been asked to dance by the men of the family party, but now several young men of the neighbourhood were bowing and asking for their hands. Naturally, most of the attention was given to Georgiana, and she, under the eagle gaze of her family, was forced to refuse their offers as she was not yet out. Mr. Bennet felt sorry for her disappointment, but admired the family protecting her so well.

His gaze turned to Jane and Bingley. They both seemed happier here at

Pemberley. He laughed to himself, wondering how they could possibly appear happier, as he had yet to witness anything resembling a frown on either one's face. Even so, Jane's serenity and Bingley's perpetual grin seemed somehow less strained.

He noticed the odd behaviour of Darcy's cousins. Both seemed to stare at Elizabeth quite frequently, in fact, all of the men seemed to be watching her, especially when she interacted with Darcy. Richard watched her closely, and Mr. Bennet noticed Darcy in turn watched Richard. Something was happening that he did not like, and if he was on better terms with his son-in-law, he would have approached him, but as it was, he could do nothing but observe.

As the strains of the final dance died away, Elizabeth leaned into William's solid form and she felt his supportive arms wrap around her. "You are exhausted, Elizabeth."

She nodded and forced herself to stand upright again before they started tongues wagging. "Yes, but thankfully it is over, at least it will be when everyone leaves."

"I will be happy to farewell our guests alone, my love. You go ahead upstairs." Darcy's concerned eyes held hers, and he brushed a fallen curl from her forehead.

"Now you know I would never do that to you William. I will be fine. Come, let us go stand by the door and give them a subtle hint to leave." She smiled and he shook his head.

UPSTAIRS, Pemberley's residents retired to their rooms. "I feel that it was a great success, Henry. What do you think?" Lady Matlock wandered into her husband's dressing room, brushing her hair as she spoke.

"I agree. We have attended the various dinners and balls that Darcy forced himself to host over the years, and while pleasant and elegant, none could compare to the atmosphere that we felt tonight. It is extraordinary what being in the presence of two such committed people can do to raise the enjoyment of the party."

Lady Matlock smiled. "They do seem to have a glow about them, do they not?"

He laughed. "It is more like the sun shining, I believe."

She sighed. "I hope someday our sons will feel something similar."

"I heard whispers of Elizabeth's kidnapping. No details, nothing of what happened to her, other than the search and the arrest of Wickham. I heard nothing of Darcy beating him, at least his people kept that quiet. But Darcy should be prepared to face questions when we return to London."

"Perhaps you should speak to him about it before we leave. We will return before them, and can begin to put out the preferred story then."

"Yes, and we should include Mark and Richard as well."

Further down the hall, Mark had retired to his separate bedchamber as he had every night of his marriage. Laura had never asked for him to remain with her. She firmly followed society's dictates that they maintain their own apartments, and after fulfilling their duties, retired elsewhere. Mark lay with his hands behind his head, first remembering Elizabeth's expression when gazing at Darcy that morning, then the sound of his cousin's voice in the sitting room, then all of the subtle and not so subtle displays of affection he witnessed during the ball and indeed throughout his stay. His final image was turning at the top of the stairs when the last guest left to see Elizabeth enfolded in Darcy's arms, her head on his chest, his resting on her hair, both with their eyes closed and swaying gently, oblivious to all. Mark's marriage was definitely one of convenience, and he never thought anything was wrong with that. Now, after watching his cousin, he wondered if he could have more with his wife.

Bingley and Jane lay together. They had given up their separate bedchambers after their last visit to Pemberley. Jane instantly fell asleep, a result of her condition and their unusual late night. Bingley was wide awake, his mind alive with thoughts of the next few days, when he would at last move into his own estate and would be the one hosting such wonderful celebrations, surrounded by his family and friends.

Kathleen and Richard had always slept together, from the first night. They climbed into the bed and he wrapped his arms around her, holding her close, lost in thought. Kathleen was also thinking. Richard had been oddly withdrawn since they left Rosings, and his characteristic joviality had been strained. The nightmares, which were lessening, seemed to have returned with a vengeance and she found herself staying awake in his arms, awaiting its nightly arrival. But today, something was different. He almost seemed to be in pain, but she did not feel that she could talk to him about it. He seemed especially nervous in Elizabeth's company, and almost wary of William. The nagging feeling that her husband was attracted to Elizabeth grew.

As Kathleen silently pondered her dark thoughts, Richard examined every second of the time he spent with Elizabeth that night. He tried to remember every feeling, every subtle nuance of both of their behaviour, attempting to determine if what he felt was love or lust, and whatever it was how to banish it without destroying his relationship with her, Darcy, and especially with his wife. He heard his father's voice. "Let her go. Keep her in your heart, but let her go." He gradually fell asleep, and within minutes, the dream began.

A familiar voice yelled, "No, no this must stop!" This dream was different, he was astride his horse, watching a battle unfold, screaming orders to his men to advance, to take the enemy. All around him were the bodies of the infantry men, bloodied, wounded, dead, and his cavalry was advancing. Bullets flew, a horse screamed and fell, crushing its rider, and still they advanced. A civilian version of himself watched from the periphery, observing the soldier Richard still pushing forward although the battle was lost. The civilian Richard called to his soldier self to stop, come back, retreat, live . . . and to his surprise, the soldier halted his advancing troops, and sat still on his horse, staring straight ahead at the unseen, distant prize. The civilian Richard stood panting; begging him to turn around, but this time his voice was joined by a second. A soft, pleading, woman's voice called the soldier back. With her words, the horseman tore his gaze from the horizon to seek the woman . . . At that moment he awoke, shaking and sweating, and opened his eyes to meet Kathleen's worried gaze.

"It is well Richard, you are safe." She stroked his brow.

He stared at her. "You are really here." He whispered. She nodded. He clutched her tightly and burst into tears, sobbing like he had not done since he was a small boy. She stroked his head, worried, frightened, and confused. Gulping and gasping he finally regained control of himself. "Forgive me, Katie."

"You have done nothing wrong, Richard. . ." She stroked his face and kissed him. "Will you tell me what tortures you so? You kept calling out, "Turn back!" Were you in a battle?"

He stared into her eyes. "Yes, it is the greatest battle of my life, but tonight, I think the tide may have turned."

"I do not understand."

"Neither do I, Katie-love, but if you will just please bear with me, I think all will be well. Will you trust me, please?' He stroked her hair from her face and held her to him. She pressed her face to his. "Yes, Richard, but will you explain it to me someday?"

"Yes, someday, when the battle is over."

NOBODY AROSE EARLY the following day. Even Darcy and Elizabeth forego their walking ritual in favour of breakfast in bed and a long soak together in their enormous bathtub. The Pemberley guests did not begin to venture downstairs until nearly noon.

Richard and Mark were the first, both leaving their wives to sleep, and with no one else about, the two brothers made their way to the empty billiards room and began a game. "I cannot remember the last time you and I were alone like this." Mark said as he set up his shot. "It seems that some family member is always present." His cue struck and the balls scattered, one sinking home in the far left corner. He moved to assess the balls and began the next shot. "How do you find marriage?"

Richard sighed. "It is wonderful and challenging all at once."

Mark laughed. "So it is, but I suspect Brother, you were wiser than I, you made a love match."

Richard startled. "Do you think so?"

Mark looked at him quizzically. "You mean you did not? I mean, aside from the fact that Kathleen brought nothing to the marriage, and she obviously was not with child, what other reason would you have to choose her? Once you inherited Rosings your options for a wife were wide open. You could have chosen the daughter of a peer and been as happy as I." This last was said with some bitterness.

"Are you unhappy?"

"Do not mind me. I made the match I was born to make. I have the marriage that brought Laura's thirty thousand pounds to Matlock. We are content with each other." He struck the cue ball again.

"I always thought it was better than that."

"So did I, but after seeing you with Kathleen, and even more so, Darcy with Elizabeth, I see the deficiencies in my lot."

"Father told me it took time for him and Mother to develop the closeness you see now."

"Yes he said the same to me." He mused, then looking up he asked, "Do you, one who does have a love match, feel inadequate around our cousin's example?"

Richard smiled, there it was again, twice his brother told him in one conversation that he was in a love match. His confidence in himself and his marriage grew. "Yes, I feel completely outdone by him. Nobody I have ever known has displayed such deep affection and I do not know that I could give myself over to it. They seem to breathe for each other. I know that Darcy is fiercely protective of her, and no one should attempt to threaten his happiness. Look at what he did to Wickham. Did you ever imagine Darcy capable of such violence, or such emotion?"

"No it was shocking. He is fiercely loyal to the family but his affection for Elizabeth . . . my God, he kisses her in public! Before the servants, without care! They display such affection, not just physical; it is as if they. . ." He sighed and looked at his brother. "Listen to me, the jealous cousin. Darcy disregarded society's dictates and he is happy."

"Can you not be happy, too? What has Laura said about Darcy? She seemed cool to it until she met Elizabeth. She now seems to have accepted her. I cannot say the same of Kathleen, but as long as she is civil, I can bear it. Does Laura seem at all . . . curious, envious of Darcy and Elizabeth's devotion?"

"I am not sure; we have not spoken of it."

"Darcy tells me that communication is the key to his happiness. Trust and communication strengthens their love. They have no secrets."

Mark raised a brow. "And do you live by that?"

"I am working on it." He admitted.

Mark leaned close to Richard. "Did you see the way Elizabeth stared at him in the fencing room?"

"It was difficult to miss." He smiled.

"Did you hear him in the sitting room?" They grinned. "What do you suppose she was doing to him?" The brothers laughed, green with envy and admiration.

"Perhaps there is something to Darcy's communication theory." Mark sank the last ball and the two brothers left the room to seek out the rest of the party.

TWO DAYS AFTER THE BALL, Bingley and Jane removed to Lyndon Hall. The Bennets were to accompany them, and stay for a few nights to see Jane's new home, then return to Longbourn. Darcy had done his best to behave civilly to Mr. Bennet for Elizabeth's sake, and was relieved to see him go, although admittedly, he had seen little of him as the man practically moved into the library. Elizabeth embraced each Bennet and Bingley with promises to write and perhaps visit soon.

With just the Fitzwilliam family as guests, the atmosphere of Pemberley relaxed considerably. One morning, Georgiana was busy with Laura and her aunt, so Elizabeth offered to show Kathleen her little oasis of summer, the conservatory.

The two women entered the humid room, fragrant with the damp earth and blooming exotic plants. "This room will keep me sane until spring comes again, I think. I never felt winter so keenly until I came here. Derbyshire is so different from Hertfordshire. Where did you grow up, Kathleen?"

"Oh, in Kent, so the Rosings winter is nothing new to me, but I would enjoy a room such as this, it does still become cold there."

They sat on a bench together. "Have things improved for you? Are you feeling more confident?"

"A little, I am afraid that I will never truly be at ease." She looked down. "I will never be like you, Elizabeth."

She laughed. "Why would you want to be?"

"You are so confident, and seem to handle everything with such skill. The open house, the family, Christmas, the ball, everything was done so well."

"I hardly did it alone. You have a staff, as well.

"You do everything so well, Elizabeth, especially your marriage. William is clearly very happy. I can see why so many men admire you."

Elizabeth was surprised. "What do you mean? Who admires me?"

Kathleen's eyes opened wide. "They all do! Have you not seen how they stare at you?"

"If they do, I have not noticed. I am afraid I only seek my husband's gaze." Kathleen studied and believed her. No, Elizabeth was not seeking anyone's attention. "Is something bothering you, Kathleen?" She asked gently.

She burst into tears. "I think Richard loves another."

Elizabeth embraced her. "Oh Kathleen! That cannot be true! He clearly loves you!"

"I thought so, but ..." She looked into Elizabeth's eyes. "I think he loves you, Elizabeth."

She gasped, not from surprise, as she knew of his old infatuation, but because he still harboured it. "What makes you think that?"

"He speaks of you with admiration, almost reverence. He became nervous when we came here. He has avoided talking to you since we arrived, but sought you out to dance, and gazed at you. Do you have any feelings for him? Has he spoken to you?" She begged her for reassurance.

"Oh Kathleen, yes I have feelings for him, but nothing more that as a cousin and friend. I have never wished for his attentions. William is the first and only man I will ever give my heart."

"And has he ever spoken to you of his feelings?" She said softly.

"Once, before I married William, he said that he wished for the kind of love he saw that I had with his cousin. I did not allow him to elaborate, but instead told him I hoped someday he would find, well, someone like you."

Kathleen stared at the floor. "Do you think he was in love with you?"

"I do not know. I do think he was envious of William and felt guilty for it. Richard has suffered greatly and silently with his army experiences. William was his only confidant. I imagine you have replaced him." She tilted her head to find Kathleen's downcast eyes.

She nodded slowly. "He has nightmares of the battles. Last night. . ." Elizabeth held her hand. She drew a breath and continued. "Last night when I was able to wake him he sobbed like a child, but when he recovered, he somehow seemed better, he said the tide had turned and I should bear with him, all would be well."

"Do you believe him?"

"I must." She looked up. "Do you really think that he loves me?"

Elizabeth squeezed her hand and smiled. "I do Kathleen. He loves, but is frightened by it."

"What about his feelings for you?

"Whatever they are, be assured that you are in no danger from me, and for him, if he has them, it seems that he may have found a way to let them go. Trust him, do as he asks, and bear with him as he struggles. I think that your marriage will come out stronger in the end. I promise you, he has never acted on his feelings for me, whatever they were or are. Never. He has always been faithful to you." She paused. "And sometime when you are sure of yourself, bring the subject up with him. Do not let this fear fester for either of you."

Kathleen wiped her eyes and hugged her friend. "Thank you, Elizabeth."

WHILE ELIZABETH AND KATHLEEN SPOKE, the men gathered in Darcy's study to discuss how they would address any questions about Elizabeth's kidnapping. Darcy was furious that he would have to speak on it at all. He wished to never think of the experience again. They agreed that the less said the better, and as the details were not let out, there was no reason to elaborate. They would only say that Elizabeth was accosted by a vagrant and the man was arrested, nothing more. Their wives would all be told the story, and hopefully the news would die quickly. Lord Matlock reminded his nephew that upon arriving in London, they could not simply hide in Darcy House. They must be seen around town, and accept invitations as a couple before Georgiana's coming out. They needed to satisfy all of those curious about Elizabeth and her spectacular catch of Darcy before they held their own ball. Darcy moaned but agreed.

When the meeting adjourned, he cornered the first footman he saw and demanded Elizabeth's location. The footman, like all of the staff, still watched over her since Wickham, and immediately told Darcy she was in the library. There he found her alone, in their chair, waiting for him. He gratefully slipped in beside her and told her of their conversation that day. William angrily confirmed Kathleen's supposition of Richard. Elizabeth was not surprised. She assured him she was ready to take on the *ton*. That only angered him again. It took a great deal of work to soothe him from his bear of a mood.

The next morning, two carriages sat outside of the door. They would all meet again in London in about five weeks. Richard was clandestinely observed by his wife, parents and cousin when he bid Elizabeth farewell. He embraced her and kissed her cheek as usual, but for the first time, he did not feel the longing he had in the past. The relief in his eyes was reflected in her smile, and she whispered so only he could hear, "Go home and love Kathleen."

He drew back and nodded. "I will, I promise." He turned to Darcy and clasped his hand. "Thank you for everything, we will see you soon."

Darcy embraced him, hoping that his cousin had finally found peace. "Take good care, Richard, I will miss you." Soon the two carriages travelling in separate directions departed, leaving Pemberley once again to the three Darcys.

Chapter 39

*S*ince returning home to Rosings three weeks earlier, Richard had plunged into his duties as Master with a new energy, seemingly determined to learn everything he could from Mr. Barnes. The two men spent countless hours together, discussing the planting designs the steward had devised. Richard was not completely unfamiliar with the process. He did pay some attention to Darcy when he accompanied him each Easter. But this time he was working on *his* estate, not his aunt's. This time it was his life at stake.

His dreams improved. They were not as violent, not as frequent, and when they occurred, he seemed somehow more conscious and was able to gain control before waking in the grip of fear. Kathleen was starting to sleep through the night as well, giving up her watch over him. His self-confidence was improving. Frequent letters from his father, brother, and Darcy giving him advice and guidance buoyed his strength. He began to feel that perhaps he *could* do well, for him and his wife.

Kathleen did as he bid, she waited, and supported him as best she could, but the knowledge of his admiration of Elizabeth was eating away at her and she determined to speak to him.

She entered his study. "Richard."

He looked up from the papers he was reading, refocused on her, and smiled. "Katie! You are a welcome diversion! What can I do for you?"

She stood before his desk and asked nervously, "Do you have time to talk with me?"

"Always, you know that. What do you need?"

She sat down and began, "Your mother asks when we expect to go to London. She wishes to make an appointment with the modiste for me."

"Ah yes, your presentation gown. You will need a great number of gowns, I suspect. I will need to visit the tailor as well." He mused, and then smiled. "I thought we would leave in a fortnight."

She nodded. "The Darcys should be in town by then."

"Yes, Darcy said they will arrive, barring any travel problems, this Saturday."

She bit her lip. "I look forward to seeing Elizabeth." She watched him carefully.

He smiled softly, now sure that he had control of his feelings for her. "So do I." He looked up at Kathleen and was dismayed to see tears. He jumped to his feet and kneeled before her chair. "Katie, what is wrong?" He tried to take her hands but she pulled away and stood and walked to the window. He began to move towards her when he heard the pained, angry, broken voice. "It is true then, you are in love with her."

"Pardon? Katie. . ."

She turned and faced him, she had to know, especially now. "Tell me the truth, Richard. I cannot bear any more." He walked to her but she put out her hand, palm up. She could not do this if he was touching her.

Richard stared at her, and then hung his head. Why now? Why would she ask him now when he thought he finally had it under control? She need never have found out . . . it was useless to speculate. She was before him. He sighed and sat behind his desk, and motioned her to the chair she occupied before. "What do you wish to know, Katie?"

"Do you love Elizabeth?"

"Yes, I do." She sobbed and put her handkerchief to her mouth, and he quickly continued. "But, you must know, I am no longer *IN* love with her. I am completely committed to you and shall remain that way until the day I die." He desperately wanted to hold her, but instinctively knew she needed the distance maintained.

She glared at him. "How can I believe you?"

He shook his head helplessly. "You must trust me. I never acted on my love for Elizabeth; even when I was convinced that I was the better man for her."

She drew a deep breath. "When did you . . ."

"Fall in love?" He sighed. "When she ate dinner at Darcy House a week after Darcy and I met her. I had not seen her since, and all that week I listened to Darcy's joyous effusions of her. I went to dinner looking for fault, and instead fell under her spell. Darcy by that time was already a changed man. I had never dreamed such a transformation was possible. You can hardly understand the unhappy, emotionally numb man he was. I could not believe he of all people could feel such deep, instant love. I think I was jealous, and wanted it for myself."

Quietly she watched him analyze himself. "You never acted on it."

"No, I could not hurt Darcy. He was smiling for the first time in years . . . since he was a boy."

"Elizabeth said that you spoke to her at Rosings."

He laughed hollowly; of course she had spoken to Elizabeth about this. "Yes, I did speak to her, and Darcy spoke to me, quite strongly as I recall."

"But you did not give up your feelings." She needed to hear every detail.

"No, it was a part of me by then." He looked up into her eyes, he was brutally honest.

"And then they married." He nodded. "And you were . . . unhappy?" He nodded again. "And then she was attacked."

"Yes, and I thought that as a soldier, I would have protected her. If she had chosen me, she never would have been so threatened. It made it more difficult to give her up. Once again, Darcy had to warn me off."

She watched him, her breathing now under control. "You met me then."

"Yes, and I admit, I was first attracted to you because I was struck by your resemblance to her."

"I remember wondering why you stared at me so."

He nodded, still not breaking his gaze. "That was why. But I soon realized that you are not Elizabeth, and exactly the woman I needed. Elizabeth belongs with Darcy. They are soul mates, as I believe we are."

"If that is the case, why did you not finally give her up when you began to feel love for me?"

"I do not know. It took me a long time to accept that the first woman I ever loved would not want me. I suppose it was a circumstance of pride. No man wishes to be rejected no matter the reason, and of course, her reason was excellent, she loves Darcy." He closed his eyes, and gathered his thoughts. Finally he met her eyes again. "Katie, I swear, I was drawn to you immediately. I thought for a long time that it was due to your resemblance to Elizabeth. I struggled with my true love for you and my phantom love for her. I felt protective of her, which made it harder to relegate my feelings to the less powerful emotion of familial love and caring. The struggle and guilt I think led to my dreams. My failure to instantly understand Rosings, and especially the very conscious knowledge of my failure to you as a dedicated husband ate at my soul. It was not until our Christmas at Pemberley, and actually the day of the ball, that I found the strength to exorcise Elizabeth from the part of my heart where you live."

The tears were slowly tracking down her face again. "What happened?" She asked urgently.

"My father spoke to me. My brother spoke to me. I watched Darcy cling to Elizabeth. I saw her deep and open love for him. I finally gave myself completely to you." He tried to convey all of his sincerity in his look, but even so, his hand moved across the desk, seeking to touch her.

She put her hands in her lap, and looked down. "I have noticed a change since we returned."

He tried to catch her eyes again. "I asked you to bear with me."

"The tide has turned." She said softly, still looking down.

"Yes." They sat in silence.

She finally met his gaze again. "I have always loved you, Richard. All of me."

He nodded and gazed into her eyes. "I can now say that you have all of me, Katie."

She stood. "I have much to think about. I will leave you now."

He stood and held out his hand. "Please stay."

"No. I will see you at dinner." She walked out of the room and left for their bedchamber.

Richard watched her go. He wanted to follow her, to wrap his arms around her, kiss her, reassure her of his true, deep, and unending feelings for her, but he let her go, and sat back down behind his desk with his head in his hands. Tears of sorrow tracked down his face. What had Darcy told him? *Communication.* Darcy regretted deeply not speaking to Elizabeth of his fears. He stood up, and wiped his cheek with the back of his hand. He would not let this rest. He would go to her now. Striding from the room, he took the stairs two at a time and soon found himself outside of the door to her bedchamber. He hesitated a moment, took a breath, and without knocking, entered.

He found Kathleen staring out of the window; it was obvious she had been crying. "Katie, please forgive me, I did not realize that you have known of my feelings for Elizabeth. I thought this was a struggle that I faced alone, and I truly know that I have conquered it."

She shook her head; she knew that he did not realize it. "I suspected it when we visited Pemberley the first time, then little things, the way your face looked when her name was mentioned, your reluctance to be near her . . . you made me feel so inadequate."

"It was not intentional." He said truthfully.

She sighed. "I know; that is what hurt. Your regard was genuine and simply flowed naturally from you.

He took her hands in his and gazed into her eyes. "I do love you Katie."

"I know." She said softly.

"You do?" He looked at her anxiously.

"Yes Richard, you would not have opened to me if you did not. You would not hold me so desperately when your dreams awaken you in the night, you would not have offered me your hand without it. You are a very good and honourable man."

He hung his head with the shame of hurting the woman he truly did love. "You know me well."

"As you know me."

He opened his arms and she fell into his embrace. She buried her face against his chest, finally feeling secure in his love, and made her decision. "I was going to wait to tell you, but I think you should know now. I am with child."

Richard stepped away to see her. "You are?" A huge smile lit up his face. "I will be a father? You are my baby's mother! Oh Katie!" He kissed her deeply, and then covered her face and hands with more kisses. She laughed, delighted with his behaviour. "When Katie, when?"

She held his face in her hands. "October." He picked her up and swung her around, grinning from ear to ear. Squealing, she demanded he put her down and smiled with true happiness; it seemed that she had finally surpassed Elizabeth. *She* would give him his child.

LAURA STOOD taking in the room. The dinner had finished and the gentlemen left for the dark panelled confines of their host's sanctum, drinking, telling lies, talking politics, boasting of their conquests, and whatever else her active imagination could conjure. She scanned the ladies around her, pretending to listen to the feathered and bejewelled women as they twittered of the latest gossip, and ripping apart women who they had never met and knew only as a daughter of this peer or that gentleman, assigning them a place of acceptance or disdain in their world.

Ordinarily she would have easily joined in, but she was married, and her husband's family had set down an edict that she was to support the inconsequential daughter of an insignificant gentleman who fell into great fortune by marrying well. She glanced at the corner where her mother-in-law was introducing Elizabeth to her friends. Laura's friends had already questioned her incessantly over the last Season, demanding that she explain how this marriage occurred. Her unmarried friends had counted on her to provide the necessary introduction to the elusive Mr. Darcy. She would have gladly performed the service if only the man had cooperated and attended events. She sighed, her cousin Darcy could have made such a brilliant match, but *he wanted love*, she thought with disbelief.

Laura's memory of Christmas at Pemberley betrayed her cold thoughts. So many little things struck her, but the image that stayed was of Darcy as he watched Elizabeth from across the music room, contemplating the portrait contained in the locket he gave her. The caress that passed between them when Elizabeth met his gaze was palpable. Laura startled out of her reverie at the sound of a woman's voice in her ear.

"I suppose that we cannot ignore Mrs. Darcy, after all, she *is* Mrs. Darcy. Tell me Laura, you spent Christmas at Pemberley. What has your new cousin done to the house? I have not heard of anyone being invited there for ages. Is Mr. Darcy ashamed of his bride's skills? Does he regret his choice?"

Laura regarded the woman and noticed the others hovering around, waiting eagerly for her cutting remarks. As much as she wished to knock down the upstart who had dared to snatch her very eligible cousin from her unhappy friends, she could feel Lady Matlock's eyes on her as she responded. "Pemberley is as lovely as it ever was. Mrs. Darcy has changed little and she was an attentive hostess." She would elaborate no further.

Dissatisfied, another woman asked, "And what of the rumours? Was she meeting a secret lover in the forest when she was attacked?"

"Certainly not!" Even Laura found that offensive. "One thing that I can say without question is that Mr. Darcy does not regret the connection, and Mrs. Darcy is committed to him."

The men rejoined them then, and many sets of feminine eyes watched as Darcy strode into the room and went straight to his wife's side. The saw him bestow a kiss upon her hand and then place it on his arm. "I cannot remember the last time my husband did that." A voice behind Laura whispered. "Is that just for show?"

"No, it is genuine." She said and looked up to see Mark watching her. She looked away and went to join Lady Matlock, leaving the rest of the ladies to make their own decisions on whether to accept or reject Elizabeth without further input from her.

The ladies of this party and every other one that the Darcys attended over the very early days of the Season observed, and drew their conclusions. Some admired her successful catch of Darcy, some despised her background, some even advanced beyond the snobbery to actually appreciate the woman, but most, at least to her face, accepted her simply because the man whose ring she wore was Fitzwilliam Darcy's, and that, it seemed, was enough.

"WILL SOMEONE PLEASE explain to me what possessed our monarch to demand three-yard long trains, feathers and bare shoulders for a presentation at court in the middle of winter?"

Darcy and Georgiana exchanged amused glances as they watched Elizabeth shift the heavy train in frustration while they practiced once again the ridiculously low curtsy. Darcy was acting the King as Elizabeth performed her irritated approach and deep curtsy, and then backed away in atypical servility. They were undecided if Elizabeth's behaviour was due to the annoyance of the act, or the condition of her body. It was the middle of February and the ladies' presentation at court was in a fortnight. They made the journey to town at the end of January, suffered through five dinner parties and the *ton's* incessant curiosity, and had just received their presentation gowns from the modiste.

"At least you do not have to wear a sword." Darcy's eyes twinkled with amusement.

"Do not even attempt to compare your measly sword to this . . . this . . ." Suddenly Elizabeth's ire was halted in midsentence and her eyes opened wide. Her hand went to her belly and she looked at Darcy. "Oh William!" She whispered.

"What is it?" He asked, on his feet and alarmed.

"I think I felt our baby!" Her face was full of wonder.

Darcy laid his hand over her middle. "What did it feel like?" He asked urgently.

"It is just as Jane said, it feels like bubbles!" She laughed ecstatically. "Wait! There it is again!" She beamed up at him. "Oh William! We are going to have a baby!" Tears of joy fell down her face as she felt the fluttering again.

Darcy pressed his hand to her, desperate to feel it himself. "I cannot feel anything through all of these clothes." He said with frustration. There was only one thing for it. He took Elizabeth's hand and excusing them from his sister, led her upstairs, where he quickly divested his laughing wife of her gown. "William, I am freezing!" She smiled up at him, watching him disrobe.

"Well, let us get under the covers, my love." He stripped back the comforter and they climbed into the bed, and wrapping his arms around her waist, placed his warm hands directly over the tiny bulge in her middle. "Now I can feel what you feel." He whispered into her ear. Curled so snugly together, he could not resist the temptation of kissing her neck, so he began nibbling on the spot below her ear that always made her moan. As her excitement grew, so did the activity of the baby, until she gasped with surprise upon feeling more fluttering. "I felt that!" Darcy exclaimed. "Oh Lizzy! I felt that!"

"Oh dear, do you think that every time you kiss me I will feel the response of this child?" She touched the spot on her belly.

Darcy smiled at her, his eyes so full of love. "Let us find out." He took her face in his hands and kissed her lips very gently, and brought his tongue to caress hers. She placed her hands over his, and they kissed tenderly for what seemed like hours. He moved his lips away from hers, suckling her neck, eliciting the soft moan that he loved so much. He stayed there, slowly torturing her with his gentle movements, while bringing his hands to fondle, ever so slowly, her enlarged and tender breasts. She was so sensitive that his feathery touch made her back arch in response. "I love you." His warm breath filled her ear, his deep voice stirring her desire. He slowly ran his hands down her body, as she began to trace her hands down his. She wrapped her arms around his waist, and caressed his back and his sweet, dimpled bottom, drawing him down onto her, covering her completely with his hard warm body.

"Oh Will, I love you." She breathed, gliding her tongue down his neck, and then drawing his flesh into her mouth, leaving behind the mark of her passion.

His mouth moved down her body, to take in her nipples. She jumped at the contact. His soft tongue laved her and then drawing her inside his mouth, he began to drink from her the way the fluttering life inside of her someday would. He stopped and looked up at her face, entranced by the pleasure he saw there. He drew himself back up to her lonely mouth and tangling his fingers into her hair, resumed his occupation of loving her lips. Satisfied that she was sufficiently sated, he returned to kissing her body.

As he moved away, she moaned, "No, come back to me." He moved back up and she urged him onto his back. "It is my turn, my love."

He smiled and watched as Elizabeth lay on top of him, running her hands over his taut muscles, revelling in the sensation of her fingers gliding up and down his tingling skin. He closed his eyes, and he felt her hair spread over his chest, knowing that soon he would feel . . . *"ah, yes!"* ...the extraordinary sensation of her warm mouth descending over his arousal. Her tongue, her lips, her hands all stroked and swirled about him, bringing a moan to his voice and constant shivers to his body. When she could feel the building tension in his movements, she moved away, giving them both a reprieve, and climbed back up to him, reclaiming his neglected lips. This time he wrapped his arms around her, and stroked her body with his hands, feeling every bit of her soft skin, and bringing his fingers to encase themselves within her folds. They drew their mouths apart, gazing at each other, knowing that it was time. He rolled and took her with him, finally coming to rest on top of her, his passion and desire evident in his eyes, his every touch explaining his love, and now upon entering her, his strong, steady thrusts telling her his devotion. They kept their eyes open, watching each other, feeling the power of their connection, building with their cries of need, begging for their mutual release, and finally collapsing, clutching each other, kissing again and again, complete.

The two lovers rolled apart and fell into their favourite embrace, she curled on her side, resting her head on his chest, and gradually regained their senses. "Thank you, my love." He whispered into her ear.

"For what, Will?" She asked, listening to the steady beat of his heart.

"For making me a papa." He gently kissed her cheek.

She looked up into his warm brown eyes and smiled. "I love you, too."

THE GREAT DAY ARRIVED. Elizabeth and Georgiana were dressed in their feathered glory and Darcy and Lord Matlock donned the ceremonial swords. Richard wore his own military sword, and laughed while giving his father and cousin words of advice on how to sit, walk and generally move without destroying the furniture or mistakenly stabbing someone. It was with a mixture of pride and sadness that Darcy watched as Georgiana, on her uncle's arm, walked down the gallery at St. James', let her train fall to the floor, kissed his cheek, and entered the Presence Chamber to curtsy to the Queen and Prince Regent. She walked in with a show of confidence that he knew was gained solely by her sister Elizabeth's work. He looked down at his wife, who smiled at him, wiping away the stray tear from his cheek. Georgiana was a child no more.

Soon it was Elizabeth's turn, and she performed her curtsy with the self-possession of a queen herself. Darcy's sadness for his sister's maturation was replaced by his swelling pride for his wife. He noted the Prince Regent's admiration for her beauty, but chose to accept it as a compliment instead of the act of a notorious rake. They waited for Richard to appear with Kathleen. After the months of anticipation, the hours of fittings and practice, the momentous event was over, and like all momentous events, it did not meet the expectations of the participants. It was over and done in the blink of an eye, like an overly planned wedding.

They all returned to Darcy House, and the party gratefully rushed upstairs to change. Lady Matlock and Lady Catherine were there waiting for them, along with Mark and Laura, and soon they were all together again, attired in more comfortable clothes and for the ladies, finally ready to eat something that day.

Lady Catherine sat, as majestic and commanding as the Queen herself, and observed as Elizabeth filled her plate with odd combinations of food from the buffet and sat down nearby. Since Anne's death, she had let go of her anger for

Elizabeth marrying Darcy. She accepted that even if he had married Anne, she knew now that her daughter still would have died. She allowed the initial undisclosed fondness she felt upon meeting Elizabeth to return, and to her niece's bewildered alarm, treated her as her own daughter.

"Elizabeth!" She barked. "What on earth are you thinking? Such combinations of food! And so much! A lady does not eat in such a manner!"

"Aunt Catherine, as you well know, I am not a lady, I am a gentleman's daughter." Elizabeth smirked at her.

Darcy and Richard grinned at each other. They were at it again. "You are trifling with me, Mrs. Darcy. I will not have it!" Turning to her nephew she narrowed her eyes and pointed at him. "Have you no control over your wife, sir?"

"None whatsoever, Aunt." Darcy smiled fondly at Elizabeth. He took her hand, and looked at her with his brows raised. She nodded. It was time. "I do know a good reason for her hunger, however." He smiled, his eyes joyous, his dimples huge, his chest puffed, he announced, "Elizabeth and I will be parents soon." He looked at her beaming face. "Not nearly soon enough, but soon." He kissed her hand lovingly.

The room was instantly filled with declarations of excitement and congratulations, and Darcy found himself the subject of much backslapping by his uncle and cousins. Lady Catherine immediately began dispensing her advice, and told Elizabeth that she was not eating nearly enough, as she was too thin.

"When are you due, Elizabeth?" Lady Matlock asked.

"I think it will be mid-August. That is why we will remove to Pemberley in April, and asked you to take Georgiana through the rest of her Season for us."

"And here I was thinking my nephew far too dedicated to his sheep and crops!" Lady Matlock laughed. She held her hand. "I assume by this announcement you have felt the quickening?"

"I am feeling it right now!" She whispered, looking up to catch Darcy's warm stare from across the room.

Lady Matlock followed her gaze. "Is he overprotective yet?" Seeing Elizabeth's blush she laughed. "Oh dear, what will we do with him when your time comes? He will be beside himself!"

"I hope that he will be beside me." Elizabeth said quietly.

"You want him there? Oh Elizabeth, I do not recommend this. One cry from you and he will faint dead away, or worse, try to take over."

Elizabeth shook her head. "I want him there. We will do this together."

Lady Matlock looked at Lady Catherine with raised brows. "Well dear, this is something I would like to see."

Darcy joined them and smiled. "Why do I have a feeling that you are discussing me?"

Elizabeth took his hand. "Hmm. Perhaps it was because we were all staring at you?" He laughed softly, then standing behind her; wrapped his arms around her waist. Kissing her curls, he rested his chin upon her head. Elizabeth leaned back against him and covered his hands with hers. Darcy smiled at the shocked expression on his aunts' faces. "Now ladies, what exactly did you have to say about me?"

"Nephew! Cease this display immediately! It is unseemly!" Lady Catherine cried.

Lady Matlock regarded them with admiration. "Oh Darcy, you are truly setting an excellent example for my sons!" They all looked over to Richard and Mark who just then happened to notice the scene before them. Mark looked to Laura for her reaction, who caught his eye then gazed down. Kathleen smiled at Richard who immediately came over to kiss her hand. Lady Matlock sighed and whispered. "Well, some progress is being made, in any case." Darcy chuckled. "So tell me, do you really intend to stay with Elizabeth when her time comes? I do not wish to frighten either of you, but it is not over in a moment, it takes hours of work, and is not without great discomfort. You will have to be prepared to see and hear your wife in a state that you can do little to alleviate. If that helplessness would make you feel overwhelmed, it is best that you keep to your library for the duration."

Darcy squeezed Elizabeth. "Aunt Elaine, although I truly have no real idea of what to expect, I cannot imagine not being with my Elizabeth anytime that she needs me. Even if all I can do is hold her hand, I will remain by her side. Whatever I may experience will be inconsequential to her labours. It is she who matters." Elizabeth looked up at him and touched his face. He met her gaze and they gently brushed their lips.

Lady Catherine watched with tears in her eyes. She was right all along, Darcy would have been a wonderful husband for her Anne, but it took Elizabeth to touch his heart and let his family see the gentle man he had buried deep inside. She cleared her throat. "Well then, Nephew. If you are determined to behave as a fool, I suppose we must support you. But if I hear of your fainting, be assured, I will never let you hear the end of it!"

Darcy laughed and hugged Elizabeth. "Of that, I have no doubt at all, Aunt Catherine."

ALEX STOOD in front of the mirror, his valet brushing his coat. This was it, the long wait was over. He had not seen Georgiana; *no, he had not spoken to Georgiana,* since Bingley's wedding, nearly nine months past. He had caught brief glimpses of her since their return to town. He was always careful to be well-hidden, having no desire to raise Darcy's ire. Through Elizabeth's letters, he learned of Georgiana's continued interest in him, and learned many useful and appreciated details, her preferences in books and music, her favourite pastimes, and most importantly, the date of her coming out. He received his invitation to her ball and responded instantly, with a request for two dances. Any two. Please.

Elizabeth was fortunately in charge of the responses, and laughed when she received Alex's request. She showed it to Georgiana, who blushed crimson. Elizabeth knew that William would never approve two dances, not at her first ball, so she gave him the supper set, thus allowing him the most time possible with her. Lord Matlock would open the ball with her, followed by Darcy, Richard, and Mark. After that she was fair game to all of the other young men who would come to win her, and her dowry.

Alex arrived at Darcy House precisely on time, and found he was one of the first guests. Darcy, Elizabeth, and Georgiana stood waiting to receive them. He approached and shook Darcy's hand. "It has been a long time, Darcy. It is good to see you."

Darcy regarded Alex appraisingly. He saw his anticipation and shook his head. His friend had kept his part of the bargain, now it was up to Georgiana. "It is good to see you, Alex. How are your parents?"

He smiled. "Very well, they send their greetings and hope to see you at our annual ball again this year."

"Perhaps, we have many events to attend with Georgiana, and we will be leaving town in April. You may need to invite Lord and Lady Matlock instead." Darcy glanced over to his aunt and uncle.

Alex followed his gaze then turned back to him. "Why are you leaving so early in the Season? Will you be returning?"

"No, we will not be returning." Seeing his questioning face he leaned in and spoke quietly. "It seems you are to be an uncle." Darcy grinned.

Alex's eyes widened. "Congratulations Darcy! That is wonderful news!" He turned to Elizabeth and kissed her hand. "I am so happy for you Elizabeth!"

"Thank you Alex!" She beamed, then turning to Georgiana she said, "Mr. Carrington, I believe you should remember my sister, Georgiana Darcy?"

Alex smiled into her blushing face. He drew a deep breath and looked into her eyes. "Miss Darcy, it is a supreme pleasure to see you again. You look absolutely lovely. May I congratulate you on your presentation?"

Georgiana, feeling the gentle pressure of Elizabeth's hand on her back gathered her confidence and looked into Alex's smiling, somewhat anxious eyes. "Thank you, sir. It was quite a memorable experience."

"I hope that I might secure a dance with you, Miss Darcy, and create a memorable experience myself." He smiled hopefully.

"Mr. Carrington, I am pleased to offer you the supper dance." She said breathlessly.

Thrilled, Alex bowed. "Thank you Miss Darcy, I look forward to it!" He looked gratefully at Elizabeth and moved on.

The house soon filled with people. Darcy became distinctly uncomfortable and relied on Elizabeth to help him through the event. In some ways, he felt that he was being just as heavily courted as Georgiana, as young men and their parents came to introduce themselves, hopeful to gain the favour of the man who would make the decisions on Georgiana's suitors

When the dancing began, Lord Matlock, as the senior member of the family, led Georgiana onto the floor. Darcy gratefully stood opposite Elizabeth and for the first time that day relaxed. "Is this ordeal over yet?" He whispered as he took Elizabeth's hand in a turn.

She laughed. "I am afraid it has only just begun, my love."

He grimaced. "This is torture. Do you realize how many men have complimented me tonight?"

"As I handled the invitations, yes, I do." She grinned.

He leaned close to her ear. "Lizzy, you once commanded me to make time pass faster. I now charge you with the same task!"

She laughed. "Forgive me William, I have not that power, but inevitably time will march on." Darcy groaned. "There is a solution, you know." He looked at her, waiting. "You could give your consent to one of them and have done with it on the first night!" She gave him a gleeful smile.

Darcy stared deeply into her eyes. "Mrs. Darcy."

Elizabeth met his gaze, still smiling. "Yes, Mr. Darcy?"

"You are provoking me to action."

"What sort of action, sir?"

"I may be forced to wipe that smirk from your lips."

"And how will you achieve that?" She raised her brow and tilted her head.

"With the firm application of mine." He growled.

"Promises, promises, Mr. Darcy." She winked at him and glided away.

Once again, Elizabeth restored his good humour during a stressful situation. With her help, he managed to tolerate the suitors and watched with equanimity as Georgiana danced with many of them.

Alex finally came to claim her hand for his dance. He smiled down at her, and tried to control the quaver in his voice. "At last Miss Darcy. I have anticipated this for so long."

"So have I, Mr. Carrington." She blushed.

They began their dance and Alex spoke to her of music. Georgiana happily talked of her love of the pianoforte, and relaxed. She found that of the many young men she had met that night, Alex was the only one with whom she felt comfortable. When the dance ended, he escorted her to supper and they spent the time in quiet conversation. They were joined by Darcy and Elizabeth, but to Alex's surprise, he was permitted to continue the conversation. Her brother did not attempt to interfere.

As the evening ended, Darcy noticed that Alex approached Georgiana to invite her to dance the final waltz with him. He was instantly angry and began to walk towards the couple. He did not want Georgiana to receive the attention that dancing twice with any particular man would bring. It was a gently applied hand on his arm that stopped him. He turned and looked down into Elizabeth's lovely eyes.

"Do not be angry with Alex, I set the dance aside for them."

He stared at her. "You know what this signals! I never danced twice with any woman until I met you!"

"Yes, my dear husband, and is it not possible that Alex has been waiting all this time to dance with his future wife? Would you have taken kindly to any other man dancing the waltz with me at the ball last year?" She smiled and gently caressed his hand.

His eyes became soft and warm. "My dear Lizzy, I do not take kindly to any other man dancing with you at any time, including tonight." He looked up and nodded his permission to Alex, and allowed him to waltz with her.

Elizabeth, now safely ensconced in his arms, smiled up at him as they floated around the ballroom. "That was very kind of you, William."

He shrugged his shoulders, admitting defeat. "I would not miss this dance with you, nor deny it to Richard, Mark, or Uncle Henry. Alex is the only other man in this room I will trust with her."

Amused with how quickly he changed his mind Elizabeth suggested, "Should we simply give them your consent now?"

Darcy smiled. "No, my love, he will have to work for it like every man." He gave her a squeeze and they laughed, twirling across the floor. He gazed tenderly down at her, "Lizzy?"

"Yes darling?"

"Do you remember what you were doing at this time exactly one year ago?" She smiled and looked into his warm gaze. "I believe that I was falling in love."

His grip of her waist grew tighter and their fingers entwined. "I believe that I had already fallen by now. Your smile a year ago; and your love today are the most treasured birthday gifts I have ever received. Thank you sweetheart."

"Will." She blinked back the tears that came so easily now, but had always been ready whenever he professed his love. The waltz ended and they came to a stop, still seeing nothing but each other. Elizabeth squeezed his hand. "Come my love, let us farewell our guests so I might add to your gift in the privacy of our chambers."

Darcy's eyes glowed. "And shall I unwrap my gift there?" He raised her gloved hand to his lips, allowing his breath to gently warm her skin.

"Mmmmm, yes." She closed her eyes, forgetting everyone around them.

"In that case my dearest wife let us urge our guests on." He smiled at her sweet expression.

She returned from her dreamy state and raised a brow. "And what method do you recommend? Putting out the candles?"

"No, too dangerous, they would trip over each other."

"Presenting their coats?" She suggested.

He smiled. "No, too much chaos, it would take forever to sort out."

"Hmm. I know! We will serve no more libations." She smiled widely.

He grinned into her dancing eyes. "I believe you have found the solution!" An hour later the guests were gone, and Darcy did enjoy unwrapping his birthday gift; very much indeed.

Chapter 40

The morning after Georgiana's coming out ball Alex sat at his parent's breakfast table staring unseeing at the rapidly cooling plate of ham and eggs before him. All he could see was the image of a perfectly lovely young woman, blushing in his arms as they waltzed the final dance together. He would be eternally grateful to Elizabeth for both secretly saving the dance for him on Georgiana's dance card, and for controlling Darcy's rather unhappy reaction when he saw them step off together. He smiled remembering his friend's angry glare almost instantly changing to a look of tender adoration at the sound of a few whispered words and a subtle caress by his wife. He hoped that he and Georgiana could share a passion like that someday.

Philip Carrington shot an amused glance at his wife. He watched with great interest his son's rapidly changing facial expressions. "Well Alex, did you enjoy Miss Darcy's ball?"

Alex startled and noticed his parents watching him with warm smiles. He could not stop the grin that overspread his face. "Yes Father, I enjoyed it very much, it was a wonderful evening."

"I am pleased to hear that, Son. How was Darcy?

Alex laughed. "He was everything expected and unexpected at the same time. He and the other gentlemen of his family take their protective roles very seriously, but surprisingly he allowed me to speak privately with her during supper. He made no attempt to interfere. I do not know if I should thank Elizabeth, or if he is remembering his own courtship."

Amanda laughed. "Oh Philip, do you remember how we wished to be alone when you courted me, and Papa was there at every turn? Whenever you left you would try to kiss my hand, and somehow my sister would always suddenly appear with an urgent directive from him. You were so frustrated!"

"I was more than frustrated, dear, I was desperate! Why do you think that I insisted on such a short engagement?"

"I thought that was Papa's decision." She looked at him with surprise.

Philip shook his head, grinning. "No indeed, I won his consent to marry you and named the wedding date. When he objected, I threatened to compromise you in a very public manner if he did not agree, and whisk you off to Gretna Green. I must have appeared serious since we married three weeks later!" Amanda gasped and laughed.

Alex's eyes were wide. This was the first time he heard this story. "I hope that I will not have to resort to such threats with Darcy. I am afraid that he is quite capable of beating me at any event, physical or mental."

Philip looked at his son seriously. "Are you not assuming something, Son? One ball does not make you a suitor. And one conversation and two dances do not make you engaged. I think that you need to reassess your attitude. After all, Alex, you are hardly the only young man interested in Miss Darcy and her thirty thousand pounds."

Alex met his father's raised brow with a small smile. "Thank you for the not so subtle reminder, Father."

"I am just performing my role as guide and critic." He smiled.

"Good, then I shall take on the role of hopeless romantic!" Amanda declared. She turned and grasped his hand. "I hope that you succeed Alex, you have waited a long time for your chance. I will be very happy to explain a lady's mind to you."

Alex squeezed her hand. "Thank you Mother, somehow I think that your advice will be the one I seek most frequently."

Amanda cast a satisfied glance at Philip. "I always appreciated how very intelligent you are Alex."

GEORGIANA AWOKE the morning after the ball with the memory of Alex's smile, laugh, and twinkling happy eyes. She hugged herself. She had the great advantage of knowing his feelings long before her ball, so all of those eager young men who tried to claim her attention failed completely. She compared every one of them to Alex, and his maturity, kindness, and relaxed, assured behaviour struck her as so much more interesting and attractive then the cocky or nervous men closer to her own age. She was also painfully aware of those men, which she was very sad to quickly realize was most of them, who were primarily interested in her dowry. Elizabeth sat down with her before the ball and explained very clearly what to expect from the gentlemen who would come to see her. The evening was not so much a romantic opportunity for her to meet the love of her life, but a very real business transaction to acquire funds for desperate families and support estates, as well as increasing status by connecting to the Darcy name. Her brother's tacit approval of Alex spoke volumes for his character and intentions. After watching the loving marriage William had made with Elizabeth, she knew that he was as concerned for her emotional future as much as her suitor's financial one.

She bathed and dressed, eventually wandering downstairs for a very late breakfast after the unprecedented late night. Upon arriving in the breakfast room she asked after the rest of the family and was told the unsurprising news that Elizabeth and William were out walking. She smiled; nothing, even an extremely abbreviated night, would keep them from their morning exercise. Upon sitting down she was presented with a salver piled high with calling cards and invitations, as well as a note from Elizabeth.

Georgiana,

Please look these over and put aside any that interest you. I have already made a list with your brother's assistance. Aunt Elaine will arrive at two o'clock and she will help us to greet all of your visitors. Of course, anyone not on our lists will not be shown in, and yes, Mr. Carrington's name has already been noted.

Elizabeth

She breathed a sigh of relief; the task would not be quite as daunting now. She was grateful for all that Elizabeth had done for her in the past year. Elizabeth selected ten young men to accept based on her observations the night before.

Darcy added two who he felt obligated to invite for at least one call due to business reasons, and otherwise reluctantly approved Elizabeth's choices. If it was up to him, Georgiana would wait several more years to enter the marriage mart. Lady Matlock also had indicated two other gentlemen who met her approval. So Georgiana, with the company of her sister and aunt, sat through fourteen visits. Alex arrived early and was very loathe leaving when his half hour was over. He saw the other men arriving and Elizabeth quietly informed him that they had identified many possible suitors and that he had some competition. He ruefully realized that his father seemed to be correct.

BY THE MIDDLE OF MARCH Darcy came to dread his morning question, "So Lizzy, what is on our agenda today?" He tried to say it with a smile, but after three weeks of nearly daily balls, dinners and other social events, both attended and hosted by the three Darcys, he had reached the end of his tolerance. His naturally shy, unsociable nature was screaming for relief. And he thought, it was only going to become worse, the Season did not really begin until after Easter, thus far they had only been attending the very preliminary events.

Elizabeth looked at him with sympathy. She was weary of the activity as well, and just wanted to go home to Pemberley. So it was with great gentleness that she told him the bad news, "We are going to St. James' tonight, William." Her heart ached seeing his miserable countenance.

"Oh no, please Lizzy, not there. Could we not miss this ball?"

"How darling? The point of being presented at court was so Georgiana, and I, for that matter, could attend events there. You know as well as I do how important this is for her, and her acceptance into society."

"I know, but it is just so . . ." He looked down.

Elizabeth squeezed his hand. "Tell me William."

He sighed and squeezed back, looking sadly into her eyes. "There are hundreds and hundreds of people. It is overcrowded, hot, candle wax drips constantly from the chandeliers, you cannot hear the conversation, and people are all over you to gain your attention. There is nowhere to hide." He ended softly.

Elizabeth regarded him, feeling his very real discomfort, and made a decision. "Perhaps Kathleen and Richard could escort Georgiana tonight."

He looked up hopefully. "Really?"

She smiled. "I am feeling very tired from all of our duties, and I think a quiet evening of rest would be best for the baby and me."

Darcy brightened instantaneously. "Yes! I will send Richard a note immediately!"

Elizabeth laughed. "Thank you, William, I feel better already!" She took his hand in hers and leaned in close to him. "What shall we do with our day now? I will not be spending hours on my hair and dress."

"Shall we take a walk? It promises to be a sunny day, perhaps we could walk down to Bond Street, or look in the book shops, or . . ."

"Or just hold hands and talk?" She smiled at his enthusiasm. "We have had very little time for ourselves since we left Pemberley."

He nodded. "Yes, if it was not for our morning exercise and sleeping," he smiled at her softly cleared throat, "I have barely seen you, well privately anyway. I miss you Lizzy." He kissed her hand.

She caressed his face. "I miss you, William. It seems we have time for everyone but ourselves."

They agreed to take a walk, and left the destination to the whims of their steps. Darcy wrote his note to Richard, and Elizabeth informed Georgiana of their change in plans. Soon they met by the front door, bundled for the cool spring day, and set off. Darcy looked down at Elizabeth and grinned. "It seems to me we were doing precisely this a year ago."

"Yes, and I must admit, my heart still skips a beat when you smile at me like that."

His smile grew. "Like what?"

Sighing she touched his face. "With those enticing dimples."

Darcy laughed. "Well my dear, I am pleased to send your heart fluttering, you send mine racing with your very fine eyes."

"Thank you my love." She hugged his arm, then touched her belly. "Would it not be wonderful if this child possessed both of our favourite features?"

"Oh my, then if we have a girl, we will have to lock her away in a tower to keep all of the suitors away." His eyes danced.

She sparkled back at him. "And if a boy, we will have to lecture him quite sternly about matchmaking mamas!"

He raised his brow and looked at her seriously. "I think we will have to do that in any case."

"Hmmm." She tilted her head and looked at him. "Have you thought of a name yet?"

"A little, have you?"

"I admit I have. You were named for your mother's family. Did you like being called Fitzwilliam?"

"Well as I do not go by it, I think you have your answer." His lips twitched and lifted in a small smile.

"Is it tradition to name the eldest son after the mother's family?"

"No, not at all, my father's name was George."

"I like that name." She said thoughtfully.

"Do you?" He regarded her pensive face. "Would you like to name a boy Bennet?"

She walked silently for several moments. "No."

He caressed her cheek and said softly, "It does not have to be about your father, it would be to honour you, Elizabeth."

She smiled up at him with shining eyes. "Thank you William." She took a breath and put forth her idea. "I think that instead of favouring one or the other, we might honour his father and grandfathers. I thought of William George Thomas Darcy."

He smiled. "I like that." He grinned mischievously. "And following your theory, if we have a girl, she would be Fanny Anne Darcy."

Elizabeth's eyes grew wide with horror. "Oh no, sir, I would not wish that on my daughter!"

"I would like a little Elizabeth someday." He said softly.

She hugged his arm, and then reached to caress his face. "Elizabeth Anne Francine Darcy?"

He was confused. "Who is Francine? I thought your mother's name is Fanny?"

"Mama could not say "Franny" when she was a child, so she became Fanny."

"Elizabeth Anne Francine, yes, but she could not be Lizzy. There is only one Lizzy." His eyes took on that possessive glint that made her heart race.

"Could we call her Beth?" She suggested.

"Yes, very nice, and a son could be Will, to avoid confusion with me." He looked lovingly into her eyes. She only called him Will at very private moments.

"Well that was easily settled! Although, I might need to think of another nickname for our son." Her steady gaze met his, and he nodded slowly in agreement.

They continued their long walk, talking about all of the neglected subjects that had been put aside in favour of the Season. They wandered into several bookshops, took tea together in a quiet shop he favoured, and enjoyed the very welcome and needed time alone.

RICHARD READ DARCY'S NOTE and started laughing. Lord Matlock looked at his wife and daughter-in-law. "Care to share, Son?"

He looked up at his father, grinning widely. "It seems that Darcy has signalled his surrender to the Season. He begs that Kathleen and I escort Georgiana to St. James' tonight."

Lord Matlock laughed, reading the letter. "How long did he last?"

"Three weeks, but if you think of the amount of socializing he has done in that time, he will not need to go out again for at least five years!" Everyone at the table joined in the laughter.

"I think that once he is a father, and Georgiana is safely married, he will be hard-pressed to ever leave Pemberley." Lady Matlock smiled.

Lord Matlock looked at his wife. "Can you blame him? Other than culture and a tailor, what does London offer him?"

"There is his club." Kathleen raised her brow and looked at Richard.

"Who needs a club when he has Elizabeth?" Lady Matlock shot him a look, and then turned to regard Kathleen. She suspected her son's fondness for Elizabeth had still not died.

Richard met his wife's gaze and grinned, "I, however, think my wife is overjoyed when I go to my club and leave her alone." Lady Matlock watched Kathleen's grin appear.

"Ah yes, my dear husband, you are quite correct, I am delighted to see the back of you." She pursed her lips and raised her brow.

"Ha!" He took her hand in his, and kissed it. "Just for that, my dear, I believe that I will have to remain by your side all day today."

She rolled her eyes. "Can I not be rid of you? Why not go and visit the Darcys? Apparently they are not busy!"

"No, my love, if Darcy has gained freedom from the ball tonight, I assure you, he will be keeping Elizabeth well occupied today."

Kathleen shook her head. "Poor woman."

Richard raised his brows. "You do not envy her being married to such a man?"

She smiled. "Well, he is quite handsome, I suppose if I were forced to, I would not object to his attentions."

Richard looked hurt. "You would not?"

She tilted her head. "Would you object to Elizabeth's?"

He smiled. "I would, without hesitation. I only love you."

Kathleen blinked back the tears that seemed to be constantly falling. "Then I suppose I will make do with only you, Richard."

Lord and Lady Matlock exchanged glances. They had seen a change coming gradually over the couple. They seemed closer, happier, and more open with each other. It seemed that Richard had indeed conquered his feelings for Elizabeth, and Kathleen knew it. Perhaps they had found a similar love.

Richard kissed her hand. "Shall we tell them the news?" She nodded.

"What news is this?" Lord Matlock demanded.

"You are to be grandparents, at the beginning of October!" He announced joyfully.

They gasped and rose to embrace each other. Questions flew and their happiness was shared by all. Richard had been dying to tell everyone about the baby since Kathleen told him, but forced himself to remain quiet, remembering the Darcys' loss and pain. That morning Kathleen had felt the quickening, and he insisted that it be a secret no longer. He could not wait to crow the news to his brother. For once, *he* was first with something.

"ALEX IS HERE." Elizabeth announced as she leaned in the doorway to Darcy's study.

He looked up from the letter he was reading and rolled his eyes. "Does he have a home? I mean, besides our sitting room?"

Elizabeth laughed and entered, closing the door behind her. She walked over to his chair and ran her fingers through his hair. He closed his eyes and sighed. "She is not alone with him, is she?"

Now Elizabeth rolled her eyes, thinking back on *their* courtship. "No, Mrs. Annesley is in the room."

"Good." He relaxed. "That feels so good, Lizzy." She smiled and continued her ministrations. "Do you think she is seeing too much of him? They are practically courting, but he has not approached me."

"I thought he had in June." She said softly.

He pinched the bridge of his nose, trying to stop the headache this subject always inspired. "I did not agree to a courtship. I said it was up to Georgiana. He has not declared himself to her."

She began gently massaging his temples. "Well clearly she has decided to accept his attentions. I think that all of the other young men have certainly realized that she only has eyes for Alex."

"This is your fault, you know." He rested his head against her growing belly.

She raised a brow. "Oh really? And how did I manage that?"

"You arranged that waltz with her at the ball. Everyone knew then that she was taken." There was an accusatory note in his voice.

Elizabeth stopped rubbing his head. "So you are telling me that a second dance scared away all of her suitors? You would prefer this house to have a constant stream of men rather than just one, and a very good friend of yours as well?"

His eyes opened and he looked up at her. "I wished for her to have a choice."

She moved away from him and crossed her arms over her chest. "Nobody is forcing her hand, William. She may reject Alex and move on to another man at any time."

He sat up and stared at her. "I think she may feel obligated to him. She knows how he put his life on hold to wait for her presentation."

"Oh really? And when did you last speak to her about this? Perhaps if you would stop burying yourself in this room and watch her with Alex, you would not be so afraid to see her happiness with him."

Darcy's voice rose. "I am *NOT* hiding in here! I have a great deal of work to do, and all of these social obligations are taking up too much time!"

Elizabeth snapped back. "Time that you were well aware had to be spent for your sister's benefit!"

He stood and began pacing. "Why, what is the point? Why must she attend these engagements if her decision is made?" He spun away and stood with his back to her, leaning on the window frame and staring at the peaceful garden full of spring blooms, deriving no comfort from the view.

Elizabeth glared at him, about to retort with a caustic remark when she saw the slight slump of his shoulders. She let out the breath she had drawn and closed her eyes to calm herself. She walked over to him and took the hand that hung limply at his side and squeezed. "It will be well, Will. You will have to let her grow up and leave home sometime." She brushed his cheek with the back of her fingers, and he sighed. He turned to embrace her, resting his head on hers.

"I know. For such a long time she was all that I had, even before Father died." They stood and held each other. "I am sorry for losing my temper, Lizzy. This is very hard for me."

"I know, darling. Forgive me for not realizing that sooner." She looked up at him. "Sometimes I forget that Georgie is more a daughter to you than a sister."

He laughed quietly. "Sometimes I forget that distinction, too." He kissed her. "Bear with me, my love. I could not do this without you."

"Well then, shall you come and greet Alex for a few minutes before returning to work?"

Darcy sighed and nodded. "It could be worse, I suppose. She could have chosen a man I dislike."

Elizabeth laughed. "And how convenient that he is already your brother!" He shook his head and kissing her hand, they left to greet their guest.

WHILE DARCY AND ELIZABETH TALKED, Alex entered the sitting room where Georgiana waited to receive him. "Good afternoon, Miss Darcy." He bowed and presented her with a bouquet of pink tulips.

"Oh how lovely! Thank you Mr. Carrington!" She held them to her face, drinking in the delicate scent of the flowers. Mrs. Annesley offered to place them in water, and left the two alone for a few moments. Alex wasted no time in advancing to her side and taking her hand to kiss her fingers. Her blush made him smile.

"I was correct!" He said with a pleased expression which covered his own blush.

"About what, sir?" She raised her eyes from the floor.

"The tulips are the exact shade of your cheeks when I touch your hand." Her blush became deeper. "Oh, well, it seems that I must bring red flowers next time." His eyes were twinkling at her.

"Mr. Carrington!"

He bent his head to hers. "Have I offended you Miss Darcy? I do not mean any harm."

"Sir, if you offend me, I will not hesitate to tell you." She lifted her chin defiantly.

He grinned. "I see that your sister has been giving you instruction on impertinence."

Georgiana's eyes opened wide. She did not realize how she had changed. "She has been a great influence on me."

Mrs. Annesley returned with the flowers in a crystal vase and the couple moved quickly apart, then sat next to each other on a small sofa. Alex glanced unhappily at the intruder, and adjusted his conversation to suit the company. "Will you be attending the Masterson's dinner party tomorrow evening?"

Georgiana sighed at his retreat to formality. "Yes, I understand that their eldest son attended Cambridge with you and William."

"Indeed, we spent many hours in company with him." Unable to resist, he became bolder. "I understand he has called on you several times?" He watched for her reaction.

Her face betrayed her surprise. "How would you know that?"

"Oh I have my sources." He said cryptically. "You seem to have received a great many callers." He again searched her face.

She huffed. "Is that not the point of a girl's Season, sir? To attract gentlemen to call on her? It would be quite sad if no man came around, would it not?"

Alex could not help but smile. "Indeed it would." His smile faded, and his face took on a worried expression.

She could see his anxiety and chose to give him a little gift. "If you were to ask my brother, he would say I have had only one gentleman caller of late, and the others have been frightened away."

Alex immediately brightened. "Is that so? And who is this frequent caller, and how were the others frightened? I hope this man has not become a nuisance?"

"No, his company is much welcomed." Georgiana dared to meet Alex's now intense stare, and she blushed anew with the touch of his hand when it crept over to lightly stroke hers. Mrs. Annesley's softly cleared throat reminded them of her presence but did nothing to calm her racing heart.

Desperate to have some privacy with her, Alex made a request. "Would you be interested in a walk in the park, Miss Darcy? It is a fine day."

She smiled widely. She had been trying to think of a way to be alone with him. "Oh yes, what a lovely idea." She turned to her companion. "Does that seem a pleasant idea, Mrs. Annesley?"

The older woman smiled knowingly. "It does indeed, Miss Darcy. Would you prefer your brother and sister walking out with you?"

Alex looked at Georgiana with panicked eyes. She stifled the laugh she felt. She no more wanted her brother as chaperone than Alex did. Elizabeth alone would be fine, but William would be breathing down their necks. "Oh no, I am sure they are too busy. I would be glad of your company."

"Certainly, Miss Darcy. I will just go and gather my things."

As soon as she left, Alex kissed Georgiana's hand. "Thank you. I enjoy your brother's company; he is one of my closest friends, however . . ."

"He does take his role of protector quite seriously, but I will never ever fault him for it. I owe him so much." She ended softly, thinking of Ramsgate, then looking up at the man she might never have known without her brother's care.

Alex watched her with concern. "Miss Darcy, are you well?" He squeezed the hand he had not relinquished.

Georgiana looked up into his worried eyes and felt a peace she had never known before. She shivered then pulled herself together. "Yes of course I am. I will just go and fetch my bonnet." She smiled and left the room, leaving Alex to wonder.

Elizabeth and Darcy arrived just in time to wish them a pleasant walk and to decline Georgiana's obviously insincere request for their company. Darcy stood at a window, watching them depart until Elizabeth took his hand and guided him back to the study. They left the door open so they would hear when the party returned.

BINGLEY SAT scowling at the letter in his hand. Jane, well over seven months pregnant, entered his study and was taken aback by the very uncharacteristic expression on his face. "Charles! Whatever is wrong?"

So angry was he that it took several more attempts and Jane's cautiously applied hand on his arm to draw him back. He blinked and looked up to her concerned gaze. "Jane, I did not see you enter!"

"Obviously, Charles. Please tell me what is wrong?"

He sighed. "It seems we are to receive an unexpected and honestly unwanted visitor. Caroline is coming, and will likely arrive today."

"Oh Charles!"

"I am sorry Jane; I do not see how we can refuse her."

Jane sank slowly into the chair opposite his desk and closed her eyes. "How long does she say she will stay?"

"She does not."

"Charles, Elizabeth and William are planning to come here in four weeks and stay until the baby comes. I want my sister with me at that time. You and I both know that William will not stay under the same roof with Caroline."

Bingley nodded and rubbed his face. "I know, Jane. Darcy is always ready to listen to me speak to him about Caroline, but he has no intention of ever spending time with her again. I will speak to her when she comes. Perhaps she only plans to stay a short time." He looked up at his wife. They both knew that was wishful thinking.

"Perhaps I should write to Elizabeth; maybe she could speak to William, and make an exception." Jane said half-heartedly.

"Please wait to do that, dear. We have four weeks. Perhaps Caroline has changed. I wish for us all to get along. I hate the thought of my sister's presence under our roof keeping the Darcys away." He was a man who hated conflict, but he saw his wife's distressed face. "I am so sorry Jane."

"Charles, I know how difficult it was for you to . . . let Caroline go her own way. You have so little family, but your aunt's letters . . . she says that Caroline is so odd, so unhappy, her rages and then times of calm. It seems so frightening!"

"Yes, but what can we do? She is not mentally incompetent, we cannot put her in Bedlam, she is angry, that is all." His frustration was apparent, and he raked his hand through his already unruly hair.

Jane sat forward on her chair and pleaded to him. "But her anger is directed to Elizabeth! She still sees her as the reason for her situation, and does she still not harbour feelings for William?"

Charles nodded. "It seems so."

"What might she do if she sees either of them?" Jane was worried.

"I cannot imagine her harming either one of them. If anything, I foresee a verbal confrontation." He added softly, "One that might cost me my best friend."

"Oh Charles, we must tell them!" She rose and came to stand next to him.

He took her hand. "Well, she is arriving today. Let us see what she is like. Let us give her a chance. Perhaps . . . perhaps all will be well. We have some time. I am truly hoping that we will all get along."

"As am I." She straightened her shoulders. "Well, if we are to have a guest, I had best alert the staff to prepare a room for her. I will not tell Elizabeth she is here." She smiled slightly, hoping for the best. "If she remains here when they come, perhaps it would be best to leave it as a surprise."

He returned her small smile. "A pleasant one, I hope." They shook their heads and returned to their duties. Bingley knew it was wrong to keep this news from Darcy, and he sincerely hoped his sister would be gone before they came. He hated the deceit. He hated being stuck in such a difficult position between his sister, and his friend and brother, and most of all, he hated being so weak. He determined to stand up to Caroline and show her he would not put up with her disruptive behaviour anymore.

Caroline arrived late that afternoon and from the number of trunks removed from the hired carriage, it appeared that she had brought everything she owned and was intending to stay for quite some time. She exited the coach and looked over Lyndon Hall with a critical eye. To anyone else it would appear a fine estate, a beautiful, well-tended park, with towering oaks lining the long drive. The house itself was about the same size as Netherfield, and as the name implied, was built for entertaining, perfect for the personality of its owner. But Caroline was disappointed. She had imagined the estate Charles would purchase to be akin to Pemberley. Lyndon Hall was not in any way comparable, not by size, or by majesty. Obviously Charles did not have good advice and was hoarding their father's money.

Bingley and Jane stepped forward. "Welcome to our home, Caroline. This is quite a surprise." He kissed her cheek.

"I hope your journey was pleasant." Jane smiled, her serene expression masking her distress, and led her into the drawing room, offering tea.

Caroline took in the room, disappointed; the furniture was of an earlier era. "The trip was a nightmare. The quality of inns is quite poor between here and Scarborough." She scanned Jane's very pregnant figure, angry that she was to be the spinster aunt. She turned to her brother. "You have a very small park and the house is much less than I expected, Charles."

Angering, he snapped at her. "What exactly did you expect Caroline? I made an exceptionally fortunate purchase with Lyndon Hall. The house came furnished, and with those savings I was able to afford an estate with lands far larger than our father's funds would otherwise have purchased. Darcy helped me quite extensively in identifying it and in negotiating the purchase. I am very proud of this estate. Nobody invited you here, Caroline. If you intend to stay, I suggest that you adjust your opinion."

Caroline stared at him in shock and Jane regarded him with pride. "I do not appreciate your tone, Charles!"

"And I do not appreciate your rude behaviour! Now, change your attitude, and we may permit you to stay." He rose and stared out of the window. It took a very great effort to stand up to Caroline, and he knew that he would not be able to fend her off for much longer.

Caroline regarded her brother's back. She really had no place to go. Her aunt had practically ordered her away from Scarborough, and repeatedly reminded her that it was time to find her own home, alone. She did not want to live by herself and knew that she needed to ingratiate herself with her brother. She also desperately hoped for the opportunity to see Mr. Darcy again. She could not let him go; her years of obsession with him had become an integral part of her being.

"Very well, Charles. I will try to appreciate your home."

Relieved, Bingley smiled. "Thank you, Caroline; I am sure that you will."

APRIL ARRIVED and Elizabeth's condition could no longer be hidden by her skirts. Her little bump had expanded to the size of ball. It was time to leave for Pemberley. Darcy was thrilled for many reasons. He was delighted to escape the Season, he was anxious to perform his duties at home, and most of all, it meant that the time was passing and he and Elizabeth would soon be parents. Georgiana's belongings were packed and the family gathered at Matlock House to welcome her and farewell the couple.

After the family dinner, the gentlemen retired to Lord Matlock's library for their port. "Well Darcy, have you any late instructions for us before relinquishing Georgiana's Season to our supervision?" Lord Matlock asked.

Darcy grimaced. "I think that she is safe in your hands, Uncle."

"Is there any gentleman in particular you favour or not?"

He sipped his drink. He had watched Georgiana and Alex carefully every time they met. Alex was at nearly every dance, called on her, took walks, attended their church, did everything he could to court her. He had never wavered. Elizabeth assured him of Georgiana's feelings and Alex's sincerity.

"Alex Carrington."

"Yes?"

Darcy sighed. "I have spoken to him. He asked for permission to court her. I have granted it." He looked miserable.

"You seem unhappy, Darcy." He just glanced at his uncle. "You do not wish to let go." He nodded, understanding.

"No, but I must. Elizabeth's father was the example of a man who could not let go. I will not be that man." He sighed. "Alex is a good man."

Lord Matlock regarded Darcy carefully. "I hope you have many sons, Darcy. I hate to see you let another girl go."

Darcy smiled. "I will be overjoyed with any child."

That evening when he said goodbye to Georgiana, he felt as if he would never see her again. Gone was the little girl he played with and then tried to protect and raise. The next time he saw her, she would be a woman, one he would have to give to another man. He kissed her goodbye and climbed into the carriage to return to his home. In the darkness he was so glad that Elizabeth was with him. He was not facing this alone.

Chapter 41

aroline stood near the window of her bedchamber, looking out at the park of Lyndon Hall. The warm spring breeze brought with it the scent of the flower beds, now bursting with colour and new life after the cold Derbyshire winter. Cold as it was, it could not compare to the harsh winter she experienced at Scarborough. There she had only the company of her Aunt Rachel, and the other older relatives who still worked there in trade, some working for her brother. The bleakness of the setting only mirrored her mood. Her despondency and then regular fits of rage drove the servants to avoid her. Her aunt, a widow in her fifties with no patience for poor behaviour, lectured her almost constantly on improving her deportment, and threatened her with homelessness if she did not change her ways. Caroline refused to change. She was sure that at any moment Louisa or Charles would remember her, and feeling guilty for her exile, send for her with offers of residence in their homes and funds to again put her back in society. But other than letters telling of their news, their annoyingly happy news she noted, no offer of hospitality was given. Louisa and Hurst seemed to be spending a great deal of time at his father's estate. Apparently his drinking was now so moderate that he was almost accused of being a teetotaller. His disposition now so lively, that his parents wished for him to live with them, and were eager to see him take the reins of the family's estate, an estate ironically smaller than Lyndon Hall.

Then there was Charles. He was now one of the landed gentry, fulfilling his father's dream to raise the Bingley name to one of respect in society. She knew that it would be his great-grandchildren who would truly be the ones to benefit from this first step into society. Their money was too new, too tainted with the smell of trade, but nonetheless, with the purchase of this land, and Jane's pregnancy, he had set the wheels in motion. He was different now; the estate had given him confidence. His marriage had given him security. He would not be easily manipulated to her needs anymore. His focus was elsewhere. But he had not completely cast her off. Until she found her own home, he still managed the income from her dowry.

She noticed Charles and Jane taking a slow stroll around the gardens. From this distance, and with the shadow of the trees, Jane resembled Elizabeth. That thought once again sent her into a fit of rage. How dare she take Mr. Darcy from her!

Caroline attempted to gain control of herself. Her plans would not come to fruition if Darcy met her and saw that she was anything but perfect. Certainly by now he had seen what a mistake he had made with Elizabeth. Certainly by now he had tired of her impertinence. She knew that Louisa was correct. Mr. Darcy would never subject himself to the shame of divorce, and the man she remembered was too proud to admit that he had made an error. She knew that barring Elizabeth's death, the position of Mistress of Pemberley was irrevocably filled. Caroline had *almost* come to peace with that. What she was still unwilling to give up was Mr. Darcy himself. Ever since that last night at Netherfield . . . she closed her eyes, reliving watching him again, imagining his movement and feeling the flood of desire spread over her, dropping her hand to rub the ache . . . she *had* to see him again. With Elizabeth pregnant, he *must* be unsatisfied. Now, perhaps, he would like her as his mistress . . . She was teetering on the edge of sanity and did not know it.

In the garden Jane and Charles walked in silence. Neither one wished to break the moment of peace. Bingley glanced at her serene expression out of the corner of his eye and squeezed the hand that lay on his arm. She looked over at him and smiled. "Jane, what is your opinion on Caroline? Do you think she has changed?"

"Well, it has not been long, but since you spoke to her when she arrived she has been quite cordial and friendly. I would say she is very pleasant. It is such a relief after reading your aunt's letters. Perhaps she simply needed to leave Scarborough. She has been there for nearly a year without seeing you." She reached over with her free hand and touched his cheek. "She must have missed you."

He looked at her hopefully. "Do you think so?"

"I do." She smiled. "Perhaps all will be well."

He nodded eagerly. "Well, there are over three more weeks before the Darcys arrive."

"I am not entirely comfortable not telling them, Charles." Jane said softly. "But I do not know what I will do if they do not come." She looked at him anxiously.

"I do not like it either, Jane, but I agree; I need them here, too." He sighed. They knew it was taking a risk to deceive them, and hoped Caroline's behaviour would continue to be pleasant. Their gaze met and they walked on.

"OH MRS. DARCY! Just look at you!" Mrs. Reynolds beamed and could not resist touching Elizabeth's belly when Darcy escorted her into Pemberley. "It is such a joy to know that soon these halls will be filled with the sound of a child's voice. You must be so very happy!" The older woman was practically in tears with her joy.

Elizabeth smiled up at her laughing husband and squeezed her housekeeper's hand. "Yes, Mrs. Reynolds we are extraordinarily happy, and are especially happy to be home now."

Mrs. Reynolds looked up to Darcy. "Now sir, you had best be taking good care of Mrs. Darcy. I will not have you overtiring her!" She glared at him.

Darcy looked at her with surprise. "Yes, madam!"

Elizabeth laughed. "Oh no, now I have two mother hens clucking at me!" Darcy blushed and Mrs. Reynolds nodded. Between them and the rest of Pemberley's staff, Elizabeth would have her every need fulfilled, whether she liked it or not.

The pair quickly settled back into their routine of running the estate. With the spring planting imminent, Darcy had much work to do with Mr. Regar before they must depart for Lyndon Hall. Elizabeth took great delight in watching the refurbishment of the long-empty nursery. Mrs. Reynolds presented her with baby clothes that she had made through the years in anticipation of a future heir to

Pemberley, and Elizabeth, upon holding the tiny garments in her hands, burst into happy tears which seemed to inspire a great round of activity for the outfits' future owner. Many times Darcy would come upstairs in search of her to find that she had fallen asleep in the great old rocker placed in the room, and would gather her up and carry her off to their honeymoon chair so he could rest with her. Both of them were enjoying this brief time of solitude.

One morning Darcy arose at dawn, and dressed. He returned to sit on the edge of the bed and found Elizabeth awake and waiting for him. "I wish that you did not have to go." She wrapped her arms around his waist.

"I wish that I did not either, but unfortunately, it is part of my duties." He kissed her head. "With this early start, Mr. Regar and I should be able to speak to all of the tenants of our plans and hopefully be home in time for dinner."

"You will be exhausted." She stroked the hair from his brow, and looked at him with concern.

Darcy laughed. "I will be fine. Now I expect you to rest."

"Oh William, I am perfectly healthy. Tell me to rest when I am as big as this house!" Her eyes sparkled at him.

"Very well, but please promise me you will not walk far or alone." He kissed her gently. "Please." Their eyes met and held.

"I promise, Will." He nodded and bent to kiss her again, then with a wave from the door, was on his way.

After a lazy morning and long bath, Elizabeth wandered downstairs to a late breakfast. She sat alone at the table, and was relieved when a footman entered with a note.

Mrs. Darcy,
I realize this is very short notice, but if you are available, I would like to invite you to come spend the day with me. I enjoyed so much meeting you and your sister, and was delighted to learn that you and Mr. Darcy had returned to Derbyshire. My coachman will wait for your answer, and will of course provide transportation.
Sincerely,
Sarah Hill

Elizabeth smiled. She remembered Mrs. Hill, a quiet, friendly woman, who seemed vastly uncomfortable in the society of the rather effusive Derbyshire ladies. She reminded her of Jane in many ways. To have her send a note requesting Elizabeth's company so soon after their return indicated either a great loneliness or at the least, a desire for a friend. A year ago, Elizabeth would have instantly agreed to the meeting and entered the coach without a thought, but now, no. She could imagine William's panic if he came home early and found her gone. She went to their study and sat down to pen her reply.

Mrs. Hill,
I would very much enjoy spending the day with you; however, I find I am unable to leave Pemberley today. If you are available, you are welcome to join me here, as my husband is away all day and I would enjoy the company. I look forward to knowing you better.

Sincerely,
Elizabeth Darcy

She sealed the note and gave it to be delivered to the Hill's coachman. She smiled. It would be wonderful to have a friend here. Jane was close, but not close enough for daily talks, and she knew the Hills lived in a country house nearby. An hour later a second note arrived, indicating that Mrs. Hill also could not leave home, but instead offered to invite both Darcys to dinner the following week. Elizabeth liked that idea even more, and sent back a note of acceptance. It was obvious that word had quickly spread that they were returned, as many other invitations began to appear throughout the day. She looked at them and sighed. They had escaped town only to be thrown back into the social rounds of Derbyshire. She was actually surprised at the number of invitations, expecting most of the prominent residents to be in London for the Season. Perhaps she and William were not the only ones anxious to return to the clean air of the countryside. Or perhaps he was not the only dedicated farmer in the area. As predicted, William did return hours earlier than he originally planned and she was pleased with her decision to stay home, particularly when he spotted her resting in a chaise on a sunny balcony and smiling broadly, swept her up in his arms and insisted he could not possibly remove all of the road dust without his wife's thorough assistance in his bath.

A few days before they were to depart for Lyndon Hall, Elizabeth was discussing household plans with Mrs. Reynolds in her own office when a maid entered with a small box, curtseyed and left. Elizabeth glanced at it and continued with her orders for household supplies when she noted her housekeeper's sad expression. "Mrs. Reynolds, are you well?"

"Yes, Mrs. Darcy." She sighed and handed her the box. "I have kept these, and had them laundered. I hope very much that they will finally be put to good use."

Elizabeth opened the box and inside she found dozens of baby items, gowns, bonnets, socks and booties, some knitted, some exquisitely embroidered, all beautiful. She looked up with a smile. "You have already given me such beautiful things; did you make these as well?"

"No, Mrs. Darcy. These clothes were made by Mr. Darcy's mother."

Her smile grew, "How wonderful! But why were they never used for William or Georgiana?"

Mrs. Reynolds wiped a tear. "Each time that Mrs. Darcy was with child, she began making new outfits. Each time she lost the child, she asked that I destroy them. I never did."

Elizabeth gasped. "These are for the ones who never came." Mrs. Reynolds nodded. "How many were there?" She said, now sadly fingering the tiny garments.

"There were six others, all after your Mr. Darcy's birth. She lost them all at about the same point . . ."

"As I did." Elizabeth finished. She looked up to Mrs. Reynolds. "Did William know that she was with child?"

"I think he knew of the first, after that loss, she no longer said anything, so I doubt that anyone but I ever knew."

"She did not tell her husband?" Mrs. Reynolds shook her head. "But why?"

Mrs. Reynolds smiled. "Mrs. Darcy suffered greatly after Mr. Darcy's birth. She took months to recover. She was a very delicate woman. I met the late Miss de Bourgh once, and they were very similar, so perhaps you have an idea there. Old Mr. Darcy did not truly realize how ill she was, as she hid it so well, and after the first miscarriage, and seeing his distress, she decided to keep the pregnancies secret until she was sure all was well. It was not until Miss Darcy's birth that her body finally gave out."

"What exactly did take her life? William has never spoken of it, although he was just a boy at the time."

"She laboured for two days with Miss Darcy. When she was finally able to complete the delivery, she was exhausted and never recovered." Mrs. Reynolds began to cry with the memory. Elizabeth held her hand and she pulled herself together. "Forgive me Mrs. Darcy. I do not mean to frighten you by telling you these things; I just thought it would please Mrs. Darcy so much in heaven if she could look down and see her grandchild wearing the clothes that she made."

Elizabeth wiped her eyes and squeezed her hand. "I think it is a wonderful idea, and you have not frightened me at all. I cannot wait to see these things on our baby where they belong, not waiting in a box. I am so glad that you saved them for our child." She rose and left the room, carrying the box up to the nursery. She carefully lifted out each item, laying them out and admiring the fine work when she felt a pair of large hands creep around her waist and warm breath on her neck, followed by lips nibbling her ear.

"What have you there, my beautiful wife?" Elizabeth leaned back into his embrace, and lost herself in the sound of his deep voice.

Shaking her head to clear it from the lovely place he was taking her, she smiled. "It is a baby gift."

"From whom?" He said, now gently caressing her swelling belly.

"Your mother." She softly said. His hands stopped and he turned her around.

"My mother?" He looked at her with confusion.

She nodded. "She made these, and they were never worn. Mrs. Reynolds saved them hoping that someday your child would use them."

Darcy looked at the garments anew, and a great dimpled smile spread over his face. "I do not know what to say, to have something my mother made be worn by our baby, I am so delighted! I will have to thank Mrs. Reynolds." He beamed. "They were never used? Why did she make them? Surely Georgiana could have worn them?"

Elizabeth had no intention of distressing him. "Perhaps they were put aside and forgotten."

He knit his brow, and then smiled. "Well, I am so happy they will be used as they were intended now." He hugged her.

"So am I, William." She tilted her head back and stood on her toes to kiss his lips.

"Mmmmmm. Lizzy, is it not time for you to take a nap?" He mumbled against her mouth.

"Will I actually experience rest, my love?" He laughed and looked down into her sparkling eyes.

He kissed her nose and taking her hand he led her into their room. "Eventually."

"WHEN SHALL WE LEAVE for Derbyshire, Thomas?" Mrs. Bennet asked as she entered her husband's library and took a seat before his desk.

Mr. Bennet regarded his excited wife from over his glasses. "I was not aware that we had been invited. Have you received a letter from one of our daughters?"

"Well, no, but Jane's confinement will soon be over. Surely she will want her mother by her side when the baby comes!" She beamed at him.

"Fanny, until we receive their invitation, I will not impose ourselves upon them. I understand that Lizzy and Mr. Darcy will be coming to stay with them and will remain until the birth."

"Oh, but Lizzy has never been present at a birth, what help can she give? It is at times like this that a girl needs her mother. I will do the same when Lizzy's time comes." She said this with great confidence.

"Mrs. Bennet, despite the fact that we have two very well-situated daughters, WE are not in possession of excess funds. We will not be making two trips to Derbyshire. Jane has indicated that they will welcome our visit in September. By that time, both of our grandchildren will have arrived, and we can enjoy meeting them together. As I know that Lizzy approves of this plan, I cannot go against it."

"But we could at least go in August so I could be with Lizzy . . ."

"No, Fanny. I will not go to Pemberley without Mr. Darcy's explicit desire." His voice held a tone of resignation to it.

Mrs. Bennet sighed, she truly wished to be with her daughters at this most frightening and wonderful moment in their lives, but was also aware that the years of her silly behaviour had most likely driven them to desire her absence. She looked at her husband. They had become so close over the last months. It was extraordinary. They were almost as happy as they had been when they first married. No, that was wrong, happier, because now they had years of shared experience between them, and knew each other so well. A new sensitivity to him had blossomed, and she sensed a great weight on his shoulders. "Thomas, what is wrong between you and Mr. Darcy?"

He startled out of his reverie. "I do not wish to discuss it Fanny."

"Please, Thomas, we have made great progress, and you are obviously sad." She got up and stood near his chair, and caressed his hair.

He sighed and rose, and taking her hand led her to the sofa near the window. Mrs. Bennet knew nothing of what he had done, or of the events at Pemberley a year before. "I will not give you all of the details. They are inconsequential now. Just suffice it to say, when Mr. Darcy asked me for permission to court Lizzy, I objected in a most cruel way. I accused him of atrocious behaviours and told Lizzy that he would be unfaithful to her in an effort to change her mind. I made great efforts to learn of his character, and when I found nothing wanting, I attempted to engage someone to try to separate them. When Mr. Darcy came and asked for my consent for their marriage, I refused . . ." He stared at the floor, then closed his eyes, the tears coming quickly. "And then I saw my family walking towards Meryton, and knew that I had one chance to still keep my daughter somehow in my life, so I ran after you. I saw the door to the church close and I ran as fast as I could to catch up and thankfully, in time to give her away to the best man I have ever known." He looked back up to his wife. "Something that I did to try and prevent their attachment led to a horrible act of violence being perpetrated upon

Lizzy. She nearly died." Mrs. Bennet gasped. "Mr. Darcy, who already had no respect for me, was desirous to end all contact with me forever. It was only our daughter who saved me from that fate. Mr. Darcy is right to hold me in disdain. I will never go to Pemberley without his express consent. I will never do anything to raise his ire again." He hung his head.

"What happened to Elizabeth?" Mrs. Bennet asked. She never admitted it, her jealousy over her daughter's monopoly of her husband's attention got in the way, but deep down, she always admired her second daughter, and truly did love her very much, even though she was not the son she had dearly hoped to have.

Mr. Bennet shook his head. "I cannot speak of it." He looked at his wife, and realized this woman before him now could bear the truth, where the Fanny Bennet of a year previous could not. He rose and went to his desk and unlocked a drawer. He removed a bundle of letters tied with a long pink ribbon, and without even needing to look, removed a very much-read letter. He walked back to the sofa and handed it to her. "I will let Elizabeth tell you." He sat back and watched as Fanny opened the letter, then saw the expression of horror and pain that crossed her face. Then he observed as the expression changed to one of admiration and contentment. She was reading her daughter's description of her husband. When she finished, she handed the letter back to her husband, and he returned it to the stack and locked it away again. "You say that you caused this to happen to her?"

He nodded. "She said that I am not culpable, but I will go to my grave believing that I am. Mr. Darcy agrees with me."

Mrs. Bennet made the greatest effort she had ever had to think and speak in a sensible, reasoned manner. "It was a year ago. She is well, happy, about to be a mother. We have been welcomed into their home, and I believe Mr. Darcy treated you with civility."

"It is more than I deserve." He said bitterly.

"And he has granted it, Thomas. I think, someday, if you continue with the course of civility you have begun with him, he may allow you to address him by his name." She smiled and grasped his hand.

He laughed. "That would be progress indeed, Fanny. You set the bar quite high!"

She smiled. It was not often she could give him a tease like that. "Well then, it seems we will spend the summer at Longbourn. That is well; surely we can spend that time finding suitable young men for Mary and Kitty!"

Mr. Bennet groaned. "You will never rest, madam!" He kissed her hand and she bustled out of the room. He sat back behind the desk, lost in thoughts of his daughters.

LORD MATLOCK regarded the nervous countenance of Georgiana's suitor. Alex had been invited to dine at Matlock House for the first time and meet officially the rest of the family. They were all there, all of the Fitzwilliams, including Aunt Catherine. Georgiana was just as nervous as he, not that she was afraid he would not do well, but because she knew the Fitzwilliams were all very fond of disconcerting unsuspecting people.

"May I thank you again, sir, for inviting me to your home this evening." Alex said, addressing the Earl.

"From what I understand, Mr. Carrington, you have been here many times before." Lord Matlock watched Alex squirm uncomfortably.

"Uh, I, yes, I have been fond of this street, and have, uh, often found myself walking this way." He swallowed under his piercing gaze.

"And riding, and staring. . ." Richard added with his brow raised.

"Just what did you find fascinating?" Mark asked, turning to look at his cousin's suitor.

Alex's eyes travelled from one man to the next. *What do I do now?* He thought desperately. "This is unfair, you know. At least if Darcy was here, I would have a friend in the room."

"Ha!" Richard laughed. "Friend or no, Darcy is extraordinarily protective of the women in his life, which number two, one blonde, one brunette. He charged us to care for one while he is devoted to the other. No sir, I doubt that you would be spared the inquisition if he were present."

Lord Matlock nodded and pointed his glass of port at Alex. "He is quite right, you know. Darcy would sooner rip your heart out than see Georgiana harmed in any way. And of course my son here," He indicated Richard, "still is very much in possession of his sword."

"And knows how to use it." Richard added with a taut smile.

Mark laughed. "Enough! I think you have warned him enough." He turned to Alex. "You have been given Darcy's permission to court our cousin, which is an extraordinary endorsement. What we want to know is why you wish for her. She is very young, yet."

Alex felt defensive. "Yes, she is, but if Darcy and Elizabeth felt that she was too young or immature to wed, they would not have introduced her to society this Season. It was as much their decision as hers."

Mark nodded. "Granted, but you have not answered the question. Why Georgiana? Surely you have not been without female companionship. Why her?"

Alex stood and paced around the room, aware of the eyes upon his back. He finally turned and faced the inquisitional board. "You are correct, I have hardly been bereft of companionship of one sort or another, and when I was younger, I found the company of ladies to be, exciting, challenging perhaps, however, I found that as I grew older I wanted more than a pretty face or pleasing form to decorate my arm. I wanted more." He passed by the three men, each in quite different marriages. "I am not insanely rich, like a certain relative of yours." He paused and they smiled at his reference to Darcy. "But I am, or rather, will be, in possession of a fair-sized estate and a desirable income. I am not, therefore, free of the matchmaking mamas. I know of society's dictate for me to choose a woman with a dowry that will increase the value of my estate, and to choose her dispassionately, but after seeing my parents' marriage, I felt disinclined to make a marriage of convenience, yet, not brave enough to risk the censure of society. I am not of the highest circles and frankly could not really risk it."

Mark looked down. He *was* of the highest circles, and *did* make such a marriage, and regretted it. Alex continued, "I watched as friend after friend married, for various reasons, but out of ten, perhaps one was a love match, and few of the others blossomed into more than a friendship." He sighed. "And then I saw Darcy. He found the most extraordinary woman, and did not let anything get in his way." He looked and saw the three men with wistful expressions, all for different reasons. "I was taken with Georgiana when I spotted her one day in the company of her aunt. I knew immediately that she was not artificial like the ladies of the *ton.* Perhaps it was her youth, and not yet being exposed to the simpering behaviour, but I felt almost instinctively that her kindness, her being was, somehow, untainted, pure, and was naturally so, and unlikely to change." He looked down in frustration. "I wanted that. I wanted that kindness to be extended to me. I knew that as Darcy's sister she was exposed to things that other women would never experience, so her mind was broadened and challenged. Then knowing Elizabeth, and the influence she would have on her, well I was sure that she would be magnificent by the time she came out, and I was correct. Georgiana is both beautiful and fascinating. How could I let that slip through my fingers?" He faced Lord Matlock.

"You cannot." He said quietly.

"Do you love her?" Richard asked.

"Or do you love the ideal that you think she represents?" Mark added.

Alex sighed. "That is the final question that I must answer before I present my suit."

"Well then sir, if that day comes, we will certainly know that you took into account possibilities that most men never consider. So, I suggest that we return to the ladies now, and you can continue your courtship. I know that Georgiana is anxiously awaiting you. She, it seems, has made a decision." He looked at Alex's startled face significantly, and led the way out of the room.

THE LADIES SETTLED into the music room, tea was poured, the servants departed, and a blanket of silence fell over them. Georgiana anxiously looked around and wished profoundly that Elizabeth was there. Lady Matlock spoke first. "Mr. Carrington seems to be a very pleasant young man."

Georgiana looked up gratefully. "Oh yes, he is. I have been introduced to so many gentlemen since my presentation, and not one has compared to him."

"He seems fond of his parents and home." Kathleen offered.

Again Georgiana smiled and eagerly agreed. "I have not met his parents yet, but William and Elizabeth like them very much."

Laura was watching the excited smile of her cousin. "Well, it is a step down for you, but considering William's choice, perhaps it is the best you can expect."

Lady Matlock looked at her daughter-in-law sharply. "What do you mean?"

Laura shrugged and adjusted her gown before meeting her gaze. "Before William married so far below himself, I would have expected Georgiana to be married into a titled family or at least to a landowner of equal status to her brother. However it seems the Darcy name has fallen in consequence, if her suitor is a man of only seven thousand a year."

"Honestly Laura, some of the ideas that come out of your mouth!" Lady Matlock looked at her with frustration. She sent a glance to Lady Catherine, who had surprisingly not weighed in as yet. She was focusing on Georgiana.

Kathleen took Georgiana's hand. "There is nothing wrong with Mr. Carrington. It is very clear that he cares for you, and I would hardly call seven thousand a trifling income. Why, Rosings brings in eight thousand, and I recall Mark telling Richard he could have married almost any woman, but he admired that Richard chose to marry me for love." She smiled.

"He did not say that!" Laura stared at her sister.

"He certainly did!" Kathleen glared at her.

Georgiana drew herself up and jumped into the fray. "How can you say that Elizabeth was a poor choice for William? They love each other and she has changed him so much. He is so happy now!"

Laura moved her glare from Kathleen to her cousin. "There is more to marriage than love."

"Do you mean money?" Georgiana asked.

"Money, power, connection, it was the reason I married as I did."

Lady Matlock laughed coldly, "Yes, and it is obvious by how very happy you both are. I am grateful that George Darcy helped us to realize the importance of a love match, or Darcy would never have found Elizabeth and would be as happy as you are now."

"I am content." She said with narrowed eyes.

"Where are my grandchildren, then?" Lady Matlock lifted her brow.

"I do not seem to recall you objecting to your son's choice at the wedding." Laura replied icily.

"That was before you turned from a pleasant young woman to a status-obsessed shrew!" She shot back

Kathleen jumped in. "Mr. Carrington's estate is quite large."

"It is nothing to Pemberley." Laura said dismissively, still shooting daggers at her mother-in-law.

"Neither is Matlock, but you do not hear me complaining." Lady Matlock met her gaze.

"You married an Earl. That makes up for the smaller estate."

Georgiana had heard enough of the fight. "I do not care of his estate!" Lady Catherine's brow rose with interest. Georgiana closed her eyes, remembering and finally understanding Elizabeth's description of love. "Mr. Carrington . . ." She paused, gathering her thoughts and determination. "Mr. Carrington makes me happy; he brings me a feeling of regard, trust, safety, and joy. I want to care for him, and fulfil his dreams, and I hope to share my dreams with him. I think that I need him to feel complete. I want to give myself to him. No amount of money could every buy that feeling! A title or status is meaningless when you are home alone with the person you married! I know that. I have witnessed first-hand what a true passionate and loving marriage is, and that is what I want for myself. I hope that someday Mr. Carrington will give me that opportunity. I will never settle for a marriage of convenience when I can be loved!" Georgiana gasped, spent from expressing herself so forcefully, but quickly straightened her back and looked around the room. Elizabeth would not crumple at this moment, so neither would she.

Kathleen and Lady Matlock smiled at her with approval. Laura stared at her, facing the raw truth of her empty marriage, and wondering if it could ever approach the shocking description she just heard. Lady Catherine was the one who finally broke the silence.

"Well, Niece. For a very long time I thought as she did." She nodded towards Laura and returned her gaze to Georgiana. "I wished for my daughter's entire lifetime that she make a marriage of convenience to your brother. Not once did I consider either of their opinions on the matter because feelings such as love are not important in our world. The only thing that mattered was keeping the money in the family and advancing the name. It was why I married, it was why your aunt married, and it was why your mother married. Of all of us, I refused to allow the marriage to grow beyond the business contract that it was. I provided a daughter, but became so disgusted with my husband's drinking and mistresses that I refused to provide his heir. The lack of affection hardened me to him. My marriage fortunately ended when his habits caught up with him." She sniffed. "I suppose that I never gave the marriage a chance to become more than it was. He did make overtures at the beginning, but my heart remained cold, which likely drove him to the habits I so abhorred. I recognize the same behaviour in you, Laura. I suggest that you change things now while there is still time." She addressed her red-faced niece and returned her attention to Georgiana. "I have observed your brother and his wife, and although I wish that such a gentleman would have married my Anne, I know that only Elizabeth could have coaxed his true self to emerge from the mask that society forced him to wear. I would be truly a cruel woman to deny him that which is so obviously what he needed, and I cannot deny the same of you. If your Mr. Carrington is of the same calibre of man as Darcy, you would do well to secure him, and be glad of it."

"Thank you, Aunt Catherine, I will!" Georgiana rose and went to embrace her.

Lady Catherine accepted her kiss on the cheek then batted her away. "Enough of this display young lady; go and resume your seat. Excess of emotion is not to be displayed in such a public setting. It would do well for you to remind your brother and sister of that!" She huffed and rearranged her gown.

At that moment the door opened and the men returned. Alex's eyes went straight to find Georgiana's, and seeing her distress he instantly was at her side. He took her hands and said urgently, "Miss Darcy, are you well?"

She looked up into his concerned gaze and smiled brilliantly up at him. "I am now."

He gasped at seeing for the first time passion in her eyes for him and returned her smile full-force. He kissed her hand. "I am so very glad."

The sound of laughter broke the spell. "Georgiana! Enough of this! Be seated immediately!" Lady Catherine's irritated voice filled the room. Georgiana and Alex blushed and let go of each other, but did not break their gaze.

"Yes Aunt, anything you say."

Chapter 42

*D*arcy and Elizabeth were surprised upon arriving at Lyndon Hall to be met not by their hosts, but by the housekeeper. "I am so sorry, Mr. and Mrs. Darcy, but Mrs. Bingley is lying down and Mr. Bingley was called out to address a problem on the estate. I will show you to your rooms."

Elizabeth smiled. "That is quite all right Mrs. Pritchett; I can certainly understand my sister's fatigue and my brother's duties. Please show us where we are to stay."

Soon they were in their chambers and the trunks were being noisily delivered to the dressing rooms. Elizabeth turned to Darcy, "William, do you mind if I follow Jane's example and lie down for a little while?"

He looked at her with concern. "Are you tired? I am so sorry Lizzy. I should have let you sleep in the carriage."

She leaned into his arms. "Mmmm, we were much more agreeably occupied." She smiled up at him and caressed his chest.

Darcy looked down at her, whispering. "If we were not currently surrounded by servants . . ."

Elizabeth laughed and stood on her toes to kiss his chin. "Yes, I know my love, I know." She took his hand. "How will you occupy yourself while I rest?"

He kissed her hand then wrapped a long curl around his finger. "I have a letter to write to my solicitor. I think that I will pursue the investment in steam engines that we were discussing. I will ask him to look into both railways and industrial uses. That, along with the investments in mining and in your Uncle Gardiner's business that I have already made, will help to diversify our income. I do not wish for all of our monies to be dependent on interest and the whims of the weather and the yields from our farms and livestock."

Elizabeth nodded her head and reached to brush one of his unruly locks from his brow; they spent many hours discussing the future and ways to secure it for their children. "That is wise William, not just for us, but for Pemberley. I am happy that you have made this decision."

"Yes, but do not let the other landowners hear of it! They will steal my ideas!" His eyes twinkled and he leaned down to kiss her. "I will be in the library if you awaken and wish for my company."

"Do you think there are any books there?" She grinned.

He laughed. "I certainly hope so; it will be a very long visit if the shelves are empty!" He hugged her tightly and kissed her again. "Rest, my love. I will see you soon."

Darcy left Elizabeth to her nap and after asking a footman, found the library. He wrote several letters, and then took to perusing the small collection of books on the shelves. He saw that he had been working over an hour, and he knew that

Elizabeth would likely sleep a little longer, so he settled in an armchair with his selection, an apparently unread treatise on the benefits of crop rotation, and soon his eyelids grew heavy.

Caroline learned from her maid that the Darcys had arrived and that Mrs. Darcy slept in her room while Mr. Darcy worked in the library. Thrilled to hear he was alone, she examined her appearance and entered the silent room where she saw him soundly sleeping in the chair, a book falling from his hands. Caroline stood still and watched him for some minutes, drinking in his handsome features. It had been *so* long. She considered how to approach him.

She called his name and saw that he would not wake. Turning, she closed the library door and advanced, now breathing in the intoxicating scent that she remembered from the night when he was making love to her at Netherfield. *No, to his wife*, she reminded herself. *NO, to me! I should be his wife!* She was suddenly awash in the memory and she wished to prove to him she was the better choice.

She approached his sleeping form and drew near enough to feel his warm breath on her face as he slept deeply. She leaned closer and closer, then shaking with anticipation, moistened her lips and brushed them across his mouth. A wave of overwhelming desire spread throughout her body. Her breath ragged, she drew back. He had not moved. She leaned close again, feeling the heat of his skin next to her lips, and studied his peaceful, handsome features. The dark lashes of his closed eyes fluttered slightly in his dream, and she nearly gasped. At last it was time to make him her own. All of the months, the years of dreaming were over, she would finally feel what she had watched and wanted. She lightly held his face in her trembling hands, and lowered her mouth to caress his, kissing him again, and this time he responded.

"Lizzy" he whispered.

The book dropped to the floor and his hands came up. Caroline suddenly felt herself drawn onto his lap, encased tightly in his arms, her mouth the subject of deep, passionate kisses. Her heart was pounding. It was all coming true! She felt one of his hands come around to touch her breast, as the other caressed her ankle and glided up her leg to stroke her thigh. She moaned, and his tongue entered her mouth to touch hers. The kisses became more demanding, and she joyously responded, wrapping her arms around his neck and pressing her body against his, when suddenly everything stopped.

To Darcy something did not feel right. Even before she was with child, Elizabeth's breasts were full; her lips were soft, and her taste, so very sweet. The woman he was caressing had no figure, thin lips, and tasted, bitter. Darcy's eyes flew open and he found himself staring into the passion-filled face of Caroline Bingley, who was revelling in the feel of his arousal pressing urgently against her bottom. Darcy instantly rose, dropping Caroline in an undignified heap on the floor. He strode rapidly across the room, spotted the closed, and he noted, locked library door, and opened it wide. He then quickly turned to face the woman who was unsteadily rising to her feet.

"What is the meaning of this Miss Bingley?" His face was red with rage. "Explain yourself!"

She stared at him with confusion. "I . . . I thought that you wanted me . . ."

"Why would I want *YOU*?" He stared at her, incensed, incredulous, and nauseous.

"*YOU* kissed *ME!*" She accused him.

He looked at her in disbelief. "I was asleep and thought you were my wife!"

She watched as he poured a large glass of port and took a huge swallow, as if he was trying to rid himself of her taste.

She was mortified, but unwilling to accept the truth of his rejection, and decided she must present her plan now. "I wish to offer myself to you as your mistress." Darcy's eyes grew wider. "Your wife is with child, she will not be able to accommodate your needs. I will come to live at Pemberley, and . . ."

"ARE YOU INSANE?" Darcy bellowed at her.

Into this arrived Elizabeth. She had come downstairs from her nap to be greeted by the sound of her husband's voice raised in fury, and the sight of servants standing in shock in the hallways. They scattered at her approach. She hurried into the room and was brought to a standstill by the site of Caroline. Elizabeth took one look at Darcy's frightening face and Caroline's dishevelled appearance and knew something terrible had occurred.

"William? Are you well?" She moved to where he was gulping down the rest of the port. He never drank like that. She took the glass from his hand and stared into his eyes.

He coughed and shuddered from the great amount of alcohol then took her hand. "I am very sorry Elizabeth, apparently I fell asleep, and Miss Bingley took the opportunity to close and lock the door . . . and kiss me."

Her eyes grew wide. "SHE DID *WHAT*?!" She spun around in fury and faced the other woman.

Caroline jealously took in her very pregnant form and became defiant. "Well he obviously enjoyed it because he dragged me onto his lap and kissed me back!" She stared at him then looked at Elizabeth with triumph.

"*THAT* was because I thought you were my wife!" He threw back at her. He turned quickly to Elizabeth. "I was asleep and did not open my eyes. I truly thought you had come to wake me, Lizzy. I am so very sorry." He held her hand tightly, staring anxiously into her eyes.

"I understand, William, I know enough of your reactions to me to envision exactly what you did. You have nothing for which to apologize."

He drew her to his chest, "Thank you darling."

Caroline stared, *Would nothing separate them?* Infuriated, she screeched. "But he wanted ME!"

The Darcys broke apart and rounded on Caroline. Elizabeth's eyes burned into the woman. "Why are you here Miss Bingley? I thought you lived in Scarborough?"

Caroline's face grew red. "My aunt suggested I come to aid Jane through the birth."

Elizabeth's voice dripped with sarcasm as she moved close enough that her pregnant belly brushed against Caroline. "Ah, and so that naturally includes accosting my sleeping husband? How fortunate Jane is to have such admirable assistance!"

Darcy held onto Elizabeth, and pulled her back, both keeping her from launching herself onto Caroline and keeping himself from personally strangling her. Bingley, learning that his guests were in the library, entered the tension-filled room and asked what had happened.

Darcy glared and said through gritted teeth, "Once again Bingley your sister has behaved in a horrific manner and attempted to come between me and my wife. If we had known she was here we would not have come. I believe her display today justifies my stance. Once again I must put to you this charge, either she goes or we do." Darcy held Elizabeth tighter.

Bingley stared in disbelief, and looked between the two of them, blood or friendship. He had no doubt that Caroline was guilty of whatever happened. He had allowed himself to be blinded into complacency by his wishful thinking. "I am sorry Caroline, but I am afraid you must leave. Please have your things packed and I will have a carriage prepared to take you to London in the morning. I gave up the lease on the townhouse, so you will have to stay with the Hursts. I obviously cannot trust you any longer. I hoped that you had changed. I was a fool to do so." His sadness and disappointment were obvious.

"Charles! You believe them over me?" She suddenly saw all of her desires collapsing around her.

"Yes Caroline, Darcy is my brother, and I believe him. Now please pack your things and leave us in peace." His face was pained but determined. "I will contact my solicitor and have your dowry released to you. The Hursts may help you find a home, or not. I wash my hands of you."

Caroline was incredulous. "You cannot be serious!"

"I am Caroline. I am a fool for believing you could ever change. I had such hopes for you finding your happiness, and you had so many opportunities. Instead you . . . I do not know what happened to you. I have done my best by you. I am finished."

Caroline held her head up high and strode to the door. She turned and glared at her brother then directed her gaze to Elizabeth, and down to her child. Darcy held her protectively. Caroline's eyes met his and held, staring coldly at him, and then she turned and left. It was unnerving, and Darcy did not know what to make of her, so he gripped Elizabeth tighter.

Charles turned to Darcy and asked for the entire story.

He did not like relating the details, especially with Elizabeth there, but it was her warm presence that gave him the ability to speak and reined in his anger. When finished, he apologized to her again.

Bingley apologized to both of them. "Caroline has been here for a month and I truly thought that she had improved. If I had any idea that she would try to interfere with you again, I would have sent her away. I apologize for not honouring your request to never stay under the same roof with her. Please forgive me."

"Forgive you?" Darcy stared at him, his expression a mixture of anger and frustration. "Bingley, I do not understand. Why would you allow us to come here blindly, knowing my feelings about Miss Bingley? I know how much Jane and Elizabeth wanted to be together for the birth of your child, it would have been a very difficult decision to make, and I admit, I would not have anticipated it at all, but in the end, I would have likely agreed to come for the sake of our wives. But to have us blindsided like this, I am sorry Bingley, but I feel that our friendship has been betrayed. Why would you not tell us? At the very least, Elizabeth and I could have been told of your sister's state of mind, and we might have been prepared. You gave us no opportunity to decide our own course." He looked at his friend's sunken shoulders, but still could not feel sorry for him. "I truly thought you had learned to assert yourself over her machinations. I thought you had become your own man. I am happy to see you finally break with her, but how can I trust you again? I felt this way for good reason." He was not shouting as he did with Caroline, but the anger was evident in his voice. "I am deeply disappointed with you, as I am sure Elizabeth is with Jane." He looked down to his wife, who nodded to him.

"I cannot believe she would not warn me." Elizabeth was so hurt. It was not the first time that Jane had not supported her, and she did not understand why.

"She wished to, I wanted to keep it secret." Bingley said, turning to her. "Please direct your anger to me." Elizabeth simply looked sadly at him; she knew the fault was as much Jane's as his.

"Bingley, you knew that your sister nursed an obsession with me. Your aunt's letters indicated she was angry with Elizabeth. How could you allow us to enter this home without any warning, or give us the ability to stay away? I am grateful she chose to accost me. I shudder to imagine what she might have done if she had chosen to enter our bedchamber while Elizabeth slept alone."

Elizabeth's eyes widened and her hand went to her mouth. "Oh William, she would not have hurt me!"

Darcy's eyes filled with emotion and he took her hand. "I believe very seriously that she would." Elizabeth gasped, and then thought of Caroline's stare as she left the library. Darcy turned back to Bingley. "If it was not so late in the day, and Elizabeth was not with child, I would leave here immediately, but I will not risk her or our child by travelling now. In the morning, however . . ."

"Please Darcy, please do not leave. Do not let my foolishness end our friendship." Darcy's face remained stony. Bingley sighed, his face pained. "What would you do Darcy? What would you do if this was Georgiana? Could you have turned her away if she came to your door with nowhere to go? Tell me. Please. What would you do?" He stared down at the floor. "I should have warned you, that is correct, and I understand your anger, and after this display, I finally realize she should never be near you or Elizabeth again. If she is ever here in my home again, I will inform you. I honestly never anticipated that she was capable of what she did here today. I do not know if she is mentally unbalanced, she seemed to be doing so well here this past month. She will be gone in the morning. Please, do not let this destroy our friendship, or indeed, our family."

Darcy felt the warm, steady pressure of Elizabeth's hand on his back, and looked down at her, absorbing her support. "What should we do William? I am angry and disappointed with Jane, but I have no desire to be estranged from her. I have already had that experience with my father." He looked back up to his old friend and closing his eyes took some moments to think clearly and order his thoughts. His disappointment was intense, but most of his anger was spent on Caroline.

"I do not know what I would have done, but I do know that I wish to value our friendship and family more than I wish to nurse a grievance against you. Never do this again to us Bingley; such an act would be unforgivable." His reluctant concession was made purely because he could now fully understand why Elizabeth tried so hard to convince him to tolerate her father. It was easier to be angry when there was no bond. Darcy made it very clear that they would not be joining the

Bingleys for any meals or other activities until Caroline was gone, and he would make sure that the lock on their bedchamber was in good working order before they retired. He also said that he wanted to talk again about what had happened in the morning after they all had time to calm.

With whispered words of thanks, Bingley left to inform Jane of the situation and arrange for the carriage. An express was sent that afternoon to the Hursts warning them of Caroline's imminent arrival. Bingley, with Darcy's permission, indicated the reason for her hasty removal. They should know what was coming their way. He did not know what else to do. After Bingley departed the couple embraced and sighed.

"Lizzy?" Darcy stood with his cheek resting on her head.

"Yes William?" Her round belly kept her from hugging him face to face, but she did her best.

"Do you believe me? I truly did not encourage her." He whispered.

She tightened her embrace. "Yes William, I do believe you. All is well."

"Thank you." He said quietly in her ear. She laughed softly. He drew back to regard her. "What is it?"

"I truly will never forget seeing you desperately washing out your mouth with the port."

He chuckled, relaxing. "If I could have gargled, I would have." She laughed and squeezed him. "It was a foul taste, I assure you; nothing like my Lizzy." He kissed her gently. "Sweetheart, could we go upstairs and rest some more?"

Elizabeth looked at him, a small smile on her lips. "You wish to replace a bad memory with a good one?"

He kissed her. "Yes, my love, please?"

"Well, you did say please . . ." He laughed with relief, and holding hands, they returned to their chambers to reaffirm their love. The door was decidedly locked.

IN THE MORNING the sound of a carriage awakened Elizabeth. Curious, she extricated herself from William, who was spooned against her. She slipped on her robe and walked to the window, looking out at the scene below. Caroline's luggage was being loaded into the coach. She was standing outside having what appeared to be angry words with her brother. He offered his hand to help her up the step and she spurned it, grasping the handhold and climbing inside herself. He shut the door, and tried to say something through the open window, but it must not have met with success as he quickly stepped away and signalled the driver to walk on. He stood watching the retreating carriage until it was no longer in view, then with slumped shoulders, an unusually downcast Charles Bingley turned to enter his home. Elizabeth drew a sigh of relief and was about to walk away when she saw Jane come out of the house and embrace him. She nodded, that was what Jane should do. A pair of hands encircled her waist and she looked up to see William watching the scene.

"She is gone?" Elizabeth nodded. "Thank God, I could not stop thinking of her harming you." They stayed in their silent embrace, holding each other tighter, wondering if Caroline was truly capable of such violence. Neither would tell the other of hearing the door handle turn during the night.

They watched their sister and brother and Elizabeth broke the quiet, "I think Miss Bingley's behaviour is the only unhappy thing in Jane and Charles' world."

"They do seem to live a perfect existence, always happy, always serene, never, ever arguing." He gently kissed her ear and nuzzled her neck. "Do you wish that we lived that way, Lizzy?"

She leaned back against him, feeling his hard body and the security of his strong arms around her. "I honestly do not think that I could live a life of no emotion, William. One cannot always be happy, and the sad or difficult times make us appreciate the happy ones more. Jane's unending serenity frustrated me, and I cannot help wondering if sometimes she was hiding her true feelings. I think that it would become quite a burden to always have to be so annoyingly peaceful, or in the case of Charles, buoyant."

"But you are happy with our life, even when we endure our little arguments or suffer at the hands of our own relatives or the influence of the outside world?" He turned her around and took her hands in his, softly caressing them, raising them to his lips while looking deeply in her eyes.

She was melting with his gentle ministrations. "Yes, William, I am very happy, warts and all. I would like to think that our times of difficulty are over, but I am too realistic to believe that. However, I would not trade our marriage for anyone else's. Why do you need to ask?"

He drew her against him, and gently kissed her. "Oh, Lizzy, just bear with me, I will forever need your reassurance that you are happy."

"Are you still insecure, Will?"

"I do not know if it is insecurity now. Perhaps it is that after a year of being loved, I am now worried that it could somehow be taken away."

She caressed his cheek. "My pregnancy frightens you, and Jane's imminent delivery is making it worse."

He nodded, getting to the truth. "Yes."

There was nothing she could say that would make his fear disappear; nothing but the birth of their child. In the meantime, she would just have to love him. "Come." She took his hand and led him to the bed. They removed their robes and climbed in. They embraced and began kissing slowly, very slowly, caressing each other. Darcy lay on his side and pulled her to him, and smiled as he felt the baby kick his belly. "Ow!"

Elizabeth laughed, "Imagine it from my side of things!" He laughed, stroking her face, smiling into her eyes. "I love you, Elizabeth."

She returned his caress, "I love you my William."

He kissed her again. "Roll over sweetheart."

He helped her to turn away from him. "I miss you lying on me, Will. I miss feeling your weight pressing me down into the bed, and being overwhelmed by your body. It will be a long time before I can feel that absolute security again."

He embraced her and gently kissed beneath her ear. "Oh, Lizzy, I miss that feeling too, but for now, let me try to bring it back for you. You are secure no matter how I hold you." His arms came around her and she felt his arousal pressing against her bottom. She lifted her leg and he pushed into her, joining together in their rhythm of love.

When they finished Darcy kept her wrapped in his arms and whispered. "Did I make you feel safe, Lizzy?"

She reached up behind her and caressed his face. "Always."

AFTER FINALLY RISING, the Darcys took a long walk around the park, stopping in a certain grove of trees for a short visit, and then returned to the house to see their hosts for the first time since the incident in the library. During their walk Darcy confessed that his friendship with Bingley had received a painful blow, and he was unsure how to proceed. He stated that had it been Elizabeth who was accosted, he would have shown no mercy to Bingley, and they would have spent the night at an inn, never to return. Elizabeth told him of her struggle with her feelings for Jane. She was just as confused. She told him that if Caroline had done anything to hurt him, Elizabeth would have given her the sound thrashing that she deserved. He had no doubt of it at all.

They both felt manipulated and betrayed. Important information had been deliberately kept from them. The Darcys were forced to accept a situation because others had decided that it was the best course to take, and suited their needs. Forgiveness was difficult to find, but neither one wished to return to Pemberley. Such an action would cause a nearly irreparable breach in their family. They agreed that conversation was needed.

The couples sat in awkward silence as the servants set out the tea and cake. Jane poured out and when everyone was served, Darcy and Elizabeth exchanged glances. It was obvious that they would have to begin.

Elizabeth spoke in a calm, clear voice. "We would like to try and understand why you would not tell us that Caroline was here. Of all people, you should have understood our feelings about her, and were clearly informed by your aunt what her feelings were towards us." She searched their faces. "Please explain this to us."

Jane looked at Bingley and spoke. "We really wanted to tell you, but we were so afraid that you would not come. I wanted so much to have you here with me, Lizzy, and Caroline's behaviour was so . . . pleasant and kind. We were sure that after you saw her, everything would be well." She leaned forward. "We truly saw nothing that would tell us she would act in such a way."

Elizabeth's brow creased. "But Jane, that is not the point. You knew that we did not want to be exposed to her, why could you not respect our wishes? At least give us the information so we could make our own decision. If you so wanted our company, why would you not support our obviously justified feelings?"

Jane looked down and then up. "It is so hard when you marry. You must balance the needs of two families. Caroline was homeless, what were we to do? I was not sure that you would have come if we told you."

"Perhaps that is true, but it does not excuse letting us come in unprepared." Elizabeth looked at her sadly and Jane dropped her eyes. She simply could not understand, nothing terrible had ever happened to her, until Caroline.

Darcy turned his gaze on Bingley. "I thought that I had made myself clear on this Bingley. Why did you not respect our friendship enough to tell us that she was here?"

Bingley ran his hand through his hair. "I know how much it means to Jane to have Elizabeth with her when the baby comes. She will not speak of it but I know she is terrified." He took Jane's hand and kissed it. Her eyes filled with tears. He looked back at Darcy. "You are entirely justified in your anger. It was selfish of us, I understand, but please do not leave us. I know that I need you with me Darcy. I cannot . . ." He choked. Darcy watched as his friend displayed all of the fear that he was personally keeping buried about losing Elizabeth when she gave birth. He looked over to her and saw that she was watching Jane, whose mask of serenity was finally removed. They looked at each other and touched hands. Darcy turned to Bingley.

"I need you to know how very angry and disappointed I am and I expect to always be informed in future if your sister is in residence. It is beyond me why you simply did not set her up in a home somewhere and been done with it then. In any case, if she does come to stay with you, we will NOT be visiting then, no matter the circumstances." He watched his friend until Bingley looked up at him. "However, I do understand your fears, and we will stay."

"Thank you Darcy." Bingley said with emotion. They shook hands and Elizabeth and Jane embraced, whispering to each other. It was tenuous and fragile, and the Darcys were unsatisfied, but the family remained intact.

A WEEK LATER Jane and Elizabeth were sitting on a shaded porch when with a cry, Jane's water broke. Word was immediately sent to summon the midwife, and Bingley and Darcy, who were riding, were intercepted. Bingley had no desire to be present at the birth, but held her hand until her excruciating cries became unbearable then ran from the room, white as a ghost.

Elizabeth went to her own equally frightened husband and took his hand. "I will stay here with Jane, William; perhaps you and Charles could go wait in his library or play billiards. This may take many hours." Jane's scream rent the air.

"Lizzy, is she well?" His eyes were wide with fear, and darted to stare at the closed door to the bedchamber.

Elizabeth tried to reassure him, but she was just as frightened for her sister. "She will be. Now go. I will come when there is news." They kissed, and Darcy hugged her, almost desperately, and then left to find Bingley.

Elizabeth returned to the birthing room, and held Jane's hand, giving her the calm assurance she would want, while taking careful note of everything around her; preparing herself for her approaching day.

Darcy tried to keep Bingley occupied, but eventually, he found that giving him wine; and encouraging sleep was the best solution. He was left to his own dark thoughts. Memories of his mother wasting away after Georgiana's birth crossed his mind. Despite the distance from the birthing room, he could still discern Jane's cries, and they chilled him. She was not his wife, but he still worried for her. He could not imagine how he would feel when it was Elizabeth's voice. He was frightened to be in the birthing room, to see her pain, to hear her cries, and God forbid, witness her or their baby's death. But he realized after sitting and helplessly listening to Jane, and remembering the hellish day a year ago when Elizabeth was missing after Wickham's attack, he would far rather be present, knowing for certain what was happening, than to sit and torture himself wondering how she fared. His understanding for Charles wanting them present, regardless of Caroline's residence and their objections, became clearer.

Hours later, an exhausted Jane finally pushed out her daughter and collapsed crying into her sister's arms. Elizabeth left the room and wearily went in search of the men. She found them, Bingley a blithering fool barely holding his glass, and William, the picture of tension, staring at the floor. He spotted Elizabeth's gown and looked up. "Is it over?"

"Yes. Jane is well, and so is the baby." She smiled and looked to Bingley, who awakened from his stupor.

"Jane?"

"Go to her Charles, she and your daughter would like to see you."

"A daughter?" Bingley's smile lit up the room, and he leapt to his feet, wrung Darcy's outstretched hand, kissed Elizabeth full on the lips and ran out the door.

Elizabeth and Darcy looked at each other and laughed. Tears of relief and exhaustion fell from their eyes, and they held each other tightly. "I know that you were frightened William, but I do hope that you will stay with me when my time comes."

He kissed her gently. "There is nowhere else in the world I should be."

ALEX AND GEORGIANA took a walk together after dinner at his parents' home. He was delighted that Lord Matlock allowed the evening. He was proving to be a very considerate guardian, in fact, he felt as if Georgiana's uncle was pushing him to get on with it.

Georgiana held Alex's arm, enjoying the feel of his muscle under her hand. He brought his free hand up to cover hers and she did not pull away. He then entwined their fingers, and noted her blush with happiness.

"Did you enjoy dinner, Miss Darcy?"

"Oh yes, I especially enjoyed meeting your parents. Your father reminds me of mine, and you look so much like your mother." She smiled up at him.

Alex smiled back, considering. After two months of courtship, and three months of the Season, he was sure that he would soon propose to her. There was no better woman to ask to be his wife. He loved her dearly. She had only the week before trusted him with her greatest secret and it only made him grateful she had been saved from a life of misery to keep her free to find him. It was time to trust her with his own secret. "It is odd that you should think that."

She tilted her head. "Why?"

He moved to a bench and they sat, and he took her hands in his. "Miss Darcy, I was . . . taken in . . . I am not Philip and Amanda Carrington's son."

She looked at him with great surprise. "You are not?"

"Yes, my parents could not have children of their own and when they learned of a gentleman's child being abandoned, they adopted me as their own. But it is assumed that I am their child in truth so that I may be my father's heir. It is a very great secret."

She smiled at him broadly, "How wonderful! How fortunate you were! Why would the gentleman not want you?"

It was Alex's turn to be surprised, he expected her to be shocked, disappointed, but happy, no; that was a surprise. "Surely you know that it is not uncommon, Miss Darcy."

She smiled ruefully and shook her head. "I am sheltered, am I not? But Elizabeth has told me of such things."

He thought that she did this to prepare Georgiana for his truth, and silently thanked her for it. "What did you think of what she told you?"

"I thought it horrible to knowingly abandon your child, without at least ever providing for it, even if it was illegitimate. Do you know your birth parents?"

"My natural mother died having me, but yes, I do know my blood father. I have met him twice, but have not revealed my identity to him."

"Why not?" She could not imagine not wanting to know her father.

"Many reasons, I do not wish to dishonour the parents who saved my life and love me as their own, and we must maintain the illusion that I am their legitimate child so that I may inherit the estate, and . . . my blood father has done things which disappoint me greatly. I have seen behaviours in him that I share and have endeavoured to change."

"Does my brother know of this?"

Alex nodded. "Yes, as does Elizabeth."

Georgiana looked at him, then down at the ground. "You have always called my sister by her Christian name."

He furrowed his brow and tried to see under her bonnet. "Yes, she asked me to do so."

"From the beginning?" Georgiana said softly.

"Almost."

She closed her eyes and asked the question that had been nagging at her. "Were you ever interested in courting her?"

He smiled, realizing the problem. "No, fortunately. You see Georgiana, Elizabeth is my sister."

She stared, not understanding. "Elizabeth is your sister? But . . . Does that not mean . . . Is Mr. Bennet . . .?"

"Mr. Thomas Bennet is my father. Elizabeth is my half-sister."

Georgiana gasped. "Why did she not tell me?"

"She said it was my story to tell. Does this change anything between us, Georgiana?" He looked at her, trying to read her emotions.

She said sharply, "Why should it?"

He smiled, relieved. "No reason, I just wanted to be sure, you see, this was my greatest secret, and if you can bear it, then maybe you can be willing to listen to what I have to say now."

Alex knelt down before Georgiana and held her trembling hands in his. He looked into her wide, beautiful blue eyes, and spoke his heart, "Georgiana, I have been struck by you since the morning we met in the millinery shop, and I spoke to your brother a year ago, telling him of my hopes for us. He told me he had only one objection, the difference in our ages, and said I must wait for you to come out and experience your Season. I now wish to tell you, Georgiana, that I love you very dearly. I have known that you would be the partner in life that I have dreamed about and I wish for you to be at my side in everything, everyday, forever. Will you accept this old man, Georgiana? Will you please marry me?"

Georgiana smiled at him ecstatically. "Oh yes! Yes! I dreamed of and hoped for you ever since the day we met, every time I saw you standing, staring up at the windows of Matlock House, and all those long months I had to wait to see you again. And now that I truly know you, and you know and accept my foolish behaviour of the past, I can say without a doubt that I love you, and I wish to be your wife!" He rose and pulled her up into his embrace. "And it will be good for such an old man to have a young wife to care for him!"

Alex laughed. "Indeed it shall my love!" He smiled into her eyes and finally kissed her waiting lips. "Thank you." He breathed a sigh of relief. "I have worked on that speech for days!"

She laughed, and brushed the dirt from his trousers. "Your valet will thank you for choosing a dry patch in which to kneel."

He hugged her and offered his arm. They began to walk back to the house. "Do you have any suggestions for approaching your brother?"

She smiled. "He looks fierce, but he is really very sweet."

Chapter 43

*D*arcy sat back in his chair and regarded his friend's nervous countenance. Alex cleared his throat and wiped his sweating palms on his breeches, waiting for his response. "I do not suppose it will be necessary to ask of your income or prospects. What do you plan to provide for her in the settlement?"

"I will provide whatever you feel is appropriate. I thought we could work out the details together." He began twisting the ring on his finger.

"Georgiana is a sweet and loving woman, Alex."

"I will treasure her."

"You will do more than that. You once told me that you wanted a wife who would keep you on your toes. She has learned much from Elizabeth, and she has grown greatly in confidence this past year." He paused. "I have learned a great deal since marrying. You must do more than treasure your wife. You must respect her and talk to her. Never let a misunderstanding or fear sit without discussion. It will grow in proportion and push you apart. Include her in decisions that affect her, and ask for her opinions in things that are important to you. Value more than her beauty. Value her mind and heart. If you do this, you will be happy, as I am with your sister."

Alex nodded. "You are describing my parents' marriage. They were an excellent example. I will be thrilled to have a marriage with Georgiana that equals or hopefully exceeds theirs."

Darcy watched him, letting him suffer a little longer. He rose, and Alex was instantly on his feet. Darcy held out his hand and Alex took it. "You have my consent and blessing, Alex. Once again, we are brothers."

Letting out a great breath he finally smiled. "Thank you Darcy, I love her dearly."

"If I did not think so, I would never have given my consent." He smiled sadly. He had given his sister away. He fulfilled his father's charge; she would marry for love and be safe. He could not ask for a better husband for her. "Well, let us go tell the ladies."

The men left the room and walked out to a porch shaded by an ancient wisteria vine. It was cool and inviting. Elizabeth sat amongst cushions, holding Georgiana's hand. They looked up expectantly, and Alex could not contain his joy. He rushed over and taking her hands, pulled her up and grinned.

Georgiana looked to Darcy who smiled slightly, "I have given my consent Georgie, congratulations."

"Oh William, thank you!" She hugged him and kissed his cheek. She turned and hugged Elizabeth, who remained seated and beamed up at her. She spun around to face Alex and blushed. He took her hand and kissed it.

"Miss Darcy, Georgiana, would you do me the honour of showing me the gardens of Pemberley?"

Georgiana forced herself to look up from her slippers and met his loving gaze. "Yes Alex, I would enjoy that."

They excused themselves and left. Darcy heavily lowered himself onto the chaise next to Elizabeth. "That was such a difficult experience, Lizzy." He wrapped his arm around her. "I think Uncle Henry was correct. We should hope for boys to spare my heart from enduring this again."

Elizabeth laughed, running her fingers through his hair then entwining them with his. "I can bear that darling, if this child would make a decision to be born."

Darcy chuckled and caressed her growing belly. "Soon."

THE DARCYS SPENT many evenings talking about what had happened at Lyndon Hall, not Caroline's actual assault upon the sleeping Darcy, but her intentions behind it. Her claimed desire to live at Pemberley and become his mistress was frightening. No woman in her right mind would offer to be kept in that way, certainly not one as socially ambitious as Caroline Bingley once was. Elizabeth suggested that after spending so many years connecting herself with William, the shock of his marriage left her unable to contemplate starting over again to search for a suitable husband. Darcy swore that he had never done anything to encourage her attentions, and did not understand why she did not simply work her wiles on some man who needed her dowry. She likely could have been settled years ago with a man of Hurst's status. Elizabeth pointed out that she thought of herself as one of the first circles, and refused to face the fact that she was nothing more than a well-dowered tradesman's daughter. She saw her brother's friendship with Darcy and was dazzled by all that he had.

"I suppose it makes sense that she would be angry with me for being your wife, and I imagine that kissing you was acting out some sort of fantasy, but to think that you would offer her a place in our home?" Elizabeth was still amazed.

"Lizzy, I believe completely that her wish to enter Pemberley was to do you some harm." Darcy said seriously. "Remember last year she spoke to her sister about my divorcing you, and Mrs. Hurst telling her that I would never do such a thing." He took her hand.

"But you seem to think that she would . . . oh William, not . . . not . . ." She stared at him and could read the fear in his eyes. "I heard what sounded like the knob on the chamber door turn during the night." She whispered.

He stared at her. "So did I."

The grip of their hands tightened. There was no doubt that the hand turning the knob was Caroline's, whether her intentions were to look, or to act in some way, and upon whom, was open for frightening conjecture. "Jane and Charles could not have known of the extent of her madness." She said in a numb tone.

"No, but were they turning a blind eye or merely naive? They always wish for peace above everything. They hide from conflict. They are selfish in their behaviour. Bingley has always been a good friend, and when I met him, he was the balm I needed. He provided the spark of optimism and happiness in my life that was missing. I think, I know, that you have entirely replaced him, except in the obvious matters of gentlemanly pursuits and concerns." He laughed slightly. "I think you know more of estate affairs than he does."

"Thank you. That is a great compliment." She tilted her head. "Have you outgrown your need for him?"

Darcy studied her for a few moments, thinking over his answer. "Have you outgrown your need for Jane?"

She smiled. "You are avoiding your answer, sir, but I will accept your parry. Yes, I have outgrown her. I do not rely on her for advice, as she is too far away. I do not rely on her for a woman's company, I have Georgiana for a while longer, and I have Mrs. Hill and the other various ladies I have befriended nearby. I think that perhaps we could invite Mary or Kitty to come stay with us in the future; I have neglected those sisters long enough. So to answer your question, yes, I find Jane slipping backwards in her growth, frustrating in her avoidance of any difficulty, and confusing in her behaviour, but I love her because for all of my life until I met you, she was all I had. She was my only source of comfort in a very difficult household. That is why after what happened at Lyndon Hall, I could not reject her. She will always be my sister, and my friend, but the days of absolute trust and unquestioned loyalty are over. She damaged that relationship by showing several times that her concerns were far greater than relieving even a small amount of mine."

He leaned over and kissed the tears off of her cheek. It was a hard realization to voice. "I think that I feel similarly about Bingley. My trust has been shaken, but he is still my friend. It will never be as close as it once was, but I think that is probably wise. He will never be his own man unless he is forced to be on his own. I will not do what he did to me. I will remain available should he need help or advice, and I will accept him as my brother and friend, but no, I believe that my respect for him is irreparably damaged."

"So inviting them here for our child's birth. . ." She stopped, unsure what to say.

He kissed her hand. "Is acceptable. If they are willing to come, I am willing to accept whatever support they are capable of giving. Is that what you needed to hear?"

Their eyes met. "Yes. I just wanted to be sure that you would not be . . . hidden behind your mask when they come."

He laughed. "I promise; you will only see that mask again when you force me to attend a large gathering."

She laughed with him. "I will remember that!"

JANE AND BINGLEY ARRIVED with their two-month-old daughter Angela. They would stay at Pemberley until the birth, which was expected within two weeks. The Darcys had left Lyndon Hall the day after her birth, and due to the conditions of both mother and mother-to-be, no visits were planned. They remained cordial, and with the two months apart, many letters were exchanged so that when they met again at Pemberley, they were able to do so as family and friends, just as the Darcys intended.

Bingley was amazed to find Darcy so calm. He was forever hovering near Elizabeth, but he was not pacing or tearing his hair out. He was pleased and relieved by Darcy's offer to spend some time alone. They were standing at the edge of the lake, enjoying a morning of fishing. Darcy refused to be any farther from the house than that. The harvest would have to come in without him this year.

"I was a bundle of nerves at this point Darcy, and I expected to find you in the same state. Explain yourself!" He smiled, seeing Darcy affect a look of superiority, and glad to see that his friend was accepting of his tease.

"It is simple Bingley. I have had the doctor in residence here for the last two days, the local midwife has no other babies expected within the next month, and she lives in Lambton. When Elizabeth's time comes, I know that she will have the best of care." He smiled; proud of his planning.

Bingley grinned. "I want to see how smug you look when you hear Elizabeth's cry." He looked at him closely. "Are you sure that you wish to be present? It was all I could do to stay with Jane as long as I did, and I am grateful that you kept me sedated through the worst of it." He cast his line out, and watched it sink.

Darcy watched as well, and said thoughtfully, "Almost exactly a year ago I stood in this spot, fishing with Mr. Gardiner. We were discussing Elizabeth's miscarriage. He assured me that even though we lost our first, we would someday be successful." He closed his eyes, remembering that sad time. He looked into his friend's face. "I vowed then that if we were so blessed as to have another child, I would not miss a moment of it. I want to support Elizabeth, and see the wonder of my child enter the world." He smiled. "I may be calm now, but I expect to be panicking then. I imagine it will be Elizabeth who reassures me, as she always does at the worst of times."

Bingley pulled in his line and cast again. He thought of his inability to stay with Jane. "I envy you your marriage."

"Are you unhappy?" Darcy asked with concern.

"No, not at all." He smiled. "I have exactly what I always wished for. Peace, serenity, but sometimes I look at you and Elizabeth, and how you are so . . . intense together in every aspect. You both feel so much, and your love is undisguised when you are at home, well, anywhere really."

"Should it be? Where else should we be open in our feelings if not at home?"

"I am putting this badly."

"Yes, you are."

"We both married for love."

"Yes."

"But yours seems so much deeper."

Darcy deliberated how to answer him. He knew very well that their marriages were vastly different; in fact he knew that his marriage was exceptionally unusual in society as a whole. But how could he explain the power of his and Elizabeth's relationship to someone who would likely never experience or even understand such a bond? Who in fact was not capable of achieving it, not necessarily because he was a lesser person, but because he and Jane were such different people? He settled on an answer that he hoped would bring Bingley comfort without sounding superior.

"Ours has been tested through many trials. It forced us to grow and learn to support each other, perhaps faster than a typically married couple would. Certainly your experience with Miss Bingley has been a trial for your marriage. Has it not forced you to cling together, support each other?"

Bingley looked at him with surprise. "Yes, it has. We have had to rely on each other and learn to speak our feelings."

Darcy smiled, relieved that his words had the intended result. "You see, you and Jane are growing stronger together. It will simply take you longer. Do not be in a hurry to suffer, enjoy your peace. And you should also remember that although my marriage appears different than yours, you are still in a love match, which is far more than the majority of couples can claim in our society."

"Thank you Darcy."

Darcy hesitated, he disliked the subject but he knew his friend had no one else to talk to about it, and he *did* need to know the answers, so he asked, "How are things with Miss Bingley?" He watched as Bingley's happy face darkened.

He sighed. "I do not know. After her latest performance in London. . ." He looked at Darcy, "You have heard about it?" Darcy shook his head. Bingley sighed again. "After she left Lyndon Hall she was determined to take part in the Season. She bought several gowns, and chose a white one, and followed the scandalous practice of wetting down the fabric to make it appear . . . transparent." He said the words as if they had a bad taste. "She somehow found some friends to escort her to a ball, and when her wrap was removed, her appearance caused such an uproar that she was forced to leave immediately. The carriage had already left, not expecting them back for hours. Her friends denied knowing her and refused to help, and she was forced to walk through the streets of London until she finally found a hack to take her back to the Hurst's home where she was staying. A notice was in all of the gossip columns the next day about her, and Hurst demanded that she leave his home. It was finally clear to her that she could never live in London again, and she returned to Scarborough. My aunt took her in on the condition that she finds her own home immediately. She has taken a cottage with a small staff. She is humiliated."

Darcy listened to the tale, fascinated. "And will she be able to maintain herself in this place with the income from her fortune?"

"Yes, if she lives modestly. I doubt that she will ever marry." Bingley shook his head at his sister's disgrace.

"I am sorry, Bingley." Darcy was at a loss. Caroline's behaviour was all of her own doing; she had been given endless opportunities to mend her ways. He deeply suspected her sanity.

"Well, there is nothing to be done for it now." He smiled slightly at Darcy, "But the experience has made the Hurst marriage stronger, and I see now that it has had the same effect on mine. So maybe Caroline has done some good in the world, if not for her."

Darcy shook his head. "You are the eternal optimist." He wondered if Bingley was being wilfully blind. He hesitated again, but knew that he had to ask. "Have you heard any more of her feelings towards . . ." He stopped.

"You and Elizabeth?" Bingley asked. Darcy nodded. "She did say something to Louisa when she was in town, speaking of you with great, almost possessive affection."

"And of Elizabeth?" He demanded.

Bingley paused. "She indicated that Elizabeth was not worthy of you."

Darcy's chest tightened. "Elizabeth and I both heard the knob on our chamber door being turned her last night at Lyndon Hall." Darcy closed his eyes. "Please keep us informed of her movements." He opened them again to see Bingley watching him with a worried expression.

"I will Darcy, I understand now."

Darcy gripped his arm and said very seriously. "She is unbalanced. Watch her. You must not let this rest."

JANE, ELIZABETH, AND GEORGIANA sat together, cooing at baby Angela. "Lizzy, you are enormous!"

"Thank you, Jane." Elizabeth said wryly, attempting to find a comfortable position.

"Oh, you know that was not an insult!" She touched her sister's belly. "Are you sure you are not due today?"

"I wish I were." She smiled, her relationship with her sister was warm, but she doubted it would ever be as close as it once was again, but she loved her, and that was what mattered. "Please distract me ladies. Talk of something besides my expanding waist!"

"We have decided on a wedding date." Georgiana burst out. She was dying to tell them. "I received a letter from Alex this morning. He spoke with his parents and visited his attorney in town for the settlement, and will be back here to meet with William in eight days." She smiled with anticipation. "We will marry in the Pemberley chapel at the end of September, on the 27th." She looked at Elizabeth. "That should give you time to recover from the birth, will it not?"

"Oh yes, that should give me at least six weeks. I am sorry that Richard and Kathleen will be unable to attend, as she is due about then. Just how elaborate a ceremony do you wish for, Georgiana?"

"I want a wedding just like yours, Elizabeth!" She effused.

Elizabeth tilted her head and looked at her sister, her brow furrowed. "I truly doubt that, Georgiana."

"No, I mean very simple. I do not want hordes of people, and as both of us have very small families, I just want us and a simple wedding breakfast."

She nodded and smiled. "That sounds lovely. I think that we can manage that very nicely."

"Papa will be visiting us then." Jane said quietly, and then looked up to meet Elizabeth's eyes. "Will he be welcome at Pemberley?"

She looked at her steadily for a moment. "Yes, through letters, my relationship and subsequently William's tolerance of him has improved. You must realize that it takes a great deal of time to heal the very deep wounds inflicted upon a person due to the selfish, deliberate behaviour of another." She watched her sister's expression as the words sunk in. "Trust is a precious gift which must be earned." Jane blushed and looked down. Elizabeth hoped her point was made.

Georgiana's beaming smile suddenly disappeared. "Do you think, Elizabeth, do you think that your father should . . . should he know about Alex? I know that it is a great secret, but . . . perhaps they should truly meet."

Elizabeth looked at Jane who raised her shoulders. "I really do not know. I have always left it to Alex's discretion who should know. One thing that I do expect is Mama to see the resemblance between the two of them. She mentioned it when they first met, but she was distracted by Jane's wedding announcement and then he left. The second time she saw him was at Jane's wedding, and she was so overwhelmed then that she did not say anything at all. This time, it is not one of her daughters marrying. She will have time to observe; especially now when she and Papa are courting, I suspect that his resemblance to the Thomas Bennet of her youth will strike her very quickly."

Georgiana nodded. "I will speak to him about this when he comes. Perhaps it is time to reveal the truth. We are all bound to see each other from time to time, and it would be odd if all of us but your parents know the truth." She looked at the two sisters. It was a discussion that they all knew would arise eventually. It seemed that the time had finally come. They could not ignore the irony that Mr. Bennet would be present at his son's wedding.

A WEEK LATER, Darcy and Elizabeth sat in their imposing chair in the master bedchamber. The doors to the balcony were wide open; the night breeze blew the drapes and helped cool the perpetually hot Elizabeth. Despite her warmth, she would not relinquish her favourite activity, cuddling with Darcy. They sat together, she in a night dress, he in a shirt and breeches, their eyes closed, when suddenly the distinct sound of "*pop*" as from a cork rent the air.

Their eyes opened and Darcy looked at her with confusion. "Did you hear that?"

"Yes." She said, equally confused.

"Darling, I might sound foolish, but I swear that sound came from you." He regarded her closely.

"I would concur. Suddenly I feel like a bottle of champagne." She bit her lip. "Do you think that it could be starting?"

"Do you feel anything?" He asked urgently.

"No, nothing at all."

"Are you sure?"

"William, I think that I would know if I felt something, and I have no doubt that I will not hesitate to express it quite clearly when I do." She said, exasperated with his silly questions.

He grinned. "That is true. Should I call the doctor?"

"Well, he has been enjoying his stay for a fortnight now. Why not ask his opinion?" She smiled and shook her head.

Darcy extricated himself from the chair and walked to the door. He told the footman in the hallway to summon the doctor. Doctor Howard arrived and hearing their story agreed that labour had begun, but it could be hours before anything of significance might occur. There was no need to panic.

The midwife was summoned, and the doctor recommended that Elizabeth attempt to sleep until the pains began. Darcy helped her onto the bed in the Mistress' bedchamber, which had been prepared for the birth, and climbed in next to her, spooning his body with hers. He wrapped his arms around her, and held her hands, caressing them. They remained silent, but he could feel her body trembling next to his.

"Lizzy, are you frightened?" He spoke softly to her.

In a shaking voice she whispered. "Yes."

"I will stay with you through all of this, darling. What frightens you?" He was trying his hardest to be comforting, when in his heart, he was just as afraid. Childbirth always carried a great deal of risk for mother and child. He entwined his fingers with hers, lending his strength with his grasp.

"I was there, and saw everything that happened with Jane, it is just . . . I suppose it is the unknown." She confessed.

Darcy closed his eyes and tried to ignore his own growing fear. "Lizzy, I want you to know how much I love you. How much I need you, and how very proud I am of you." He hugged her to him and kissed her.

She felt his damp face pressed to hers, and felt her courage rising. "William, I know that you are worried about my survival, please do not. I will be well. I promise that if you stay by my side in this, I will never leave you alone. I love you." She squeezed the hands clutching her tightly. As always, she became stronger when she felt his need for her assurance.

They stayed in their embrace for hours, eventually falling into a light sleep. The cramps became pains, and the pains became excruciating. True to his word, Darcy stayed with her throughout. At first he supported her as they walked the hallways, then held her hands and took the punishment of her grip as each contraction came and went. Jane wiped her brow, brought her water, and comforted her as much as she could; telling her what to expect next, but Darcy was not relinquishing his position of primary caretaker for a moment. Jane watched the couple with admiration.

The midwife, Mrs. Jones, arrived and was not at all pleased to see him in the room. "Dr. Howard, I hope that you will ask this man to leave us. This is no place for him."

Darcy did not take kindly to being spoken of as if he were not there. "Madam, I appreciate your concern for my behaviour, but I assure you, I will be remaining for the duration." He fixed his most imperious glare upon her and she did not even flinch.

Dr. Howard watched the standoff for a few moments. "Mrs. Jones, I have seen Mr. Darcy's reaction to times of stress concerning his wife. I will vouch for his steadiness."

She humphed. "Then you can move him out of my way when he faints!" She directed another scathing look at Darcy and began muttering under her breath as she set out her tools of the trade, oils for soothing and lubrication, snuff to help with pushing and expelling the afterbirth, wine and a bottle of laudanum if Elizabeth became hysterical, forceps, a block of wood wrapped in cloth, twine and scissors, and many other equally mysterious and somewhat frightening items that kept the Darcys hands tightly entwined. Elizabeth, at least, had seen the array before with Jane, but Darcy was a novice, and deeply frightened. He prayed through each contraction that God give Elizabeth the strength to endure the pain and survive along with the babe. He prayed for the strength to help her as best he could.

When the midwife finally declared her ready to push, there was no question of sending him from the room. His glare matched Mrs. Jones' for fire and obstinacy. After examining her progress one last time, unhappily with Darcy present, she directed Elizabeth to rise from the bed and seat herself in the birthing chair, but it was Darcy who managed the movement. He helped her from the bed, he walked her to the chair, he arranged her nightdress, and he determined where he would station himself and how he would support her, sitting behind, his arm around her shoulders. Jane held one hand while he gripped the other. Her screams of pain were shattering to him, but he forced himself to encourage her cries. He resisted the urge to run away, she needed him.

Elizabeth completely focused on his eyes. It hurt *so* much. She listened to his directions, reminding her to breathe, and demanding that she cry out. She wished to spare him but he would not allow it. He forced himself to suppress the desperate need to make the pain stop, he knew that it was natural, but it killed him to see her tears and be helpless to stop it.

He stayed there, moving his body so that he could stare into her eyes. His deep, ever present, loving gaze held her, strengthened her, and his words of encouragement and devotion lifted her through that final, thankful moment when the intense pain suddenly ended, and the baby was born. Darcy heard none of the exclamations of the others in the room, including the baby's strong cry. He was completely concentrated on Elizabeth. When her expression of excruciating pain changed to one of undeniable relief, his heart soared. It was over. He joyfully took her face in his hands and kissed her repeatedly, their tears mixing together as they celebrated with relief and whispered declarations of love the end of the ordeal. It was only then that they looked up to see Doctor Howard holding a bundle in his arms and a happy smile on his face. "Congratulations Mr. and Mrs. Darcy. You have a son!"

The baby, big by any standards, but enormous considering the size of his mother, was washed and handed to Elizabeth. She lifted the cloth and examined his face, the shock of dark curls on his head, and the suddenly open eyes, so deep, dark, and brown, and she cried. "He is you, William!"

She beamed up at Darcy, and he smiled; that dazzling, dimpled smile, and wrapped his arm around her. He tentatively stroked his son's hand, and delighted in his instant grasp of his finger.

"Oh Lizzy, he is both of us." He whispered. Darcy tore his shining, teary eyes from his son and gazed at his glowing, exhausted wife. "You have never been more beautiful, my love." He kissed her gently.

Elizabeth laughed and stroked his stubbled face. "And you, my dear love, have never been so blind!" He laughed and lovingly kissed her again.

"Enough of that, sir." Dr. Howard said with a grin. "Mrs. Darcy still has some work to do." Darcy broke away and looked at Elizabeth, whose face reflected the pain of a new cramp.

"What is wrong?" He took her hand and watched as the baby was whisked out of her arms by Mrs. Reynolds. "Lizzy?" He looked back at the doctor.

"Nothing is wrong, she must deliver the afterbirth." The midwife massaged her belly and with a cry and one last push it was over.

Elizabeth opened her eyes to Darcy's worried gaze and smiled wearily. Dr. Howard and Jane left the room. The new parents stayed gazing at each other, oblivious to the midwife cleaning Elizabeth. After a fresh nightdress was slipped over her and the padding tied in place, Mrs. Jones said that Elizabeth was ready to move to the bed. She began to stand, but Darcy refused to let her move.

"William, I can walk a few steps!" She protested.

"No, Mrs. Darcy. You will not." Before she could say more he carefully lifted her, holding her close to his chest, and kissed her forehead. "You have done quite enough for one day, my lovely wife."

She cuddled against him and smiled. "Will you remain a mother hen forever, Mr. Darcy?"

He smiled down into her sleepy face. "Forever."

Darcy carefully settled Elizabeth into the bed, and directed Mrs. Reynolds to place the baby back into her arms. He then walked around the bed, kicked off his slippers and reclined beside her, wrapping his two most precious possessions in his protective embrace. The three lay with their eyes closed. "You all may leave us now." His whispered command arose.

Mrs. Reynolds and Mrs. Jones exchanged amused glances, the servants hurriedly removed all evidence of the birth, and soon the new family was left to sleep in peace.

When Jane left the room, she found Georgiana and Charles in the nursery, he clutching their baby girl. "Is it over?" He whispered worriedly.

Jane sank into a chair and watched him slowly rocking. "Yes, we have a beautiful nephew. He is sleeping with Lizzy and William." Georgiana squealed and ran from the room to begin writing letters.

Charles smiled as she ran out the door. "The Heir of Pemberley!" He grinned. "Your mother will be ecstatic."

She nodded. "I am afraid our little Angela will not receive nearly the adulation Lizzy's son will from his grandmother."

Charles raised his brows. "How fortunate for Angela . . . and us!"

"Charles!" Jane shook her head then asked softly. "Are you jealous?"

"Of Darcy for his heir?" Charles looked at her then down at his peaceful daughter. "No Jane, we have a beautiful healthy child. That is all that matters. Someday our heir will be born." He kissed her cheek and then looked at his wife. "Or maybe she already has been. We have no entailment, and I have no plans to create one." Angela woke and began to fuss, and Charles rose to hand her to Jane. "I will call her nurse and then we will go to sleep."

While the Darcy family slept, Mrs. Reynolds crept in to take the newborn and place him in the cradle next to the bed. When she turned, she saw that Darcy already had pulled Elizabeth tightly to him. She looked closely and realized he was not sleeping, and saw tears tracking down his cheeks before he buried his face in her neck. She noticed his shoulders starting to shake and she quickly slipped out of the room, saying a prayer of thanksgiving as she closed the door behind her.

After four quiet hours, the young master awoke and made his desires known in a very vocal way, startling Elizabeth and thoroughly alarming his father. "What is wrong?" He sat up then looked around the room in confusion.

Elizabeth laid a hand on his arm. "William, he is hungry. Could you please bring him to me?"

He stared with wide eyes. "You wish me to lift him?"

She laughed. "Well, if you do not I will climb out of this bed and . . ."

He jumped up immediately. "No, no, no, I will go."

Darcy approached the wailing baby and spoke to him seriously. "Now Wills, bear with your Papa, and I promise not to drop you."

Elizabeth covered her mouth to muffle her laughter and watched as William worked out the best method for tackling his task. His hands were so large, he could have lifted him in any way and not made a difference, but he finally made a decision, scooped him up, and clutched him to his chest. His triumphant face beamed at Elizabeth. "Now what do I do?"

She smiled. "Unless you intend to feed him, Will, I believe that you should bring him here." Walking very slowly he gently laid the baby in Elizabeth's arms.

"I did it!"

She laughed and kissed him as he sat on the edge of the bed. "Yes, now let us see if I know what to do." She opened her nightdress and placed the baby to her breast, coaxing him with the nipple and gently stroking his cheek while speaking to him softly. It took several tries, but he caught on, and the room filled with the soft humming of a baby being fed.

"What does it feel like?" Darcy asked as he watched in fascination.

"It is not unlike your attempts," he blushed, "but with a far different purpose." She gave William a teary smile as they watched their baby feed. Darcy stroked the dark curly hair.

"Are you sure that you wish to nurse him yourself? It is not expected of you. Jane has a wet nurse."

"I wish to William. I do." She looked at him with determination in her eyes.

He sighed. "Will you at least let me employ the wet nurse Mrs. Reynolds found? For the night time? I want you to sleep."

He looked worriedly at her. Elizabeth held the fingers that were stroking hers. "You mean you want my attention solely on you?" She pursed her lips.

He quickly protested. "I did not say that, Lizzy. I *do* want you to be rested." He then shyly looked into her amused eyes. "But of course, I cannot give you up either." He added sheepishly.

"Ah. I suspected as much. I just wanted to hear you say it." She smiled and closed her eyes with contentment. "Well, if you can keep me from rising when he cries, the nurse will have employment." She opened her eyes and sparkled at him. "Of course, that means that you will not be rushing to look at him either."

He smiled and shook his head. "You know me too well."

"I know that you want the people you love to be safe." Elizabeth looked down at their boy then back to him.

He leaned forward and kissed her tenderly. Darcy rose and settled back into the bed next to her, embracing his family. "Safe in my arms."

"SIR, THIS LETTER JUST ARRIVED by the Pemberley messenger." The butler bowed and handed Lord Matlock the envelope.

"Well, I imagine we know what this is!" He grinned at Lady Matlock, who sat forward on her chair.

"Do not keep us in suspense Henry, open it!"

He laughed and broke the seal, reading silently, and then looked at his son. "It seems that you owe me five pounds, Mark."

"A boy!" Mark cried. "Well done, Darcy!"

"I would say well done Elizabeth." Lady Matlock gazed pointedly at her eldest son. She turned to her husband. "An heir, how wonderful! What does he say?"

Lord Matlock smiled at his wife and read aloud. "William and Elizabeth welcomed William George Thomas Darcy into the world yesterday morning. He is a strapping lad with black curls, brown eyes, and an extraordinary wail. He is healthy and whole and his mother is beautiful and tired, but very happy and well. He looks forward to our arrival in a few weeks for Georgiana's wedding when he will introduce his heir to his questionable relations." He laughed. "Darcy was giddy when he penned this!"

Lady Matlock held out her hand for the letter and read it, smiling. "Oh I am so happy for them! I think that they could care less if it was a boy or girl, but it is good to have this burden done for them." She looked up and saw Mark gazing at his wife. Inspired by the examples of their cousins and brother, and the not too subtle hints of their parents and Aunt Catherine, they had made great efforts over the past months to improve their marriage beyond one of convenience.

"Well in a short time it will be Kathleen and Richard's turn. I hope she will hold on until after the wedding, we will have to leave soon after the breakfast for Rosings, Henry."

"Are you sure that we are wanted?" Lord Matlock asked with a smirk.

She was affronted. "Kathleen's mother is passed. Of course she wants me."

Mark met his father's twinkling eyes. "It seems Elizabeth did well without her mother's presence . . . ."

She sniffed. "Her sister was there."

"Of course, Elaine." Lord Matlock agreed.

"I hope that you will be with me when my time comes." Laura said softly.

The room became silent. "Laura, do you . . . do you have something to tell me?" Mark stared at her, unwilling to believe what he thought she had said.

Laura met his gaze. "I am with child, Mark."

"Really?" His smile was slow but was spreading rapidly. "When will . . . how long . . .?"

"I believe it will be in March, near the end of the month." She smiled.

"You are . . . two months along?" He said as he walked to her and grasped her hands. She nodded. "How long have you known?"

"I became convinced only this morning. Are you pleased, Mark?" She looked at him hopefully.

"Am I pleased?" He laughed and pulled her up and into his arms. "Of course I am! I am thrilled!" He kissed her cheek. "Thank you, Laura!"

Lord and Lady Matlock rose and congratulated them. "I will be honoured to be with you, Laura." She hugged her.

Laura whispered in her ear. "Thank you. Thank you for forcing me to change before it was too late."

The two women regarded each other and embraced again. "You are forever welcome, my dear." Lord Matlock called for champagne to be opened, to toast the new Heir of Pemberley, and the hoped for Heir of Matlock.

Chapter 44

*A*lex's carriage arrived two days after the baby's birth. Georgiana was standing outside on the steps, excitedly waiting for his carriage to come to a rest and almost outran the footman who rushed forward to open the door and pull down the steps. "Alex!" She threw her arms around his neck and kissed him.

"Georgie!" He embraced her tightly then forced himself to let go. "Sweetheart, if your brother sees us he will beat me raw!"

"Oh, he is holding his son or Elizabeth, or more likely both. He has no time to spare for us." She hugged him again.

He laughed at her persistence. "It is a boy then, wonderful! Tell me about this new nephew of ours."

"Oh Alex, he is the most handsome young man!" Georgiana took his hand and dragged him into the house. "Come, they are waiting to see you!"

"Could I change clothes, first?" He protested.

"No! Come on!" She pulled at him enthusiastically.

"You do realize I am older than you. All of this activity might leave me exhausted."

Georgiana stopped and stared at him. "That does not bode well for our honeymoon."

Alex's eyes opened wide. Georgiana smiled and pulled him along much more willingly. They arrived at the nursery and knocking, she cautiously opened the door. She looked at Alex and they entered. Elizabeth and Darcy were sitting next to each other in rockers, holding hands, the baby on Elizabeth's lap. Darcy rose and shook Alex's proffered hand. "Alex, welcome, may I introduce you to our son?"

Alex smiled at his friend and brother, "Congratulations Darcy, Georgiana told me the news the moment I arrived." He leaned to kiss Elizabeth's cheek.

"Welcome Alex!" She smiled.

"You look radiant, Elizabeth." He peeked at the swaddled bundle in her lap. "He is a handsome young man. Obviously he takes after our side." He winked at her and stood to grin at his friend.

"It will not work, Alex. Nothing would make me happier than to see our son resemble his mother." Darcy looked down at them, his eyes were shining, and his chest was puffed with pride.

"Besotted!" Alex laughed and grinned at them all. "Now, if you do not mind, I would like to make myself presentable. Darcy, whenever you feel you can tear yourself away, I have the settlement for you to sign."

"We have weeks before the wedding."

Alex regarded this new man and shook his head in bemused surprise. "Besotted!" He laughed again and Georgiana led him from the room.

DARCY ATTEMPTED to concentrate on the enormous pile of letters that had accumulated on his desk over the three weeks since fatherhood had made its welcome and permanent intrusion into his life. Concentration, however; was difficult when his attention was perpetually distracted by his wife, who seemed perfectly at ease answering notes of congratulations with her right hand, while, cuddled securely on her left arm was their son, who stared at her in rapt attention. Elizabeth looked up, feeling two identical pairs of intense brown eyes staring at her and smiled, first indulgently at one young man, then lovingly at the other. Darcy's heart lurched and he met her expression with his own smile, then sighing, bent back to work. How he could possibly love her more was beyond him, but that mark had been exceeded most thoroughly. He had experienced many moments of panic in the past weeks. Elizabeth developed a fever the morning after the birth, and Darcy felt the horrible fear that he would lose her and be left alone to raise their son. Thankfully she recovered quickly and was fine by the next day, but it only served to make him more protective. Despite the employment of the wet nurse for the night, both he and Elizabeth would rise to check on his breathing, or to care for him at the slightest sound. For the first week, Darcy absolutely refused to let her walk or venture from their chambers. Of course, Elizabeth eventually rebelled, and just the day before, when he finally gave in to his duties and left to work in his study, the first thing she did was dress and walk downstairs. At least she tried, before becoming dizzy and sitting down on the great marble staircase. She addressed the worried queries of a footman, who obviously was not fooled by her assurances, and immediately set off to alert Darcy. He came striding out of his study in time to see Elizabeth walking out the front door.

"Lizzy!" He called, but when he exited, she could not be seen. "Where did she go?" He said to himself, not a little angry with worry. He started to descend the steps to search for her when a musical voice caught his ear.

"William, what are you looking for?"

He turned and there she was, sitting on a bench directly behind him, her back against the sun-warmed stone of the house, her curls blowing slightly with the breeze. He let out a breath. "I lost you."

She shook her head and held out her hand. "How could you lose me when I am right by the door?"

He took a seat beside her, and grasped her hand. "Jenkins said that you grew faint and were sitting on the stairs. Why would you get up, Lizzy? You should be in bed!"

"No, I needed some sunshine and fresh air." She smiled at his never-ending worry. It had been three weeks, after all!

"There is a balcony off our chambers." He said stubbornly.

She caressed his face. "I needed to escape."

His brow furrowed. "From what?"

"Oh, William, do you realize how long it has been since I could simply stand and walk? I needed this." He remained unconvinced. "I need to test my limits, and I need exercise to regain my strength so I can care for you and Wills properly." She gave his hand a squeeze. "Do you have time to escort me on a stroll in the garden?"

He looked at her raised brows and beguiling smile and sighed. "You promise you will not ever walk alone?"

"I promise. If you cannot come, I will coax Georgiana to join me, at least until I am fully recovered, and then we will address the subject again." She peeked up at his lowered head. "Will that do?"

"I suppose." He said grudgingly, he had no intention of ever letting her go alone anywhere again. He looked into her smiling eyes and stood. "Shall we, my love?"

They set off on a stroll through the nearby gardens, now colourful with the flowers of the coming autumn. The nip in the air, the breeze, and the changing leaves suited to reinvigorate them both after the long confinement. She looked up at his contented face, and felt a desire to tease him. "I was thinking, William, I will have to go into Lambton soon."

"What do you need? Surely we could send a servant?" He smiled down at her.

"Well, now that I am a mother, I suppose that I really should start wearing a lace cap. I have not worn one since we married, but . . ." Any further thoughts were immediately stopped by Darcy's arms holding her to him and his lips descending upon hers.

"No. *MY* wife will not cover her beauty with such a thing. If someone wants proof of your wedded state, they may look at your hand. If they wish to see that you are a mother, they may see our son. Your hair was meant to be seen. I will buy you combs, ribbons, jewels or feathers to decorate your hair, I will even accompany you to the milliner's to purchase hats and bonnets to wear outside of our home, but please do not ask me to see you in a cap."

Elizabeth laughed and kissed the lips that hovered over hers and smiled up into his serious eyes. "But William, it is also meant to keep my head warm!"

"Was your head cold before you married, my love?" His lips began wandering over her face and neck.

"No, I suppose it was not." She said, closing her eyes and feeling a familiar ache returning to her recovering body.

"Then please indulge my desire. I have no doubt that my eccentricity will become quite fashionable before long." His lips travelled lower to taste her shoulder.

"Oh my, William, you are reading the fashion magazines?" She whispered breathlessly.

"Of course not. We do not need them. *You* shall set the fashion." His breath was coming in rasps, and his hands began to travel over her form. Her waist was almost back to its former state, but her breasts were tender and enlarged by their new duty. "Oh Lizzy, how much longer must we wait?"

"Three weeks, my love."

"The moment you are recovered, find me." He stared into her eyes. "The second you are ready."

Elizabeth swallowed and felt the burn of his desire as he ran his hands over her, and nodded. "I will."

THE IMPOSING CARRIAGE rolled up to the entrance of Rosings, and for the first time in over a year, Lady Catherine de Bourgh entered her former home. Her old housekeeper led her to the drawing room where the very pregnant Kathleen rested on a sofa, her swollen feet propped on pillows. The older woman looked around the room. Gone were the ornate decorations. Now the room held a brightness, a happiness that Lady Catherine never achieved as her goal was to display her wealth, not to create a comfortable home. Kathleen moved to rise and Lady Catherine stopped her.

"Stay seated Mrs. Fitzwilliam. I will not have you risking your well-being for a courtesy."

"Thank you Aunt Catherine. Without my husband's assistance, I am afraid that rising from a chair has become a quite undignified process." She smiled and indicated a chair, "Please be seated. I hope that your journey was comfortable."

"It was. My carriage was made for that purpose. Nonetheless, I am pleased to take this much shorter trip than the journey to Pemberley would have been."

"Is that why you decided not to attend Georgiana and Alex's wedding?"

Lady Catherine regarded the young woman in silence, and then spoke. "No. I am here because my daughter's wish in giving Rosings to your husband was for him to marry and fill these halls with the sound of children's voices, and make this place a home. From what I see already, the transformation is well underway. I wish to be here to witness Anne's dreams come to fruition." She blinked back a tear and resumed her fierce expression.

Kathleen understood this woman's desire to show no weakness and did not make notice of her emotion. "Well Richard and I are delighted to have you here. We expect that his parents will arrive in time for the birth. They plan to leave for Rosings directly from Pemberley after the wedding, although, if this child chooses to appear sooner, I will not protest!"

"From what I remember of my experience, I understand your desire to see this process end." Softening she nodded to her legs. "You will be pleased to see that you indeed will have feet again very quickly."

Kathleen smiled and laughed with surprise at her unexpected levity. "Thank you; I do harbour hopes of that!"

Richard entered the room, smiling at hearing Kathleen's laughter. "Aunt Catherine! Welcome!" He came and kissed the proffered fingers.

"Where have you been, Nephew?" She demanded.

He rolled his eyes at Kathleen. "I have been attending to estate affairs. Our harvest is underway."

She nodded her acceptance of his explanation. "And how is the harvest?"

"Excellent. My steward, in fact, my entire family has taken me under their collective wing and has been of great help. I have learned a great deal this year."

She regarded him. "What think you of the Heir of Pemberley?"

"We were delighted to hear of Wills' birth. Georgiana and Darcy both wrote to us with the wonderful news. I hope that our child will have the opportunity to see his older cousin often." He paused and smiled. "Of course, Elizabeth's sister gave birth to a daughter recently, so I am not sure if a marriage has been arranged between those cousins yet. We may be too late to join Pemberley and Rosings, if we have a daughter, that is."

Kathleen closed her eyes at his humour. She knew that Richard could not resist jabbing his aunt.

"You know Anne and Darcy would have been a brilliant match." She huffed. "But, I have formed the opinion that arranged marriages are not always ideal. I hope that you keep that in mind, Fitzwilliam!"

"Yes, Aunt Catherine, I hope that our child will follow his parents' example." He sat next to Kathleen and kissed her hand.

She watched the tenderness and softened for a moment, then barked. "Humph. Well, show me to my room, Fitzwilliam!"

"Of course." He jumped to his feet and offering his arm to her and a grin to his wife, led the way upstairs.

Six days later, Lady Catherine was indeed present in the room where she once gave birth, holding Kathleen's hand while Charlotte wiped her brow. Richard paced outside of the room, endeavouring to ignore his wife's cries by devising increasingly painful ways to dispatch Mr. Collins, who felt it was his duty to honour his patron and to stand by him at this most extraordinary time.

Unable to bear the effusions of the obsequious man any longer, he strode to the bedroom door, pulled it open and stepped in. He stood in open-mouthed shock. He could feel Collins attempting to see past him, turned, casting a melting glare upon him, and slammed the door in his face.

Lady Catherine looked up from her position and demanded, "What are you doing here, Fitzwilliam! This is no place for you! Be gone!"

Richard took in the scene, Kathleen on the birthing chair, her head bent, eyes tightly shut, a block of wood clenched in her teeth. His aunt on one side, Charlotte on the other, the midwife crouched at her feet. His eyes searched the room for something to focus upon besides his wife's contorted face, when a wrenching scream tore from her. "Katie?" He stuttered, and he did as any strong, confident, experienced soldier would, and promptly collapsed with a floor-shaking thud.

Kathleen panted, the wood fallen from her mouth. "What was that?" She whispered in the reprieve between contractions.

Lady Catherine raised a satisfied brow at her comatose nephew. "*That* my dear, is the weaker sex facing his truth."

"You have the right of that, my Lady." The midwife nodded, casting a disgusted look at the fallen man.

"Is. . . Is he . . . well?" Kathleen groaned out.

"He is much better off than he was in my husband's company, I think." Charlotte said, looking at him sympathetically.

Lady Catherine rolled her eyes. "I look forward to writing to Darcy of this." Kathleen gripped her hand again. She gave her niece a motherly smile. "Come now, my dear, you are nearly there."

Kathleen's labour was blessedly short, and within only four hours, she delivered a healthy, golden-haired girl, named Anne Kathleen Fitzwilliam. Her husband was revived upon hearing the energetic cries of his daughter and was so delighted he kissed his aunt and swung Charlotte around in a joyful spin. Soon enough he settled next to Kathleen on the bed to delight in his new family. Lady Catherine sent an express to Darcy with the news of the birth and his cousin's reaction. He would never hear the end of it.

ELIZABETH WATCHED, her heart swelling, as William tenderly kissed Wills and lay him down for the night. It was a ritual they began spontaneously on his third day of life. Elizabeth would sit in the rocker, feeding him, singing and cooing, while his eyes slowly drifted closed. Darcy would rise from his seat; and lifting him from her arms, hold his son to his face, murmur some secret, kiss, and place him safely to sleep. This night when William turned back, she held out her hand to him and smiled. "Come." She said softly.

"Lizzy?" He was unsure of her intentions. It was not quite six weeks since the birth, and she had said . . . he saw the familiar, deeply missed, look of welcome in her eyes and drew a quick breath.

"Come." She repeated, and led him from the nursery and through her bedchamber, back to his, where they had not slept since Wills' arrival. He closed the door behind him and watched, his heart pounding, as Elizabeth's hair cascaded down around her shoulders with the slow removal of the pins. She looked nowhere but into his eyes, and her fingers began to unbutton her gown. Trembling, he stepped forward, touching her hand. "Are you sure, darling? I do not wish to harm you." He was trying so hard to control his rapidly building desire, just in case he was misreading her actions, or she changed her mind, or . . .

"Love me William, I need you." She caressed his dear face.

"Oh Lizzy, yes, I need you, too." He pulled her to him and tangled one hand in her hair while the other held her body securely to his. He searched her face one last time for reassurance, then gratefully lowered his head and possessed those beautiful rosy lips with his own. His body screamed for him to ravage her, to strip off the unnecessary clothing, and throw her onto the bed, leap upon her warm, yielding body, and vigorously drive his aching, swollen manhood deep, deep inside of her until he roared with his rapture and she fell back in a molten lake of euphoric pleasure. He wanted to hear her beg him to satisfy her, he wanted her to crave his body, he wanted . . . oh God . . . he wanted to feel his gloriously beautiful wife cling to him and desire him as desperately as he needed her. He tore his lips from hers and looked into her half-closed eyes, and saw what she wanted. She wanted to be loved; he knew that expression so well. She wanted it to be slow, affectionate, and tender. This first time together, this first time when they could lie face to face in so very long, she wanted him to love her, not take her, the time for that sort of lovemaking would come another night, and he was more than willing to give her the pleasure she desired.

They slowly undressed each other, taking their time. As each item fell away, their lips tasted the newly exposed skin, first her sweet shoulders, then his delicious neck, her swollen breasts and his taut, muscular chest. Their hands glided over their bodies, pushing aside the unwanted barriers until they stood naked, gazing at their lover, then embraced, tightly entwined, anticipating their reunion. "I have missed this, sweetheart." He murmured in her hair.

"So have I." She said, and he felt some tears on his chest.

He looked down. "Lizzy?"

"Do I . . . does my body still please you?" She said in a quiet voice. "I know that I have changed, my hips are wider, and my stomach is not quite flat as yet, and my breasts are so swollen and they leak, and . . ." Her ramblings were halted by his lips. He was right, she needed to be loved and reassured. He scooped her up and lay her down in the bed and immediately lay on top of her; *that* was a feeling that *they both* craved.

He kissed her softly. "My dearest Elizabeth, your body, your entire being pleases me. You are more beautiful now than you have ever been." His hands caressed her sides. "Your hips are even more delightfully curved than ever, and have given me more to hold." He ran his tongue from her lips, down her neck, between her breasts to her stomach, where he kissed and caressed her slightly rounded belly. "Your shape is lovely, and if it never becomes flat again, I do not care, because I know the gift that grew inside of you." His mouth rose to her breasts where he licked and suckled the tender nipples, swallowing and revelling in the taste of his wife's milk. "Your breasts have always been a favourite of mine my love; and you cannot possibly think that I would object to there being more of them for me to enjoy." His mouth travelled to the other, suckling it and relieving the uncomfortable pressure. He moved back up and settled his weight back on top of her. Her arms encircled him while he held her face in his hands. He smiled into her worried eyes. "Have I convinced you, my Lizzy? Or do I need to do more?"

"More." She whispered.

"As you wish." His lips hovered over hers for a moment, then seeing the light of desire in her eyes, began kissing her deeply. Her response was as fervent as he hoped it would be, and soon they both were caressing each other, urging their bodies closer together. Elizabeth opened her legs and he fell naturally in between. Unable to wait longer, he rose to his knees and touched her, feeling the wetness. He plunged his fingers into her core, watching for any sign of discomfort, but instead saw her pleading eyes. He smiled and with no more hesitation, entered his Elizabeth, and made her his all over again. Her response was every bit as passionate as he dreamed. Their bodies slid and melded together. His thrusts, at first long and slow, gave in to the primal need to rise to the fevered vigour that a man craves. Elizabeth met his strokes and devoured his lips with kisses that reaffirmed the ardent, unending love that she held for her man. Their motion went on and on, building upon and exceeding the memories of every past encounter, when finally Darcy heard that longed for cry from his lover's lips, begging him to give her everything he had, and with his cry of joyous release, he felt her body clasp his, and take his essence deep inside, as her ecstatic kisses covered his face in her own surrender.

Panting he shakily pushed up from her. "Oh, Lizzy, I missed you so much!" He kissed her and rolled to his side, bringing her clinging form with him, and surrounded her with his tight embrace.

She smiled and looked up at him. "I have wanted to do this for weeks."

"You have?" He ran his hands over her. "But you have been so tired and sore."

"Well, yes, of course, but all of those nights we spent loving each other with our lips and hands, I anticipated when we could once again be one body." She hugged him. "As much as I adore your tender ministrations, my love, I needed to feel you inside of me again. I see that you agree?" She laughed at his vigorously nodding head and then grew serious, asking quietly, "Did it feel the same?"

Darcy knew exactly to what she referred. "It felt better." He stroked her face and kissed her.

She looked up, searching his face, and finally relaxed, cuddling into his chest to hear his slowing heartbeat. "Yes, it did." He chuckled and kissed her hair, and pulling the covers over them, settled down to a long night of needed rest. This night, the nurse would finally perform her duties.

THE CARRIAGES BEGAN ARRIVING, carrying the guests for the wedding of Georgiana Darcy to Alex Carrington. First were the carriages from Matlock, bearing the Fitzwilliams. Alex's parents came next. Alex and Georgiana would be leaving immediately after the wedding to the cottage for their honeymoon. It was still warm enough to enjoy the beautiful scenery there before the weather changed. The Carringtons had many friends, but few relatives, and since this was a family affair only, Alex's parents would be the only official members of his family to be present, at least with the exception of his Bennet family. Jane and Bingley's carriage, followed by their Bennet houseguests' carriage were the last to arrive. Kitty was in school, so Mary was the only sister to come with them. The reactions heard from that last arrival to Pemberley were just as excited and effusive as they were at Christmas, but they were all careful to restrain themselves in the presence of their host.

When Mr. Bennet emerged from his carriage, he was greeted by Elizabeth, beaming, holding baby Wills in her arms. Darcy was standing next to her, proudly looking down at his son, his hand resting gently on his wife's shoulder. He looked up when his in-laws approached. "Oh Lizzy! You have your son! Oh Mr. Darcy! How proud you must be! My Lizzy has fulfilled her duty and given you an heir! Oh my clever, clever girl!" She kissed her daughter's cheek and stroked the soft baby face. Elizabeth blushed and looked down at the ground. It was William's gentle voice that brought her back.

"Yes, Mrs. Bennet, we are delighted to have our son, but I would have been overjoyed with any child. I hope with all my heart that our next is a daughter just like her Mama." He looked into her eyes, full of love for her.

Mr. Bennet took in the scene with great emotion. "I am delighted to meet my grandson at last." He kissed Elizabeth's cheek. "You look beautiful, my dear." He turned to Darcy and addressed him formally. "Congratulations, Mr. Darcy."

Darcy held out his hand. "Thank you sir, please call me Darcy."

Mr. Bennet looked at him, trying to read his face, but Darcy displayed nothing but his usual solemn demeanour. He gratefully took the offered hand. "I would be honoured sir, and I hope you will call me Bennet."

Darcy nodded, and looked at Elizabeth. Her eyes were full of tears. They had all come such a long way.

Later, after dinner when everyone was gathered together in the music room listening to Georgiana play, Mrs. Bennet sat staring at Alex. She tapped Mr. Bennet's leg. "You know Thomas, I had forgotten, but I remember thinking the first time I saw Mr. Carrington that he resembled you in your youth. Do you not think so?"

Mr. Bennet looked at her with surprise. "I thought the same thing, Fanny."

Elizabeth heard the conversation and squeezed William's hand. He nodded and signalling Alex, he turned to Mr. Bennet. "Bennet, I wonder if you would care to join me in the library for a few minutes?"

"You do not have to ask me to do that twice, sir! Please, lead the way!" The men rose, and Elizabeth, Alex and Mr. Carrington followed them.

They arrived in the enormous room, and surprised, Mr. Bennet saw that they were not alone. "What is this?" He asked, first looking to Darcy then catching Elizabeth's eye.

She walked to him, and laid a hand on his arm. "Please sit down, Papa. We have something to tell you."

"All of you?" He asked, confused.

"Yes, Bennet, this involves all of us to some degree." Darcy looked to Alex. They had agreed that if at any point during their stay, someone recognized the resemblance between Mr. Bennet and Alex, the truth would finally be told. It was decided that Darcy would be the calm moderator of the discussion. "Sir, I believe you have recognized that you resemble Alex."

"Yes," he said slowly.

"Alex has given me permission to tell this story." He looked to Elizabeth, and she rose and took his hand. "Alex is the adopted son of Philip and Amanda Carrington."

"Adopted?" He looked at Alex with surprise.

"Yes sir." He answered, and looked with pride at Philip.

"Approximately nine and twenty years ago, a young chambermaid, a niece of the cook to the Carrington family came to her seeking help. She had been dismissed from her position with the Markham family when she was found to be with child by a gentleman friend of the Markham's son. She came to her aunt to find employment." At the sound of the name Markham, Mr. Bennet's eyes opened wide. "The cook brought the situation to Amanda's attention, who told her husband. They knew that after many years of trying, their hopes of having children of their own were impossible. They decided to take in this rejected child of a gentleman and raise him or her as their heir. Alex was the child born to the maid. Before the girl died in childbirth, she testified to the name of the baby's father." Everyone in the room looked at Mr. Bennet, who only had eyes for Alex.

"You are my son?" He whispered.

"Yes, sir." Alex looked straight at him.

The two stared at each other, while the room remained silent. "I knew that the maid was with child when I came to visit again. She claimed that it was mine, but I did not believe her. I thought that it was a ruse to try to extract funds from a convenient source. I had no way of knowing for sure. I wondered over the years, but I never tried to find out the truth. I never saw Markham again after graduation. My father died and I had to assume his duties. I no longer had time for the frivolities of youth. Soon I married Fanny, and we began our family." He looked into Alex's eyes. "You are my heir."

Alex shook his head. "No sir, I am not. I will not dishonour the man who rescued, raised and loved me." He looked to Philip, who had tears of pride in his eyes. "I am the heir of Philip and Amanda Carrington."

Mr. Bennet closed his eyes, sadly acknowledging the truth. "You are, of course, correct. You have made the proper choice." He looked at him, "I would like the opportunity to know you."

"As I would you, sir. I would like to know my blood history, so that I can tell it to my children."

"Thank you for that, sir." He blinked back a tear, and felt Elizabeth's hand in his. He looked at her. "How long have you known?"

"William told me when we were at Rosings. Philip and Amanda realized who Jane and I were when we were at their ball, and asked to speak to William about it.

They were concerned with Alex's attraction to Jane." She smiled at him, and he shook his head.

"It seems that I am very much attracted to women with blond hair and big blue eyes." Everyone laughed, breaking the tension.

"So when you came to Longbourn . . ." Mr. Bennet addressed him.

"It was to meet my birth father."

"I must have made a wonderful impression." He smiled sardonically.

Alex's smile was exactly the same. "It was . . . memorable."

"I would like to know you, Mr. Carrington." Mr. Bennet said softly. "I cannot make up for not taking responsibility for you, but I can try to be your friend, if you would like."

Alex looked at his father, then his sister, and his friend, finally turning to Mr. Bennet. "Please call me Alex, and yes, I would like that as well."

The two men rose and shook hands. Elizabeth kissed first her father, then her brother. Mr. Bennet offered his hand to Philip. "Thank you sir, you have raised a fine son. I doubt that I could have done better, and probably would have done much worse. He is fortunate to have you as his father."

"Thank you, sir." Philip placed his hand on Alex's shoulder. "I will leave you two alone. I think that you have much to discuss." He looked at the two men once more, and exited the room with the rest of the group.

Alex and Mr. Bennet stared at each other for a minute, and then sank down into their chairs. "Well, sir, where shall we begin?" Mr. Bennet asked.

"At the beginning, sir. Tell me all." The men stayed in the library until the very early hours of the morning. They both left with a new understanding of themselves.

"GEORGIANA MAY I SPEAK TO YOU?" Darcy asked. He was standing, a little nervously, at the door to her bedchamber. Georgiana was supervising the packing of her clothes, separating out the things she would take on her honeymoon from the things that would be sent to Kingston Hall, where she and Alex would live when they were not at the Carrington townhouse in London.

"Of course, William, please come in." She dismissed her maid and led him into the small sitting room adjacent to the emptying dressing room.

Darcy took a seat and looked about the room. Was it only two years ago that he had everything redecorated in an effort to please his depressed sister after Ramsgate? And now the event that he feared would never happen for her was about to take place, and he was going to see her married. He cleared his throat, and attempted to control his emotion. "Georgie, I . . ." He looked down, he fiddled with his cuff, he ran his fingers through his hair, and then looked up to his sister's understanding blue eyes. "I do not think that we will have the opportunity to speak alone again like this. The wedding preparations, small as they are, seem to be taking over, and well, I just wanted to tell you how very proud I am of you, and I know that you will have a happy life with Alex. You could not have accepted a better man." He let out a breath, and looked at his twisting hands.

"William. Thank you." She stared down at her own hands; the two siblings were identical in their native shyness, although both had been touched by the same woman to achieve the ability to express themselves. Georgiana gathered her rapidly forming thoughts. "I know that I have chosen a wonderful man, and with the example that you and Elizabeth have shown me, I hope to achieve a similar felicity in my marriage. Alex has stated the same hopes, as he has seen you and his own parents' enduring relationship. I knew after seeing your happiness that I would only marry for the same reasons." She drew a deep breath.

"I . . . I shall miss you Georgie. Pemberley will be lacking without you, but I always knew that someday you would leave. It is just, you must understand; you were the only family I had for a very long time. After Mother died, I . . . I consoled myself by taking care of you, at least, when I was home from school. It was good to know that I would be coming home to see your happy welcoming face, someone who loved me without reservation. For many years when I was at Cambridge, seeing you was the only reason I returned. After father changed, and began talking to me, it was . . . wonderful to feel like a family, and see your happiness making us both smile. When he died, you were all that I had left, and I was determined to do well by you. If I did not have Elizabeth, and now Wills, I . . . I do not know how I could have faced your wedding day." He looked up at her, his eyes bright with emotion, his hands twisting together. Georgiana understood how hard it was for him to talk about his feelings, as she was afflicted the same way.

She sat beside him, taking his hands. "I could not have been blessed with a better brother, and I could not have accepted any man's offer until I knew that you were loved and not alone. I would have gladly stayed at Pemberley all my life rather than leave you." She hugged him. "I thank you for everything you have done for me, my entire life; some things more than others." They exchanged a look, knowing she meant Wickham. "I love you William, and though I will be another man's wife, I will always be your little sister. You have not lost me."

Darcy smiled. "You are correct; I just wanted to tell you . . . that I love you too." He kissed her cheek and hugged her. "Now, go finish your packing. I am sure that Alex is impatiently waiting for your return to his side." He stood and squeezed her hand. "We are both blessed with finding our soul mates."

"And what a surprise that they were brother and sister!" She laughed.

Darcy chuckled. "Just like us!" He smiled and feeling much better, went in search of his wife.

DARCY AND ELIZABETH STOOD on the steps of Pemberley and waved a tearful goodbye as Georgiana and Alex departed for their honeymoon amid a shower of shoes from the servants. He looked down at his glowing wife, and she reached up, caressing his cheek. "She is very happy, William."

"I know." He whispered.

"Let's go visit our son. I think that our guests can entertain themselves for the time being." She took his hand and led him inside and up to the nursery. They entered the room and dismissed the nurse. Elizabeth lifted little Wills from his cradle and the couple walked back to their bedchamber, settling into their favourite chair.

"I think that he looks like you, Lizzy." Darcy started the familiar argument.

"I do not have dimples, sir. You do, at least when you care to show them, you do." She teased.

"Do I not smile enough for you?" He asked as he raised his brow.

"Well, you smile more than you once did. It does not seem to be a struggle to coax one from you anymore." She grinned, her eyes sparkling up at him.

"It is hard to believe that I ever was that man, Lizzy. I am so grateful for you taking pity on me that momentous birthday at the theatre." He wrapped his arms around her and their son, and rested his hands over hers.

"That was not pity sir; it was the joy of a challenge, and fascination with your beautiful eyes." She entwined her fingers with his. "I am just thrilled that you allowed yourself to accept my challenge and respond. I have often wondered what moved you that day. It certainly was not in your nature to respond in such a way."

"I do not think it was in your nature to issue such a challenge, dear Lizzy." He whispered, nuzzling her neck.

She closed her eyes, and moved her head to allow him room to brush his lips. "You do not?" She asked softly.

"No, but I do think that whenever you see that I need you, you have always ignored the urge to hold yourself back, and instead jumped to reassure me. I think that was what you were doing that night." His gently kissed her ear.

She lifted her head. "But I did not know you then."

"Yes you did. You dreamed of me, remember?" His smiling eyes twinkled.

"So I did. But you have neatly avoided explaining your behaviour, sir." She raised her brows.

"Ah, you are far too clever, my love." He hugged her tightly to him. "Well, now you must know, I dreamed of you, too."

"You did? What was this dream?" She asked curiously.

He gently caressed her cheek and looked deeply into her eyes. "I dreamed of meeting a lady who would fill my heart with joy, my soul with peace, and my life with love. I knew that I would recognize her instantly when she smiled at me. I knew that when I first looked into her eyes, I would feel the connection and that when this happened, my life would be transformed, and that I should do everything in my power to win her heart, because without her, my life would continue as the lonely, empty existence it had been up to that wonderful day."

"And you saw me." She whispered, in awe of his tale.

"And you saw me." He repeated, leaning down to tenderly kiss her lips.

"I love you, my William."

"I love you, my dearest Elizabeth."

Epilogue

The two men on horseback appeared to be identical. Both sat straight, proud, with fine athletic figures and apparent ease. Dark, intense eyes scanned the fields, the older man, distinguishable only because of his gray-streaked hair and deeply incised laugh lines around his eyes, looked at his mirror, and a warm smile spread over his face. "Well Son, are you ready to take on your assignment?"

William Darcy, Wills to his family, drew a breath and nodded at his father, and inwardly chuckled as he saw the excitement that he was so obviously trying to repress. He found it hard to believe sometimes the descriptions his mother and other family members gave of his father in his younger years, when he never smiled, was never happy, and could not consider displaying any emotion other than that of a very solemn, sedate, man. He did still have that look about him, especially in a crowded room, but the image he had of his father at home was one of great happiness and joy, particularly when in the company of his mother.

"Yes, I think that I will enjoy this challenge to plan next year's crops. With this year's harvest now complete, I will have all winter to think it through, and decide what grew well and what should be changed."

Darcy nodded. "Very good, but remember, I expect your report by Christmas, so that we can refine it if necessary."

"Of course, Father." Wills looked at him, and shook his head. "Now that I am five and twenty, I find it all the more extraordinary that you were Master of Pemberley at two and twenty. I do not think that I would have been capable of taking it on, or making it what it is today. The crops are such a small part of the whole. I would have been overwhelmed."

Darcy smiled. "You do not know that. Never say never, Wills. I rose to the challenge because I had to. Just be grateful it did not happen that way for you."

"I will make you proud, sir."

"You always have." Darcy looked away, feeling his chest swell. He was so very proud of this boy, this man.

The two worked their way back to the stables, dismounted, and walked into the house. They were met at the door by their housekeeper, Mrs. Henderson, the granddaughter of Mrs. Reynolds. Darcy smiled as a maid took his hat. "Where might I find my wife, Mrs. Henderson?"

"Oh sir, Mrs. Darcy has not returned from her walk yet."

Darcy felt a jolt and spoke sharply, "She has not returned? How late is she?"

"She is an hour past her time, sir." She cringed. She knew what was coming, and sure enough, there was the look of panic in her master's eyes, the one that always came when he thought Mrs. Darcy was in any danger, real or imagined. "I am sure she will be right home, sir. It is a lovely day for walking." She tried to reassure him, but knew it was an exercise in futility.

Trying to control his voice he asked, "What path did she take?"

"The lake path, sir." He nodded and taking his hat back from the maid, turned and began walking out the door.

"Father, where are you going? She is fine, she always is." Wills tried. "I will come with you."

Darcy met his son's gaze. "No Son, she is *not* always fine. I will go and find her. You should get to work." He turned and left the house to mount a fresh horse and begin his search. His chest tight, the old feeling of fear was rising in him.

Wills went to his rooms and changed from his riding clothes and descended to the study his father had given him when he came of age. It was actually meant to be the mistress's study, but his mother had moved into his father's when she moved into Pemberley, just over twenty six years ago. He sat down behind the desk and thought of his father's expression and wondered at it. His cousin Richard Fitzwilliam only that past summer had told him the story of his mother's abduction. That was their first trial, but so many other times his parents' marriage had been tested. He was old enough to remember his father sobbing at her bedside several times, after accidents, deaths, and his mother's voice, begging him to come back to her when he lay in that same bed. They were chilling times, which always led back to the extraordinary marriage they had. He hoped he would someday find a wife he could love as his parents obviously did. Like his father, he was unhappy with the pretence of society. He looked up at the sound of a horse as it galloped by on the drive, and saw his father set off on his search. His face did not hide the worry that Wills could easily see, even at such a distance. *Mama is fine Papa, you will see.*

"Lizzy!" Darcy called as he rode slowly down the path. His eyes darted around, searching for any sign of her. "Lizzy, where are you?" He kept on, pausing slightly at the old spot where Wickham had attacked, then, unable to stop himself, reined in the horse and dismounted, forcing himself to look over the edge of the cliff to see if she lay by the stream below. Letting out a stale breath at seeing nothing more than the placidly flowing water, he returned to his horse. "Lizzy!" He called again. This time he thought that he heard a voice. Kicking his mount, he continued on, looking, looking, then relief.

"There you are!" He jumped down and throwing the reins over a branch, rushed to her.

Elizabeth smiled up at him from her seat on a fallen tree, still just as lovely as she was the first time he saw her. "I knew you would come for me." She caressed his face, seeing the fear there. "I am so sorry for worrying you."

Darcy sat on the log and brushed the back of his fingers across her cheek. "Are you well? What has kept you?"

Ruefully she pulled up her skirt and showed him her swollen ankle. "I had an altercation with a root that had the impertinence as to grow across the path." She pointed to a spot not too far away. "I considered limping back, but I thought my dear husband would not be happy about that, surely he would come to rescue me before too long."

Darcy was already removing his tie and took her foot in his hand, moving the ankle to be sure it was not broken, then quickly bound it up. He did not say a word. Elizabeth knew that he was trying hard not to say exactly what was on his mind, and further knew that he would anyway.

"Lizzy, I do not want you walking alone again." She smiled. If she could have laid a bet, she would have won. He gently set her foot down and then lifting her up in his lap, he kissed her. He looked seriously down at her; and said softly, "Please stop torturing me like this."

"Will, I do not walk to torture you. I walk for exercise." She stroked his cheek. "I could just as easily demand that you stop riding."

"You would never do that, besides, Wills is always with me." Holding her close, he buried his face against her throat. "Wills thought you were fine."

"But he offered to come with you?" She asked, and felt his nod. "He is a good boy."

"He is hardly a boy anymore, Lizzy." He whispered, letting his fears go now that she was in his arms.

"They will always be my little boys, just as Beth will be my little girl, even though she is married." She kissed his cheek. "I wish . . ."

He held her tighter. "What do you wish, sweetheart?"

"Never mind." She whispered.

"You wish that we had more children." He looked up at her wistful face.

She nodded. "It was not for lack of trying, was it?" She laughed and hugged him. He smiled at her. Their many losses had been so hard on them both, sometimes he wondered if it was something from his Fitzwilliam side that had to do with it, Richard only had two, and Mark managed three.

"I should not complain, our three are wonderful, and taking in Kitty's has been a joy. But soon they will be grown and leave us, too." She paused. "Sometimes I look at Jane and I am jealous." She admitted.

"Would you truly wish to have birthed twelve children?" Darcy asked, now brushing back a stray curl, and laughed when she made a face in horror. He kissed her cheek. "I am just so happy that they finally had their boy."

Elizabeth wiped a tear and laughed. "Poor baby Charles. He will be spoiled and overprotected. We must make sure to look out for him, William."

He nodded. "We will." She kissed his lips, "I think, my dear Elizabeth that what you are feeling are the pangs of a mother who just married off her daughter." He smiled and his eyes regained their twinkle.

She pursed her lips. "Oh, and you did not hole up in the library at the thought of your baby girl leaving home!"

"I do not deny that at all! I am merely making an observation of you." He hugged her tightly to him. "Wills will never leave us."

Snuggling into his chest, she listened to his steady heartbeat, and relaxed. "I could not bear to lose him, too." She whispered. His chuckle rumbled in her ear. "Georgiana's Bess is engaged, did I tell you? No, the letter just came today. The first of her three to marry, Alex will undoubtedly be asking you for advice on giving up his only daughter."

"No doubt." Darcy smiled. "He did say something about trying for another. Perhaps it is not too late for us." He brushed her lips seductively. It was time to cheer her.

She smiled. She was not formed for melancholy. "Mr. Darcy, what exactly do you have in mind?" Her eyes were lit up and sparkling, seeing the old familiar desire in his.

"I think, my beautiful, luscious, fascinating wife; that I wish to ravage you most thoroughly." He began nibbling her neck, on that particular spot that made her so very happy. Elizabeth drew his head up to hers and kissing his hungry lips moaned, "Ohhhhh Will, yes, please, yes."

Several hours later, Wills Darcy looked up from his work to see his father galloping past the window, beaming, while his laughing mother was held tightly in his arms. He smiled, shook his head, and returned to work.

The End

About the Author

Linda Wells worked for years in the environmental engineering world until she traded her career as a geographer for one as a mom to a challenging and really great son. After seeing the 2005 production of *Pride and Prejudice*, she bought a copy of Jane Austen's masterpiece and fell under the spell of her unforgettable characters and story. Eventually, a story of her own started nagging at her until she finally wrote it down. It has become a wonderful and rewarding experience to stretch her imagination, and with ideas for new stories still nagging at her, she hopes to write many more.

If you would like to contact Linda, she would be happy to hear from you: Lindawellsbooknut@gmail.com or you may find her on Facebook, as well.

Books by Linda Wells:

Chance Encounters

Fate and Consequences

Perfect Fit

Memory

Imperative